done ✓

The Teacup Novellas

—The Collection—

Diane Moody

Copyright © 2013 Diane Moody
All rights reserved.
ISBN-13: 978-1494209360

Published by
OBT·Bookz

Cover design by Hannah Moody

These novellas are works of fiction. Names, characters, places, and incidents are either the product of the author's imagination or are used fictitiously. Any resemblance to actual events, locales, organizations, or persons living or dead is entirely coincidental and beyond the intent of either the author or the publisher.

In memory of my beloved aunt,
Lucille McKeag Hale
who taught me to appreciate
the little pleasures in life,
one teacup at a time.

CONTENTS

Preface

Lucy Alexander has a hopeless case of writer's block. But all that changes when her handsome UPS guy delivers a box of vintage teacups from the estate of her namesake and beloved Aunt Lucille. Happy memories of tea parties they shared when Lucy was young flood her mind. And with them, the forgotten stories her aunt loved to tell over tea and Scottish shortbread. Colorful tales of fascinating characters woven together with the undeniable power of love. Some were true, most weren't, but it was her aunt's extraordinary gift of storytelling that first ignited Lucy's passion to write. Though still grieving the recent loss of her aunt, Lucy unwraps the fragile cups and saucers, and with them, a flood of memories and story ideas.

So begins the premise for *The Teacup Novellas.*

When I was a young girl, I spent a couple of weeks in Chicago with my Uncle Harold and Aunt Lucille. To me they seemed larger than life, and lived in the biggest city I'd ever visited. From beginning to end, those weeks felt magical. I still have the charm bracelet she bought me at Marshall Field's and on it, a tiny replica of the store's famous green clock. We bought fabric in the fashion district and strolled the aisles of the fresh market beneath the overhead tracks of the subway called the El. They took me to Drury Lane, my first theater-in-the-round where we saw *Everybody Loves Opal.* We spent a weekend at a resort in nearby Wisconsin, and to this day, I can still smell the piney woods surrounding that beautiful lodge. Uncle Harold taught me how to drink coffee, and oh my—how grown up I felt! He showed me around his beautiful flower gardens and shared secrets of his green thumb. I loved how he'd often break into song, reprising glorious show tunes he'd sung in local theater productions.

Theirs was a love that filled their home and overflowed to those around them. At my young age, I didn't have a clue about romance, but that summer I saw it lived out in everyday life in a thousand different ways.

I think it was the stories they told that I remember most of all. Colorful narratives of everyday life that were anything but ordinary. I would later realize it wasn't so much the *content* of the stories as the way in which they were told. I remember sitting spellbound as I listened to their captivating dialogues and vivid word pictures, all generously flavored with that familiar Chicago accent.

I'm not sure how I ended up with Aunt Lucille's teacup collection, but I'm so glad I have them.

For years they've collected dust, and sadly, a few got chipped in the moves we've made along the way. Then one day, when the kids were grown and I finally had time to pursue my dream of writing, I noticed a cup and saucer sitting on a nearby end table. I remembered my aunt and her extraordinary passion for life, and a thought drifted through my mind.

If teacups could talk . . .

And so it is that Lucy Alexander, the fictional author inspired by her Aunt Lucille, shares many memories and affections for her aunt as I do for mine. Alas, that's where Lucy and I part company. For while our story lines may intersect now and then, I am not Lucy and she is not me.

Though we both love a good chai latte.

Blessings,
Diane
November 2013

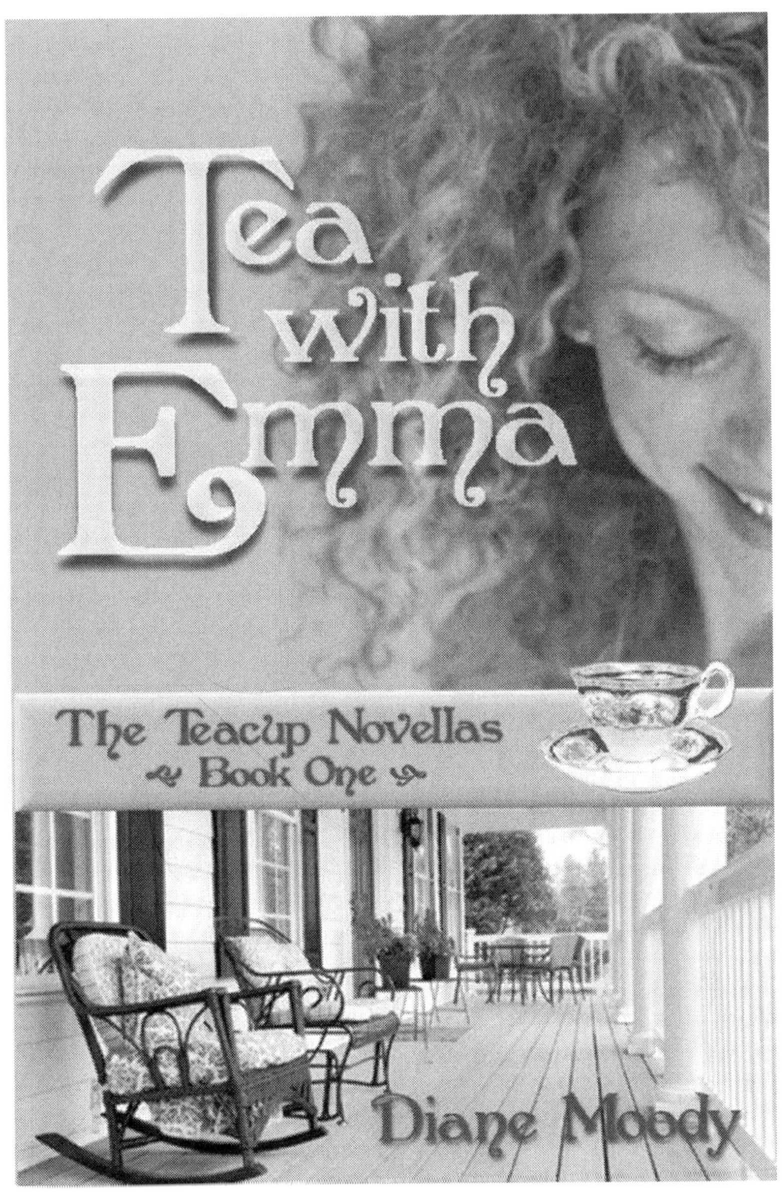

Don't miss a sampling of recipes
from The Chawton Tea Room
located at the end of the Book One!

"It's such happiness when good people get together—
and they always do."

—from Jane Austen's *Emma*

Many are the plans in a man's heart,
but it is the Lord's purpose that prevails.

Proverbs 19: 21

Prologue

Another interruption. Great. Just great.

"Can't a body get five stinkin' minutes without a phone call or someone knocking at the stupid door?" I muttered, my teeth clenched. "Hold your shorts. I'm coming!"

I shoved my office chair back from my cluttered desk, avoiding eye contact with the calendar hanging above my mess. September lurked a few pages back, breathing down my neck. Only three months to go and not a chapter written. If Samantha made one more inference about "writer's block" in that graveled editor's voice of hers, I would throw my keyboard at her in a New York minute. Never mind that she was 3000 miles away in the aforementioned Big Apple.

I quickly finger-combed my wild hair before throwing open the front door. "Hey, Mark," I greeted, sounding much more cheerful than I felt. "Sorry it took me so long."

"No problem, Lucy. Buried in another novel?" My UPS guy smiled as he keyed in something on the big scanner gadget in his hands. I noticed a medium-sized box resting on the weathered bench beside my front door.

"I wish. Can't seem to get this one off the ground." I signed the gadget using the special pen he handed me. Samantha was a stickler for receipts, insisting on delivery confirmation, so I was used to this little ritual. Except I noticed this one wasn't from her. It was from my dad.

I glanced up just in time to find Mark staring at me. His eyes quickly darted back to the scanner as I passed it back to him. Normally I looked forward to his deliveries. Even though his visits were brief, in typical UPS oh-so-rushed fashion, he'd always been friendly. Always asked about the books he delivered fresh from my publishing house. Once, when he was ahead of schedule, he even sat down on my wicker porch chair and waited while I opened a box of my newest release, an Australian romantic comedy. I signed one for him to send to his sister who was living in Sydney at the time.

Did I mention he's also a dead ringer for that guy who played Sawyer on *LOST?* Yeah. That guy.

"Working on another sappy love story?"

Our running joke. He assumed I wrote strictly romance. Probably a sexist remark, but I always gave him a pass on it. Getting lost in those killer dimples for a couple minutes seemed like a fair trade-off.

Most of the time, that is. Today? Not so much. I felt irritable and tired, and I needed to get back to work. So I played along. "Yeah, nothing but sap. All that yucky, mushy stuff. You know—hey, how are you, I think I love you, will you marry me, happily ever after stuff. Same old, same old."

He lifted the box easily and handed it to me. "Hey, don't knock it 'til you've tried it. Sometimes that yucky, mushy stuff can be good medicine." He tossed me a wink as he turned to go.

"I'll remember that. Have a good one, Mark." I couldn't help but notice the tanned muscular calves as he sprinted down the driveway. Gotta love the warm summer months when the UPS guys wear those manly brown shorts . . .

"You too, Lucy. Happy writing!"

The box felt surprisingly light. As I made my way back in the house, I admired Dad's perfect handwriting. Normally I didn't have to sign for anything from him, so I was intrigued. *Dad, what are you up to now?*

I'd missed his call the other night and only now realized I'd never listened to my voice mail or called him back. When he called, I'd been in the midst of another Migraine Hell, third time this week, and chose to keep the pillow over my head rather than be sociable. He was always a good sport.

"Gertie, whatcha think?" I asked my Scottie as I set the box on the kitchen table. She wagged her tail vigorously, cocking her head to one side to study the mysterious box. "What would Dad be sending us? Another weather radio to protect us from the storms?" I grabbed some scissors out of the kitchen drawer and snipped the packaging tape. "Another deadbolt for our back door?" Gertie barked. I scratched behind her left ear. "I'll take that as a no. Hmm, perhaps a case of Mace to carry on my next trip to New York?" Two barks. She knows him well.

With the tape sliced, I opened the box, pawing through an enormous supply of Styrofoam popcorn. "Good grief, Dad. What could possibly need this much packing?"

My hands searched through mounds of the white stuff until I touched something wrapped in tissue paper. I pulled it out, knowing immediately what it was.

Tears stung my eyes. For a moment, I had trouble finding my next breath. I blinked away the moisture blurring my vision and unwrapped the many layers of tissue. A delicate bone china teacup, with tiny hand-painted flowers in rose and amber resting against airy green fronds. Ornate oval frames scrolled in gold surrounded each small cluster of flowers here and there. Behind all of them, a deep red-on-red design contrasted against the cup's creamy white background. A narrow gilded leave-like pattern rimmed the scalloped edge of the cup. Sophisticated and elegant, every hand-painted brush stroke more beautiful than the next.

"Aunt Lucille . . ." Her name escaped my lips. As I closed my eyes, I saw her. Seated across from me at the miniature table in the guest room she'd decorated just for me. Her red hair, always in a perfect updo of curls with a big bow in the back, wouldn't dare allow even a hint of gray. Never mind the stash of *Just My Shade* in "Light Auburn #2" I'd discovered in the bathroom cabinet. Her secret was safe with me.

She always took time first thing every morning to apply makeup to her pale complexion. A little reinforcement to the eyebrows, a dash of blue shadow on her crinkled lids, a wisp or two of mascara to her fine lashes. Then came the rouge she so loved, kissing those powder-dusted cheeks. And the ever-present *Parisian Rhapsody* highlighting her lips, always the perfect companion for the bright shades of purple and turquoise she loved to wear.

In my mind, I watched as she lifted the cup I now held in my hand, her pinky raised, taking a sip of hot chamomile. I watched a much younger version of myself mimic her every move. We had tea parties in my room every afternoon at four o'clock—tea with cinnamon scones or wedges of her mouth-watering Scottish shortbread. She'd collected vintage teacups from her travels all over the world. Each cup and saucer had a story—anecdotes she eagerly shared with me, her eyes aglow with memories of exotic trips abroad.

It was the summer of my tenth year. My parents were overseas for a conference, and I had been so thrilled to take my first airplane ride to Chicago. There I would stay with my aunt and uncle while Mom and Dad were away. Aunt Lucille's only child, my cousin Stephen, was off at college. And for those four glorious weeks in July, I was the daughter she'd never had.

And I *adored* her.

She spoiled me rotten, and I loved every moment of it. We toured museums. We browsed the wondrous aisles of Marshall Field's downtown. We explored fabric shops tucked in the Garment District of the Windy City. We went to a theater in the round.

And twice a week, we shopped at the fresh market downtown, buying luscious fat blueberries and strawberries, seedless watermelons, asparagus and pole beans, and the biggest, juiciest tomatoes I'd ever seen. Lucille was an accomplished cook, and I loved sitting atop the stool in her kitchen, watching her work her magic on dishes I'd never heard of before, let alone tasted. Best of all, I got to witness the miraculous assembly of her Hazelnut Almond Torte, an extraordinary masterpiece with twelve layers that took three days to make—a cake for which she was famous.

I caught myself licking my lips, remembering the blended flavors of that incredible delicacy.

I looked down, fingering the exquisite cup cradled in my hands. "I remember," I whispered, recalling its story. When Lucille was younger, she'd found this little treasure in a quaint shop in England near Jane Austen's hometown. My aunt *loved* to read. And her love of books was highly contagious that summer. She told me all about Miss Austen, the English author whose famous Regency romances had captured hearts for centuries. That summer Aunt Lucille bought me my first Jane Austen book—a delightful comedy called *Emma.*

It was the beginning of my life-long love affair with the written word.

Just one month ago today, my father called to tell me his sister, my precious aunt and namesake, had died in her sleep.

The funeral was a blur to me now. I returned a few days later, leaving Mom and Dad to sort through her will and all of her possessions along with Stephen and his family. I was already way behind deadline before I left for the funeral. When I returned, I plowed into a brick wall instead of a manuscript. I must have deleted at least a dozen false starts, each one as bad as the one before it. I just couldn't settle into a story line I liked. I began to hate the characters that kept vying for my attention and gladly deleted them off the page. Which, of course, left me with nothing but empty pages.

I just couldn't find my mojo. Whatever the heck that was. Something was missing. And as I marked each day off the calendar, the pressure mounted, making my creative juices quite literally disappear. I wondered if they'd left for good.

That was three weeks ago.

An envelope floated to the surface of all that popcorn. I opened it, reading Dad's short note. "Lucille specified in her will that these teacups were to go to you. I know you'll cherish them as much as she did. Love, Dad."

As I carefully finished unwrapping each of the cups and their matching saucers, I kept thinking back to those tea parties with Aunt Lucille. The delicious chats we had. Her endearing patience as I rattled on and on about my serious crush on Rodney. Or was it Jared? The spell-binding stories she shared about the handsome Northwestern student who courted her, married her, then enlisted in the Army Infantry after the Japanese bombed Pearl Harbor. I always hung on her every word.

Oh my goodness.

That's it!

These teacups! The stories . . .

Suddenly my head began to explode with ideas. Lots of them. I set the cup down and stared at it. Then I grabbed my head between my hands and closed my eyes. A whole library of movie-like scenes fast-forwarded through the camera lens inside my mind.

A hopeless romantic in a modern-day twist to Jane Austen's *Emma* . . . in Austin?

A misfit couple of journalists thrown together . . . on the *Oregon* coast?

A fresh start in a small town . . . and a pastor who rides a Harley?

And a familiar love story set against the heartbreaking backdrop of World War II.

"STOP!"

Gertie started barking, no doubt wondering why I'd yelled. I dropped into the kitchen chair, staring off into that no-man's land where authors often discover their characters. They paraded by, one after another, already outfitted in their respective costumes, each trying to tell me something about themselves.

Each one carrying a teacup on a saucer.

Hands down, the strangest thing that's ever happened to me.

My eyes tracked back over to the collection of my aunt's teacups. Don't laugh, but I'm pretty sure I could hear their voices calling out to me. Some even had English accents. As if teacups could talk.

As if teacups could talk . . .

I grabbed the first cup and saucer I'd held, the one with the red and gold design, and took it to the sink. I washed and rinsed both pieces, then carefully dried them. I heated some water in my stainless steel teapot, and a few minutes later, a bag of Lipton tea brewed in the dainty cup I carried back to my office. I cleared the clutter and set it down, allowing it to brew a few minutes more as I opened a new file on my computer.

If teacups could talk . . .

I was amused to find those characters had all followed me into my little office. We were a bit cramped, but that's okay. We needed to get to know each other up close and personal. It was also rather noisy, what with them all still chatting among themselves.

She should tell our story first. It was our idea, after all . . .

It's the renegade wheel off my luggage. You don't want to know . . .

Okay, don't be alarmed but I smell smoke in your clothes.

Anyone bring the Glenn Miller records?

Mentally, I told them all to zip it so I could think. Even Gertie yipped as she hopped up onto her favorite chair. She sniffed the air suspiciously then nestled into her afghan. Did she notice our imaginary guests as well? Their whispers floating around the room?

"Hush!" I scolded them. "I mean it. Not one more word from any of you. We have work to do."

I took a sip of the steaming tea, almost crossing my eyes as I studied the details of the tiny paint strokes along the rim of the cup. Then I gently put it back on its saucer, rolled up my sleeves, and starting typing.

Tea with Emma
A novella by Lucy Alexander

Chapter 1

British Airways flight 6732 from London Heathrow banked effortlessly toward the south, beginning its initial decent to Austin-Bergstrom International Airport. Maddie Cooper awoke, aware of the slight change in altitude. She lifted the window shade to peek at the horizon, now tilted at a perfect forty-five degree angle.

She gently touched the shoulder of her friend seated beside her. "Lanie, wake up. We're almost home. We're about to—" A vigorous yawn eclipsed her statement.

"Right, Maddie, like I was supposed to understand that?" Elaine Morgan, known by all her friends as Lanie, clasped her fingers behind her neck, twisting her head back and forth. "Massive crick here. What time is it?"

"About 6:00 p.m. Eastern. We're right on time."

"Would the British have it any other way?" Lanie's attempt at a stodgy English accent triggered the usual laughter.

Maddie arched a brow in that unspoken language between close friends, chiding the pitiful mimic.

"I say, old girl, are you mocking me?" Lanie continued, still stretching her neck.

"Indeed. I am most assuredly mocking you. I shan't deny it a moment longer." Maddie affected each syllable in her best English aristocratic imitation. "A fortnight in Jane Austen's very world begs me do justice to Her Majesty the Queen's native tongue. T'was not my intent to offend you. T'was only my desire to cause you mirth."

"I mirth! I mirth! Enough already!" Lanie begged in a thick Southern drawl. Their joined laughter rang louder than intended. The seat in front of Maddie abruptly snapped upright. She and Lanie tried to squelch any further outbursts, but the resulting effort caused Maddie to snort, triggering more suppressed laughter.

The passenger in front of them jerked around the seat to face them with a harsh glare.

"Sorry," Maddie mouthed sheepishly at him.

"Is it just me," Maddie whispered into Lanie's ear, "or do you feel like a child reprimanded by a crotchety old school teacher? Only he's not *that* old. He can't be that much older than us, can he? What a jerk."

Lanie smirked, dismissing the man's rude behavior with a flip of her wrist. She continued massaging the pain in her neck. "Oh, Maddie, didn't we have the most wonderful time? I feel like we've been time traveling in another era. I just wish we could've stayed forever, don't you?"

Maddie closed her eyes, reliving the sights and experiences of the past fourteen days on their official Jane Austen tour. "I do, but I'm determined to bring that whole mystique back with us to Austin." She opened her eyes, turning toward Lanie. "Am I crazy to try this? Do you think I can actually pull off an authentic English tea room?"

She reached for the carry-on bag below her seat. She unzipped it, digging through its contents before carefully lifting the flowered box.

"What are you doing? We're about to land, silly."

"I know. I can't help it." She unlatched the tray table and let it down, then set the box on it. Maddie untied the string and opened the box, lifting the tissue-covered object onto the tray. She peeled back the layers of paper, finally unveiling the fussy teacup and its matching saucer. "It's just as beautiful as I remember."

"That it is."

She traced her finger along the rim of the cup, the gold sparkling in the sunlight streaming through the small window. "Have you ever seen anything so fine? Look at these hand-painted flowers. Can't you just imagine the Queen herself sipping tea from this very cup?"

Lanie drank from an imaginary cup, her pinky held high. "I assure you, my dear," she announced, the accent dripping, "had these royal lips touched that royal cup, you would never have been able to afford it."

"Is that so?" Maddie raised her teacup to toast Lanie's air-copy. "Well, please don't tell that adorable man at the gift shop where I bought it. He assured me it had 'history from the palace'—wink, wink."

Lanie picked up the saucer, examining its design. "Those winks can be translated: 'If you believe that, I've got some swamp land to sell you in Wales.'"

"Surely you jest!"

"What, you've never heard of gators and crocs in the English countryside?"

"Lanie."

"Maddie."

She waved her off, then rewrapped the cup and saucer and returned them to the box. "Doesn't matter. I'm so excited, it's all I can think about."

"The teacup?"

"No, eeijt, the tea room. I can't remember being so sure of anything in all my life. A Jane Austen tea room in Austin, Texas. I mean, think about it. It's got to be destiny! And I know Nana will be excited too, once I share all my ideas with her. I'll do my research, I'll study all about the different teas and pastries, and we'll design everything down to the last detail. I can see it all in my head already. Patrons will think they've literally stepped into Chawton Cottage.

"Tell me I'm not dreaming, Lanie. Can I do it? Will you help me?"

"Of course you can, and of course I'll help, silly. It's just what Austin needs. And no one could do it better than you. Just don't forget your promise to let me work there, m'dear." The pitiful accent was back. "I'll be a real asset to you, I will!"

"The job is yours but lose the Eliza Doolittle, will you?"

"Deal."

"I still can't believe Nana surprised us with this dream trip, can you?"

Lanie yawned again. "She's amazing. And I think it's so funny how she conspired with Jonathan to make all the tour arrangements for us. Who knew he could pull all that together?"

"That part doesn't surprise me at all. He can do anything. He may be her attorney, but I've watched their friendship grow the last few years. He treats her—I don't know, really special. Don't you think?" Maddie smiled, envisioning dear Jonathan, his rim of white hair and the half-glasses permanently riding low on his prominent nose.

She ventured down a whimsical path she'd been traveling a lot lately. Her divine call as a matchmaker was becoming clearer with each passing day. *I'm not sure how to do it, but somehow I'm going to get those two together. I'm quite certain this is what God wants me to do. Help people find their soul mates.*

"Hello? Anyone in there?"

Maddie blinked out of her musings and picked up here she left off. "Jonathan positively *adores* her. All she has to do is reach for the phone and he comes running. But still, I'm blown away that she wanted to do this for us. It's just too much."

Lanie cocked her head and glared at her. "Too much? Look, you've taken care of her for almost eight years now. You've had more career offers than most people have in a lifetime, yet you shelved all of them to look after Nana after her stroke. You're a saint and an angel, and she knows it. She was thrilled to do this for you. It's not that big of a leap to figure it out. She's just grateful, Maddie. Really, really grateful." She pinched her friend's elbow. "I'm just glad I got to tag along."

"Ouch! Stop that!" Maddie rubbed her elbow with great flair. "Enough with the pinching, okay? Besides, you make me sound like

Mother Teresa. Easy on the accolades or that regency bonnet I bought in Southampton will never fit."

Lanie blew out a weary sigh. "But I'm serious! You're an inspiration to everyone who knows you." She looped her arm through Maddie's on the armrest. "Me included. Not a bad birthday present either, that's for sure. But then, a girl doesn't turn thirty every day."

"Shhh!" Maddie ducked down in her seat. "You don't have to broadcast it to the entire plane."

Lanie rolled her eyes. "What's to hide? You're smart, you're beautiful, you've got *great* hair, you're the most thoughtful and compassionate person I know. So what if you're still single and seriously geriatric?"

"Stop!" Maddie growled playfully, smacking Lanie's elbow and bringing on a fresh wave of giggles.

"DO. YOU. MIND!"

The Pierce Brosnan accent emerged from the contorted, infuriated face of the Scrooge peering over his seat at them.

Maddie blinked as her imagination took immediate flight onto the big screen. She, playing the part of Jane Austen's *Emma,* being reprimanded by the handsome Mr. Knightley as they practiced archery, dressed in regal finery. Only *this* Mr. Knightley had thick brown hair with the slightest curl in it—a bit unruly perhaps—framing a frighteningly serious face. She noticed a few streaks of gray, surprising on someone so young. Only the faintest hint of laugh lines fanned his startling blue eyes. *As if he once knew laughter—but not in a long, long time . . .*

"In case you haven't noticed, no one else on this aircraft is even remotely interested in your incessant chatter and ridiculous cackling." The Brit spoke in angered tones barely above a whisper. His biting words snapped Maddie back to reality.

"I suggest you attempt to contain yourselves for the remaining moments of this flight or I shall ask the flight attendant to sequester both of you to the loo. Am I making myself quite clear?" His eyes blazed first at Lanie then at Maddie.

Neither moved or made a sound.

"Well? Am I?" he demanded.

"Quite. Yes. Quite." Maddie's words sounded stilted even to her own ears. She took a deep breath and exhaled slowly. "We'll try. We really shall try. Absolutely. Our deepest apologies. Deepest. Truly." *Oh no. Please tell me I didn't say that with an accent? He'll think I'm mocking him.* She clamped her mouth shut and forced a pathetic smile.

Lanie elbowed her, casting an agitated glance before turning to face the intruder. "Listen, Ebenezer, I don't know who you think you are, but unless you own this big bird, what gives you the right to—"

Maddie returned the jab.

"OW!"

"Please accept our apologies," Maddie interrupted with no trace of an accent. "We won't disturb you again."

Lanie glared at her. Maddie returned a plastered smile, raising her eyebrows to communicate in their silent language again: *Not. Another. Word.*

The man disappeared behind the seatback, his exasperated sigh drifting between the seats.

Lanie rolled her eyes again, slouching down in her seat. "Well, that was fun," she whispered. "Sounds to me like *someone* got up on the wrong side of the island this morning."

Half an hour later, the exhausted travelers gathered their belongings from the overhead compartments and exited the plane. Maddie and Lanie carefully avoided eye contact, or any other kind of contact, with Sir Scrooge. Through the terminal they kept a safe distance as they made their way to the baggage area.

"Maddie, look—it's him," Lanie grunted as they reached their carousel. "Get a load of all those bags. He must have paid a fortune in extra baggage fees. He's got more luggage than we do combined." She snorted. "The man travels like a girl."

They broke into laughter again, more from fatigue than anything else, and watched his every move. Scrooge followed the sound until he spotted them, his jaw clenching at the sight of them. Visibly irritated, he looked away, busying himself as he counted all his bags. A uniformed skycap approached him, then began loading the bags onto a cart.

"What's his problem anyway?" Maddie wondered, shaking off the distraction.

"Look, Maddie. Here comes your last suitcase. C'mon, let's go. I'm beat."

Maddie stepped through the crowd and reached for her bag, then stacked it atop her bigger one. Popping the handle up, she tilted the bags, rolling them behind her as she followed Lanie toward the exit doors. Lanie stopped short as her unsecured bags toppled over, spilling into everyone's path. Maddie quickly helped her gather the scattered bags, moving them out of the way. "You know, it wouldn't hurt to use the straps to—"

"Stupid bags. I knew better than to borrow these from Alice."

"I'll get this one, let's just go." Maddie grabbed a smaller bag. Just as the automated doors slid open, she glanced up to see a man in an expensive dark suit holding a printed sign bearing the burnt orange University of Texas logo:

DR. IAN GRANT

"Over here—I'm Dr. Grant."

At the sound of the familiar English accent, Maddie turned around just as Scrooge handed off his bags to the skycap and headed toward the man in the suit.

"Welcome, Dr. Grant! I'm Howard Martin, head of the English department at the University of Texas. We've chatted on the phone."

Scrooge extended his hand toward Martin who grasped it heartily. "Right. Of course. Nice to meet you in person at last, Dr. Martin."

"On behalf of the University, I welcome you to the United States and to our great state of Texas. We are most excited about your upcoming year with us. I trust you had a good flight?"

"Oh great," Maddie muttered under her breath. "We've ruffled the feathers of a visiting professor."

Lanie moaned. "Well, I guess I can kiss my raise goodbye," she whined, concerned about her job as an assistant librarian on campus. Even as the words left her mouth, her bags fell over again, this time sending a broken wheel skittering with lightning speed across the tiled floor. Maddie and Lanie watched in horror as the renegade wheel headed right for Scrooge as if on missile lock.

"No! No! No!" Maddie cried in a hoarse whisper.

Lanie grabbed her bags then pushed Maddie, rushing for the automated doors. "Move it, Maddie. We've gotta get out of here. Hurry!" Just as the doors slid open again, they heard the distinctive cry of a man who'd lost his footing.

"Ahhhhhhh—" *Thunk!*

"Dr. Grant! Are you all right?"

Maddie leaned back to look through the closing doors as the commotion erupted in their wake. "But shouldn't we—"

Lanie propelled Maddie through the doors, then with thumb and forefinger bracing her lips, let loose an ear-piercing whistle.

"TAXI!"

Chapter 2

"Ian, please let me know if you need anything else. I'm so sorry about all this," Howard Martin apologized for the umpteenth time since the fiasco at the airport. "Are you sure I can't arrange for a nurse to assist you? It won't be any bother at all, and the University would, of course—"

"Howard, I'll be right as rain in no time. I've lived alone long enough to know how to take care of myself. But thank you." Ian limped to the door with the aid of his crutches, compliments of the hospital emergency room.

"Well, then, I'll leave you be. You have my number if you need anything. Please don't hesitate to call."

"I will. Thank you, Howard."

Martin backed out the front door, casting another mournful glance at Ian's injured foot before heading down the bricked sidewalk to his car. Ian used one of his crutches to shove the heavy door closed then wrestled his way back to the living area just off the foyer. He dropped into the soft leather chair, tossing his crutches on the floor beside him, then propped his booted foot on the matching ottoman.

"It's a bad sprain, Dr. Grant, but the x-rays show no broken bones. Just stay off your feet as much as possible and keep that foot elevated." The ER physician had wrapped Ian's right ankle and heel in a figure eight with miles of Ace Bandage.

Now, with his eyes resting on the oversized boot covering his throbbing foot, Ian blew out a frustrated sigh and dropped his head back against the chair. "Splendid."

With only the ticking of the grandfather clock in the background, he closed his eyes and tried to figure out how he would prepare for his classes, navigate his way to and from the campus, or manage the simple things like showering and dressing. It was kind of Howard to offer to send help, but the last thing he wanted was some overzealous nurse smothering him day and night.

"Blast those ridiculous girls!" Ian punched the arm of the chair with his fist.

He'd seen them bothering with their bags as Martin arrived and made his introductions. It was bad enough to endure the flight from London with those two constantly twittering behind him. If he had heard one more word about Jane Austen, he would surely have lost his mind. *A few days in England and they fancy themselves experts on the entire life and works of Miss Austen. Typical Yanks.*

After arriving at the airport, they seemed to appear everywhere he turned in the terminal. *Hard to miss the two of them. The dark-haired hippy with her long flowing skirt and stupendous floppy hat. The nerve of the woman, trying to tell me off. Absolutely appalling.*

And how could you miss the tall one with her all those strawberry curls . . . or were they reddish blonde? He remembered the wisps of those curls dancing as she walked, glistening in the bright sky-lit terminal. Even through his tirade on the plane, he'd noticed her fair skin with the faintest of freckles sprinkled across a perfect nose.

Ian shook the image from his head disturbed by the thoughts. *Good heavens, what's the matter with me? Must be the painkillers they gave me at the hospital.* But the imprint of her face continued drifting through his mind . . . her peculiar attempt at a smile after he'd chastised her on the flight. *Were those eyes hazel or were they green? Green. Definitely green. I've never seen eyes so vibrant and alive. So . . . sincere?*

He felt his facial muscles relax for the first time all day. With a grunt, he rubbed his face. *Women are nothing but trouble, be it here or across the pond. It must be in their Yankee DNA.*

Ian grabbed his crutches again and clumsily lifted himself off the chair. He wanted to check out his lodgings. Howard had described Bradford House, the university's residence for visiting professors, as "comfortable and nicely appointed." Indeed. He was pleased with his surroundings—the hardwood floors, the expensive leather furniture and works of art. Quite obvious the university took pride in housing guests here. The house, located in prestigious Hyde Park, was built in the late 1800s, according to Howard, but its caregivers had certainly outdone themselves keeping it up to date.

He continued his slow awkward tour of the downstairs, relieved to find the master suite on the first floor. King-size bed. Whirlpool tub in the master bath. An oversized desk beneath a large window in the study. And at the back of the house, a modern kitchen fit for a king and well stocked at that. He grabbed a chilled bottle of water from the refrigerator, snatched a handful of red grapes, and hobbled back to the bedroom.

An hour later, after a long hot bath, Ian fell into bed. With the BBC on mute on the bedroom's large flat-screen television, he sunk deeper into the embrace of the soft sheets, finally giving in to his fatigue. Falling into a deep sleep in mere moments, he was surprised when none other than Jane Austen herself showed up. She turned out the light on the bedside lamp and clicked off the remote. *Wait—how did she know how to do that?* She tucked him into bed, much as his mother had done when he was just a lad. And just like Mum, she planted a gentle kiss on his brow. He looked full into her face—a face surrounded by wispy curls of strawberry blonde, adorned with a sprinkling of freckles across a perfect nose, warm green eyes, and smiling lips . . .

Good night, Jane.

Good night, Ian.

"Nana!"

Maddie flew across the foyer and into the sitting room where her grandmother sat reading. "Oh Nana, we had the most amazing time! You should have come with us! You would have *loved* it!" She knelt beside Rachel Cooper, engulfing her grandmother in an enormous bear hug.

"Oh good heavens, Madeline! You're about to choke the stuffing out of me, dear." The slow, careful cadence of her words warmed Maddie's heart.

"I don't care! I've missed you *so much,* and I have so much to tell you, and I don't even know where to start and—wait—how are you feeling? Are you okay?" Maddie leaned back, taking in the full sight of her sweet Nana. Her eyes raced over the thick white hair, gathered into an elegant chignon. She searched her grandmother's ever-smiling eyes, always filled with life and love . . . the gentle wrinkles around her mouth, still lopsided from the paralyzing effects of the stroke. She noticed Nana's favorite summer shawl draped over her shoulders, a perfect match to her lavender blouse and slacks. The hint of lilacs, her grandmother's familiar scent, reminded Maddie she was home again where she belonged. "Oh, you look perfectly wonderful!"

"I feel perfectly wonderful, sweetheart. Now, sit. I want to hear everything. But first tell me why you're so late? I expected you almost three hours ago."

Maddie fell onto the sofa beside Nana's chair, kicking off her shoes and tucking her feet beneath her. "I'm sorry. I should have called. Lanie arrived home to a crisis, and—"

"Mercy, what now? That poor child lives in eternal calamity."

Maddie rubbed her eyes and yawned. "You're not going to believe this. Alice was supposed to take care of Mr. Darcy. Well, apparently—being the selfish roommate that she is—she neglected to feed the poor cat and he *died.*"

"Oh no. Mr. Darcy is dead?"

"We're guessing Alice must have spent most of the last fourteen days at her worthless boyfriend's apartment. Left poor Mr. Darcy all alone without so much as a morsel. And Nana, you know how much Lanie loved that kitten! She couldn't stop crying, *I* couldn't stop crying because *she* was crying—all the while, Alice acting like it wasn't her fault that he died. Can you believe the audacity?"

Tears pooled in Nana's tired eyes. "Dear Lanie. I can't even imagine how upset she must have been."

"Lanie was devastated. She kicked Alice out, told her to come back tomorrow for her things, then we buried poor Mr. Darcy."

"She must be heartbroken."

"Beyond heartbroken, but she wanted some time to herself, so she insisted I come on home. I guess she needs to grieve."

"Call and check on her first thing in the morning, will you?" Nana unlocked her wheelchair and pressed the lever to drive herself across the room. "Now you stay right there. I'll go see if Gretchen will make us some tea."

Maddie stretched out on the sofa. "So, how did it work out with Gretchen? And please don't tell me you're going to hire her permanently and kick me out." Maddie reached out to grasp her grandmother's hand as she rolled by.

"Gretchen is a sweetheart. But you're my Maddie. Need I say more?" Nana winked and rolled out of the room.

"Tea . . ." Maddie sat up, the entrepreneurial fires reigniting. "Nana, wait up! There's something I need to talk to you about."

Lanie pulled the last tissue from her box of Kleenex and blew her nose. The male voice from the speaker on her laptop beckoned.

"Lanie, I'm so sorry. It's killing me to hear you cry like this."

She wiped her nose again, thankful Jeff couldn't actually see her in this state. Granted, he'd never actually *seen* her at all. At least not in person. They'd been cyber-friends for several months now, but had never met face-to-face. Video-chatting via Skype was their usual method of communication. But on a night like this, she'd opted against the video, simply talking through the audio version.

"I just can't seem to stop the tears, y'know? And yet I'm so angry, I could just BITE somebody!" she growled, holding back another sob.

"Totally understandable. A helpless little kitten, left all alone? I mean, who *does* something like that? What was she thinking? Where did you find this roommate anyway—the heartless store?"

"Not funny. Actually, she found me. Before my previous roommate Selena graduated, she told Alice about the apartment. They had some classes together or something. So Selena all but promised her she could move in with me once she moved out. I guess I should have checked her out better, but it was just so much easier than having to post ads for a new roommate or put the word out."

Jeff blew out a long sigh. "So you didn't notice the she-devil horns when she first showed up?"

Lanie wiped the remains of her mascara from her eyes. "No, she seemed fine. A little distant, but that's actually not a bad thing for a roommate. I wasn't looking for a gal-pal, just someone to help pay the rent. Guess I should have been a little more selective."

"I'd say that's a slight understatement, wouldn't you?"

"No kidding." She could hear the tapping on his keyboard when he answered.

"Are you busy? I'm sorry, I've taken up way too much of your time." She sat up, trying not to be hurt by his obvious distraction.

"No, not at all, Lanie. I just had something I needed to order. I'm done. Sorry about that."

She rubbed her face, suddenly exhausted. "Well, I probably need to get to bed. It's after 2:00 here. I've got to get up in a few hours to go to work. I haven't even unpacked yet."

"Don't go. Besides, it's only midnight here in California. We've got worlds of time."

She could hear something pouring over ice through the speaker. "Yeah, well, you can't exactly *give* me those two hours between us. What's that you're drinking?"

"I'd give you those two hours if I could, though. Just so you know. And it's Dr. Pepper, since you asked. I had a craving."

"Mmm. I haven't had a Dr. Pepper since we left for England, and the fridge is bare. Could you bring one over?"

"Wish I could. But mostly I wish I could give you a hug right now."

Lanie closed her eyes, trying to imagine how that would feel. This stranger she'd never met, so kind. So understanding of her broken heart. Oh, to be able to feel his arms around her . . . right here, right now.

"That would be nice, Jeff."

She heard him inhale a deep breath, then slowly let it out. "Someday, Lanie. Someday."

"G'night, Jeff."

"G'night, Lanie."

Chapter 3

Ian tightened the belt of his robe before opening the heavy front door. As he maneuvered the crutches to propel himself through the door, the heat and humidity swallowed him whole. *So this is autumn in Texas. Ghastly hot. And to think school starts Monday. Feels more like summer holiday.*

He spotted the folded newspaper on the sidewalk near the street and started toward it. The wide porch gracing the front of the house sat atop ten broad steps. For a moment, he contemplated forgetting it. As he'd told Howard, he could read the *London Times* online, but he much preferred to hold a newspaper in his own hands. He liked the smell of the ink and the rustle of the pages. He also wanted to be more cognizant of his Austin surroundings by a daily browsing of the local paper. Determined, he reached for the handrail and slowly hopped down on his good foot, one step at a time using only one crutch.

"There now. That wasn't so hard, was it?" He limped up the brick path, leaning heavily on the crutch. Looking around, he noticed the houses were all quite old but in excellent shape. A canopy of trees covered the narrow street. An American flag snapped in the warm breeze at the house next door. Ian might have smiled at the Rockwellesque feel of it all, but he wasn't in the mood. It was too hot. Besides, yesterday's angst still gnawed at him. Grasping the crutch with one hand, he leaned over to grab the paper.

"It's you!"

A woman's voice startled him. Losing his balance, he hung onto the crutch for dear life while trying desperately not to put any weight on his bad foot. Hopping around like an eejit, he finally regained his balance and stopped the dreadful dance.

"Oh no! I'm so sorry—I didn't mean to scare you!"

The voice edged closer. Ian whipped his head around in time to see a flash of pastel pink crossing the street—an ankle-length cotton robe hovering over outlandish fluffy pink slippers.

"Here, let me help you," she begged, picking up the newspaper.

"No, that's not necessary," he snapped, holding his hand up to stop the intruder. "I'm quite all ri—" The oxygen whooshed from his lungs when he recognized the fountain of blondish-red curls. The green eyes blinked back at him innocently. A growl erupted. "It's—*you!*"

Her eyes widened as a shy smile slowly crept across her face. *She thinks I'm happy to see her! The woman is positively delusional!*

"Yes, I'm the one from the airplane yesterday and—"

"I know exactly who you are!" he grunted. "And don't think I'm not well aware of the fact it was the wheel off *your* suitcase that gave me *this!*" Ian pointed to his bandaged foot. He could feel the vein on his neck pulsing.

"Actually, no, it was Lanie's wheel. You see—"

"It doesn't matter! I knew the two of you were trouble the minute you got on that plane. All that non-stop prattling and ridiculous giggling. Outrageous behavior for women your age. Absolutely outrageous! And if that weren't enough, you go fumbling through the terminal, dropping your bags, causing mayhem—and breaking my foot!" He straightened, as if just pronouncing them guilty as charged in a court of law. He snatched the paper from her and started clomping back toward the steps.

"But if you'll just let me explain, I'm sure you'll see that it was just an accident! I was horrified when that wheel came off and starting rolling toward you!"

Ian stopped in his tracks without turning. He jerked his head to face her. "Do you mean to tell me you *knew* the wheel had come off? You saw it rolling toward me yet said nothing?"

"I—I, well you see—"

"Barbaric. Positively *barbaric!* You Americans have a lot to learn about common decency. You should be ashamed of yourself." He hadn't noticed he'd gotten in her face, mere inches from her. The realization stopped him cold.

She dropped her head, lifting a palm to her forehead. When she looked up, her eyes glistened in the morning light. "I'm so sorry," she began quietly. "I wanted to do something—say something, but Lanie thought we should—look, it doesn't matter what happened. It was wrong of us. I'm trying to apologize as best I know how. I had no idea you might break your foot. Is it terribly painful? Are you all right?"

Ian fought the urge to surrender. He fought the melting sensation drifting through him. He was much too close to her; her face even more lovely than he remembered. Not breathtaking or gorgeous, but a natural kind of beauty. Still, he mustn't be swayed by her mere appearance. "Yes, it's quite painful. I hardly slept at all last night, no thanks to you."

She leaned over, studying the boot on his injured foot. "They didn't put a cast on it? That's odd. I thought a break usually necessitated a—"

"Yes, well, actually it isn't *completely* broken. Just sprained. But a *bad* sprain. *Very* bad. And quite the inconvenience, too. I'm to start classes Monday and now look at me." He lifted his chin in defiance and turned back toward the house again.

"So that's why you're here at the guest house. You're a visiting professor, aren't you?"

The sound of her voice was too close. *Good grief, she's following me.* "Yes, I am."

"What will you teach, Dr. Grant?"

He stopped, turning again to face her. "How on earth could you possibly know my name?"

A lazy smile tilted the right corner of her mouth. "That little sign, remember? The one Dr. Martin was holding when he greeted you. Had your name on it? Hard to miss."

He shook his head, weary of the conversation. "Yes, well, why don't you scurry on home and leave me alone. I have work to do."

She darted in front of him. "The least I can do is help you up the stairs. Here, take my arm," she offered, raising her elbow toward him.

"I'll do no such thing! I came down, I can most certainly go back up."

She pulled her arm back. "You're a stubborn one, aren't you? Are all the English so obstinate?"

"Good day, Miss—"

"Cooper. Madeline Cooper. Though my friends call me Maddie."

"Miss Cooper. Now if you'll please honor my request and leave."

She turned toward the street, scuffing those fluffy pink slippers on the brick sidewalk. "As you wish, Dr. Grant. My grandmother and I live just across the street there. If you need help, please don't hesitate to ask. We won't bite . . . unless it's contagious."

Maddie closed the door, then peeked through the sheers at the house across the street. Dr. Grant—*Ian*—was still struggling up the porch steps. A snort escaped as Maddie watched. *One more step, dear grumpy man, and you're home free . . . there you go. I knew you could do it.* She smiled, watching him straighten himself, looking around though carefully avoiding a glance in her direction. He hobbled into the house and slammed the door.

She continued spying, her mind whirling over the encounter. "You're awfully young to be a visiting professor, Dr. Grant," she mused out loud. "Most of those guys are old as the hills, with hair coming out of their ears and nose. I'm guessing you can't be more than thirty-eight? Thirty-nine? Forty tops. So how did you end up in the Lonestar State at our little ol' prestigious university?"

With her thoughts lost on the mysterious guest living across the street, she suddenly noticed he'd pulled back the curtains in the front room, peering out the window, looking straight at her. She darted out of sight, her heart pounding.

"Well, well, well, Dr. Grant. Seems you're not the tough guy you pretend to be, now are you?"

Later, Maddie rinsed the last of the breakfast dishes and placed it in the rack to dry. "Nana, don't you think it's providential that this Dr. Grant was on the same plane, that we had that, uh, 'unfortunate' situation arise so that we met, and now I find out that he's living right across the street at Bradford House? I mean, what are the odds of that? It's like God dropped him into my lap 'for such a time as this.' For me—Madeline Cooper—to find the perfect soul mate for him. If ever there was a man whose very essence cried out for female companionship, it is Dr. Ian Grant. And I'm just the one to find him that perfect companion!"

Nana laughed heartily. "Oh honey, I hate to disappoint you but your name is Madeline, *not* Queen Esther. You do live in another realm, don't you?"

Nana's gentle chuckle filled the room. Maddie poured them both another cup of tea then joined her grandmother at the kitchen table. "I have no idea what you mean. I'm as sane as the next person." She couldn't camouflage the grin tugging at her lips.

Nana stirred cream into her teacup and continued. "Sane indeed. If I'd had any idea you'd come back from England with your head filled with all these grandiose, romantic notions, I might have thought twice about sending you in the first place. I fear you've been bitten by some idyllic Jane Austen bug but good. Might I remind you this isn't eighteenth century England, and there are no fancy balls or elaborate picnics here in Austin. I don't mean to burst your bubble, dear, but playing the matchmaker can be quite a dangerous task. And surely you remember Emma's disastrous results?"

"Now, Nana, where's your sense of adventure? Why should Jane Austen have all the fun? I believe this trip was ordained by God. In fact, I'm quite certain of it."

At that pronouncement, Nana laughed out loud.

Undaunted, Maddie continued. "I am! I believe with all my heart that God exposed me to Jane Austen's world through that tour, gave me a genuine taste of her life and her utter romantic *genius,* then sent me home to bring a touch of her to all of us here. That's why I'm the obvious choice to find a mate for Dr. Grant, and that's why I'm going to open this tea room. Oh, Nana, won't it be fun? I can hardly wait until we open!"

Nana wiped her lips with the cloth napkin. "Oh, you'll liven it up, all right. You always do. But as for our new neighbor Dr. Grant, why try to find him a girlfriend? Why don't you just invite him over for dinner? Maybe *you're* his perfect soul mate."

Maddie snorted, spilling her tea. "Now *that's* funny. You should see his disdain every time he looks at me. He'd limp all the way back to England if he thought I had my sights on him. But thanks for the laugh, Nana. That's a good one."

Nana backed her chair away from the table and buzzed over to the counter where she set her empty cup and saucer. "You're much too picky, Madeline. One of these days you need to climb down out of that ivory tower and take a look around you. And don't think I don't know what all this nonsense about matchmaking is about."

She pulled alongside Maddie, reaching out to stroke her hair with her good hand. "Just because your father was a sorry example of a gentleman—and an unaffectionate one at that—does *not* mean that all men are out to hurt you. Playing Cupid to avoid a relationship of your own can only lead to trouble, sweetheart."

Maddie looked down at her hands, uncomfortable with the conversation. Nana patted her granddaughter's cheek, then pressed the lever to move her wheelchair toward the door. "And that's all I'm going to say about that right now."

"Wait, Nana. We still need to talk about the tea room. I want to make sure you're one hundred percent behind the idea. I can't do it without your help, and for the record, I *won't* do it without you."

She followed her grandmother down the hall to the living room. She loved watching her maneuver the automated wheelchair around the house with all the expertise of a Daytona 500 race car driver. Only a tad slower.

"I'm already ten steps ahead of you, dear. Not only am I behind you and looking forward to our little adventure, I've already called Jonathan and invited him to dinner tonight to discuss our plans. He'll need to help us with the financial arrangements and legal aspects. Besides, I value his opinions and want his input on this."

Dear Jonathan . . . what a perfect couple they'd make. Maybe we'll add a little candlelight to set the mood tonight. I'll pick up some fresh flowers and—

"Which reminds me. Why don't you call Lanie and invite her to join us. Maybe we can help get her mind off poor Mr. Darcy."

"That's a wonderful idea. Oh Nana, have I told you lately how much I love you? There's no place on earth I'd rather be than right here with you." She hugged her grandmother then placed a loud, wet kiss on her wrinkled cheek.

"Oh for heaven's sake, Madeline. You'll smear my rouge." She teasingly waved her away. "But sit down for a minute. There's something else I want to discuss with you. I've done a lot of thinking while you were gone, and I think we're due for a bit of a change, you and I."

Chapter 4

Maddie pulled the upholstered ottoman directly in front of her grandmother's wheelchair and plopped down on it. "Change? What kind of change?"

"Last night, I did a lot of thinking, and I made a decision about something. Madeline, there hasn't been a day go by that I haven't loved having you here with me. After your dear mother passed away when you were only four, then your father made himself so scarce all the time—"

"Nana, it's okay. You've been the best parent a child could ask for."

"Let me finish, dear. I raised him to know better. George knows he's not done right by you, spending so much time in Hong Kong. No business is more important than family, Madeline. You remember that in the years ahead. And if you ever find a young man worthy of your love only to find out his work is his god, then you *run!* Do you hear me? You run like the wind."

Maddie watched as her grandmother grew more animated, despite her slow, methodical speech pattern. It was a familiar topic of discussion, one that Nana brought up often, though usually around the holidays when George Cooper called from overseas with his litany of excuses why he wouldn't be able to come home. Years ago Maddie had learned to close the door on her feelings about the father she hardly knew. She knew her grandmother still grieved that he had abandoned his child so soon after her mother's death.

But for Maddie, all she ever knew was the love of her adoring grandmother, and that was enough. Rachel Cooper was there for Maddie when she learned to ride a bike, when she had her tonsils out, when she shopped for her first bra, and when she sang her first solo in the Christmas program. She was right there when Maddie struggled with peer pressure in high school, when she eventually graduated with honors—and when her college sweetheart found someone new, leaving her heart shattered.

When Nana suffered a massive stroke just weeks after Maddie graduated from UT, there was no question in Maddie's mind who would take care of her. Never looking back, she learned the necessary skills to care for a stroke victim paralyzed on one side, otherwise known as "unilateral" paralysis. She learned to bathe her, to use the automated lift to get her in and out of bed. She helped her exercise, hoping to help her regain the use of her left arm and leg. And more than anything, she tried to return the gift of love—a lifetime of love.

"So what's this big decision you've made?"

Nana reached for her hand and Maddie gave it willingly. "No one could have cared for me better. Most children, let alone grandchildren, would just shut their loved ones away in some institution, but you stayed with me. I'll never forget it, sweetheart. But the time has come for you to move on."

"No! Stop talking like that." Maddie pulled her hand back, crossing her arms tightly across her chest. "I don't think I like the direction this is going."

Nana laughed easily. "Well, if you think I'm offering to check myself into some old folks home, you're wrong. I've simply decided to ask Gretchen to stay on with us. To live here with us. I want her to take care of all those mundane tasks—the bathing, the dressing, the lifting here and there, the cooking and cleaning—and let you simply be my granddaughter again. My *live-in* granddaughter, of course."

A whoosh of air rushed from Maddie's lungs. "Oh, is that all?" She grabbed Nana's good hand. "I thought you were kicking me out! Good heavens, don't ever do that again. You scared me half to death!"

"I think it's the best of both worlds. I already love that dear girl like she's one of my own. She's efficient and cheerful, and we get along famously. And oh my, how she loves the Lord. We've shared the dearest prayer times together. Besides, I hate for you to have to do all those things for me. You need a life of your own. We should have done this years ago. And it will free you up so that you can open your tea room—"

"*Our* tea room."

"Yes, of course. *Our* tea room. So what do you think?"

"I think it's smashing, my dear. I think it's ex*traor*dinary." Lacing her words with her contrived English accent, Maddie jumped up, lunging for another hug.

"Oh dear, here comes the accent again," Nana moaned, buried in the exaggerated embrace.

Maddie leaned back. "Yes, and do get used to it, love, for I shall practice it day and night to put myself in the proper mindset for our very proper English tea room."

"And just what have you decided to call this very proper English tea room?"

"What do you think of *The Chawton Tea Room*?" Maddie studied her grandmother's face.

"Named for Jane Austen's home? I think it's perfect."

"Do you? Given, that's where the idea first occurred to me?"

"Absolutely. Then *The Chawton Tea Room* it is. And Maddie, don't forget to pray about all this, dear. Remember what the Bible says—'In all thy ways acknowledge Him and He shall direct your path.' Give this tea room to Him and see what He has in store for you."

"Not to worry, Nana. God is all over this. I'm sure of it."

"He's across the street? Right *now?*"

Lanie and Maddie peeked out the living room window at the stately brick home across the street. The last traces of sunlight cast golden shadows across the four white pillars bedecking the spacious front porch. "Where else would he be? He's on crutches. And I feel terrible about it, Lanie. It's all our fault. We never should have run off like that. What were we thinking?"

"Doesn't bother me in the least." Lanie continued snooping, hoping for any sign of movement. "That's what he gets for being so rude to us. What a jerk. That reminds me—I almost forgot . . ." Lanie reached for her purse and dug out the copy of *The Daily Texan.* "Get a load of this, will you?"

"Oh my goodness." With Lanie leaning over her shoulder, Maddie scanned the headlines of the school newspaper. "'Texas Welcomes Dr. Ian Grant' . . . And look, there's our very own Scrooge in a flowing black robe walking across Oxford's historic campus. Do you believe this?" Maddie's voice trailed off as she stared at the second picture, a head shot of the professor. "He's much better looking than this, don't you think?"

"That's what I told Amanda, which, of course, sent her into vapors. She's already asked me to introduce him to her."

Maddie lowered the paper. "Your boss wants you to introduce her to him? Not gonna happen. She way too flirtatious for him."

Lanie shot her a questioning glance then peeked back out the window. "He must be some kind of big cheese in the English literary field. Everybody's talking about him."

"Ooh! Right up our alley. He's probably an expert on Jane Austen. We should drop by for a chat sometime. Better yet, invite him to our next book club meeting." Maddie wiggled her eyebrows.

Lanie's face deadpanned. "I think *not.* Are you out of your mind? Have you already forgotten how rude he was to us on that plane? Never mind that we broke his foot. The farther we stay from him, the better, Maddie. Besides, I probably shouldn't mention this, but—"

"But of course you will because we keep no secrets," Maddie finished, still staring at the picture of Ian Grant.

"Okay, but just remember—this is nothing but gossip, so there's a good chance it's bogus at the very least."

"Out with it."

Lanie moved to the sofa, kicking off her shoes. "I can't believe I'm repeating Amanda's gossip. Oh well. Apparently, a few years ago, our dear Dr. Grant was jilted at the altar. As in, literally *at the altar.* Rumor is he's a bit of a stuffed shirt because of it." She smirked a half-smile. "At least we know *that* part is true."

Maddie took a seat in the easy chair, staring off into space as her mind chased a romantic rabbit.

"Oh no you don't," Lanie chided. "I know that look in your eyes. Don't even *think* about it, Maddie."

"Think about what?"

"Whatever you're thinking. Just forget it."

"But don't you see? He *needs* us. He needs our help to find him that special someone who can take away the hurt and show him what real love is all about. It's what we do best."

Lanie covered her face with her hands, moaning. "Leave me out of this. You're asking for nothing but trouble. *Big* trouble. He's a lose-lose, any way you figure it."

"He just needs a little TLC, that's all. I could tell this morning when we talked. He's covering for something. I could see it in his eyes. He tries to come across tough and uncaring, but it's just an act." She poked the paper with her forefinger. "And now we know why."

Lanie tilted her head. "Wait. You talked to him this morning?"

"That's what I wanted to tell you. I went out to get the paper, and there he was, across the street doing the same thing. Only he's on crutches! Crutches that *we* put him on, Lanie." Maddie looked toward the front window, nodding her head as if bearing the heavy mantle of guilt for them both.

"Phhhht, don't pull me into your little pity party. I feel no guilt whatsoever. So what did he say? Was he still mean and grizzly?"

Maddie faced her again. "No, though I think I scared him a little."

"You? Imagine that."

"Stop it. I simply offered to help him up the porch steps, which he refused. But get this—when I came back in, I peeked through the sheers and saw him *peeking back* at me through the blinds of his living room! How funny is that?"

"Our Mr. Scrooge? Playing look-see through the window? Well, what do you know."

Maddie brushed the wrinkles out of her apron then stood up again. "It's just a matter of time, Lanie. Just a matter of time. They're all putty in my hands, you know."

Lanie smacked her forehead with the heel of her hand. "Not again. Maddie, when are you going to learn? Reading *Emma* does not qualify you as some sort of love guru. I hate to be the one to break it to you, but girl, you are *not* a matchmaker."

Maddie planted fists on hips. "I am too! Need I remind you about Jana and Doug? Hmmm? They married exactly six months after I introduced them."

"And divorced a year later. Not exactly a successful match, if you ask me."

Maddie waved her off. "What happens after they marry is not my concern. Now stop trying to dampen my spirits."

"Thank goodness I found Jeff on my own, *without* your help. Did I tell you he called last night? We talked until two in the morning. Maddie, he was *so* wonderful comforting me about Mr. Darcy. I was so distraught, I couldn't stop crying. I kept seeing his furry little body, all limp in that box we buried him in. That poor little guy . . . he didn't deserve it." Lanie's eyes grew shiny with tears as her chin began to tremble.

She sniffed, wiping her eyes with her thumbs, then looked back up at Maddie. "But Jeff—he just let me talk and cry, and then he knew exactly what to say. It was like he was right there hugging me or something. I think I could really fall for this guy. He's everything I've been looking for. He really is."

Maddie didn't miss the dreamy look in Lanie's eyes. "But the fact is, he *wasn't* there. He was across the country. He's just a cyber romance, Lanie. Nothing more. I don't understand you at all. You don't even *know* this guy. He could be some—"

"Okay, okay. I've heard your lecture before. Same song, same verse. Give it a rest. Besides, how dangerous can he be? I met him in a Jane Austen chat room. Not exactly predator territory."

"Like that means anything? You don't know! He could be some major pervert just stalking the chat room. And even if he is a Jane fan, you have to admit—most of those guys are seriously needy geeks. Think about it. Have you ever met a good looking guy with a decent personality who would even *consider* watching a Jane Austen flick with you?"

Lanie peeked back out the window, avoiding eye contact with Maddie. "Did I mention he sent me flowers today? Last night I actually got my feelings hurt, thinking he was working or something as we talked. I could hear him typing on his keyboard. Turns out he was online ordering *two dozen roses* for me. They were delivered first thing this morning. They're so beautiful, Maddie."

"Like perverts don't know how to charm a girl?" Maddie rolled her eyes. "C'mon, Lanie. Don't be so gullible!"

Lanie plugged her ears with her forefingers. "I'm not listening anymore," she answered in sing-song. "Can't hear a word you sa-ay!"

"Fine!" Maddie shouted. Then realizing Lanie was still singing, she walked over and pulled the plugs on her friend. "Stop being a baby and come help me finish getting dinner ready. Jonathan will be here any minute."

The sing-song continued as Lanie followed her into the kitchen. "I'll be glad to he-elp, but no more lec-tures, 'cause I don't wanna hear the-em!"

Chapter 5

"Maddie, that was positively scrumptious."

Jonathan Spencer's compliment pleased Maddie as she cleared the dishes from the dining room table. "Why, thank you, Jonathan. Always a pleasure to have you join us." She tossed a wink at Nana.

"You're as good a cook as Rachel, but don't tell her I said that," he whispered loudly.

"I heard that," Nana jested, right beside him.

Lanie gathered the remaining dishes from the table. "We all know Maddie stole all Nana's recipes so we know precisely where the credit lies. Right, Nana?"

"Goodness knows I have no use for them," Nana quirked with a laugh. "I'm just pleased Madeline does them justice. Which brings us back to our discussion. Jonathan, do you really think Madeline's business endeavor can be up and running in just two or three months? Seems awfully fast to me."

"I see no problem with the zoning permit," Jonathan answered. "This section of the neighborhood is transitioning to homes with businesses—*Crayton's Antique Shoppe*, *The Book Nook*—all similar concepts with proprietors living on the premises. But as for the fast track schedule, I suppose that all depends on Maddie."

Maddie refilled everyone's teacups before joining them again at the table. She'd honored Jonathan tonight by setting her new favorite at his place, the cup and saucer she'd brought home from England. She would forever associate the set she bought in Chawton village with her dream; its deep red and gold design and tiny flowers on a pristine white background, a visible reminder. She smiled as she sat back down, still admiring the cup even as Jonathan stirred sugar into it.

"Nana, I *know* we can do it. I've already ordered my books on English tea. I'll study everything I need to know as fast as I can. I've already scoured the internet for information, recipes, that sort of thing. I'll only be making a few of the pastries initially, experimenting with some new ones and making some of your favorites as well. The finger sandwiches are a cinch. Oh, remind me to let you sample my cranberry chicken salad panini tomorrow. I found the most amazing recipe. It calls for dried cranberries, chopped walnuts, chopped scallions, and several other things, mayo of course. Then you layer it on some sourdough bread with a sassy little smear of Brie and of all things, apricot preserves. Oh my goodness, the flavors just explode in your mouth!"

"I'm stuffed to the gills," Jonathan added, "but that does sound awfully good. I might have to happen by around lunch time tomorrow." He danced his unruly eyebrows up and down with delight.

Nana's half-smile lifted as her eyes twinkled. "You know you're welcome to stop by anytime, Jonathan. And I'm quite sure we'll need another taste-tester, won't we, Madeline?"

"Of course!" Maddie scratched above her brow, trying to remember her train of thought. "Where was I before I got distracted with that recipe? Oh! I know. I was just going to say that by the time we get the minor renovations finished, we should be ready to go."

"For the record, I vote for these chess squares to be on the menu." Jonathan helped himself to another of the gooey golden bars.

"Jonathan, I think I speak for all of us when I say we couldn't do *any* of this without your sophisticated and experienced palate," Maddie teased, drumming her fingers on the edge of the table. "As for these, we'll dub them 'Spencer's Chess Squares' in your honor."

"Well now!" Jonathan beamed.

"Back to the task at hand, honey. Lanie's going to help you with the marketing, printing, that sort of thing?" Nana inquired.

"Yes. She's a whiz at layout and already has tons of ideas for advertising, don't you, Lanie?"

"You'll love what we come up with, Nana. I promise. It's going to have a very English feel to it, top to bottom. And I've got a friend helping me design a simple website. Gotta have a web presence, you know."

Maddie jumped back in. "Then I'll do the decorating—tablecloths, window treatments, even personalized aprons for all of us. I can see it all in my head—it's just a matter of pulling it all together. It's going to be *fabulous!*"

Lanie took another sip of tea, then set the cup back on the delicate saucer. "Back up a sec, Maddie. Nana's got a good point. What's the rush?"

"Yes, Maddie, why the hurry?" Jonathan asked. "We definitely want this to be done right, so where's the fire?"

Maddie wiped her mouth with her cloth napkin, blushing at the question. "No fire. Just a—I don't know—a driving desire to do it. *Now.* I've been searching for years for something to pour myself into. I'm not sure I can explain it. I just feel such an urgency on so many different levels about this. Ever since our trip to England, it's as if I've been *called* to do it—almost like a ministry. That probably sounds crazy, but it makes perfect sense to me. I guess I'm just asking you all to indulge me a little here. The sooner we open, the better." She punctuated her request with an asking smile.

"Then that's what we shall do," Nana responded. Extending her hand to Jonathan, she instructed him, "Whatever it costs, whatever she needs, Jonathan. And you heard her—the sooner, the better."

He wrapped her good hand in his, leaning over to kiss it. "Then, as Rachel so aptly put it, that's what we shall do, ladies." He patted her hand then turned to Lanie and Maddie. "We'll get started right away on the remodeling in here and in the kitchen. And I know just the man for the job—Brad Chapman. He's a contractor. Dependable, trustworthy, and he gets the job done."

"I think I know who he is," Lanie said. "Big guy? Nice tan? Thick black hair? Dimples?"

Maddie slowly tracked her attention. "So Lanie. Quite the information source on the new handyman, are we?"

"Stop with the insinuations, Maddie. I saw him at Home Depot a few weeks ago. It was no big deal. I happened to follow him out of the store and saw him get into a pickup, one of those big fancy kinds with a sign painted on the door—'Brad Chapman Construction.' No mystery, no romance, so put away your Cupid arrows, girl."

Maddie cocked her eyebrow anyway. "All the more reason to get this ball rolling!"

Ian leaned back in his chair, pushing away from the desk. His head ached from too many hours poring over his notes. He knew he could teach this subject in his sleep. *So why all the frustration?* Grabbing the crutches, he went through the routine, lifting himself from the chair and limping down the hall toward the kitchen. He stood in front of the large stainless steel refrigerator with the door open, welcoming the cool air against his skin. He reached for a chilled bottle of Pellegrino and closed the door. Moments later, seated on a wicker chair on the wide front porch, he tried to ignore the humid night air and just relax.

Resting against the soft padded cushions on the wicker, he pulled out the bottle and took a long swig of the sparkling water. The bite of the cold, bubbly liquid refreshed him instantly. He looked around, taking in the nighttime sights and sounds of the neighborhood. A dog barked in the distance. A whiff of fried chicken drifted from somewhere, and he realized he'd forgotten to eat.

When he finally allowed his eyes to venture across the street, he noticed extra cars in the driveway and lights in the front room on the left side of the house. *Must be dinner guests.* He couldn't make out any more than that through the sheers, only several folks sitting around a table appearing to have a good time. *Discussing nuclear physics, no doubt.* He chuckled at his sarcasm.

A breeze rustled the leaves above him, a sound Ian found soothing along with the faint chirping of crickets. He let his eyes close and crossed his arms across his chest. In a matter of moments, he drifted off to sleep.

He had no idea how long he'd been asleep when a commotion across the street woke him. The guests were apparently leaving—an older gentleman getting into a newer model Cadillac, and a younger, shorter one heading for a nondescript sedan parked at the curb. *Ah, the other partner in crime.*

Ian scooted down in the chair, hoping they wouldn't see him sitting on the dark porch. He could see—*Madeline, was it?*—standing at the top of her porch waving goodbye to them. When they drove off, she started back toward the front door, then did a double-take looking straight across the street at him.

"Don't see me, don't see me," he whispered, willing her back into the house. As if on cue, she paused a moment then stepped into the house. Ian blew out the breath he'd been holding, thankful she hadn't seen him.

Just as he was beginning to relax a few moments later, her door opened. Before he could move a muscle, she was half-way across the street.

"Hi neighbor. Warm night, isn't it?"

Please don't come over here and—

"I don't know where my manners are, Dr. Grant. We had guests for dinner, and I should have invited you as well."

He could see something in her hands as she gracefully walked up the steps to his porch. She was wearing a white sleeveless blouse over a pair of faded blue jeans. He couldn't help noticing how nice she looked in that blouse, her curls bouncing off the collar's edge.

"No need to apologize. I couldn't have come."

"Couldn't or wouldn't?" She sat down on the wicker swing adjacent to his chair.

"Tell me, Miss—"

"Maddie Cooper. Remember?"

"Of course. Tell me, Miss Cooper, are all American women as forward as you?"

She smiled, and he hated the way it warmed him.

"I don't consider myself forward at all, Dr. Grant. Or may I call you Ian?"

He had no clue how to respond so he didn't.

"I'm not forward, Ian. Just trying to be hospitable. Neighborly. You're in a new country, in new surroundings, all alone . . ." She pointed to his foot propped up on the small wicker table. "You're infirmed—"

"Thanks to you and your accomplice."

She dipped her head briefly. "Point well taken. All the more reason I should have invited you to dinner. But since I didn't, the least I can do is share a few of our leftovers. I hope that's not considered bad manners in England?" Her eyes sparkled even in the moonlight, accompanying her hopeful smile.

"Well, I . . . it's not considered . . . but—"

"Good. Then I shall leave them with you. Just pop the Chicken Crescents in the microwave for about a minute. There's also a Waldorf salad—apples, nuts, celery—and a couple of chess squares. I hope you like them. I'll put this in the kitchen for you then you can eat whenever you like."

With that, she disappeared inside the house. *The audacity. She just walks in like she owns the place. These Yanks have a lot to learn about etiquette.* Moments later she returned.

"It wasn't necessary. You needn't have bothered." He tried to sound pleasant enough but somehow it didn't come out that way.

She made her way to the top of the steps and began her descent. "Goodnight, Ian."

He blinked, unsure what to make of her, what to say. She turned her head, casting one final smile before crossing the street.

Goodnight . . . Maddie.

Chapter 6

Maddie lifted the kettle of hot water to fill the Spode teapot to warm it properly. Carefully sloshing the water inside before pouring it back out, she then measured the loose tea leaves into the infuser filling the air with a delightful aroma. Taking the kettle of gently boiling water again from the stove's burner, she refilled the teapot.

"There. Now we'll let it steep for six minutes then give it a try. Are you ready?"

Nana smiled, visibly happy to be Maddie's guinea pig as she practiced her new skills. "Ready when you are."

Maddie picked up one of the delicately painted teacups. "Aren't these beautiful?"

"They truly are. Who could have known that my little hobby, collecting teacups from around the world, would someday come in handy for you like this?"

"Are you sure you're okay with us using them? You know there's a good chance a few might get chipped or broken."

"Good heavens, yes. What good are they stored away in the attic or collecting dust around here? And a chip here and there only adds character—to teacups *and* old ladies," she mused, pointing to her useless left arm.

"You're a character, all right. I've known that my whole life," Maddie teased.

"I'm only trying to keep up with *you,* young lady." Nana laughed again, her crooked smile as enchanting as ever.

"I've got a couple dozen new ones on order from that little shop in Chawton. The place where I found that gorgeous cup and saucer I brought back with me?"

"I love the deep, rich shades of red on that one. Plus, you know I'm always partial to the ones with gold touches. It's absolutely stunning."

"Isn't it though? Although the ones I've ordered are a variety—all different kinds. No two alike."

"That makes each one so special."

"Okay, okay, let's get back to work here. Is your cup still warm? According to my research, the best 'cuppa' is one that is served in a warmed teacup."

"Warmed and ready to go," Nana obliged. "What flavor are we having today?"

"This is an English Breakfast Tea. Pour your cream first, Nana. That's the proper way—*before* I pour the tea."

"I know. I remember." Nana poured a splash of cream into her cup then set the chilled creamer back on the table. "Hope we finish this before the workers get here. They're like a bunch of bulls in a china shop." She chuckled. "A *real* china shop, in this case."

Nothing pleased Maddie more than the sound of her grandmother's laughter. Coming from one who could have chosen never to laugh again, it was music to her ears. She checked her watch. "Six minutes exactly. Any longer and we risk a bitter tea. That's because the longer it steeps, the better the chance for Tannin to be extracted from the tea leaves. 'Bitter stuff, that Tannin.'"

"I was wondering when the accent would show up," Nana feigned.

"Hush. This is a Taylors of Harrogate tea. Their teas were voted *Best Cup of Tea in England.* I've decided to use them exclusively. And if I've done my homework correctly and made this pot to specifications, it should be superb. *Utterly superb.*"

"Yes, *Eliza.*"

"Only the best for our customers, right? Okay, here we go."

Maddie poured from the hand-painted teapot, first into Nana's cup, then into her own. Following each sip, they discussed the flavor and quality of the tea giving today's sample two thumbs up. Maddie added their comments to the list of other flavors they'd sampled over the past week.

Finally, she sat back to read over her notes. "Seems we both enjoyed the Earl Grey, the English breakfast, the Lemon and Herb Tisane, and the Scottish Breakfast tea. I liked the Peppermint Tisane, you did not. You liked the Raspberry and Rosehip Tisane, I did not. And we both *loved* the Yorkshire Gold. And during the holidays we'll offer the Spiced Christmas tea—remember how good it smelled?"

"My goodness, what a lot of teas to keep up with. How will your customers—"

"*Our* customers."

"How will *our* customers know what to choose?"

"Lanie will include a description of each flavor we offer on a page in our menu. She's already doing a mock-up for us. I'm hoping she'll bring a rough draft when she stops by after work. I found some gorgeous watercolors of teacups and English gardens, that sort of thing, by an art student at UT. She was thrilled when I offered to pay her for the prints to use on our menu. We'll write a blurb about her on the back. Remind me to show those to you later, will you?"

Nana pushed the lever to roll her chair back. "I will, but for now you must excuse me. I think I'll go rest for a while."

"I'll help you lie down," Maddie followed, taking their cups to the sink.

"You'll do no such thing. Gretchen will be happy to help me. Gretchen?" she called, rolling into the hall.

"Right here, Rachel. Ready for your morning nap?"

Maddie watched as the plump, cheerful nurse greeted Nana with a ready smile. In the weeks since her return from England, she'd come to love the newest member of their family. Gretchen's warm personality made for a relaxed atmosphere despite the chaos of all the renovations. Maddie couldn't imagine how they'd managed without her all these years.

"Sweet dreams, Nana. I'll go over our sandwich menu with you after lunch, okay?"

"Howdy, Miss Cooper."

"Oh!" Maddie turned as Brad Chapman walked through the back door. "Oh, hello, Brad—I didn't hear the door open. You gave me a start! How are you this morning?"

Clearing the table, Maddie took a good look at her contractor. He was definitely a man to behold—tall, muscular, tanned, and unusually polite. Quite the gentleman, in fact.

"Fine, thank you. And you?"

"Fine as well," she answered playfully. "Would you like a cup of tea? I have a delightful English Breakfast tea that's quite good."

Brad's face broadened in a smile. "That's kind of you to ask, Miss Cooper. But no, I'll have to pass. I want to finish that built-in hutch this morning before I start in here. The industrial refrigerator and stove should be delivered today."

"Oh, that's great! I can't wait to see how they're going to fit."

"They'll fit real good, Miss Cooper. You have my word. Now if you'll excuse me, I'll head on into the dining room to work. The rest of the crew should be here any minute." He tipped his ball cap, a gesture she always found amusing, and disappeared into the hall.

Yes, Mr. Chapman, I do believe it's time I arrange a little rendezvous for you with Miss Lanie Morgan . . .

As Maddie continued washing the dishes, she remembered how Lanie had scoffed at her the first time she mentioned setting the two of them up.

"Are you crazy? A guy like that? Interested in a girl like me? What are you, blind? Besides, Maddie, I think I may be falling in love with Jeff. He says, and I quote, he's 'crazy about me.' Isn't that incredible?

And he writes the *most* romantic emails. I've saved every one of them. I've never met anyone quite like him."

"That's because you've never *met* him!" Maddie recognized the love-struck look in Lanie's eyes, and it made her shudder. She wasn't about to let her best friend fall for some nerd permanently affixed to his computer. "C'mon, Lanie, don't be ridiculous. Online romances are a joke. Brad Chapman is the real deal. Not to mention the fact that he's *here,* not off in cyberspace oblivion. I mean, c'mon, Lanie. Have you *looked* at the guy?"

Maddie knew best, if only Lanie would listen to her! She'd initiated several "coincidental" meetings between Lanie and Brad, inviting her to stop by on the way home from work knowing Brad would still be working. She'd insist they sit down for a cup of tea together before he left. His deep voice and quick sense of humor always made for a good time. Gradually, over the course of time, Lanie had warmed to the idea, responding to Brad's good manners and easy laugh.

No overtures of romance yet, but that will come if I do my part. Her mind wandered along a similar path until it landed right across the street.

And then there's the elusive Dr. Grant. There's got to be someone I can send his way. Maddie hadn't seen much of her new neighbor. Occasionally she'd wave as he left the house for the campus. He had traded his crutches for a cane, still limping as he made his way down the sidewalk. Sometimes he returned her wave, but most often not. She had ventured over to visit him a couple of times, but he'd maintained the same wall of defense. Several times she'd left a basket of cookies or muffins on his porch table. She would send him an invitation for her grand opening, but doubted seriously he would show up. *Unless . . . unless I can find someone to accompany the stodgy professor?*

Maddie snapped out of her musings and dried her hands on her apron, acknowledging the smile on her face. Her thoughts skipped back to Lanie and Brad, the vision of a candlelit dinner . . .

"You 'n me, God. We're quite a team."

Several weeks later, Maddie crossed the commons of the UT campus headed for Perry-Castañeda Library. In an hour she would meet with Lanie on her lunch break to go over advertising copy for the tea room. Until then, she hoped to do some research about Chawton to verify what she'd learned while touring Jane Austen's quaint English cottage. Knowing the library's layout, she quickly made her way to the sixth floor which housed the English literature section.

Browsing the familiar shelves, she found a couple of books then looked for a table. As she rounded the corner, she was startled to see her neighbor seated at a long table, pouring over a thick volume beneath a green desk light.

"Why, hello Ian," she greeted nonchalantly. Depositing her books across from him, she pulled out a chair and sat down.

Deep in thought, he finally looked up. "Oh, yes well, hello." His eyes darted around, much like those of a trapped animal, then back to his book. Maddie noticed a blush creeping up his face. He sighed impatiently then grunted, "What brings you here, Miss Cooper?"

He remembered my name. "Just doing some research for my tea room. I've decided to name it *The Chawton Tea Room* in honor of—"

"For your beloved Miss Austen's home in Chawton, just outside of Alton, Hampshire." He never looked up, tossing the comment at her like discarded change. "Big surprise there."

Maddie wasn't sure what to make of it. *You're not going to provoke me, Ian Grant.* "Regardless, I wanted to tell you I'll be sending you an invitation once we're ready to open. Probably sometime in early November."

Ian turned a page, clearly attempting to ignore her.

"I hope you'll join us. And, just so you know, you're more than welcome to bring someone."

Nothing.

"A friend. A date. Whatever."

He leveled his eyes at her, shutting the thick volume with a loud thud. "A date? Miss Cooper, I am not—"

"Oh, why must you keep playing the martyr? I've apologized every way I know how. I've made every effort to show my remorse." She paused for effect, then folded her hands on top of her open book. "I simply want to be friends. Is that too much to ask?" she added quietly.

"Why on earth would you care to be friends with me? Just because I'm residing across the lane from you does not demand we be *chummy.*"

Maddie pushed her hair out of her face. "Because I can sense your loneliness. I see the sadness in your eyes, and I want somehow to make you feel more at home here."

Ian stood, grabbing his book. "Is that a proposition, Miss Cooper? You think I'm so lonely, I'd accept your company just so I won't be 'lonely' anymore? You're even more delusional than I thought."

"No, wait! That's not what I meant at all!" Maddie whispered loudly, standing as he started to walk away. "Please! This is exactly what I'm talking about—why must you still be so angry with me? And why must you reject my gesture of friendship—and that's *all* it is, Ian. Nothing more, I assure you."

He paused, then turned to look at her. Maddie felt his blue eyes bore into her soul, but she fought the urge to look away. *Why oh why must he be so handsome?* As he stepped toward her, she felt her heart pounding inside her chest.

Finally, standing mere inches from her, he opened his mouth to speak, then stopped. His eyes searched hers as if conflicted. Then his stern countenance softened before he broke eye contact and blew out another sigh. "Look, Miss Cooper—"

"Maddie."

A sad smile attempted to reach his eyes. "I don't wish to be rude. But I'm not . . . you see, it's simply that . . ." He exhaled, standing straighter. The vulnerability vanished. "I appreciate the invitation, but I'm much too busy. Good day."

She watched him limp away, somewhat relieved to see he no longer used a cane, but disappointed in the exchange. *Oh, what must I do to reach you, Ian Grant? And how can I help heal your wounded heart if you won't break down that wall and let me in?*

Let someone *else* in, that is.

Chapter 7

Ian Grant gathered his papers from the podium. "Test on chapter eight tomorrow. Papers on Samuel Johnson are due next Friday. And yes, that is the day after Halloween, but I'll make no exceptions for hung-over ghosts and goblins. Consider yourself warned. Good day." His students filed out of the lecture hall, the usual cluster of those wishing for his attention gathering around him. Normally, he would try to spark the students in debate about his lecture, but today he had plans.

"You'll have to excuse me. I'll be available in the conference room for further discussion after three o'clock this afternoon. Now if you'll make way, please."

The chatter followed him out of the classroom and down the hall, gradually dissipating as he stepped into his office. His assistant, Jennifer Simms, stood as he rushed by her desk.

"Dr. Martin called. He says they're ready for you over at the luncheon. And here are your phone messages."

After depositing his briefcase and books on his desk, he whisked back through the outer office. "Just put those on my desk, please. And give Howard a ring. Tell him I'll be there in less than five."

"Yes, Dr. Grant."

"I'll be back around two-thirty. See you then."

He headed across the commons toward the administrative building. Howard had insisted Ian attend the luncheon for faculty members in the English department. Not one for social gatherings, Ian would have preferred his usual sandwich in his office, but Howard would not be deterred.

Relieved to be rid of the cane, Ian hurried his pace despite the pesky limp. His foot was still a tad tender, but much improved. He hoped the doctor would give him clearance to start running again soon. He had missed his morning runs dreadfully.

Ian made his way to the private dining room in the rear of the building on the first floor. He could hear the clinking of silver on fine china and the low murmur typical of academicians in social settings.

"Ian! Over here, my good man. Nice to have you join us." Howard Martin closed the space between them, extending his hand.

"Thank you, Howard. You promised a good meal, so here I am,"

Ian teased, shaking hands. "As long as it's not one of those ghastly casseroles so popular in the cafeteria, I'm a happy chap."

"Not a chance," Martin chuckled. "Prime rib that will melt in your mouth. But first I want to introduce you to some of our other new staff members."

Ian played the game, exchanging pleasantries. Some were names familiar to him, others not. Soon they were all seated and lunch was served. The food was top shelf as promised, much to Ian's surprise. Even the generous slice of New York cheesecake caught his fancy, urging him to leave room for a taste.

Halfway through his meal, Howard interrupted the quiet conversation, scooting his chair back and stepping toward the entrance behind Ian. "Ah, there she is—Melissa, how good of you to come!"

"Howard! So good to see you again! How is Roberta?"

Ian stopped chewing, his fork suspended in mid-air. *It can't be.* He tried to swallow, lowering the utensil to his plate, then attempted to wipe his mouth with the linen napkin. Ian braced himself as the chatter neared him. Only then did he notice the empty seat across the table.

"Ladies and gentlemen, please allow me to introduce our new interim professor who will be taking Dr. Smith's classes until he is able to return from the Anderson Clinic. This is Dr. Melissa Phillips, formerly of Vanderbilt University, bringing us her expertise on women authors of the eighteenth century."

The men at the table stood as Dr. Phillips followed Howard to the empty seat next to him. "Please, gentlemen, have a seat. I apologize for my late arrival. There was a nasty pileup on the interstate and it simply couldn't be helped."

Ian stood half-way, the prime rib lodged in his throat refusing to go down. Once seated again, he reached for the crystal glass of iced water, praying for relief and avoiding eye contact.

"Dr. Phillips, I'm sure you know many of your colleagues around the table. Allow me to make formal introductions." Howard went around the table, thankfully starting the other direction, giving Ian time to compose himself. He felt the heat on his face.

"And finally, Dr. Ian Grant, our esteemed visiting professor on loan to us from Oxford University."

"Ian?"

He coughed, finally clearing his throat, then lifted his eyes to meet hers. "Melissa, nice to see you."

"What a surprise—I had no idea you were here in Austin. I'm—it's nice to see you again."

"Yes, well. Here we are." The heat continued to scorch his face.

Smile. Force the smile. "I too had no idea you were joining the faculty here." He pinned Howard with a look to kill.

"Oh dear," Howard groaned, his eyes darting back and forth between them, obviously remembering too late the former relationship between his two guests. "That is to say, I, uh, yes, well. You see, Dr. Phillips was gracious enough to shorten her sabbatical to cover Dr. Smith's classes. We have no idea how long his chemo-therapy treatment will last, and since Melissa was in the area working on her new book, we were fortunate to convince her to take a couple of his classes." He stopped rambling for a moment then added, "Well now, isn't this nice?"

The conversation resumed, others dominating Melissa's attention, much to Ian's relief. His heart pounded, the hot anger quickly racing through his veins. Teeth clenched, he fought the eruption of old memories and still-open wounds. For the remainder of the meal, he picked at his food, chastising himself for letting her affect him this way after all these years.

The tall pillar of cheesecake remained untouched.

Maddie gazed around her new kitchen. The freshly painted walls in a soft yellow called *Butter Cream* created the perfect, soothing ambience she would need for her culinary efforts. The white lace curtains allowed plenty of sunshine to stream through the pane-glass windows. She ran her hand over the cool marble countertop on the huge center island, dreaming of the delicacies she would create here. Appreciating the new cabinets banking the walls, she realized what a miracle Brad had pulled off in just a matter of weeks.

"Brad!" She looked at her watch then grabbed the phone, quickly dialing Lanie's number.

"Lanie, where are you? He'll be back in just a few minutes! I thought you were going to be here for tea?"

"I'm coming, I'm sorry! I was talking with Jeff and lost track of time."

Maddie felt her teeth grinding. "Lanie, will you forget about him? I really think Brad likes you. So hurry up! I want you here before he gets back. Get your sweet bum over here!"

She hung up the phone, again irritated by the mention of the California nerd. *I'm finally getting you and Brad connected and here you go, wasting more time with that stupid geek. When will you ever learn to trust me, girl?*

Her gentle nudges to bring Lanie and Brad together had gone according to plan. She'd actually been hearing less about Jeff and more about the handsome contractor from her friend. "I have to admit he's fun to be with," Lanie had admitted on more than one occasion. "He's got the funniest sense of humor. And is he buff or what?"

Maddie observed the growing excitement in Lanie's eyes each time she *happened* to stop by when he was done for the day. She loved watching her respond to his impeccable manners. Their laughter over tea or lemonade filled Maddie's heart with joy. *Just a matter of time, those two.*

Half an hour later, Maddie heard Lanie's voice at the front door.

"Maddie, I'm here! Sorry I'm late. I was on fumes and had to stop for gas which took way longer than it should have. Maddie? Hello?"

"Back here, Lanie. Come see my new appliances!"

Squealing like a school girl, Maddie greeted her best friend with a hug. "Look! Our refrigerator and stove were just delivered! Aren't they unbelievable?"

"Oh wow, they're *huge*—you could store a side of beef in there."

"Well, hi Lanie. How are you?"

Lanie lit up at the sound of Brad's voice. "Fine, Brad. How about you?"

Maddie watched her take in Brad's appearance. His worn jeans fit him like a glove as did the white t-shirt stretched across his chest. *Show me any computer geek who looks this good.*

Brad tipped his ball cap and started for the door. "I'm good. But if you two will excuse me, I need to be going."

"No! Brad, wait," Maddie said. "I was hoping you'd have tea with us today."

"Thank you, but I have a meeting with an architect in about an hour. I appreciate the offer, though. See you tomorrow. Bye, Lanie," he said, giving her a wink before closing the door.

"Did you see that?" Maddie whispered. "He winked at you! Lanie, hurry—run out there and catch him before he leaves!"

"Why? What would I say?" She peeked out the door.

"Invite him to meet you at Starbucks later. Tell him you have something you want to talk to him about. Anything! Just go. Go!" Maddie pushed her out the door then dashed to the open window overlooking Brad's truck. She hid out of sight, peeking through the curtains.

"Brad! Wait up!"

Maddie watched as Lanie hurried down the driveway, catching up to him just as he climbed in the cab of his pickup.

"What's up?" he asked, tossing his cap on the passenger seat and ruffling his hair.

Ask him, Lanie. Ask him. Be brave, girlfriend!

"I was just wondering, would you—well, if you're not too busy sometime, could we—could I buy you a cup of coffee at Starbucks later tonight? There's something I'd like to talk to you about."

Atta girl! You did it!

"I'm afraid not."

Maddie's heart sunk. *What?*

"Oh, that's okay," Lanie answered. "No problem. Just thought I'd—"

"I can't let *you* buy, but I'd be happy to meet you later at Starbucks. My treat."

Maddie shot her fists in the air. *Yessss!*

"How does eight-thirty work for you?"

Lanie smiled, laughing her response. "Eight-thirty would be lovely. See you there."

Maddie danced a jig around the kitchen island. "Do I know a match when I see it? Am I a genius or what? Move over, Emma Woodhouse. You have met your match." She laughed out loud. "Met your match. Get it? Oh I'm good. I'm *really* good."

Ian wrung out the white washcloth, its steam swirling into the air. He placed it back across his forehead then sunk deeper into the tub. The whirlpool jets pounded his body, matching the rhythm of his throbbing temples. He shook his head, trying to block it all out. Trying to wipe her from his memory . . . all over again.

Another pounding woke him from his drowsy melancholy. He turned off the jets, listening. Someone was knocking on the door, the doorbell chiming repeatedly. "Go away!" Still the knocking continued, the doorbell incessant.

"All right, all right. I'm coming." He toweled off then wrapped his robe around him before heading down the hall, leaving wet footprints on the hardwood floor. He stopped cold. Melissa stood on the other side of the door, her face visible through the beveled glass inset.

He turned around. "I'm not home."

The knocking continued. "Ian, let me in. We have to talk."

"No we don't. I'm not here. Remember?"

"Ian!"

"Halloween's not until next week. You'll have to come back."

"Stop acting like a child and open this door."

How dare she! He bolted for the door, throwing it open. "What could you possibly want?"

"I—just let me in. We have to talk."

"I don't think so."

She lifted her chin in defiance, pushing the door open wider then stepping by him. "Stop this ridiculous behavior. We can at least be civil toward one another."

"Can we?"

"Of course we can. And for heaven's sake, close the door. You're in a bath robe in case you haven't noticed."

Without breaking eye contact, he shoved the door. The resulting slam felt good as he strode past her into the living room. "So what is it you want to say to me, Dr. Halston—or wait, *Phillips,* is it now?" Ian claimed the easy chair beside the fire-place, propping his foot on the ottoman. "Married, are we?"

"Five years. With a four-year old daughter named Isabelle." She walked across the room, placed her purse on the sofa, then took a seat.

"How nice. Isn't that just lovely. And here I thought all this time you didn't much like the idea of marriage. What with all that *commitment* rubbish and what not. Silly, silly me. I'm *so* very happy for you. In fact, if I wasn't so busy, I'd ask to see pictures, but alas, I just *don't* have the time." He drilled her with his eyes, hoping to make her squirm.

She studied her fingers. He didn't miss the large oval diamond on her left hand. "Ian, I never meant to—"

"Spare me. I don't want to hear it. Not a word, Melissa."

She looked up again with pleading eyes. "You never responded after I sent you all those letters. I hoped you would, though I know it must have been painful."

"Painful? You left me *standing* at the altar! In front of all our friends and family, standing there like a complete and utter fool. And you think it might have been *painful?* Your mother appears at the back of the church only to say you've 'changed your mind' and there won't be a wedding after all. I haven't a clue in the world why anyone should think it might be *painful* for me? Least of all YOU!"

"Ian, calm down and listen to me."

"No. I will not listen to you."

"Fine. Don't listen. But there are things I must say to you. I *couldn't* marry you. Our engagement was my parents' wish and not mine. Surely you know that. The college professor marrying the daughter of the chancellor. I tried to deny my feelings, tried to make everyone happy, but in the end, I couldn't go through with it. The dress, the flowers, the music—suddenly it all hit me—it was nothing but a charade to please everyone but me. I *adored* you, Ian, truly I did. But I didn't love you. I mean, not in that way. It wouldn't have been fair to you. Not fair at all."

He stared into the fire, refusing to look at her.

"You never read my letters, did you?"

He shook his head, despising the sting in his eyes.

"You must have hated me all these years. I can't blame you, of course. What I did was deplorable."

"Quite."

"That's why I was so surprised to see you today. I thought you surely hated all Americans after what I did. Yet here you were, back teaching in the states again."

She stood and walked toward the front windows. "I'm not asking for your forgiveness. I'm in no position to do that after all these years." She turned to face him. "But here we are, both in the same town, working on the same campus. In *Texas* of all places. There must be some way we can at least be cordial to one another."

The grandfather clock ticked quietly. He closed his eyes, willing them to clear. After several moments, he realized she was seated again across from him.

"Ian."

Her voice, graveled with emotion, pricked at his heart. He inhaled loudly, pulling his feet off the ottoman. "Not to worry, Dr. *Phillips.* I assure you I'll remain completely professional at all times." He stood, walking toward the foyer. "Now, if you'll excuse me, my bath water is getting cold."

She followed him to the door, pausing as she neared him. He leveled his gaze at her, steeling the storm of emotions inside.

"Ian? Please?" she whispered, a lone tear cascading down her face.

"Good night, Melissa."

The silence was palpable. Finally, she reached out her hand against his face then pressed a long kiss against his cheek. With that, she left, descending the porch stairs into the night.

Chapter 8

Maddie watched the car pull away from the curb in front of Bradford House. Sitting on her porch, she pulled her sweater around her against the evening chill, and reached for her cup of tea. Her pulse quickened, replaying the scene in her mind. She'd felt like an intruder when the door across the street had opened. But had she moved to go inside, she surely would have been noticed. The backlighting of the foyer chandelier had cast Ian and his lady friend in silhouettes as if some Hollywood director had created the romantic effect.

She fought the desire to be happy for the professor, hoping he might have some secret love after all. But there was something about the exchange that told her otherwise.

He was in his bath robe. Rather familiar apparel for a mere acquaintance. Who is she? And why didn't he respond when she kissed him?

The cell phone in her sweater pocket vibrated. "Hello?"

"Maddie, you won't believe what has happened. Jeff and I had a horrible fight. I told him I was going to meet Brad for coffee, and he got so upset! *Really* upset. What am I going to do?"

Lanie's sniffles filled her ear. Maddie looked at her watch. "Wait, aren't you supposed to be meeting Brad right now?"

"I know. I was just getting ready to leave when Jeff Skyped me. Oh why did I even tell him? I had no idea he would mind. And now I may have lost him forever. Maddie, I can't see Brad right now. I'm a wreck!"

Lanie blew her nose, causing Maddie to distance the tiny cell phone from her ear. "No! You have to go! Lanie, Brad is probably already there waiting for you. And besides, if Jeff is such a wimp that a little thing like coffee with a friend upsets him, do you really want a relationship with someone like that? Of course not. Now, go wash your face, get in your car and get over to Starbucks. Go!"

Maddie turned off her phone, slipping it back in her pocket. "Oh Lord, what am I going to do with these people? If they'd just listen to me—to You, I mean."

"Lanie! I was beginning to worry I'd misunderstood when we were to meet. Hey, are you okay?" Brad stood, pulling the bistro chair out for her.

She took a seat, avoiding his eyes. "Um, sure. I just, I think maybe I have a little cold coming on or something. Or maybe allergies. I must look awful."

"Not at all. I was just about to order a cappuccino. Would you like one?"

"Sure. Whatever you're having is fine with me."

Brad placed their order at the counter, smiling back at her a couple of times while waiting for the barista to make their drinks. Lanie used the time to sneak a peek in her compact, applying a dab of powder beneath her eyes to hide the redness. Brad returned a few minutes later, setting their drinks on the table.

"Thank you." She popped the lid off her cup. "It smells wonderful."

"It'll probably keep us up all night, but who cares, right?"

Lanie tried to laugh. "Right. Who cares?"

Brad took a sip, then wiped the whipped cream from his upper lip with a napkin. "So what is it you wanted to talk to me about?"

Lanie looked into his sable brown eyes, studied his broad smile and strong jaw line, and wondered what he must think of her. He was strikingly handsome. *He's probably Mr. October on some calendar of hunky Texas construction guys. What's he doing here with someone like me? Maddie, why did you put me up to this?*

"Lanie?"

"Oh, sorry. Um, well—wait, didn't you say you had something to ask me too? You go first. I insist." *Good thinking. Buy some time.*

"All right, if that's your preference. See, the thing is, I've been working for your friend Maddie now for almost two months. And I've noticed, no matter what time of day or night I'm there, she never seems to have—well, what I mean is—is Maddie seeing anyone?"

"What?" Lanie blinked.

"Is Maddie dating anyone right now? Because if she's not, I was thinking about asking her out."

"Maddie? You want to ask Maddie out?"

His smile vanished. "Why? Is there something wrong with that? Is she married or something?"

"No! Maddie's not married!" Lanie heard the harsh response leave her lips. *Deep breath. Think. Think! He's not interested in me. He likes Maddie. How could I have been so blind?*

"So . . . is there some reason I shouldn't ask her out? Do you think she'd go if I did?"

Lanie stared at him. Same beautiful brown eyes. Same masculine jaw line. Same kind smile. *What an idiot I am. To even think he might go for the plain and simple. Oh no! Someone with looks like his? Of course he'd fall for someone beautiful. I'm such an idiot!*

Lanie stood up, grabbing her purse from the table. She forced a smile. "Yes, Brad. I think Maddie would *love* to go out with you. In a heartbeat! But I just remembered I, uh, I left a candle burning in my apartment. Don't want to burn down the building." She swallowed a sob. "Thank you for the cappuccino. Really." She dashed for the door, biting her lip to hold back the dam inside.

"But Lanie, wait! What did you want to talk to me about?"

"He WHAT?!"

Maddie jumped to her feet. Lanie's words slammed into her like a freight train. "You can't be serious! He asked you about *me*? Oh no, no! This is all wrong!"

Lanie collapsed on the sofa, burying her face in her hands. "This is all your fault. I knew better than to listen to you!" She looked up, her tear-streaked face breaking Maddie's heart. "All these afternoon teas together, all these coincidental encounters and—" She blew her nose into her tissue.

"Oh Lanie, I feel terrible!"

Lanie honked again into a fresh tissue. "*You* feel terrible? Oh, please. Pardon me if I have no sympathy for you right now."

Maddie slid beside her on the sofa, wrapping her arm over her shoulder. "No, Lanie, I didn't mean that. Well, yes, of course I did! This *is* all my fault. I should never have pushed you into something you weren't ready for."

Lanie pushed away from her. "Something I wasn't *ready* for? No, Maddie. I will *never* be ready for someone to manipulate my feelings like that. I came so close to spilling my guts, asking Brad if he'd like to go out some time. Asking him if he would consider dating me. Do you have any idea how embarrassing that would have been for me? I *never* ask guys out! You know that. But because you kept pushing and arranging all these happenstance meetings, and telling me how even a gorgeous man like that 'can see a good heart' like mine—wasn't that how you put it? Because we both know a guy like that could *never* be attracted to a wall flower like me, right?"

"Lanie, no! I never said that. You've got it all wrong!" Maddie cried openly, her own tears spilling done her cheeks. "You're my best friend in the whole world! I would never do anything to hurt you! You must surely know that?"

Lanie stood up and stomped across the room. "Never hurt me? Well, let's see. If I have my accounting correct tonight, this makes *two* relationships you've ruined for me. Not just Brad, who was obviously never interested in me in the first place, but let's not forget Jeff. Maddie, you may think he's some computer geek, but the fact is, I care for him. And up until tonight, he cared for me. In fact, I hadn't told you this because I knew you didn't want to hear it. But last week, he told me he loved me. Imagine that. Some guy out there—*loves* me!" Lanie sobbed. "At least he did until tonight.

"So excuse me, Madeline Cooper, if I take a permanent pass on your so-called friendship. I've had just about all of you I can stand! I am DONE with you!" She slammed the door, rattling the windows and pictures hanging on the wall.

"Good heavens! What happened?"

The whir of Nana's wheelchair rounded the corner. "Oh Nana, I've made such a horrible mess of things. Lanie will never speak to me again as long as she lives."

The whole miserable story spilled out through Maddie's tears, her grandmother listening patiently until there was nothing left to say. She reached for Maddie's hand, brought it to her lips and kissed it gently.

"Madeline, it's time you and I had a little heart to heart."

"I'm such a wretch!"

"Yes, you are. We *all* are from time to time. The question is, what are you going to do about it? Will you keep making the same mistakes over and over, or will you learn from them?"

"But all I ever meant to do was help Lanie find happiness. She's never been in a serious relationship before. Doesn't she deserve a little happiness?"

"Did she *ask* you to find happiness for her, dear?"

Maddie wiped her eyes with the embroidered handkerchief her grandmother had loaned her. "No, but she never would."

"And correct me if I'm wrong, but don't I recall Lanie lighting up like a Christmas tree each time she mentions this fellow she met on her computer? A fellow Jane Austen admirer? Why, they must have so much in common. So many things to talk about."

"You don't understand. She's never *met* him. He's probably some ugly, wimpy little nerd who can't find love any other way."

"Oh, so you've met him?'

"No, of course not."

The silence passed between them until Maddie finally looked up at her grandmother, realizing she was trying to make a point. "What?"

"Sweetheart, the Bible says, 'Many are the plans in a man's heart, but it is the Lord's purpose that prevails.'"

"But that's just it! I felt God calling me to this ministry, helping people find love. And I've prayed every step of the way. We've had a partnership, of sorts, me and God."

"Have you now." It wasn't a question, but a spoken doubt.

Maddie thought back through the past weeks, remembering her talks with the Lord. She quickly realized that's *all* they were. She talked to God, mostly telling Him what her plans were, rarely asking about His.

Nana reached out to push back the dampened hair from Maddie's face. "I'll leave you to think about that awhile. And let me suggest one more thing. Perhaps you need to give Lanie a little credit. She's a bright girl. She'll know love when she finds it. *Without* your help."

Chapter 9

Ian slapped his alarm clock, groaning at the red digits. Six o'clock. Suddenly he remembered why he'd planned to get up so early. He jumped out of bed and dressed quickly in his sweats and running shoes. After a swig of orange juice, he headed for the front door, anxious to stretch out his muscles and commence his long-awaited run.

Just inside the door, a large manila envelope rested on the floor just below the mail slot. Ian clenched his jaw, seeing his name in the familiar script. *Can't you just leave well enough alone?*

He tore open the envelope, dumping its contents onto the table beside the door. Two identical FOB keys on a BMW key ring fell out. "What in the . . . good heavens!" He opened the door, stunned to find the black Beamer he had bought Melissa as a wedding present sitting in the driveway. "Now I know she's lost her mind."

Unfolding the letter, his eyes raced through the paragraphs.

Dear Ian,

I had hoped we might find some peace at long last, but I'm afraid I've only caused you more unhappiness. Unfortunately, we have unfinished business and I know no other way to handle it.

Once I heard you'd returned to England after I called off the wedding, I had no idea how to return the car. When you refused to answer my letters, I finally decided to put the car in storage back in Nashville and deal with it later. There it remained until our recent move here. My husband never understood why I didn't just sell it, but I knew it wasn't mine to sell.

The enclosed papers make it yours again, along with the keys. If you'll do nothing else, please accept the car that rightfully belongs to you.

There's something else I must tell you. Not long ago, I gave my heart to the Lord, Ian. It has made all the difference in my life. But one thing I have learned is that unforgiveness will destroy you. As the saying goes, "To forgive is to set a prisoner free and discover that the prisoner was you."

I pray you will find it in your heart to forgive me, Ian,

whether we ever speak again or not. God alone can help you let go of the bitterness you hold against me and learn to love again.

As God is my witness, that is my prayer for you.

Melissa

Ian dropped the letter on the table and stepped outside. Taking a seat on top of the porch stairs, he stared at the pristine automobile. A rush of memories coursed through his mind tugging his emotions along for the ride. The internal battles he'd fought. The mind games. The burning heat of bitterness poisoning his every thought.

So many years. So many wasted years.

And then Melissa's words repeated themselves. *To forgive is to set a prisoner free and discover that the prisoner was you.* And without a moment's hesitation, he knew. He just *knew.* The time had finally come.

As his feet pounded the sidewalks of Hyde Park, Ian reflected on those lost years. The blasted restlessness that forever ate away at him. The hopelessness that covered him like a hot blanket on a blistering summer's day. And the brusqueness for which he'd become known, a characteristic so utterly unfamiliar to his personality—at least until Melissa so publicly humiliated him. It had settled upon him so completely, he'd been unable to shake it. All these years later, it still plagued him, like the all-encompassing role of an actor playing the part of an ill-tempered grouch. But unlike an actor merely playing a part, he couldn't let go of the stranger he'd become.

As he turned the corner and trekked his way through the quaint neighborhood, Ian realized something was going on inside him. Quite an odd feeling, actually. He pushed himself harder, ignoring the slight remnant of pain in his foot, and allowed himself to search his heart for answers.

Could it be Melissa was right? Had theirs had been an engagement of social peer pressure and not a legitimate result of true love? *No, of course not. I loved her dearly. With all my heart.*

But even as the thought marched through his head, he knew it wasn't completely true. He cared for her. Deeply. There was never any question of that. And perhaps at some point that affection grew into love. But was it the kind of love that would have lasted a lifetime? Was it worthy of the vow he nearly took—*til death do us part?*

A strange ache washed over him. He slowed to a trot, wondering why he felt this way. Then it hit him.

Good heavens. It's true.

And just that fast, he knew. Without a trace of doubt, he knew

Melissa was right. They had almost married for all the wrong reasons.

If she hadn't been the chancellor's daughter, I never would have asked her out in the first place. If we hadn't dazzled the university community as the "perfect couple," I would never have proposed.

Ouch. The realization smarted like a slap in the face. Sure, Melissa was beautiful. And smart. And funny. But she was also a daddy's girl. And Daddy still ruled, no matter where she might have roosted. At the time, the attention and notoriety made it all intoxicating and appealing. At least on some level. And if he was completely honest, he'd fantasized about climbing the academic ladder and one day succeeding his father-in-law as chancellor of prestigious Vanderbilt University.

But now, with the cleansing clarity of unabashed truth rushing through his veins, he knew he never could have lived in Dr. Halston's domineering shadow. Perhaps the marriage would have lasted a year or two. But only if he became a dutiful, family puppet.

He slowed, coming to a stop, more winded than he'd been in years. He leaned over, hands on his knees as he tried to catch his breath. He closed his eyes, imagining Melissa in her wedding gown that fated day. He pictured her in the bridal suite at the church, standing before a full-length mirror. He watched as her eyes, hidden beneath the veil, slowly tracked upward until she faced herself directly in the reflection.

She knew. She knew . . .

And she couldn't do it to me.

She loved me enough to let me go.

Ian stood, then stumbled against a nearby tree as a sob escaped from his throat, catching him completely off guard. *Dear God, she knew. She did it for* me. *And all these years I've hated her, despised her for embarrassing me. Oh God, forgive me. How did I get it all so wrong?*

He slid down the tree, landing in a heap on the dying grass. He dropped his head in his hands and felt the tears fall. He couldn't find the words, but somehow he knew God heard his heart. Filled with shame, he could only ask for forgiveness, over and over. For hating her. For wasting so many years of his life filled with that hate. And for spreading a little of it on everyone he met.

To forgive is to set a prisoner free and discover that the prisoner was you. The words echoed through his soul again. But this time, they felt less like an indictment and more like a soothing balm.

He leaned his head back against the tree, looking up through the almost-bare branches. A breeze danced through the remaining leaves, seeming to shake them just for good measure. As he squinted against the morning sun, he watched one of the shriveled, surviving leaves give up the fight and let go. It floated downward, first this way then that, finally coming to rest just beside him.

A sign. A vivid picture.

He'd let go too. After all these years, he'd finally let go. He was no longer a prisoner of his own making anymore.

He was *free*.

He picked up the leaf and twirled it by the stem, uttering a prayer of thanks. It had been a long, long time since he'd prayed. In fact, he couldn't remember the last time. But in his new-found freedom, he felt surprisingly close to the God he'd ignored for so many decades. As if the Almighty Himself was listening to every word he prayed. Especially the ones he eventually whispered as he invited God back into his life.

Half an hour and a phone call later, Ian Grant experienced the incomparable sweet release of complete forgiveness and a new beginning.

Maddie and Lanie kept a cool distance in the days following their heated exchange. Maddie tried several times to apologize, but Lanie always cut her off. "We can maintain a professional partnership, Maddie, but our friendship is over. I'll do whatever you need me to do for the grand opening. But please honor my wishes and don't confuse our professional relationship with our former friendship." They had slid into an odd place, one Maddie could barely tolerate. But with only four days left before they opened, it would have to do.

Late one afternoon, Brad hung around the kitchen. "Maddie, do you have a minute?"

"Sure," she answered, pushing the curls out of her face and tucking them back under her bandana. "What can I do for you?"

He leaned against the island, running his hand along the smooth granite edge. "I was just wondering if you'd consider having dinner with me sometime. I've enjoyed getting to know you, and I thought maybe—"

"Oh, Brad, that's really sweet." She turned her back to him, busying herself with the dirty stack of cookie sheets in the oversized sink. "But y'know, with the opening coming up, and everything I still have to do, I just wouldn't possibly have time."

"Oh," he said, then paused. When he didn't say more, she turned her head to see what he was doing. He shuffled his feet then folded his arms across his chest. "Well, I can understand that. In fact, I assumed you'd need some time. Of course, I meant *after* the opening. I suppose I should have said that, huh? Once you've had some time to get used to your new routine. No rush."

Maddie dried her hands on her apron and turned around to face him again. "Well, uh . . . the thing is . . ." She stopped cold, her eyes glued to his lazy smile that warmed his brown eyes. She caught herself staring, studying the tiny flecks of gold in those brown eyes. *What is wrong with me?!* She coughed, continuing to mentally scold herself.

He reached across the space between them, brushing the same renegade curl out of her eyes. When his fingers touched her brow, a shot of electricity bolted through her. *Where did* THAT *come from?*

"Maddie, I'd be lying if I said I wasn't attracted to you. In fact, I've been trying to get the nerve to ask you out for quite a while now. Guess I'm just a little slow when it comes to that sort of thing."

She closed her eyes and sighed. "But Brad, I just thought maybe you and Lanie—"

"Me and Lanie? What gave you that idea?"

She opened her eyes again. "Oh, I don't know. I guess I just fancy myself a bit of a matchmaker." She grabbed a hand towel, absently wiping a phantom spot on the counter. "I just thought the two of you might have a lot in common. Or something. And Lanie is such a sweetheart, I just thought maybe—"

He scratched a spot above his right eyebrow. "Wait a second. Did you . . . was that night Lanie met me at Starbucks—was that your doing? Did you put her up to that?"

She focused on another spot on the countertop. "Well, see, I thought—"

"Oh no," he groaned. He let his head fall back, shaking it. "She said she had something to ask me. She was going to ask me out, wasn't she?" He leveled his gaze at her.

"Um, well actually—"

"Maddie?"

She dropped the hand towel and stuffed her fidgeting hands in her apron pockets. "Yes. Yes, I *suggested* she talk to you. But all I did was give her a little nudge. Brad, she was really hoping you'd agree to start going out with her."

"*She* was hoping? Or *you* were hoping? Which is it? Because I really never got that impression from her. Not once."

They stared at each other until Maddie could no longer stand it. "Okay, *I* was hoping. But it's only because I know Lanie so well! We've known each other our whole lives. And she's such an *amazing* person. But guys never give her a chance because she's . . . because she doesn't come across that interested, y'know? She's more into books and computers. *Way* too interested in computers, if you ask me."

He let out a loud sigh. "Good grief, Maddie. Do you know what you've done?" He rubbed the back of his neck. "That night at Starbucks, before she had a chance to ask me out, I asked her about *you.* I asked if she thought you might go out with me."

"I know."

"What do you mean, you know? She told you?"

"We tell each other everything. We're best friends. Or at least we *were.* She hasn't spoken to me since that night. Well, not in anything but a professional capacity, anyway. And only when she has to concerning the business."

He shook his head again. "Wow. She's that upset about it? I wondered why I hadn't seen her around much."

"Oh," Maddie croaked, avoiding his eyes on her. "Well, it wasn't *just* that."

"What? What else have you done?" He stepped closer, definitely invading her comfort zone.

"Well, the thing is, she was already kind of involved with someone else."

"What? Why would you even think of putting her up to ask me out if she was already dating someone else?"

She blew out a huff in frustration. "Because she wasn't 'dating' someone else. He's just a cyber-boyfriend. And that's all it is. She's never even met him. She Skypes with him all the time, but what kind of a relationship comes from that? Besides, he's a geek. He's not her type."

"You've met him but she hasn't?"

"Why does everyone just assume I've met him? No, of course not. He lives in California."

"Yet you know enough about him to know he's not your best friend's 'type'?"

She stole a quick peek at him, unnerved by the disappointment registering in those brown eyes. For a split second, she tried to figure out what cologne he was wearing, then she realized it wasn't the time or place for that sort of thing. *Get a grip, Maddie. You're in hot water here.*

He turned, drumming his fingers impatiently on the counter as he slowly made his way to the back door. "I don't know, Maddie. Seems to me you should mind your own business and let others figure out their own lives."

"I know. It's just a character flaw, I guess. Nana lectures me about it all the time."

He opened the back door without turning around. "Maybe you should start listening to her," he said, quietly closing the door behind him.

Maddie bit her lip, wondering why she couldn't get it right. Brad had everything in the world to offer. *What* was *that cologne? He smelled so good tonight. And that smile. I could get lost in that smile for a couple centuries. And what was it about those eyes . . .*

So why didn't she just agree to have dinner with him? Why *wasn't* she interested in him like that? She didn't have a clue. Of course, now that she'd blown it, he'd probably never even think to ask her out.

In the days that followed, he was the perfect gentleman. Distant, but polite, just as he'd always been. For that she was sadly grateful.

Even if she didn't deserve it.

Chapter 10

As the opening neared, Jonathan became a fixture at the house, helping with even the smallest details. Maddie watched the growing fondness in his eyes for her grandmother, but she clung to the scriptures Nana had shared with her, knowing God was more than able to make a match if there was one to be made.

But Ian Grant was another story.

She spotted the mystery woman's car in the Bradford House driveway more times than she cared to think about, though she never saw her again. The situation confounded her. The temptation to walk across the street and knock on that door gnawed at her. *Who is she and what is she to you anyway, Dr. Grant?*

Of course it was none of her business. What troubled her even more was the wound it had left in her heart, an ache that bothered her every time she saw that car. *But why? What concern is it to me?*

Now, on this unusually cold November morning, as she unloaded the groceries from her car, the sight of that car infuriated her. *At eight o'clock on a Saturday morning? It's a disgrace.*

"Good morning!"

Maddie turned to see Ian slowing from a run, approaching her driveway.

"Hello." She headed for the porch with her groceries, aware of his winded breath right behind her.

"I thought you should know the doctor has given me a clean slate. Says the foot is as good as new."

She turned to face him just as he pulled the hem of his sweatshirt up to wipe his face. *Goodness. Who knew such a build was hiding beneath that crabby-professor façade he has going?* She turned before he could see her blush.

"Feels great to run again."

"That's nice. I'm happy for you." She continued up the steps, then set the bags on the porch.

"I understand your tea room will be opening soon." He looked up at her, his eyes narrowed against the morning sun. The mere sight of him irritated her.

"Yes, we plan to open Wednesday afternoon. I mailed the

invitations this morning. You should be receiving one, regardless of our previous conversation."

"Good," he responded eagerly. "I'm glad you reconsidered. Well, then. I shall look forward to it." He smiled.

He's smiling? Maddie studied him, perplexed by the transformation on his face. *And he wants to come to my grand opening? What happened to your stuffed shirt, Dr. Grant? At the dry cleaners?*

"Good. We'll be pleased to have you."

"Excellent. Until then." This time the smile lit up his whole face. A new look for him.

He tossed a wave then jogged across the street and ran up the steps two at a time. Maddie abruptly turned her back. The last thing she wanted to see was a welcome-home kiss at the front door from his mistress. Instead, she lugged her bags inside and slammed the door.

And wondered why she wanted to cry.

"Madeline, may I help you? I've put your grandmother to bed for the night. Could you use a hand?"

The sound of Gretchen's pleasant voice soothed the knots in Maddie's stomach. "Oh Gretchen, that would be wonderful. I've got two more pans of these chess squares to cut, I need to glaze all those loaves of poppyseed bread now that they're cooled, and the first batch of blueberry scones are ready to take out of the oven. Could you take them out and put them on the cooling racks?"

"Wouldn't mind a bit. Your grandmother is so proud of you, sweetheart. I think she's as excited about tomorrow as you are." Gretchen's easy laugh softly blanketed the room. "We've got her new dress all pressed and ready. She'll be a vision for your grand opening tomorrow. I promise."

Maddie blew a wisp of hair out of her eyes then rinsed her hands before cutting more of the gooey squares. "Gretchen, do you think she's up to this? Do you think it might all be too much for her?"

"Not at all! She'll be your greatest asset, you watch. And I don't want you to worry about her a 'tall. I'll keep a close eye to make sure she's not overdoing it. If she is, I'll take her back to her room to rest a spell."

Maddie lifted the empty pan, dumping it into the sudsy water in the sink. "You're an angel. You have no idea what a tremendous relief it is having you here." She tore off a big sheet of clear wrap then covered the platter of chess squares.

"Maddie, here are the menus."

Lanie walked into the kitchen, a large box balanced on her hip. "I had them print fifty, thinking you could add more as you need them."

Maddie fought the disturbing tug, the same pull she felt each time she heard the strange monotone in Lanie's voice. She cleared her throat before responding. "Are you pleased with them?"

"Very. Take a look." She opened the box, handing Maddie the finished product of their collaboration.

"Oh Lanie, they're—*beautiful!* These are amazing!" Maddie leaned in to give her a hug, but stopped, realizing her mistake. She moved to the kitchen table, focusing instead on the exquisite art work and layout of their menu.

"I just can't believe it's really happening, can you? Remember that day at Chawton Cottage, touring Jane Austen's home? And we had this idea for a tea room, right here in Austin? Remember how we laughed, thinking how proud Jane would be of us?"

A guarded smile. "I remember."

Maddie watched, visualizing the same scenes no doubt playing through Lanie's mind—their unforgettable trip with all its thrills and fantasies. But just as quickly, Lanie blinked it all away.

"I'll be back early in the morning. Good night, Gretchen. Maddie."

Lanie let herself out the back door. Maddie stared after her, losing the battle with the war raging inside her. She excused herself, asking Gretchen to close the kitchen down for the night. She grabbed her sweater from the closet, wrapped a knitted scarf around her neck, then let herself out the front door. Lanie's red taillights disappeared down the street just as the dam broke.

Maddie wept, reliving the grief all over again, wondering if it was truly the end of their life-long friendship. She'd tried to give Lanie space and time to get over the pain of that night. But now, weeks later, it was obvious their relationship was doomed. The fatigue and stress of the grand opening overwhelmed her, sending wave upon wave of tears. She cried so hard, she was afraid she might throw up.

"Excuse me, but is this the home of Maddie Cooper?"

Maddie looked up from her cocoon on the wicker loveseat, searching for the source of the voice. She wiped her face. "Who wants to know?"

Chapter 11

My name is Jeffrey Townsend. I need to speak to Maddie, if she's home."

"Excuse me?"

"Are you Maddie?" He stepped off the sidewalk, following the brick path to the porch.

How do I know that name? The lamp in the living room window cast just enough light on the tall stranger dressed in sweater and jeans, a jaunty hat covering his thick curly brown hair.

Maddie slipped the kerchief off her head and wiped her nose with it, embarrassed to think how she must look even in the shadows on the porch. "Um, yes. I'm sorry, do I know you?"

He climbed the steps, tilting his head to see her better. "I'm Jeffrey Townsend. I'm an English fellow at UCLA and a member of the Jane Austen Society of America. And I'm in love with Lanie Morgan."

He stepped onto the porch, digging his hands into his pockets. "Do you know me now?" His eyebrows arched.

Maddie gasped to see the man behind the dreaded name standing on her porch. "Jeff? *Lanie's* Jeff?"

"Well, I had hoped so at one point. But that all depends on you."

"Me? What are you talking about?"

He walked over to the empty chair beside her and sat down. She could make out his features beneath the stylish cap—surprised to find one of the kindest faces she'd ever seen. Dimples the size of Texas and eyes that sparkled even in the darkness of night.

"A few weeks ago, Lanie and I had a fight because of you."

"I know. It was horrible of me and I—"

"Yes, it *was* horrible of you. I believe Lanie was falling in love with me until you intruded and pushed her into the arms of someone who rejected her. I could deal with that—in fact, I have to say I was relieved he wasn't interested in her. His loss, my gain, I guess you could say," he continued. "Only Lanie didn't see it that way at all. She was shaken by the whole thing, said she felt 'unworthy' of me, that I 'deserved better than someone so easily led astray by a mere infatuation.' Now she won't even talk to me. She quit signing online; she won't return my phone calls . . ."

When he paused, Maddie blew out a long, weary sigh. Seconds passed before she spoke. "Jeff, I don't know what to say. I've screwed up *everything*—for you, for Lanie—and for the friendship I've cherished since I was a little girl. Lanie is the best friend I've ever had. But now all that's changed because of what I did. She won't talk about it—refuses to accept my apology. I'm at a total loss. I—I don't know what to do." Fresh tears stung her eyes.

Jeff leaned forward. "Really? I had no idea. Lanie used to talk about you all the time. I didn't know she'd shut you out too. This is worse than I thought."

She could only nod her head, quietly weeping.

"Maddie, I came over here first because I wanted to meet you for myself. See if you really were as heartless as I had imagined."

His words felt like a slap to the face. Maddie cried out, dropping her head in her hands. Her sobs drifted through the night air like the siren on an ambulance.

"No! No," he insisted, touching her arm. "I didn't mean to upset you! The thing is, I envisioned you as this manipulative witch of a friend—"

Her sobs escalated to a full scale wail.

"No! No, you're taking this all wrong! It's obvious you're not like that *at all!* I can tell you love Lanie as much as I do. And the way I see it, there's only one thing to do. I'm going to see her right now and straighten this all out. For *all* of us."

He jumped up, rushing off as Maddie stood in his wake. He stopped at the top of the stairs. "Oh, forgive my manners," he laughed, hurrying back to hug her. "It's nice to meet you, Maddie Cooper. And I look forward to getting to know you."

With that, he ran down the stairs and across the lawn to a car she hadn't noticed. "Oh, by the way—where does Lanie live?"

Maddie shouted the easy directions then watched him pull away from the curb. "Jeff? Computer geek Jeff? Looks like *that?*" She drew a ragged breath and started back inside when she heard a car door slam. For a moment she thought he'd returned, but immediately spotted the black car parked in the driveway at Bradford House.

"Madeline? Is that you?"

Ian leaned around the car, looking toward her.

No, no, no—please don't come over here!

He strolled across the street. "I was hoping I might see you tonight. I wanted to offer my best wishes for your grand opening tomorrow. I'm sure it will be a smashing success. Getting a bit of fresh air, are you? You must be positively exhausted. What, with all the preparations."

Ian slowly climbed the steps, a warm smile spreading across his face. *Oh, why does he have to be so handsome?* Maddie wiped her face, sniffing the flood from her nose. Her breaths came in wild hiccups. "Exhausted? Look at me! There's nothing left. *Nothing,*" she squeaked, unleashing the floodgates again.

He blinked, eyes wide open. "Surely it can't be as bad as all that?"

"Oh, I *assure* you it is! I'm so tired, I haven't a clue what else needs to be done before tomorrow. And now my best friend hates me . . . she *hates* me!" She nodded vigorously, affirming the truth of her words as they spilled out faster and faster like some runaway train. The waterworks in her nose continued to run like a broken faucet. "Then Jeff the Computer Geek shows up at my doorstep, professing his love for my aforementioned former best friend, who's apparently shunned his affection because *I* interfered and pushed her into the arms of Brad the Contractor who, as it turns out, was more interested in *me,* when all the while I thought he might be a good match for Lanie, which of course devastated her."

She stopped to wipe her nose, wailing again. He offered his handkerchief. She cried harder at the kindness, accepted, and immediately blew into it with an earsplitting honk.

She sighed heavily, nodding her head with renewed vigor. "Oh, it *devastated* her. Not because Brad didn't want *her* but that he wanted *me,* when I'd literally pushed her at him and because of my stupid misreading of all that, now she'll refuse to ever get married and Jeff will die of a broken heart and—and—and now *you* show up, the man who *blasted* me on the airplane then rebuffed my every attempt at kindness . . . Now you show up in the middle of the night, as nice as you please, offering me your handkerchief and your best wishes for success tomorrow? ARE YOU CRAZY?!"

"Great Scott! Take a breath, will you?" Ian loosened the scarf about his neck, his skin suddenly damp and clammy. "I feel as though I've stepped into one of those soap operas on your American telly. But surely—"

She dissolved into unrestrained blubbering. Not knowing what else to do, Ian pulled her into his arms. He felt her melt at once into his embrace. "There now, there now, Maddie."

She cried even harder, the sobs shaking her body. Finally, she murmured against his shoulder. "I was so sure God called me to help others find love. And just look what's happened. I've ruined *everyone's* life."

He simply held her, stroking her hair, whispering quietly in her ear. "Shhh . . . don't cry, Madeline. Don't cry."

"I must be a sight," she moaned. She stole another look at him, her nose red and her lashes wet. "I—I don't know what to say. Thank you. Apparently I needed a shoulder to cry on."

He pulled her closer into his embrace, tucking her head beneath his chin. "Maddie, I have a confession to make."

"You do?"

"I've wanted to hold you like this . . . for some time now."

She pulled back, her face etched with confusion. "What? I don't understand."

"I'm afraid there's quite a lot you don't understand about me. But if you'll give me a chance, I'd like to change that." He led her to the wicker loveseat, then sat beside her, taking both her hands in his.

"I was an absolute beast to you on that plane. It was inexcusable. And I'm afraid it set us off to a very bad start. You see, it's only been a couple of weeks since—since my eyes were opened, if you will, so that I could see what a contemptuous, insolent man I'd become. It's a long story, but suffice it to say, that's all gone now. I've learned how desperately important it is to learn how to forgive. And I wish very much to offer my apologies for my previous behavior and ask for a new start."

She stared at him. A hiccup quirked her body.

"I know, I know. But you must believe me—I *am* a changed man."

She blinked, then looked over his shoulder. "That must make your girlfriend very happy."

"Girlfriend? But I don't—" He followed her line of vision, his eyes landing on the BMW across the street. "Ohhh . . . . no, that's not what . . . oh my, then you must have seen—"

"I was sitting here on the porch that night. You opened the door and then she kissed you so tenderly, and, well, I just assumed, since the car is there all the time now—"

"Maddie," he chuckled. "You're quite mistaken. I assure you no one is living with me, nor do I have a 'girlfriend.'"

"You don't? I mean, you don't! I mean—*oh . . .*" Her face crimsoned. "Because to be perfectly honest," she looked back into his eyes, "and I think it's time I learn to be perfectly honest, don't' you? Then I would have to tell you—"

He pulled her into his arms again, silencing her with the kiss he could no longer hold back. Maddie responded, slow at first, then with such eagerness, it took his breath away. At last, when he pulled away and looked at her, he discovered the most enchanting smile on her face and eyes gazing back at him with unabashed pleasure.

"No girlfriend," he breathed, kissing her forehead. "Unless . . ."

"Wait—Ian," she gasped, pulling back abruptly, running her hands through her hair. "You don't even know me. Yet you say you've wanted to hold me? I don't understand." She searched his eyes for meaning.

"Oh, but you're wrong." Ian traced her jaw with his thumb. "I know a great deal about you, Miss Cooper. I know that you've cared for your grandmother selflessly for many years." He smiled. "And yes, I overheard that part on the plane."

"How very rude of you, Dr. Grant," she teased.

"I know that you love your grandmother very much. I've seen you on this porch with her, singing together while you arrange flowers, consulting her with every stem you add. Having tea together, working crossword puzzles together. And I've watched how you lavish her with your kisses and smother her with your hugs.

"I've seen how you treat the work crew over here. Some of them don't even speak English, yet I've watched you serve them elaborate picnics here on the front porch." He tipped her chin to face him closer. "And I have it on good authority that you often leave baskets of muffins and cookies on the doorstep of perfect strangers. Even ill-tempered ones who never offer so much as a thank you. Quite delicious pastries, I might add. Not a single crumb survived."

"Ian, I don't know what to say." She nestled her head against his chest, burrowing deeper into his arms. She felt her heart beating against his. *I could stay right here for a lifetime.*

"That's easy," he whispered into her hair. "Just say you'll do me the honor of allowing me to court you as a proper English gentleman who'd love nothing more than to spend a lifetime getting to know you, Maddie Cooper."

Chapter 12

The grand opening of *The Chawton Tea Room* was a huge success. By eleven, it was necessary for Lanie to take names as the customers far outnumbered the available seating. Every nook and cranny of the downstairs filled with patrons who enjoyed a traditional English tea menu and browsed the many Jane Austen artifacts and books decorating the festive tea room. The local newspaper covered the event, promising to splash the smiles of delighted customers on its pages the next day.

But no one was happier than Maddie Cooper. Early that morning, Lanie and Jeff appeared in her kitchen, faces beaming. In a flurry of apologies and cries of joy, Lanie and Maddie mended their friendship, thanks to the persistent diplomacy of a certain California computer geek. And when Lanie announced their engagement, Maddie's shout of joy could surely be heard down the block.

"Oh, Lanie! Nothing could make me happier! Nothing! This is spectacular! And to think you did it in *spite* of me!"

"Miracles never cease, eh, Maddie?" Lanie laughed, hugging her best friend again.

Jeff hugged Maddie as well, as if they'd been friends for years, promising he would take good care of Lanie. "Oh, and Maddie? In case you're interested, I've got a whole computer lab full of friends I could introduce you to."

Her mouth fell open until she realized he was kidding. "Oh yeah, really funny. No, I think all efforts of matchmaking should hereby cease and desist. Agreed?"

"Agreed," they shouted in unison.

"Besides," Maddie added, "I'm not really in the market. But that's all I'm going to say about that." Her eyes danced mischievously. "Hey! We've got a tea room to open today! We've got work to do!"

"Maddie?" Lanie drawled, cocking her head to one side. "Is there something you need to tell me?"

"Yes! Lots and lots! But there's no time now. Here, put on your apron and get to work. Jeff? Would you like to jump in and help too?" She handed him one of the bib aprons she'd designed—the *Chawton Tea Room* logo monogrammed against a classic English chintz background, and handed Lanie one as well.

"Consider it done," Jeff offered, already pulling an apron over his head. "Just put me to work."

"I knew I'd love him," Maddie teased.

"So did I, girlfriend. So did I." Lanie planted a kiss on Jeff's cheek, which quickly blushed a soft shade of crimson, and nuzzled into his embrace.

Jonathan arrived an hour later with an enormous bouquet of pale pink roses smothered in baby's breath. "For the belle of the ball, my dear," he announced, kneeling beside Nana and kissing her freshly-rouged cheek. "At your service, today and forever, Rachel Cooper." Nana's eyes sparkled in ready adoration. Maddie wasn't sure what to make of those two, but had a feeling about them—one which now she gladly kept to herself.

A few moments later, one more early bird arrived at the front door.

"Ian!" Maddie felt the heat on her cheeks as she returned his smile.

"Forgive me if I'm intruding at this hour. I wondered—well, I thought perhaps I could be of assistance to you somehow today. Maybe pour a spot of tea, clear a dish or two, park a car or mop the floor . . ."

Maddie snuggled into his extended arms, wrapping her arms around his neck as she kissed him firmly on the lips.

"Well, now! I take that as a yes?" He kissed her back, this time more gently, taking his time.

At last, Maddie pulled back. "But of course you may assist, Dr. Grant," she intoned. "How could I possibly welcome my guests to an authentic English tea without the presence of an authentic Englishman?"

"Well there you have it!" Ian backed out of her embrace, taking a deep bow.

Maddie introduced Ian to Nana and Jonathan then reacquainted him with Lanie. He begged Lanie's forgiveness, taking her hand into his. She burst into laughter, then pulled him into a hug. In her best English accent, she responded, "Jolly good form, Ian Grant. Jolly good form!"

"Thank you, my dear girl, but do us all a favor today and leave the accent to *me*. Will you?"

"Gladly, old chap. Gladly."

They all shared more laughter before scattering in different directions, jumping into the tasks at hand.

Hours later, after *The Chawton Tea Room* closed its doors on its first day of business, a small after-party gathered around the kitchen table. With fresh pots of tea and the few remaining pastries before them, the group basked in the glory of the day. Maddie leaned against Ian, sighing with pleasure. "We did it. We actually did it."

Lanie raised her cup. "To Maddie, for making dreams come true."

"Here, here!" they answered in unison.

Nana joined in the toasts. "To Lanie, for finding it in your heart to forgive a dear friend, and finding love in the process."

Jeff kissed Lanie's cheek as another "here, here!" rang out.

Jonathan lifted his teacup. "To Rachel, whose quiet strength and courage inspire us all."

"Here, here!"

Ian cleared his throat, raising his teacup as well. Maddie smiled when she realized it was the same cup she'd brought back from Chawton Village in England. The very same cup she'd unwrapped to admire on the flight home, seated behind a quite irritable Scrooge of a professor who'd scolded her and Lanie for their "incessant chatter." She dipped her head, pressing her lips together to keep from laughing out loud at the memory. Could that cranky Englishman actually be the warm and caring man seated beside her now, his fingers snuggly entangled with hers below the table?

"Lanie. Maddie. Mrs. Cooper?" Ian began. "I salute you for your success today. Jane Austen could not have done it better herself. Take that from a true Englishman."

"Here, here!"

He took a sip then turned to Maddie, bringing her hand to his lips, then speaking just to her, barely above a whisper. "To new life, new friends, and new beginnings." Then, with his eyes locked on hers, he bestowed a long gentle kiss on her hand.

Leaning over, Maddie placed a perfect kiss against his warm lips.

"Here, here, Ian Grant," she whispered. "Here, here."

Epilogue

With ridiculously exaggerated flair, I typed the last two words on the page:

The End

I punched my fists straight up in the air. "YESSSSSS! I'm fi-nished. I'm fi-nished. I'm fi-nal-ly fi-nal-ly fi-nished!" I cranked up the volume on my laptop speakers and jumped up from my desk chair. As Michael Jackson's eccentric voice quirked the first lyrics of *Thriller,* I mimicked his famous moves, complete with ghoulish expressions and syncopated side steps—even throwing in an ad-libbed moonwalk across my hardwood floor. That October weekend we all used Shirley's Wii to learn the King of Pop's dance moves had really paid off. I didn't miss a beat.

Gertie jumped off her chair and twirled beside me, barking along for good measure. The two of us zombie-walked our way to the kitchen where I pulled a pint of Blue Bell Mint Chocolate Chip from the freezer. The dancing continued while I pried open the lid on the little carton then grabbed a spoon out of the drawer. Multi-tasking never felt better.

As with anything I attempt to accomplish these days, I was interrupted by the ringing of my doorbell. I dug out a scoop of the minty green ice cream and savored it as I headed toward the door. I did a modified zombie-walk down the hall with Gertie traipsing along behind me. I was about to open the door when I peered through the curtains and saw my UPS guy laughing. Make that *guffawing.*

I dropped my head then opened the door. "Okay. Fine. So you saw me dancing."

"You do a wicked *Thriller,* Lucy. Where'd you learn to dance like that?"

I admit it. I love his dimples. I truly do. But even those sweet craters couldn't distract my embarrassment. "It's a long story and you don't have the time. Hand it over."

He handed the small carton to me, then shook his head, still laughing at my pitiful zombie. I had to admit it was a great laugh. The kind you feel all the way from your abs up. And might I just add, I'm quite sure that UPS-issue brown uniform shirt was hiding some killer abs. Not that I've seen them.

"Okay, okay, you've had your laugh, big guy. Where do I sign?"

"No need to sign for this one. You've just got me trained to make it personal, with or with a signature request. Besides, you're always the highlight of my day."

"Yeah, well, you must be starved for entertainment."

"Oh, I don't know. I know how to have a good time now and then."

He smiled that crooked smile again. Like the cheek on the right forgot to pull up as much as the one on the left. He had no idea how cute that is.

My face heated, so I avoided eye contact. "Well, then, there you go. Have a good one, Mark. See you next time."

"Sure thing. And give my best to Michael." A wink and off he went, doing his best Michael in a silly falsetto.

I rolled my eyes, shut the door, and tossed the package on the side table. Just another case of tea. After doing my research on Maddie's behalf, I'd grown partial to her preferred brand, Taylors of Harrogate. I liked ordering it by the case because . . . well, if you must know, it's one more excuse for the guy in brown to stop by. But let's just keep that between you and me, okay? I smiled and shook my head, continuing down the hall.

We walked back into the kitchen, my funny black Scottie tapping her nails on the hardwood as she tried to keep up, her long tongue hanging out the side of her mouth. I snatched the carton of Blue Bell and scooped out another bite of that heavenly blend of flavors when my cell chirped. I wouldn't have heard it, but it was the part in *Thriller* where it's mostly rhythm and percussion playing over and over. I dug in the front pocket of my jeans for my cell, debating whether or not I'd answer it. *Samantha Graham*. My editor. Crap. I had to take this.

I made my way back to my office and turned Michael down a few decibels. "Sam! It's finished. You're gonna love it. And we made deadline with time to spare!"

I was greeted with her usual cough, a raspy tribute to her two-pack-a-day habit. I pulled the cell away from my ear. A natural reflex, somehow sure if I don't, my ear will be grossly baptized. Ew?

"You know those things are gonna kill you one of these days," I reminded her. Again.

One final hack followed by a deep breath. "I know, I know. I don't want to hear it. So you're finally done. Why don't I see it in my inbox?"

"Because you caught me in my Celebratory Ritual. Some things can't be rushed. You know that."

"Ah, that explains Michael in the background. Was that *Thriller*?"

"I love that about you, Sam. You don't have a clue who's in the White House or which team won the Super Bowl, but you know your Michael Jackson. You're a regular Motown groupie."

Another cough. Another deep breath. Then three clicks and an expletive.

"Your lighter still not working? Could be a sign to stop, you know."

She ignored me. "When the song ends and you finish your ice cream, will you please send me your manuscript? I don't need to remind you we have less than twenty-four hours until the official deadline."

"It's worth the wait, I promise you. This one—I don't even know how to explain it. It wrote itself. I just tapped the keys. Never had that happen before." I thought back to the day my aunt's teacups arrived and the flood of memories and ideas that seemed to float out of that box. "This one was truly a gift. I'm dedicating it to Lucille's memory."

"Ironic, since it was her funeral that put you so far behind schedule."

I remembered Samantha's stern lecture (that's putting it nicely) when I insisted on flying to Chicago for Lucille's memorial service. As if a silly deadline would keep me from being with my family at a time like that? "Be nice. I adored her."

"Yeah, fine, whatever. Look, Lucy, just hurry up and send me what you've got. The design team is giving me grief here. Since you threw out the original story line, they've got to start from scratch, which puts them behind before they begin."

"Giving you grief, are they? What's that saying—*what goes around, comes around*? No problem. I'll have it to you in ten."

"Ciao mein." Click.

"Ciao mein yourself," I grumbled, dropping my cell back in my pocket. I took another lick of ice cream and reached for my keyboard. A couple of quick strokes and my sweet baby was up, up, and away in cyberspace, mere seconds from landing in Samantha's Manhattan inbox. Mission accomplished.

I curled up in Gertie's chair, much to her delight. She hopped up to join me, settling in with a final sigh of pleasure. I scratched the back of her neck as my mind wandered. Sam had short-circuited my celebration, but that was okay. I was already drifting into Phase Two of my post-manuscript ritual—the major let-down as I say goodbye to my characters. You live with these people, crawl around inside their heads for months on end, put every word in their mouths, only to close the book on them. So to speak. It's just hard.

That said, I felt a glimmer of excitement at the prospect of starting the next novella in the series. I usually take a couple of weeks off between projects, but I couldn't wait to get started. I gnawed at my lower lip, then gave in. I jumped up and reached over to pick up the red and gold teacup and saucer resting on the decorative shelf above my desk. It had served as my inspiration through the entire book I just completed. But it was time to move on.

I padded down the hall to the dining room and opened the door to my china cabinet. The sunlight streamed through the windows striping broad, bright lines across the room. Still, I turned the switch inside the cabinet door, illuminating the shelves and their precious contents. A slow smile crept across my face as I returned the cup and saucer to the empty spot on the second shelf. Alongside it, Aunt Lucille's teacups were displayed in all their elegance, like so many members of the royal family all vying for my attention. I'd felt so honored to receive them after she passed away, especially knowing she'd included instructions in her will for them to go directly to me. Even the cabinet that now housed them was a gift from her, another surprise inheritance that arrived a couple months ago. As I touched each and every cup, I felt Lucille's presence so near, I could swear I caught a whiff of her beloved Chanel No. 5.

"Well, that makes it official. You're here with me. That means you have to help me pick the next one."

I studied them all, trying to remember which design had sparked the story line buzzing around in my head. The plots all came to me so quickly that first day, but I neglected to jot myself a note as to which teacup set beckoned which story. But I knew she'd tell me.

"It's an unusual plot. Not something you'd ever see coming. Which means it must be unique and—ah! Now I remember. This is the one."

Tiny hand-painted bows in cobalt blue, very simple, each tied with an even smaller gold ribbon, all linked together in a unique net pattern, airy on a white background. The cup and saucer were both rimmed in gold as well, with an eyelet-like edging inside the cup. The cup handle was painted in a matching cobalt blue with just a touch of gold. I remember Aunt Lucille telling me about this famous Russian design, the *Lomonosov Cobalt Net.* I lifted it from the shelf even as the characters of my new story came to mind. "This is it. The one that mends a broken heart. It's perfect."

And just as I did the first time, I made a pot of tea and poured the steaming brew into my new cup of inspiration. I headed back to my office and set the cup beside my keyboard. Browsing through my music files, I found the collection I wanted—*Sounds of the Sea.* I loved these songs, all accompanied by the lapping of waves against the beach and the call of sea gulls in the distance. Soothing. Comforting somehow. I closed my eyes and could almost feel the ocean breeze against my skin. Smell the salt air. A couple more minutes of this, and I would surely drift off to sleep.

But the story couldn't wait. Far away on the coast of Oregon, drama hovered restlessly in that salty night air. Lots and lots of drama, along with all that smoke and the wail of sirens in the distance . . .

Time to work. I sat up, took a sip of tea, and began typing my first page . . .

Keri! The Blankenship cabin is on fire! Get over here. Now!"

Oh, this is gonna be good.

A Sampling of Recipes
from
THE CHAWTON TEA ROOM

Spencer's Chess Squares

Box of yellow cake mix (non-pudding)
4 eggs
16 ounces powdered sugar
1 stick butter, melted
8 ounces cream cheese
2 teaspoons lemon juice

Preheat oven to 350°.
Spray 9x13 cake pan or Pyrex with no-stick spray. Mix dry cake mix, butter, and one egg. Spread in cake pan. Mix cream cheese, three eggs, powdered sugar, and lemon juice. Bake at 350° for 40 minutes or until crust is just golden brown. Cool completely before cutting into one inch squares. Store in air-tight container. Makes 24 squares.

Old World Raspberry Bars

A recipe from Teresa Nardozzi

2¼ cups all-purpose flour
1 cup sugar
1 cup chopped pecans
1 cup butter, softened (2 sticks)
1 egg
10 ounce jar raspberry preserves

Preheat oven to 350°.
In a large mixing bowl, combine all the ingredients except preserves. Beat at low speed, scraping bowl often, until well mixed, about 2-3 minutes. Reserve 1½cups of the mixture and set aside.

Press remaining mixture into greased 8-inch square pan. Spread preserves to within 1/2-inch from edge. Crumble reserved mixture over preserves. Bake for 40-50 minutes or until lightly browned. Cool completely before cutting into bars.

Blueberry Scones

What's a tea party without yummy scones?

2 cups all-purpose flour
¼ cup brown sugar, packed
1 tablespoon baking powder
¼ teaspoon salt
¼ cup butter, chilled
1 cup fresh blueberries, rinsed and dried
¾ cup half-and-half cream
1 egg

Preheat oven to 375°.
Cut butter into mixture of flour, sugar, baking powder, and salt. Add blueberries and toss to mix thoroughly. In another bowl, beat together cream and egg, then slowly pour this into the dry ingredients, stirring with rubber scraper until dough forms. Knead gently until it comes together, no more than three or four times. Do not over-work! Divide dough in half. On lightly floured board, shape each half into a 6-inch round. Cut into 6 wedges. Bake on ungreased cookie sheet about 20 minutes until golden brown. Serve warm.

Poppyseed Bread

A show-stopper every time!

3 cups all-purpose flour
1½ cups milk
2½ cups sugar
3 eggs
1½ teaspoons vanilla
1½ tablespoons poppyseeds
1½ teaspoons baking powder
1½ teaspoons salt
1 cup plus 2 tablespoons vegetable oil
1½ teaspoons almond extract

Preheat oven to 350°.
Combine all ingredients in large bowl. Beat 2 minutes. Pour into 2 large or 4 mini-loaf pans (greased and floured). Bake 1 hour at 350 degrees (50 minutes for mini-loaf pans).

GLAZE:
¼ cup orange juice
2 teaspoons melted butter
¾ cup powdered sugar

Spoon glaze over loaves immediately in pans and let cool completely.

Nana's Crescent Chicken Squares
Makes 4 servings

1 3-ounce package cream cheese, softened
3 tablespoons butter, melted
2 cups cooked cubed chicken
1/4 teaspoon salt
1/8 teaspoon pepper
2 tablespoons milk
1 tablespoon minced onion
1 teaspoon Nature's Seasons (or spice of your preference)
1 tablespoon chopped pimento, optional
1 8-ounce can refrigerated crescent dinner rolls
3/4 cup seasoned croutons, crushed

Preheat oven to 350°.
In medium bowl, blend cream cheese and 2 tablespoons butter until smooth. Add chicken, salt, pepper, milk, onion, seasoning spice and pimento (optional). Mix well.
Separate crescent dough into 4 rectangles; firmly press perforations to seal. Spoon about 1/2 cup chicken mixture onto center of each rectangle of dough. Pull 4 corners of dough to top center of chicken mixture, twist slightly and seal edges. Brush tops with remaining butter, melted; sprinkle crouton crumbs on top of each square. Place on ungreased baking sheet. Bake at 350° for 20-25 minutes or until golden brown.

Ambrosia Fruit Salad

1 cup pineapple tidbits in their own juice
1 cup mandarin oranges
1 cup mini-marshmallows
1 cup sour cream
1 cup coconut

Mix all ingredients and chill thoroughly before serving.

Cranberry Chicken Salad Paninis
The chicken salad can also be prepared and served on a bed of salad greens.

3 cups cooked and cooled chicken, chopped
3 stalks celery, finely chopped
½ cup dried cranberries
½ cup chopped walnuts
¼ cup finely chopped scallions
1 cup Hellman's mayonnaise
2 tablespoons white wine vinegar
1 tablespoons lemon juice
2 tablespoons Dijon mustard
Salt and pepper to taste
6 (½ ounce) slices Brie cheese
8 slices sourdough bread
¾ cup apricot preserves

Preheat panini press or indoor grill.

Combine chicken, celery, mayonnaise, scallions, cranberries, vinegar, lemon juice, mustard, salt, and pepper and mix well. Assemble sandwiches by layering four slices of bread with the chicken salad filling, topping each with a slice of Brie and preserves (divided evenly). Top with remaining bread. Lightly butter one side of sandwich and place that side down onto heated panini press, then lightly butter topside of each sandwich. Cook each sandwich in the panini press until bread crisps and turns light gold.

Tea Punch
For a nice chilled and refreshing beverage.

8 regular tea bags or 1 family size tea bag (enough to brew 1 gallon)
6 ounce pink lemonade frozen concentrate, thawed
6 ounce orange juice frozen concentrate, thawed
2 cups sugar

Bring 4 cups of water to boil. Take off heat and brew tea for exactly 4 minutes. Remove tea bags. Add sugar and stir thoroughly until melted. Add lemonade and orange juice and enough water to make 1 gallon. Chill, then stir each time before serving.

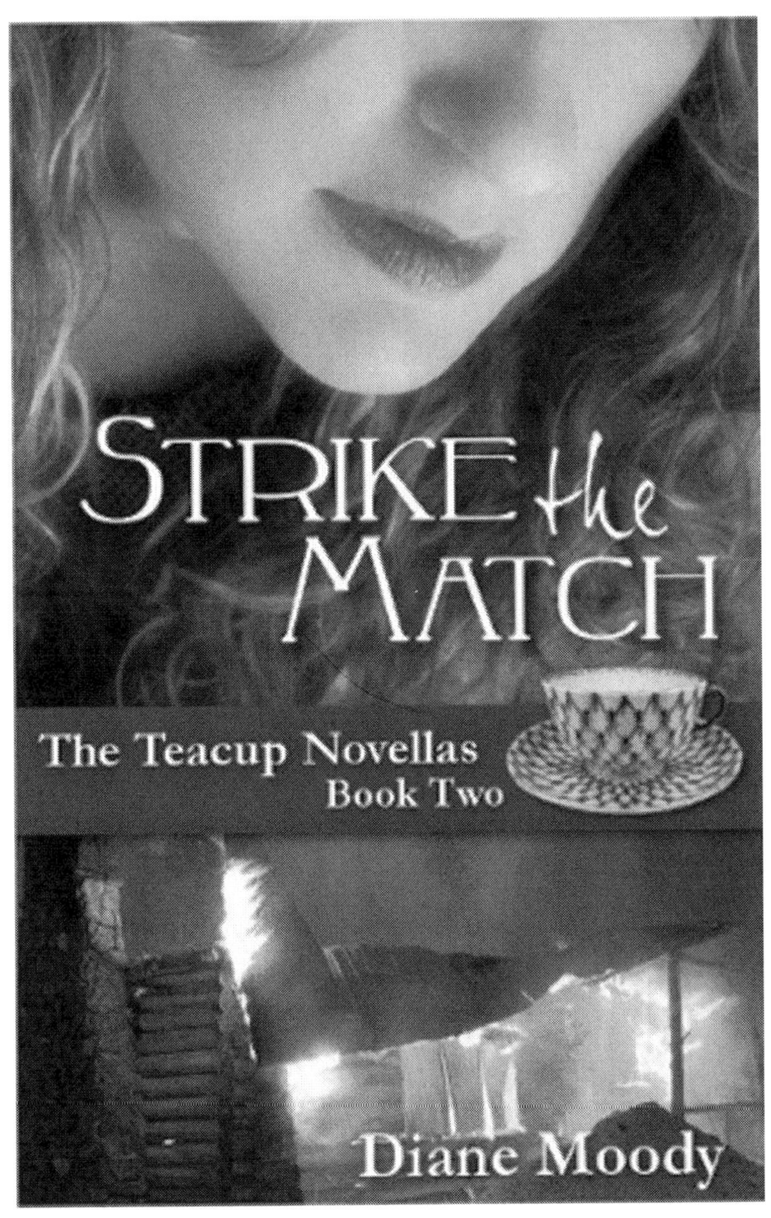
STRIKE the MATCH
The Teacup Novellas
Book Two
Diane Moody

To Sally Wilson

For introducing me to your
beautiful state of Oregon,
for sharing this love of writing
And always inspiring me,
but most of all for being such a
forever friend.

Love is a fire.
But whether it is going to warm your hearth
or burn down your house,
you can never tell.
— Joan Crawford

Love bears all things, believes all things,
hopes all things, endures all things.
Love never fails.
— I Corinthians 13: 7a

Prologue

I blew my nose and reached for another Kleenex. A whole fleet of them dotted my desk, wadded up like so many wilted white roses. This was ridiculous. You'd think I just lost a best friend or something. Why so many tears, you ask? I just finished writing a particularly touching scene in my newest novella. One of my main characters just got hurt, and I could literally see him lying there in the hospital bed . . . such a dear man. He was only trying to help!

Okay, okay. I know. I get way too carried away. I can't help it. My characters are closer to me than some members of my own family. After all, I crafted them. I gave them life, as it were. Of course I'd be invested. Involved. Face it, they do nothing without me telling them to. So if one of them gets hurt, it only makes sense—

"Lucy? You home?"

Speak of the devil. My brother.

"Back here, Chad. In my office." Gertie leaped off her chair, her nails tapping like a drum cadence against the hardwood floor as she flew down the hall.

"There's my girl! Hey Gertie!"

Those two. If anything ever happens to me, I don't need to worry about my sweet Scottie. Chad spoils her rotten. He'd steal her in a heartbeat if he thought he could get away with it. I can hear the love-fest getting closer.

Chad filled the door frame of my office. Still scratching Gert behind the ears, he looked up, his eyes immediately tracking to my desk and all my used tissues. "Oh no. Let me guess. Another gushy love scene?"

"No," I protested. "I've got a cold." I plucked up each and every one and moved past him toward the bathroom where I quickly deposited them in the trash. I'd left my office trash can in the garage. Or somewhere.

"Doesn't sound like a cold to me."

"Did I ask you?"

Gertie jumped up against his knees, begging for more attention. "Well, no. And come to mention it, you don't look so hot."

I planted my hand on my hip and blew my hair out of my face. "You always did have that natural charm thing going. Any other observations you'd like to make? Is that why you're here? To bolster my self-esteem?"

He smiled and gathered me into a hug. "Nah, I just came by to say hi."

"Hi," I mumbled, my mouth smashed against his chest. He smelled really good. Must have just showered.

He pulled back. "I was just worried about you. Hadn't seen you in a few days. Where've you been?"

I pulled another ratty tissue out of my jeans pocket and wiped my nose. "Here. Where did you think? I never go anywhere."

"Oh, but you go lots of places. A few weeks ago you were in Austin with Jane Austen, right? And I think this week you mentioned something about Oregon, is it?"

"Very funny." I shuffled past him making my way to the kitchen. "Want some tea?"

"Sure. Sounds good." He and Gert followed me down the hall. "Coast of Oregon, that's it. Some fictional town on the coast of Oregon. Something about a fire and a journalist and a student home from college. Oh—that's why you were crying? Did the journalist break the college girl's heart? Wait—did she 'carry a torch for him'? Get it? The fire? Carry a torch?"

"Chad, it never ceases to amaze me how funny you *aren't*. Besides, you know I don't like discussing my plots with you. Can we talk about something else? How's school?"

My brother teaches history at the local high school. The kids are all smitten with him. And not just because of his good looks. He makes history fun and fascinating. They can't get enough. He even started a history club that's bigger than the marching band. You have to admit that's pretty rare. They take field trips to museums in DC and visit a lot of the battlefields around Virginia.

He loves those kids. He has such a passion for his students, which only makes them love him more. Well, not *love* love. He's extremely careful about those schoolgirl crushes that often sprout up in his classes. Smart man, that brother of mine.

"School's great. But that's not why I'm here."

I handed him his favorite mug filled with the steaming tea. "Then pray tell why you are here, dear brother mine."

"I want you to join me for dinner. Saturday night. Fitzgerald's." He looked at me with eyes feigning innocence.

I poured tea into my own teacup. The Russian one that I was using in my current novella. Gorgeous design. Delicate blue netting on a white background, as if tied with simple gilded bows. I stirred in some cream and watched it swirl around before blending into that perfect shade of caramel.

"Hello?"

I looked up. "What?"

"I realize the tea is far more interesting than I could ever be, but I asked you a question. Would you join me for dinner Saturday night?"

"What's the catch?" I asked, then blew on my tea.

"Who said there's a catch?"

"Chad. It's not my birthday. It's not *your* birthday. It's not a holiday. You never ask me out to dinner. There's got to be a catch." I looked over my glasses at him, pinning him with my best accusatory glare.

"Okay, fine. There's someone I'd like you to meet. I've got a date. I thought we could—"

"Nope. No way. I don't do double dates. Not with you. Not with anyone. End of discussion."

He slapped his palms on my countertop. "Lucy, why are you so stubborn?! What could possibly be the harm in going out for a nice meal with your brother and a couple of other people?"

I flashed him a palm. "Not happening."

"When was the last time you had a date? Had cell phones been invented yet? Were eight-tracks still in your stereo? C'mon, sis. Humor me."

I blew out a huff for effect. "I have no interest in going out, sitting around and making small talk with some stranger while—"

"He's not a stranger."

"—you sit and make goo-goo eyes with some girl." I stopped, setting my cup down. "What do you mean he's not a stranger?"

"It's someone you know."

I blinked. "Well, why didn't you say so? Who is it?"

"I don't know if I should say. You're making this all so difficult. Maybe he deserves better. Maybe I should find someone who actually wants to go out with him."

"Chad, I swear. I'm gonna hurt you."

Gertie barked. Twice.

Chad reached down to pet her. "See? Even Gertie's upset with you."

"Fine. I don't want to know." I slammed a drawer shut then stomped toward the refrigerator. I opened it, unsure what I was looking for. Ah. Leftover fruit salad. I grabbed the bowl and ripped off the plastic covering while shutting the refrigerator with my rear end.

Chad reached for a strawberry, but I batted his hand away. Our eyes locked.

"Y'know, for someone who doesn't get out much, sis, you sure don't seem very grateful."

"Who said I need help finding dates? That's what I want to know. Why is it your business to beg some poor guy to go out with your 'pitiful' sister?" I plopped down on the opposite stool at the counter and chomped down on a slice of fresh pineapple.

"First, he's not some 'poor guy.' Second, I didn't 'beg' him to take you out. He asked *me* about *you*. Okay? And third, it's my business because I care about you. You sit home night after night, so absorbed in your stories, you never even think about doing something fun for a change. Seriously, Lucy, your characters have more of a life than you do! How sad is that? And it's not like you couldn't get a date, you just haven't made any effort in, what—a decade?"

I ran my hands through my hair then rested my chin on my fist. "Who is it, Chad?"

"Mark Christopher. Your UPS guy."

My heart skipped a beat. At least I think that's what it was. Mark? My hunky UPS guy? Mark asked my brother about *me*? No way. I lifted my head to pin another stare on him.

"How in the world would you even know who my UPS guy is?"

He grabbed the biggest strawberry in the bowl and tossed it in his mouth. "Easy. We both work out at the Y. I see him there several times a week."

I let that one work itself through my brain cells. I could easily see Mark working out, what with him being so buff and all. And Chad was a die-hard when it came to staying in shape. It's what caused all his female students to bat their mascara-drenched eyes at him.

Huh. Mark and Chad. Working out together. Small world.

"He's in great shape. The guy's an ox. He can lift—"

"And what, he just came up to you and said, 'So you're Lucy's brother, I wanna ask her out?'"

Chad's lips turned up in that smile of his. "Well, not word-for-word, but yeah. More or less."

"Huh."

"Yeah. Huh. Seems you have an admirer, little sister."

"And he wants to go out with me. Saturday night."

"That's a fact."

"I haven't got a thing to wear."

He jumped up. "That's it. I give up. Try to do a favor and what do I get? Nothing but grief. Honestly, Luce, you're worse than my students."

My mind fingered through my closet. "Wait. I've got that little black dress. I haven't worn it since—"

"We'll pick you up at seven." He jumped up and started to leave the room. "Oh, and sis?"

"Yeah?"

"Try to get over your cold by then, okay? That red-eye-snotty-nose thing is *not* a good look on you."

I threw a blueberry at him, which bounced off his retreating derriere and dropped on the floor tiles.

"See you Saturday!" his voice echoed down the hall.

I cleaned up the kitchen and decided I should get back to work. I'm not quite sure why, but I found myself strolling by the front door, stealing glances out the beveled glass. Y'know, just in case a brown truck should drive by . . . or maybe stop by to make a delivery. Or something.

A few minutes later I was reviewing my last couple of pages. I loved writing these stories. Ever since I'd received my Aunt Lucille's teacup collection, I'd been a writing machine—each of those cups inspiring romantic tales in all kinds of settings. Some were stories that popped into my own imagination as I studied these porcelain works of art. Others sprang from all the fascinating stories she'd shared with me so many years ago during those magical afternoon tea parties.

My finger traced the Russian teacup, with its unusual blue and gold netting design. A smile curled its way up my face as I warmed back into my story. I loved these characters. *Loved* them. And suddenly, I knew just what needed to happen next . . .

Chapter 1

"Keri! The Blankenship cabin is on fire! Get over here. Now!"

Keri McMillan strained to see her alarm clock. Three-fifteen in the morning. "No, no, no! This can't be happening!" she shouted into the phone. She threw back her covers and jumped out of bed. "Carson, did you call the fire department?"

"They're already here. Hurry, Keri!"

"On my way." She flew into her closet, grabbed her clothes and dashed into the bathroom. A minute later she was dressed and rushing outside into the frigid Oregon night.

Oh God, no! Please let them save it!

Tires squealing, she stomped the accelerator and headed for the construction site, consumed with dread. The Blankenship's cabin was her dad's latest design, intended to be a high-end showcase for his log cabin company. Perched high atop a bluff overlooking the Pacific, the luxury home was just one week shy of opening its doors to the new owners with plenty of time left to decorate for the holidays.

Keri's mind raced, a storm of thoughts and emotions swirling in her head. She'd only been home from school for three days, returning after first semester finals during her second year at New York University. With dwindling funds, Keri decided to move home for a year, work for her dad, and stockpile every penny she earned. She was determined to fill her savings account then head back to complete her degree in journalism.

As she pulled up to the raging fire, she couldn't help but think her dreams were going up in smoke before her eyes. Fire trucks flanked the back of the house, their hoses attempting to douse the flames that licked the sky from the enormous two-story structure. Keri's heart pounded as tears burned her eyes.

I've got to call Dad.

As she reached for her cell phone, someone banged on her window. Keri jumped then pushed open the door. "Carson, you scared me half to death!

"Sorry, Keri, I was just—"

"What happened? How did it start?" She stepped out of her vehicle.

"Don't know yet." Her dad's construction chief rubbed his face with his hands. "A neighbor called the fire department, then Bill called me first chance he got. He knew this was one of ours. It's bad, Keri. Real bad."

She wrapped her arm around his thick waist. Carson had been with her dad from the start when they first launched McMillan Log Homes twenty years ago. She wanted to comfort him but couldn't think of a thing to say. He hung his arm around her shoulders, releasing a long, tired sigh.

"We called the Blankenships, but all we got was their voice mail. Apparently they're still in Europe. We'll keep trying."

"Carson, I've got to call Dad. He needs to come home."

"I know. I was just hoping the guys could put this out before any major damage was done. Too late for that now, I guess."

She looked at the emerging shell of the massive home, sickened by the sight of it. The lump in her throat hindered a response. Keri climbed back in her car, pressed the auto-dial number for her dad's cell phone, and closed her eyes.

Grant Dawson hit the brakes on his SUV and grabbed his camera. His windshield reflected the blaze roaring against the black December sky. His mind began framing the best pictures, the captions catapulting through his head. He could see the bold print on his front page. NEW OCEANSIDE ESTATE DESTROYED BY FIRE. *No, too blah.* DREAMS SHATTERED BY MIDNIGHT BLAZE. *Too cheesy? Maybe—*

"Grant! Over here!"

He couldn't help but smile. Nita Sanders, in all her glory. Pink foam curlers wrapped with her bright white hair peeked out beneath a wool scarf. Green flannel pajamas flashed from beneath her winter coat, tucked into oversized yellow galoshes. He was tempted to snap a picture just to get a rise out of her, but it hardly seemed appropriate at a time like this. When he moved here six months ago, Nita was the first person in this tight-knit coastal town to befriend him. She had welcomed him with uncommon hospitality, taking him in like one of her own.

He pressed his lips together to hide the smirk. "Nita, what brings you out on this beautiful night?"

She whacked him on the arm. "The fire, you big lug! Do I need to remind you that's my house just across the road? I heard all the sirens and got over here fast as I could. It's also my brothers—"

"Aunt Nita!"

Grant noticed the young woman approaching them as they made their way toward the inferno. Surprised, he did an immediate double-take. He'd never seen her before. The blustery wind whipped a mass of light brown curls around a face etched with worry. Her skin was flawless, her eyes sparkling with tears in the surreal glow of the blaze. He forced his gaze away from her, not wanting to be caught staring.

This must be the niece Nita's been babbling about so much. The journalism student, home from school and none too happy about it. No doubt a Christiane Amanpour or Ashleigh Banfield wannabe.

Weeks ago, Nita had broached the subject, batting her merry eyes at him. "Grant, couldn't you just tell her a thing or two about the business? Show her the ropes? She's so disappointed about having to come home. Maybe you could hire her part-time to help out with the paper."

Since then, every time she'd brought up the subject, he'd envisioned some pimple-faced, gawky coed wearing black-rimmed glasses, nipping at his heels, bugging him to death with a million questions.

What was her name? Sherry? No, Carrie. That's right. Carrie. Like the freak from the Stephen King movie. Sheesh, I hope she doesn't destroy Waterford Bay with her telekinetic powers.

He watched Nita hug her very un-Sissy Spacek niece, then quickly moved away from them, anxious to avoid the inevitable introduction.

"Sweetie, did you call your father?"

"Yes. He's on his way home. He's devastated. He actually broke down over the phone, Nita. You know Dad—he never does that. I can't even imagine what he'll do when he sees what's left of this."

Nita pulled her close, hugging her tight. "Honey, he'll survive. He always does. I stood beside him, holding you in my arms when we buried your sweet mother. You were just five days old. If he can survive that, he'll get through this. God will see him through."

Keri took a deep breath, pushing the thoughts from her mind. "C'mon, let's see what Bill can tell us."

They tromped through the mud, stepping over a tangled web of hoses. The local fire chief watched as his men took control of the blaze. Keri was relieved to see most of the flames almost extinguished, despite the waves of smoke still billowing into the air. "Bill, any idea what started it?" She covered her nose and mouth with her knitted muffler.

Bill Gregory shook his head. "We won't know until it's out and we can investigate. The structure was fully engulfed by the time we got here. Good thing Bertie next door called when she did. With this wind and all these trees around here, we could have lost a lot of homes tonight. Where's your dad?"

"He's in Sacramento bidding on a job, but he's on his way home now. He should be back early this afternoon."

Nita coughed. "*If* he doesn't get stopped for speeding. Mercy, that brother of mine has a lead foot."

Bill gnawed on his signature toothpick. "Oh, he'll be here by noon, if I know Tyler. You can count on that, Nita."

A loud crack ripped through the night air.

"GET BACK! MOVE IT! MOVE IT!"

As the warning cut through the chaos, Keri felt herself propelled backward. Bill shoved her and Nita away from the house with startling force as a sickening crash exploded behind them. All three landed in the mud beside Keri's car. Bill scrambled away from them, barking orders and demanding a headcount of his men.

Keri sat up to see what had happened. The entire second floor had pancaked onto the first floor, leaving only the stone fireplace standing like a lone statue draped in a whirlwind of sparks, smoke, and debris.

"Nita! Are you okay?" She crawled to her aunt's side.

"I think so, honey. Although it's the first time in my life I'm thankful for the extra padding on my back side. Help me up, will you?"

"Here, let me," someone offered. "Nita, are you all right?"

Keri didn't recognize the voice of the man helping her aunt back on her feet. A dark baseball cap covered his head, but she could see still see his thick salt and pepper hair. *Heavy on the salt.* A fancy Nikon hung from a strap around his neck over a blue squall jacket.

"I'm fine, I think. Good heavens, what a mess!" Nita pulled the scarf from her head and wiped her muddy hands on it. "And Keri, look at you—covered head to toe."

Keri looked down at her jeans and jacket, completely covered in brown slime. She held out her hands, unsure where to wipe them.

"Here," the man said, digging a bandana from his back pocket then handing it to her.

She reached for it, finally looking up into his face. He was younger than she'd thought. The hair had fooled her. He couldn't be more than thirty, maybe thirty-two? But it was his eyes that stopped her. She wasn't expecting them to be that blue, even in the mere reflection of all the flashing lights. And there was genuine concern in them, too. *Who is this guy?*

As if her thoughts were overheard, Nita answered. "Oh Keri, honey, you haven't met Grant yet, have you? This is Grant Dawson, the editor of our local paper. I write a column for him now and then, though I think he mostly keeps me on out of pity. Grant, this is my niece, Keri McMillan. The one I told you about."

She wiped the mud off her hand as best she could then extended it toward him. For a split second, he didn't respond. *Hello? I'm holding my hand out here?*

He took it briefly, gave it a quick shake. "Nice to meet you, but I need to see what happened over there. If you'll excuse me."

They stared after him, Keri still rubbing her hands on his bandana. "Friendly guy."

Nita used her scarf to wipe off some of the mud on Keri's face. "Who, Grant? Oh, normally he's a teddy bear. Just focused. Used to be a big shot reporter for the *L.A. Times*. Got tired of the politics and rat race, and moved here a little over six months ago. Took over *the Waterford Weekly* when Ed Furley decided to retire and move to Florida. Grant was a writer, not a publisher, but he's learned fast. Does a nice job with our little paper."

Keri watched him taking pictures of the wreckage. "He left one of the biggest papers in the country to come *here* and run a small-town weekly? What an idiot."

"A kinda handsome idiot, though, don't you think? I've always thought he looked like that dear reporter from NBC. You know—the one who died over in Iraq, God rest his soul. What was his name? David something . . ."

"David Bloom?"

"David Bloom! So you see it too, the resemblance?"

Keri studied her aunt's face. Perfectly manicured eyebrows danced in mischief on a genteel face betraying her age. "Nita? Forget it."

"I'm just saying—"

"No, *I'm* just saying—I'm not interested, don't go there, and don't bring it up again. Got it?"

Nita's face melted in disappointment. "Oh sure, fine. Take away all my fun."

Keri grabbed her aunt's elbow and steered her toward her car. "I'm not home for fun, Nita. I'm home to work and save money.

Period." She stopped, turning to face the smoldering cabin. "Let's just hope Dad's insurance is paid up."

"Well, if not, you could always go to work for the local paper." Nita planted a kiss on her cheek. "In fact, I've already talked to Grant about hiring you while you're home. Might be a good chance to get your feet wet and—"

"You're impossible."

"I know. That's why you love me, though. Now come along. Let's go get cleaned up then I'll make us some breakfast." She turned back. "Maybe I should invite Grant to join—"

"Not gonna happen. Move it." Keri gently pushed her aunt toward the car. As Nita grumbled her way to Keri's vehicle, Keri took one last look at the smoky skeleton of the once-beautiful log home and sighed.

"Oh Daddy, I'm so sorry."

Chapter 2

Grant leaned closer to the computer screen, studying the thumbnail images of the pictures he took at the fire. *Good job, Dawson, good job.* He selected ten pictures, a variety of different shots of both the burning cabin and the firefighters he interviewed. He would narrow it down to five pictures to sprinkle throughout his story.

Satisfied, he stretched, happy to have so much done this early in the day. Normally, he'd trek over to Chandlers for an espresso to kick-start his morning. But the pouring rain and chilly temperatures convinced him to settle for a cup of his own brew. He made his way back to the small kitchen area of the old house that served as the office for the *Waterford Weekly.*

Scooping the coffee beans into the grinder, he realized he was smiling. Not so many months ago, he would have already popped a handful of pills by this time of day. The relentless pressure of working for a paper like the *Times* had taken its toll. At first, he'd loved it. The chase for the hot story, the killer pace of the office and constant deadlines, the opportunity to travel—heady stuff for a kid just out of college. Landing a dream job at a major newspaper was the biggest adrenaline hit he'd ever known.

But in less than ten years he'd had enough. The glitz that initially lured him into the job only frustrated him. He was constantly at odds with his bosses, usually fighting over political philosophies and the resulting pressures to give his stories an "edge." But that was only part of it. Even now, more than six months later, he tried not to think about it, the loss just too painful.

"Anybody home?"

"Back here, Pop."

He heard the slow footfalls of his father ambling down the hall. Shep Dawson appeared in the doorway, his raincoat dripping on the hardwood floor.

"Whoa there, Hoss, let's get that coat and hat off you. You're puddling the real estate, old man."

Shep's lopsided grin barely lifted one side of his mouth. "S'pose you're right."

Grant helped his father out of the heavy slicker and weathered captain's hat. "I'll put these on the back porch rockers. Grab yourself a cup of coffee there. Cream and sugar's on the counter."

"Well . . . okay," Shep mumbled.

Grant draped his dad's rain gear on the covered porch then joined him in the tiny kitchen. "To what do I owe this honor?" He reached for his Dodgers mug. "You haven't been to town in weeks, Pop."

Shep shuffled toward Grant's office, heading for the easy chair facing his son's desk. "You left early. Didn't come back. Just wondered."

Grant stirred cream into his coffee then plopped down in his desk chair. It amused him endlessly that his dad never used the telephone. Instead of trekking to town, something his father hated to do, he could have picked up the phone. But Shep Dawson was a man of few words. The telephone—forget the convenience of a cell phone—was nothing but a nuisance to him.

"Sorry. I should've called you. There was a big house fire up on the bluff. That new luxury cabin Tyler McMillan's outfit built. Got a call about three o'clock this morning. Afterward, I came here and got started on the story. Paper goes out tomorrow, and I knew this had to be our lead."

His dad nodded, sipped his coffee again.

The grandfather clock in the corner ticked in rhythm, the only sound between them. He studied his father, still surprised by this unusual visit. Shep was a loner. As captain of a whale-watching vessel for Oregon's tourist industry, he stayed mostly to himself. His buddy, Joe Trent, played host to the many guests on Shep's whaler always entertaining them with plenty of enthusiasm, humor, and more knowledge of the whales of these waters than anyone else along this coast. Shep simply took care of the boat, steering her to the favorite waters of the gray whale.

Grant was used to his father's silence. It was just his way. When he'd left his job in Los Angeles, his dad offered for him to move in with him and live aboard *The Sarah Jane,* his 64-foot Grand Banks Alaskan docked at the Waterford Bay Marina. They'd always been close, but Grant knew his father liked his solitude. Always had. At least since Grant's mother died of breast cancer fifteen years ago. Sarah Jane Dawson.

He'd thanked his father for the offer, insisting he needed to live closer to the office in town. He'd bought a cabin just off Main Street and happily called it home, giving both himself and his dad the privacy they both needed. Still, he made sure to check on his dad on a regular basis, usually driving out to *The Sarah Jane* two or three times a week for a game of chess or a slow conversation under the stars.

They'd settled into a quiet routine together. And it was just what Grant needed at this point in his life. Peace and quiet.

"Bad?"

"Bad what?"

"Bad fire?"

"Oh." Grant smiled. "Yes. A total loss. The owners were supposed to move in sometime next week, I believe."

"Strangers?"

"No. They're from Idaho, I think, but they used to summer here a lot. Apparently decided to build a permanent home here. It's a shame, too. That was some place. You'd have loved it. A whole bank of windows on both levels overlooking the ocean, wrap-around porch. Incredible view. Now it's gone."

"How?"

"How what?"

"How'd it start?"

"They don't know yet. Bill said there'd be an investigation. I'd hate to think it was arson, but who knows."

Shep nodded again. The clock ticked on.

Grant finished his coffee and leaned back in his chair. "No charters today with all this rain?"

Shep shook his head.

"So what are your plans for the day?"

Shep shrugged. "Need Fig Newtons. Oatmeal."

"Tell you what. You pick up your groceries, let me do a little more work here, then we'll meet over at Chandlers for a couple of cinnamon rolls. My treat."

His father stood up, dug a hand deep into the pocket of his worn pants. "Well—"

Grant scooted his chair back and stood up. "Oh, c'mon. It won't kill you, Pop. If anyone tries to bite you, I'll whomp 'em with my baseball bat. Fair enough?" He took the empty cup from his father and deposited both on the kitchen counter.

Shep headed for the back porch. "We'll see."

"No good. I'll see you there at nine sharp. Don't make me come looking for you."

"Well sir . . ."

The back door slammed, punctuating the old man's signature retort, his answer to everything.

Grant chuckled at the familiar peculiarities of his father, loving him all the more for it. He poured himself another cup of coffee. If he worked hard he could have the new layout ready to roll in another hour. He looked out the workroom window to see sheets of rain parading down the street. He still wasn't used to this weather.

Especially on press day. Paper and ink weren't too fond of humidity in the hundred percentile range. Could be another long night.

As he took his seat, he reached for the mouse to scan through the pictures again. He scrolled through them to make sure he hadn't missed anything important. A face popped out at him. *How did I miss this one?*

He clicked on the thumbnail image to see the bigger version of Keri McMillan talking to Bill. Grant remembered the shot now. He'd used his zoom lens, focusing on the moisture of her lips to bring her into perfect clarity. Her hand was suspended above her hair. He remembered that she'd grabbed a fistful of those curls in apparent frustration at Bill's remarks shortly after he took the picture. He clicked on the zoom icon, making Keri's image even bigger. She was without question beautiful. The lines of her jaw, her slender nose. Olive-green eyes filled with emotion. Even in the darkness, he'd noticed her teeth. She hadn't smiled once, but as she'd talked, he could see they were perfect and straight and white.

So her teeth are nice. She's not a horse, Dawson. Get a grip.

He leaned forward, looking closer at the computer screen. Tears were pooled in those dark green eyes.

It disturbed him to look at her in such obvious pain.

It disturbed him even more that it *disturbed* him at all.

"Feel better?"

Keri toweled off her hair. "Much better. Thanks."

"Our clothes are in the wash. They'll be ready by the time we finish breakfast. Here, have some coffee. NO, Muffy! Get down!"

The ball of fur bouncing at Keri's feet took a sudden beeline for the sofa, diving under its plaid skirt.

"What *was* that?"

"That's my naughty, naughty little girl. She's a rescue from the pound, but I'm about to take her back if she doesn't start minding me. I've had her about three months now, I guess. And I've decided she's schizophrenic."

Keri leveled her eyes at her aunt. "A schizophrenic dog?"

"Oh very. When she's playful like this, I call her Muffy. Cute as a button. But sometimes she's rowdy and acts almost like a man with an attitude, if you can imagine. That's when I call her—*him*—Jock. Then there's the demure side of her when she thinks she's some best-of-show poodle or something. I call her Fifi on those days.

And then there's Pedro—"

"Let me guess. Spirited and hyper like a Chihuahua."

"Very good!" Nita beamed. "But she's mostly Shih Tzu. She just doesn't know it."

"A schizo-Shih Tzu. Now there's a mouthful."

Nita dropped her head back and roared with laughter. "Oh, that's perfect, Keri! I must remember to use that in my column next week. 'A schizo-Shih Tzu'—love it!"

Keri sipped her coffee. "Mmm, this is really good. Thanks, Nita." Keri wrapped the towel around her head. The soft pink robe felt heavenly against her skin. "I might just have to steal this from you. I'd forgotten how much I love chenille."

"Take it, honey. I've got plenty more where that came from. Now sit. I'll have these eggs cooked in a jiffy. I put some cream cheese in them for you."

"You remembered. You're too good to me, Aunt Nita." Keri took a seat at the counter, releasing a heavy sigh.

Nita turned, still stirring the gooey egg mixture with a wooden spoon. "Now, Keri, you've got to let this go. It's all going to work out. We need to be thankful that no one was hurt tonight. And thank goodness the Blankenships hadn't moved in yet. Think of what *could* have happened."

Keri dropped her head in her hands with a moan. "I didn't even think of that."

"You didn't? That was the first thought I had when I saw those flames. I thanked God no one was sleeping in that house yet."

Keri looked up, shaking her head. "What kind of horrible person am I? That thought never crossed my mind. All I could think of was Dad, and how much this would upset him. And . . ."

"And?"

She took another sip of the steaming coffee and set the mug back on the counter. "And how it would affect *me*. If it would affect how much Dad could pay me this year." She rubbed her face. "How's that for compassion?"

Nita scraped the eggs out of the black iron skillet onto two separate plates, then pulled a tray of biscuits from the oven. She set them on the stove. "Grab some orange juice for us, will you?"

Keri knew her aunt too well. Nita avoided answering the question Keri put out there, but she knew an answer would come. And knowing Nita, she was praying for wisdom even as she dished up bacon to put on their plates.

When they finally sat down on the bar stools, Nita unfolded the cloth napkin and laid it across her lap. Keri followed suit, knowing the ritual. Her aunt reached for her hand and bowed her head.

"Father, we thank You for Your mercy and grace. We thank You for protecting everyone tonight during this horrible fire. Lord, we trust You with every smidgen of our lives, and we're trusting You with this one as well. Bring Tyler home safely. Protect him as he travels. And prepare the Blankenships for this devastating news. May they feel Your presence even in their hour of sadness."

She squeezed Keri's hand. "And Father, please comfort my sweet Keri. Lord, cover her with Your peace and understanding. Help her to know that all things truly do work together for good for those who know and love You. Help her to trust You in the days ahead as she pursues her goals. But more than anything, Lord, help her to rest in Your open arms. Let her feel those arms around her even now.

"Thank You for Your blessings and the food for which we are about to partake. In Jesus' name, amen."

She squeezed Keri's hand again, but Keri couldn't speak.

"So eat, already! The girls tell me their food always gets cold when I pray, but I just can't help it. Prayer diarrhea, what can I say? C'mon. Take a bite."

Keri smiled as she picked up her fork. "Nita, Nita, Nita. What am I going to do with you?"

Nita shrugged with a chuckle as she buttered a fat biscuit.

"How are the girls these days? I haven't seen them yet."

"Oh my goodness, they're ornery as ever. Which is why I love them so much. Peas in a pod and all that. Stop by Chandlers on your way to the office and say hello, okay? They're all dying to hug your neck."

Keri took a bite of the enormous fluffy biscuit. "Mmmm . . . oh Aunt Nita, this is so good. I didn't know I was so hungry."

"Of course you are. You eat like a bird if I'm not around. You've lost weight, missy, and I aim to fatten you up while you're home. I'll send you back to New York absolutely waddling." Nita laughed in the warm, boisterous way Keri had always loved. How could the sound of someone's laughter bring so much comfort?

"Like I'm going to let that happen?" But she knew it would be a battle. "Then again, these eggs are to die for. No one makes them better."

They chatted over the rest of their meal and Keri even succumbed to Nita's offer of a second biscuit. Dawn was just breaking, so there was no need to rush to the office yet. Dad wouldn't be home for several more hours. After they cleaned the kitchen, they settled into the den over another cup of coffee. Muffy scampered into Nita's lap and settled in for a nap as rumble of thunder gently shook the house.

"I was wondering when that storm would arrive," Nita mused, sipping her coffee.

"Wouldn't be Oregon if it didn't storm every day." Keri lifted the framed picture from the table beside the sofa. "Oh Nita, I miss Uncle Rafe so much."

Nita smiled, setting her mug on the coffee table. "I know, sweetie. I do too. Not a day goes by that I don't talk to him, laugh with him. He's still my best friend. After all these years."

Keri caressed the pictured face of her uncle. It was Rafe Sanders who first sparked a love for journalism in Keri's heart. A war correspondent for the Associated Press, Rave had traveled all over the world covering some of the biggest stories of his time. His lively tales of daring adventures in far-off lands like Vietnam, South Africa, Iraq, and Israel had planted a burning desire in her to follow in his footsteps. She was only thirteen when he was killed in a bombing in Bosnia. The pain of his loss still haunted her, but it was also the driving force in her quest to carry on the work he loved so much.

"And oh, how he loved you, Keri." Nita's smiling eyes misted. "You were the daughter he never had. He would have given you the moon had you asked."

Keri smiled. "And didn't I know it? He spoiled me rotten. Remember that Christmas when I asked for a Belle doll from *Beauty & the Beast*?"

"How could I forget? He was in Europe and once he heard his Keri wanted that doll, there was nothing doing, but he had to get you an authentic Belle from Paris. Nothing was too good for his Keri."

"I was *so* proud of that doll! All my other friends got theirs from Wal-Mart, but not me. My Uncle Rafe made sure I had the real Belle. I was convinced he bought that doll in Belle's little village, the same one in the movie."

Keri fingered the tiny heart-shaped necklace against her skin. It was Rafe's last gift to her, on her thirteenth birthday. *You're a teenager now, princess. And a princess must have diamonds! I didn't think you'd wear a tiara to school, so I thought this would do instead.*

She'd never taken it off.

With a deep breath, she stood up, carrying her mug to the kitchen. "I've got to get moving before I fall asleep. I need to meet Carson at the office in another hour and call the insurance company."

Nita followed her, stifling a yawn. "Are you sure you don't want to take a nap first? It's going to be a long day, honey."

Keri snuggled into the arms of her aunt. "Can't. If I lie down, I'll never get up." She pecked her on the cheek, and headed for the laundry room.

Nita followed. "I'll be at the Christmas tree lot this afternoon. The trees should arrive around three or four."

Keri pulled the warm clothes from the dryer. "Is it that time already? I can't believe it."

"Good heavens, yes. In fact, we're behind schedule. Our growers had a sudden death in the family. Normally we're set up and selling the day after Thanksgiving, but what can you do? As long as we make enough to put in a new playground for the kids at church, I'm happy. Last year we had such good sales, we were able to put a new steeple on the sanctuary."

Keri folded Nita's flannel pajamas. "Still the Christmas Tree Queen of Waterford Bay, aren't you? Gotta love it." Keri disappeared into the guest room to change her clothes.

"Will we see you at Chandlers later this morning?" Nita chimed down the hall.

"Sure. I'll try to stop by after I meet with Carson," Keri answered, pulling on her jeans, still warm from the dryer. "I'm not sure what time but I'll come by. Hopefully before Dad gets back." She finished dressing and rounded the corner where her aunt leaned against the wall.

"What? Why are you looking at me like that?" she asked, pulling on her jacket.

The mischief had returned to Nita's face. "Me? Mischievous? Not a chance. Just don't forget to stop by."

With that, her aunt sashayed down the hall humming an old Tony Bennett tune. Keri couldn't place the song, but was more concerned by her aunt's elusiveness. She knew Nita had something up her sleeve.

She hoped it had nothing to do with the new editor of the local paper.

Chapter 3

In any other part of the country, a cold and rainy morning would scare away the customers. Not so at Chandlers Restaurant in Waterford Bay, Oregon. These were the mornings that filled the blue checkered tables and sold out the morning's triple batch of cinnamon rolls. The bell rang constantly as customers came and went, their chatter about the big fire buzzing from one table to the next.

"Nita, when did you say Tyler is due back?" Theta Morris asked while putting her rain bonnet back on, tying it beneath her ample chin. Theta, Arlene and Marla—Nita's "girls"—had discussed the fire for more than an hour at their usual booth, first on the right-hand side of the cozy restaurant.

"Any time now," Nita answered. "I just wish he'd get here. I'll feel better once I talk to him face to face. And I know Keri's just worried sick for him. Lord, that poor child needs her daddy's hug about now, I expect."

Arlene rose first, Theta and Marla following suit, as they so often did. "Well, you tell him we're mighty sorry and we're all praying for him."

"Let us know if there's anything we can do, will you?" Marla asked, buttoning her slicker.

"I will, dear."

Theta gave Nita a hug. "And you tell that niece of yours to stop by and see us later, okay? Goodness, hasn't that child had enough heartache for one lifetime?"

"I know," Nita sighed. "But we'll get her through this. And Tyler too. See you girls later at the tree lot. If we don't all float away first."

The three ladies slowly made their way out the front door. Nita looked at her watch, disappointed that Keri hadn't arrived in time to see her friends. Of course, Keri wasn't the only one who hadn't shown up yet . . . She'd put in a call to Grant shortly after Keri left her house, encouraging him to drop by the restaurant.

"What's up, Nita?" he'd asked.

"Oh nothing. Just thought it'd be nice to sit and chat after such a difficult morning."

He'd chuckled then promised he'd try to stop by.

She leaned over for a better look at the front door, disappointed her plans hadn't come together. She dug into her purse, foraging for her lipstick when the bell over the door rang once more.

"One cinnamon roll. That's it. And then we'll go. I promise, Dad."

A smile lifted the lips she'd just painted when she heard Grant's voice. She looked up in time to see him ushering in his father as both men shed their raincoats. Another twinge of disappointment hit her, wishing Grant had just come alone. She hadn't seen Shep in months. Rarely did. *He's such an odd duck, that one, always staying to himself. Never offering so much as a hello or how are you.*

Years ago when his wife died, she and the girls had all taken meals to him. As members of The Circle at their church, it was routine—a simple act of benevolence in times of grief. But Shep had hardly said thanks when they arrived with their piping hot dishes, the old man mumbling about them not needing to do it. They didn't get their Pyrex dishes back for over a year. One day Arlene found them stacked on the steps of the church with a short note. "Thanks. Shep."

But Nita had never held it against him, knowing he was mostly just shy. *Some people are just like that. Still, you'd think after all these years he would have been awfully lonely living out there on that boat all by himself.* When Grant arrived in town, she was shocked to find out the handsome new newspaper editor was the old man's son. Grant was outgoing, personable, and quite charming. *Must have gotten that from his mother,* she mused, watching them now.

"Good morning, Nita—again," Grant greeted as they approached a nearby table.

"Hi Grant. Nice to see you, Shep." She noticed the elder Dawson avoided eye-contact, merely nodding. "Why don't you all join me here? My girls just left and I'm not ready to leave just yet. Thought I'd wait out the downpour."

Shep shot a look of desperation at his son, one that Nita didn't miss. She chuckled silently, not at all surprised.

Grant looked back and forth between them. "Dad, okay with you if we—"

"Oh, c'mon," she said, scooting over in the booth. "I'd love the company. Besides, Clara just took a fresh pan of rolls out of the oven. Can't you smell them?"

Grant smiled and clapped his dad on the back, directing him into the other side of Nita's booth. "You drive a hard bargain. We'd love to join you, wouldn't we, Dad?"

An uneasy smile spread beneath Shep's heavy white mustache. "Well . . ."

Clara stopped by with fresh mugs of coffee before taking their order. The bell over the door rang yet again. Nita had to lean over to see around Clara, pleased to find Keri stomping her boots on the welcome mat.

"Keri, sweetie, over here," she called.

Keri made her way to the booth, then stopped abruptly when she saw the two men seated across from her aunt. "Oh, I'm sorry. I thought you were alone."

Grant stood up. "Miss McMillan."

A tight smile. "Mr. Dawson."

Nita waved her niece over to sit beside her. "Oh, for the love of Pete, can we dispense with all the formality? Grant. Grant's dad, Shep. Keri. Nita. There. We're all on a first name basis now."

Keri settled into the booth next to her aunt, wishing with all her heart she could run right back out into the rain. Like she needed another get acquainted chat with this ridiculous man and his father? She busied herself shedding her raincoat and hat, hanging them on the booth's side hook behind her.

"Well, now, isn't this nice?" Nita offered, her smile stretched wide.

Silence.

Grant cleared his throat. "Any news on the fire?"

Keri looked up at him, not wanting to discuss something so painful with this stranger. But his eyes stopped her cold. There was sincerity in those clear blue eyes. She started to answer, but nothing came out.

I really want to hate this guy. He threw away everything I've wanted my entire life. A perfect job with one of the top newspapers in the country. To come here? To this tiny excuse for a town with its pathetic little newspaper?

Instead pressed her lips together and toyed with the napkin. "No. Dad called a few minutes ago. He's only about a half hour out." She turned to her aunt. "That's why I stopped by. I wanted you to come back to the site with me. I think we should both be there when he arrives."

"Mind if I come along?" Grant asked, interrupting. "If there's any news, I'd like to include it in my feature on the story."

Keri took a deep breath, trying not to show her aggravation. She leveled a gaze at him, choosing her words carefully. "Our conversation will be private. But it's a free country. Do what you have to do. Just stay out of the way."

"Keri!" Nita laughed nervously. "That's a little harsh, don't you think? Grant is only trying to do his job."

Keri shrugged, digging her thumbnail into a blue line on the tablecloth. "It's been a long day. What can I say?"

"Oh honey, don't let it get to you. Once you see your father, I'm sure you'll feel better."

"My apologies," Grant said quietly. "I realize this is hard on you. On all of you."

Keri blew out a sigh. "No, I'm the one who needs to apologize." She stole a brief look at him. "Sorry."

He nodded, apparently accepting her apology. "I'm sure you'll learn more once your dad gets here and has a chance to talk with the insurance folks. In cases of suspected arson, it usually—"

Keri felt her teeth grinding. "I'm sure we'll handle it, Mr. Dawson."

"Grant."

"Whatever. Dad is perfectly capable of dealing with the insurance people." She took a sip of coffee hoping he'd get the hint. *It's none of your business.*

"Honey, Grant is just trying to help," Nita added quietly.

Keri ignored her. "Besides, don't you have a paper to publish?"

She watched his eyebrows rise along with a shrug and upheld hands. "Message delivered. Loud and clear."

Clara returned with a plate full of rolls and topped off their coffee. "Enjoy."

Grant grabbed the ticket and stuffed it in his pocket. "Ladies? May I?" He lifted one of the hot confections onto a small serving plate and handed it to Nita.

As he started to dish a second one, Keri held up her hand. "Thanks, but I'll take a pass. I'm still full from your breakfast, Nita."

Her aunt took a bite and wiped her mouth. "What's one got to do with the other?" She barked a laugh and cut another piece of the gooey roll.

Keri smiled, then caught Grant's dad stealing a look at her aunt. She noticed the slightest upward twitch in that bushy mustache of his. When his eyes tracked to Keri's, his weathered face reddened before he quickly busied himself with another sip of coffee. Keri remembered the scruffy whaleboat captain from her high school days. All the kids at school thought he was mute, as he never spoke a word on his rare visits to town. They conjured up all kinds of stories to explain his silence, including a crazy tale about a whale rising up out of the water and lunging at the captain as he stood on the deck of his boat. "Bit the tongue right off him," the adolescent legend claimed. Then, just a couple of years ago she was shocked to hear him say hello one day as they passed on the street.

Grant interrupted her thoughts. “Look, I honestly meant no harm. And I certainly don’t want to intrude on your family at a time like this. Just do me one favor.”

Keri traced the rim of her coffee mug. “And what would that be?”

“Let me know if there’s anything I can do to help. I mean that. Anything at all.”

She studied his face again, wanting to throw back a sarcastic response in light of his pseudo-attempt at compassion. But Keri couldn’t find it in her. *Maybe I’m just exhausted. Maybe I just need to sleep or something. I can’t even think straight right now.* But hard as she tried, she couldn’t think of a thing to say. She took another deep breath and tried to smile, quite sure it never reached her eyes.

Nita cleared her throat. “Well, now that you mention it, Grant, would you give some thought to the possibility of Keri working for you at the paper?”

“Aunt Nita! I wouldn’t—”

“Oh come on now, Keri. You know it’s unlikely your father will be able to hire you now. So why not just make lemonade out of your madness and get some experience working for a real newspaper?”

“Lemonade out of my madness? I don’t even know how to respond to that. And for the record, I would hardly call *The Waterford Weekly* a ‘real newspaper.’ Give me a break. It’s nothing more than a silly little rag. Always has been.”

Nita squeezed her hand. “Keri, that’s out of line. Grant has done a wonderful job with our paper, and if I was you, I’d watch my tongue before saying something so rude.” She looked across the table. “Grant, I apologize for my niece. She’s normally a very kind and considerate young lady.”

Keri blew out a huff. “Fine. I’m rude. I’m out of line. I’m sorry. I believe I mentioned it’s already been a really long day. So if you’ll excuse me,” she said, gathering her rain gear and standing up, “I need to get out to the site. Shep, it was nice to meet you after all these years.”

He nodded.

“Nita, as soon as you’re done here, drive up to the Blankenship’s . . . or what’s left of it. Dad should arrive shortly.”

Nita leveled a look at her, exhaling. “Will do, honey.”

Keri pushed her hat on her head and climbed into her raincoat, not making eye contact with Grant. “Mr. Dawson.”

“Keri.”

Chapter 4

"Oh Daddy." She fell into her father's embrace, trying so hard not to cry. He needed her to be strong. She inhaled the comforting fatherly scent, catching a trace of his familiar aftershave and a hint of the cigar that always surfaced when he got stressed. She was thankful the rain had stopped so she could hug him, unencumbered by an umbrella.

"How're you doing, pumpkin?" He held on tight longer than usual, kissing the top of her head.

"I'm okay, Dad." She pulled back just enough to look up into his face. "The question is, how are *you*?"

He rubbed his nose against her forehead, then stepped to her side, tucking her safely under his arm. "It was bad enough on the drive home, trying to imagine it all. But seeing this . . . I just can't believe it." His voice broke.

Keri fought the lump surfacing in her throat. "I know. I see it with my own eyes, but I still don't believe it. I'm almost glad you weren't here to see the flames. It was surreal." She tightened her arm around his waist. "And heartbreaking."

He inhaled, obviously trying to buck up his emotion. "That it is, sweetheart." He took hold of her hand and walked toward the huge skeleton still draped in whiffs of smoke here and there. "I talked to our insurance folks on the way in. They can't close the investigation until they determine whether or not it was arson. And they can't pay me until the investigation is closed." He sighed. "Typical insurance red tape."

"You think it could be arson? Who would do such a thing?"

Before Tyler could answer, Carson pulled up and stepped out of his pickup. "Lord have mercy, what a mess."

Tyler gave his foreman a quick hug, shaking his head continually. "What a mess. What a loss."

They talked at length trying to decide what to do until a cause was determined.

"The crew said not to worry about them, Tyler. In fact, I think they're more worried about you. They know how much you had at stake here."

Tyler took a quick swipe of his eyes and let out a long sigh. "We need to take care of them, Carson. Any chance we could go ahead and give them their Christmas bonuses just to tide them over?"

Carson winced. "I'm not sure you want to do that, Tyler. At least until you get some answers. You may not have the funds for that bonus."

Another long sigh.

Keri couldn't bear seeing her father in such pain. She wandered away from them, stepping under the yellow crime scene tape that stretched around the perimeter of the home. Eventually she approached the once beautiful stone fireplace, now blackened with smoke. She searched her heart, wishing she had some encouraging words of wisdom to offer her father and his foreman. A sick feeling rolled through her stomach.

She'd seen more than just disappointment and heartache in her father's eyes. She'd heard more than mere frustration or stress in the tone of his voice. *Despair. That's what it is. Dad's never been the kind to let despair overcome him. So why now? Sure, his show house is destroyed, but he can build again, right?*

She kicked absently at the soggy ash on the ruined floor beneath her as her thoughts continued on a downward spiral. *Nita's right. He probably can't afford to pay me as planned. I'll work for him, but I can't expect a dime. He'll need every dime he can find.*

Nita's van pulled up. Her aunt stepped out of the vehicle, immediately into the waiting arms of her brother. Keri was glad to be out of hearing distance. She wasn't sure how much longer she could hold it in. She watched as Nita held onto her brother, quite sure she was crying as evidenced by the familiar handkerchief he held out to her. They talked a while longer before Nita called out to her.

"Sweetie, I told your father I'll cook an early dinner at your house tonight, okay? We'll regroup and talk through all this then."

Keri closed the gap between them. "Sure, Nita. I'll be home later to help. Call if you need me to pick up anything. "

"Sure thing," Nita answered. "Carson, you're welcome to join us."

"Thanks, Nita. I'll try to stop by."

"Bye y'all. Just take a big ol' deep breath. We'll get through this. God's with us. He always is."

She drove off, leaving a dull ache in Keri's heart. If only she believed like her aunt believed. Instead, all she could think was—how could a loving God let something like this happen?

Keri cleared away the dinner dishes as Nita cut generous slices of apple pie and topped them with vanilla ice cream. "Sweetie, how about giving us all a refill with that decaf?"

Keri topped off their mugs and sat back down at the cozy kitchen table with them. They continued the troubled conversation.

"Any word from Bud?" Carson asked. Bud Curtis had been Waterford Bay's sheriff for more than twenty years.

"He asked us to stay off the property as much as possible so we don't tamper with any potential evidence."

Keri hoped they hadn't destroyed any evidence when they'd been on the property earlier. "So he thinks it's arson?"

"No, he didn't say that. Just trying to be careful until the insurance folks get here and get a look."

Nita set her mug down. "Seems to me they should be here by now. Where are they coming from, China?"

Keri noticed her dad's lame attempt to smile. "No, they're wrapping up an investigation in Portland. Pretty bad one, from what I hear. Storage area at Powell's. Completely destroyed."

"Oh no," Keri moaned, remembering long afternoons browsing the famous bookstore. "Any damage to the bookstore itself?"

"Couldn't tell you. I just wish those folks would hurry up and get here. I can't stand the suspense much longer." He pinched the bridge of his nose then rubbed his eyes.

"Why, Dad? I mean, I realize you need to know what caused the fire and find out what the insurance will pay. But what aren't you telling me?"

He wrapped his hands around his coffee mug, his brow taking a dive. "What haven't I told you? A lot. Because I haven't wanted you to worry."

Nita quietly set her fork back on her pie plate. Carson sat perfectly still. Keri felt sure someone had sucked the oxygen out of the room. "Dad, what is it?"

"Well, sweetheart, the fact is . . . if this turns out badly, I could be facing bankruptcy."

Now the oxygen disappeared from her body as well. "What? How can that be? Yours is one of the most successful log cabin companies in Oregon! Surely one fire can't put you out of business?"

Tyler closed his eyes. "Normally, it wouldn't. But these aren't normal times."

"The economy has flattened our sales for the last five years, Keri," Carson added. "We kept building, kept hoping it would turn around. Instead it got worse."

"But that's the nature of construction, isn't it?" Keri heard the fear in her own voice. She took a deep breath. "I mean, you've weathered the ups and downs before. Why is this any different?"

Tyler scraped at the pie's crust with his fork. "Because it's just bad, honey. Real bad."

Nita placed her hand gently over her brother's. "Ty, you'll get through this. I know God will see you through."

"Sis, I wish I could believe that. But the problem is, I sunk everything into the Blankenship project. *Everything.* All my cash was tied up in it. Every penny. I'm up to my eyeballs on this one."

Keri couldn't even blink. Now it all made sense. The despair. Her father hadn't just seen one of his projects go up in smoke; he was watching his entire livelihood disappear in that smoke as well.

She couldn't breathe, seeing her father react this way. She slowly stood up, taking her half-eaten dessert to the kitchen counter. A thousand thoughts pelted her mind as she absently scraped the pastry into the garbage disposal. How had it come to this? How had her father backed himself into such an impossible corner? What on earth would they do if he lost his business?

She looked out the window into the darkness outside. Troubling images flashed through her mind. Then it hit her. She realized what she was staring at . . . the delicate saucer sitting on the windowsill.

"Dad, where's Mom's cup?"

Silence.

She turned around. Her dad avoided her eyes and covered his face with his hands. "I broke it, Keri."

The last trace of oxygen, gone. "Wha—"

"It was an accident. I was cleaning the window. I should've moved the cup and saucer first, but I just wasn't thinking. It shattered into a thousand pieces. I'm so sorry."

She continued staring at him, swallowing hard against the pain in her chest. *Don't say anything. He's had enough trouble for one day. Let it go. Just let it go . . .*

Nita came to her side. "We didn't want to tell you, sweetie. We know how much it meant to you. Your father's felt awful about this for weeks now."

Tyler raised his head, his eyes glistening.

She dropped the dish rag and excused herself, heading for the front door.

"Keri, don't leave. Let's talk about—"

She grabbed her coat and ran out the door just as the dam inside her heart broke.

Grant flipped on the windshield wipers, hoping the last remnant of wiper fluid would clean up the mess marring his view. He'd told his father he'd be over after he put the paper to rest. He was looking forward to unwinding with his dad for a couple of hours. He loved the drive, especially at night, with the harbor lights reflecting across the choppy black waves. The sight of the lighthouse this close was still a thrill even after all these months. There was just something alluring and mysterious and . . .

His thoughts were interrupted by the headlights of a vehicle parked at the base of the lighthouse. *Is that Keri's car?* He quickly pulled off the road barely making the entrance to the lighthouse parking lot. He pulled up alongside the black Jeep Cherokee, curious when he found it empty. He stepped out of his truck and, finding the door unlocked, opened the car door and turned off the headlights. Thankful for the lighted sidewalk, he made his way toward the overlook area on the other side of the structure.

He heard her before he saw her.

"Keri? Are you okay?"

She jumped, startled by his voice, even over the roar of the waves below. She quickly wiped at her eyes, and turned her back to him.

"What do you want?"

He held his tongue, wondering what in the world he'd ever done to deserve such a constant stream of irritation. It would be so easy to snap back at her. Still, the sight of her tears reflecting in the lights made him refrain. "I was driving out to Dad's and saw your car parked out front here."

"So? Is there a law against visiting a lighthouse after dark?" She blew her nose and took an aggravated breath.

"No law that I know of. But you left your headlights on. I was afraid it would run down your battery."

She finally looked up at him. "Oh. Well. You didn't have to do that, but thanks. I'll go turn them off."

"Already did. But you should lock your car, you know. Even in Waterford Bay we have crime from time to time."

"Thank you for that news flash, Mr. Big Time Reporter. I'll try to remember that."

He moved closer, then took a seat on the other end of the park bench she was sitting on. "Are you okay?"

He waited for another snippy reply. It didn't come. He cocked his head to one side for a better angle. "Keri?"

"It's all I had of her."

"What? Had of who?"

"My mother. That cup and saucer were the only heirlooms of hers I had."

"Did you lose them?"

"No. But Dad accidentally broke the cup. It shattered."

He had no clue what was wrong but one thing he had no question about. This was not the same Keri he'd sparred with earlier. She was broken.

"I'm sorry to hear that. Nita told me your mother died when you were born. I'm sure it wasn't easy growing up without her." He looked out at the dark expanse of water, giving her time to respond. When she didn't, he asked, "Would you like to tell me about it?"

She looked at him for a split second then away. "Uncle Rafe, Aunt Nita's husband, was a war correspondent back in the seventies. He was in Yugoslavia, behind the Iron Curtain, reporting for the Associated Press. My mother was around twenty at the time. She worked at the hotel where he was staying. Uncle Rafe never met a stranger and he became friends with her. He was already married to Nita by then, so he was like a big brother to my mom. He said they'd talk for hours in the evening when she got off work.

"It must have been hard for her, living in a communist state where people just vanished in the night. Her own grandparents had been gunned down when she was younger. She lived in constant fear. She tried to get her parents to leave, but they were too afraid.

"Then one day, she asked Uncle Rafe if he would help her escape to the United States."

"Pretty gutsy thing to do at her age," Grant commented.

"They tell me she was a pretty gutsy girl, even back then. Rafe pulled some strings, used his connections, and engineered a very elaborate plan to help her escape. Literally, in the dark of night, he snuck her out of the country. Like something out of a spy novel, you know? He brought her back here. He and Nita took her under their wings and became her sponsors. She was eventually granted political asylum. She owed her life to them."

"And the cup and saucer? Something she brought with her?" Grant asked.

"The *only* thing she brought. Other than a couple changes of clothes. She wrapped it in a sweater in a small bag. It made the trip without a single chip." She took a deep breath and continued. "It was a part of her family's dinnerware. A beautiful hand painted design by Lomonosov. Rafe said she wanted something to remember her parents, and they let her take a single cup and saucer. She knew she'd never see them again."

Keri wrapped her knitted scarf more tightly around her neck. "Her name was Nadia. They tell me it was love at first sight when my dad first met her. He was a couple years older, but he was a goner the minute they met. They were married three months later. Nita told me it was the happiest she'd ever seen Tyler. A few months later, they found out they were going to have me." She smiled. "Nita said that was the second happiest she'd ever seen Dad."

A moment passed. The breeze blew her hair around her face before she pushed it back out of her eyes. She dug in her pocket and pulled out a tiny red band that she used to pull her curls into a thick pony tail. "Mom died after giving birth to me," she said quietly, looking out across the dark waves.

He said nothing, giving her time to say what was on her mind.

"Nita told me Dad poured his heart into his business. Buried himself in it. I mean, he was always there for me, but it was hard for him, I'm sure. As I grew older, I loved helping out when I could. I guess it was good therapy for both of us. Which is why his company means so much to him. To both of us . . ."

He started to say something and let it pass. He knew she was hurting but he couldn't help it. He liked being here, listening to her, learning more about her.

"It took me a long time to get over the whole guilt thing. If it hadn't been for me, Mom would still be alive today."

"Keri, surely you don't —"

She waved him off. "I know, I know. But try telling that to a young child when she finds out her mother dies giving birth to her. Pretty hard stuff for a kid. But eventually I understood. Still—"

"What happened to Rafe? Didn't he die overseas?"

"Yeah. Fifteen years later, he was sent back to cover the Bosnian war. Same country, just torn into several different pieces. He stayed in the same hotel where he'd met my mother. One night, rebels bombed the hotel, knowing there were lots of foreign correspondents staying there. Uncle Rafe was killed in the attack."

"Nita must have been devastated," Grant said.

"She was. Broke her heart. But she has the strongest faith of anyone I've ever known. She says those first few years after Uncle Rafe was killed, she had to rely on her faith just to make it through every day. And she did.

"I, on the other hand, didn't take it as well. I adored my uncle. He had spoiled me rotten, for all kinds of reasons. And I took full advantage of him, of course." Another slight smile. "I couldn't believe God took my mother, then had the gall to take my favorite uncle. I was pretty convinced God hated me."

"You don't believe that now, do you?"

"Mostly I try not to think about it. Or God."

Grant shifted on the bench, facing her. Someday he'd like to talk to her about that. But not tonight. "So tell me about this cup and saucer. What did it look like?"

"The design has all these intertwining lines in cobalt that look like they're tied with tiny little bows in 22 karat gold. In fact it's called *Cobalt Net* because it resembles netting." She continued describing it in detail to the point he could almost see it. He couldn't imagine how it must have felt to find out something so precious was gone now. Especially after a day like today.

"I could take one look at that cup and saucer and instantly feel close to my mother. I never knew her, of course, except for the stories Rafe and Nita told me. And Dad, when he could talk about her. Aunt Nita told me the light went out of his soul the day she died." She tried to smile, her lips trembling. "But she always said I was the one who put it back for him."

Grant merely nodded, not wishing to interrupt her.

He watched her face begin to crumble. A haunting moan from deep inside gradually grew louder until she could no longer hold it in. She sobbed, the sound of it breaking his own heart. Without thinking, he scooted to her side, wrapping his arm around her shoulders. She buried her head against his, the sobs still shaking her in his arms. He wasn't sure how long they stayed that way.

As her tears began to slow, she pulled a few inches away from him. "I'm so sorry. I guess I just couldn't hold it in any longer."

"Like you reminded me earlier, 'it's been a day.'"

She wiped her face with the back of her hands. He handed her his handkerchief, another blue bandana.

"It's clean. I promise."

She wiped her eyes and nose, then refolded the handkerchief. "I still have your bandana from last night. I promise I'll get these back to you. After I wash them."

"No problem. Glad to help."

"I guess that's it. First the fire. Then finding out Dad could lose his company. Then he tells me Mom's cup was smashed to pieces . . ."

"Wait. What do you mean, your dad could lose his company?"

Something flashed through her eyes before she looked down. "I probably shouldn't say anything. It's just a bad situation . . . apparently the Blankenship home was make-or-break for him."

They sat in silence. Grant tried to imagine what it would feel like to lose so much in one day. After a lifetime already marred with loss.

"I'm sorry. Sorry for your dad. His business. And for you as well."

"Me? Because I'm slobbering over a piece of china?"

"No, not that. I know you were counting on working for your dad."

Keri stiffened her back and looked away. "Well, who knows, that could still work out. Maybe. I don't know."

"Hey, why don't we both just cut to the chase and admit it. We need each other."

Her head snapped up as she looked at him. "What's that supposed to mean?"

"Exactly what it sounds like. I need some help. You need a job. Money is no object, so I know I can afford you. You're interested in journalism. How better to learn the ropes than by jumping in feet first? We need each other. Plain and simple."

She opened her mouth, then shut it. Opened it again and shut it again.

"What's so hard? Just say yes."

She jerked her head, looking away from him. He watched her shoulders move up and down as she took several breaths. Was she trying to make a decision? Or was she trying to figure out how to say no? They hadn't exactly gotten along very well.

At least not until now.

Chapter 5

A couple days later, Grant made sure he got to the office early. Keri would arrive at 8:00 for her first day on the job. He had mixed feelings about it. On the one hand, he'd found himself thinking about her way more than he should. Even under normal circumstances. But something was still bugging her. Something about *him*. He still didn't have a clue why she seemed to constantly bristle whenever they interacted.

Except for that night at the lighthouse.

A smile warmed his face as he remembered. The warmth of her tears against his skin. The scent of lavender in her hair, its silkiness soft against his hand as he'd gently stroked those curls as he tried to calm her.

"Knock it off, Dawson," he said aloud to himself. He made a fresh pot of coffee and tried to gather his thoughts as it brewed.

On the other hand, she's hurting. And she really does need a job.

Grant had called the sheriff on his way to the office.

"Arson," Bud Tomlinson had said. "There was enough kerosene out there to burn the whole town. Which accounts for how fast it went up."

"Have you talked to Tyler yet?" Grant had asked.

"Yeah, he was here when I got the call from the insurance folks. The investigation is still ongoing, but their initial findings left no doubt about the cause of the fire."

He poured himself a steaming cup of coffee and headed back to his desk, trying once again to come up with a game plan. He wanted to help her out. He just wished his intentions were solely from a working point of view.

He heard the back door open. "Back here!" he called.

Keri appeared at his door, her expression stoic. She looked around like she was observing something utterly and completely disgusting.

Well, so much for a good start.

"Good morning. How are you?"

Sad eyes made their way back to him. "Fine. I had no idea this was such a tiny office. It looks bigger from the outside."

And so much for trying to make a good impression.

"Well, for now it's all the room we need. Someday, who knows, maybe we'll grow into—"

"The L.A. Times? Somehow I doubt that."

He bit his tongue. "Which is fine. Sometimes smaller is better."

She made no attempt to hide the rolling of her eyes.

"Have a seat, Keri. Would you like some coffee?"

She took a seat. "No thanks."

He sat back down, tenting his fingers, elbows planted on his desk. "Well, then, first I'd like to talk about the general operation around here, then I'll show you around—"

"That should take, what—a minute? Two?"

He leveled his gaze at her, opting not to respond. When the silence grew uncomfortable, he continued, filling her in on the day-to-day routine, the weekly schedule with a Friday morning release, and an overview of tasks he'd like her to handle.

"I'm not five, you know. I was on staff for the WSN, the—"

"The Washington Square News. NYU's campus paper. I'm familiar with it. Quite a prestigious college paper."

"Then you know I have plenty of experience working for a major newspaper. At least, compared to this."

It was the dismissive wave of her hand as she'd said it that set his teeth on edge. "Okay, fine. You're a veteran reporter. I get it. I'm sure you know way more than I ever will. But this is a different beast. Yes, it's smaller. But it's MINE. And I'd like at least of modicum of respect if you're going to work here. Unless it's beneath you to waste your precious time."

She held up her hands, closing her eyes. "Fine. I'll keep my comments to myself. Let's just get on with it.

"Fine."

"Fine."

They stared at each other, unblinking, the tension crackling through the space between them.

Keri fought the urge to bolt. This was ridiculous. If he hadn't offered such a ridiculously generous salary—which she jumped at, eager to fill her collegiate coffers and get back to school—she would never have stepped foot in this office. It wasn't really *that* bad. In fact, she found it rather quaint and appealing. But she couldn't fight the brewing anger as she watched him sitting behind that old, beat-up excuse for a desk, knowing he should never have walked away from a prominent paper like the Times. It irked her. To the core.

She knew her salary was way over the top, and she also knew he'd done it out of pity for her predicament. But she wasn't stupid. If he was dumb enough to fork out that kind of money for a rookie reporter—WSN experience notwithstanding—then she would gladly take the money and run.

If I can just keep my mouth shut.

"As I was saying," he continued, "I would like to get your feet wet, not just reporting, but in the production area as well. It's a bit archaic at the moment. Though I'm hoping to upgrade next year."

"Fine." She studied the blue of his eyes, trying to decide if they were really that blue or perhaps contacts with some color added. Not that it mattered to her.

"And you never know. Some day you may find yourself in an even smaller town with an even smaller press, and you'll need to know how to make it sing."

Don't roll your eyes. Make him think you're falling for this line of bull. She wondered why his hair was so heavily sprinkled with gray. Not that there was anything wrong with it. *It actually adds an air of class. Or something. He's probably a lot younger than I first thought. Not all that much older than I am.* She wondered if he'd ever considered Grecian Formula or one of those gray-removing hair products. Then she realized she was glad he hadn't. She liked the touches of gray.

Then she wondered why she'd wondered at all.

"And then we'll get you involved in distribution and marketing at some point. Let you get out there and sell some ads. Give you get a taste of that as well."

"Wonderful."

He shot a look at her, narrowing his eyes.

"What?"

He continued to stare at her.

"Look, let's just get on with it. I'm sure you have a whole list there on that desk somewhere, an entire agenda of assignments you want me to cover. Real hard copy stuff."

He blinked, saying nothing.

She stood up, rearranging her scarf. "Surely there's a school bake sale that needs immediate coverage? Or maybe a load of mums arriving at Elizabeth's florist shop across the street? Maybe a flapjack eating contest in the works? Oh wait, let me guess. A new shipment of Hardy Boy books getting the spotlight at the library? Want me to scoot right over and interview Myrla?" She mimicked a runner's arms moving back and forth, keeping pace. "Hey, time's a wasting, boss! Chop chop! There's a whole big world of news waiting out there, so let's get this party started!"

He tilted his head at a forty-five degree angle as he tapped a black Bic pen on his desk blotter. "Are you done?"

"Hey, I haven't even *started*."

He shoved his chair back and stood up, bracing both hands on his desk. "Keri? Knock. It. Off."

His tone caught her short.

"I am one breath away from kicking those cute little sarcastic dimples of yours out that door. How DARE you come in here, mocking my paper! I offered you a job out of the goodness of my heart, mostly because your Aunt Nita asked me to months ago. Long before I stumbled into you at that fire last week. And let's not forget that hefty salary I stupidly offered to pay you. A salary which, I might add, I am seriously reconsidering at the moment. I'm real sorry you've had such a rough time and things aren't going the way you'd planned. But you either button up that smart mouth of yours and quit copping such an attitude, or you can go crawling over to Chandlers and see if Clara needs help washing dishes." He straightened, holding up his forefinger and thumb less than a quarter inch apart. "Because I am this close to wishing I'd never met you, Keri McMillan."

She couldn't breathe. Her eyes felt like saucers plastered on her face. "I—"

His eyes pierced hers, obliterating every thought from her mind.

Finally, Grant slowly sat back down in his chair. She quietly moved back to the chair she'd occupied, sliding back on the seat while wishing she could somehow disappear beneath it. *What have I done? How could I be so thoughtless? And when did I become so obnoxious?*

"Now, if it's not too much to ask, I'd like to tell you what *I* had in mind for your first assignment."

She lowered her head while nodding, unable to look him in the eye.

"I would like for you to immerse yourself in the investigation of the Blankenship fire."

She raised her head, searching his eyes. *Is he dishing it back at me? Is this some kind of joke?*

"No one knows the situation better. No one knows this town like you do. No one understands the dynamics and the implications better. Can you be unbiased? No way. Is there anyone more motivated? Not a chance."

She swallowed, a lump the size of Mt. Hood sticking in her throat. Emotion burned her eyes and she tried hard not to give in to the tears.

"I don't know what to say. I—"

"A simple thank you would be really nice about now."

She couldn't believe he hadn't made good on his threat to give her the boot. And now this? She took a deep breath and said the words, meaning them.

"Thank you."

"Not so hard, was it? Okay, let's get to work. Here's what I want you to do."

She sat in her car, her forehead resting against the steering wheel. The conversation with Grant played over and over in Keri's mind. She vowed to offer him a serious apology. Soon. Okay, eventually. She hardly recognized that person who'd sat across his desk, hurling insults like some acerbic late-night comic. She cringed, promising herself to try harder. To cut him some slack.

But right now she had a job to do. He'd spelled it out: build a list of suspects.

He'd explained his background in investigative reporting. He'd offered tips and suggestions. She'd bit back some of the retorts that crossed her mind, trying hard to focus on the task at hand. At some point the realization hit her. If she could control her attitude and keep her mouth shut, she might actually *learn* something from Grant Dawson.

Whether she liked it or not.

She stepped out of her Jeep and made her way up the steps to the sheriff's office. "Bud, can I have a minute?"

"Hi there, Keri. Come on in. My time is your time."

"Thanks. I've taken a temporary job at the paper working for Grant Dawson. He's asked me to look into the Blankenship fire."

"Well, now. Never figured you to be the sleuthing type, but more power to you. How can I help?"

Bud Tomlinson pointed to the extra chair in his office. She took a seat. "If I asked for names, who would you consider at the top of the list of possible suspects?"

He sat down behind his desk. "You don't beat around the bush, do you? I like that. Well, of course any time there's trouble in Waterford Bay, Zack Clayton is always at the top of the list."

"Zack?" she said, scribbling his name on her notepad. "He's still causing trouble?"

"Did he ever *stop* causing trouble?" He quirked a smile.

"What kind of trouble?"

"Mostly small stuff. Nothing major. Petty theft, shoplifting, vandalism—"

"Wasn't he the one who inked the indoor pool at the high school a few years ago?"

"Seems our boy had a problem with the P.E. teacher. And vice versa."

"Must have been quite a problem. Anything in his file involving arson?"

Bud smiled at her as he reached for the file already open on his desk. "You don't miss much, do you? Let's see here. Shoplifting, shoplifting, vandalism—he has a real fondness for liquid soap. Likes to put red dye in it and dump it in the town fountain." He continued browsing the file, flipping page after page. "More shoplifting—mostly cigarettes, mind you. He's also quite the graffiti artist. Doesn't even try to hide his tracks anymore. Messed up some buildings, cars, other private property. We've lost count on those.

"But no arson. Wait . . . I take that back. Looks like a couple of minor incidents way back. He was only fourteen at the time, so it's not on his official record. Juvenile stuff. Suspect in a fire at an abandoned barn down at the end of Forest Lane. No charges were pressed. But his name showed up on the list of suspects."

"Anything else?"

"Yes, another case that was never solved. A small row boat in flames found adrift off the shore. Traces of kerosene were found on some of the charred pieces of its hull. Someone saw his truck near the marina shortly before. He said. She said. No solid proof."

"Let me guess. He was under age. No official record."

"Atta girl."

"Have you spoken to him since the Blankenship fire? Does he have an alibi?"

"Oh, Zack always has an alibi. But they're all his friends. Liars, every one of 'em. But we're checking it out."

"Bud, do you think Zack burned down that cabin?"

He leaned back, hooking his ankle over his other knee. "I don't know. It's still early in the investigation. We'll see what turns up."

"Anyone else under suspicion?"

"No. Least wise, no one to speak of. How about I give you a call if I hear anything?"

"Fair enough," she said, standing. "Thanks for your time."

Chapter 6

"Hey Dad. What brings you to town?" Grant clicked on SAVE to make sure he didn't lose the article he'd almost finished.

"Oh . . ."

"Take a load off. Want something to drink?"

"No. Thanks."

"You in town on an errand or just stopping by to say hello?"

Grant looked up from his desk when his father didn't answer. He was used to his father's peculiar ways, but almost did a double-take. Shep had a goofy grin on his face.

"Cornstarch."

"Cornstarch?"

The grin settled back into a more Shep-like subtle smile. "Cornstarch. Plumb out."

Grant chuckled at his dad's quirky behavior. "What do you need cornstarch for?"

"Oh . . . I don't know."

Their eyes met. Shep blinked and looked away.

"Never know."

"Never know what?"

"When you might need some."

"Ah," Grant followed. "True."

"And tea."

"Well, now. One can never have enough tea in the house."

Shep nodded.

"Oh, that reminds me . . ." Grant stopped himself before saying anything more. He jotted himself a note on an orange Post-it: *Teacup.*

"What's that?" his father asked.

"Nothing. Just something I've been intending to look up online. Some research."

"On tea?"

He smiled. "Something like that."

His dad moseyed down the hall, his boots scraping on the hardwood floors. "Something else you need, Pop?"

"No."

"Okay if I get back to work?"

Shep passed back by his door going the other direction. "Yep."

"I'll stop by tonight. My turn to win at chess."

"We'll see."

Grant heard the door close with a click. He loved living near his father again after all these years. Shep Dawson never failed to bring a smile to his lips.

"Cornstarch?" He threw his head back laughing. *Yesterday it was pistachio nuts. The day before, vanilla wafers.*

He wasn't sure, but something was going on behind his father's mysterious gray eyes. He'd bet his life on it.

Then another thought drifted through his mind. It came unbeckoned and unwelcome. Was it possible his father was drifting into the Netherlands of dementia? He shook off the thought, refusing to give it a landing strip in his mind or on his heart.

Keri put her Jeep in park at the rear of the burnt cabin. She needed some fresh air, time to think. She looked through the windshield at the skeletal structure, still in disbelief.

By now, she should have been helping her father finalize the paper work preparing for the transfer of ownership to the Blankenships. They should be tying up loose ends, putting the final touches on the cabin. She should be ordering a huge "welcome home" poinsettia to greet the new homeowners to their oceanside cabin.

Instead, she was staring at what was left of it. Next to nothing.

She noticed a pickup parked to the side of the lot, almost out of sight. Curious, she got out of her car and stepped under the yellow crime scene tape. Keri spotted a young man standing in what should have been the family room.

"Hello?"

He turned suddenly. "Oh—hi. You're . . . Keri, right?"

"And you're Matt Blankenship. It's been a long time."

He started toward her, stepping carefully through the ash. "Oh. Yeah, right." He waved his arm toward the skeleton of the house behind him. "I just got in town. Came to see what's left of our house."

She reached out, briefly placing her hand on his forearm. "I'm so sorry, Matt. I've been so consumed with worry for my father, for his business . . . I never stopped and thought about you and your parents. Have they returned from Europe yet? They must be heartbroken."

He looked back at the ruins. "Yeah, they're pretty upset. Last I heard, they were trying to get home as fast as they could, but the flights . . . I don't know. Could be a few more days yet."

She hurt for him. She remembered something about him losing his twin brother a long time ago, but since the family only vacationed here, she didn't know anything more than that. And now this.

She tried to make small talk. "So what have you been doing all these years? I've been off at school, but it's been, what? —five? Six years? Where have you been keeping yourself?"

"School. Work. Y'know, around."

"Where did you go to school?"

He turned back to face her. "You sure ask a lot of questions. What are you, a reporter or something?" He smiled, but she noticed it didn't quite reach his eyes.

She laughed. "Well, yeah, actually I am. Just started working for the *Waterford Weekly*. I took a year off from school. Anyway, I'm just looking around. Trying to put together a story."

He stared at her. For the briefest moment, it made her uncomfortable. Then she remembered he'd always seemed kind of creepy. When the Blankenships would roll in for the summer, Matt always tried too hard to fit in with the other kids in town. He was the kid always doing cannonballs off the high dive, soaking the girls sunbathing in the pool lounge chairs. He bragged incessantly about his family's money and all their cars and vacations. Which only alienated him from the locals who quickly wearied of his silly antics and constant bragging.

His brother Sam had been the complete opposite. More of a bookworm who didn't often come to the pool or hang out with the other kids. Smart as a whip from what she'd always heard.

"Hello?"

She blinked out of the memories. "I'm sorry, what did you say?"

"I asked if you'd heard anything about the fire. Do they know what caused it?"

"Arson."

"Arson?" He seemed genuinely surprised. "Why would anyone want to burn our house down?"

"That's the million dollar question. Or, I guess *two* million would be more accurate. Your parents spared no expense." She turned to look over the ruined property, shielding her eyes. "It really was a stunning house."

A burst of wind suddenly kicked up, blowing ash in their faces. They both coughed and turned from the gust. "Whoa," she said, wiping her eyes. "Not a good day for contacts."

"Or long hair," he quipped, pulling a band off his wrist to tie his unruly head of hair into a pony tail. "So do they have any suspects?"

Keri realized she shouldn't say any more, recalling Bud's request to keep their conversation confidential. Except for her dad. And Grant.

"You should probably check in with Bud. Sheriff Tomlinson. He'd probably like to talk to you if you haven't stopped by the station yet."

"Me? Why me?"

"Since your parents aren't here yet, I'm sure he'd like to brief you about every-thing that's happened."

"Oh. Okay, I'll stop by his office. That's actually why I'm in town. On their behalf. Til they can get here. They asked me to see what's been happening since the fire."

"I'm sure they appreciate that."

"Well, I've gotta run. Errands and stuff. And I'll stop by to talk to the sheriff. Nice to see you again." He reached out to shake her hand. The gesture seemed awkward, but she shook it anyway.

"You too, Matt. And I'm really sorry about your house. I think you would have loved it."

He pressed his lips together and nodded, then walked briskly to his truck.

Keri decided to look around. The perpetual Oregon dampness seemed to be dissipating with the sunshine they'd enjoyed over the last couple of days. It was certainly easier to investigate without all the muddy ash. She walked slowly, looking for anything out of the ordinary despite knowing the authorities had sifted through it all repeatedly. She wandered around for a while then made her way back to the enormous stone hearth and wiped away a spot to sit down. She took a seat, dusted the sooty ash off her hands, then rested her elbows on her knees.

Think, Keri, think. Who had motive to destroy this place? No one around here really knows the Blankenships that well. Doesn't make sense they'd have any enemies to speak of. And Zack? She tried to picture the troubled kid everyone thought of as the town loser. The last time she saw him he had a pitiful excuse for a beard, if that's what you'd even call it. Dark circles under vacant eyes. Pale skin stretched across his bony face. Long stringy hair, usually pulled back in a tight pony tail that hung half-way down his back. Zack had clearly never bothered with shampoo more than a couple times a month. The image made her skin crawl. How can someone live like that, filthy and aimless, year after year? Course, his mother ran off with Blake Simpson when Zack was just a snot-nosed kid. His dad did what he could, raising his son in a decrepit double-wide out south of town.

But surely after all these years Zack didn't think he could get away with something this big? Knowing he was at the top of Bud's list for every single crime in town? Doesn't make sense. Still, if Bud has him at the top of his list of suspects, I can't just dismiss him. And there were those two cases of arson on his unofficial record . . .

She sat up, breathing in the crisp, cool air. She shielded her eyes against the bright sunlight, trying to think. Another breeze kicked up the ash and she quickly covered her eyes. When it settled, she blinked away the particles in her eyes and looked down at her feet and found her sneakers covered with the gray stuff. She stomped her feet, trying to shake off the ash. Something caught her eye. The tiniest glimpse of red. She nudged it with the toe of her shoe. It looked like a piece of cording of some kind. But very thin. She couldn't imagine what it might be, a length no longer than an inch and a half. It was smoked-tainted but clearly a shade of red. She bent down for a closer look, wondering how the investigators would have missed it.

C'mon, you're not exactly Lara Croft here. You're way out of your league. If the authorities thought it was important, they would have bagged it. Still, she hesitated, wondering if she should touch it. *Why didn't I think to grab some latex gloves? Definitely* not *something Laura would forget.*

"Keri, is that you?"

She stood up, startled to hear her name. Bertie Crowder was heading toward her, one slow step at a time with the aid of her cane. "Hey Bertie. Nice to see you."

The elderly woman, who lived next door to the Blankenship's property, stopped at the yellow tape. It was Bertie who'd made the 911 call the night of the fire.

"I heard you were back in town. Nita told me you were home for a spell, gonna work for your daddy. Such a shame, isn't it?" She looked over the remnant of the cabin. "I still can't believe that big old house is gone before those poor people even had a chance to move in."

Keri walked toward her. "I know. It's hard to believe something so big could burn down so fast. Had you met the Blankenships?"

"Oh my, yes, Sweet couple. They were really looking forward to moving here."

Keri brushed her hands against her jeans. "Bertie, did you ever see anyone hanging around here who didn't belong? Strangers? Kids?"

"Well, now, you know it's difficult for me to see much through the trees between our properties. Course, once the leaves fell, I've had a little better view. But can't say I recall seeing anything out of the ordinary. I know most of your dad's workers. Know their vehicles and what not. Nothing out of the ordinary comes to mind."

"Any locals? Maybe some nosy town folk who wanted a sneak peak at the big log cabin going up on the cliff?"

Bertie looked beyond Keri at the ocean view bordering what had been the front of the cabin. "Oh honey, my memory's not that good any more. There were a few from time to time, but I can't recollect who."

"That's okay. But if you remember, would you give me a call? You've got Dad's number at the house, right?"

"Sure thing."

"Thanks, Bertie. I've gotta run."

"Good to have you back, Keri. Tell your daddy I'm sure sorry about this."

"Will do."

A headache had started crawling up the base of Keri's neck and she needed to take something before it got worse. She contemplated raiding Nita's medicine cabinet across the street, but decided not to. She'd be too tempted to stretch out and take a nap after such a busy day.

Besides, there was the whole report-in-to-the-boss thing. *Good little reporterette that I am.*

As she opened the door to her Jeep, she noticed Bertie waving her down.

"You know, Keri, I didn't think to mention Jerry Winkler."

"What about him?"

"Well, I see him drive by here a lot. But I know he's working on a house down the street so that's nothing unusual. I know he and your dad are friends and I always just assumed he was slowing down as he passed to see how your dad's project was coming along. Still, I thought I should mention it. Probably nothing."

Keri didn't correct the kindly woman. Jerry and her father were *not* friends and hadn't been for many years. But if the guy had a reconstruction project a couple blocks down the road, he had every right to be in the neighborhood. Still, it was something to mention to her dad.

And her boss, of course.

Chapter 7

"Oh my, aren't these beautiful! And just take a whiff of those pine needles." Nita pressed her nose in the fragrant needles and inhaled again along with Arlene. "That has to be one of the most heavenly scents on this earth. Oh, this year might be one of our best sales ever! Why, we could sell enough trees to pay for *two* playgrounds for the church!"

"Well, I still think we should use the funds to update the church kitchen, but what do I know. I'm only the church cook."

"Arlene, enough with the whining. The committee voted on the playground. We'll do the kitchen next year. Now help me hang these wreaths."

The trees had arrived late in the day, making the volunteers scurry around to get set up before the sun went down. They were more than a week behind schedule but relieved the trees finally showed up.

Nita loved this time of year and especially loved the tree sale. Everyone was always in such good spirits and sharing holiday cheer. Plus, it was a great way to see people she didn't share pews with as theirs was the only tree lot in town. She leaned over to grab another stack of fresh wreaths. When she stood back up, she gasped, the wreaths dropping from her hands. Shep Dawson stood right in front of her.

"Good heavens, Shep! You like to scared me half to death!" She patted her heart, trying to catch her breath. "Where did you come from?"

He pointed behind him. "Yonder."

"I meant, where did you—oh, never mind. Is there something I can help you with?"

He smiled. It was a most peculiar smile, barely visible beneath that big white mustache. Oh, what she would give to have a go at that hairy mess with a pair of clippers. He turned, looking around at the trees and the other volunteers.

Oh for heaven sake. It was an easy question. "Shep?"

He turned back to face her, his eyes slowly finding hers again. "No, ma'am."

"No ma'am?"

Another lopsided smile.

"Mr. Dawson, I'm kind of busy right now," she said, trying to hide her aggravation. This was the third time this week she'd run into him. Which was most unusual for a man who rarely came to town. Each time he'd ambled up to her, uttered one or two words—literally—before wandering off again.

She squatted down, gathering the pile of wreaths she'd dropped.

He stooped down to help. "Shep."

She looked up at him, his weathered face just a few inches from hers. "I beg your pardon?"

"Shep'll do. No need to call me Mr. Dawson."

She plastered a smile on her face. "Well, then. Shep. What is it I can help you with?"

He grabbed the last wreath then took the rest out of her hands. "I was just . . . well, I thought . . ."

She waited, wondering if New Year's would come and go before he finished the sentence. "You thought what?" She took a wreath from him and hung it on the wall of reinforced chicken wire hanging behind their makeshift counter. He followed her lead, hanging some of the wreaths. When they'd finished, she stood back. "There now. That looks great. Thank you for your help."

He nodded, his face crinkling around his smile.

"Would you like some hot cider?" she asked reaching for a paper cup.

"No, ma'am. But thank you."

She put the cup back and buried her hands in her coat pockets. "Okay, then. Well, it was nice to see you."

He nodded.

"If you'll excuse me, I need to finish setting up so we can open for business."

He nodded. Again.

A bizarre thought popped into her head. "Shep, would you be interested in helping out here at the tree lot this year?"

He blinked. Several times.

"I just thought . . . well, I've seen you in town a lot lately. I thought maybe you'd like to give a hand. We're getting such a late start this year, which means we'll be awfully busy."

"Well sir . . ."

She waited for more. None came. "It's actually a lot of fun."

"Not much good with folks."

That's an understatement . . . "That's okay. You wouldn't have to sell the trees. Maybe just help keep the trees stocked, tie them on the top of folks' cars if they need help. That sort of thing."

He looked off in the distance. His mustache twitched as he chewed on the side of his lip. Or so she supposed. She felt sure he was trying to put together enough words for an excuse of some sort.

"Well, it was just an idea. No harm in asking," she said, trying to sound indifferent. *Why can't he just go back to his boat and quit wasting my time?*

"Okay."

"Okay?"

"Uh huh."

"Uh huh, you'd like to help out, or uh huh, it was just an idea?" *For the love of Pete, mister, spit it out!*

"I'll help."

She was sure the shock registered on her face. *Well, bust my garters. I never . . .*

"Start now?"

"You want to start now?" Nita asked, still in disbelief.

"Okay."

She smiled, feeling like they'd made a major breakthrough. In what, she had no idea.

"Well then. That's great. Let me get Theodore to show you around, show you the ropes."

She passed him off to her fellow volunteer, confident he'd have more luck communicating with Shep than she did. "That is the strangest man I have ever met. You could die of old age waiting for him to finish a thought."

"What's that?" Arlene asked, setting the cash box under the covered table.

"Oh never mind. Can you mind the fort for a few minutes? I'd like to run over to Tyler's and make sure he and Keri eat a hot meal. If I don't make them sit and eat, they'll grab one of those nasty corn dogs at the convenience store and call it dinner."

"Sure enough. We've got plenty of help. Take your time."

She buttoned her coat and took one final look at their newest volunteer just as he turned to look over his shoulder at her. She waved, watching his face crimson as he nodded in response.

"Never thought I'd see the day," she mumbled, heading toward her car.

"Keri, just because you've known him all your life, you can't dismiss him as a suspect. In fact, at this point, everyone's a suspect. You have to start from that point of view."

"What about 'innocent until proven guilty'?" she asked, obviously fighting the familiar frustration that seemed to always lurk between them. "Isn't that a basic premise? This is still America, last I checked."

"You're right, but as an investigative reporter, you start with a list of suspects then eliminate them as you verify your facts. And you can't eliminate Jerry just because you know him."

"No offense, Grant, but you didn't grow up here. You don't know these people. Dad and Jerry may have had their differences over the years, but Jerry would never do something like this."

"Yeah? And you know this how? Because he used to bounce you on his knee when you were little? Because he joined the family for Thanksgiving dinner? Bought you Barbie dolls back in the day?"

"No," she answered defensively. "But he *was* like family. I know the guy. He just wouldn't do something like this."

Grant leaned back in his chair. "But am I right in remembering Nita told me he and your dad had a nasty falling out a while back? Ten years or so?"

"Yes."

"Why was that?"

Her eyes narrowed as she exhaled. "Jerry went through a tough time. His daughter was accidentally killed by a drunk driver. His wife left him. He . . . changed."

"How? How did he change?"

She folded her arms across her chest. "He started drinking."

"Ironic, isn't it? People whose lives or loved ones are damaged or killed by drunk drivers turn into drunks themselves? Go figure."

She huffed, ignoring him. "Dad caught him drunk on the job one too many times. He warned him, Jerry promised to do better, but didn't. Then his workmanship started to suffer. Dad couldn't rely on him to do a good job any more. He tried to help him, tried to get him into a recovery program, but the harder he tried, the more defensive Jerry became. Finally, Dad had to let him go. Jerry started his own construction company a short time later."

"So he's in competition with your father now?"

"I wouldn't call it 'competition,' though he probably thinks so. Everyone knows his work is second-rate. But he undercuts Dad, bidding low on jobs. Folks who want cheap go to Jerry. Those who prefer quality hire Dad. At least, they did before the economy tanked."

"I know it hurt your Dad's business. Jerry's too?"

"I have no idea. I'd assume so."

"Is there still bad blood between them?"

"Dad got over it years ago. I mean, he had to do what he had to do. He's got good men working for him now. It's not like he's still fretting over all of it."

"And Jerry?"

She paused for a minute. Grant wondered how much she really knew about her dad's nemesis. He could almost hear the debate going on in her head, trying to determine if there was any possible way Jerry would do something so despicable to his former friend.

"I honestly don't know. He's a loose cannon. Shoots his mouth off a lot. Or so I'm told. I haven't seen him since I left for school a couple years ago."

Grant stood up and came around his desk. She stood and followed him down the short hallway. "Keep him on the list. Talk to your dad about him. See what he thinks. Did you ever track down Zack?"

Keri started toward the back door. "Not yet. I'll try to find him tomorrow. Any word from the Blankenships?"

"Not that I know of. Why do you ask?"

"I forgot to tell you I ran into their son Matt out at the site this morning."

"Didn't know they had a son."

"Yeah, he's doing what he can until they can get back here. They're stuck overseas somewhere. Something about problems getting flights because of weather. It's strange. Until I saw him, I hadn't even thought about how they'd all react to losing their new home." She looked down, rubbing her wrist. "I guess I've been pretty self-absorbed, worried about my own situation. And Dad's too. Hadn't even stopped to think about them losing their dream home."

"How old is Matt?"

"Oh, probably a couple of years older than I am. He said he's in school some-where. Though I don't think he ever said where. He was pretty distraught. Anxious for his folks to get home, I'd imagine."

"Learn anything from him?"

"No. He seemed amused that I was trying to find out who burned his house down."

"Well, put him on the list."

"You're kidding, right? It's his house. Why would he burn down his own home?"

"Which is the exact question you need to ask yourself as you look into it. Put him on the list, Keri."

She rolled her eyes—something he was getting used to by now. Even when she got under his skin with all her annoying antics, he couldn't fight the attraction.

He didn't like it, but he couldn't help it.

"You're the boss," she groaned, heading down the steps.

"That, I am. Keep in touch."

She paused at the bottom of the steps. He leaned against the door jamb, folding his arms across his chest.

She stood there, not turning around. "Grant, I—"

"Yes?"

She twisted her head, looking up at him. Her brow furrowed as she started to say something, then stopped. "Nothing. Good night."

"Good night, Keri. See you tomorrow."

Chapter 8

"Soup's on! I'm not going to call you all again."

Nita set a third bowl of chowder on the table as Keri and Tyler shuffled into the kitchen, then sliced a loaf of bread she'd baked that morning. "Sorry, Sis. Just finishing up a call with Bud."

Keri took a seat. "Any news?"

A weary smile lifted a corner of his mouth. "Not really. Except I hear there's a new reporter in town who's been rather busy today."

She buttered a thick wedge of bread. "It's no big deal, Dad. Just helping Grant over at the paper. Not exactly the *New York Times*."

"Well, I think it's wonderful," Nita added. "You and Grant will make a great team. You mark my words."

"There's no 'team' in the making here, Aunt Nita. I'm just working for him. Temporarily, I might add."

"So what did you do on your first day on the job?" Tyler asked, digging his spoon into the creamy chowder.

"Grant asked me to look into the fire investigation. See if we might help speed up the process."

"Is that so? And how do you plan to do that?"

"I'm putting together a list of suspects."

"Suspects?" Nita asked, taking a seat. "Goodness, how do you even start on something like that?"

"Oh, I'm just nosing around. Asking questions here and there. Had an interesting conversation with your neighbor, Aunt Nita. Bertie stopped by while I was over at the site poking around."

"Bertie's on your list of suspects?" Tyler asked with a chuckle. "Might as well mark her off, pumpkin. She's too busy watching her soap operas. No time for arson."

Nita laughed out loud. "That's for sure. Between her soaps and her naps, she wouldn't have a moment to spare. Certainly not long enough to torch a house like the Blankenships'. Trust me on that." She tossed her brother a wink.

"Very funny, you two. No, she's not a suspect. Give me a little credit. I simply asked if she'd seen any strangers or kids hanging around the neighborhood. She couldn't recall anything. Although, she flagged me down as I was leaving, saying she'd seen Jerry's truck drive by quite often."

"I've seen him pass by too," Tyler said. "He's working on a house down the road. Makes sense he'd drive back and forth on his way there."

"Which I explained to Grant. But he seems to think everyone's a suspect until proven innocent. Aunt Nita, why didn't you warn me how stubborn he is? The man drives me nuts."

"Grant? He's not stubborn. Doesn't have a stubborn bone in his body. I don't know what you're talking about."

Keri made a face at her but said nothing more about him. "Dad, in your heart of hearts, do you think Jerry would ever pull something like this to get even with you? Do you think he's capable of such a thing?"

Tyler finished a mouthful. "Jerry? No. He's harmless. His bark is far worse than his bite. We're still not on speaking terms, but that's his choice, not mine."

"Well, he's still downright rude to me whenever our paths cross in town," Nita added. "I'm sorry for his losses, for the rough road he's had, but that's no excuse for his behavior. He needs to grow up and get over it."

Keri folded her napkin. "I have to say, Dad, I remember some pretty ugly arguments between you and Jerry when I was younger. First time I heard language like that."

"I never—"

"I know. Not you, Dad. Him. He's got quite a mouth when he's tanked up."

"True. He deals with a lot of anger issues. Still does, from what I'm told. But that doesn't make him an arsonist," Tyler said. "You can cross him off your list, sweetheart."

"I guess. But Grant will want me to talk to him face to face. Any idea where I can find him?"

"One of my guys told me he's been in Portland for a few days. I'll try to find out when he's due back in town, if that would help."

"Speaking of Grant," Nita interrupted. "I meant to tell you. It's the oddest thing. His father keeps showing up. All over town. What's that all about? Everybody knows Shep Dawson only comes to town about twice a year. His semi-annual grocery run. Suddenly he's everywhere I turn. Has Grant mentioned anything about that to you, sweetie? I'm wondering if the old guy might be losing it."

Keri scraped the last of the chowder from her bowl. "No. He hasn't mentioned it. Maybe Shep's working on something in town on his days off."

"Yeah, or maybe he's taking speech lessons," Tyler teased. "You know, as in how-to-talk-to-people?"

Keri smiled. "Maybe he enrolled in one of those adult education classes. Like *How to Win Friends and Influence People.* Might do him some good. Or . . . "

Nita took the bait. "Or what?"

"Or maybe he's got a *crush* on someone in town. Maybe he's sweet on a certain someone. You know, like a girlfriend?" She waggled her eyebrows at her aunt.

Nita nailed her niece with a look. "Keri Nadia McMillan. You bite your tongue. Why, I wouldn't give that old man the time of day if I was the last person on earth. He's actually starting to get on my last nerve, if you want to know the truth. I almost wet myself today when he snuck up on me at the tree lot."

Tyler leaned over to his daughter. "Methinks she doth protest too much?"

"Methinks ditto," Keri added.

Nita pushed her chair back, standing up. She grabbed their empty bowls. "I'll hear none of that from the two of you. This is the thanks I get for making you a home cooked meal?"

Tyler joined her by the sink, wrapping his arm over her shoulder. "Ah, we're just kidding, Sis. Feels kinda good to have something to laugh about after everything that's happened. Don't you think?"

She bent her knee sideways behind her, kicking his backside.

"Ouch! What's the matter, did we hit a little too close to home with our romantic musings?"

Keri brought their empty glasses to the sink. "Methinks, methinks, methinks . . ."

"Enough!" Nita tossed the hand towel on the counter and headed toward the front door. "I've got to go home and feed Muffy. At least *she'll* treat me with a little respect."

The door slammed behind her.

Father and daughter made eye contact then broke into unrestrained laughter.

"After all these years . . ." Tyler chuckled. "Whodathunkit?"

Keri watched her father, pleased to see him relaxed and smiling again. But in the blink of an eye, something changed. He winced, taking a deep breath then slowly blowing it out.

"Dad?"

He flexed his hand, open and shut, open and shut. Then he gasped, his face contorted with pain.

"Dad! What's wrong?" She rushed to his side, quickly placing her hand on his forehead. "You're all clammy."

He pulled her hand off his head then wrapped it between his own hands. "Nothing, sweetheart. Probably just indigestion."

"Isn't that what most people say right before they have a heart attack?"

He closed his eyes, attempting a smile. "Very funny."

"I'm serious. Tell me what you're feeling. Why did you flex your hand like that?"

He pulled his left hand into a fist. "I don't know. Just a reaction, I suppose. Stop worrying. I'm fine."

"But isn't it the left arm that usually—"

"Keri, I'm fine. How about pouring me another glass of iced tea?"

She looked at him, studying the familiar creases in his face. There were several new ones, mostly carved by worry, she supposed. He didn't look good. No matter what he said.

She exhaled, getting him the cold drink. "When was the last time you had a checkup?"

"Well, let's see, Nurse Nancy . . ."

"Stop. Seriously, Dad, I'm worried about you. Didn't anyone ever tell you stress can kill?"

"Stress? What makes you think I'm under stress?"

She handed him the glass and sat on the floor at the foot his leather recliner. Flashes of dread sparked through her. Images of her father on a gurney. A monitor beeping in a hospital room. Friends gathered in a cemetery. She swallowed hard, fighting off the unbidden fears.

"Don't tease. It's nothing to joke about." She took hold of his hand, leaning her cheek into his open palm. "You're my only dad. I don't want to lose you."

He stroked her hair. "I'm not going anywhere, pumpkin. I'll always be here for you."

A tear broke free, rolling down her cheek and into his hand. He tipped her chin, turning her face toward him. "That's a promise, okay? So no tears."

She sniffed, then lunged into his arms. "I love you, Dad."

"Love you too, sweetheart."

She clung to him for several moments. She leaned back when he began to talk.

"I've tried really hard, but I know I haven't been the best father."

"Stop. I won't listen to that kind of talk."

He pushed a curl from her face. "You're so much like your mother in so many ways. Always looking out for everyone but yourself. Taking everyone else's problems to heart." He sighed. "I miss her so much, Keri. And I grieve every day of my life that you never had the chance to know her."

"I know her, Dad. From the pictures. From all the memories you've shared with me through the years. Things Uncle Rave used to tell me. And Aunt Nita. It's not the same, but it's all I've known. You've been the best father a girl could ever ask for. So lose the guilt. It doesn't suit you."

"Is that so?" He squeezed her hand, his countenance growing serious again. "If we lose the business, how will we get you back to that fancy school of yours?"

She pressed her palm against his cheek. "Stop. Don't even think about that now. That will all work out. Eventually. There's no law that says I have to graduate before I'm thirty. Forty, yes. But not thirty."

"Maybe not, but I don't want to ruin your dreams any longer than I have to."

"You're not ruining my dreams! So knock it off. It's a delay. That's all. Enough about school, okay?"

He took a sip of his tea. "I'm just glad Grant could find some work for you. He's a fine young man. You do a good job for him, okay?"

"Yeah, yeah."

He tilted his head. "You could do worse, you know."

"What do you mean? A worse job?"

"No, that's not what I meant."

She pegged him with a scrutinized stare. "Don't go there. One matchmaker in the family is enough. Don't you dare give me double trouble. And for the record, it ain't happening."

He didn't answer, just smiled. A tired smile, but a smile nonetheless.

Keri wiped the remaining tears from her face. "We'll get through this, Dad. Don't you worry about me. We'll be okay."

"That's my girl."

His cell phone rang as he mussed her hair. He checked the caller I.D. "I have no idea who this is." He clicked to receive the call anyway. "This is Tyler McMillan."

He must have pressed speaker-phone. She could hear the anxious voice through the line. "Tyler, this is Grant Dawson. I tried to call Keri but it keeps going to voice mail."

She reached for her cell phone. Dead. She must have forgotten to charge it.

"She's right here—"

"No, I don't have time. Tyler, you and Keri need to get to the hospital. My dad's been injured. There's been another fire."

Chapter 9

Keri and her father rushed through the emergency room doors. They stopped at the desk, asking where they could find Grant. The receptionist said she'd let him know they were here.

"Tyler! Keri! I came as soon as I heard!" Nita rushed to their side, unwrapping the knitted scarf from her neck. "Is it true? Was Shep blown out of the building?"

"What?" Keri gasped. "Where did you hear that? He was *blown* from a building?"

"There you are," Grant called out, approaching them. "Thanks for coming."

Nita grabbed him in a bear hug. "Oh honey, how's your daddy? Is he okay?"

"We don't know yet. He's still unconscious."

Nita buried her head against his shoulder. "Oh, that dear old man!" Her shoulders shook as she began to sob. "I was so ugly and impatient with him today and all but shooed him away like nothing more than a pesky mosquito. And now he's lying in there at death's door." Another sob.

"Nita, we don't know that," Grant said, trying to calm her.

Keri and her father exchanged glances at Nita's unexpected reaction, along with a very surprised Grant Dawson. Grant held her at arm's length. "Now Nita, why are you so—"

"I'll never forgive myself if he . . . if he should—"

"What happened?" Keri interrupted, turning toward Grant. "Aunt Nita said he was blown from a building?"

Grant raked his hand through his hair. "That's right. There was a fire at the newspaper office. Bud said Dad placed a 911 call to report a small blaze in the back room near the press. Apparently there was some kind of explosion by the time Bill and his crew got there. They're guessing the fire reached some of the chemicals in there. They found him lying in the grass several yards from the building."

Nita wailed, falling into her brother's arms. Keri couldn't figure out why she was carrying on to such an extreme, but there were too many other pressing questions. "What was Shep doing at your office this time of night?"

Grant shook his head. "I have no idea. I'd left the office earlier, ran a couple of errands before heading out to his place. We were supposed to play some chess tonight. I assumed he was home. I was almost to the marina when I got the call from Bill."

"Oh my dear Lord."

All eyes turned to Nita.

"He must have stayed at the tree lot," she croaked.

Grant placed a hand at her elbow. "What was Dad doing at the tree lot?"

Nita's chin trembled, tears spilled down her cheeks. "It's all my fault. He kept showing up, day after day. I never could get him to spill the beans, explain why he kept hanging around. Then, before I knew it, I heard myself inviting him to help out this year. You know, volunteer along with the rest of us selling trees."

"My dad?" Grant scoffed. "You're kidding, right? He's not a people person. That's the last place he'd want to be."

The puzzle pieces suddenly fell in place in Keri's mind. The time she'd caught Shep staring at Nita over his coffee mug that morning at Chandler's. Nita mentioning how Shep kept showing up at the tree lot. Shep, who rarely ever came to town. Could it be those "romantic musings" she and her father had voiced earlier tonight at dinner had been right on the mark?

Apparently so.

Shep Dawson had a thing for Aunt Nita.

What d'you know?

"I know, Grant," Nita whispered. "But he seemed very pleased I'd asked. It shocked me too. In fact, he was still there when I left tonight. I'd stopped by the lot after dinner to make sure things were okay. He seemed to be genuinely enjoying himself. Not saying much, of course." Her chin wobbled again. "He's a man of few words, that father of yours."

Grant rubbed his face. "That's an understatement. So you think he just happened to drive by the office on his way home and perhaps spotted the blaze?"

"Your guess is as good as mine," Nita said before blowing her nose.

"What has the doctor said?" Tyler asked.

"Not much. Until Dad comes around, there's not a lot they can do. Thankfully, he wasn't burned. Bill seemed to think that explosion may have actually saved his life, blowing him clear of the fire. And believe it or not, he doesn't seem to have any broken bones. Though I'm sure he'll be awfully sore and bruised."

"Is there anything you need?" Keri asked. She had the strangest urge to give him a hug, even though it seemed totally inappropriate. He was her boss, after all. Still, she wished there was something she could do to ease the worry etched on his face.

"Actually, there is. Would you mind checking back with Bill and see what he's found out? His guys got the fire out relatively fast. Still, it occurs to me that two fires in less than two weeks in our little town . . . well, something stinks. And it's not just the smoke."

Keri nodded. "Sure. I'll run over to the station and talk to him."

He leaned over to whisper in her ear. "We need to narrow that list of yours. Help me find who did this, Keri."

Her heart pounded. Whether it was his nearness, the warmth of his breath on her ear, or the emotion in his request, she couldn't be sure. Suddenly she embraced him, wishing she could take away his pain. "Go take care of your father. We'll find whoever did this. I promise."

He pulled back, searching her eyes. Then he turned and slowly walked down the hall.

"Well, sir . . . "

"Dad!" Grant stifled the sob caught in his throat as relief flooded over him. He leaned over, hugging his father. "Thank God! Are you okay? You gave us quite a scare last night."

Shep struggled to swallow then looked around. "Hospital?"

"Yes. Do you know how you got here? Do you remember what happened?"

His father closed his eyes. For a moment, Grant thought he'd drifted back asleep.

"Fire."

A second wave of relief fell over Grant. *He's cognizant. He's okay.* "Yes. There was a fire at the office."

Silence.

"Dad, I'm so glad you're okay."

"Don't feel okay."

Grant smiled. "I'm sure you'll be fine. You just need to take it easy for a while."

A page sounded out in the hall summoning assistance STAT.

"Truck."

He could barely hear his father's voice. "What's that? Did you see a truck?"

Shep nodded, his eyes still closed. "Dark out. Hard to see."

"Could you tell if it was a pickup? Or some kind of delivery van? Something bigger?"

"Pickup. Dark."

Grant tried to think, tried to remember who drove pickups, but the information wouldn't present itself. He'd almost lost his father. His only living relative. The investigation could wait. At least for now.

Nita appeared at the door. "They told me I could come back for a few moments. Is that okay?" She looked beyond Grant to see Shep. "Oh Shep, you're alive!" she whimpered, approaching the side of his bed. "You poor dear man. I'm so, *so* sorry."

Grant watched her lift his father's bandaged hand to her lips, pressing a gentle kiss on it. He stretched for a better view of his dad, curious at his reaction. Shep grinned from ear to ear as if he'd just won the lottery.

If I wasn't seeing it with my own eyes, I wouldn't believe it. Son of a gun.

As Nita's soft cries continued, he thought for sure Shep would say something.

Not a word. He just lay there, like a star-struck teenager meeting his favorite movie star for the first time.

"You okay, Nita?" Grant asked.

She quickly composed herself, dabbing her eyes with a handkerchief. "I'm fine, honey. I'm just so glad he's all right." Her shoulders slowly began to shudder again as she fell apart again.

He watched as his father's hand slowly reached for Nita's. She looked down at him, obviously surprised by the gesture.

But nowhere *near* as surprised as Grant.

Grant backed toward the door. "I think I'll . . ." Words failed him as he watched Nita lean over and plant a long, gentle kiss on his father's brow.

He slipped out the door, mumbling. "Don't mind me, I'll just be the one roaming the hall . . . in search of some electric shock . . . since I'm clearly the one here who's delirious."

Chapter 10

Keri stepped carefully through the debris. The office of the *Waterford Weekly* was a mess, but the damage was mostly contained to the back part of the old house. The press would need a proper burial, but better it than Shep. A chill raced down her back as she visualized Grant's strange but kind old father looking so fragile in his hospital bed. She'd stopped by to check on him first thing this morning, relieved to find him out of the ER, moved to his own room.

She'd hoped for a chance to talk to Grant, but was surprised instead to find her aunt at Shep's bedside. Any doubts she may have had about a budding romance between those two had immediately been laid to rest. She couldn't help the smile that kept tugging at her mouth as she listened to her aunt update her on Shep's progress. Nita kept patting his hand, stroking his wayward hair as she told Keri about the doctor's visit earlier in the morning.

"Shep's gonna be just fine. Another couple days of observation here, then he can go home. I told Dr. Richards we'd all be sure he got plenty of TLC to help him recover." She looked back at Grant's father. "Isn't that right, Shep?"

His chin seemed to disappear under the bushy mustache but it was plain as day he was smiling. He dipped his head in a nod of affirmation, his eyes still glued to Nita.

Keri chuckled, thinking about the warm chemistry between the two of them and how pleased she was they'd found a second chance at romance.

Or who knows. Maybe even something more.

"Keri, over here," Grant called, waving her over to the back steps.

"Is it okay for me to walk through this?"

"No problem. This time around, the insurance guys were close by. As you know all too well, I'm sure."

"Yeah, I'm afraid I do. But I'm glad you didn't have to wait as long as we did. What did they determine?"

"This was an easy one. A clear case of arson. Same as the cabin. Our arsonist isn't very imaginative. Kerosene seems to be his weapon of choice."

She walked up the steps looking at the chaos strewn across the yard. As she made her final step onto the back porch, his arm circled her waist, drawing her near. "Thanks, Keri."

"For what?"

He rested his chin on her head. "For just being here. For me. For Dad. I can't believe how close I came to losing him." He chuckled. "He's such a private man. It's hard to feel close to him. Always has been. I mean, I know he loves me. I never doubted that. We really are close in our own strange way. But I never heard him say the words. It's just his way. Still, last night made me realize how much I desperately love him and always have. I think I needed to *know* that. Just wish it hadn't been this way."

She lifted her eyes to look into those baby blues. "I just stopped by the hospital to see him. He looks great. I can't believe he escaped with so few injuries. Not a burn on his body."

He turned, taking hold of her elbow as he directed her into the damaged office. "Watch your step," he warned. "It's truly a miracle. Not a doubt in my mind God was watching over him. How else can you explain it?"

"Maybe, but that same logic flies in the face of innocent people who get hurt or badly burned or killed every day." *Where did* that *come from?* The words had raced out of her mouth before she even thought them.

He stopped short, turning to face her. A flicker of sadness passed through his eyes. "True. I suppose. One of these days, I hope we can talk through our differing views of faith." He pushed his hair off his forehead. "But for now, we've got work to do."

The front office had sustained only minimal damage; he'd obviously finished putting most of the room back in order. He grabbed a chair for Keri then leaned against the edge of his large vintage desk. She noticed a box with some kind of strange foreign postage sitting on his desk. The return address looked Russian but she couldn't be sure since she was reading upside down. He must have seen her staring at it and turned to following her gaze. He quickly shoved the small box behind him.

"What's that?"

"Nothing. Not a thing. Just something . . ." He moved behind his desk and deposited the box in a lower desk drawer. When he stood back up, his face was flushed.

"Grant, what was—"

"So have you talked to Bill?" he asked, taking his place in front of the desk again, his face still blushing.

What was that all about?

She shook it off, trying to concentrate on the matter at hand.

"After I left the hospital last night, I went to see him," Keri said. "He's *extremely* concerned about these fires."

"I'm sure he is. We all are."

"He thinks we have a serious danger lurking around town. Of course, I wasn't surprised at his sense of urgency to get to the bottom of this. We tossed around some ideas. Talked about some possible suspects—"

"Any conclusions?"

She exhaled slowly. "Nothing specific. I'm going to see if I can find Zack after I leave here. I'd like to have a little chat with him today. I'd also like to talk to a couple of his so-called alibis."

"Be careful, Keri. That kid is trouble."

"I know. I'll be okay." She twisted her neck from side to side, feeling it pop. "I've also got a call into Jerry's office, trying to find out if he's back in town. I thought I saw his truck over on Martin Lane, but I can't be sure. If he's in town, I want a face-to-face with him."

"Maybe I should come along. Something about all this . . . I just don't want anything to happen to you."

An awkward silence fell between them. She looked down, toying with her mittens.

"Wait," he started. "Did you say you thought you saw his truck?"

"Yeah. He drives a black Dodge Ram. Why do you ask?"

He was silent. She could see the wheels turning in his mind.

"Because the only thing Dad saw last night was a dark pickup. He noticed it turning the corner right before he saw the glow of the fire in the window back there." He tipped his head in the direction of the press room.

Their eyes met, the questions obvious.

"I'll make sure I talk to Jerry today. It's a small town. I'll find him."

"Good idea. Sure you don't need me to tag along?"

She stood, pulling on her mittens. "No, I'll be fine. I've known Jerry my whole life, Grant. Even if he's involved in this somehow, he'd never do anything to harm me."

"Never say never," he added, squeezing her shoulder.

"I'll be in touch. In the meantime, you should clean this place. It's a pig's sty," she teased.

"Yes, ma'am. Anything else you'd like me to do?"

She started out the door then turned back. "Yeah. Find out what's going on with your dad and my aunt. I'm a little curious about all that."

He laughed. "You and me both, Keri. You and me both."

Keri turned off Main Street, headed toward The Bayside, a bar on the outskirts of town. Bud had told her Zack could be found there just about any time day or night. Whenever he wasn't spray-painting shopping carts or sidewalks, or stealing cigarettes, that is. She'd been in the honky-tonk only a couple of times, both times looking for some of her dad's crew late on Friday afternoons. It was a favorite hangout for local construction workers. Bud had told her Zack spent his time there bragging to the other regulars about his many varied "accomplishments," in between video games, a round of pool, and an occasional attempt at darts.

"Well, look what the cat dragged in. As I live and breathe, it's Waterford Bay's little miss ray of sunshine."

It took a moment for her eyes to adjust to the dim lighting of The Bayside, but Keri would know that voice anywhere. The creepiness factor notwithstanding, she was relieved to know she wouldn't have to spend all day trying to find the town's biggest loser. Just as Bud had predicted, Zack Clayton was holding court in his home away from home. *Or maybe it* is *his home.* Keri found the thought fitting somehow.

"Hey Zack. How's it going?" she asked, making her way toward him across the sticky floor. The air was thick with smoke, one of the only establishments in town that still allowed smoking under some ridiculous city ordinance. Of course it wasn't just the stench of stale cigarette smoke that gagged her. Keri had no doubt the flavors of fried catfish, chicken, and French Fries were indistinguishable once they came out of the oil in the Bayside's deep fryer. She guessed the oil hadn't been changed in a good six months. Or more.

But it was the reek of body odor that made her want to turn and leave. The closer she got to Zack, the worse it got. Evidently, his busy schedule didn't allow for personal hygiene. She tried to breathe through her mouth. Either that or hurl on his filthy boots.

"Well, a whole heckuva lot better now that *you* stopped by." He set down his near-empty mug of beer, and turned on the stool to give her his full attention. "What brings you here, missy? I thought you was off at some fancy college back east? Yet here you are, slumming with the boys back home."

Most likely he thought his smile was appealing, but something about the stained teeth and dirty hair just ruined the whole magic for Keri. And there was that nasty "aroma" still wafting through the air.

"Zack, Bud tells me he talked to you about that fire out at the Blankenship place."

He let out a loud whoop of a holler and slammed his palm flat on the bar. “Not you too, little missy? I told that stupid cop I wasn’t anywhere near that place that night!” He grabbed his beer, finishing it with a loud belch. “And that’s all I got to say about that.”

She tried to act nonchalant. “Well, sure, Zack. He told me that. I was just wondering if you’d heard anything. Like maybe somebody told you something or saw something. Being as how you weren’t anywhere near that place that night.”

His smile faded. “Nah, I didn’t hear nothin’. My guys was all with me at my place. We was playing poker.” A lewd expression flamed his face. “Course, if *you’da* been there, we’da played some *strip* poker.”

Keri rolled her eyes. “Yeah, I’m real sorry I missed that. But—”

“Not half as sorry as I am.”

She pinned him with a stare. “Zack, c’mon. Think. You had to hear something. You know people. Somebody in this town has talked about that fire and chances are you would’ve heard them say it. Work with me, here, would you?”

He tugged at a curl on her shoulder. “Oh I’ll work with you all night long, sweet thing.”

She batted his hand away. “Fine. You don’t know anything about the Blankenship fire. What about the fire at the newspaper office?”

He ordered another brew. “You want one?”

She tilted her head to one side. “No thank you. Ten o’clock is a little early for my taste buds. Now back to my question. Know anything about that fire? Hear anything?”

The bartender took his empty mug, replacing it with a frost-covered full one. He slurped a long swallow, then wiped the foam from his sad excuse for a mustache. “Nope. Don’t know nothin’ about that one either. How come you askin’ all these questions? You a cop now? Where’s your uniform?”

“I’m working for the paper.”

“Oh, that’s a real shame. You come back to town, go to work for the paper, and it goes up in smoke.” Another grin crawled up in face. “Wait, that cabin was your daddy’s, wasn’t it? He built that one, didn’t he? Whoa. That’s a real shame. You’re two for two. I’m thinking Bud oughta be asking *you* all these questions. Kinda coinky-dinky, don’t you think? You got a big ol’ lighter in that fancy bag of yours?”

What a waste of time.

“Maybe some matches and a little kerosene?”

How could he know about the kerosene? Bill and Bud kept that information private. She and her dad knew about it. And Grant. But details like that hadn’t been shared in public. She was sure of it. She quickly guarded her thoughts, masking her expression. “No, I’m afraid not. Only some lipstick and breath mints. Hey, what—”

“Here’s an idea. How about tossin’ me one of them breath mints then let me sample some of that lipstick. On your lips, of course.”

“Not happening. What kind of pickup do you drive?”

“It’s a Ford—wait, who says I drive a pickup?”

“Just a hunch.”

He studied her with those bloodshot eyes. She studied him back, disgusted but undeterred.

“Who cares what kind of truck I drive?”

“No reason. Just curious. What color is it?”

“Well, I guess that’s for me to know and you to find out, Keri. Course, if you’d like to come hang out at my place a while, I’d be happy to take you for a little drive in my truck. Let you find out for yourself what *color* it is.”

She narrowed her eyes at him, weary of the game. “You stole my backpack in sixth grade, didn’t you?”

“Well, duh? I stole everybody’s backpack. It was one of my defining middle school characteristics. You wanna come over to my place and see if you can pick it out? I kept ‘em all, y’know.”

“Yeah?”

“Course. They’re called souvenirs in my line of work.” He laughed again, this one full of wheeze and phlegm.

Keri pressed her lips together, not sure she could keep her stomach down. “Fascinating though it is, I’ve got to run. But I may stop by sometime. You still live in that double-wide out on Lynn Lane with your dad?”

“Yeah. But just me and Duke. My dad croaked a few years ago. So the trailer’s all mine now. I own it free and clear.”

“Who’s Duke?”

“My rottweiler.”

“Of course it is.”

She turned to leave, already wondering how fast she could get home and take a hot shower to wash off the stench of this place. And him.

“Bye now, little missy. You come on out sometime and meet ol’ Duke.”

Sure thing. Right about the time hell freezes over . . .

Chapter 11

With that hot shower still front and center on her mind, Keri rounded the last corner onto her street and immediately spotted Jerry Winkler's familiar black truck sitting in the driveway. "Must be my lucky day," she said out loud. Grant would label it a divine appointment, but Keri simply thanked her lucky stars for making her job easier today.

Then her stomach tightened. *Jerry's here to talk to Dad. This can't be good.*

Before she even opened the door, she heard her father's voice.

"It wasn't me, Jerry. I swear I never said that! Not to anyone! Why won't you listen to me?"

A string of Jerry's expletives peppered the air as she opened the door. They both turned as she walked into the kitchen.

"And you can tell your stupid daughter to mind her own business!" Jerry growled.

Tyler backed toward her, his hands raised in warning. "Leave her out of it. She's just doing her job. Like I said before, if you have nothing to hide, then you have nothing to fear."

"I'm not *afraid* of anything, McMillan. Least of all you. But if one more of my guys tells me he's heard I'm the lead suspect in the fire that burned down that Blankenship monstrosity, then it's you and me." He stepped into Tyler's path, his nose not an inch from her father's. "Just like old times, Tyler. You and me."

The two men glared at each other, their chests heaving with each angry breath. Finally, Jerry turned, taking a step toward Keri. He pointed an index finger in her face, closing the gap between them. "And you, young lady." He paused, as if needing a moment to contain his wrath.

She could feel his breath on her face. It reeked of alcohol.

At this hour of the morning?

"You'd better watch your step." He lifted a curl, wrapping it around his finger. "I sure wouldn't want to see anything happen to that pretty little face of yours."

She jerked her head back, dislodging the strand from his grasp. "You don't scare me, Jerry. I know you're just a big teddy bear underneath all that whiskey bravado."

He stared at her for a moment before throwing his head back to roar with laughter. "Oh Keri, you always were quite the vixen. Even as a little girl. A spitfire just looking for a fight." His smile waned. "But like I said. Watch your step. Seems to be a lot of matchbooks around town just begging for a light."

He pushed passed her and left, slamming the door behind him.

"Well, that was—" She turned only to discover her father was no longer standing where he'd been. "Daddy!"

He fell back against his recliner before landing on the hardwood floor, his face ashen. His eyes rolled back in his head. "Keri—"

"DADDY!"

She dropped to his side. "I'm calling 911. Just stay still. Don't move!"

In less than half an hour, Keri found herself back in the ER waiting room. She paced, angry they wouldn't let her back to see her father. The ambulance had arrived less than five minutes after she'd called, thanks to the proximity of the fire station to their home. Keri had tried to hold herself together as they strapped an oxygen mask on her father's face and checked his vitals. Before she could even utter a prayer, they were loading him into the ambulance, rattling off all kinds of stats and informing the ER of their imminent arrival.

Now, all she could see in her mind was the pasty white skin on his face as he'd fallen. If Jerry Winkler walked through the door right now, she was absolutely positive she could kill him. With her bare hands.

How dare he talk to Dad like that! Dad never thought for a minute Jerry was behind the fires. After all he's put Dad through, you'd think he might realize it's not Dad who's causing his life to fall apart. It's his own fault. Nobody to blame but himself.

"Keri, where is he? Where's Tyler?" Nita rushed through the automated doors coming from the interior of the hospital. "Have you seen him since you called me?"

She fell into her aunt's open arms. "No, they won't let me go back there. I'm about to lose my mind! Oh Nita, he looked *so bad* . . . I thought . . . I thought I'd lost him."

Nita hugged her hard. "Now Keri, let's don't jump to conclusions. That father of yours is made of steel. He probably just let himself get dehydrated or something. Maybe he forgot to eat. You two don't have a clue how to take care of yourselves. I've got a mind to move in and rule your roost with an iron fist." Her eyes softened. "Or at least my cast iron skillet."

Keri pulled back, wiping her eyes. "Aunt Nita, this is serious. He didn't just pass out because he skipped breakfast. Something is seriously wrong with him. The other night, he got all clammy and lightheaded. He kept rubbing his left arm and flexing his wrist."

"What? Why didn't you tell me?"

"Because that's when we got the call from Grant that Shep had been hurt. We got here as fast as we could. Then in all the mayhem, and then the fire . . . it just slipped my mind. And of course he never said another word about it." She looked up, feeling the tears sting her eyes. "I'm a *horrible* daughter! How could I forget something like that? He's my own father . . ."

Nita gathered her back in her arms. "Now, you just stop that. We've all been under an enormous amount of pressure these last few weeks. It's a wonder we aren't all back there alongside Tyler being treated for stress. Or whatever it is he's experiencing right now." She leaned back, pushing Keri's wild curls from her face. "We'll just pray he's going to be okay. God's watching over him in there. He'll take care of him."

Dr. Richards approached them, looping his stethoscope back around his neck.

"Oh there he is," Nita said. "Dr. Richards, how's my brother?"

He reached out, putting his arm over Keri's shoulder and grabbing Nita's hand. "I'm afraid it's not good news. Tyler needs surgery. Right away."

"What?!" Keri cried.

"What kind of surgery?" Nita asked.

"He's got major blockage in two arteries. We need to take care of those immediately. I know he's been under a lot of pressure lately. Chances are, all that stress has just aggravated a condition that's been going on for some time. Tyler's not too faithful with his physicals. I haven't seen him in more than eight years, according to my records."

"And don't think he won't be hearing about *that*," Nita snapped. "You can be sure I'll give him a piece of my mind on the subject and start making sure he sees you on a regular basis."

"I'm sure you will, Nita. But for now, we need to get him into surgery." He squeezed both their hands and turned to leave. "We'll let you back to see him before we take him upstairs to the OR. Then you can move to the waiting room up there. I'll make sure someone keeps you updated on his progress."

Keri watched him walk through the doors, her vision blurred with tears.

Nita pulled her to a nearby row of seats and gently lowered her into one. "Keri, he'll be fine. I believe with all my heart, he'll be just fine."

Keri slowly turned to look into her aunt's worried eyes. "If only I believed that."

Nita's brow deepened. "Oh sweetheart, I know it's hard. But don't lose faith. Don't you let go of your faith."

What faith?

Chapter 12

Keri slowly took a seat on the weathered bench. The breeze was biting cold this morning but she didn't care. It was like she hadn't taken a breath all day. She'd always come here, to this bench beneath the lighthouse. It was her own personal haven where she could allow her mind to go places she normally kept carefully guarded. The steady rhythm of the waves lapping against the shore below had always soothed her soul.

But never as much as today.

Her father made it through surgery fine. The relief at hearing those words from Dr. Richards' mouth had been the best news she'd ever heard. She'd spent the afternoon at her father's bedside, though he mostly slept. Nita popped in and out, dividing her time between Tyler's room and Shep's. When her dad finally came around enough to talk, she wept openly, blubbering her relief that he'd made it through surgery.

As the tears began to slow, she'd vowed to bring Jerry to justice. She'd never known such deep, consuming fury. She'd experienced heartache and sadness before. Lots of it. And she'd faced disappointment too many times to count. But this was different. There was a burning anger deep inside her toward this pathetic waste of humanity who'd come much too close to taking her father from her. Dad had learned to handle Jerry through the years. She would not be so forgiving. If it was the last thing she ever did, she would make sure he paid for all he'd done.

"Sweetheart, please. Don't talk like that." He'd closed his eyes but continued. "I can't lie here worrying about you confronting him. You have to promise me you won't do that."

She'd bitten her lip, debating whether to lie or make the promise.

"I can't get well if I'm worrying about you stirring it up with Jerry again."

That's all it took. She'd promised, knowing her father's recovery was all that mattered.

She'd promised. But she hadn't liked it.

Now, as the wind howled around her, she took deep cleansing breaths, trying to let the ocean air rid her of the toxic anger eating her up inside.

Let it go, she told herself. *You promised. You have to let it go. At least until Dad's better.*

It took a conscious effort and wasn't easy, but she tried to get her mind off Jerry and the fires and the losses—and *near* losses—they'd suffered.

Just focus on the gratitude. Show some serious appreciation. Dad's okay and that's all that matters.

Moments passed until she sensed a shift in her thoughts and feelings.

Thank you, God.

Her eyes popped open. Had she said that aloud?

Where did that come from?

But she knew. It came from a heart overflowing with gratitude. She blew out a hard breath, feeling genuine relief for owning up to the truth of it—that Nita had prayed and God had brought her father through his surgery.

I'm here for you, Keri.

This time she jumped up and looked around. The voice was so close, so intimate . . . but there was no one there.

Or was there?

I love you.

The three words echoed over and over through her spirit. Pinpoints of heat pricked her eyes just before the tears began to fall. She didn't even try to stop them.

She knew exactly Who it was. And instead of putting up her customary defenses, she welcomed Him with everything inside her. Moments passed. She felt the strong breeze on her face, heard the rush of the surf below, the cry of seagulls in the distance.

She had no idea how long she'd been sitting there when she felt something wash over her. Something different. Strange. She wasn't quite sure what to do with it or even what to think about it. But it felt good. Really good. As if she'd been covered with a soft, warm blanket wrapped in peace. How was that even possible with everything that was going on? Yet there it was. Real and comforting, filling her with a sense of security she'd never experienced. Not even close.

The sound of footsteps approaching pulled her back to reality.

"You know we've got to stop meeting like this."

She turned, watching the wind whip those salt and peppers strands of hair peeking out beneath his ball cap. "Seems my private little hideout isn't so private anymore."

He stopped just before reaching her, the smile fading from his face. "Oh. Keri, I'm sorry. I didn't—"

"Grant, I'm kidding." She patted the bench beside her. "Have a seat."

"Whoa. You had me worried there for a minute."

"Sorry. Didn't mean it that way. This has always been where I come when I need to think. Or just air out my brain." She dug her hands in her coat pockets. "But it's hardly private property. So were you following me or just in the neighborhood again?"

He'd sat down closer than she expected. He seemed to be searching her eyes, then slowly looped his arm through hers. "I was just heading out to Dad's to pick up a few things for him. He gets nervous if he's without his pipe for any length of time."

"His pipe? They won't let him smoke in the hospital, you know."

"Oh, that's no problem. He hasn't lit the thing in years. Just likes the feel of it in his mouth. Maybe you've noticed he's a bit on the peculiar side?"

Keri smiled. "Your dad? Peculiar? No, I guess I never noticed."

"Liar."

She laughed quietly. "I'm glad he's okay, Grant."

He snuggled closer, taking a deep breath as he looked out on the pounding surf below them. "Me too." He stole a look sideways. "Are you okay?"

"Me?"

"Yeah. You said you come out here to think. If you need to talk, I'm all ears."

A chorus of sea gulls flying by reminded her of the moments just before he showed up when a new-found sense of calm had eased all the anxieties she'd been fighting.

"Grant, I'm not entirely sure, but I think maybe God just spoke to me."

He turned to face her. "Really? How do you mean?"

She tried to explain it. The words hadn't been audible, but she'd heard them just the same. Felt them in her heart. So real. So heartfelt.

She wasn't even embarrassed to tell him. Everything in his eyes, every expression on that handsome face, welcomed what she was saying.

Almost as if he'd been waiting to hear them.

He pulled his arm free then wrapped it over her shoulder, drawing her close to him. "Oh Keri, you have no idea how happy I am to hear you say this. I've been praying for you."

She sniffled. "You have?"

She felt him nod his head. "As much as you pushed me off at first—wait, why exactly *did* you push me off so hard?" He leaned closer. "Because you must admit, you really couldn't stand me. Barely tolerated being in the same room with me. What was all that about?"

She pulled back a little, avoiding his eyes. "Uh . . . well, I think we just got off to a bad start."

He laughed. "Ya think?"

"Hey, I couldn't help it." She huffed. "Okay, you really want to hear this?"

"Yes, I really do."

"You represented *everything* I've ever wanted—a job with one of the leading newspapers in the country. Ever since I was a little girl, I've wanted to be a reporter. Work on the big stories of the day for a leading news outlet. That's why I had to put off going to college for so many years, because I had to save up so I could go to NYU and get my degree from one of the top journalism schools in the country."

She stood up, then took a few steps closer to the railing overlooking the ocean. "It broke my heart to have to leave before I finished. But it was *so* expensive. Far more than I'd estimated. And I just ran out of money. I tried working several different jobs—you know, the usual—Starbucks, odd jobs around campus, tutoring . . . but I finally realized all of those paychecks combined could never pay as much as working for my dad here. Besides, he needed my help.

"Of course I had no idea how bad things had become with his business. He didn't have the heart to tell me. He knew I was counting on my old job here. And I had no clue the economy had affected his company so badly. I should have realized it, looking back. But I was so consumed with my school work and my own financial mess, I never once thought about *his* situation.

"He'd already been forced to lay off some of his crew. That absolutely killed him. But neither he nor Nita said a word about that when I finally told them I was coming home to work for a year." She turned back toward him with a sad smile. "Ever the thoughtful daughter."

He stood, reaching for her hand. "I'm sure they were both trying to protect you. They knew how disappointed you were about having to take a year off. If you only knew how many times your aunt nagged me about hiring you."

"Seriously? I mean, I knew she had spoken to you. But 'nagged' you?"

He smiled. "Afraid so."

She buried her face in her other hand. "Now I'm really embarrassed."

"Don't be. Course, if I'd had any idea Nita's niece was so smart and beautiful and such a brilliant journalist—"

"Oh please."

"I'm serious!" He lifted her chin. "You weren't at all what I expected. So you see I was happily surprised to meet you that night the cabin burned. Even if the circumstances weren't the greatest. Whereas you, on the other hand, were clearly unimpressed by this loser who walked away from the L.A. Times and chose instead a small town weekly."

She averted her eyes again, this time blowing out a slow breath. "Yeah, well . . . sometimes you have to get to know someone to really appreciate them."

"Well, now. We're making progress. You 'appreciate' me, do you?"

They sat back down on the bench, his arm returning to its place over her shoulder.

"Grant, I have to know. Why *did* you walk away from the Times? I mean, who does that? People spend their whole lives wishing for a place at that table. I was *so angry* when Nita told me about that. I could barely stand to talk to you. But looking back, I guess I should have at least asked to hear your side of the story."

"Yes, I believe they teach that in Introduction to Journalism, don't they?"

"Very funny."

"Keri, sometimes what you wish for turns out to be anything *but* what you wished for. Meaning, sometimes that 'dream job'—isn't. And that's what happened to me. I was lucky. I had a professor in college who really liked my work and put in a good word for me to a friend of his at the Times. It's like I skipped the ladder altogether and went straight to the head of the line. And don't think I didn't realize what an unbelievable stroke of luck that was.

"At first I loved it. I was fascinated with every aspect of it. The adrenaline was incredibly addicting. I couldn't stand my days off. All I wanted was to be out there on the front lines of the news, witnessing the big stories, interviewing all the players making the news. It's all I cared about. Eventually, I moved into investigative journalism, and then it got even more addictive. I couldn't stand not to be working on the cases. Doing the interviews. Keeping up with the minute-by-minute developments. Following the leads.

"And I was good at it. Really good at it."

"Yeah? So, just how good at it were you, Mr. Dawson?" she asked playfully.

"Pulitzer-Prize-good-at-it, Miss McMillan."

"Yeah right," she smirked.

He nodded slowly, his eyebrows rising to validate the point. "I'd be happy to show it to you sometime. As long as you don't bite my head off in the meantime."

She felt her jaw drop as her eyes locked on his. And then she felt it again. The slow burn in her gut as envy and frustration and outrage all boiled together.

"Now I really don't understand!" She pulled away from him, taking his arm off her shoulder. "How could you walk away from that? How could you turn your back on a *Pulitzer* and come here? To this?!

"You really *are* the idiot I thought you were. I was right. Oh, I was right about you."

"Hey, settle down, Keri."

"No! Don't tell me to settle down!" She jumped up, backing away from him. "What's the matter with you? How dare you throw away a perfectly good career? Don't you see? Don't you get it?"

"Yes, I think I do."

She paused. "What's that supposed to mean?"

"It means, you think I've stomped on *your* dream because I walked away from mine."

She stared at him. "That's exactly what I think! It's like you wadded it up and tossed it in the trash can and then made sure it ended up in some disgusting landfill! It's SO UNFAIR!"

"But the dream died for me."

"How? How did the dream die?"

He gripped the rail, looking down below at the foaming surf. "Like I said, dreams aren't always what you think they are. Sure, it was exciting and stimulating and rewarding . . . at first. Then it became exhausting. I said it was an addiction because it was. I started popping pills to stay awake and keep on task. Then I'd have to take sleeping pills because I couldn't sleep. Then I'd be so stressed and exhausted, I'd do anything to relax and get away from it for a while. Everyone I worked with fought the same demons, so happy hour became part of our daily schedule. We'd drink and discuss our work and drink and talk half the night away. Combine all that booze with all the pills I was popping? Not a good combination."

"So what, you had to go into rehab? Even so, couldn't you just clean yourself up and go back? Try to be more disciplined?"

He scoffed, choosing to ignore the sarcasm. "I suppose."

"Why didn't you, then?"

"I simply got burned out, Keri. It happens."

"Grant, you have a PULITZER. Wasn't that even the slightest motivation to get back in there and try again? I just don't understand how you could—"

"No, you *don't* understand. Because you can't. You weren't there, putting up with the political agendas hiding around every corner. You weren't there to see good people brought down hard and ugly by those with self-serving agendas. You weren't there, having your ethics compromised at every turn just to get the story. You weren't there, watching every relationship you attempted go down the drain because you were too wrapped up in your job to give anyone a chance to get close. And you weren't there when your best friend overdosed because the lie he was forced to write caused a young girl to take her own life . . ."

He stopped abruptly, panting after the words spilled out, still suspended in the wintry puff of air between them. He blinked several times and stole a look at her. Then he looked away, embarrassed. "I'm sorry. I didn't mean to—"

She pulled off her mitten and touched her fingers to his lips. "Don't. I'm the one who owes you an apology. Again. I . . . I had no idea, Grant."

He took a deep breath and pulled her into his arms. They stood that way for several minutes. She felt like such an utter fool trying to tell this good and decent man how he should have lived his life.

"No, you had no idea. There's no way you could."

She burrowed deeper into his embrace. "I'm so sorry."

The wind kicked up again, the roar of the waves making it impossible to speak. Moments passed.

"Well, it's not something they teach you in school."

"Apparently not."

"Besides," he began, leaning back to look at her, "if I'd stayed in L.A., how would I ever have met Nita's feisty little niece?"

She smiled. "I'm not sure. Maybe we should investigate."

He leaned his forehead against hers, cupping her face in his hands. "My thoughts exactly." And then he kissed her, his lips warm and gentle . . . and in no hurry whatsoever. She wrapped her arms around his waist, holding on for dear life as she felt that blanket of peace and security surround her once again.

Then, without the slightest hint of disappointment, she realized those dreams she'd been clinging to for so many years had just shifted. In a whole new direction.

The thought surprised her. Actually it shocked her.

But that conversation would have to wait because she'd also made another discovery.

Grant Dawson's kisses could take her breath away.

And then some.

Chapter 13

Her encounter with Grant at the lighthouse left Keri breathless and dizzy. They'd walked back to their cars and Grant had left her with a final kiss before driving off to his dad's boat. She was having trouble getting her brain to function with any semblance of normalcy, so she opted to stop by the sheriff's office. She needed to talk to Bud about her encounter with Zack, but she needed the infamously strong coffee they brewed at the station even more.

Still, the sweetness of her stolen moments in Grant's arms couldn't be dismissed just yet. First, she'd experienced that unexpected moment when the Lord had spoken to her heart. Then the long, heartfelt conversation with a man she never once had imagined as anything more than her boss. And an irritating one at that. *Funny how things change . . .*

"Now that's a refreshing sight if ever I saw one," Bud said, waving at her from behind the counter of the messy outer office.

"What's that?" Keri asked, heading straight for the coffee urn.

"That big ol' smile on your face. Wouldn't have expected to see that today, what with your dad in the hospital and all."

She poured the thick black brew into a clean mug then doused it with creamer. She hoped the heat she felt in her face would diminish before she had to face him again. "Oh, just amused about something. That's all." She kept her head down, focusing on her swirling coffee.

"Come have a sit. Let's compare notes."

They moved into his office. "I'm afraid I'm more confused than anything else, Bud."

"How so?"

"I talked to Zack. Didn't learn any more than you did, I'm sure. But I definitely get the feeling he's capable. He's got prison written all over him. I'm not sure he wouldn't be better off tucked in safe and secure at the state pen over in Salem."

"True, but we've got to have something solid to get him in there. Believe me, I've tried for years."

She took a sip, grimacing at the strength of her coffee despite the heavy dose of creamer. "Whoa. You guys don't kid around with this stuff."

"Helps get the job done."

"I guess it does. Hey, Bud. I need your help. I really think Jerry Winkler could be our guy. You already know about his fight with Dad the other night."

"Yeah, I talked to Tyler. He filled me in. Sounds like quite a showdown."

Keri bit her lip, trying to find her words. "What can we do to bring him in? Do you have to have a warrant or something? Is there any way you can do a polygraph on him? I have a feeling—"

"Hold on, Keri. I think you're getting ahead of yourself here."

"You know as well as I do he's dangerous! Did Dad tell you his comment about 'all the matchbooks' around town? How else can you interpret that but a threat?"

Bud's chair creaked as he leaned back and tented his fingers. "Keri, I know there's bad blood between Jerry and Tyler."

"You should have seen him, Bud. He scared me to death! It's like he's this ticking time bomb, just waiting for something to set him off."

"I get it. I know. I've known the man for years. But that's hardly enough cause to bring him in. But I'll talk to him. I'd ask you to come along but—"

"Don't bother. Dad pretty much made me swear not to cross paths with him. And it's probably a good thing. I might not be able to control myself. I'd like to punch his lights out or maybe—"

"I did not hear that," he quipped, holding his hands against his ears. "Not a good idea to tell the sheriff of your intent to physically harm someone. Even if you have good cause."

Keri laughed and set her mug on his desk. "Point taken. So let me ask you. Have you learned anything new in the investigation? Anything you can share with me?"

He sat up and began rustling papers on his desk. "Well, let's take a look. Seems to me there was . . . oh, I remember now. He reached for a plastic bag, holding it by the corner. "I don't guess you have any idea what this is, do you?'

She reached for the bag, noticing the dirty red string inside. "I think I saw this out at the site the other day."

"You did?" He tilted his head. "When was that?"

She traced the string through the plastic realizing it was much heavier than mere string. Something more like— "Wait. This looks like a strand of one of those elastic pony tail holders." She grabbed the one out of her hair and held it up in her hand. "Like one of these." It was only then that she realized hers was red also.

Bud pursed his lips. "Ah. That explains it then. Must be one of yours."

Something in the back of her mind began to spin. But what?

"Then again . . ." Bud began, tapping the eraser end of his pencil on his blotter.

She looked up at him. "What?"

"Doesn't Zack wear that greasy mess of hair of his in a ponytail most of the time? Do guys use these too?"

"Sure. They don't exactly make 'his and her' pony tail holders. And guys usually wear this plain kind, without any decoration."

They stared at each other, thinking. Something just out of reach in her mind nagged her. But what? *Who else wears a pony tail?* "I'm trying to think if any of the guys in Dad's crew have long hair but most of them wear it short or even shave their heads."

"And you're sure that's not yours? I mean, it's red just like yours."

"They come in all kinds of colors. Mostly black and navy and red, but they could be any color." She closed her eyes, trying to think if she'd had her hair pulled back when she was at the site. The night of the fire, she hadn't had time to do anything with her hair. After she got Carson's call, she'd quickly dressed, but she didn't remember pulling her hair back. Besides, that night she never got near the hearth where she'd seen this . . .

"Oh my gosh."

"What?"

"I remember when I saw this. It was a few days after the fire. I'd gone out there to the site to nose around. Grant had just hired me and asked me to start probing into the fire, come up with a list of suspects. I drove up and found Matt Blankenship at the cabin."

"Matt? What was Matt doing there?"

"He said his folks were having trouble getting back from Europe."

"I know, Keri. We've been in constant communication with them since the fire. They just flew into Portland late last night. Should be in town later today."

"Matt said he'd come in town on their behalf to check out the damage. He said—"

Keri jumped at the sound of Bud's chair scraping against the floor as he stood abruptly. "Keri, when was the last time you saw Matt?"

"What? I just told you. That morning at the cabin."

"When? What day was that?"

"I don't know, it must have been . . . it was Tuesday. Same day I started working for Grant. Wait—it was right after I came by and talked to you that morning. Remember?"

"I remember. So?"

"After I left here, I drove out to the cabin. Just to look around. Matt was already there. When I pulled up I saw—" She gasped, jumping to her feet. "Bud! Matt drives a pickup! A dark pickup! Remember, Shep said he saw a dark pickup leaving the *Weekly* office just before he saw the fire?"

"Focus, Keri. Focus. Back to Matt. You saw him at the cabin and he had a black pickup?"

"I saw it parked around back. Or I mean, front. The front of the cabin. But it wasn't black, it was navy. A navy blue pickup . . ."

The memory raced through her mind. The surprise at finding him there. The compassion she'd felt toward him about the loss of his new home. The awkward conversation . . .

She gasped again. "Bud!" Her eyes tracked up to his. "It was really windy that day. A big gust of wind came up, blowing all that ash in our faces . . . and once I'd cleared my eyes, I looked up just as Matt took *a red band* off his wrist and pulled back his hair into a pony tail."

Bud started to say something, but she stopped him.

"But wait. That was *after* he left that I saw this in the ash near the fireplace." She picked up the evidence bag again, looking at the singed remnant. "I sat on the hearth and toed my sneakers in the ash. That's when it caught my eye. So it couldn't have been Matt's because I'd just seen him put it in his hair."

Bud tried to interrupt but she continued, dropping the plastic bag and stretching the band she'd just taken out of her hair. "But of course, when you buy these, you buy them in a pack of a dozen or so. And they usually come in an assortment of colors."

"Keri—"

"And if he's like me, he keeps extras in his pocket or on his wrist."

Bud came around the desk and held his palm in her face. "Keri! Listen to me!"

She blinked, snapping her head up to face him.

"The Blankenships haven't talked to Matt in years. They're estranged. Some kind of huge fight they had years ago. He'd threatened his mother, and his father kicked him out."

"But why was he . . . oh. Oh! Oh my gosh—he burned their house down."

"I think we've found our guy."

Keri rushed after the sheriff as he hurried out the door, barking orders at his deputies.

"I'm coming with you."

He turned and grabbed her by the shoulders. "No ma'am, you

most certainly are not. Your father would have my hide if I put you in any kind of danger. You either sit tight here or go check in on your father. But whatever you do, do NOT interfere. And that's an order."

She bit her lip as he turned to leave, knowing he was right. "Be careful, Bud. I'll be at the hospital with Dad. Call me if you find him."

He nodded just before ducking into his cruiser.

A few minutes later, Keri stopped by the paper to talk to Grant. As she walked up the back steps of the building, she remembered he'd headed out to Shep's boat after leaving her at the lighthouse. She tried to call him on his cell but it went straight to voice mail. Instead of leaving a message, she called her aunt, assuming she'd be at Shep's side and maybe she'd know where to find him.

"Hey sweetie. No, he's not here. He called from Shep's place with a couple of questions for his dad. Then he said he was going by Chandlers to pick up some of Clara's meatloaf and mashed potatoes for Shep. Our patient is a bit cranky about the hospital food he's been served here."

"Okay, tell you what. If you hear from him, tell him I need to talk to him as soon as possible. He's not answering his cell."

Nita hooted. "That's because he dropped it in the john in Shep's bathroom here at the hospital. I couldn't help laughing but he was *not* happy about it. Oh what a sight that was!" Nita continued to chuckle. Keri could hear her chatting with Shep in the background.

"AUNT NITA!"

"What? Good heavens, Keri, what's the matter? You sound upset."

"I'm fine. But I've got to talk to him. In fact, I think I'll stop by Chandlers and see if I can catch him there." She hurried down the steps and back into her car.

"All right, sweetie. I'll tell him in case you miss him."

Keri snapped off her phone and turned her key in the ignition. A few moments later, she pulled up in front of Chandlers, disappointed she couldn't find Grant's car in the parking lot.

That's when she saw it.

The dark pickup parked toward the back of the lot. A navy blue pickup.

Her heart raced. She knew she should wait. She knew she should call Bud. But without a second thought she got out of her Jeep and hurried to the front door. When she entered, she spotted him immediately, sitting up at the front counter.

What should I do? What should I say? Oh God, help me out here.

"Hi Keri," Clara called from the window to the kitchen. "How are you?"

Matt turned, looking over his shoulder at her. He nodded, studying her as he continued to eat.

She was quite certain he could see the fear in her eyes, hear her heart pounding in her chest. *He knows that I know. There's no way that he knows that I know. But he knows. I'm sure of it.*

But it made no sense. She told herself to calm down, breathe normally, and stop acting like such an amateur. Even if she was one.

"Hi, Matt. Nice to see you again."

He just nodded then took a sip of his Coke.

"Keri, are you here to pick up that order Nita called in?"

"Uh, yeah. That's why I'm here." She shot Matt a plastic smile. "Picking up food. For a friend."

He took another bite of his burger, indifferent.

She slowly made her way to his side, biting back the huge lump of fear in her throat before climbing up onto the stool. She left a stool between them. "I haven't seen your folks yet, Matt. Did they make it back yet?" She prayed he didn't hear that nervous crack in her voice.

He didn't turn to look at her, instead focusing on the fries he was pushing through a puddle of ketchup. "Not yet."

"Really? I would have thought they'd made it home by now. I mean, it can't take *that* long to fly home. Even with the storms. I read once where—"

"They'll be here soon enough. Why?"

"Why what?"

He chomped down on the messy fries, taking his time to chew. Finally, "Why you need to know where my parents are?"

"Oh. Well. I was just, uh . . . Dad needs to talk to them. He's got a lot to discuss with them, you know. So many decisions to make now that . . . now that, uh . . ."

He reached for his Coke again, his eyes sliding sideways toward her.

She pushed her hands into her coat pockets to hide the trembling. "Anyway, if you hear from them . . ."

He blinked.

Her fingers grasped something in her pocket. *The elastic hair band.* She felt the heat creep up her face as an idea immediately took shape in her mind. She swallowed hard again, her eyes briefly closing. Then she locked eyes with him as she pulled the red band from her pocket and placed it next to his plate on the counter.

He looked at it, his brow dipping slightly. “What’s that?”

“What do you think it is?” She cringed, hearing the waver in her voice again.

He pushed his plate back then wiped his mouth with a wrinkled paper napkin. “I don’t have a clue. Why don’t you tell me?”

She leaned to one side for a better view of his hair. “Oh, I think you know what it is. Especially since there’s one just like it holding your pony tail in place.”

He looked ahead, shaking his head slightly. “Okay. What’s this all about? Is this some kind of game? Because I’m really not in the mood.”

“It’s no game, Matt.” She pushed her own hair out of her eyes and leveled them at him. “The investigators found the burned remnants of one of these out at what’s left of your parents’ house.”

He shrugged, his body language saying, “So?”

“Just like the one you were wearing that day I saw you out there. Just like the one you’re wearing now.”

He suddenly spun on the stool to face her. “Are you making some kind of accusation here?”

She stepped down off her stool, backing away. “Maybe.”

“Because you had better have something more than that if you’re saying what I think you’re saying.”

Keri tried to steel her nerves. “You never told me you were estranged from your parents.”

His eyes narrowed almost imperceptively but he said nothing.

“You said you were checking on the house on their behalf. But you haven’t talked to them in years. Not since . . .”

He stood up, nearing her. “Not since what?

Her heart pounded, her chest heaving in response. “Since you threatened your mother. Something about a big falling out.”

“And you think because I had an argument with my parents I would come all the way back to Oregon just to torch their dream house?”

She let the theory hang in the air, knowing it was true. Even his cocky demeanor couldn’t hide the guilt written on his face.

He stepped even closer, grabbing her elbow in his hand, squeezing hard. “I asked, is that what you think?” he growled under his breath.

“Actually, it’s what we all think.”

Matt stepped back, Keri’s elbow still in his grasp. The sheriff and his deputy stood just inside the door of the café, their hands on their holstered weapons.

"Matt, why don't you let go of Keri and let's have us a little chat."

Keri yelped as Matt's fingers dug into her skin.

"Let her go, Matt. Let's don't make this any more complicated than it already is."

He started to move sideways, his back to the row of stools at the counter, as he drug Keri along with him. "Stay back. You guys don't know what you're talking about. I had nothing to do with those fires."

"Fires?" Bud echoed, emphasizing the 's' on the end of the word.

"Bud, please . . . help me," Keri croaked, pulling away from Matt.

He tugged harder, jerking her closer to him as he continued moving backward toward the kitchen area.

"You've got nothing on me. A stupid piece of a hair band? Are you kidding me? That could belong to anyone. Even your little keystone cop here. Ever think about that?"

"She had no motive. In fact, she had a lot to lose in that fire. Same as her dad. You, on the other hand, have an ongoing feud with your parents."

As if on cue, a middle-aged couple entered the door behind the sheriff and his deputy. Keri recognized them immediately.

"Matt? What are you doing? What's going on here?"

Matt grabbed Keri's other elbow, shoving her in front of him like a human shield. She felt his hot bursts of breath on her neck. *Oh God, please don't let me die.*

The man stepped beside Bud. "Matt, let her go. Whatever this is about, we can handle it. You don't want to hurt anyone else."

"Oh, that's rich coming from you, Dad. 'Anyone *else*'? You just confirmed what I've known all these years."

"Stop, Matt. Just stop it," his mother begged.

"Yeah, Mom, like that's gonna happen. You guys crack me up. You come in here like you're going to rescue the damsel in distress and save the day. Please. Don't make me laugh."

But there was no laughter in his voice. Keri could feel him shaking and knew it wasn't from fear. The anger in his voice was unmistakable.

"We know you burned the house down, Matt," his father continued, a barely-contained rage edging his voice. "The sheriff told us everything, including your attempt to blow up the newspaper office. You've done enough damage for a lifetime. Don't add more to it. Just let her go."

Matt kept pulling as he and Keri moved closer and closer to the kitchen. "Sam's death wasn't my fault. He jumped off that bridge. I didn't push him. But you never believed me. He was your 'sweet Sam', the good twin. He could do no wrong, and I could do no right. Same as it's always been."

"We never said that!" his mother cried.

"You didn't HAVE to! I got the message loud and clear. But never more obvious when Sam died and you just couldn't bring yourself to believe it might have been his fault. Oh no, it had to be MY fault.

"Well, to hell with the both of you. The good son is gone. All you've got left is ME. And just because my face is identical to his, you couldn't stand to be around me. Couldn't stand to even look at your only remaining child. How do you think that made me feel? Huh? "You ABANDONED me!" he bellowed. Keri heard the emotion overtaking his accusation. "You kicked me out like I was nothing more than a mangy, flea-bitten dog! You closed out my trust fund, made sure I had no way to live and then wiped me from your memory. All because you blamed me for Sam's death, but IT WASN'T MY FAULT!" He paused, a groan rushing from somewhere inside him. "I *LOVED* SAM. He was MY BROTHER!"

Keri closed her eyes, praying for an escape. He was out of control, his fury bleeding through every word." He stopped again, panting hard.

"Well, fine. Just fine. I don't need you. I don't need either one of you." He started moving faster, backing toward the swinging doors into the kitchen. "And who cares about your stupid house? Serves you right. You can go live in a cave for all I—"

WHACK!

The sound reverberated through the café as Matt collapsed in a heap on the ground. Grant stood in the kitchen door, the oversized cast iron skillet still clutched in his raised hands. He locked eyes with Keri, her face still frozen with shock, then dropped the skillet as he stepped over Matt's body and wrapped her in his arms.

"Grant!" she cried as tears of relief streamed down her face.

He held her so tight, she thought he would suffocate her. "You're okay! You're okay. Oh thank God. Keri, I was so afraid he was going to—"

She wept against his shoulder, shuddering in his embrace.

"Shhh, it's okay. I'm here now, Keri. I'm here.

She said nothing as she clung to him, her face still buried.

"I'm right here. I'll *always* be here for you."

Chapter 14

One week later

"I have an idea."

"Well good morning to you too," Grant teased as Keri entered his office. "And congratulations, Miss McMillan. The whole town is buzzing about your cover story."

Keri grabbed the paper off his desk. Her face lit up as she scanned her story and saw her byline beneath the title. "Wow! This is even cooler than I'd imagined." She looked up at him, her face glowing.

He laughed, going to her side. "I should hope so. It's the biggest story this town has seen in decades, and it's all yours." He wrapped his arm around her waist. "And I couldn't be more proud." He planted a kiss on her head.

"I still can't believe it. How it all happened. How it all just fell into my lap like this."

He took her hand, leading her back toward the makeshift kitchen. "Don't be so modest. You worked hard on the case, you helped crack it, and that front page is just icing on the cake."

He poured her a mug of fresh coffee then one for himself. The kitchen had suffered damage, but the construction crew was able to salvage most of the cabinets and countertop. The press was another story. Fortunately, a Portland print shop helped them get the paper out on time, putting a rush on the job. Grant was already thinking in terms of replacing the outdated press and moving the *Waterford Weekly* into the 21st century.

"Wait, what idea? You said you had an idea?"

Keri finished sipping the hot brew as they leaned against the newly refurbished countertops. "I have a great idea. Shep is supposed to get released tomorrow, right?"

"Yeah. It's about time. They kept him a lot longer than they originally planned. That ticker of his needed some testing. Thank God he's gonna be okay."

"I know. Same for Dad. Although I wish they'd kept *him* longer. Why do hospitals boot the surgery patients a couple days after they cut them open, but keep old guys for days on end running countless tests? We should do a story on that. Investigate the practice of—"

"Okay, fine. We'll do that. Back to the question. What's this idea of yours?"

"Oh, right. I was thinking we should decorate his boat. As a welcome home gift for him."

"Yeah?"

"Well, sure! Think about it, Grant. Your dad has been such a loner all these years. Then he finally works up the courage to come to town and lo and behold, if he doesn't get a bad case of the schoolboy crush on my Aunt Nita."

"I'll admit, they're pretty cute together. Though I'm still in shock over it." He threw his head back laughing. "Never thought I'd live to see the day."

Keri smiled. "Exactly. So it's really more than just a homecoming. It's more like—I don't know, like a new beginning for him. A new chapter in his life. And Nita too. I've never seen her so radiant and so devoted. Well, not since Uncle Rafe died. And I'm so happy for her. For both of them. So what do you say?"

"Define 'decorate' . . ."

The sun was just setting as they drove the final mile from the hospital to Shep's boat. Keri sat shotgun up front with Grant, while Nita sat in the backseat with Shep, her hands wrapped around his. Keri couldn't stop smiling. Watching the two of them dote on each other was one of the sweetest things she'd witnessed in years. Quite the mother hen, Nita hadn't stopped doting on Shep since the minute he came to in the hospital. Sneaking in treats, keeping him supplied with books and magazines, fussing over him all day long until he fell asleep each night—even hanging a fresh pine wreath on his bathroom door.

Not that Shep minded. He followed her every move with those puppy-dog eyes. He never stopped smiling when she was around. Even when she brought her clippers from home and gave his hair and mustache a long-overdue trimming. Everyone stopped and raved about his new look, and Keri caught him more than once sneaking a pleased peek in the hand mirror Nita had brought him.

Keri reached for Grant's hand, giving it a gentle squeeze as they passed the lighthouse. He tossed her a wink, acknowledging the memory of their stolen moments up there. Had it only been a week since they'd finally shared from their hearts up there?

As Grant made the final turn toward the boat dock, the *Sarah Jane* came into view. Miniature white lights stretched from stern to stem, accenting every line of the vessel, sparkling in the reflection of the water. An enormous Douglas fir covered in lights stood on the deck, like a beacon of Christmas cheer. A long banner stretched across the starboard side of the pilothouse: "WELCOME HOME, SHEP!"

"Oh my goodness!" Nita gasped. "Shep, do you see? Isn't it beautiful?"

Keri glanced in the rearview mirror above her, watching Shep's face. His chin wobbled as his smile disappeared behind his neatly trimmed but still bushy mustache. The lights reflecting in his eyes revealed a shimmer of tears.

Grant squeezed her hand again, his eyes still darting back and forth between the road ahead and the scene in the backseat through his rearview mirror.

Nita buried her head against Shep's shoulder. "I think that's just the sweetest thing I ever saw, don't you, Shep?"

Of course he didn't respond. At least not verbally. Instead, a tear broke free, cascading down his weathered face before disappearing into his mustache.

Once they'd boarded the vessel, Keri and Grant seated Shep and Nita at a table set for four, complete with tablecloth and small votive candles. The flames struggled in the breeze, but remained lit, thanks to the surprisingly calmer weather. In moments, Grant and Keri brought up the dinner they'd left warming in the galley. Pecan-crusted flounder, baked potatoes, a fresh tossed salad, and garlic bread. They dined beneath the stars, the conversation happy and festive.

"Well sir . . ." They waited. Keri was used to Shep's ways now, his "well sir" now a familiar precursor when he had something to say.

He looked around the table, then ducked his eyes before turning toward Nita. He reached for her hand. "Well sir . . ."

"What's on your mind, Pop?" Grant finally prodded.

"Oh . . ."

"Out with it, Shep," Nita urged. "You're among family here. Spit it out, sweetheart."

His eyes darted around again, then he looked out across the water, taking in the reflection of the lights bouncing on the waves. Finally, he turned back to Nita and smiled.

"Marry me."

Nita's expression went from shock to questioning to tender affection. She tilted her head as her eyes filled and a smile stretched across her face. "Oh Shep, I would be *honored* to marry you." She searched his face with expectation, obviously waiting for a response.

He quirked a smile, dipped his head again. "Well sir, then."

They all laughed, then Nita jumped up to smother him with hugs and kisses.

Grant stood as well, holding his hand out to Keri. "How about we take a walk, Miss McMillan?"

Keri rose. "I'd love to, Mr. Dawson."

They left the lovebirds and made their way off the *Sarah Jane,* then down the marina and onto the beach. They couldn't help giggling, still shocked at the sudden proposal. A quarter of a mile down the beach they came to a fire pit still stocked with the remnants of someone else's fire. Grant quickly relit the logs , then he took a seat beside Keri on a log a couple feet from the fire. They snuggled close together against the night air.

"I'm not sure anything could ever surprise me again. Not after *that* shocker."

She burrowed against him. "Can you believe it? Goodness, those two didn't waste any time, did they?"

"Yeah, but I guess at their age, time is everything."

"True," she echoed. "I'm so happy. For both of them.

"Me too, Keri. The change your aunt has made in my dad . . . it's nothing short of a miracle. And I couldn't be happier for them."

They sat in silence, staring into the fire, warming to its glow. Keri tried to remember if she'd ever been this happy, and for the life of her, couldn't. She looked up at Grant, so filled with love for this man she'd grown to love. Hard to imagine she'd once despised him. She remembered the first time they'd met, the night the Blankenship cabin burned to the ground. How she'd hated him and hated his witty little exchange with her aunt that night. How she'd fought him, the small town publisher with a Pulitzer collecting dust somewhere. What a loser, she'd thought.

How could that man be the same one here, sitting beside her, filling her heart with so much love?

Talk about a miracle.

"Oh, I almost forgot." Grant reached into the oversized pocket of his squall jacket. He handed her a small package, wrapped in Christmas paper and tied with a red ribbon.

"What's this?" she smiled. "You're a little early for Christmas, aren't you?"

"It's not really a Christmas gift. But that's the only wrapping paper I could find. Go on. Open it."

She looked at him quizzically, and started unwrapping the small box. She lifted the lid, finding an object heavily wrapped in tissue. When she finally pulled the last of the tissue free, her breath caught. In her hands, she held a teacup—a Cobalt Net Lomonosov porcelain. The exact same design of her mother's heirloom. Her mouth fell open. "How" she mouthed, unable to speak.

"How'd I find it?"

She nodded, still speechless.

He pushed a curl from her eyes. "Easy. I'm a reporter. I investigated."

"But—"

"Don't you remember that night at the lighthouse? When you were so upset after finding out your mom's teacup had accidentally been shattered?"

She nodded slowly, a tear falling from her eyes.

He brushed it away with his thumb. "Well, I decided to see if I could find one. Of course, I knew it could never replace hers. Of course not. But at least it could *represent* her. So instead of seeing that empty saucer and the loss it represented, I thought maybe a replacement might help keep her memory alive."

She pulled the teacup close to her, cradling it against her chest. "Grant, I don't know what to say. This is the kindest thing anyone's ever done for me."

"Then that settles it. My work is done."

She carefully wrapped the cup back in the tissue and placed it back in the box before wrapping her arms around his neck. "I can never thank you enough," she whispered. "You'll never know how much this means to me."

He held her face in his hands, then gently kissed her. Not once. Not twice. In fact, at some point he lost count. He slowly pulled his hands from her face and wrapped her snuggly in his arms, pulling back to face her. "I love you, Keri."

She gulped back a sob of pure joy. "I love you too, Grant. And I think I have for a very long time now."

He brushed another tear from her cheek. A moment passed as the glow of the fire reflected in their eyes.

Finally, Grant turned, tucking her under his arm as they faced the fire again. "Well sir . . ." he croaked, mimicking his father's favorite line.

She laughed. "You do that well. Shep would be impressed."

He chuckled. "Well sir . . ." he repeated.

She sat up to look at him. "I said, you do that—"

"Marry me."

For the second time in five minutes, she was speechless.

"Well sir . . . I think we should make it a double."

"What?" she whispered.

"I think we should make it a double ceremony." His eyes warmed as a smile crept across his face. "Marry me, Keri McMillan, and make me the happiest man in the world."

Her eyes searched his, her brow dipped briefly in question, then she grabbed him, shouting, "Yes! Yes, I'll marry you!"

They laughed, they kissed, and then they kissed a little more.

"Ahoy, there!" came a voice from the *Sarah Jane.* "What's all the racket out there?" Nita shouted. "You'll wake the whales!"

"Then let 'em wake up! WE'RE GETTING MARRIED!" Grant shouted.

"Shep! Did you hear that! Grant said they're getting married too!"

Silence followed, the waves lapping against the beach the only response.

Then, from across the water . . .

"Well sir . . . that's nice . . . that's real nice."

Epilogue

I couldn't help it. Not that I tried. If I had a mirror positioned over my desk, I'm sure the smile reflected in it would be slap-dog silly. But hey, I make no apologies. I *love* how this one ended. A double wedding! How fun would that be?! It was hard not to add another chapter and celebrate the happy occasion with my characters, but sometimes you just know when to close . . . Isn't that a line from some Kenny Rogers song?

Speaking of songs . . . I leaned over, searching for MJ's *Thriller* on my iPod, ready to commence my own celebration ritual. Even now I could hear the mint chocolate chip calling my name from the freezer . . . *Luuuuucccyyyyy!*

My cell rang before I could crank up the opening rift of my favorite Michael Jackson song. "Hello?"

"Hey, sis. Just wanted to let you know we're running a few minutes late."

Eh?

"Apparently Beth had some kind of *wardrobe malfunction.*"

Lucy could hear a giggling female in the background. "Beth? Who's Beth?"

"Elizabeth Frazier. She teaches with me, remember? Anyway, she's appropriately dressed now and we should be at your place in—"

Oh no. No no no no no!

"—about twenty minutes."

No no no! Tell me I did not—

"Mark's gonna meet us at your place, so he should be there any time now."

I stood up, searching for the note on my calendar. And there it was: *Friday night – double date/ Mark*

No no no no no!

"Sis? You there?"

"Yeah, sure. No-problem-I'll-be-ready-when-you-get-here-bye."

I threw the phone on my desk and ran down the hall, grabbing the bathroom doorframe as I accidentally slid past it. Socks on hardwood. Risky business.

You don't even want to know the dialogue going through my head as I showered, blew my hair dry, did a drive-by with my make-up, and rushed in my closet to find my black dress. I started to dig through my underwear drawer for a pair of black hose, when I suddenly stopped. *No one wears hose any more, do they?*

I took a quick assessment of my scrawny legs, immediately noticing the ugly scar down the front of my right shin from a shaving mishap last week. *Lovely.* I blew my hair out of my eyes, cracked open the L'eggs egg and starting pulling on a pair of black hose. At least they had a pattern in them—thankfully, not fishnets.

I grabbed my heels and raced back to the bathroom. I'd just lathered up with my Extra-Brightening Crest when the doorbell rang.

"Ahlbeyarinamint!" I shouted before spitting.

Yeah. Like he understood that?

A quick rinse, a final brush through the hair, a spritz of cologne, and I was ready. I grabbed my gauzy black shawl, draped it over my shoulders, stepped into my strappy black heels and tried to find some semblance of poise in me as I walked toward the front door.

Deep breath. Relax . . . I closed my eyes for just a moment then fixed a genuine smile on my face before opening the door.

And there he was. My Mark.

A smile as big as Boston on his face.

A huge bouquet of flowers in his hands.

Dressed in his UPS browns.

Brown shirt.

Brown shorts.

Brown socks.

"Oh." It slipped out. Honest. I didn't mean to say it out loud. But even I could hear the tinge of disappointment in that tiny little word.

"Hi, Lucy."

I blinked. Three, maybe four times. I simply couldn't find the words . . . My imagination kicked in as I watched us walk into Fitzgerald's. We made our entrance, passing linen-covered tables set with crystal and fine china, aglow with soft candlelight, as easy jazz played on a Bose sound system . . . with every eye riveted on the man in brown escorting the girl in the little black dress.

I blinked again, realizing my eyes had traveled downward from his sweet smile, to that shirt, those shorts, and those socks.

His eyes followed mine. "Oh—yeah, I know. I'm still in uniform."

I swallowed. As an author, I'm paid to piece together words that communicate. But I have to tell you—I got nothing here.

"No! Oh, you think . . ." He laughed, throwing his head back. "No,

I'm not here for our *date*, Lucy!" He laughed again. It was a great laugh.

A wheeze flew out of me on a gust of relief. "Oh!" I laughed in return, trying to act nonchalant. "Oh, sure. I knew that. Really . . . duh?!

"Oh Lucy, I swear—I'd *never* dress like this for a date." He chuckled this time. "I promise I'd never do that to you. See, I was on my way home to change when I got a call from our dispatcher. My buddy's truck broke down on the interstate and I've got to go help him transfer his load into my truck, then finish the deliveries. It'll take hours. I didn't want to just call, so I swung by on my way out there. Oh, and I just got off the phone with your brother, explaining what happened. I'm so sorry, Lucy. I was really looking forward to going out with you tonight."

She leaned against the door jamb, wrapping one ankle around the other. *He came to tell me face to face. How sweet is that?*

He handed her the bouquet. "Any chance you'd give me a rain check? Say, Sunday night?"

And so it was, my first date with my handsome UPS guy was postponed.

After we said our goodbyes, I kicked off my heels and padded into the kitchen to put the flowers in a vase. Truth be told, I wasn't *that* disappointed. Now I'd have time to anticipate our date the right way. I'd set the alarm on my cell phone on Sunday afternoon to remind me. I'd take a long hot bubble bath, do my nails, maybe try an updo.

I took my beautiful bouquet back to my office and pushed aside some clutter on my desk to give them the priority they deserved. I sat down, propped my feet on the ottoman, and welcomed Gertie who also seemed pleased my plans had changed.

"Gertie, life can be funny sometimes. You just never know what you'll find at the front door."

I noticed the Lomonosov teacup and saucer sitting beside my keyboard. I'd washed it that morning, still admiring its glistening blue and gold netting-like design. I couldn't believe it was time to put it back on the shelf.

It's hard, finishing a story. Sure, the sense of accomplishment feels great. It feels *amazing*. But then there's the necessary letting go . . . having to step back out of the story line and say goodbye to my characters. That's the part I hate. It always feels a little like I'm packing them up in a shoebox and sticking them in the attic. Not exactly a fitting farewell for people who made my story come alive! Could I really walk away without witnessing Grant and Keri's double-wedding with Shep and Nita? Would Keri ever finish her degree? Or would she and Grant start a family? Would Tyler's business recover? So many unanswered questions.

And yet, ask any author how they determine where to end a story and they'll tell you. *You just know.*

I sat there pondering my next adventure. *Time to pick another teacup and begin another story.*

I already knew which was next. That interesting cup and saucer with the mysterious history . . . at least, a history I'd soon create for it. So many secrets in that one. I couldn't wait to unveil them.

I reached for the cup, blew the dust from its interior, and listened to the sound of a motorcycle roaring through my mind on its way to that quaint little Tennessee town . . .

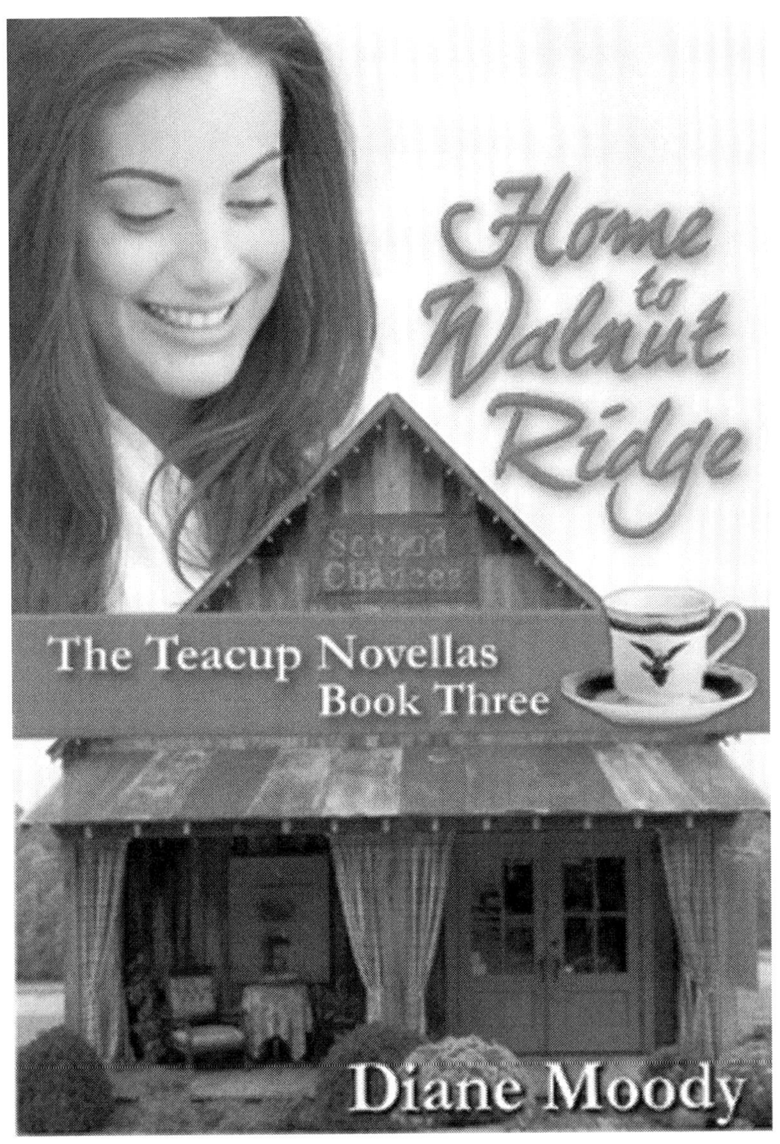
Home to Walnut Ridge
Second Chances
The Teacup Novellas
Book Three
Diane Moody

To Sharon Jacob

For your amazing gifts of
inspiration and restoration;
For always seeing the potential beauty
in old furniture (and people too);
For your contagious passion for life,
and your sweet, gentle spirit . . .
How blessed I am to be your friend.

If you do a good job for others,
you heal yourself at the same time,
because a dose of joy is a spiritual cure.
—Dietrich Bonhoeffer

On the third day, He will restore us
that we may live in His presence.
Hosea 6:2b

Prologue

It's Monday morning and I desperately need to get to work. A few minutes ago, I made a fresh pot of Earl Grey and poured it into a unique and intriguing teacup. It's a part of the collection of teacups I inherited recently from my beloved Aunt Lucille. And just like when I wrote my two previous novellas inspired by these family heirlooms, I can already feel her smiling down on me as I begin this newest tale.

So why am I still staring at a blank page on my laptop screen? Why am I having so much trouble staying focused this morning? Well, if you must know, I'll tell you.

Last night, at long last, I went out to dinner with Mark Christopher, my hunky UPS guy. And we had the most *wonderful* time.

Actually, it was what you'd call a rain-check date after a false start on Saturday night when I *completely* forgot about our double date with my brother and his girlfriend until the last possible minute; at which point I busted tail to get myself ready just in the nick of time, only to have Mark show up in his company browns telling me he had a work emergency and needed a rain check . . .

Wait. I think that last paragraph might just qualify as the second longest run-on sentence on earth. The first, of course, penned by Victor Hugo on numerous pages in his masterpiece, *Les Miserables.* I once tried to read the unabridged version, but finally gave up after dear Victor took an entire page for one sentence. One sentence! Now, I love Jean Valjean as much as the next guy, but Victor—a little brevity is not a bad thing now and then. Just sayin'.

But I digress.

Bottom line, I should be in the deep end of my next novella by now, but instead I'm chasing rabbits here, there, and everywhere while suffering from a severe case of what I shall call the Monday Morning Mushbrain. And if I'm honest, this sheer lack of discipline all points back to last night's date with Mark. So why not cut to the chase and just blame it on him?

I really can't remember the last time I went out on a bona fide date. My brother Chad says the characters in my books have more of a life than I do. And I think that's the problem. I get lost in all these colorful stories, and I'm consumed with their dramas. I get weak-kneed telling their sweet love stories and describing their breathtaking romances.

Then some Joe the Loser wants to take me out for gas station corn dogs and call it a date? No, thank you. Give me fiction. I'm much more comfortable in the LaLa Land of storytelling.

Still, I admit I was rather enchanted when I heard Mark wanted to go out with me. I knew he was a nice guy, and I'd always enjoyed his delivery visits. But frankly, since I work at home and never bother with the whole hair and make-up thing before "going to the office" each day, he always catches me *beauty-challenged,* shall we say. Not exactly a guy-magnet, if you know what I mean. On the other hand, his adorable dimples and tanned muscular calves have always caught my eye. And did I mention he has a great laugh?

Yes, but where was I? Oh, yes. The date.

Can I just say that Mark is quite possibly the nicest guy I've ever met? That sounds so clichéd, but I'm pretty sure they broke the mold with this one. How do I know? As an author, I keep an ongoing list of character traits and descriptions in a little notebook I keep stashed in my purse. Let's just say I had to sit on my hands so as not to write down all the thoughtful things he said, the sound of his easy laughter, and his subtle kindnesses. Like when I came to the door wearing the exact same dress and shawl as the night before when he'd rain-checked me. I felt awkward about it, but right away, he smiled.

"Wow, Lucy, you look *amazing.* Is it okay if I tell you I was really hoping you'd wear that little black dress again?"

"You had me at *wow,* big guy."

Okay, no. I didn't say that. Honest.

But see what I mean? And I think what I enjoyed most about Mark was his positive outlook on life. Not in a fake cheesy kind of way (think four-for-a-dollar powdered mac 'n cheese mix). It's just who he is. He looks for the best in people and situations. It made me realize how rare that is these days. Which made me feel pretty darn lucky to have those baby blues looking my way last night.

After dinner, we walked to a little pub down the street. He casually took my hand then spoke my love language— "Best bread pudding on the planet," he said. "Lucy, it will rock your world."

He was right. We shared a serving big enough for four NFL linebackers.

"I think I just found my new office," I said. "I could set up shop right here in this booth with my trusty laptop, downing four or five of these decadent bad boys every day. Would you swing by with your forklift to pick me up after work?"

And there was that laugh again. I decided then and there that Mark's unrestrained laughter was one of the happiest, most contagious sounds I'd ever heard. And that's why, without so much as a thought, I leaned over and kissed him.

I have *no* idea what came over me. And for the record, I've never done anything like that before. Ever! It just seemed so perfect, so right. And guess what he said, after our perfect, first kiss?

"Whoa . . . thanks, Lucy."

Be still, my heart.

Which is why I'm not worth squat today. Which is why I can't stop smiling and looking forward to seeing him again. Which is why I'm addicted to Amazon's two-day free delivery—by way of UPS.

But enough with the excuses. Time to work. No, really.

And as much as I've procrastinated this time, I'm really looking forward to writing this next novella. There's a "story within the story" this time around and that always makes it fun. A little history, a little mystery, a little romance . . . throw in a Harley or two, and I'm ready to roll.

So to speak.

Chapter 1

With a deep cleansing breath, Tracey Collins closed her eyes. The decision had come quickly once she'd finally been honest with herself. She'd known all along this was what she needed to do. *How naive I've been,* she thought. *How easily I've been fooled, thinking I could ignore the constant warning bells sounding off in my head. Thinking I could withstand the subtle overtures day after day.*

Gently shaking her head to banish the thoughts, she opened her eyes and placed her hands on her laptop keyboard. And as she did, Tracey's mind flashed back to the reception she'd attended last night at the White House. Standing at the beverage bar, she'd just stirred cream into her coffee when he approached her, his voice hushed.

"Tracey, you look *amazing* tonight."

The warmth of his breath so near her neck had sent a shiver skittering down her spine. Refusing to acknowledge Morgan's presence, she'd smiled at the waiter and thanked him for the coffee, buying herself a moment. Turning around to face the other guests in the East Room, she'd avoided eye contact with him. "I sent your draft of the Ledford Bill to Senator Crawford's assistant before I left the office. She assured me he'd take a look at it and get back to you tomorrow."

"Tracey, I don't want to shop talk tonight," he said, still facing the bar, his arm brushing gently against hers as he took a sip of his wine. "C'mon. I just gave you a compliment. Don't you want to tell me how handsome I look?" he'd said, arching his eyebrows.

She'd continued, doing her best to ignore him. "Also, I went over everything with Paul to get him up to speed on the projects needing attention while I'm away."

He blew out a sigh. "So you're still planning to take the next couple of weeks off?"

She leveled her gaze at him. "Yes, Morgan. I'm taking the next couple of weeks off. You've known that for three months now."

He looked sideways at her, his glass at his lips. "I know, but I was kind of hoping you'd change your mind."

"Give me a break, Morgan. You sound more like a spoiled child than a United States Senator."

"The two aren't mutually exclusive, you know," he teased.

She started to walk away. "Very funny."

"Wait," he said, catching her arm.

She glanced down at his hand then faced him directly. "Do you mind?" she whispered.

"It's just that there's something we need to discuss before you leave." He motioned her toward a corner of the room by a large floral arrangement.

"Fine, but make it fast. There are several people here I need to speak with tonight."

He led the way, lowering his voice. "I was hoping you'd come back to the office with me tonight."

She studied his face, alarmed by the unmistakable look in his eyes. She'd seen it before, a gaze so tender, so inviting.

It would be so easy . . .

And so, so wrong.

Morgan Thompson had always stood for things she believed in. He fought for causes she was passionate about. Family Rights. Religious liberty. The ongoing battle against those who would stomp on the Constitution. When he hired her fresh out of Vanderbilt's grad school, his alma-mater, she worked tirelessly beside him while getting her feet wet learning how things worked inside the Beltway.

Staring into those warm blue eyes, she knew precisely why he wanted her to go back to the office with him. She tucked her hair behind her ear and looked away. "Morgan—"

"Hey, you know I hate it when you use that tone with me."

"That's because you know what I'm going to say."

He leaned closer. "Please, Tracey. How many ways can I say it? I *need* you."

She wadded up the small embossed beverage napkin then stuffed it in her half-empty cup. She returned her eyes to his. "No, Morgan. Not tonight. Not ever. Go home to your *wife*." She shoved the cup and saucer into his hand and turned to walk away.

She'd cried all the way home. Not from a broken heart, but because of the implications of his invitation. He'd never been *so* transparent. Had she somehow inadvertently encouraged him? Morgan Thompson—the face of family values in Washington—what could he *possibly* be thinking to come on to her like that? Did he just assume she'd fall for him and no one would ever know?

As if *any* secret was safe in Washington?

But worst of all was the intense betrayal washing through her. Amanda Thompson had welcomed Tracey to Washington the day she arrived, taking her under her wing, helping her navigate the perilous waters of the nation's capital. But more than that, Amanda was her friend. They attended the same Bible study at church. They baked together. They shopped together. Tracey had twice stayed with their kids when Morgan and Amanda had last-minute trips come up.

Now, as her flight headed homeward, she couldn't help but wonder. *How has it come to this? Has he lost his mind?*

She shook her head again, trying to refocus on the task before her.

Morgan,

I've done a lot of thinking since last night, and there's something I need to do. I should have told you this in person before I left town, but the coward in me won the toss, so I'm writing you instead. We've both known this day would come. I wanted so badly to believe I could maintain a professional relationship and continue working alongside you for as long as you remain in Washington. However, it's quite obvious that's no longer possible.

If I've done anything to cause you to think of me in any way other than professionally, I can assure you it was unintentional. Over the past several months, I've asked you repeatedly to stop making advances toward me. In all honesty, I should have reported such harassment. But out of respect for Amanda, I decided not to do so. Your wife is my best friend, Morgan. Are you really that heartless?

You've given me no other choice, so please accept this as my two-week notice. I have no plans to return to Washington. I'll be in touch with Paul to finalize my departure from the office and square things away with personnel.

In the beginning, it was an honor and privilege to serve with you. That's no longer the case. I truly hope you'll find your way back to the man you used to be. You owe that to Amanda, to your kids, to your constituents, but most of all, to the God you purport to serve.

Tracey

Tracey keyed in the address of Morgan's personal email account and clicked SEND. There was one more note she needed to write. She quickly opened a new message page and began typing.

Amanda,

I owe you a long phone call and an explanation, but for now, I just wanted you to know I'm resigning from my job as Morgan's assistant for personal reasons . . .

Her hands froze on the keyboard. *For personal reasons? How benign that sounds. Amanda knows me too well. She'll pick up the phone and call the minute she reads those words, then pelt me with a thousand questions.*

Tracey wasn't ready for that. She quickly deleted the email, shut down her laptop, and slipped it back into her leather bag. A long sigh eased from her lips as she rested her head against the seat back and looked out the small oval window beside her. No sooner had she done so than the calm voice of the pilot interrupted her thoughts.

"Ladies and gentlemen, we're on final approach to Nashville International Airport . . ."

He continued the usual announcement which was followed by the obligatory end-of-flight instructions by one of the flight attendants. But Tracey tuned them out. She leaned closer to the window, wishing the autumn landscape below would refresh her weary soul. She felt detached. Strangely adrift. As if she'd finally broken free of the tangled mess lodged somewhere in the vicinity of her heart.

So why is there so much sadness creeping through my veins?

As the 737 gently banked toward home, Tracey uttered a silent prayer.

Oh God, what have I done?

"Tracey Jo! Over here!"

She heard her father's voice just as she grabbed her bag from the conveyor belt. Turning to search him out, she found herself buried in a bear hug, his familiar laughter encircling them.

"Oh, sweetheart! It's so good to see you!"

Tracey clung to him, her face buried against his chest. "Hi, Daddy. It's good to be home!"

As she pulled back, she got her first look at him. "Dad! What—I mean, how . . . good heavens, *look* at you!"

"Yeah, I know—my hair's a little longer than last time you saw me. Right?"

"That's a *huge* understatement." When he turned his head, she all but gasped. "You have a *ponytail*?!"

Buddy Collins flashed her his signature crooked smile and dancing eyes. He flipped his head back and forth, causing the long salt and pepper mane to whip from shoulder to shoulder. "Pretty cool, huh?" He hoisted the smaller bag over his shoulder and grabbed the handle to her rolling suitcase, starting toward the sliding doors. "C'mon. I've got a surprise for you."

She followed him, eyes still wide as she looked over this strange new version of the father she loved. He wore a black leather jacket with some kind of insignia on the back. His faded blue jeans were frayed at the hems over black boots studded with silver.

He turned around, stopped abruptly, and tilted his head to one side looking back at her. "What? Did you forget something?"

"No, no I got—Dad, what's happened to you?"

"To me? What do you mean?"

"The last time I saw you, your hair was a bit shaggy, but—"

He started walking again. "Ah, sweetie, it's no big deal. I just thought it'd be fun to grow it out—"

"And when was the last time you shaved?"

He jutted his chin out, showing off his close-cropped white beard. "Not bad, eh? I just got tired of the routine. It's a nuisance, having to shave every morning, sometimes twice a day. I figured, who cares if I have a few whiskers?"

"I know, but—"

"I mean, it's not as if I'm gonna have a bunch of nosy deacons calling to complain about it. Know what I mean?"

She finally caught up with him just as sunlight glistened off the general vicinity of his ear. She stopped, grabbing his arm and pulling him to a stop. "Is that . . . is that an *earring*?!"

He parked the rolling bag and reached for his earlobe. "Yeah! You like it?"

She blinked, unable to speak.

"Half a carat. It's the stone from your mother's wedding ring."

"What?!"

"Well, sure! She left it behind when she took off with that home-wrecker. And I figured, why let a perfectly good diamond go to waste? So I took it into town, had a jeweler yank the stone and make me some *bling* with it. I like to think of it as a fitting symbol of my new life. My own little declaration of independence, if you catch my drift."

"That's *Mom's* diamond?"

"Not anymore!" His guffaw rolled across the parking lot as he reached for the luggage handle.

Still aghast, Tracey slowly started following him again. The last time she'd seen her father—*had it been a year?* —he was better, but nothing like the larger-than-life guy he'd always been. Known for his abiding faith and contagious sense of humor, Buddy Collins never met a stranger. But that had all changed a couple of years ago when their mother up and left him. Then a few weeks later, the church he'd pastored for more than twenty years let him go when a handful of deacon bullies deemed him "unfit to serve."

The double punch decked him hard, sending him into a severe depression. Tracey and her sister Alex were devastated for their father and seriously concerned. Alex—short for Alexandra—moved back into the family home with him not long afterward. Since then, she'd kept Tracey informed of some recent "changes" but hadn't been specific.

Still, watching his easy gait and that swinging ponytail, Tracey had to admit it was good to see him happy again. She looked forward to a long chat on the way home to find out where all these changes had come from.

And that way we keep the conversation on him, not me. Perfect.

Tracey switched her leather bag to the other shoulder. "Dad, where's the car?"

He whipped around, his face lit up. "That's the surprise!"

"What do you mean?"

He took a few steps to the right, put her bags down, and posed like Vanna White—at a huge motorcycle. "Ta da! Tracey Jo, meet Stella. Stella, meet Tracey Jo!"

"You have GOT to be kidding."

"Ain't she a beauty?! She's a 2007 Harley-Davidson Touring Road King Classic. Paid extra for the Pacific Blue Pearl color. Worth every penny. Check out those white wall tires. Sweet, huh?"

"Dad, this isn't funny. In the least."

His face fell. "Ah, sweetie, don't spoil my fun! I could hardly wait for Stella to meet you!"

"There's no way I'm riding a motorcycle forty-five miles to Jacobs Mill."

"But I've—"

"No. I said no. I meant no." She snatched the handle of her rolling bag and tried to grab the one off his shoulder.

He held it tight, pulling away from her. "Tracey Jo, *please.* It'll be fun! Look, I even borrowed this Sport Trailer for us to stash your bags." He unlocked the fancy three-wheeled trailer and started loading her things. "See? Worlds of room. And here's your helmet."

"Dad, I don't—"

He put it on her head, oblivious to her protests, explaining the proper way to strap it on. "We can even talk! Here's your built-in microphone. Just keep that turned on, and we can jabber all the way home. Cool, huh?"

Tracey stared at him, uncomfortable with the helmet pressing against the tortoiseshell barrette holding her long brown hair up off her shoulders. She pulled the helmet off her head. Her father sighed wearily, visibly disappointed, then reached out to take the helmet from her hands.

She held tight, refusing to give it up. He looked up at her. Narrowing her eyes, she cocked her head to one side. "Patience . . ." she scolded. Then, tucking the helmet under her arm, she reached up and unclipped the barrette, releasing her hair. She pulled the helmet back on.

"There. That's better. What are we waiting for?"

Chapter 2

Exiting the airport, Tracey could hear her screams grow louder as the Harley gained speed up the entrance ramp to I40. She clung to him, her eyes squeezed shut behind the protective sunglasses, and her arms in a grip lock around his ribcage.

"Tracey Jo! I can't breathe! Ease up on that grip, will ya?"

"I CAN'T! I'LL FALL OFF!"

She heard the sound of his laughter over the roar of the engine. He raised his voice just enough for her to hear him. "You're not gonna fall off. But we're heading into some heavy traffic, so I'm gonna need a little oxygen to get us through it, okay?"

She tried to relax her grip.

"Yeah, that's better, but a little more, sweetie. C'mon, you can do it."

Visibly shaking, she consciously made the effort to stop squeezing his middle.

"Atta girl. Now sit back and enjoy the ride!" The Harley roared to life as they blended in with six lanes heading into Nashville.

She cracked open one eye, peeking just long enough to see the mass of cars, trucks, and tractor-trailers crowded around them. "DAD! CAN'T YOU TAKE A BACK ROAD AND GET US OFF THE INTERSTATE?"

"First of all, you don't have to shout. You are right in my ear. I can hear you just fine. Second, you just need to take a nice deep breath and trust me. We'll be out of the thick of it in just a few minutes. We'll hop on I65 and head south to home. The traffic will ease up. You'll see."

She swallowed hard and talked herself into opening both eyes this time. She darted her eyes to her right hoping to see the skyline of Nashville, but a semi eclipsed her view. Its side showed the façade of a Cracker Barrel restaurant, complete with a row of rocking chairs out front. She'd always loved the cozy restaurants and their familiar menu of good Southern cooking. But at the moment, those rockers seemed much too close for comfort. She looked the other way just as they started up the ramp that arced high then banked them south.

I will not scream. I will not scream . . .

When her breathing finally started returning to normal, she tried to keep her mind off the vehicles zooming past them. “Why do you call her Stella?”

“It’s from that old Marlon Brando movie. You know, the one where he stands outside her window and yells, ‘STELLAAAAA!’”

“Okay, but what’s that got to do with a Harley?”

“Absolutely nothing. I just enjoy yelling, ‘STELLA!’ every time I see my girl.”

As Stella ate up the pavement beneath them, her father chatted about sights they passed along the way. Soon the congested traffic unknotted itself, giving them plenty of room on the road. As the sprawling commercial areas gave way to neighborhoods then farmland, she felt the tension slowly slipping away. She let her eyes feast on the stunning fall palette coloring the rolling hillsides beneath a perfect blue sky. Here and there she’d see cattle grazing and flocks of birds flying in perfect formation.

The wind sailing around her soothed her soul and sent her mind down an unexpected path. How long had it been since she stopped to notice the landscape around her? Washington offered spectacular displays of the changing seasons, but the frantic pace had somehow blinded her to it. That same frantic pace had robbed her of a personal life, zapped her energy, and sent her home exhausted every night. When had she lost that initial zeal? What happened to the excitement that once propelled her to work each morning? When had she lost that camaraderie she’d always enjoyed with her friends at church and at the office?

With each question floating through her mind, she saw his face, and she knew. The disillusionment hadn’t come from the projects she’d so passionately worked on or the long days she put in. It was all because of him.

Tracey shook off the stress that had trickled back in, instead taking another deep breath, willing the fresh air to somehow repair what was damaged inside her. *I’m gonna be okay. Right, Lord? I didn’t just leave D.C.; I’m walking away from my life there. I lost my way. Open my heart to something new. Show me what You want me to do.*

Tracey let her mind wander imagining all kinds of possibilities ahead of her. Still she couldn’t imagine anything that didn’t involve politics. She decided optimism would surely come later. For now, she just wanted to go home.

Forty-five minutes later they rolled into Jacobs Mill. The small town located just a few miles east of I-65 seemed to welcome her with open arms. The row of Bradford Pear trees on Neely’s Lane almost took her breath away, their deep crimson leaves making quite a show this year. As they turned onto Main Street, it seemed nothing much had changed, and that made her smile. Barrows Hardware Store, the cozy log cabin library, Emma’s Coffee Shop, Dorsey’s Barbershop,

The Depot—the town's only pub—they all looked just as she remembered them.

Tracey leaned slightly to her right to see around her dad. Here, the four blocks of Main Street came to a three-way stop, but straight ahead—Walnut Ridge.

Home.

Tracey smiled again as she looked up at their 190-year-old home sitting high above town on 45 of the plantation's original 500 acres. The two-story home had been in her family since it was first built by her father's ancestors. With its two wings flanking the original structure, four white columns, six working fireplaces, wide front porch, and seven outbuildings, Walnut Ridge had been the hub of Jacobs Mill from its beginning.

As they rolled up the long driveway, Tracey felt her heart swell at the sight of the magnificent oak tree that sheltered the front of her home. She hugged him hard, this time from sheer joy. "Oh Daddy, it's so good to be home."

They rolled to a stop at the bottom of the porch steps, pulled off their helmets, and climbed off the Harley.

"If I hadn't seen it with my own eyes, I wouldn't believe it!"

At the sound of her sister's voice, she ran up the steps. "Alex!"

"Tracey, Tracey, Tracey!" Alex cried, embracing her little sister. "I can't believe you let him drive you home on that thing!"

Buddy beamed. "Are you kidding? She loved it! Didn't you, Tracey Jo?"

"Not so much at first, but I have to say—"

"You don't have to say another word," he said, joining them at the top of the steps. "I rest my case. Now c'mon, big family hug here." He wrapped them both in his strong arms and planted a noisy kiss on both their cheeks.

"I made us some tea," Alex said, pulling back. "Y'all have a seat, and I'll be right back."

He squeezed her shoulder and hustled back down the steps. "Thanks, honey, but I've got to skedaddle."

"Dad, you just got here!"

"I know, but I've gotta check on my Elders. They're helping over at the city park. I'll be back in time for dinner."

"Elders?" Tracey whispered.

"Tell you later," Alex mumbled, tossing a wink as she turned to go back inside.

Buddy bounced back up the steps. "Here're your bags, Tracey Jo. You need me to run them up to your room?"

"No, I'll take them later. Thanks anyway."

"Good. See you tonight." He hooked his elbow around her neck and pulled her close enough for another peck on the cheek. "Good to have you home, sweetheart!"

A moment later, he brought the Harley to life and took off down the long winding drive.

Alex backed out the front door then let it slam shut, a wooden tray with two glasses, a pitcher of tea, and a small basket of sugar cookies in her hands. "So Biker Buddy took off, did he?"

Tracey grabbed a cookie and took a seat on one of the cushioned wicker rockers. "Good grief, Alex. You said he'd changed, but seriously—who *is* that guy with the ponytail?"

Alex sat down and poured their glasses of tea. "The ponytail, I'm used to. It's the—"

"Earring? I almost passed out when I saw it! Buddy Collins got his *ear* pierced?!"

"I'm sure he told you where the diamond came from." Alex took a sip of tea.

Tracey tucked one leg beneath the other and leaned back. "With great pleasure, I might add. I'm sure Mom could care less, but don't you think it's a bit juvenile on his part?"

"Oh, I don't know. Though I admit I was upset about it at first."

"How come you never told me?"

"Because I didn't want to bother you with it. To be honest, I thought it was just a phase he was going through. First the Harley, then the hair and the beard . . . I kept thinking one day he'd come downstairs looking like the clean-cut Buddy Collins we've always known."

"You mean like the *Pastor* Buddy Collins we used to know?"

Alex stopped and slowly turned to face her. "Yeah, I guess that's what I kept hoping for."

Tracey looked out across the sweeping lawn as a breeze swirled some leaves down the hill. "That guy's never coming back, Sis."

"I know."

Tracey studied her sister's profile. She had always envied Alex's thick blonde hair, even her wispy bangs. She had their father's smile and compassionate eyes, though Alex's glistened a deep sable. The ever-present readers gave her a sophisticated but somehow endearing look. Hers was a sister everyone loved.

Alex had always been the Martha in their family, always trying to stay a step ahead, anticipating everyone else's needs. Hers was the shoulder Tracey had cried on when Randy Simmons broke her heart in sixth grade. It was Alex who always baked the cake or cupcakes for her birthday parties. And when she was older, Alex was the one who explained the facts of life to her. For as long as she could remember, Alex had been more of a mother to her than Mom ever was.

Which was good since their mom never seemed to have much time for them when they were growing up. Or any time, come to think of it.

"And I have to say, I'm not sure I *want* that guy to come back."

Alex turned to look at her. "Why not?"

"Well, think about it. He devoted his life to that church for twenty years. He was at their beck and call, day in and day out."

"But he loved it, Trace."

"I know he did. And they loved him. But the first hint of trouble with Mom, and what did they do? They kicked him out the door."

Alex took another sip of tea but said nothing.

"All those years he gave to them. Then at the worst time of his life, when Mom humiliated him by taking off like she did, instead of supporting him in his time of need, they gave him the boot."

"You know it wasn't like that. It was—"

"Dad did nothing wrong. They punished him for something Mom did. It isn't right."

"Why are we rehashing all this again? We've been over it a thousand times before."

Tracey blew out a huff. "I know, I know. But it still irks me."

Alex reached over and covered Tracey's hand with her own. "You've got to let it go, Sis. Dad did, so you need to forgive them and move on."

Tracey picked at the polish on her thumbnail. "Dad may have forgiven them, but it took a long time before he could."

"I know. I don't know what we would have done if Uncle Rob hadn't shown up."

"Of all people, who would have ever thought Uncle Rob would be the one to get through to Dad."

Alex smiled. "The Lord certainly moves in mysterious ways. But dragging Dad out of the house on that road trip was exactly what he needed."

"Remember how funny he looked perched behind Uncle Rob on his motorcycle?" They both laughed out loud. "I thought for sure he'd fall off before he got to the end of Main Street."

"And he looked *so* serious, sitting ramrod straight, with his hands clamped to Sam's waist but at arm's length?"

They simultaneously mocked the pose then laughed at themselves.

"My, how far he's come now," Tracey chuckled. "He looks like he's ridden all his life."

Alex grabbed a cookie and turned to face her sister. "Enough about Dad. Tell me about you. I can't believe we've got you home for two whole weeks! What do you want to do while you're home? Any plans?"

Tracey's thoughts jumbled at the sudden question. She took a long sip of tea, wondering what she should say. "Well, to be honest—"

"Out with it, already!"

"I don't know, Alex. Mostly, I just need a break. I want to unplug, sleep late, maybe do a little cooking—" Her cell phone chirped, interrupting her wish list.

"So much for unplugging," Alex added.

Tracey silenced the tone as she saw Morgan's name on the small screen. "Yeah, I might have to keep this thing buried somewhere. I really need to be unreachable."

"Do you need to take that call?"

"No. I absolutely do *not* have to take it." She slipped the phone back in her pocket. "So where were we?"

"You were telling me what you want to do while you're home."

She waved her off. "I'm here. I'm home. That's good enough for me."

"Good! And since you mentioned cooking, come on in and help me get dinner ready," Alex said, standing. "I made apple cobbler for dessert."

"Yum! I think I gained five pounds from just visualizing it."

Alex took her empty glass. "Which you could stand to gain. You're too thin, Trace. I've got to fatten you up while you're home. But first I'll help you get settled up in your room."

Tracey opened the door for her. "Martha, Martha, Martha. I'm pretty sure I can handle that by myself. You go. I'll be down in a few minutes."

"Deal. And stop calling me Martha. You know I don't like that."

"Sure thing, Martha—I mean, *Alexandra*."

"Thank you, *Tracey Jolene*."

Chapter 3

Buddy wiped his mouth with his napkin. "Alex, I believe this may be the best meatloaf you ever made. And I'm not just saying that."

Alex passed the biscuits to Tracey. "You say that every time I serve it, Dad. You just love it because it's Granny Jo's recipe. You grew up on it."

Buddy smiled. "Maybe, but I still say yours is the best."

"It's the chili sauce. I use chili sauce instead of the ketchup in Granny's recipe. Gives it a little more flavor."

"See?" He nodded toward Tracey. "Do I know my meatloaf or what? Your mother didn't have a clue how to make a meatloaf. I hope Mr. Movie Mogul likes dining out because he'll starve if he's living off Regina's cooking."

Alex rolled her eyes. "Dad, let's not—"

"I'm just saying, it's a good thing he's got money. He probably hired a chef after the first time she cooked dinner for him."

"How's Mom doing?" Tracey asked her sister. "Have you heard from her lately?"

"She actually called last week."

Buddy's head snapped up as he stopped chewing.

"Really?" Tracey asked.

Alex smirked. "She wanted to let me know she was about to have a tummy tuck."

Buddy guffawed, falling back in his chair.

"You're kidding, right?" Tracey asked.

Alex took her time sipping her coffee. "Apparently Jared likes her thin, and she's put on a little weight."

Buddy continued laughing, wiping his eyes with his napkin. "Seriously, you can't make this stuff up. Your mother never weighed more than a hundred pounds her whole life. Jared must go for the anorexic look." He tossed an exaggerated shudder.

Tracey ignored him. "Didn't she just have some cosmetic work done last year?"

"Just a brow lift and a lip plump. Nothing major."

Buddy composed himself though a smile still lit his handsome face. "Girls, you have no idea how often I thank God that He sent your mother away from us."

Tracey flinched. "Daddy, don't say that."

"But it's true, Tracey Jo. I know God doesn't ever like to see a marriage end in divorce. But the truth is, just because two people get married doesn't mean God *ordained* that marriage. I knew when I married your mother that she had little use for the Lord. When I gave my heart to Christ a couple years later, she didn't seem to mind. But when I felt God calling me into the ministry, she let me know she sure didn't hear God calling her to be a pastor's wife."

"But she stayed with you," Tracey said. "All those years, she stayed."

"Well, you girls had come along by then. I think somewhere in that selfish heart of hers, she knew you girls needed her to stay. I'll give her that much. You were both well on your own before she took off."

When he grew silent, Tracey and Alex shared a silent glance. They both knew that despite all the bravado, he still had a soft spot in his heart for their mother. It had come as a complete shock to both of them. She'd called each of them, explaining the whole sordid story of reconnecting with her childhood sweetheart. Jared Blakely had searched her out on Facebook, of all places. He said he'd never forgotten her and had to see her again. An A-list agent in Hollywood, he wasted no time sending his private jet for her.

At the time, Buddy was overseas in Thailand on a month-long mission trip. He knew nothing about it until he got home. By then, Blakely had wined and dined Regina, lavishing her with expensive gifts and introducing her to some of the biggest names in Hollywood. It was the perfect escape she'd been looking for. She filed for divorce immediately, and didn't even bother coming home to pack her things. Apparently, she had all she needed in Beverly Hills.

Alex and Tracey had taken the news hard, stunned by their mother's brash disregard for their father's feelings and the implications it would have for him. She'd minced no words, saying she'd paid her dues and was glad to finally be rid of Jacobs Mill, the church, and yes, even Buddy. "He bored me to tears," she liked to say.

Tracey flew home to be with her father even though her sister still lived in town. Alex had taught at the elementary school in Jacobs Mill for twelve years, a respected and cherished member of the community. Though she'd never married, she'd bought a cottage a few miles south of town where she lived happily in a home cluttered with books and travel guides to places she'd visited and dreamed of visiting.

But when Buddy Collins came back to find his wife gone and his deacons murmuring for his dismissal, he lost it. He'd slipped into such a deep depression, the girls quietly had him admitted to Vanderbilt Hospital in Nashville. Several weeks later, they'd brought him home, and Alex moved back into Walnut Ridge.

Now, as Tracey passed her father another biscuit, she tried to move the conversation back to safer ground. "Well, all I have to say is, thank God for Alex and Uncle Rob."

Buddy blinked away the moisture in his eyes, his smile slow but sincere. "And I do thank God for them. And for you too, sweetheart. Every day."

Alex lifted the bowl. "Who wants more mashed potatoes?"

Tracey reached for it. "I do, Sis. I can't remember the last time I had mashed potatoes."

"Did you tell her your news?"

Tracey and Alex turned simultaneously toward their father. When Tracey realized he was addressing her sister, she slowly caught her breath, thankful the question wasn't aimed at her. "What news?" she asked.

"I assume you're referring to my early retirement?"

"You retired? But Alex, you're only thirty-four!"

Alex glared at her over her glasses. "And thank you so much, little sister, for reminding me. But this has nothing to do with my age."

Buddy wiped his mouth with his napkin. "Tell her how you let ol' Deacon Stone have it."

"Alex? What did you do?"

Her sister toyed with a green bean. "Oh, nothing really. I just refused to bow at the altar of the almighty ruler baron of Jacobs Mill."

"Meaning?"

"Meaning," Buddy answered, "that among other things, your sister threatened to rat him out for swindling all these old folks around here out of their property."

"Dad, you know that's not what hap—"

"How on earth did you get involved in *that*?" Tracey stared at her.

Alex placed her silverware on her dinner plate. "That's a long story for another day."

"Go on, Alex. Tell her," Buddy pressed.

She stood, gathering their dishes. "No, Dad, I really don't want to talk about all that tonight."

"But what will you do?" Tracey asked. "Are you looking for another teaching position?"

Her sister scoffed. "No point in that, not as long as Deacon's still on the School Board."

"I'm so sorry. I had no idea."

"Don't be sorry. Besides, I think I've decided to make a new start. Do something different for a while. Someday I may go back to teaching, but in the meantime, take a look under the tablecloth."

Buddy looked at her then at Tracey then back at Alex. "What are you talking about?"

"Here, let me show you." She set the dishes back down and reached down to pull the cloth back.

"Is this a new table?" Tracey asked.

"No. Look closer."

Buddy moved his tea glass out of the way and pulled the cloth back on his side. "Well, I'll be. That's our old table, isn't it? What'd you do to it?"

Alex cocked her head to one side. "Gee, Dad, thanks for the vote of confidence."

Tracey studied the finish on the surface of the large oblong table, then leaned over to look beneath at its elaborate legs. The old cherry finish had been painted over with a creamy ivory paint of some kind then distressed in all the right places to show some of the dark cherry. "This is *beautiful*, Sis. Isn't this what they call shabby chic? Who did it for you?"

"Nobody. I did it myself."

Tracey sat back up. "You did it *yourself*? When did you—did you take a class or something?"

"No, I learned how to do it from one of those HGTV shows. I'd been wanting to do something with this old table for a long time. It was all scuffed up and scratched and desperately needed refinishing. But I wanted something different, so I got some paint and voila! New table."

"She's right, Alex," Buddy said. "This looks great. How come I never noticed it before?"

Alex picked up the dishes again. "Oh, I don't know, Dad. Could it be you're a bit décor-challenged? Which would explain why you've probably never noticed the hutch over there and the armoire back in the den."

Tracey and her father got up to check out the other pieces of furniture. "This is amazing, Alex!" Tracey said, admiring the hutch. Its broad counter, doors, and open cabinets all finished to match the dining table. "Seriously, when did you do all this?"

"Couple of weeks ago, I think," Alex answered, following them into the den. "It was when you were on that trip to New Orleans, Dad."

"No kidding? These are fantastic, Alex."

"Oh, and check out the armoire," Tracey added. "It's gorgeous! How'd you get this look? Paint it black then sand it?"

"Actually it's a color called *Typewriter.* That's pine under there, so I use a milk paint that gives it a natural chippy look. I love this paint because basically, it distresses itself. It's really fun because every piece responds differently."

Tracey looked more closely, running her finger along the inset panels of the armoire's door. "So, is this what you meant when you said you wanted to do something different?"

"Actually, it's *exactly* what I meant. I'm thinking of opening a little shop, then try my hand at buying and refinishing furniture. I've been going to yard sales and estate sales, picking up pieces here and there, then working on them in my spare time. Believe it or not, I've had some interest in them from friends of mine, parents of my school kids, a few others. So, Dad . . . I was thinking about remodeling the big smokehouse for my shop. It's right on the road and big enough for a workshop in back and a showroom up front. What do you think?"

"I think it's a great idea!" Buddy wrapped his arm around her shoulders. "Oh!" he said, snapping his fingers. "And I know just who to help us turn that old shack into a cozy little place for your business—my Elders!"

"Who are these elders you keep talking about?" Tracey asked. "Do you mean the deacons from church?"

"Good heavens, no!" Buddy laughed. "*My* Elders. That's what I call the guys I work with. Haven't I told you about them?"

"No one ever tells me anything, apparently," Tracey said.

Buddy sat down on the hearth. "My biker buddies. But they're more than that. We do things for people. Help 'em out when they need help. Odd jobs, big jobs, you name it."

Tracey dropped into the wingback chair beside the fireplace. "What, like a business?"

"Not at all. It's a ministry. After Rob brought me back from that first road trip, I knew I needed to find a new ministry for my life. I'd met all these guys who like to ride, but a lot of them, like me, had way too much time on their hands. Some are retired, some are all but homeless. Some have problems they're dealing with—some have done time, some are battling addictions and what not. Some of them . . . well, like me, some of them just needed a reason to get up in the morning.

"And one morning, I was out there on the back porch having my coffee and reading my Bible, and it came to me—almost like God just spoke it into my mind. I knew these guys all had talents of one kind or another. And right there, as if the whole idea just rolled out before me like a great big panoramic vision, I could see us putting our heads and hands together to help those in need."

He scratched the beard under his chin. "It's a strange

phenomenon. I never felt more alive than when I was over in Thailand on that mission trip. And it wasn't just when we *told* folks about Jesus. It was more about *being* Jesus to those people who had no idea who He was. We built homes for them. We dug wells so they could have fresh water. We had a medical team that taught them about health and hygiene.

"See, it would've been a wasted trip if we just dropped in on those folks, told them about a Man who lived thousands of years ago and died on a cross so they could live, then took off again. Sure, that's the message we wanted to tell them. But we did it by getting to know them, by investing our time and resources in them. We didn't just *tell* them, we demonstrated the love of Christ through our actions."

Tracey could hear the passion in his voice as he talked and see it in his blue eyes that danced on a face warmed with compassion. She'd always thought his ready smile and kind, gentle eyes comprised the most compassionate face on earth. But it had been a long, long time since she'd seen him so engaged and excited. "So you and these guys—your Elders—you just look for things to do? Do you advertise online or in the paper?"

"We haven't had to. As soon as we finish one job, another one comes along. Sometimes lots of 'em. It's the craziest thing. Course, I know where all these jobs come from." He nodded toward the ceiling. "'I know from whence my help comes,' so to speak."

Alex took a seat on the arm of the sofa. "Dad, I'd love the help, and I know the guys would do a great job, but you said it yourself—what you all do is ministry. I'm not exactly an old widow needing her grass mowed."

"Obviously not, but who's to say which task is a job and which job is a ministry? As I recall, you didn't bat an eye when I came back from the hospital. You moved back in here, took care of me, made sure I didn't off myself—"

"Dad! Don't say—"

"I'm just sayin', sweetheart, that sometimes we do things because we simply feel led by God to do them. Besides, I've been wanting to do something with that old smokehouse for years. I can't think of a better project. I'm excited about this!"

"Yeah?"

"What's not to like? The way I see it, we're both on similar journeys. I give these guys fresh starts, you give your furniture a new life. Looks like we're all about second chances, y'know?"

"Dad! That's the perfect name for my shop—*Second Chances*."

"It's perfect, Alex," Tracey added. "Just perfect."

Buddy jumped up. "I can't wait to get my guys on this. Do you have time to take a walk-through in the smokehouse tomorrow? Maybe sketch out some ideas?"

"Well, sure," Alex said, her face beaming as she glanced over at Tracey. Her smile fell. "But maybe we should wait—"

"Don't wait on my account," Tracey argued. "Besides, it sounds like fun. Why not let me help too? And maybe you could teach me some of your magic. Show me how you transform your little beasts into beauties."

"I'd love to, Trace. We can work on a piece or two, but I don't want to tie up your whole vacation on all this."

Tracey felt her face warm. "Well, now that you mention it," she began, then cleared her throat. She stopped and looked back toward the kitchen. "How about we put on a fresh pot of coffee and dish up some of that cobbler? There's something I need to tell you both."

Chapter 4

"I can tell you one thing right here and now," Buddy snapped, angrily stirring his coffee. "I've got a mind to hop on Stella, drive up to Washington, and tell Senator Whistlebritches just what he can do with those 'family values' of his."

"Dad, that kind of talk doesn't help," Alex said.

"Maybe not, but it would sure feel good to smack that pretty boy's face into the next county." He punched his fist into his open hand.

"Dad, please. Alex is right. And you and I both know you'd never do any such thing."

"Yeah, yeah, I know. Tracey Jo, does his wife know anything about all this?"

"No, at least I don't think so." The thought hadn't occurred to her. Could Amanda have picked up on anything? Morgan hadn't been very discreet lately. Then again, he'd never been out of line when the three of them were together. "No, I seriously doubt it. We're—" Tracey glanced down, watching her finger crush a piece of the cobbler's crust. She quickly dusted the crumbs off her hands. "The thing is, I love Amanda. I don't *ever* want her to know about this. It would break her heart."

"Yes, it would," Buddy said quietly. "Take that from one who's been there."

Alex patted her father's hand then turned to her sister. "So he doesn't know yet that you're not coming back?"

"I wrote him an email on the plane giving my two-week notice."

"Good for you," Buddy said.

"The problem is, it's more difficult than that. There are procedures for leaving jobs like mine. There are exit reviews and debriefings and confidential information that has to be—"

"Something tells me Dick Nixon didn't have an 'exit review'," Buddy grumbled.

Alex peered over her readers. "Not helping, Dad. Okay?"

"Fine. But all I'm saying is, don't make this so hard on yourself, Tracey Jo. You've got enough to deal with on an emotional level. Deal with the rest of it later."

"What about your things?" Alex asked.

"I could probably just send for them. Ask my landlord to have them boxed up and shipped to me."

Buddy slapped his hand on the table. "No need. I'll grab a couple of my Elders, and we'll take care of it. All we'll need are your keys."

"You and your Elders," Tracey teased. "What am I gonna do with you guys?"

"Oh, you'll love us. I guarantee it. You won't be able to help yourself."

Tracey walked over to hug him. "Thanks, Daddy. I love you."

"Right backatcha, sweetheart."

Back in her old bedroom, Tracey slept like a rock. *There's something intrinsically soothing about having the same sheets and blankets and quilts piled over you that you slept under when you were a child,* she mused. She smiled at the thought and rolled over on her back, yawning as she gazed at the clock which read 9:45.

I haven't slept this late in years. This is heaven . . .

She reached for her cell phone on the bedside table and unplugged it from the charger. The face lit up showing twelve more missed calls since she went to bed. She flopped her head back on the pillow, debating whether she should look at the list of names. She gave in and scrolled down the list. *Just as I thought. Morgan, Morgan, Morgan . . . after ten calls, could you not get the hint?*

Then she saw Amanda's name, and her heart skipped a beat. She pressed the link for her voicemail and listened, bracing herself. There was no way to skip directly down to Amanda's message, so she listened to Morgan's first message—a fabricated reason for calling, nothing more. She skipped through the rest of his messages, hearing only snippets of each until she came to Amanda's.

"Hey girl! Morgan said you've already left town on your vacation! I thought we were going to have coffee this morning before you left? Well, knowing me I got the times mixed up and missed my chance to say goodbye. I'll miss you terribly, but I know you need some time at home. Call me sometime if you feel like chatting—oh, hold on. Someone wants to say hi."

"Oh no, I don't—" Tracey stopped herself, realizing she was talking to a machine.

"Hi, Taycee!"

Tracey smiled with relief as she listened to the voice of three-year-old Aaron Thompson.

"Where are you go? Come see me, Taycee. Come my house?"

She pressed her lips together, visualizing the little guy in Amanda's arms, his big brown eyes and thick head of blond hair so like his mother's.

"Mommy, why Taycee not talk?"

"Because she's gone bye-bye. Okay, Tracey, I'm jamming up your voicemail. Well, have fun, okay? I'm already missing you! Love you! Bye."

Tracey clicked off her phone and dropped it on the covers. "Oh Amanda . . . I hate this. Hate. It."

"HEY!" her dad yelled from down the hall. "Are you gonna sleep all day?"

"I just might. Who wants to know?"

"Nobody. Go back to sleep. But if you miss us, come on down to the smokehouse. The Elders are here. I left the coffee pot on. Grab a cup and come on down."

"We'll see."

At the sound of his footsteps going down the long staircase, Tracey decided to get up and take a shower. Fifteen minutes later, with her wet hair piled up on her head with a clip, she threw on a pair of worn jeans and a plaid flannel shirt she found in her closet. She made her way downstairs thinking she might make some toast before she went down the hill.

"Hello."

She jumped, missed the last step, and grabbed the banister to keep from falling.

"I'm so sorry!" he said, reaching for her elbow. "I didn't mean to startle you."

"No, it's okay—I just didn't know—"

She looked up at the man behind the voice and found herself staring into the face of . . . *an angel?* Backlit with sunlight from the open side door, a bright aura seemed to surround him. For a moment, she wondered if she'd actually fallen, cracked her head open, died, and this was the angel Gabriel escorting her through the pearly gates.

"Are you all right?" he asked, kneeling beside her.

"I, uh . . . I think so. Who *are* you?"

"I'm Noah Bennett, a friend of Buddy's."

She blinked. "Do I know you?"

"No, we've never met. But I'm guessing you're Tracey."

"Yeah, that's me." She tried to stand and he rose with her, his hand supporting her arm.

"Listen, I'm sorry. We're kind of used to coming and going around here. Buddy's always told us to make ourselves at home."

"That definitely sounds like my dad." She stopped and turned to face him as she connected the dots. "Oh, you must be one of the Elders."

His smile spread into deep dimples beneath a day's growth of dark whiskers. His messy hair, the color of dark chocolate, wasn't particularly long. His eyes were clear, somewhere between a green and light brown. *Hazel?*

"That's what he likes to call us. Which I've always thought was a bit strange considering—" he paused, his brows lifting. "Well, that whole church thing and all." The angel's face colored as he looked away.

Tracey couldn't help snickering. "Yeah, you've gotta love 'that whole church thing.' But please don't be embarrassed on my account." She rounded the corner heading into the kitchen. "It's ancient history. Besides, Grace Church had deacons, not elders. I'm sure it's some kind of personal joke that he dubs you all his Elders."

"Here, allow me." He opened the cabinet and reached for two mugs, then filled them both from the large urn.

She made her way to the refrigerator for cream. "What happened to Mr. Coffee and his pot?"

He handed her a mug. "It was forever running out, so Buddy bought the urn. Said it was the kind they had at the church."

She poured cream into her coffee and offered him the carton, which he waved off. She put it back in the refrigerator. "You and the guys come here a lot?"

He chuckled softly. "You could say that. We try to be respectful and not abuse his generosity. Especially for Alex's sake."

"Good to know. I'm sure she appreciates that." She could just imagine her sister playing hostess to a house full of ragamuffins. Although, she noted, the tall man leaning against the counter could never be called a ragamuffin. An angel? Definitely.

Suddenly, she realized he was staring at her over his mug as he took a sip. "Yes, well," she said, "I was about to head down to the smokehouse, so if you'll excuse me."

"I'll join you. I was on my way there when Buddy sent me up here for coffee. After you," he said, holding his hand out like a perfect gentleman. He followed her through the hall then stepped ahead to open the screen door for her.

"Thanks."

"You're most welcome. It's a beautiful morning, isn't it? I've always loved fall."

"Me too. In fact, it's my favorite time of year at Walnut Ridge. Well, except maybe for winter when it snows."

"Ah, true. You can't beat a Tennessee snowfall."

She pushed a renegade strand of hair out of her eyes and looked at him. "You don't sound much like a Tennessean."

"That's because I'm from Virginia."

"Oh?"

"And Connecticut, North Carolina, and New York. Pretty much in that order."

"You move around a lot."

"Used to. Not so much anymore."

She pulled a bright yellow leaf from an American elm tree and twirled its short stem in her hand. "What brought you to Tennessee?"

He looked away. "Oh, this and that. Needed a change of scenery, I suppose."

"Lot of that going around." She smiled briefly then took a sip of coffee. "So do you just hang out here with the guys? Or do you have a job? Family?"

"Actually, I do have a job. I'm a roadie, but I'm between gigs right now."

"A roadie? Like with musicians?"

"Right. Tour buses and a different town every night. That pretty much sums it up."

"Wow, that's got to be exciting, huh?"

"Sometimes. It's nice to see different parts of the world. But it can be rough at times. A drag, y'know? Same thing day after day, night after night."

"Then why do you do it?"

"Because it's what I do."

Wondering what that meant, she turned to face him. He smiled back at her, but it was the kind of smile a guy slaps on his face when he's said all he's going to say.

"Noah!" Buddy shouted. "I was wondering what happened to you. I see you met my daughter."

As they approached the back of the old building, Noah finished the rest of his coffee, then said, "I had the pleasure, yes. Though I'm afraid I gave her a bit of a start."

Tracey stepped into her father's outstretched arms. "Morning, Daddy."

"Morning, sweetheart." He held her close, then kissed the top of her head. "Y'all come in and take a look. Alex is so excited, she's like a kid in a candy shop. Except there's no candy. Just a lot of dust and ancient cobwebs."

They followed him through the rustic back door. She could already smell the familiar smoky scent. "Daddy, how long's it been since they stopped curing meat in here?"

"Ah, this old shack hasn't been used for smoking meat since the fifties, I guess. Long before you were born."

"Maybe so, but I sure remember the smell. Always makes me think of Granddaddy's barbecues. Like he used to say, 'that was some good eatin'.'"

Alex came through the front door with several guys. She brushed her hands on her jeans. "Tracey! What do you think? Isn't it perfect?"

"Yeah, I mean, it needs a lot of work, but I can see some possibilities."

"Where are my manners?" she said. "Have you met the Elders yet?"

"She met Noah up at the house," Buddy said. "Let me introduce you to the rest of my guys. This half-pint here is Earl Givens, but we call him Stump."

Tracey shook hands as her eyes trailed the long way up to the face of a gentle giant. He had to be at least six-eight, maybe six-ten, with the breadth to support every inch. "Well, hello up there. I'm Tracey. Nice to meet you, Earl." He pulled his hat off which had covered a mass of thick, black-brown hair. His beard covered most of his face and reached somewhere near mid-chest.

"Pleasure's all mine, Miss Tracey. It's okay if you wanna call me Stump. It don't matter none to me."

"Good to know."

"And this good man here is Greg Sells. He goes by Gristle."

"Gristle?" Tracey asked as she shook hands with the young African-American.

"My mama called me that ev' since I was just a lil' snot-nosed kid. Said I was always tough like that chewy stuff you sometimes get on a steak. Not that *we* ever ate no steak. Mamma just liked ev'body *thinkin'* we dined on t-bones and rib-eyes. Name just stuck."

"Well, Gristle, if it's good enough for your mama, it's fine by me. Nice to meet you."

"You ev' bit as pretty as they says you was."

"Now, don't you start charmin' my girl like that, Gristle," Buddy said. "And certainly not while I'm standing right here."

"Trace, you'll have to watch out for Gristle," Alex chimed in. "He could charm the trunk off an elephant."

"Ah, go on. Y'all know I'm just playin' w'cha."

Buddy tossed Gristle a pair of work gloves then glanced back at Tracey. "You'll never find a man more gifted with a saw. Puts on his tunes and I mean, he tears it up." Buddy turned to the last one, a stocky young man with a shock of wild red hair. "And this is Hank Biddle."

He reminded her of the troll dolls they sold at flea markets. Tracey took his outstretched hand. "Wait—let me guess. They call you Red, right?"

"No ma'am," he said, looking somewhat bewildered. "Folks just call me Hank Biddle."

"Well. Okay then, Hank Biddle, nice to make your acquaintance."

He didn't respond. Just stared at her like she'd sprouted a third eye on her forehead.

"Hank's your man if you need any sweeping," Buddy added, patting the redhead on his shoulder. "He's got a real knack for knowing how to clean things up in a jiffy. We couldn't manage without him."

"I was head of maintenance at State," he announced.

"Really? I had lots of friends who went to State," Tracey said.

His brows drew close together, but he said nothing.

"Ah, she means Tennessee State University," Gristle said. "Nah, Miss Tracey, he wadn't at no college. He was at—"

"Never mind that, Gristle," Buddy interrupted. "How about you and Stump go take a look outside and see which limbs need to be trimmed off that big elm tree."

"Sho'nuff, Buddy. We on it."

"Noah, come tell us what you think," Alex said. "Any ideas for turning this decrepit old building into a quaint little shop with a workroom toward the back?"

For the next hour, they tossed around ideas, brainstorming how to best use the space available. Tracey remembered her grandfather once telling her that the original smokehouse, a stone's throw from the kitchen wing at Walnut Ridge, was used only for the family. The "new" larger smokehouse where they now stood, was added a few years later when the plantation had begun to flourish. By that time, the family had sold off part of Walnut Ridge to a friend in need. As a result, the spacious smokehouse sat on the county road that bordered the east property line. Then, almost a century later during the depression, Hiram Collins doubled the size of the building. With so many of the townspeople and those in neighboring counties in need, he wanted a place where folks could stop by and pick up a slab of bacon or some ground beef or stew meat.

Tracey loved the story, picturing her great, great grandfather graciously providing for those who had little or nothing. "God doesn't bless us to spoil us," he was known for saying. "He blesses us so that we might bless others." Looking at the men around her, it seemed Buddy Collins was carrying on the family legacy. Tracey felt a lump in her throat, so filled with love for her father and the incredible miracle that had taken place in his own life. Here, decades later, Buddy blessed his Elders and by doing so, showed them how to bless others.

"Those are some great ideas, Noah," Alex said, interrupting Tracey's thoughts. "When do you think y'all might get started?"

He scratched his head for a moment. "How about this afternoon?"

Chapter 5

Noah let himself in the back door of the cottage and tossed his keys on the kitchen table. He grabbed an apple from the bowl on the counter and took a bite as he kicked off his boots. The face of Buddy's younger daughter drifted into mind. Funny, he'd never given much thought to the one called Tracey Jo who worked in Washington. He wasn't sure why he'd assumed she was the nerdy type, all caught up in politics. He realized she was *anything* but nerdy. Still, she was just home for a week or two. He doubted he'd see much more of her.

His mind switched gears, brimming with ideas for the smokehouse conversion. When Buddy first mentioned the idea, he wasn't sure if he should commit to helping. He still hadn't heard back from Dawson's people about the concerts they had scheduled between now and the holidays. Last he heard, Beau Dawson was having some kind of problem with his vocal cords and his doctors hadn't signed off for him to go back on the road yet. Noah wondered if the problem was indeed medical or if Dawson was having marital problems again.

None of it mattered to Noah. He wasn't invested in their lives, as such. He was nothing more than hired help. Most folks in the business just knew him as "Beau Dawson's guitar guy" and didn't bother with his name. Which suited Noah just fine. He'd lived in that world of who's-who once and didn't miss it.

He iced down a glass of water and took a seat on the sofa, stretching his legs out on the coffee table. He really liked it here at the cottage. When Buddy first offered the place to him, he told him thanks but no thanks. At the time, he'd been unattached from anyone and anything for quite a while. He wasn't ready to be tied down, least of all to a place of his own. Then, the more he thought about it, the more the idea grew on him.

He'd liked Buddy from the first time they met on a weekend bike trip over to the Blue Ridge Mountains. A couple of the other roadies were Harley riders and invited him on one of their weekend trips. Noah had learned to love the open road and never passed up a chance to ride. On that particular trip, he'd been curious about the guy everyone called Buddy. He seemed genuine, but you never know about the religious ones. Buddy wasn't obnoxious about all that, but it slipped into conversation now and then. For some reason, coming from this guy with the fun-loving smile and white ponytail, it seemed natural. Just a part of who he was.

Noah sunk down into the leather sofa and rested his head against the cushion. His mind drifted back to that first night they'd talked beside a fire pit on the campground where they stopped for the night. Buddy had asked him where he was from. He'd mentioned growing up in Virginia, and how much he loved playing sports. Undergraduate degree from Florida State and his graduate work at Harvard Law School.

"Harvard!" Buddy had marveled. "Didn't realize I was in the presence of an Ivy Leaguer."

"I keep that to myself most of the time," Noah had said. "That's all ancient history now."

"Really? You never practiced law after graduating?"

"I did. For a while."

"Where was that, if you don't mind my asking?"

"New York City. I had a lot of doors opened to me along the way."

Buddy had waited, probably expecting some kind of explanation. Noah hesitated, then realized the guy seemed sincerely interested. And so he began telling him his story. About his successes on Wall Street as a finance attorney. About his wife who he'd married the day after graduation from law school. About their life together in the Big Apple.

And then he'd stopped. The break in his voice seemed as good a sign as any to draw the line. Why burden a stranger with all that?

"Noah, you probably don't know this, but I used to be a pastor."

"Oh?"

"I'm not doing that anymore, but I still have a good ear, and I still do a good bit of counseling now and then. Which means, my friend, I still know how to tell when someone's burdened with heartache." He'd leveled his gaze at Noah. "So if you need someone to talk to, son, I'd be honored to listen."

Noah remembered staring at Buddy, seeing the kindness in his eyes as the reflection of the fire danced around them. He had a feeling the man looking at him could surely see all the way to his soul.

"Melissa . . ." he'd whispered.

"Your wife?"

Noah nodded because he couldn't speak. Buddy seemed to have all the time in the world. When Noah dug in his pocket for his handkerchief, Buddy had patted his knee. As if to say *take as long as you need.* When he could, he tried again.

He told Buddy of the April day he'd been tied up in court with a judge who had a serious God-complex. Noah knew if he had left, the case would be thrown out, and his firm would reassign him to the mailroom. He'd texted Melissa, apologizing profusely and promising he'd meet her at the address she'd sent him as soon as he could. She had found the perfect loft for them to buy in Soho, and wanted him to see it so they could make an offer before someone else snapped it up. Hopefully, they'd wait until he got there. Her text came back immediately—*HURRY!*

A half-hour later he'd dashed from the court house in the pouring rain and flagged down a cab. He was soaked by the time one stopped. As soon as he settled into the back seat, he dialed her repeatedly but couldn't reach her.

"Traffic was at a standstill," he'd told Buddy. "I was about to crawl out of my skin, and I remember yelling at the cab driver to turn at the next light and take a different way. He yelled back, but I couldn't understand a single word . . . I remember shouting at him, telling him if he was gonna live and work in the U.S., he should learn the blasted language."

Noah looked up at Buddy. "Though in a somewhat more colorful choice of words."

Buddy smiled.

"I finally gave up, threw some money at him and decided to make a run for it. And that's when . . . that's when . . . I saw her . . ."

Buddy waited several moments, then quietly asked, "You saw her?"

Noah shook his head. "Not her. Her car." He cleared his throat and tried again. "Or what was left of it."

"Oh no," Buddy groaned.

Noah attempted a smile. "She'd always loved Volkswagen Beetles. I'd given it to her two years earlier on her birthday. It was bright red. I ordered a vanity plate—*My Lil' Bug.* And Melissa, she always kept a bunch of daisies in the little vase on the dash. She loved daisies. And she really loved that car." He swallowed hard. "So I knew immediately it was hers. The driver's side had been broadsided by a delivery truck that ran a red light. The truck driver, a bicycle courier, and Melissa were all killed."

Lost in the fog of those memories, Noah startled as his ringing cell phone pulled him back to the present. Alex's number appeared on the phone's small screen. Noah almost answered, then stopped. Instead, he silenced the ring without connecting the call. She and Buddy had invited him up to the house for dinner as they often did. He'd actually intended to go. But the lingering trace of melancholy drifting through him gave him pause.

He tapped the phone against his forehead and closed his eyes. He couldn't put it in words, this sadness that sometimes washed over him. Sometimes he could almost visualize it—like thick ribbons of fog seeping through a crack in his armor, or drifting like a mighty wave through an open door. Eerie, dark, snaking through him until it reached fingers around his heart and squeezed—tighter and tighter until he could hardly breathe. He'd learned to fight it, mentally slamming the door on the despair before it overwhelmed him and left him drained and despondent. Again.

Noah opened his eyes and slowly exhaled. He hated these moments and knew the easiest way to keep them at bay was by doing something else, going somewhere, escaping. It was why he loved his Harley. He raked his fingers through his hair and got up, tossing the half-eaten apple into the trash. He retrieved his phone and listened to Alex's message.

"Hey, Noah, it's Alex. I wasn't sure if you were coming up to dinner or not, but just wanted you to know we're having fried catfish tonight. Hope you'll come. We'll eat about seven. Bye."

He felt a smile tugging at his face. Buddy and Alex always seemed to be there when he needed them. Even on voicemail. Alex knew how much he loved catfish. He sent her a text, then hopped in the shower, hoping to wash away the dust and filth from the smokehouse.

And if he was lucky, maybe some of the fog in his heart while he was at it.

"Noah, c'mon in!" Buddy chimed as he walked through the back door into the kitchen. "We were about to give up on you."

Tracey slid the last biscuit into the basket and looked up as their guest arrived. His eyes met hers, but before she could say hello, she couldn't help noticing how handsome he looked. He wore a blue chambray shirt beneath a navy cable knit sweater. The blues brought out the green in his eyes. She smiled. "Hello, Noah."

"Hi, Tracey. I hope I didn't hold up dinner. I figured the least I could do was clean up after crawling under the smokehouse half the day."

"And you don't clean up half bad for a Yankee," Buddy teased, carrying a dish of pan fries. "Grab that bowl of fried okra. I'm starving!"

Alex walked in from the dining room. "Noah! I'm glad you came. What can I get you to drink?"

"Iced tea would be great."

Tracey covered the biscuits and turned toward the dining room just as Noah turned to do the same. "Whoa! Sorry—" she said, jostling their cargo. A few pieces of okra spilled from Noah's dish onto the floor. She leaned down. "I'll get them."

"No, let me," he said, squatting. "I'm such a klutz—" At that precise moment, they bumped foreheads. "I'm *so* sorry! Are you okay?" He reached out to steady her.

Tracey laughed, rubbing her forehead and trying to ignore his hand on her elbow. "I think so. Though I'm beginning to wonder about—well, you know—this morning, when we—"

"Oh, yeah. That." He chuckled as his face reddened. "I suppose I should have warned you that I've never been good at introductions."

"No problem." She threw the fallen okra into the trash. "I have quite a history of falling down stairs, if that makes you feel good."

"Well, now that you mention it—"

"Will you two stop with the chatter and get the food on the table?" Alex squawked. "I'd like us to eat before it all gets cold."

They gathered around the dining room table, placing the remaining dishes in the center of the cloth-covered table.

"Where are all the others?" Noah asked.

Buddy held out Alex's chair before taking his seat at the head of the table. "Tonight's their bowling league in town."

"Ah, I forgot," Noah said, pulling Tracey's chair out for her.

"Thank you."

As Noah took his seat across from her, Buddy reached out his hands and they followed, holding hands around the table. "Father, for Your incomparable goodness and blessings, we thank You. Bless my daughters for the meal they've prepared. It's in Your name we pray, Lord."

"Amen," they said in unison.

Over dinner, they discussed the day's accomplishments, making a few more suggestions along the way. Tracey watched Alex bubbling over with ideas, pleased to find her sister so animated and excited about the prospects of her new business. It saddened her to think she'd walked away from teaching because of the town bully. Deacon Stone had always been a pain, but she was tired of him hurting the people she loved. First Dad, now Alex. Not to mention the countless others in town he'd squashed like so many bugs beneath his big fat thumb.

She looked up and caught Noah watching her. She smiled before taking a sip of tea, curious about the two little lines between his eyebrows. Frown lines? Worry lines? And yet, his was a kind face. Alex said something amusing which caught his attention. He smiled but didn't laugh.

Tracey forked a piece of the steaming catfish and gazed at her sister as she took a bite. That moment, something slowly occurred to her. She'd often wondered why no one had ever swept Alex off her feet and married her. She was so full of life and funny, so thoughtful, and the hardest working person she'd ever known. As she let her eyes drift back toward Noah, she wondered if there might be something there? She hadn't had a chance to ask Alex about Noah—to find out what brought him to Jacobs Mill, how long he'd been around, and if he had a wife or family. She noticed he wasn't wearing a ring. And obviously, if he had a home, he'd be having dinner there now, not here. She tore off a piece of biscuit and made a mental note to talk to Alex after dinner.

Nothing would make her happier than to see her big sister fall in love and marry.

"So what do you think, Tracey?"

She glanced up to find them all looking at her. "I'm sorry, what was the question?"

"Pay attention, Sis!" Alex said. "Noah asked what you thought of extending the front porch of the smokehouse a couple feet wider and building an awning over it. That would give it a covered porch where we could have some rocking chairs, hang some ferns—make it a really inviting entrance where people could also sit and visit."

"Great idea," Tracey answered. "And that would make it so easy to decorate for the seasons. You know, hay bales and pumpkins and cornstalks in the fall, Christmas lights and fresh garlands strung with lights—"

"Oh, Trace, that's a GREAT idea!" Alex cried. "Noah, we've got to get this done! I'm so excited!"

"Sweetheart, let the man finish his dinner first, okay?" Buddy said. "You worked him all day, I think he deserves a little peace and quiet while he eats. Isn't that right, Noah?"

"Buddy, I've been around Walnut Ridge long enough to know—there's *never* 'a little peace and quiet' when the Collins get together."

"Yeah, Dad, you heard him. So Noah, how early can we get started in the morning? If I have breakfast ready at five, will that work for you?"

"Five o'clock?" Tracey moaned. "Isn't that awfully early?"

"Okay, fine. We'll make it six!"

Chapter 6

After an enormous Southern breakfast of scrambled eggs, bacon and sausage, grits, biscuits, and a piping hot urn full of strong coffee, the team headed down the hill to get started on the smokehouse makeover. Tracey insisted on cleaning up the kitchen so Alex could go with them. Her sister had been up bright and early, banging around pots and pans long before the sun came up. Rinsing off the breakfast dishes, Tracey smiled, finding her sister's enthusiasm highly contagious. Much to her surprise, Tracey's thoughts had been filled with visions of the new shop as she drifted off to sleep the night before.

Her smile faded when she realized what a drastic change that was. How many nights had she lain awake consumed with the stress of her job? And yet, that was nothing compared to the angst that had hovered over her night and day as she contemplated how on earth to keep the job she loved while constantly having to fight off Morgan's subtle nuances.

As she dried the large cast iron skillet and stored it back in the cabinet, she silently thanked God for this new distraction. On her flight home, Tracey had wondered how she would get through the first few weeks away from D.C. She was certain the whole mess she'd left behind would constantly eat at her and drain away all her energy. Her conscious decision to check her cell for messages only once a day had worked wonders. What a relief to be untethered from it. From that life.

Instead, here she was, anxious to get started in something she'd never even thought about before. To turn pieces of discarded junk into one-of-a-kind treasures. To work alongside Alex, filling the old smokehouse with these treasures, then open their door for business. She felt invigorated! She couldn't begin to understand why she was so eager to do it. Then again, maybe she *did* know. It was new. It was different. It was an about-face to everything she'd ever done before. And it was all about making old things new.

Tracey noted the symbolism, felt it touch deep in her heart.

It was everywhere. Her father's new life—so radically different from that of the small-town pastor he'd once been. His band of Elders, men whose lives had been transformed as a direct result of Buddy's own metamorphosis. She was anxious to meet the rest of them, curious to hear all their stories and find out how their lives had changed. Noah's And Alex. *Dear Alex.* At a time when anyone else would be filled with bitterness and spite at the hand that was dealt her, Alex dusted the whole situation off her shoulders and chose to look forward.

A lesson I'd do well to learn. Thanks for raising the bar, Sis.

Tracey filled a large thermos with coffee, grabbed a sleeve of Styrofoam cups, and headed outside. The brisk fresh air filled her lungs, making her grateful for the old Vanderbilt sweatshirt she'd thrown on over her blouse. Septembers in Tennessee had a mind of their own. Warm one day, chilly the next. She enjoyed the walk down the hill, hearing the breeze rustle through the leaves. How she'd loved growing up here, raking up mountains of leaves then flying into them from the swing Dad had hung from their oak tree's massive branches. If she closed her eyes, she could probably still hear the little girl giggles as she and Alex took turns on that swing, like a soundtrack from her childhood. She could smell the intoxicating aroma of the leaves Dad always set to burn just over the hill. One of her all-time favorite scents.

Yes, it's good to be home.

As she neared the smokehouse, she found the men hard at work clearing out rubble, pulling off rotted planks of wood, and lots of other dirty work.

"Hey, guys," she said, holding up the thermos. "I'll have this inside if you need a cup. Just come on in, okay?"

"Sure thing, Miss Tracey," Gristle said, using his forearm to wipe some dirt from his chin. "That's real nice. We thank you."

"No problem, Gristle. Looks like you're making headway out here."

"Yes, ma'am, we are," Stump said as she passed by him. "Mighty fine breakfast you and Miss Alex served this morning."

"It was our pleasure, Stump. Nice having you join us."

Just before she stepped up to the back door, she noticed an unfamiliar face. She smiled at him, but he didn't smile back. Just gave her a nod. She tucked the bag of cups under her arm and extended her hand toward him. "I don't believe we've met. I'm Tracey Collins."

He nodded again, brushed his gloved hand against his jeans, then shook her hand.

"Miss Tracey, that's Lester," Stump said. "We don't know what his last name is. He don't talk much."

Tracey looked back at the scraggly beard and ruddy complexion of the man as he shook some dirt off his worn boots. He looked to be in his mid-thirties, but she wondered if he might be younger with a lot of wear and tear from a rough life.

"He's harmless," Gristle said. "Don't mind him none, Miss Tracey."

She turned back toward Lester, surprised to find he'd walked off.

"He just like that. Keeps to hisseff. He don't mean no nuthin' by it."

"Thanks, Gristle," she said, stepping up to the building. "I was afraid I'd offended him somehow."

"He an odd one, but Buddy sees sumpin' in him. He likes Buddy."

"Good to know," she said then slipped inside. There, a bank of temporary light stands bathed the room in a surreal light.

"Oh, Trace! You're here!" Alex said. "Come here! I've got to show you something!"

Tracey found a rough-hewn bench against one wall and set the thermos and bag of cups on it. "What is it?"

Alex grabbed her sleeve and pulled her toward the front of the building. As they approached a section of an interior wall that had been partially ripped out, Noah stepped through the front door. "Did Alex show you what we found?"

"She was just about to," Tracey said. "You both look like you're about to pop. What did you find, Jimmy Hoffa's body?"

"No, silly." Alex squatted down and unwrapped some kind of old cloth. Tracey kneeled beside her. "Look at this." Carefully, as if handling the Hope Diamond, Alex lifted an old teacup from the cloth. "Isn't it beautiful?"

Noah kneeled beside them. "We found it in the wall here. It was wrapped in this long piece of cloth, wound around and around. Obviously to protect it. Which worked, since it's in perfect condition."

"And look, Trace," Alex said in a near whisper. "The saucer was wrapped separately but just as carefully. Not a fracture or crack on it. They're both perfect."

Tracey held the saucer in one hand, gently fingering it with the other. "So why would someone store their fine china in the wall of a smokehouse? I wonder who put it here?"

Noah held one of the cloths in his hand. "I'm no expert, but that looks like some kind of crest." He pointed to the design on the cup. "Much more regal than I would expect to find in most Tennessee homes." He carefully turned it over. "Unfortunately, there's no stamp by the china company. That would help, at least to know where it came from originally."

"I still don't understand why these were in the wall," Tracey said.

Alex carefully began rewrapping the cloth around the teacup. "I don't either, but I bet we can Google it and find out. But it sure adds to the mystique of this place, doesn't it? I've always wished the walls at Walnut Ridge could talk. Now maybe they will!"

"In the meantime, I'd suggest taking these up to the house and storing them somewhere so they don't get broken," Noah said. "In fact, I promised Buddy I'd meet him there. He's got another generator for these lights until we get an electrician to wire the place. If you'll trust me with them, I'll put them in your dining room hutch."

Alex helped him wrap the saucer. "Good idea. In fact, let's put them in my backpack there so they'll be easier to carry."

They placed the fragile dishes gently into the canvas bag and sent Noah on his way.

"Okay, Sis. I brought some of Dad's work gloves, so put me to work."

Side by side, Alex and Tracey pulled down cobwebs, swept the filthy floor, and continued prepping the interior for more serious work. Nasty work, but Tracey loved it.

She leaned over to look out the back door before lowering her voice. "I've been wanting to ask you about Noah. He told me he met Dad on one of his biker weekends and that he's a roadie of some kind, but not much else. What's his story?"

Alex didn't even bother looking up from her work. "Well, there's not a whole lot more to tell. He's been in the area a year or so, give or take. From what Dad said, he used to be some big financial attorney in New York, but gave it all up after his wife died."

"He's a *widower*?"

"That's usually what they call a man who loses his wife," Alex said.

"I know, but—well, how did she die? Cancer?"

Alex stood back up and arched her back. "No, she was killed in some kind of accident."

"That's so sad," Tracey said. "I mean, he's so young."

Alex blew a strand of hair out of her face. "I know. It's hard to imagine, isn't it? He still struggles, from time to time. He disappears now and then, and not just when he's on tour with those musicians. He'll just take off on his bike, and we won't see him for a week or two."

"Where do you think he goes?"

"No idea. I'm guessing he just gets on the road and goes. Maybe it helps clear his thoughts. Who knows. But he's come a long, long way since Dad more or less took him under his wing. They're really close, as you probably noticed."

"Which explains why he's living in your cottage."

"When I moved back to the house to help Dad, it just seemed like I was supposed to stay. So I stayed. Left most of my things down at the cottage, in case I ever change my mind. But it was stupid to have it sitting there empty when Noah didn't have a place to hang his hat."

Tracey picked a piece of straw off her sister's shirt. "So, tell me. How well have you gotten to know him? He seems really comfortable around you."

Alex clumsily scratched her ear with the oversized glove on her hand. "What do you mean? The guy eats dinner with us occasionally, he does odd jobs around the house, helps Dad with his ministry projects, and they bike together now and then. Yeah, I know him a little more than the others, but why do you ask?"

"Oh, I don't know. I was just hoping maybe you and he—"

"Oh, for crying out loud, Trace," Alex whispered hoarsely. "If you're asking if I have a crush on him—"

"No! I just thought maybe you and he might have gone out for dinner or a movie or something."

Alex laughed. "Who are you, Cupid?" Then, after glancing through the back door to make sure no one was listening, she said, "No, little sister, I do not have a crush on him, and we have not been out on a date together. He's a wonderful guy who's survived an unspeakable tragedy. Sometimes a guy like that just needs a sense of security and friendship. The last thing he needs is romance."

"Oh no," Tracey croaked, grabbing her arm. "Look out front."

Deacon Stone was making his way up the front steps, his signature mustache and aviator sunglasses in place.

"Quick, Trace! Lock the door!"

"I would but there's no lock. Want me to body-slam it shut?"

The town's self-appointed unofficial boss stepped inside the smokehouse, took off his sunglasses, and looked around the room. "Ladies, ladies, what have we here?"

"Gee, Deacon, I don't recall asking you to stop by," Alex said, brushing her bangs aside then planting her hand on her hip. "To what do we owe this pleasure?"

He tucked the glasses in his shirt pocket, taking his time as he nosed around the large room. "Oh, you know, just stopping by to say hello, Miss Collins."

His saccharine tone irritated Tracey, but she tamped down a burning desire to spit on his fancy leather boots. She'd never liked his Tom Selleck mustache, especially since everyone had long told him he resembled the older actor. Tracey didn't see it, forever distracted by a rather large mole just below his left nostril. Plus, Deacon's personality certainly didn't match that of the famous actor. She let out a huff. "What do you want?"

"I heard you were back in town, Tracey Jo." He chuckled, still glancing around. "I've always found it amusing how our national politicians vote themselves big fat salaries, then find every excuse they can to take a vacation. Not just our elected officials like your boss, Morgan Thompson. But staff like you as well. Must be nice."

"Tracey asked you a question," Alex stepped closer to him. "What *do* you want?"

"Well then, I'll get right to it. I couldn't help but notice all the commotion around this old building. You're obviously not tearing it down. Looks to me like you're into some kind of renovation or such?"

"Could be," Alex said. "But I sure don't see how that concerns you, so if you don't mind—"

"Actually it does concern me. As a member of the City Council, I don't recall seeing any kind of paperwork about this particular building. I inquired of our City Manager as to whether you'd applied for a building permit. Faye said she's seen nothing of the kind. So I suppose you could say I'm here on official city business. Because if you've got any plans whatsoever for this ol' shack, you'd best stop right now. Nothing happens in Jacobs Mill without approval of our City Council." He plastered a smile on his face and waited for a response. "It would be wise to remember that."

Tracey saw anger smoldering in her sister's eyes. Not tears—more like Vesuvius on the brink of eruption. She stepped between them. "Deacon, why don't you just cart yourself down to Faye's office and have you a nice little pow wow. We're busy here."

His gaze moved slowly to hers. Another fake smile. "Did your sister here tell you the School Board had to ask for her resignation? She flagrantly broke school rules and wasn't the least bit shy about it. She'd been warned about it before. She knew she was in violation of—"

"Are you done?" Tracey snapped.

Alex pushed Tracey out of the way. "Deacon, so help me, if you don't get out of here this minute—"

"What? What exactly are you going to do, Miss Collins?" He stretched himself to his full height, a good four or five inches taller than Alex. "Hmm?"

Alex inhaled and slowly let it out, trying to control her temper. "I mean it, Deacon. GET. OUT."

He laughed. Tracey couldn't believe it. The man actually threw his head back and laughed.

Tracey blocked Alex just as she reached out to shove him.

They turned at the sound of footsteps behind them. Noah, Gristle, Stump, Lester the quiet one, and even Hank the redhead gathered slowly around them. Tracey noted the glint in Noah's eyes, but he didn't say a word.

"Well, well," Deacon said, his tone once again laced with sweetness. "I see we have us a party here."

None of the Elders said a word. They just stared at him, their message unmistakable.

"I see then, well, I'll be on my way," Deacon said, turning to leave. "Miss Collins, you just let me know if there's any way we can be of service—" He stopped as he opened the door, glancing over his shoulder "—With whatever it is you all are up to here." His mustached smile didn't quite reach the disdain in his eyes. He turned and made his way out the door and down the steps.

Alex let out a long, graveled groan. "I mean to tell you, if *that man*—"

"Alex, what's going on?" Noah asked.

Tracey answered before Alex could. "Just an old bully flexing his muscles. Nothing new about that."

Alex let her head drop back, her eyes closed. "I can't tell you how badly I wanted to smack that fat gnarly mole right off his face."

A snort sounded behind them. They all turned to find Lester snickering with a crooked smile. A split-second later they all broke into laughter.

Everyone except Alex. "No, I can't laugh. I won't. There's nothing funny about that jerk. Nothing."

As their laughter settled, Tracey put her arm around her sister. "Oh, c'mon, Sis. You can't let him get to you. That's exactly what he wants. But you know what?"

Alex huffed and tossed her a glare. "What?"

"I think he just met his match," she said, nodding her head at the guys around them.

They looked at each other as if considering the idea.

"You want me to go slash his tires, Miss Alex?" Stump asked, completely serious.

"No, how 'bout I go teach him a *thang or two* about manners?" Gristle gestured with great flair. "That dude think he *all* that. And I'm tellin' you right now, he *ain't*."

Tracey looked at Alex. "Y'know, I have to agree. Don't you?"

They all laughed, then Noah planted his hands on his hips and shook his head. "That may be, guys, but you don't want to cross him."

"Ah, c'mon, now!" Gristle cried. "Where's the fun in *that*?"

"Noah's right." Stump folded his arms across his massive chest. "You can't let him scare ya away, but you sure don't wanna get him all hot 'n bothered. Just let it go so as he'll leave you alone, Miss Alex."

"Easier said than done, Stump. I've still got battle scars from that one."

He stepped closer to her, rested his hand on her shoulder as an easy expression warmed his bearded face. "Well, don't you worry yourself none. We gotcha covered."

Alex exhaled, relieved, and looked up at him. "Good to know. Thanks, Stump."

Tracey looked at him, this tall, tall man, and decided beneath all that hair and height and breadth was a big soft heart. The thought eased her own tension.

"Okay, show's over, let's get back to work," Alex said, clapping her hands.

The men stood there, not moving.

"What?"

"Nothin', Miss Alex, 'ceptin' we only came in fo' a cup of coffee," Gristle mumbled. "That okay wid' you?"

Chapter 7

While Buddy and Noah rigged up additional temporary lighting, the girls told him about Deacon's visit. He assured them he would handle the permits *and* Deacon Stone. Tracey could see the immediate relief in her sister's face. She reminded herself to ask Alex sometime about the whole sordid story of her retirement—which clearly wasn't.

The day had been exhausting, but productive. The Elders took off at four-thirty when Alex thanked them and sent them on their way. Alex had told Tracey they all had their own places and liked their privacy, which was why she didn't offer them dinner every night of the week. Just on occasion.

The three of them ate a quiet dinner together, then both Dad and Alex called it an early night. Tracey was tired, but rarely ever went to bed early. Her D.C. hours had left an indelible mark on her sleep patterns.

Besides, there was something she wanted to do. She made herself a hot cup of tea, slipped her laptop under her arm, and headed for the back porch. As much as she loved the grand front porch at Walnut Ridge, the large screened-in back porch was her haven. Cozy and intimate for its size, it was the perfect spot to get lost in a good book or stretch out on the cushioned sofa for an afternoon nap. Several years ago, Buddy added a stone fireplace on the east side of the porch, making it even more inviting on nights like this.

Tracey built a small fire like her father had taught her years ago. Satisfied, she trekked back inside for one more thing, then returned, placing the fragile, wrapped items on the wicker coffee table. She unwrapped them, first the cup then the saucer, and turned on the small lamp on the table beside her. All day, thoughts of their unexpected discovery had needled her.

Carefully holding each piece up to the light, she studied the design. Basically, both pieces had a white background edged in gold and a deep, dark shade of red—no, now that she looked at it in the light, more like a dark maroon or magenta. A white twisted rope pattern set inside the gold band rimmed both cup and saucer. Below that, a quarter-inch band of the dark maroon with a single row of tiny gold dots circled the pieces.

And on the face of the cup, an eagle with its wings outstretched, its head turned to the left with the faintest wash of yellow behind it—

almost as if the sun glowed behind it. What looked to be an olive branch was gripped in the eagle's talons atop a shield of sorts with muted red and white vertical stripes below, topped by a horizontal band of navy blue. *How odd that the shield leans to the left just ever so slightly,* she thought. Protruding from the upper right edge of the shield were four or five arrows.

She wondered if it were some kind of colonial design. Something about it seemed familiar, but she just couldn't put her finger on it. The eagle, the red, white, and blue shield, the olive branch—

"Good evening, Tracey."

"Ah!" She caught herself, juggling the cup but saving it. "Noah! You've got to stop sneaking up on me like that. I almost dropped the cup we found today."

As she set it down, he came around to the back entrance of the screened-in porch and opened the door. "I'm so sorry—really. I promise I'm not trying to spook you."

"I know, but—maybe I should give you bells to wear around your neck so I'll hear you coming."

He smiled. "I hope not. Never been one for wearing dog collars."

"Well, never say never," she said, pushing her hair back out of her face. "Was there something you needed?"

As he approached the sitting area, Tracey noticed he'd changed into an olive-green sweater and a clean pair of jeans, his hair still damp from a shower.

"Please, have a seat. I didn't mean to interrupt. I saw the light back here and decided to take my chances and see if anyone was up."

"Oh? Did you need Dad or Alex? I doubt they're asleep yet."

"No, please don't disturb them." He pointed to the rocker adjacent to the sofa. "Mind if I join you?"

"Please, have a seat. Would you like a cup of tea? Or I could make some coffee."

"No, I think I've had enough caffeine for one day." He sat down and gently set the chair rocking, his glance moving to the cup and saucer on the table. "Apparently we're both on the same wavelength. When I got back to the cottage, I couldn't stop thinking about them. Where they came from—"

"—and who put them there?" Tracey added. "Me too. I was just about to go online to see what I could find out."

He chuckled softly. "Like minds. I did the same thing, but I've misplaced my charger and my laptop's out of juice. I'm bad about that sort of thing. That's why I came up to the house. I wanted to take a better look at the pieces." He leaned forward, pointing at the cup. "Do you mind?"

"No, not at all."

He lifted the cup then leaned back in the lamplight. "So what have you found out?"

"Nothing, yet. I'm curious about that crest or whatever it is. What do you make of the symbols on it?"

He held the face of the cup up to the light on the table between them. "I actually had a thought about that. I thought it looked like some kind of crest or coat of arms, but it occurred to me it might be something else. It almost looks as if it could be some kind of official china. I can imagine it in a place setting at the governor's mansion for some kind of state dinner, can't you?"

"At the *Tennessee* governor's mansion?" she quipped. "I doubt it. I'm sure those cups have some gaudy orange and white design. Go Vols and all that."

He smiled. "You're probably right. But since you're a Vandy grad, I doubt you'd approve. You'd expect something gold and black."

"Well, of course. Much more elegant for the governor's mansion, in my opinion." She reached for the saucer, inadvertently pulling the linen wrapping along with it. As she did so, something fluttered to the floor. "I wonder what that is?"

"I'll get it." Noah set the cup on the table between them and reached for a torn piece of paper. "Whoa. Where did this come from?" He transferred it to his other hand, holding it in his palm. "Looks like parchment or something."

Tracey set the saucer down and leaned over for a closer look. "Has to be parchment. Can you make out what it says?"

He moved it closer to the light. "Hard to read. The ink is really faded." He looked up at her. "Do you have a magnifying glass handy?"

"Dad keeps one in the kitchen. I'll get it."

"I'll come with you. I think we need better light." He followed her, blinking when Tracey flipped on the lights over the kitchen counter. "Much better. Let's take a look."

They sat side by side on the tall bar stools. Noah carefully laid the small note on the counter and held the magnifying glass over it.

"Wow, this must be really old," Tracey whispered in awe, just before gasping. "Noah, look!" Leaning closer, she pointed at the last line of the note. "That's a date—*April 29, 1863.* Can that be right?"

"Whoa . . ."

"What do the words say? There," she pointed. "Is that an F or a P?

"I think it's a P," he answered reverently. "I think it says, *For safe—"*

"For safe-keeping?"

"*For safe-keeping . . . until the—*"

"*—until the war is over!* That has to be the Civil War!"

He turned, their faces just inches apart. "Do you realize what that means?"

She turned at his question, looking into his eyes. "What?" When he simply stared at her without answering, she asked again. "Do I realize what *what* means?"

A moment more then he looked back at the small piece of parchment. "It means this note was written around 150 years ago."

Still watching him, she pressed. "You were going to say something else."

"I was?"

"Noah?"

He glanced briefly at her then back at the note. "Nothing. I guess I was just overly excited or something."

She wasn't convinced.

"I think these must be someone's initials. And if I'm not mistaken, it's CJC."

She leaned in closer, taking the magnifying glass from his hand. The capital letters were in script and rather swirly, but she had to agree. "CJC. Has to be one of my ancestors, wouldn't you think? The last C most likely stands for Collins."

"Probably. No way to know for sure, but it's a place to start." He leaned back and folded his arms across his chest. "Do you have some kind of record of family names?"

"There's an old family Bible with that sort of thing, but I think it's up in the attic."

"Probably not the best time for us to be rooting around up there," he said, carefully picking up the note again.

"I guess you're right." Tracey hopped down from the stool. Maybe I can look for it in the morning."

"Have you got a Ziploc bag we could put this in? We should probably try to keep it as sterile as possible."

She pulled a plastic bag from a drawer and opened it for him to drop the parchment in. "Hey, I bet Mrs. Sadie over at the library would have some old records. She's quite the historian."

He followed her out to the back porch. "Should we take her the cup and saucer?"

She sat back down, tucking her feet under her as she picked up her laptop. "I suppose. But I'm not sure I can wait. Let's see if we can find out something about the china." She looked up at him. "Are you in a hurry?"

"No. Are you sure you don't mind me sticking around?"

"Not at all. We're in this thing together, right?"

"Yes, I suppose we are," he said, smiling. "In which case, do you mind if I—?" He motioned to the sofa beside her so he could see the laptop screen.

"Have a seat." As he sat down, she caught a whiff of his cologne and decided it suited him. After powering up her laptop, the screen came to life. A chat screen popped up. *Morgan: Trace, are you there?* She quickly closed the chat and felt her face warm.

"If you need to answer that, I can go," Noah said, starting to get up.

Tracey grabbed his sleeve and pulled him back. "No need. Now let's see. What should I Google—teacup?"

Noah leaned back, wondering why she hadn't answered the chat notice from her boss. It seemed a little odd that a U.S. Senator would use chat to communicate with his staff. *Then again, what do I know?*

"Try using Google Images first," he said. "That way you'll see the pictures, not just a listing."

"Okay."

"And type in 'teacup with eagle crest' and see what you get."

The monitor filled with pictures of all kinds of teacups, teacup-sized puppies, crests, and even a teacup-sized piglet or two.

"This is going to take forever," Tracey mumbled, scrolling through the images.

"Stop," Noah said, placing his hand on hers over the mouse. "Scroll back up."

"Why? What did you see?"

"Do you mind if I take the mouse for a moment?"

She took her hand off the device. "Sure. But tell me what you—"

"There," he said, clicking on an image. As an enlarged image filled the screen, he slowly turned his face toward hers. "We're going about this all wrong."

"What?" she asked, meeting his eyes.

Intensely aware of her closeness, he reached up and gently turned her face back toward the screen. "That."

"Okay, it's a—oh my *gosh,*" she croaked, turning to face him again. "It's a *presidential seal*?"

He smiled. "Yes, it is. Now keep that thought. If the note we found from your great-great-great-uncle-Craggie is authentic, and the date is right . . ." He arched his eyebrows encouraging her to connect the dots.

She gasped, both hands flying to her cheeks. "It's . . . it's—"

"It's entirely possible that teacup and saucer over there came from the White House." He paused. "Which was occupied at the time by—"

"ABRAHAM LINCOLN!"

He laughed out loud, cupping his hand over her mouth. "Well, yes, but must you announce it to the whole world?"

Tracey grasped his hand over her mouth and drew it away. "*Abraham Lincoln* could have sipped tea from that cup?!" she whisper-squealed.

"Yes, I think that's quite possible."

He couldn't take his eyes off her. The discovery may have been breathtaking, but no more so than the young woman sitting beside him. From the moment he met her, Noah had been intrigued. Her quiet confidence. Her warm and ready smile creating the perfect frame for eyes the color of dark caramel. Her hair—a deep, rich brunette, always shining, reaching well below her shoulders.

As she stared into his eyes, he could tell her mind was far away. "What are you thinking?" he asked.

"I'm imagining a much younger version of the White House. I'm there in the State Dining Room where President and Mrs. Lincoln are hosting their guests. And everyone's seated at decorated tables, all set with this same china." He watched as she blinked back to the present.

"Then again," he said quietly.

"Yes?"

He tipped his forehead down to touch hers. "Then again, it *could* have been Mary Todd."

"Mary Todd?"

"Mrs. Lincoln. *She* could have sipped from that cup over there, not Abe."

"Ah."

Their eyes seemed locked on one another . . . then the moment passed.

"Yes, well—" she said.

"Yes, well," he echoed as she turned her attention back to the screen.

"May I?" She reached for the mouse.

"Sure. Fine. Absolutely." He slid it over to her.

He watched as she keyed in *Lincoln china pattern,* then hit ENTER. The familiar images filled row after row of the exact same pattern.

"Whoa!" Noah leaned back. "I can't *believe* it!"

Tracey's smile widened as she glanced at him in utter shock. "Unbelievable," she whispered.

For the next half hour, they followed a cyber rabbit trail of pictures and information about the Lincoln china. They learned that the crest on the actual plates and bowls and platters was more detailed than the one on the teacups—a lower arc of clouds on the bottom half of the design; the nation's motto, *"E pluribus unum"* written on floating ribbons against the clouds; an arc of clouds edged by sunlight above the eagle's head and wings. They talked over each other, pointing out this anecdote and that, comparing one picture with another.

After Noah grew quiet, Tracey paused. "I've worn you out, haven't I?"

"Not at all. This is fascinating, and I'm anxious to find out how a cup and saucer from the Lincoln White House ended up in your smokehouse."

"Well, yes, there's that," she said with a tired smile.

Noah stood. "But I've got an early morning, and I need to get some rest."

She set the laptop aside and followed him to the back door. "I hadn't even noticed the fire died out. Some hostess I am."

He pushed open the screen door and turned to look back at the fireplace. "It's nice back here. I've always enjoyed my visits with Buddy out here when he builds a fire."

"I'm sure Dad's fires never die out."

"No, but you'll get the hang of it. Just takes practice."

"I'll try to remember that."

"It was fun. Thanks, Tracey. I'll see you tomorrow." He let the door tap shut behind him. "Next time I'll try to remember my dog collar." He mimed the noisy collar. "Lots of bells."

"Please do. And I'll try not to jump when I hear them."

"Good night, Tracey."

"Good night, Noah."

Chapter 8

At breakfast the next morning, it was just the three of them again. Tracey couldn't wait to tell her father and Alex about the amazing discovery she and Noah had made last night. She'd brought the cup and saucer into the kitchen, setting them on the table beside her. Knowing they'd want to see for themselves, she'd also brought her laptop along. When the moment came, she enlarged the photo of the Lincoln china and spun the screen around so they could see it.

"Ta da!"

"Oh. My. GOSH!" Alex cried.

Buddy pulled the laptop closer to him. "You've gotta be *kidding* me!" He tilted his head up so he could view it through the readers perched on his nose. "Well, for the love of Pete! Sure enough—there it is. Tracey Jo, how'd you find out? How'd you even know where to look?"

"I was studying the pieces when Noah stopped by last night, and he suggested we do a Google Image search. Then he—"

"Wait, Noah came by?" Alex asked, with raised brows. Like her father, she turned to look at Tracey through her half-glasses.

"He came over after you guys went to bed. I was out on the back porch, and he said he saw the light on. Apparently he was curious about the pieces too, but—OH! I completely forgot! Tracey jumped up and stuck her hand into the pocket of her robe. She carefully removed the Ziploc containing the note they'd found. "You will not *believe* this!"

They leaned closer. "What is it?"

"It's a note! Last night as I was unwrapping the cloth from the saucer, it fell out. I guess when we unwrapped it before, it must have stuck to the cloth. Or maybe we never completely unrolled the rest of it. Doesn't matter. Look at this."

"What's it say?" Buddy asked.

"It says, 'For safe-keeping until the war is over.' Then it's signed with the initials CJC. But look at the date—1863!"

Alex leaned closer, her hand over the faded letters and numbers. "Are you sure? It's so faded, how can you be sure?"

Tracey stepped over to the kitchen drawer and pulled out the magnifying glass. "Here."

Alex and Buddy crowded over the small piece of parchment, both looking through the magnified glass. "Oh. My. GOSH!" Alex gasped for the second time. "Dad! Look! She's right. It says 1863 just as clear as day!"

He leaned back and pushed the readers up on his head. "This is unbelievable, Tracey Jo! But who's CJC? Obviously a Collins, but—"

"I don't know and that's exactly why I'm climbing up in the attic as soon as I finish breakfast. Are all those old trunks and boxes still up there?"

"A few, but we donated most of the documents and letters to the library," Alex said, still bent over studying the note.

"What about the old family Bible? Is it still up there?"

"Yes, but I know it doesn't go back to the mid-1800s. Check with Sadie over at the library. She probably has it all documented and categorized. This kind of thing is right up her alley."

Alex finally leaned back. "Oh, she'll have a ball with this. Why don't we take this and the pieces over to her as soon as we get dressed? The library doesn't open until nine, but she's always over there by seven."

"Perfect! But don't you need to work at the smokehouse with the guys today, Alex?"

"No," their father answered instead. "It's mostly just grunt work at this stage, so the Elders can handle it. In fact, a few more of the guys are coming out today. Besides, I've got to go to City Hall and file all the permits and have a nice little chat with my favorite demon—I mean, *deacon*." He rolled his eyes and downed the last of his coffee.

"You need back up? Alex and I can go with you. Better yet, take the Elders. They scared him off yesterday, maybe they'll have the same effect today."

"No, this is between Deacon and me. And the lovely Miss Faye. Don't you girls worry about it. All that to say, the guys can handle the work today. Alex, I'll let you know if we need you. Y'all go on and see what you can find out from Sadie over at the library."

Alex stood up, gathering their dishes. "Will do, Dad."

"And whatever you do, don't drop the cup and saucer! Those must be worth a fortune!"

"He's right, Trace. We should probably find something more secure to put them in. Heavens, if I'd known these were Lincoln's, I'd never have let Noah carry them in my backpack. I'll see what I can find. I'll clean up, so you go on and get dressed."

Dad took the dishes from her. "No, *I'll* clean up so you two can get ready. Go on, scoot."

Alex kissed his bearded cheek. "You're the best. Thanks, Dad."

Tracey pecked his other cheek then headed for the stairs. "Love you, Dad."

After she showered and dried her hair, Tracey dashed on a little make-up. As she waved the wand of mascara over her lashes, she saw the face of her cell phone light up. She'd kept the tone on silent, so she'd missed all of Morgan's calls over the past couple of days. But this time it was Amanda's number that flashed. She reached for her cell, then stopped herself, slowly pulling her hand back.

"Amanda, I know we need to talk but not now," she said aloud. Returning to her make-up, she felt the familiar uneasiness. Just because she'd left Washington and thrown herself into her home and family life didn't mean she'd forgotten all she'd left behind. She couldn't imagine how Morgan must be handling it. And truth be told, she didn't really want to know.

But Amanda was a different story. She promised herself she'd either email her or call her soon. Just not yet.

As Tracey and Alex made the short walk from Walnut Ridge to the library, Noah slowed his Harley to a stop after spotting them on Main Street. He told them he was headed up to Nashville to order supplies for the renovation.

"I'll be anxious to hear what you find out. I'll stop by later today to hear what you learned."

"Come for dinner," Alex said. "I put a roast in the crockpot earlier."

"Sounds good. But only if you let me bring dessert."

Alex shielded her eyes from the morning sun. "You baking or buying?"

"Very funny. No time today, so I'll pick up something in town."

"Drive safe," Tracey said as he put his helmet back on.

"I always do. Later, ladies."

As he took off, Tracey watched over her shoulder until he drove out of sight. He looked completely different in his black leather jacket with that big black helmet on his head. *Different in a good way*, she thought. *I wouldn't mind taking a ride in that seat behind him . . .* When she turned back around, her sister was staring at her.

"What?"

"Did I say anything?"

"No."

"Well, there you go," Alex answered. "Oh look, there's Sadie's car in the parking lot."

Sadie Woolsey smiled as she unlocked the door to let them in. "How lovely to see you girls this morning. Come in, come in!"

Tracey had always loved the little log cabin that housed the town's library. The large paper maché tree towering over the children's section had always reminded her of *The Giving Tree,* one of her childhood favorites. On the other side of the room, a large fireplace warmed the cozy atmosphere and invited readers to have a seat in one of the rocking chairs before the hearth. And all around them, rows of shelves stood filled with books. She'd spent many a happy afternoon here when she was young. Good memories.

"Tracey Jo, I heard you were back for a visit. How are you?"

She placed her laptop bag carefully on the table then gave the elderly woman a hug. "I'm fine, Miss Woolsey. It's good to see you."

"How's our fine senator? We're all so proud of you up there in Washington. People say you're his right-hand man—I mean, right-hand *girl,* of course. Must be quite an honor to work with Senator Thompson."

Tracey forced a tight smile. "I suppose you're right, but let me tell you why we're here." Then, while explaining yesterday's find in the smokehouse wall, she and Alex carefully opened the bag where, instead of a laptop, the cup and saucer were each secured in bubble-wrap. They unwound the wrap, revealing the two pieces.

"My goodness, what have we here?" Sadie asked, picking up the teacup.

Tracey filled her in on last night's research. Holding the cup, she turned it so the presidential seal faced the librarian. "And that's when we put two and two together and realized—these were from *Abraham Lincoln's* White House china service."

"What?!" she gasped, dropping into the chair behind her. "You can't be serious!"

Tracey found the eighty-year-old's expression utterly priceless—her eyes wide open, her hand to her chest, the other on her rouge-dusted cheek. Alex had once commented how much Sadie Woolsey resembled the old-lady version of Kate in the movie, *Titanic.* At the time, Sadie had far fewer wrinkles than the actress. Now, her pale, paper-thin skin seemed crinkled enough they could be twins.

"It's true," Alex said, digging the Ziploc out of the bag's inside pocket. "But that's just the beginning." She placed the clear bag on the table in front of Sadie. "The real mystery is who put it there and why."

"Which is why we need your help," Tracey added.

With the help of the magnifying glass they'd brought along, they discussed the note, its date and initials.

"Oh my goodness, it's almost too much to comprehend," she said, leaning back in her chair, her hands clasped like those of a child in prayer. "It's as if the Holy Grail is right here in our grasp."

"Miss Sadie, are you okay?" Tracey asked. "Can I bring you some water?"

"Oh dear, no, I'm fine. Just a little shocked. To think that our dear President *Abraham Lincoln* could have sipped tea from this very cup . . ." She shook her head in disbelief.

Alex and Tracey laughed. "We've had that same thought. It's pretty surreal, isn't it?"

Sadie sat up straight. "Girls, you must secure these," she said in a hushed voice. "If anyone knew you had something so valuable, you could be robbed!"

"Oh, I doubt anything like that—"

"No, it's true! I read emails from my friends all the time about how easily thieves can get into your home using nothing more than a credit card. And another one told how they case your house, so you should always put your lights on timers and leave the TV on so they think someone's home." She punctuated the information with a knowing nod.

Tracey and Alex shared a smile. "We'll look into that, Miss Sadie. But what about these initials—CJC?" Alex asked, pointing back at the note. "We assume it's someone in our family, one of our ancestors. But Dad said you have most of the Collins family documents in your archives here."

"Oh, yes. I've got them . . ." She fell silent, staring at the note.

"What is it?" Alex asked.

Sadie looked up, still dazed. A moment passed then two. "I know who put these in the wall . . ." Suddenly she blinked, looking back and forth between them. "And I think I know how he came to have them!"

Chapter 9

It was well after one in the afternoon before Tracey and Alex climbed into their father's pickup truck and drove to the estate sale west of town. They chatted like magpies, discussing everything Sadie had shared with them, much of it conjecture on their part. Finally, Alex had enough.

"Okay, I think we should table any further discussion until we can talk to Dad and Noah tonight at dinner."

"I'm sorry we're late getting to the sale. We should have left Sadie to search through all those papers."

"Are you kidding? She was so excited, I thought we were going to have to put the dear soul on oxygen. If we'd left and she passed out, we'd never forgive ourselves."

"I know, but didn't you tell me you like to get to these sales early so you can have first pick?" The old Chevy pickup hit a bump in the road and sent them bouncing. "Good grief! When was the last time you had the shocks on this thing checked?"

"I think Lincoln was still in the White House," Alex quipped. "No, Sis, it's okay. We would've been completely distracted if we'd come here before going to the library. And the way I see it, no matter when I get there, if one or two sweethearts are meant to be mine, they'll still be there waiting for me. You'll see."

"By 'sweethearts' are you referring to the stuff you buy at these sales?"

Without taking her eyes off the road, Alex batted at her. "Bite your tongue, Tracey Jolene Collins! I'll have you know I do not buy *stuff*. I take in *orphans*. They may be battered and abused and showing a lot of wear and tear, but that's just because they need a little TLC."

Tracey smiled. "I've got to hand it to you. You've put your heart and soul into this, haven't you?"

Alex laughed heartily. "You have no idea. I've never had so much fun in all my life. It's positively addicting. I bring home these pitiful little souls, clean them up, pamper them, give them a fresh coat of paint, and just love on 'em. I can't wait to show you how much fun it is."

Tracey grew silent, contemplating her sister's burst of enthusiasm. Alex pinched her arm. "Ouch! Why'd you *do* that!"

"You got so quiet. What are you thinking? Did I say something wrong?"

Tracey rubbed her arm. "Geez, Alex, that hurt." For as long as she could remember, Alex had always pinched her to get her attention. It was a wonder she could ever go sleeveless after a lifetime of such abuse.

"Spit it out."

Tracey rolled her eyes. "Fine. It just occurred to me that the way you were describing the furniture you find at these sales as your 'sweethearts' is exactly how you used to talk about your students. And that made me wonder again what happened. You *loved* teaching. It was your passion. How could you let Deacon and the School Board let you go?"

Alex stared straight ahead. "First off, they didn't let me go. They fired me."

"But why? What did they accuse you of doing?"

"They accused me of proselytizing my kids. Which, of course, I did. They had warned me repeatedly; someone called the ACLU, and when I refused to stop, they axed me. End of story."

"So what exactly were you doing? How were you proselytizing?"

"Oh, the same thing I've always done. I started my class each day with prayer. I read them Bible stories every morning. I taught them about the *real* meaning of Easter, and I let them dress up and act out the story of the Nativity. Y'know—the usual hardcore proselytizing."

Tracey snickered. "Yeah, hardcore. I'm sure you ruined them for life."

"Likewise, I refused to spend a full week guilting them for 'ruining the planet' during Earth Week, opting instead to let them explore the wonders of nature and God's miraculous creation. That one got the tree huggers all hot and bothered."

"You have students who are tree huggers?"

"No, silly, their parents. Actually, it only takes one. They freak out when they hear little Susie might learn something truly horrific like . . . like how God made the woodpecker's tongue so long, it wraps around its skull when not in use. Better I should teach her how cow flatulation is destroying the ozone."

Tracey laughed. "And who doesn't love a good cow flatulation story now and then?"

"Exactly! So someone called the ACLU. The ACLU called Deacon, who got his boxers all in a wad over it. Demanded I comply with public school dictates on the subject, and then voila—pink slip."

Tracey adjusted her seatbelt so she could turn and face her sister. "But that's what I don't understand. You've *never* let them railroad you like that before. Why didn't you fight it?"

Alex made a sharp left turn onto a country road, bouncing them hard. "Ah, there it is just up ahead."

"C'mon, Alex. Answer me. Why didn't you fight them?"

She slowed the truck to a stop on the side of the road and shifted into park. "Because, little sister, they have the law on their side. Of course I knew what I was doing was against school policy. I'd always known it would happen someday, but in my heart of hearts, I just wanted my kids to know Jesus loves them. And I couldn't *not* tell them, if that makes sense."

Tracey reached out and gently squeezed her sister's arm. "I'm so sorry, Alex. They've lost the best teacher they ever had."

Alex patted her hand. "Well, somehow I doubt that, but I appreciate you saying it. But enough of that. We have babies waiting for us!"

An hour later, they loaded the last of their treasures into the back of the pickup and headed home. There, Alex and Tracey unloaded their purchases into the back part of the old barn at Walnut Ridge.

"So this is where you work," Tracey said, looking around the cluttered room. "Oh, Alex! All these pieces—I had no idea! No wonder you need a showroom for them."

Alex set a side table in the corner with some other unfinished pieces. "I told you it's a bit of an addiction on my part. Though, I prefer to think of it as my ministry. Check this one out," she said, moving a rocker out of the way to get to an usual table against the wall.

"Wait, how come there are only three legs?"

"I'm guessing it had four originally, and who knows why the other leg is M.I.A. I'm thinking about using it as a display table in the shop, so we'd just bolt it to the wall to make it stable. But look at the scroll work on these legs! It will be stunning by the time I get done with it." She looked up at Tracey with a smile. "When *we* get done with it."

"I don't know, Sis. I think you may be giving me too much credit too soon. I don't know the first thing about all this."

"Not a problem. You'll pick it up as we go along. Oh, and look at this hall tree I found at a garage sale."

"Hey, what is this?" Tracey picked up a wooden box the size of a cigar box. "This is beautiful."

"You like that? You should have seen it before. Hold on, I keep before and after pictures." She crossed the room and opened the top drawer of an old refinished filing cabinet. She fingered across the top of several folders. "Ah, here it is. See how scuffed up it was?" she said, pointing to a photo.

"Did you fix all that or just paint over it?"

Alex glanced at her over her glasses. "That's why I use a milk paint called *Miss Mustard Seed*. You don't have to prime, you don't have to sand, you just clean it then paint. Then, like I told you before, the paint just does its thing. It flakes off into what I call 'chippy goodness'—sometimes a lot, sometimes just a little. Then after it dries, you can use your fingers to help remove as much flaking as you like and let some of the original finish show through. I love it because each piece is truly unique."

"And that's all there is to it?"

"That's it, except for the top coat. I use either furniture wax or hemp oil to seal it. Gives it a really rich but soft look. Now, open it and look inside," she said, opening the lid. "I found these vintage postcards at an estate sale and thought they were the perfect contrast to the black finish. So I Mod Podged them, and—"

"What is Modge—"

"Mod Podge. It's a creamy white liquid that seals whatever you're working on then dries clear. It's like a watery Elmer's glue that spreads really well. Comes in different kinds of finishes. I used a matte finish on this one."

"Kind of like we used to decoupage when we were kids?"

"Smart girl!"

In the bottom of the box, three long black velvet trays, each slit down the middle lengthwise, were nestled side by side. Tracey rubbed her fingers along them. "Where'd you get these ring displays? I could keep all my rings in this."

"Yard sales. You can't believe what you can find." Alex closed the lid and placed Tracey's hand over it. "It's yours."

"Really?"

"Yes, really. Tracey, meet Olivia. Olivia, meet Tracey."

"You *named* it?"

Alex rearranged some of the other pieces in the room. "I name all of them. I told you, Trace," she said, looking over her shoulder, "they're my children." She danced her brows and pinned a wide smile on her face.

Tracey clutched the beautiful ebony box to her chest and looked around. "Y'know, I think I'm gonna love this."

"Told you it's contagious. Now let me introduce you to the rest of my babies."

Chapter 10

Sadie Woolsey took a seat at the table where Buddy held out her chair. "What a treat to be invited for dinner tonight. I'm honored!"

Alex placed the salad bowl on the table then sat down. "It was Tracey's idea. We decided to wait to tell Dad and Noah what you told us about the cup and saucer this morning. Then she suggested we let *you* tell them since you're the one who knows the story so well."

"Oh, it would be my pleasure," she said, her face aglow with anticipation.

"But first, let's have a word of prayer," Buddy said, encouraging them to hold hands around the table. He offered a brief thanks to the Lord before they began passing the dishes.

Noah laughed as he forked a piece of roast. "I can't wait another minute, Miss Woolsey—please, tell us your news."

"Noah, you must call me Sadie. I insist. But as for the news, let me begin at the beginning. When I saw the cup and saucer the girls brought over this morning, then learned it was from the Lincoln White House, why—I was astonished! Then they showed me the note they found signed with the initials CJC. And something starting fussing at the back of my mind. Then all of a sudden, I knew!"

Buddy set his fork on his plate. "The suspense is killing me, Sadie. Out with it!"

"Ah, but you must hear the story first." She slowly took a sip of her hot tea then set the cup back on its saucer. "You see, back in the time when Lincoln became president, the protocol was for the president's family to furnish the White House. Meaning, they supplied their own beds, tables, dinnerware, that sort of thing. The White House had very few possessions of its own because at that time, it was considered a public building. So people came and went all the time. Of course, this was long before they had any security measures like they do now. It is told that folks could be found wandering through the house any time of the day or night. Can you imagine?

"So when a president left office, oftentimes the public would just help themselves to whatever they left behind. It's told they'd even tear wallpaper from the walls and rip up pieces of carpet for souvenirs."

"Basically, they vandalized the White House?" Noah asked.

"That's precisely what they did. And that's why in 1861 when Mr. and Mrs. Lincoln moved in, they found the house in complete disrepair. As you might imagine, Mary Todd Lincoln found this quite unacceptable. And among the improvements she took upon herself to oversee was to replace the fine china, silver, and glassware. The cup and saucer the girls showed me were indeed the same pattern she chose while on a shopping spree to New York.

"The original design she found had a blue band around it. Preferring the more popular color known as *solferino*—a bright purplish-reddish shade similar to burgundy—she requested the change and placed her order which was produced by Haviland & Company in Limoges, France. Originally there were 666 pieces of this pattern which, by the way, was the first set of china used for state dinners chosen by a president's wife."

"Now, tell them how the cup and saucer ended up here at Walnut Ridge," Tracey urged.

"Trace, let her eat!" Alex said. "She's hardly had a bite. Go on, Miss Sadie. Eat your dinner before it gets cold."

The librarian thanked her and took three tiny bites of the roasted vegetables. "Oh, this is simply delicious."

Buddy took a sip of his tea. "Am I right in remembering that Mary Todd Lincoln was a difficult person to get along with?"

"I always heard she suffered from mental illness and headaches," Noah added.

"That was her reputation, I'm afraid," Alex said. "She suffered from terrible migraines, even worse after a carriage accident. I also think her severe depression was responsible for much of her behavior. But who could blame her after losing two of her children?"

"Okay, back to the cup and saucer and the note," Buddy said. "Whose initials are those?"

Tracey smiled. Her dad was a cut-to-the-chase guy who grew restless with long, drawn-out tales such as Sadie's. "Dad, be patient. She's getting there."

"Yes, well, where was I?" Sadie asked, gazing up at the ceiling. "Oh yes. Those initials. This is where the story gets truly interesting. As you know, Buddy, your father's family has lived here at Walnut Ridge since the plantation was first built in the early 1800s by Jacob Elias Collins. And, as you know, the town and its mill were named for him. I should be able to tell you how many great-great-greats he was from you, but I'm drawing a blank at the moment. Now, Jacob had a son named Eli Andrew Collins. Of course there were many other siblings, but for our interests tonight, I'll just stick to Jacob's descendants. When Eli married Celeste Parsons, their first born was a son they named Craig Jacob Collins—"

"CJC," Noah added.

Sadie's eyes twinkled as she smiled. "Yes, CJC. And what an interesting boy he was. By the time Craig was around twenty, Walnut Ridge had grown into a thriving plantation growing tobacco and raising cattle. But Craig wanted no part of it. He was a rebellious child who preferred to go by Craggie, which actually suited him better. Craggie developed a terrible case of wanderlust, so one night he took off without telling a soul, and especially not his parents. Later, they would learn, he roamed the country for several years, always picking up odd jobs along the way until he had enough money to move on. Then, around 1861 he found himself in Washington D.C."

Tracey glanced around the table. She smiled, observing her father and Noah hanging on Sadie's every word, totally mesmerized by her story. They hadn't even noticed when Alex served dessert, though they'd both taken several bites of the apple chunk cake.

Sadie continued. "By this time, Craggie had learned the ways of the world enough to know how to charm himself into any job he set his eyes on. And so it was, our own Craggie Collins found himself a butler in the Lincoln White House!"

Buddy leaned back in his chair. "Well, for heaven's sake. How on earth did he do it? I wouldn't think you could just walk up and knock on the White House door and ask for a job."

"Dad, remember what Sadie said about folks coming and going in the White House day and night?" Tracey asked. "It's not like they had guards out front and metal detectors at the door. Times were different then."

Noah finished a bite of cake. "Who knows, maybe he met someone in a pub or a boarding house. And if that's the case, then things really haven't changed that much—it's all in who you know."

"Of course, we have no way of knowing," Sadie said. "The family archives had no such information on how he got the job. What we do know is that he was quite fascinated to be a part of the White House staff. By then, I'd like to think he'd matured and knew his manners. Still, with the states at war, Craggie found himself at odds with those who walked the halls of the White House." She stopped and looked around. "Oh dear, where did I leave my valise?"

"It's probably with your coat," Alex said. "I'll get it for you."

"Yes, please, dear. Because there's something I must show you. Do you suppose we could clear away some of these dishes?"

"No problem," Tracey said as she and Noah started gathering dishes. "By the way, your apple cake was delicious, Noah."

"Wish I could take credit for it, but the compliment goes to Publix."

"Can't beat their bakery," Alex added as she handed Sadie the thin leather case.

Buddy leaned forward. "Tell us what you've got there, Sadie."

The librarian gently removed a folder and laid it on the table in front of her. She carefully opened the file and removed a page in a clear plastic sleeve. "This is a letter I found in your family's archives, Buddy." She turned it for them to see and slowly slid it across the table.

They all stood up, their chairs scraping in unison against the oak floor as they crowded to take a look.

"As you can see," Sadie began, "this is a letter signed by Craggie Collins dated May 6, 1862. It was a letter he wrote to his father who had recently written to tell Craggie that his older brother Evan had been killed in the Battle of Shiloh in early April. Evan had been the one sibling Craggie got along with before he left home. Tracey, why don't you read it for us since you and Alex had a chance to look it over with me this morning."

"Sure," Tracey said, picking up the protected page. She took her seat as Noah, Dad, and Alex leaned over her shoulders.

Dear Father,

I was so very sorry to hear that Evan had been killed in battle. I hadn't shed a single tear since I was a boy, but I confess I cried all night after receiving your letter. How I wish I'd told Evan how much he meant to me.

Even though I'm from the South, I've always liked Mr. Lincoln. He's very kind to all of us who work here. When his son Willie died back in February, President Lincoln did not return to work for almost three weeks, as he and Mrs. Lincoln suffered through their grief. We all felt the sadness in every room of this great house.

But now, as I experience my own grief—one caused by this wretched war—I find myself angry as well and fearful of my actions. Others I work with know I am from Tennessee and regularly provoke me about my allegiances. Just yesterday I nearly punched a footman for a vulgar joke he made about the Confederacy.

That is why I have decided to leave here at once and come home to Walnut Ridge. If you and Mother will have me, I want to come home.

Your son,

Craggie

Chapter 11

After Sadie left, Buddy said goodnight and went upstairs. Noah helped Alex and Tracey finish the dinner dishes, then Alex headed off to the barn to work for a while. Noah was much too wired to call it a night, so on a whim he invited Tracey to take a ride with him. She balked at first, uneasy about riding a motorcycle in the dark. The fact that she quickly came around pleased him. She borrowed Buddy's leather jacket, spare helmet, and protective eyewear, then followed Noah out to his bike.

"Wow. This is a lot bigger than Dad's. A lot more chrome, too."

"Bigger, but older than Buddy's. It's an '04 Ultra Classic, but it's got all the bells and whistles." It even has helmets with communication headsets." He then showed her how to plug into the communication port on the bike and where the switch was to activate the headset. He climbed on and helped her up onto the seat behind him. He motioned for her to hold on. "You'll probably want to—"

"Oh, I'll *definitely* want to." She leaned forward and wrapped her arms around his ribcage. "I'm new at this, you know. I practically cut off Dad's circulation on the way home from the airport."

"Good to know. If you notice my voice jumping an octave or two, you might want to ease up. Ready?"

She tightened her arms around him. "Ready."

Holding the clutch, he turned the key and powered up the Harley. It was one of his favorite sounds—like a personal, open invitation to relax. He gently eased off the clutch and slowly drove the bike down the long, winding driveway. A few minutes later they were rolling along, the cool autumn air whisking over them.

"You okay back there?"

"Doing great. You okay up there?"

Noah laughed. "I'm good, thanks. Check out that moon."

"Whoa! It's beautiful! I forgot how big those harvest moons can be."

"What, you didn't have them in D.C.?"

"Yes, wise guy. We have harvest moons in Washington. But I was always too busy to notice. Hard to take in a sight like that sequestered in an office 'til all hours."

Noah drove them out of town on the two-lane country road with no particular destination in mind. He'd never had a woman passenger before, but he decided then and there he liked it. In fact, he liked it a lot. It felt good to have Tracey's arms wrapped around him. A little strange considering they'd only known each other a few days. That, and how intimate it was, feeling her pressed against him like this.

They rode in silence for fifteen or twenty minutes until they came to a bluff overlooking a river. Slowing, he pulled off and parked. "I've never been up here before. Mind if we take a look?"

Tracey pulled off her helmet and eyewear. "This was a favorite parking spot back when I was in high school. Mind you, *I* was never up here. Dad always convinced Alex and me that if we ever did that sort of thing, he'd know. 'I'll just *know*,' he'd say. I had images of him jumping out of the bushes if I ever came up here with a guy. He sure put the fear of God in us."

Noah secured their helmets. "I guess we're safe then."

"Safe?" she asked, following him up the steps to the lookout.

He turned back, reaching for her hand. "Buddy's home in bed. I don't think you have to worry about him jumping out of the bushes."

She laughed, keeping up with him until they reached the top. A concrete wall served as a barrier to keep them from falling down the long, steep embankment below. "What a view—I had no idea we were this high up."

Tracey walked around him. "It's absolutely breathtaking. Oh my goodness, I don't know which is prettier—all the twinkling lights below or the canopy of stars above. Especially with the moon looking all fat and orange like that."

"Well, I did call ahead. Asked for something breathtaking."

She laughed quietly. "Did you now? So you planned this? Like a rendezvous or something?"

He could tell by the look on her face she hadn't meant to say that. Even in the moonlight he could tell she was embarrassed. "Ah, yes, ma'am, it surely does. I called up Dial-A-Sky and said I'd be coming up here with a beautiful young woman at—" he checked his watch— "8:55 and would they please toss out a few stars. I had to pay extra for the moon, of course. Being so big and all."

"So now you're mocking me? You and your stars and your big fat moon?"

"Not hardly. I'm not that clever. But you have to admit it was a good one."

"What, the Dial-A-Sky?"

"Subject change," Noah said, turning around so he could lean back against the wall. "I still can't get over all this business with the Lincoln teacup and your *Uncle* Craggie hiding it in the wall of the smokehouse. If I hadn't seen the letter with my own eyes and compared the handwriting to the note we found with the cup and saucer," he shook his head, "I wouldn't have believed it."

He watched Tracey looking out at the view below. "Unbelievable, isn't it? And thank goodness Sadie is such a stickler for keeping the town's archives. Imagine if we'd found that teacup and had no possible way to find out how it got there."

"She's incredible," Noah said. "She's quite the fountain of information. I keep trying to envision this Craggie fellow on his last day at the White House. What possessed him to steal that teacup? Was it just a souvenir? I find it hard to believe someone with a reputation like his would be smitten with a particular pattern of china."

Tracey chuckled. "Yeah, probably not. And from what Sadie found in her research about that china and how so many pieces of it were broken and missing—it makes you wonder if Craggie was part of those on staff who deliberately dropped a piece here or there out of spite toward Mrs. Lincoln." She shrugged. "Then again, maybe he just stole it right from under their noses."

"Which in Abe's case, was quite large." Seeing her perplexed expression, he added, "His nose. You could hide a band of gypsies under that nose of his."

She bumped against him, smiling. "Hey, have a little respect. He was our president, after all."

"Duly noted."

"Or, is it possible, as Sadie indicated, that the china really was defective," Tracey continued. "Remember she said Mrs. Lincoln replaced it with a whole new different set when her husband was re-elected? How sad that they never got to use any of it because he was assassinated."

"Somehow I doubt the First Lady gave it a thought, considering someone just *murdered* her husband."

"Duly noted."

Noah turned to face her, his hip still leaning against the wall. "So somehow, whether he just wanted a souvenir of his tenure there at the White House—"

"Or maybe he took it as proof that he'd actually worked there. Think about it. He'd always been this wild child, roaming half the country. Everybody back home probably thought he was an embarrassment to his family. There's no telling what they all thought of him."

Noah followed her lead. "Maybe it was just a last-minute whim on his way out the door. Maybe he was about to leave and noticed a tray with the cup and saucer just sitting there. So he grabs it, slips it under his jacket, and walks out the door."

Tracey nodded, a far-off look in her eyes as if imagining the entire scenario. "Then he comes home, maybe even tells his folks it was a parting gift from the Lincolns."

"But—being the *ne're-do-well* the townspeople knew him to be—maybe no one believed him. Or . . . or maybe, after all his bragging around town, he began to worry that someone might steal it."

Tracey faced him, continuing the supposition. "And Sadie said all this would have happened right about the time Craggie's father was having the new smokehouse built." She suddenly grabbed his arm, caught up in the imagery. "So he hid it in the wall because he was leaving to join the Confederate Army! Sadie told us he enlisted shortly after he got home, remember? He told his parents it was something he had to do, to fight in Evan's place."

He stared at her, a shudder rippling over him as his imagination drifted away from the image of the young man, and in its place, a deep and quite unexpected affection for the woman standing before him. She said nothing, her face still filled with wonder at the story they'd just shared. As if they'd both been there, witnessing the entire scene.

Her smile began to fade as she searched his eyes, no doubt distracted by his silence.

Kiss her . . . a voice seemed to whisper in his ear. He wondered where such a notion came from, and then he heard it again.

Kiss her!

And so he did.

He leaned down ever so slightly, his eyes still locked on hers. "Tracey . . . ?" Had he actually breathed her name? Or merely imagined it?

She hesitated only a moment. Then, "Yes?"

He swallowed, tamping down his own hesitation. "I think I'm going to kiss you." He hadn't meant for it to sound so matter-of-fact, but there it was.

Her eyes glistened in the moonlight as her face warmed with a smile. "I was hoping you would."

As his lips touched hers, something inside him shifted. Changed. Melted. Giving way to something he hadn't felt in a long, long time. Her arms slipped slowly around his waist, the familiar sound of their crinkling leather making him smile as their kiss lingered. He gathered her into his embrace, loving the warmth of her in his arms and admitting to himself he'd wanted to do this since last night on the back porch at Walnut Ridge. That he was actually holding her now beneath the stars and losing himself as she kissed him back . . . it all seemed too good to be true. And then that voice inside his head —the same one that had prompted him to kiss her—convinced him to stop all the analyzing and enjoy the moment.

And so he did.

Chapter 12

As the first rays of the morning sun crept into her room, Tracey rolled over on her back and pulled the comforter up to her chin. With her eyes still closed, she remembered Noah's first kiss last night on the bluff. Then the second and third . . . and somewhere along the way, she lost count. She smiled at the memory, still surprised how suddenly it happened, and the way her heart had skipped a beat when he wrapped her in his arms.

They'd stayed on the bluff talking until the autumn night's chill chased them home. She'd wrapped her arms around him all the way home, different somehow from the ride out there. Back at Walnut Ridge, she wasn't ready to say goodnight. Nor was he. They made hot chai lattes and sat by the fire in the den. There they talked for hours about the silliest things. His love of Jimmy Stewart movies. Her favorite indulgence—getting lost in historical novels until the wee hours of the morning. His utter disgust for sushi. Her instinctive gagging reflex at the sight and smell of Brussels sprouts, cabbage, and sauerkraut. His appreciation for a more relaxed life away from the big city. Her fondness for the old house and the chance to come home again.

When he asked what caused her to walk away from her job in Washington, she was evasive. She didn't want thoughts of Morgan to spoil their perfect evening, but somehow it all came spilling out. She'd noticed the tiny muscle on Noah's jaw twitching when she told him about that last night at the White House reception.

"You should report him, you know," he had said. "There are laws about these things."

"No, I could never do that, Noah. I couldn't do that to Amanda. Never."

Moments had passed. The old clock on the mantel slowly ticked as the fire beneath it crackled. Finally, he leaned back on the sofa and sighed. "I suppose it would be devastating—for her *and* for you. But it's not right. He was taking advantage of you. He doesn't deserve to stay in office."

"I know, but it's over now. I'm home."

"You haven't heard from him since you left?"

"Oh, I've heard from him. Last time I checked, he'd left thirty-seven voicemails and twenty-six text messages. I never answered, and I quit listening after my first night home."

"Thirty-seven voicemails? Twenty-six text messages? Tracey, that's a form of stalking. He's a U.S. Senator—doesn't he have anything better to do?"

"Can we please change the subject?"

He took her hand. "I'm sorry. Yes, by all means. Let's change the subject."

She pulled his hand free and lifted his arm around her shoulders, snuggling against him. They sat together silently for several moments. As his breathing steadied, she wondered if he was falling asleep. She turned to face him, pleased to find him gazing at her. "Can I ask you something?"

"Sure."

"After I met you the other day, I asked Alex about you."

"Must have been a brief and boring little chat."

"Not really."

"And what did Alex tell you?"

Tracey swallowed hard. "She told me you'd lost your wife."

Something in his countenance changed. She saw it in his eyes. He seemed to be holding his breath, and right away, she wished she'd never asked. When he said nothing, she did. "I'm sorry, Noah. Forget I asked."

"No," he said, quietly looking away, his eyes now fixed on the fire. "No, I . . . it's just that . . ." He pulled his arm from behind her and took both her hands in both of his. He slowly looked up at her, searching her eyes. "I've had a really nice time with you tonight, Tracey. And I really like you—I do."

He paused, briefly looking down at their hands as if searching for the right words. Her heart pounded, so afraid of what he might say next.

"I would really like to spend more evenings like this one with you. I'd like to see where that might go. But for now . . . " He blinked, moisture filling his eyes. "For now, I'd like to ask you if we could have that talk for another time." He closed his eyes, his expression pained. "If that's okay with you."

When he opened his eyes again, she pulled her hands free, then cupped his face with them. Unable to find the words, she'd simply nodded, then gently kissed him. "That's perfectly fine with me."

He'd held her quietly, then led her to the front door where he put on his jacket and with a final kiss, said goodnight.

Now, with last night's memory fresh in her mind, Tracey sat up and wondered at the whole incident. Would they have that chance to see where their relationship might lead? Or had she blown it, asking something so personal, so soon?

As her thoughts ran wild, her cell phone vibrated. Morgan. Again.

She threw back the covers and stepped into her slippers. “Senator, I have just one thing to say to you on this bright and beautiful morning—phhhbbbt!”

The old flannel-lined jacket felt good as Tracey made her way down to the barn. Ten minutes earlier she’d found a note by the coffee pot: *Got an early start this morning. I’m down at the barn so grab a cup and come join me! —Alex*

The oversized mug warmed her hands on this clear, brisk morning. She let herself drink in the sights and sounds and smells as she walked along the well-trodden path to the barn. Walnut Ridge had always been her balm, her refuge. The rustle of leaves beneath her feet reminded her how much she wasn’t missing Washington and the stress that always kept her in knots day and night. She pushed those thoughts away, not wishing to ruin such a beautiful day.

It’s so good to be home.

“It’s about time, Sleeping Beauty,” Alex teased as she set aside her paint brush. “Nice of you to join me this morning.”

Tracey hugged her with her free arm. “Just because I’m not up before the chickens doesn’t mean I’m a slacker. Look—” she said, lifting her wristwatch face up. “Five minutes after seven. Not too shabby.”

Alex placed a noisy kiss on her cheek and turned back to her paints. “Yeah, especially since you didn’t get to bed ’til after two.”

“Yeah? And how exactly do you know that?”

Alex whipped around with a broad smile on her face. “Well, kiddo, it’s not like Noah just tiptoed down the drive when he left.” She tucked a strand of hair behind her ear. “His Harley has a distinct rumble when it starts.”

“Ah. Well, I guess there’s no keeping secrets from you. But why do I feel like I’m in high school again, and you’re spying on me and one of my boyfriends?”

Alex laughed then squatted down on the floor beside the coffee table she was working on. “Nah, I left that to Mom and Dad. I was too busy reading my books.”

Tracey set her coffee cup on an upturned barrel. “Yeah, like Mom ever cared about what we did or didn't do. Y'know, I was thinking about her the other night before I went to sleep. And it dawned on me; she was probably going through menopause when all that happened."

Alex dipped her brush in the pale mustard-yellow paint and started brushing quick, efficient strokes on the coffee table. "I had the same thought a while back. Let's face it. Mom hit menopause and decided to fly to the moon. Or Hollywood, I guess. They're basically the same."

"Poor Daddy."

"Oh, Trace, stop with the poor Daddy stuff. He's fine."

"You honestly think so? I keep wondering if he's really as okay as he wants us to believe. Maybe beneath that ponytail, earring, and his proclaimed love for Stella, there's actually a broken heart that still beats for Mom. Maybe he's just hoping if he gives her enough time, she'll come back to him."

Alex glared at her. "I totally disagree. In fact, I've never seen him happier. Especially now that you're home. His little princess has returned to the castle."

Tracey grabbed a paint brush, dipped it in Alex's paint, and dashed the tip of her sister's nose with it.

"Well, aren't *you* the clown this morning?" Alex twisted around, attempting to return the favor just as Tracey jerked her head away. A long yellow streak reached from her nose to her ear. "Ah! Perfect! I always knew mustard was in your color wheel, and now we have proof!"

Tracey shrieked, her laughter bouncing against the rafters of the old barn.

"Settle down, girl. Don't make me paint you from head to toe."

"Ha! As if you could." Tracey grabbed a rag and peeked into the antique mirror they'd hung on the wall. Still snickering, she gently wiped the paint from her face.

"Okay, enough with the horse play. Get to work."

"You're not the boss of me."

"Am too."

"Are not."

"Am too." Alex raised a hand in surrender. "Okay, okay! I give up."

"Good. Because I've got work to do, and I'd appreciate it if you wouldn't keep distracting me."

"Ah, my little *seeester*, it's so good to have you home."

"Yeah, yeah. Hey, did you see the finish I put on my little step stool?"

"Yes, and it's perfect. Your first official baby. Congratulations!"

"Thank you, thank you." Tracey bowed, then held up the small stool admiring her work. The unusual bowed legs on the short white stepping stool had been a challenge. She assumed it had been left out in the rain at some point, all warped and beat up. It was the first thing she'd picked up at the estate sale, and for a dollar, she couldn't refuse it.

With Alex's help, she'd cleaned it, giving the strange little legs extra attention. Tracey used a coat of a near-black shade of gray called *Typewriter* on the legs. Then, using a true rich red shade called *Tricycle,* she painted the top of the stool to give it an interesting contrast. Once it had thoroughly dried, she distressed it, exposing some of the dark undercoat. The look had amazed her.

"And what have you named your first baby?"

"Oh. I completely forgot. Silly me." Tracey smiled. "Let's see. It's definitely a he and not a she."

"Absolutely."

"How about Stanley? A homage to his cute little legs."

"Hey, it's your call. Stanley sounds perfect."

"Stanley it is. Now what shall I work on next?"

"Wanna help me finish Fredo here? He needs another coat of *Boxwood.*"

"Ah, Fredo-the-Coffee Table." She pulled on her work smock. "Put me to work."

Tracey settled in next to her sister. "So, do you have favorites? Which of your *babies* did you like best?"

"I love them all, so I can't choose favorites. But there was a chest of drawers with a curved front that I absolutely adored. It took several days, waiting for it to speak to me and tell me what it wanted to be, what color, that sort of thing. But I was patient. Then one day I knew. She said her name was Beatrice, and she wanted a pale shade called *Linen* on top and a rich blue called *French Enamel* below. And that's what she got. I distressed her more than I usually do, but she loved it, and so did I. Then she let me know in no uncertain terms that she wanted glass knobs and pulls. And she was so right. Oh Sis, she was just *beautiful.*

"And here's the best part. I haven't mentioned this before, but I pray for each of these babies while I restore them."

"You *pray* for them? Okay . . ."

"I pray for the people who adopt them. But it was hard to let Beatrice go. Then one day my friend Gigi stopped by. She teaches with me at school. She and her husband were expecting their first child—a little boy—and she wanted some decorating ideas for her nursery. Trace, the split second she laid eyes on Beatrice, it was love at first sight! They had just painted the nursery walls a pastel shade of blue that matched the *French Enamel* just perfectly. And so it was that my Beatrice went home to care for Gigi's baby—"

"Alex, are those tears in your eyes?"

Alex put her brush down and wiped her face. "Oh, sure. I can't help it! Here I'd been praying for Beatrice, having *no* idea she would go home with my friend Gigi and be a part of her new baby's room! I love when things like that happen."

Tracey shook her head. "Who but my sister would see furniture restoration as a ministry? I love that about you, Sis."

Alex finished wiping her tears and picked up her brush, dipping it into the olive-gray-green *Boxwood* paint. "Think about it—why would God give us a passion for something unless we could somehow use it for His glory? But the whole idea of restoring something old and worn out into something new and useful didn't originate with me—God's been in the restoration business from the beginning of time."

Tracey thought for a moment. "You're right. Just look at Dad. And the rest of the Elders, for that matter."

"Speaking of which, tell me about last night. Did you have a nice time with Noah?"

Tracey couldn't help smiling. "Yeah," she nodded. "Really nice."

"Evidently. He stayed long enough."

"Well, we took a ride first, so he wasn't technically 'here' the whole time. We went out to the river bluff. My first time there, I might add."

Alex turned, her paint brush in mid-air. "Oh? Isn't that where all the kids used to go to make out?"

Tracey focused on her paint strokes. "Yeah, I guess."

"You guess?"

"Anyway, we just talked up there for a long time, then—"

"Did he kiss you?"

"What? You're awfully nosy this morning."

"Ah, so he *did* kiss you!"

"What is this, the inquisition? I'm not in high school anymore, y'know."

Alex busied herself painting again. "You like him?"

Tracey didn't answer at first. Hearing her sister's questions—well, it just felt weird. Tracey wasn't sure *she* was ready to let her mind go down that line of thinking, let alone discuss it with her sister.

Alex sat up again and looked at her. "Oh, dear."

"Oh-dear what?"

She returned to her work. "Nothing. Don't mind me."

Tracey felt her heart flutter and wondered why. Then, as she continued painting, she remembered Noah and the bluff and his first kiss . . .

And she smiled.

Chapter 13

Noah had just returned from another trip to the home improvement store when Buddy approached him on the porch of the smokehouse.

"Noah, I'm glad you're back. We just got word Mrs. Oglesby needs some help. That big ol' black walnut tree in her back yard finally keeled over. Made quite a mess of her garage."

"How can I help?"

"I'd like to leave most of the guys here to finish dry-walling, but I thought I'd get Gristle and Stump to bring their chainsaws and take care of the tree. You up for some minor roof repairs? I thought we could patch it up from the inside and get some shingles back on there before another storm rolls through."

"Works for me. When do you want to head over?"

"Soon as we can. Let's grab some of those shingles we had left over from the Farley's roof. I think they're in the barn if I'm not mistaken."

Noah felt a catch of apprehension knowing Tracey was probably at the barn working with Alex. He hadn't seen her since last night—well, this morning. He couldn't believe they'd stayed up half the night. He hadn't slept much when he finally got to bed, unable to get her off his mind. Over and over, he wished he hadn't reacted the way he did when she asked about Melissa. He thought he'd finally started living again, that the worst was all behind him—right up until Tracey asked him about the wife he'd lost. He could only hope she understood. She seemed to handle it okay last night.

He only wished *he* had handled it as well. Instead, the images of his wife, the wreck, and all those dark months he'd lost to grief played over and over like a slideshow through his mind . . . and sprinkled among them, flashes of Tracey's smile and the memory of how good she felt in his arms. He tried to shake it off before seeing her again. Especially in front of Buddy and Alex.

A few minutes later, Buddy backed the pickup to the barn door and they got out.

Buddy stepped into the barn. "How's it going, sweetheart?"

Alex dusted off her hands on her smock. "Hi, Dad. Hey, Noah. What are you two doing here?"

"Just stopped by to pick up some shingles." As Buddy told her about Mrs. Oglesby's roof problem, Noah noticed Tracey coming from the back of the cluttered barn. When she looked up and saw him, she smiled.

"Hi, Noah."

"Hi, Tracey."

He could almost feel the abrupt silence in the air as Buddy and Alex just stood there looking at them. By the grin on Alex's face, he knew Tracey must have told her about their evening together. But how much had she told her?

Awkward.

"Well, then," Tracey finally said, "what's this about Mrs. Oglesby?"

Buddy explained the situation again and the plan to fix her roof. "We'll just load up some of those shingles back here then be out of your way."

"You're not in our way," Alex said. "In fact, take Tracey with you. She can help. Might be fun for her to see you and the Elders in action."

Tracey turned to her sister with her back to Noah. By the tilt of her head, he could only imagine the look she was giving Alex. Just as quickly, she turned back around with an exaggerated smile plastered on her face. "I'd love to. Let me get some gloves, and I'll meet you in the truck."

"Good," Noah said. He returned Alex's smile. "Good."

"You said that," Alex said.

"I know. Well, bye for now."

"Bye, Noah."

An hour later, Gristle and Stump had most of the tree limbs off the roof and had started cutting them for firewood. After making the repairs inside the garage, Noah and Buddy helped Tracey up onto the roof, and the three of them set to work pulling off the damaged shingles. Once that was done, they started hammering the new shingles in place.

At first, conversation had been difficult with the chainsaws buzzing below. Eventually Gristle and Stump finished and started stacking the logs.

Tracey reached for another shingle. "How often do you all do this sort of thing, helping folks out when they have emergencies?"

"All the time," Buddy answered. "When I started getting to know these guys on the bike trips, I kept feeling like I needed to do something." He hammered a few times and continued. "It felt like God was telling me to reach out to them, but in a specific way.

Problem was, I couldn't figure out what that meant. So for the longest time I just kept praying, waiting for some kind of sign or direction from the Lord. Well, as you are well aware, my dear daughter," he said with a smile, "sometimes I'm a little slow on the draw. It finally dawned on me that one of the things that had helped me so much after my world caved in was taking my eyes off my own troubles and looking for other folks who needed a hand. Best medicine on the planet.

"And that's when I decided to give these guys a dose of that medicine. The Bible says that helping widows and orphans in their time of distress is one of the 'purest forms of religion.' So I made a few calls, mostly to the older residents here in Jacobs Mill asking them to let me know if they had any odd jobs or projects they needed help with. I started getting requests, so I made a simple offer to some of the guys asking if they could help out. And little by little we got a reputation for doing these jobs well and efficiently." Buddy held up his hammer. "I kept thinking, with every nail we hit or tree we clear away, we're demonstrating the love of Christ, pure and simple." He tossed her a wink and banged his hammer down to prove his point.

Noah finished hammering a shingle and looked over at Tracey. "I wish you could have seen some of those little old ladies when we first rolled up their driveways on our Harleys." He and Buddy laughed. "I guess they thought the Hells Angels had arrived. They'd peek out from behind their curtains, probably convinced we were there to trash the place."

"Then after a while, they'd warm up to us," Buddy added. "Course, they all knew *me*, and let me know right up front they wished I'd cut my hair and shave my beard." He shook his head as he smiled. "But God love 'em, every single one of them gave my guys a chance. Took a while, but they finally learned to look beyond the loud motorcycles and shaggy appearances and just accept them for who they are."

Noah wiped his forehead with his bandana. "You should have seen the day Mrs. Peterson tiptoed out of her house carrying lemonade out to 'her boys' as she called us. You could tell she was still nervous about us by the way the ice in those glasses kept rattling—" Noah re-enacted the widow's trembling hands carrying an imaginary tray. "I thought she might just die from fright then and there."

"Oh, poor Mrs. Peterson!" Tracey chuckled. "But how sweet of her to do that, even though you all must have terrified her."

Buddy hooted. "Glory, by the time we finished painting her house, she was sending *her boys* home with pecan pies and watermelon and fried chicken—you never saw such a love fest." He paused, slowly lowering his hammer. "But I'll never forget the day

Stump leaned *waaaay* down to give her a hug, then swept her right off her feet and twirled her around in a circle."

Tracey laughed so hard, Noah was afraid she might fall off the roof. "Knowing Mrs. Peterson, I bet she shrieked with delight!"

"Oh, you should have seen that dear old soul," Buddy said. "To this day, she has a standing invitation for Stump to come for Tuesday night dinner. Those two are a sight to behold." He paused for a moment, looking down across the yard where Stump and Gristle were still piling the tree logs. "But Tracey . . ."

When he paused, both Noah and Tracey looked up at him. Noah could see the moisture in his eyes and the slight tremble of his lips.

"Tracey, what that woman has done for that big giant of a man—well, I can hardly find words for it. He came from such an *awful* background. No daddy. A mom who didn't want him. Kicked around from one orphanage to another. And you can only imagine how all the other kids treated him, like he was some kind of freak. A horrible life from the day he was born. Stuff I won't share because I consider it confidential as his friend and pastor, but also because it's the stuff of nightmares."

"When I first met him," Noah began, "he scared me to death. Mean as a snake and every word out of his mouth was—well, 'vulgar' doesn't even come close."

"He kept everybody at a distance," Buddy continued. "Nobody liked him and most of them hated when he'd show up for our rides. But y'know, after a while you'd catch him pretending not to listen when we'd talk about the Lord. And trust me, Tracey Jo, these conversations about the Lord were nothing like you'd hear at church. Oh, no sir, not even close."

Noah reached for more nails. "Yeah, it could get pretty raunchy. Definitely not for the faint of heart."

"Then slowly but surely," Buddy continued, "he just—I guess the best way to put it, he just started to melt. His walls started crumbling down. He still didn't say much, but you could just tell he wasn't so angry and ready to bite your head off every time you were around him.

"Not long after that, we had a big storm come through. Tornados hopping all over the county. The boys and I immediately jumped into action, helping at the homes that had suffered the worst damage. And lo and behold—there was Stump. Never said a word, just started working with us, side by side. And after that, he was just one of us."

"You said Mrs. Peterson—"

"Oh, yeah. By the time we painted her house, Stump had come a long, long way. But he still held back. You could just tell. He and I had talked by then, and I'd told him how much God loved him, and how his past was all behind him if he'd let Jesus have his future. But he just couldn't seem to believe it. But then that tiny little wisp of a woman started having him come to dinner once a week . . ."

Noah smiled at Tracey after they both noticed the tears spilling down Buddy's cheeks.

"Go on, Daddy. Tell me what happened."

He wiped his eyes and blew his nose then started again. "Never saw anything like it. She just loved on him. Cared for him. *Mothered* him." Buddy stopped again, then just gave in to it and let the tears flow. "And Tracey, all that love just got up inside Stump's heart and dissolved every last ounce of resistance he'd been holding onto. He and Mrs. Peterson got down on their knees—right there in her kitchen—and ol' Stump gave his heart to Jesus. And he has never been the same. Oh, he's still shaggy on the outside, but he's just a big ol' teddy bear in here." Buddy tapped on his heart, laughing through his tears. "Lord! Look at me, blubbering like a kid who just lost his marbles. Which might be closer to the truth than we know." He laughed again, wiping his eyes. "I just can't help it when I start talking about all the miracles God's been doing in the lives of my guys."

"Dad, that may be the sweetest story I've heard in years. I love what you've done for your guys—your *Elders.*"

"No, it wasn't me, Tracey Jo. It was God. All God. Every bit of it."

"Don't let his humility fool you," Noah said. "He always tells us it's the Holy Spirit that convicts us, not him. But without your dad here, none of us would be here doing this. We'd all still be screwed up and . . . messed up."

"Noah, I'm only doing what God led me to do. When my brother Rob dragged my sorry carcass out of the house a couple years ago, I'd pretty much lost the will to live. And he told me I basically had two choices. I could spend the rest of my life feeling sorry for myself and building a monument of hate to those who'd 'done me wrong' as he put it. Or I could get off my keister, kick out of that self-imposed prison of pity, and start over. Make a fresh start.

"Here he was, my own brother, telling *me* how to let God give me another chance. Rob, my crazy biker beach bum brother from Naples, Florida, telling me—the pastor—about forgiveness and purpose and the unconditional grace and love of Christ." Buddy raised his hands in the air. "Ah, the strange and mysterious ways of Almighty God whose wonders never cease! Can I get an amen, brothers and sisters?"

Tracey laughed and shouted, "Hallelujah, amen!"

"I'll second that hallelujah and raise you two more," Noah quipped.

"Daddy, how come you never told me all this before? I wish I'd known."

"Well, sweetheart, as I recall you haven't been around much."

"Ouch?"

"No, I didn't mean it that way. I'm just saying you were living your life, and I was living mine. It is what it is. But as the great Paul Harvey used to say, 'and now you know the rest of the story.' And that's what matters most."

Tracey put down her hammer and carefully crawled up to where her father sat on the ridge of the roof. She scooted beneath his arm and wrapped hers around him. "I love you, Daddy. I'm so proud of you."

Not wishing to impose on their private moment, Noah bit his lip and looked away. He also didn't want them to see the dam threatening to burst just beneath the surface inside him. It unnerved him, this inability to keep his feelings under control. He vowed to spend some time back at the cottage and try to get his emotions in check.

He pounded another nail then gazed over at Tracey as she made her way back to her work spot. Just then she looked up. And as she did, the kindest possible expression seemed to glow on her face. As if she were telling him—*it's gonna be okay. Trust me.*

And oh, how he wanted to believe her.

Chapter 14

That night after dinner, Tracey turned on her laptop and opened her email. She'd avoided it as long as she could. She knew Morgan wasn't stupid enough to put anything in writing, short of a cryptic "office" issue that he needed to discuss with her. Sure enough, as the new emails flooded her inbox she saw his name on a handful. Reading the first one confirmed what she'd expected. He needed to ask her something about her notes on that matter with Senator Crawford and would she please give him a call.

Not happening.

She browsed through the rest of them, nothing urgent popping out. Most everyone assumed she was still on vacation and had the decency not to bother her. But she couldn't stop thinking about the voicemail Amanda had left the day Tracey flew home. She prayed Amanda would never have to know why she was leaving her job with Morgan. Sometimes, while lost in her thoughts as she painted, she tried to think of a way to explain her reasons without lying, but without having to tell her best friend the blunt truth.

Tracey took a deep breath and blew it out, then offered up a prayer for guidance. Then she opened a new email and started typing.

Dear Amanda,

I'm so sorry I forgot about meeting you for breakfast the day I left! I had so much to wrap up before leaving town, and honestly, it just slipped my mind. A thousand apologies. And please tell Aaron how sorry I am that I missed his call. You can just tell him Aunt Taycee lost her mind and has gone away in hopes of finding it. Or something.

I'm having such a great time here with Dad and Alex. The weather has been gorgeous. Alex is opening a new shop where she can sell the amazing vintage furniture pieces she's been restoring. Amanda, you would love what she's doing. I've never seen her so happy. And yes, she's no longer teaching . . . long story, which I'll explain another time. I've been helping her and loving every minute of it.

You'd also be happy to know I've met someone . . . He's one of Dad's friends (my age, thankfully!) and it's been really nice getting to know him. I'd forgotten what it was like to go out on an actual date again. His name is Noah, and I know you'd love him. We'll see what happens next.

Tracey's hands rested on the keyboard. She started and stopped three times, carefully deleting lines she couldn't finish, words that felt untrue. She mentioned the possibility of staying longer than she'd planned, then quickly erased those words too. She knew Amanda would have called or texted or written if Morgan had told her she quit, so she certainly didn't want to go there. Fifteen minutes of starts and stops came and went. *Oh, for heaven's sake. She's my best friend! Why can't I just—*

But of course she couldn't. She would deal with it when she had to. Tonight was not the time.

I hope you've had a great week. I miss you, but thanks for under-standing why I'm keeping my phone off and not checking email. I just really needed this break. Take care and keep me in your prayers.

Love you,

Tracey

She prayed another prayer—this one for Amanda. *She needs it more than I do, that's for sure.* Tracey closed her laptop and set it aside.

"TRACEY JO?"

She smiled, remembering all the years her dad had called up the stairs just like that. She padded to the top of the stairs. "What do you need, Dad?"

"Me? Not a thing. But Noah's here." He quirked a silly grin and danced his eyebrows. "Just thought you might want to know."

"Yeah?" she said with feigned indifference.

"He's out in the kitchen. Why don't you come down and say hello?"

She grinned. "Why didn't you say so? I'll be down in a sec."

She dashed into her bathroom and brushed her teeth, brushed out her hair, and put on some lip gloss. A minute later she went downstairs.

Noah stood up from the kitchen table as she entered. "Hi, Tracey."

His sheepish grin tickled her, knowing it had everything to do with her dad's presence. "Hey, Noah. I would've thought you'd had enough of the two of us after spending half the day with us on Mrs. Oglesby's roof."

His smile widened. "You'd think, wouldn't you?"

She smiled back. Then they both looked at Buddy.

"Oh. Okay, I think I'll go upstairs and read for a while." He stood up and grabbed his cup of coffee. "If that's okay with the two of you?"

"Fine with me, Dad."

"Fine with me too, Buddy."

"Well then, it's unanimous. G'night, you two."

He headed for the kitchen door, his old slippers slapping against the oak floor. Just before leaving, he turned and gave Noah a nod of the head. Another smile and he was gone.

Tracey reached for a mug from the cabinet and poured herself a cup of coffee. "What was that all about?"

Noah sat back down at the table, his hands wrapped around his mug. "Ah, you know your dad. Nothing, really."

"Nothing really, huh? Want me to warm you up?"

Startled, he looked at her with the strangest expression. Then his eyes landed on the coffee pot in her hand. "Oh . . . sure. Please."

Tracey snickered. "My, my, Mr. Bennett. Surely you didn't think—"

"Well, surely I did." He raised his cup, a guilty smile on his face.

"You did?" She topped off his coffee and put the carafe back on the burner.

As she turned around, he reached for her hand and silently led her into the den. She had hoped he might come by tonight. Her thoughts seemed to be consumed with Noah and wanting to see him again.

Preferably alone.

She couldn't help it. She was thrilled he'd come to see her, and even happier he'd led her back to the same exact spot where they'd been the night before. They set their coffee cups on the table and took a seat on the sofa.

Same sofa. Same fire blazing on the hearth. Same heart pounding inside her chest.

He put his arm around her shoulder and pulled her close. "Wow, you smell *really* good."

"I could say the same for you," she said, lifting her face to his. "In fact, you clean up pretty nice for a roofer."

"I try."

"You succeed."

He took a deep breath and let out a long, contented sigh. "It was nice having you out there with us today. You're not much of a roofer, but—"

"Hey! I think I kept up with you and Dad, so what's the problem?"

"Just kidding. The thing is . . ."

"Yes? The thing is . . ?"

"Tracey, ever since last night, I haven't been able to think straight. I know I got kind of, well . . . the thing is—"

"There's that *thing* again. Out with it, Noah."

"I can't stop thinking about you." He shrugged. "There I said it. "I can't. I tried, but I can't."

She laughed, momentarily dropping her head to her chest. Finally, leaning back and pushing her hair out of her face, she looked up. "Ah, that's too funny, because *the thing is* . . ." she paused, prolonging the anxious look in his eyes, "*this* is all *I've* thought about today." She placed her lips on his and felt a wave of butterflies skitter through her stomach as he wrapped her in his arms and kissed her back.

Tracey felt herself relax in his arms, feeling the warmth of his body so close to hers, loving the scent of his clean skin against her face. It felt so right—so secure, so perfect. As his kisses grew more intense, she felt something else. A desire so unlike anything she'd ever known before. It was too much, too good, too soon—but she didn't care.

Slow down, slow down, slow down!

Tracey stopped herself, pulling away, startling both of them.

"What's wrong?" he breathed. "Did I do something—?"

"No." She placed her hand against his chest. "No, not at all. I just . . ."

I just feel myself falling for you, and the thought of that scares me!

She'd never been in love. Lots of boyfriends. Lots of kicks, but never anything like this . . . "Whoa."

"Whoa?" The hint of alarm in his eyes calmed her, made her smile.

"Whoa. I'm, uh, I think maybe I was just getting a little too . . . carried away." She ducked her eyes, embarrassed.

He didn't say anything but slowly tucked her back under his arm and leaned his head against hers. "Well, then. We'll just have to work on that. Take things a little slower."

Whew. Tracey wondered why it seemed like she was on a roller coaster every time she was with Noah. It didn't make sense, but at the same time, she could tell she was falling for him. Falling hard. And that concerned her.

"Probably a good idea," she said, putting those thoughts aside. She reached for her coffee and handed his to him.

Noah took a sip. "There's something I want to ask you."

"Oh?"

"A bunch of the guys are going on a ride on Saturday, and I was wondering if you'd like to come along. With me, I mean."

She smiled, relieved that they'd changed the subject. "Is that why Dad was acting so goofy a few minutes ago?"

He set his mug down, chuckling. "Yeah. I'd asked him if he thought you might like to go. Obviously, he does."

"Will I be the only female on this little adventure?"

"I don't know. Maybe? But you won't be the first. Gristle mentioned bringing someone he's been seeing."

"Gristle's seeing someone? Have you met her?"

"No, but to hear him you'd think she's part Beyoncé, part Mother Teresa."

Tracey laughed. "Now there are two names you don't often see together."

"I know, which is why I'm actually curious to meet her."

"Me too. But tell me where you all are headed Saturday. Will I get saddle sores from hours and hours of riding?"

"No way," he said, a smile forming. "As I recall, you didn't seem to mind last night."

"No, but that was a short little hop."

"We're heading over to Natchez Trace Parkway and riding down to Tupclo."

"That's pretty far, isn't it?"

"Not to a biker."

She narrowed her eyes. "Is that some kind of dare?"

His raised a brow. "Not unless you'd like it to be."

She wasn't at all sure she was up to it, but Tracey wasn't about to let him know that. She raised her chin, shooting him more confidence than she felt. "Sure, I'll go. What time do we leave?"

"Early. So don't keep me up half the night on Friday. I'll need my rest. Never a good thing to doze off behind the wheel."

"Before sunrise or after?"

He tugged at a strand of her hair. "Neither. We leave right at sunrisc.

"Not a problem."

"One more question."

"Now what?" she teased.

"Do you have plans tomorrow night?"

"I don't think so. Why?"

"There's somewhere I'd like to take you. But we'll need to see if

Buddy would loan us his car."

"As long as it's not his ratty old pickup, I'm fine with that."

"Exactly. I was hoping for something a little more comfortable."

"I'm sure he won't mind. But where are you taking me?"

"It's for me to know and you to find out. Dinner's involved, just so you know."

"Blue jeans or ball gown?"

He tilted his head. "More like something in-between."

"Ah. Then I'll send my boa out to be cleaned."

Chapter 15

The team was making considerable progress on the smokehouse. The electricians had wired the shop and added plenty of recessed lighting per Alex's wishes. The plumbers had set all the water pipes in place to provide running water, and the carpenters had successfully replaced the interior walls and cathedral ceiling with mismatched weathered planks to retain the vintage look. Similar weathered planks were used on the floor of the large front porch. And behind the building, a covered deck would provide room as a gathering area. Just beyond the deck, the Elders built a fire pit which the girls surrounded with primitive chairs and colorful cushions to encourage customers to relax and chat.

As Tracey and Alex entered the shop from the back door, they could barely contain themselves.

"I cannot believe how much they've done in such a short amount of time. Look at this place!"

Tracey could already feel the ambiance coming together even before the final touches had been added. The large back room would be their studio, out of sight to the customers behind a new wall separating the two rooms. With plenty of cabinets to store their materials and a large workbench in the center of the room, they would have a perfect work environment. Noah had suggested a couple of skylights cut in the roof to give them natural light in addition to the track lighting directly above the workbench.

The front showroom with its pitched ceiling made the room feel open and airy, giving them ample space for the constant flow of pieces they'd stage. She and Alex had ordered bright pillows and rugs to soften the room, as well as long curtains made of vintage fabrics to dress the windows. Alex found a ridiculously good deal on some quirky lamps to set on tables here and there giving the room a cozy feel. Up in the attic at Walnut Ridge, they'd found some surprisingly well-preserved upholstered chairs to use for seating as customers contemplated their purchases.

Tucked in the back right corner of the shop, the checkout counter offered endless possibilities. The spacious wooden counter Stump built them would provide plenty of room to wrap purchases. Slotted nooks beneath would house all their supplies. At an estate sale, the girls found a tall square pillar which they decided to use as a caddy for the brown paper sacks, twine, and assorted colors of tissue paper they'd use to bag smaller purchases. Tracey refinished it in a creamy sage and attached vintage decorative hooks to the sides and front. Perfect.

They continued wandering through the shop, making notes of display ideas and items that still needed attention. Gradually, they made their way out the front door and into the small lawn where they could stand back and take it all in. Tracey suggested the possibility of hanging floor-to-ceiling curtains made of outdoor fabric on each of the posts to "frame" the porch and make it feel more welcoming. They decided to put a few rustic rockers and chairs cushioned in coordinating fabrics, as well as seasonal flowers and greenery to cheer the entrance.

As they turned to admire the storefront, they noticed Hank and Lester up top, securing the awning that would cover the front porch. Alex and Tracey hadn't decided quite what to do, whether to purchase a fabric awning or go with more of the aged wooden slats. Then early that morning, Hank and Lester had surprised them by showing up with a pile of rusted sheets of corrugated metal. The look would give the awning a more rustic appearance. Alex and Tracey had been skeptical, but once the two Elders started putting it together, the girls both loved it.

Tracey marveled now, watching the shop take on an entirely different look. "Who knew rusty old metal could add so much charm?"

Alex leaned close, speaking out of the side of her mouth. "Seriously, Sis, don't you wonder how on earth those two came up with such a thing?"

Tracey snickered. "Oh, to have been a fly on the wall for *that* discussion. Can't you just hear it?" She and Alex played the parts, keeping their voices low.

"Copper?"

"Yep."

"Awning."

"Sure."

"The dump?"

"Why not."

The sisters laughed, causing Lester and Hank to look up from their work.

"Looks great, guys! We love it!" Alex cheered.

"Totally makes the look of the shop," Tracey added. "You guys are geniuses!"

The two awkward young men tried to hide their smiles but didn't succeed. Without a word, they went back to work.

Buddy and Noah came around the corner to join the girls.

"I've got to hand it to you," Buddy said, observing the dramatic changes on the old smokehouse. "You guys have outdone yourselves on this one."

"Who, us?" Hank asked.

"Well, not just you—*all* of you. It's been a team effort from the first day. Just look at how far we've come in a matter of days! Noah, have you ever seen anything like it?"

He smiled, shaking his head. "Not even close. I feel like we're on one of those makeover shows on TV where a team comes in and completely overhauls a house in one week."

"Ah, those guys?" Stump came up behind them, giving Buddy a pat on the back. "We'd give those turkeys a run for their money. Course, we don't have a hundred folks workin' behind the scenes, so it's taken a little longer, but they ain't got nothin' on us."

"Still, it's amazing," Noah said. "Absolutely amazing."

Buddy scratched the back of his head. "Now, if I can just convince Deacon to come around. He's determined to find some piddlysquat ordinance on the books to keep us from opening as a business. You wouldn't believe the lame attempts he's made so far." He put his worn baseball cap on his head backwards. "I honestly believe that man's entire purpose in life is to make me miserable. His sole reason for walking on this earth."

"I keep askin'—you want us to pay him a visit?" Stump offered. "All you've gotta do is ask."

"No, but thanks for offering—again. I learned a long time ago to let the Lord fight my battles. He can handle them much better than I ever could. Things always seem to work out better when He's calling the shots."

"I keep meaning to ask," Noah began. "Why's he called Deacon? That's surely not his real name?"

"Nah, his real name is Deke. But once he took over as chairman of the deacons at the church, folks just started calling him Deacon. He rather liked the title."

"Enough about Deacon," Tracey said. "Dad, the workbench in the back studio looks incredible! I can't wait to get all our paints and materials in there. "

"And the sooner the better," Alex added. "Our babies are complaining about the cold nights out in the barn. They'll love the nice warm heat up here."

Buddy snapped his fingers and looked at his daughters. "That reminds me, did DeAnne Barlowe find you two?"

"Yes!" Alex said. "She told us you sent her down to the barn.

Would you believe she bought that dining table and six chairs we just got in? We haven't even started refinishing them yet!"

"She told us she was heading up to Nashville to buy something for her renovated dining room," Tracey added, "but then she heard we were opening a shop, so she stopped by to see us first."

Alex continued. "She was thrilled because this way she got to pick out the color and finish to match her decor. And she paid us full price—on the spot! She even said she was going to show before-and-after pictures on her blog and tell everyone about us. Did you know she has over 10,000 blog followers?"

"What's a blog follower?"

They all turned to look up at Lester on the roof. When no one said a word, Tracey intervened. "A blog is an online journal. Like if you kept a journal—say, a journal about your hobbies or your work or maybe just a place to share the books you've read. Then you post it online and other people read it and make comments on it. It's a popular means of social networking."

Lester stared at her, blinking twice before scratching his chin. "But I don't have a hobby."

"Oh, well, you don't have to have a hobby to blog," Alex said. "Trace was just using that as an—"

"And I don't like to read."

"No, Lester," Buddy said, chuckling. "See, all she was trying to say was—"

"And I don't have an online either." Lester went back to work, turning his back to them. Apparently, he was through with the conversation.

"Okay, then!" Buddy laughed as he turned to go. "Well, I've got to skedaddle. Pray for my meeting with Deacon so I don't punch his lights out. Noah, you still have those boxing gloves I loaned you?"

"Sure thing. Stop by the cottage if you want to pick them up. They're on the coffee table right next to my sword."

Buddy turned around, walking backwards toward his bike. "Hey, now—a sword duel with Deacon. That has possibilities!"

Alex turned to go back into the shop. "Bye, Dad. Good luck."

Just then Gristle rolled up on his Harley and parked right beside Buddy's bike. "What's this? Some kinda party goin' on and no one calls me?"

"You just about missed me," Buddy said, putting his helmet on. "You okay? We were wondering where you were this morning."

Gristle took off his helmet and stepped off his bike. "Well, I needed to catch a *class* this morning, if you know what I mean." He glanced at Buddy sheepishly.

"Ah." Buddy reached over to grab Gristle's shoulder. "Good for you."

Tracey looked at Noah with questioning eyes.

"A.A.," he mouthed with a smile.

"Oh," she said silently.

"Mr. Daniels been calling you again?" Buddy asked.

"Yeah, he sho 'nuff been callin'. That dude must got me on speed dial. Called me a good *six times* 'fore I got up and just left. I never answered. I wanted to, but I didn't."

Tracey looked back to Noah for help.

"*Jack* Daniels," he mouthed.

"Oh," she mouthed again.

"But don't you worry none, Buddy. I called my girl, and we found us a church service to go to. Good thing it was a Wednesday night, huh?"

"Good for you." Buddy wrapped his arm over Gristle's shoulders. "I like this girl already. When do we get to meet her?"

Gristle looked over at Noah and Tracey. "That's what I was wantin' to ask. Okay if I bring her along Saturday?" He flashed a goofy smile. "Maleeka, she *loves* my bike."

"Maleeka?" Tracey said. "What a beautiful name."

"Yes it is, Miss Tracey, but it ain't half as pretty as she is."

"Ah, that's so sweet. I hope you'll bring her. I'm riding with Noah, so it'll be nice to have at least one other female on the trip."

"Tell her we'd love to have her join us," Buddy said just before keying his ignition. "Just don't be late!" With a salute off of his helmet, he turned the bike and headed out.

"I goin' park my bike out back and get to work," Gristle said. "Okay wid' you if I start varnishin' that workbench?"

"That'd be great," Noah said. "I'll go wipe it down for you. Varnish is already inside."

"Perfect. See you later, Miss Tracey."

"Bye, Gristle. I'm looking forward to meeting Maleeka on Saturday."

The goofy grin returned as Gristle cranked his bike to life again. "Ah, you goin' like her. She' sumpin' else."

As Gristle took off, Tracey tugged on the bill of Noah's ball cap. "I've got to get down to the barn and help Alex. We've still got a lot of work to do."

"You sure you've got time to go to dinner with me tonight?" he asked.

As Tracey turned to go, she folded her arms across her chest as a cool breeze kicked up the fallen leaves around them. "For you? I'll make time. Dad said we could take his car. I think I heard him vacuuming it out early this morning. How funny is that?"

Noah stepped up on the porch. "A man and his machines. It's a beautiful thing. Pick you up about five, okay?"

"I'll be ready," she said. "Me 'n my boa."

"You mean, you and your *beau*?"

Tracey smiled as he disappeared inside the shop.

Me and my beau?

Even better.

Chapter 16

Noah still hadn't told Tracey where they were going. Taking the long, winding mountainous road heading east, he'd easily dodged all her questions. They'd been driving just over an hour when he pulled into the gravel parking lot.

"This is it?"

"This is it," he answered, sliding the Buick Regal into an open space. "I promise you're going to love it. Welcome to High Point."

He opened the car door for her then took her hand as they made their way toward the enormous three-story stone mansion with the cobblestone roof. "Looks like it belongs back east. In those old neighborhoods in New York."

"New York, eh?"

"So what's the big secret? Why didn't you just tell me about this place?"

"Ah, you'll just have to wait and see. This old house has all kinds of secrets to tell."

They stepped under the covered entrance and through the heavy arched front door. Inside, a hostess greeted them, acknowledged Noah's reservation, then led them to a room with lots of windows, low lights, and a large stone fireplace toward the back. Seating them in the corner beside the hearth, she left menus with them and said their waiter would be with them shortly.

"Interesting place, Noah."

He watched as Tracey looked around the room, taking in the tablecloths, folded napkins standing like pyramids on plates, candlelight on each table, and the fire crackling just beside them.

Her face glowed with curiosity. "It's positively magical in here."

After their waiter served their drinks and took their orders, Tracey crossed her arms and leaned her elbows on the table. "All right. Out with it. What's so mysterious about this place?"

He smiled, reaching for her hand. "High Point has quite a history. You are sitting in a home once built and owned by Al Capone."

"Right. And that couple over there is Bonnie and Clyde."

"Now, Tracey," he chided like a patient school teacher. "In fact, this was a stopping point for the famous mob boss as he traveled from Chicago down to Florida. Capone had it built in 1929. Supposedly there's a whole system of underground tunnels beneath us that helped Capone transport his liquor during Prohibition. I don't know if it's true or not, but supposedly, there's a layer of sand between the floor here and the tunnels below to stop any bullets from penetrating."

"So you're really serious? This really belonged to Capone?"

"I've also heard he built the house for one of his mistresses. Which was convenient, of course, since it was right on his way to Florida."

He watched Tracey study the room again, this time with believing eyes. Turning to look out the windows, Noah noticed the sun had set and the growing darkness outside had engulfed the back patio area in an eerie shroud of fog.

She looked back at him. "Seems like they should be playing the theme from *The Godfather* instead of Tony Bennett."

The waiter returned with their dinners—a bourbon-marinated rib-eye served with a fully-loaded baked potato and Caesar salad for Noah; a filet mignon served with a burgundy mushroom sauce, accompanied by steamed asparagus with hollandaise and an applewood spinach salad for Tracey.

"This is *so good*," Tracey said, slicing off another bite of her steak. "How did you find this place?"

"One day I was out for a ride by myself, and I pulled off here in Monteagle for gas. When I asked the guy at the counter where he'd recommend for dinner, it was either McDonald's or 'a real swanky place' up the road, as he put it. It was about this time of day, so I decided to check it out. One of the best meals I've had in years. And you can't beat the ambiance."

Tracey touched her napkin to her lips. "So you just hop on your Harley and go for rides whenever the mood hits?"

Noah felt a stab near his heart, unsettled that she'd unknowingly hit so close to home. That was exactly what he did—take to the open road whenever the memories and thoughts threatened to overwhelm him.

"Noah?"

"Something like that." His smile didn't feel legit, but it would have to do. Glimpsing the concern in her eyes, he busied himself with a sip of water. *Change the subject. Quick.*

"What have you heard from Miss Sadie? Anything new about the Lincoln cup and saucer?"

She rested her fork back on her plate. "I can't believe I forgot to tell you! She stopped by the house early this morning to tell me she'd contacted the Smithsonian. You should have seen her, Noah. Her face was wild with excitement again, just like it was that first day she found out about the cup and saucer."

"What did they tell her? The folks at the Smithsonian."

"They said they'll send a team to investigate and determine whether it really is an original. Apparently, it's quite common for companies to make reproductions of presidential china patterns. Sadie said the person she talked to wasn't convinced ours were authentic. That's why she's so eager for them to see for themselves. And not just the teacup and saucer, but the note and letter from Craggie Collins as well."

"If they validate its authenticity, will you donate it to the Smithsonian?"

"I'm not sure. Alex, Dad, and I haven't had time to talk through all of that yet."

"I suppose not, with everything else going on."

They talked about the progress on the shop and possible time frames for its opening, what else needed to be done, and the ideas Tracey and Alex had for decorating once it was ready. Noah loved the way her eyes lit up when she described the new business and all the potential it held.

"I didn't have a chance to talk to Buddy after his meeting with Deacon and Faye, did you?"

The sparkle in her eyes quickly faded as she relayed Buddy's comments when he got home.

"Never mind that our shop will bring people to town who've never been there before. We have plans to advertise throughout the mid-south. We've been working with a friend to design a website for us, and we'll use all the usual social media networks to get the word out, showcase our pieces, and all that. So you'd think Deacon would be pleased at the prospect of having folks discover our little town, and visit the other shops and restaurants. But no—instead he's trying every possible angle to stop us from opening. It makes no sense."

The waiter cleared their dishes and Noah ordered coffee and dessert, though Tracey said she couldn't eat another bite. "But wait until you taste this grilled pound cake. You won't believe it."

The waiter returned with an enormous slice of the grilled confection, a generous mound of vanilla bean ice cream resting on top, all drizzled with a caramel sauce.

"There's enough here for four people, let alone two!"

He handed her a fork. "Oh, I think I can handle it. Here, just taste it." He held the bite to her lips.

A moment later, she closed her eyes. "Oh, that is just decadent."

"Told you."

"Hand me the other fork. I think I suddenly found room for this."

Later, as they finished their coffee, Noah mustered his courage and took her hand. "This is nice. I'm glad we came."

"Me too." She breathed in slowly, then let out a long sigh. "Even though I've only been back a few days, it seems like months now. I can't tell you how much I needed an evening like this." She smiled, her eyes sparkling in the candlelight. "I'm glad you brought me here."

Noah rubbed his thumb slowly against the back of her hand. "Tracey, I need you to know that . . ." He'd rehearsed this in his mind before they left Jacobs Mill. Now, at the perfect moment to say what he wanted to say, the words eluded him.

Tracey leaned forward. "What is it?"

He gave her a nervous smile and pushed through the jitters wreaking havoc with his gut. "I just wanted to say that . . . I'm really thankful we met. I certainly never saw it coming. Ever since I've known Buddy, I've heard about you. I guess you know he's really proud of both his daughters. He talks about you all the time."

"Really?" she asked, tilting her head.

"To listen to him, you pretty much run Washington."

She laughed. "Yeah, I can see him saying that. He's never understood my fascination with politics, but that paternal pride sometimes works overtime. Dad's always been a cheerleader for Alex and me. He's definitely got the gift of encouragement."

"Clearly," Noah agreed. "Which is why all of us stick around. When I'm on the road now, I can't wait to get back and see what Buddy's got going—who needs a helping hand, where he's headed on his road trips. Definitely a contagious personality."

She smiled. "That's my daddy. Everybody *loves* Buddy Collins. Well, except for Deacon and his cronies."

"Yeah, but he's the exception." He swallowed hard and continued. "I guess what I'm trying to say is, until I met you, I didn't think I could ever . . . I mean, I wasn't sure anyone would ever . . ."

Her brows rose as she waited for him to spit it out. *Why is this so hard?*

"Anyone would ever what, Noah?"

He sighed. "I didn't think I'd ever have these feelings again. I thought I'd live the rest of my life on my own. Unattached. Because to love again would just be—"

"—too much of a risk?"

"Yes. Too much of a risk. I'm not sure I'd survive if something happened again. If, well, if something were to happen to you. To us."

She looked deeply into his eyes, her face filled with compassion. "Noah, life doesn't offer guarantees. It just doesn't." She looked down at their hands. "Someday, when you're ready, I want you to tell me all about Melissa. It's important to me."

He looked up, hoping she wasn't expecting him to go *there*. Not tonight. He felt instant relief when she continued.

"But until then, promise me something."

"And what would that be?"

"Promise me you'll just take this—take *us*—one day at a time. Because for now, that's all we need. Dad always drilled it into our heads that each day is a gift from the Lord, and he's right."

He nodded, grateful she seemed to understand his hesitancy.

"Noah, I've really enjoyed getting to know you, too. It's been a long time since I . . . well, since I cared for someone the way I care for you." Her smile widened as a touch of mischief sparkled in her eyes. "And I'd be lying if I said I didn't melt like butter whenever you kiss me."

"Good to know," he said, returning her smile.

"But we *both* need to take this slowly. There's no reason to rush into something more. So let's take the pressure off and just take it one day at a time. Fair enough?"

He felt a wave of relief drift over him. "Fair enough," he said, leaning over to place a slow kiss on the top of her hand. "Fair enough."

After paying the waiter, Noah and Tracey took a short tour of the mansion then made their way to the door. The hostess thanked them for coming then opened the arched door for them. As she did, a dense fog rushed into the entry area like a dark and hungry serpent.

"Oh my goodness," Tracey said. "I've never see that happen before, have you?"

Noah stepped back, speechless. The fog sweeping into this old house . . . just like the living, thriving cloud of darkness that so often curled its way into his heart. How often had he experienced this exact phenomenon? What he now saw with his eyes—a visual façade of the flood of depression that so often crept into his soul. A chill raced from head to toe, making him shudder.

Tracey touched his arm. "Are you okay?"

He looked at her hand, and for a moment wondered who it belonged to.

She pulled him aside as another couple passed by, stepping out into the eerie abyss. He watched them, dreading having to walk through it himself.

"Noah, what's wrong?"

He closed his eyes just for a moment, searching for something—anything—to grasp onto as the chilling darkness tugged at his heart.

"Noah!" Tracey whispered urgently. She placed her hands on his face, cupping his cheeks. "Noah, *look* at me. What is it?"

When he opened his eyes, he saw compassion and strength in her countenance. He breathed again, unaware he'd been holding his breath. *Let her be your anchor.* The words drifted through his mind like a soothing balm.

"I'm okay," he said, placing his hands atop hers. "I'm sorry. I'm not really sure what . . . came over me." But, of course he did. "Let's go home."

She smiled, though concern shadowed her eyes. "I'm ready if you are."

He held onto her as they navigated through the thick fog, unable to spot Buddy's Buick until they were right upon it. Slowly pulling out of the parking lot, they made little headway down the winding, mountainous road, unable to see much of anything beyond the Buick hood ornament. The first half hour was treacherous. He kicked himself, thinking they should have waited out the heavy blanket of fog. Now, on this two-lane road, there was no turning back.

Tracey rolled down her window, keeping her eyes locked on the yellow line separating the road from the shoulder. Noah kept his eyes glued to the center line. By the time they finally slipped out of the cloud, he was exhausted. Just a few miles from home, it began to rain. They said little the rest of the way, even when Tracey reached for his hand and gave it a gentle squeeze.

Back at Walnut Ridge, Tracey had snuggled into his arms for a hug at the door before they parted. "It was unforgettable, Noah. The food, that historic old house, the bizarre ride home . . . what a night." She leaned up to kiss him on his cheek, then she was gone.

On his way back to the cottage, he wondered how such a perfect evening had been so quickly hijacked by the familiar, gripping oppression. He'd wanted tonight to be special—a chance to tell Tracey how much he liked her, how he found himself thinking of her first thing in the morning and the last thing at night. But he wasn't sure he conveyed any of that to her. Instead, he'd been consumed with fighting off the haunting tug in the most fragile place in his heart.

Maybe he was fooling himself. Maybe Melissa would forever live on, her memory so deeply imprinted into his soul, leaving no room for anyone else. Guilt gnawed at his gut, once again plaguing him with the peculiar thread of unfaithfulness to his wife.

As he unlocked the cottage door, Noah pushed everything out of his mind, trying to pinpoint his sole focus on the image of Tracey's face and the comfort he'd found there.

If only that were enough.

Chapter 17

The next couple of days flew by. Tracey couldn't get the strange night out of her mind, but did her best to sidestep her concerns as she and Alex worked long hours to finish the pieces to showcase in the shop. Occasionally they'd stop for a quick bite, but little else. She'd asked Alex if it was okay for her to take Saturday off, even asking if her sister would like to go along. Alex gave her *the look.*

"But why not?" Tracey gently sanded the first coat of an armoire. "Think how nice it would be to take a break. All that fresh air in your lungs? C'mon, Alex, please?"

Alex continued painting an old rocker. "First, I'm not a biker. Never have been. Never will be."

"But how do you—"

"Second, I would much rather stay here and have a day with no interruptions. I'll cue up one of my audio books and lose myself here with my kids."

"I know, but wouldn't you—"

"And third—" she looked up briefly, her eyes narrowing as she scratched her nose, "I have *no* idea what I was going to say. But thank you for asking, sister dearest. You go, have fun, enjoy the ride, and don't worry about me."

"I'm not worried about you. I'd just like to see you do something fun now and then. All you ever do is work."

"I disagree, but the bottom line is, I'm having a blast doing this, Tracey. I *love* it. And I would not enjoy this trip. To be honest, I still hate motorcycles. I have to pray my sanity back every time Dad takes off on Stella. I've seen the remains of too many motorcycle accidents on the news. I can't get those images out of my mind. I could never 'enjoy' spending a day on one." She feigned a shiver. "Never, never, ncvcr."

"Okay, okay." Tracey blew her hair out of her eyes. "I get it. No motorcycles. But would you just spend some time away from all this while we're gone? If you won't do it for yourself, do it for me."

"Why would I do it for you?"

"Because I asked!" Tracey teased. "I forgot how stubborn you are!"

Alex touched up a couple spots on the rocker then balanced her brush across the top of the paint can. "Ah, I'm just stubborn because that's what you expect me to be. I'm just a little teddy bear. You know that."

"Yeah, right."

Alex stood up, stretching her arms over her head. "Trace, is everything okay with you and Noah? I haven't seen him up at the house much these past couple of days."

Tracey pushed the annoying strands of hair from her face with the back of her wrist. "We're fine. Not that we're a *we*. To be honest, I'm not quite sure what we are."

"Are you okay with that? Not knowing?"

"I think so. I'm just trying to give him space until he's—" She looked up at her sister standing over her. "Until he's ready for *us* to be an *us*. If that makes sense."

Alex brushed the hair out of Tracey's face, tucking it beneath the bandana her sister wore. "It makes perfect sense. And I'm glad you're willing to give him that space. He'll come around. Eventually."

"You really think so? Sometimes I see this far-away look in his eyes, and I wonder."

Alex squatted beside her. "Yes, Trace. I believe he'll come around. And I think you're just the person to be there for him when he does."

Just before sunrise on Saturday, the bikers gathered at Walnut Ridge. As Tracey stepped out on the front porch, she watched as most of them busily buffed the finish on their Harleys. Buddy opened the door and joined her.

"Why are they all polishing their bikes now? Won't they just get dirty once they get on the road?"

Buddy handed her his extra pair of protective sunglasses. "It's a biker thing, sweetie. It's like those show dog competitions on TV. You always see their owners fussing over them at the last minute, brushing their coats to perfection. That's exactly how we feel about our Harleys. I suppose it's a pride thing, wanting our machines to glisten in the sunlight. Look real sleek and classy while we're on the road. Besides," he said, heading down the steps, "Stella never lets me ride until she feels adequately pampered."

Tracey followed her father down the steps. "So why aren't you over there dusting her off?"

He grinned. "Stella likes to get up early. I gave her the spa treatment before any of these yokels showed up. She's pristine and raring to go, don't you think?"

Tracey admired his glistening bike, shaking her head. "Stella, Stella, Stella. You are one lucky girl."

Noah joined them, wiping his hands on a cloth. "Morning, Tracey."

"Hi, Noah. Hey, that reminds me. I never asked—do you have a name for your bike?"

He smiled. "Sure."

She waited, he said nothing. "Okay . . . is it a secret or would you mind telling me?"

"Bike."

"Bike?"

"What? You don't like Bike?"

She laughed, pinching his elbow which made him howl. "Bike. Such a creative, clever name for such a beautiful, sleek Harley." She put her arm around his waist as he wrapped his arm around her.

"I thought you'd like it." He looked down into her eyes. "You ready?"

"As ready as I'll ever be."

Noah explained the protocol for group rides like this. Tracey was fascinated to learn how safety-conscious they were.

"Your dad's riding lead today. That means he'll ride at the head of the pack, staying to the left side of the lane. The rest of us stagger behind him—right, left, right, left. Now, if you were riding solo and it was your first time, you'd ride in that second slot just to the right behind the lead. That way, we'd have you surrounded should anything go wrong."

"But since I'm with you, I won't be treated like a newbie?"

"That's right. Just before we start up, Buddy will determine what hand signals we'll use today. It's important to know those."

"What kind of hand signals?"

Noah extended his hand down toward the ground and pointed. "If you see Buddy or anyone do this, it means there's something in the road that could be hazardous. Like pieces of tires, debris, that sort of thing. When he extends his left hand at a forty-five degree angle and moves his hand up and down, low like this, it means slow down. He may see something ahead that you can't see, so you obey his lead."

"I always have," Tracey quipped.

He went through several other hand signals. Speed up, ride in a single line instead of two by two, stop, left turn, right turn, and pull off the road.

"Well, all I can say is I'm glad you know what you're doing. I'd be lost before we even left the driveway."

"You'll get the hang of it. And you need to know the hand signals as well as I do. Keeps us both alert so we don't take any chances." He mounted his bike and motioned for her to do the same. "Hop on."

She started to the helmet on.

"Hold off with that until Buddy gives his instructions."

"Oh, okay." Tracey casually climbed onto her seat in back. "Is it true what they call these back seats?" she asked with a smile.

He chuckled. "I'm afraid so. How about we call it a *princess seat* today instead?"

"Much better."

Just then, a bike roared up the driveway. Tracey recognized the older model black Road King, knowing immediately it was Gristle. A young woman rode behind him covered head to toe in black leather. He pulled up beside them and cut his engine. Gristle pulled off his helmet.

"Will someone *please* tell this pretty young thang that it is NOT cool to be late for a HOG ride?! GLORY, if the sistah don't take fo-EV-ah to doll up her pretty lil' seff and make me LATE!"

She pulled off her helmet, a radiant smile filling her face. "Don't you all be listenin' to him. He was supposed to *call* me at six to make sure I was up. But did he call? No, he did not. It's a miracle we got here at all!" She laughed, climbing off the bike. "Hey, bikers! Since Gregory forgot to introduce me, I'll just do it myself. I'm Maleeka. And thanks for waiting for us."

Gregory? Then Tracey remembered Gristle's real name—Greg Sells. She leaned over, extending her hand. "Hi, Maleeka. I'm Tracey, and this is Noah."

The introductions were made quickly through the dozen or so other riders, all men. Tracey knew most of them, introduced herself to those she didn't. All the while Gristle carried on and on about his girlfriend's disregard for biker protocol.

"I'm so glad you're here, Tracey," Maleeka said, climbing back on Gristle's bike. "Gregory told me there'd be another girlfriend here today."

Tracey blushed at the term knowing Noah heard it. She caught a slight tilt of a smile before he turned back around. "I'm glad you came too, Maleeka."

"Okay, listen up!" Buddy called. "Looks like a beautiful day for a ride. Let's go over our hand signals just to make sure we're all on the same page."

He demonstrated the various gestures, many like the ones Noah had just shown her. After a few minutes, Buddy said. "Looks like we're ready to ride. Let's have a word of prayer."

For a moment, Tracey was surprised. It seemed odd for a bunch of bikers to bow their heads in prayer before taking off. Then she realized Buddy Collins would never miss an opportunity to pray before something like this.

"Father, thank You for this spectacular fall morning. We ask for Your hedge of protection as we ride today. Give us safe roads and sweet, sweet travel. And as we ride, help us be mindful of the beauty surrounding us. The changing leaves. The wildlife. The clear blue skies. Help us ride with a mindset of praise and thanks for You and the glory of Your creation all around us. We give this day to You, Lord. And the people said?"

"AMEN!"

"Let's ride!"

As soon as helmets were in place, the bikes came to life, their roar eclipsing all other sounds on what had been a quiet Saturday morning. *Boom boom boom! Boom boom boom!* Tracey got goose bumps, feeling the rumble of the engine beneath her as it rocked the bike. With so many other engines revving to life, it felt like the ground beneath them literally trembled.

Even with the thunder of so much noise all around them, she noticed the unique sound of the engines. Adjusting her headset, she asked Noah why.

"It's Harley's trademark sound—*potato-potato-potato.* I love it, don't you?"

She smiled, watching Maleeka grab handfuls of Gristle's black leather jacket, her eyes already squeezed shut behind her sunglasses. Tracey chuckled, remembering her first ride with her father not so long ago. Buddy led them all down the long driveway, everyone taking their place behind him just as Noah had described. Turning out of the drive onto the road, the cycles roared even louder, announcing their departure to the sleepy little town.

As Noah pulled out onto the road, he took his place in the line-up and accelerated. Tracey couldn't believe how exhilarating it was to be a part of this. "HEY, NOAH!" she shouted. "I *LOVE* THIS!"

"You don't have to shout, Tracey! Remember?" She watched his helmet shake side to side and imagined him rolling his eyes.

She laughed. "Sorry about that! I can't help it. This is GREAT!"

Just as they were about to pass Emma's Coffee Shop, she noticed someone holding a Styrofoam cup in one hand and making a bunch of animated motions toward the bikers with the other. As they passed, she recognized Deacon Stone—his face purple with rage, his mouth in angry motion. She could only imagine the contempt spewing out of his mouth.

She shouldn't have, but she couldn't help it. As they passed, she waved at the gnarly old guy and with a big smile shouted, "GOOD MORNING, DEACON!"

He clamped his mouth shut and threw the coffee cup down on the ground sending a splash of brown all over the sidewalk.

"What's his problem?" Noah asked.

"He's just hateful, that's all."

"Obviously. But what's that all about?"

Tracey leaned back, proud of herself for no longer needing to clutch Noah's back. "Actually, it's kind of a long story."

"We've got nothing but time," he said, turning his head so she could see his smile.

"I think it all stems back to years ago—maybe ten or fifteen; I've lost track. Deacon has a son named Thad. Only child. And all along, I guess Deacon assumed Thad would grow up and work in the family real estate office. Problem was, Thad had no interest in real estate. And if you ask me, I bet he mostly just wanted to work *anywhere* but with his dad.

"Thad was a smart kid. Really popular too. Quarterback of the football team, pitched for the baseball team. But he couldn't handle all his dad's constant pressure. So during his senior year in high school, he started visiting Dad at the church, asking advice on what to do with his life and how to follow his own interests when all the while his dad never let up on him. Dad counseled Thad, trying to help him find out what the Lord wanted him to do. And in the end, Thad wanted to go to Middle Tennessee State. He'd had all kinds of offers for football scholarships. Then, without telling his father, he signed with MTSU.

"When the news came out, Deacon was furious. He stormed into Dad's office and accused him of undermining Deacon's role as a father, of telling his kid to go against his father's wishes—all that stuff. Apparently, it was pretty ugly because Dad refused to tell us what Deacon said to him that day. And ever since then, Deacon's had it out for Dad."

"The man sure knows how to hold a grudge," Noah said.

"It's more than that, really," Tracey continued. "He's so shady in all his real estate dealings. It's no secret, but everyone's afraid of him, so nobody's ever blown the whistle on him."

"Every town has its bully, I guess."

"I guess so. What really irks me is how he takes advantage of so many of our older folks. He's been quietly buying up property for years. All of it's legal, or so they say. But it's completely unethical. He approaches senior adults when they're either in some kind of grief over losing a spouse, or facing some kind of medical or financial bind. He 'buys' their house from them for pennies on the dollar, then lets them live in their own homes rent-free until they die."

"What a guy. He's all heart, isn't he?"

"He makes me sick. He's conned so many widows in this area, it's obscene. But so far nobody's been able to prosecute him. He stays just within the law, like I said. But he's knowingly taking advantage of these people. Dad's tried for years to put an end to it, but Deacon always finds a way out. He really is a snake. I hate the guy for all the grief he's given Dad over the years. I just wish he'd drop dead and give the whole town some peace for a change."

"That's a little harsh, don't you think? Wishing him dead?"

"Probably. But still . . ."

They rode in silence for a while. An hour into their trip, they turned onto the Natchez Trace Parkway. The historic, winding, two-lane road stretched 444 miles from Nashville, cutting through the northwest corner of Alabama, and ending at Natchez, Mississippi. With the autumn leaves at their peak, the drive was breathtaking. Here and there they'd spot deer grazing in wide, open fields. Now and then, Noah pointed out chicken hawks in flight, and once they even saw a bald eagle.

Tracey closed her eyes, breathing in the crisp, cool air as it rushed past her. She tried to remember what it was like working in the pressure cooker that was Washington D.C. She smiled broadly when she realized it had been several days since she'd given her life there more than a passing thought. *How quickly I've grown accustomed to this life,* she thought. *And I love it. I honestly love it. This is where I belong.*

She opened her eyes again, realizing how much Noah was a part of those feelings. Tracey tried to keep her emotions in check—at least until she knew it was safe to let go of her heart and love him the way she wanted to. *Give him time,* she reminded herself. *Give him time.*

"What're you smiling at back there?" he asked, breaking her thoughts.

Thankful for the sunglasses that hid her eyes, she quipped, "None of your business."

She could see his face in the rearview mirror and watched him smile. She reached up, placing her hand at his waist, deciding to leave it there a while. As if reading her mind, he placed his gloved hand over hers, apparently deciding to leave it there a while too.

Not a bad way to spend an autumn day . . .

Chapter 18

Tracey was surprised how quickly the miles flew beneath them. They'd stopped only once at an overlook for a rest break before continuing their ride to Tupelo. She and Noah talked at times, but for the most part they'd ridden along listening to a random assortment of tunes over the Harley's radio piped through their headsets.

They stopped for lunch, taking a short detour on Highway 20 to Florence, Alabama. There, they feasted on platters of fried catfish, shrimp, slaw, and hush puppies, while sipping sweet tea. Afterward, they headed back to the Parkway and once again enjoyed the bright blue skies above as they traveled.

Tracey closed her eyes and felt herself drifting off to sleep. "I can't keep my eyes open."

"Me neither," Noah teased. "Wake me up when we get there."

Her eyes flew open. "No! Don't even talk like that!"

"Just kidding. Remember, I usually ride solo, so I'm used to long distances without interruption. You go ahead and fall asleep. I'll wake you if you start to fall off, deal?"

"You have a really sick sense of humor, you know that?"

As they rounded a curve in the road, the line of hand signals cautioned them to slow down and come to a stop.

"What's the matter?" Tracey asked, placing her hand on Noah's shoulder.

"Looks like there may be an accident up ahead."

As the bikers all came to a stop on the two-lane highway, they couldn't see ahead because of an incline and bend in the road. All they could see were a dozen or more vehicles stopped in front of them.

"Can you see anything?" Gristle called out from behind them.

"Nothing," Noah said as he and Tracey stepped off their bike. "I'll go see what I can find out."

"I'll come with you," Gristle said, handing his helmet to Maleeka. "Now, you stay here and stay outta the road, you got that?"

"Why? How come I can't—"

"I'll keep you company," Tracey said as the guys walked away. An uneasy feeling crept under her skin.

"I don't know about you, but I *needed* another break," Maleeka said, twisting and turning. "How they do this—all these miles on these motorcycles? Least in a car you can move around now and then."

"Ah, but think how much more—"

"Oh, this can't be good," Maleeka said, looking over Tracey's shoulder. "Here comes an ambulance and a police car."

The emergency vehicles cut their sirens as they came closer, their lights still flashing. Shortly after passing them on the shoulder of the road, they came to a stop. They could hear other sirens in the distance. Tracey and Maleeka started walking toward the crash scene, forgetting their promise to stay behind. As they crested the hill, they could see three mangled and twisted vehicles sitting at odd angles, on and off the road. Shattered glass covered the road along with bent bumpers and broken tail lights. The biting smell of gasoline filled the air.

"Oh good Lord, what a mess, what a MESS," Maleeka said, taking the words out of Tracey's mouth.

People surrounded the vehicles, including most of Buddy's Elders, distinctive in their black leather jackets. She shielded her eyes from the sun, looking for her father and Noah. They appeared to be speaking to someone in a small red car that had flipped upside down. Buddy turned and shouted to the paramedics, motioning for them to hurry.

When she looked up, Noah was no longer in view. She assumed he was on the other side of the vehicle. Another ambulance arrived, its siren making short, loud chirps as though to say, *get out of the way!* Two more squad cars filed in behind it.

As the emergency personnel rushed toward the accident, the policemen began corralling the onlookers, pushing them back to a safer distance.

"Maleeka, do you see Noah?"

"No, I see Gregory and Buddy and some of the other guys, but not Noah."

A fire truck arrived, its blaring siren filling her soul with dread. As it pulled into the grassy median alongside the wreckage, Tracey prayed silently. She watched in disbelief as the emergency personnel pulled a young child from inside the small red compact. Still inside, a woman screamed for her baby. *Why aren't they getting her out too?*

She felt Maleeka's hand take her own, clasping it tight. "Oh, dear Jesus, help these people!" Tracey joined her in silent prayer, thankful to close her eyes to the scene below.

Eternity seemed to pass before the crash victims were loaded into ambulances and driven away. Gradually, the Elders made their way back to their bikes, none of them speaking. Gristle took Maleeka in his arms as tears tracked down his face.

"The mama, she didn't make it. She gone," he cried quietly.

Tracey rushed past them, searching for Buddy and Noah. She finally spotted them off the side of the road. Noah sat on a guardrail, his head in his hands. Buddy stood over him, his hands on Noah's shoulders. Dread washed over her again. Then, just as she neared them, Buddy held up his hand, shaking his head. The message was clear.

She stopped in her tracks, nodding a silent response. Wrapping her arms around herself, she bowed her head and continued to pray. *Oh God . . .*

Suddenly, she heard footsteps and looked up. "Noah?"

He didn't look at her, but briefly squeezed her shoulder as he walked by. She turned to follow him, then felt another strong hand stop her.

"Give him a minute, Tracey Jo," her father said, putting his arm over her shoulder.

"Is he okay?" When her father said nothing, she turned to look in his eyes and found them moist. "Daddy, what's wrong?"

They walked slowly back toward the other bikers. "I don't believe in ghosts, but I think sudden triggers can evoke all kinds of memories and images that haunt our souls. The young woman in the car . . ."

"Reminded him of Melissa?"

"Yes." He said nothing for a moment or two. "I assume he's told you about her accident?"

They stopped alongside Stella. "No, not yet. He promised to tell me at some point. Alex told me he'd lost his wife in an accident."

Buddy gathered her into his arms. "Yes, he did. And on that day, his wife was driving a small red car."

"Oh, no."

"Be patient with him, sweetie. He just needs a little space right now."

Noah felt like a short bungee cord was wound tightly around his chest. He had experienced the sensation before, but now was not the time for breathing exercises or stretching out until it passed. As Noah approached his Harley, he put one hand on the handlebar and one on the seat to steady himself. He closed his eyes, trying desperately to shut out the glassy stare of the young woman in the small red car. Her seat belt had tethered her to the driver's seat, suspending her from the roof of the upside-down vehicle. She was pinned at an awkward angle, unable to move her head against the smashed-in car door.

She had screamed for her child, unable to see the paramedics carefully unhooking the child seat where her little one was secured. As the toddler was safely removed from the back seat of the car, the mother's screams had continued, begging to know if her daughter was okay. Buddy and Noah had tried to calm her as other paramedics worked to free her.

As Buddy continued murmuring his reassurances, she suddenly fell silent. Noah had leaned in, pressing his fingers to her neck but finding no pulse there. He tried again and again. Nothing.

After the paramedics asked him to step aside, they too were unable to find a pulse. Noah's eyes had been riveted to the vacant eyes of the young woman, his own emotions crashing in on him. He'd turned away and rushed off to a nearby tree where he lost his lunch. Buddy had been at his side immediately.

"You'll be okay," he'd said calmly, handing him his handkerchief. "Take some deep breaths, Noah. It will pass. Let it pass."

Buddy led him to the guard rail where he'd tried to breathe again, but nothing seemed to help. When Tracey had called out to him, he couldn't think. The sun was too bright. Too many eyes were looking his way. *I have to get out of here. Now.* He'd hurried by her, knowing he couldn't speak and thankful that Buddy was there for her.

The roaring riptide of emotions threatened to roll over him and drag him under.

He picked up the extra helmet, quickly stepped over to set it on Stella, then got on his own bike and cranked it up.

Gristle reached over to pat him on the back. "Noah? You okay, bro?"

Noah pulled away, holding his hands up, shaking his head.

Suddenly, Tracey was there, Buddy right behind her. The look on her face pulled the imaginary bungee cord tighter around his chest.

"Noah, where are you going?"

"C'mon, Noah. Don't leave," Buddy said.

"Back off!" Noah snapped, hating the sound of his voice.

They froze, all staring at him.

"*Please* don't go," Tracey pleaded with tears in her eyes.

He pushed his sunglasses in place. "I'm . . . I have to . . . I'm sorry." He turned his bike the way they'd come, and roared off as fast as he could, refusing to glance in his rearview mirror.

Chapter 19

A week passed. Noah hadn't called. He wasn't taking Buddy's calls. Apparently, he wasn't taking anyone's calls. Tracey had stopped listening for the sound of his Harley and wondered if he'd ever return. She wasn't angry that he left. Both Buddy and Alex had told her he often took off like this, sometimes for weeks at a time. They'd learned to give him his space. Tracey was trying, but the consuming worry seemed to eat at her day and night. She knew he could take care of himself, but it was the condition of his heart that concerned her most of all. He'd come so close to letting her in. But now? It all felt like a distant memory.

Tracey busied herself finishing pieces for the shop which was almost completed. Their upcoming grand opening gave her less than a week to go. The deadline enabled her to focus all her efforts and thoughts into getting the place ready. But late at night, after a long soak in the tub, the emptiness of Noah's continued absence loomed all around her.

On one such night, she padded downstairs to make herself some hot tea. She was surprised to find her father still up, reading in the den by the fire.

"You'd think after all these years, I'd know the sound of my daughters' footsteps," he said, placing the bookmark between pages. "I thought for sure you were Alex."

"Sorry, Dad. What are you doing still up?"

"Couldn't sleep. Came down for hot tea. There's still some in the kitchen if you'd like it."

"You must've read my mind. I'll be right back."

Tracey made her way to the kitchen, filled her mug with tea, then joined her father back in the den. She took a seat beside him on the sofa. "What are you reading?"

"C. S. Lewis."

"Your favorite."

"True. I wish I possessed even one one-hundredth of his wisdom. Maybe then life would make more sense."

"Well, for what it's worth, I think you do all right," she said.

He closed the book and turned toward her, quirking a smile.

"Lewis once said, 'You can never get a cup of tea large enough or a book long enough to suit me.' I'd have to agree. Wouldn't you?"

She nodded then blew on her tea.

"So what's got you up so late after a long day's work?" he asked.

Tracey took a sip then shrugged. "A little this, a little that. I'm excited about the store opening. It's been good, having something to keep me busy."

"Alex says you have a real knack for restoring furniture."

Tracey smiled. "You know Alex. Always the encourager."

"Maybe so, but I can see for myself she's right."

"Still, I just can't . . . no matter how hard I try, I can't—"

"You can't stop worrying about Noah?"

She blew out a weary sigh. "I can't stop worrying about Noah."

He squeezed her shoulder. "He'll be back. You'll see."

"Dad, it's not just that. I thought I'd been so careful not to let my feelings for him rush ahead of me. We both agreed to take it slow, one day at a time. And yet, there's not one trace of doubt in my mind that I'm in love with him." It seemed strange, hearing herself say those words out loud.

His wide smile slowly deepened. "If you're expecting to find shock on my face, don't waste your time."

She reached out and took his hand. "I know. It's not as if I've tried to hide my feelings. I'm just not quite sure what to do with them at this point."

Her father rested his head back on the sofa. "I think you just keep doing what you're doing, and try not to overanalyze it."

"Easier said than done."

"True. But if I've learned anything these past few years, I've learned that worrying myself to death over this or that doesn't help a thing."

"I still remember that sermon you preached on worry back when I was in high school," Tracey began.

"And here, all this time, I thought all you ever did in church was pass notes with your friends and giggle."

"Most of the time, but occasionally I listened."

Buddy tugged at a lock of her hair. "You were saying?"

"I remember the analogy you gave, comparing worry to a rocking chair. 'It keeps you moving but doesn't get you anywhere.' I never forgot that."

"A great word picture, isn't it?"

Tracey nodded. "Yes, and I feel as if I've put a million miles on that rocker since Noah took off."

Buddy took another sip of tea. "For what it's worth, when I can't seem to stop worrying, I always go back to one of my favorite scriptures. Philippians four, verses six and seven. 'Do not be anxious about anything, but in everything by prayer and supplication with thanksgiving, let your requests be made known to God. And the peace of God, which surpasses all understanding, will guard your hearts and your minds in Christ Jesus.' That's a mighty powerful promise, if you ask me."

"I know, Dad. I just wish I could live that out, you know? It sounds like the perfect antidote for worry, but something inside me just can't let go enough to really buy into it completely."

"It's about trust, Tracey Jo."

"I know. But it's amazing how often that particular word picture gets blurred."

"It's a hard lesson to learn—trusting God completely. Especially when it comes to relationships with others."

"Speaking of which," she said, turning to face him again. "Where do things stand with Deacon and the City Council on our permits? Is that what the meeting is about tomorrow night?"

Buddy ran his hand through his hair. "I'm afraid so. It's their monthly meeting, which means it's open to the public. I figure it's the only way I can get a fair hearing by the entire council without Deacon blocking me. I'm sure he'll put up a fight, but he doesn't have a leg to stand on. There's no reason for him to block these permits, which means it's sheer vindication on his part."

"So what happens if he has convinced everyone else on the council to block the permits?"

"That, my dear, is when I cling to those verses we just talked about and put my trust in God. I have to trust He'll be able to do what I can't."

Tracey stood up and stretched. "Guess I need to do the same where Noah is concerned."

She leaned over and kissed her father on the top of his head.

"God will never let you down. That much I know for sure. G'night, sweetheart."

"Good night, Daddy."

Alex stepped back to admire Tracey's work. Her latest project, two matching bedside tables, boasted three pastel shades highlighting the wainscoted detail on the front of each table.

"I cannot believe what a natural you are at this. Had I known, we should have done this years ago. Think how much fun we've missed!"

Tracey stood up, twisting to stretch her aching back muscles. "I doubt I'd be able to stand up straight now if we'd been doing this for years. I can't wait to be up at the shop where we'll have a worktable and stools. Much more of this and we'll both be in traction, Sis."

The loud rumble of a Harley drew closer to the barn. Tracey stopped to listen, then sighed when she recognized the familiar sound of her father's bike.

"Trace, I'm sorry," Alex said, rubbing her sister's shoulder. "One of these days it'll be Noah's you hear."

"But not today." Tracey set aside one of the tall narrow tables and wiped her hands on her apron.

Buddy stepped into the barn. "Ah, my two favorite girls. How's it going?"

"You look nice, Daddy. What's the—"

Alex jumped. "Oh my goodness—what time is it?!"

Buddy checked his watch. "It's a little after six. I thought you two were planning to come to the meeting tonight."

Tracey yanked at the strings on her apron. "We completely lost track of time! When does it start?"

"City Council meets at 6:30 sharp. Think you can make it?"

Alex threw off her apron, then stopped herself to pick it up and hang it where it belonged. "Daddy, just go. We'll be there!"

Twenty-two minutes later, Tracey and Alex dashed down the hill toward the town's small City Hall. Even before they got there, they could see a line of people waiting to get in. When they reached the end of the line, Alex tried to catch her breath. "What's going on? Why are you all out here?"

Tina Redmon's face lit up. "Are you kidding? The showdown between your dad and Deacon Stone! Everybody's talking about it. We'll be lucky if we can squeeze in the back of the room."

Alex grabbed Tracey's arm and pulled her along. "Make way, make way! Family coming through. C'mon, people, let us through." Slowly but surely, the sisters pushed through those in line and the crowd standing in the outer hall of the small building.

Suddenly, Stump appeared before them. "Miss Alex, Miss Tracey, Buddy said for me to bring you girls in. He saved you seats on the front row with him."

Alex stood on her tiptoes and pecked the big guy on his cheek. Thankfully, he had leaned down so she could place her lips on the small patch of his face that *wasn't* bearded. "Thanks, Stump! You're our hero."

He smiled as he showed them the way. Just as they took their seats, Deacon started pounding his gavel. Their father gave them each a hug and a kiss on the cheek.

"Ladies and gentlemen, take your seats and come to order." Deacon continued pounding the gavel, his face pinched in a scowl.

"Looks like Ginny Stone's been feeding her husband persimmons again," Alex whispered.

Tracey smiled but was much too nervous to laugh. She spotted her father's knee bouncing at a rapid rate, so quickly stilled it with her hand. "Dad. It's gonna be okay."

"Oh. Sorry, sweetheart." He put his hand over hers. "I'm good. Really. Just ready to get this over with."

"Ladies and gentlemen, that will be enough!" Deacon pounded the gavel three more times and held it up as he waited for the audience to give him their full attention. When the murmurs died down, he placed the gavel back in its holder. "That's better. This City Council meeting has now come to order. My colleagues and I wish to remind you that we will maintain complete decorum during this meeting. If, for any reason, we find the actions of this gathering to be of a disruptive manner, we will clear the room. I trust all of you will comply."

Tracey studied the six other council members, three on each side of Deacon, who, of course, was council chairman. They were all people she'd known her whole life. Good, decent people with one exception—they all kowtowed to Deacon Stone. Which, of course, is how they got themselves elected to this council year after year. *How does he do it? Are the elections rigged? Surely after all these years, someone would have blown the whistle if that were the case. The real question is why. Why would anyone be so driven to rule a tiny community like Jacobs Mill? Big fish, little pond? Really? Are you that starved for power, Deacon Stone?*

"At the top of our agenda this evening is the matter of the residential property owned by Buddy Collins. Mr. Collins, on behalf of his daughters, has requested a proprietary change of zoning for a shack on his property—"

"Oh brother," Alex groaned.

"—which he prefers to now be zoned for retail business. The council has denied Mr. Collins' request on numerous occasions for the simple reason that we have rules against such things. These rules are in place to prevent folks from turning their homes into businesses and thereby detracting from their neighbors' property values."

Tracey listened, marveling at the tone in Deacon's voice. Just a good old boy looking out for everyone's best interest. Like Andy Griffith explaining to Aunt Bee why she can't sell her prized pickled beets from her kitchen. *No wonder so many fall for Deacon's bull. Who doesn't love Andy Griffith?*

"Who among us would want Lennie Flickerman to move his auto mechanic shop right next door to their home? Who among us would want Avery Cramer to open his fish bait shop right beside our front porch? Or who among us would want Birdy Simpson to move her beauty shop into the house next door? Of course, none of us would. That's because we respect one another's property and have each other's best interest at heart.

"It's really a very simple case of protecting our fair city against those who would ruin it. First, a store selling beat-up, secondhand furniture—"

Tracey noticed her sister's fingers clenching and unclenching. On the other side, she saw both her father's knees bouncing in rhythm now. She closed her eyes and uttered a prayer for both of them.

"—and what's next? A thrift store? A Wal-Mart? A Jiffy Lube? Why, Jacobs Mill would be nothing but another tacky stop on the interstate! And I know not a one of you here want that to happen."

To his far right, council member Flossy McMills leaned over to her microphone. "Deacon, I think we should—"

"Now, Flossy, remember our protocol. We do not interrupt one another."

"Yes, but—"

"You can have your say when I'm finished."

Flossy blinked and busied herself with a paper clip.

"The point is, ladies and gentlemen, we all know what's going on here. Our town has quite a history of having to deal with this family and their ilk. Why, who hasn't heard Buddy and his hooligans roaring through town on those enormous motorcycles? Which, by the way, are in direct violation of the noise ordinance."

"Is he talking about us?"

They all turned when Hank Biddle spoke aloud to Stump.

"I believe he is," Stump answered, glaring across the room at Deacon.

"We gonna let him talk about us like that?" Hank continued.

Buddy stood up and turned to face his Elders, all standing across the back of the room. "Guys? Let's keep this civil, okay?"

The Elders looked back and forth at each other, then finally shook their heads in agreement. "If you say so, Buddy."

"Thank you." Buddy turned back to face Deacon. "Look, I can't sit here and let you turn this into another personal vendetta for whatever it is you hold against me and my family."

Deacon slammed the gavel down. "You'll have your turn to speak, Buddy. Now take your seat."

"Let him speak!" someone yelled from the outer hallway.

Deacon slammed the gavel again until the room grew quiet. "I think we can all see what we're dealing with here. And as chairman of this council, I for one will not sit idly by while ANYONE tries to degrade our little town by refusing to obey the rules and laws that were set in place for the good of all."

"Is he gonna shut up and let the rest of us have a chance to speak?" Alex whispered in her father's ear, loud enough for those around her to snicker.

Deacon slammed his gavel down, his face reddening. "Miss Collins, did I not make myself clear that we would not abide disruption of any sort in our proceedings this evening?"

"Sure you did, Deacon," Alex shot back. "I was just wondering how long you're gonna listen to yourself bloviate before letting some of the rest of us have our say. Isn't that why we're here?"

A ripple of restrained laughter rolled across the room. Deacon adjusted his glasses and turned his direction to Buddy. "I see your daughter Alex is as caustic as ever. I suppose that's no great surprise. Apparently, the apple doesn't fall far from the tree."

Buddy turned toward his daughter. "Actually, she just took the words right out of my mouth. Thanks, honey."

"No problem, Dad."

The polite chuckles sent another wave through the room.

Deacon straightened the pile of papers in front of him. "Well, I see no need to take any more time. As anyone can see, this is an open-and-shut case. The Collins wish to change zoning. The Council stands on the laws on our books which prohibit such a change. There's really no use in—"

"Let them have their say!" Sadie Woolsey warbled in a shout from the other side of the room. "Deacon, you know perfectly well it's in the bylaws that folks can speak their mind before a final vote is taken. I'd be more than happy to read the pertinent bylaws if you've forgotten them."

"Now, Miss Sadie, there's no need to—"

She raised a booklet in the air. "I have the bylaws right here."

"I'm sure you do, but we're all adults here. I believe we can—"

"I'm glad you see it that way," she said. "Now who'll speak first?" She turned to look around, her back to the chairman whose face crimsoned even more.

"Miss Sadie, please take a seat before—"

"I'll speak first," Alex said, already making her way to the microphone at the front of the short aisle. She tapped the mike. "Is this thing on?"

Deacon let out a loud sigh as he groaned, "Yes, Miss Collins, I'm afraid it is."

"Good. I'll make this short and sweet."

Tracey watched her sister with fascination. Alex wasn't the least bit flustered, looking each council member in the eye as she spoke.

"Ladies and gentlemen, *we* all know what this is about. As most of you know, the 'shack' Deacon is referring to is, in fact, the old smokehouse that has been on our property since the mid-1800s. As many of you know, my great-great grandfather later opened that smokehouse to the public during the depression to give the folks of Jacobs Mill food when they had none. Fortunately, there were no 'laws on the books' prohibiting his benevolence.

"Several weeks ago when we started renovating that property to turn it into a storefront, Dad complied with all the paperwork and petitioned for the zone change."

"Yes, well, Miss Collins," Deacon said, stifling a fake yawn. "You have as yet to tell us anything we don't already know."

Alex smiled sweetly. "I'm getting there. But please, go ahead and take a nap if you're bored. We'll wake you when we're done."

Laughter erupted then quickly abated with the glare on the chairman's face. "Miss Collins, I will not warn you—"

"Yeah, yeah, I heard you the first time. Now. Where was I?" Alex snapped her fingers. "Ah, I remember. As I said, Daddy petitioned for a zone change. Deacon sat on it. Even refused to discuss it with his fellow council members here. We're about to open for business, and yet our esteemed, self-appointed town *dictator*—"

"That's enough!" Deacon shouted, pounding the gavel over and over.

"—has handled this simple request—"

"I said that's ENOUGH!"

"—the same way he handles everything in Jacobs Mill. By bullying everyone on this council the same way he's bullied me and my father and everyone else in—"

"MISS COLLINS! I SAID SIT DOWN!"

Everyone froze. The gavel fell to the floor as Deacon clutched at his chest. His purpled face quickly drained of all color. "I said . . ." His eyes rolled back in his head just before he fell backwards, hitting his head against the credenza behind him then slumping to the ground.

For a split second, no one moved.

"SOMEBODY GET THE PARAMEDICS NEXT DOOR!"

Suddenly, the room exploded into action as people rushed toward the front to help the fallen chairman. Others backed away in shock. Buddy, Tracey, and Alex joined the other council members who knelt beside Deacon. Seeing the blood pooling beneath his head, Buddy yanked out his bandana and placed it gently beneath Deacon's head.

"Where's Ginny? Is she here?" Alex called back to the crowd, looking for Deacon's wife.

"No. She's in Texas with the grandkids!" Flossy cried, standing beside her chair at the table. "Should I call her?"

Just then paramedics from the Fire Station rushed into the room. "Clear out, folks! Give us room!"

Tracey backed away from the knot of council members circling Deacon. As she looked up, she saw Stump calmly urging everyone to leave the room.

"That's it, nice and quiet like," he said. A few of the townsfolk looked at him with suspicious eyes, but followed his instructions.

"Do as he says," Mrs. Peterson instructed, appearing beside her big friend. "Let's gather ourselves outside."

With the paramedics checking Deacon's vitals, Tracey and her sister stepped back to give them room.

"Can you believe this?" Tracey whispered.

When her sister didn't respond, she turned to find out why. Alex's eyes were glued to the back of the room.

"No, I can't believe this," she whispered. "And neither will you when you turn around."

Alarmed by the look on her sister's face, Tracey turned around. There, standing amidst the outgoing flow of the crowd, stood Noah.

Chapter 20

Moments before, Noah had arrived at City Hall just in time to witness Deacon's outburst and fall. He'd rolled back in town a few minutes earlier, stopping by Walnut Ridge in hopes of seeing Tracey. But the house was empty, as were the shop and barn. Not until he drove down Main Street had he seen the crowd and stopped to ask what was happening. Someone he didn't know had told him the Collins were having a showdown with Deacon and the City Council.

He'd parked his bike and elbowed his way through the crowded outer room. Squeezing into the council room, he'd spotted Alex at the microphone, though her back was turned. He searched for Tracey, finding her up on the front row with Buddy. Then, before he'd even caught his breath, Deacon collapsed.

As the room cleared out, he pushed his way through the last of the townsfolk as he made his way toward Tracey and Alex. This wasn't at all how he'd planned to face Tracey after his absence. As she turned to face him, he swallowed hard. Closing the space between them, he then stopped.

"Hello, Tracey."

"Noah, when . . . where did you . . ." Her expression seemed to crumble, a mix of emotions rushing through her eyes. He held out his arms, not knowing what to say, wishing her into his embrace. As a tear slipped down her cheek, she stepped closer—close enough that he could wrap his arms around her.

He buried his face in her hair. "Tracey, I'm *so* sorry."

He felt a hand cover his and looked up to see Alex, her eyes pooled with tears as she simply nodded then passed by them. Buddy followed, giving him a hearty pat on his back along with a knowing wink before he joined Alex.

Tracey looked up at him. "I wasn't sure I'd ever see you again," she said, her voice rasped with emotion.

He pushed a strand of hair from her eyes and wiped her tears away with his thumb. "I wasn't sure you'd ever *want* to see me ever again."

A nervous chuckle escaped as a smile tugged at her lips. "Noah, I want you to know—"

He put his forefinger against her lips. "Shh, not here. Not now. Can we go somewhere and talk?"

A paramedic interrupted them, guiding a gurney down the aisle. "Might be best for you folks to join the others outside."

"Sure thing," Noah said, reaching for Tracey's hand.

She didn't move, her gaze turned to those assisting Deacon. "Noah, do you remember that day we left on the ride when I said I wished Deacon would just drop dead?"

Noah put his arm over her shoulder and steered her away. "You didn't mean it."

"I know, but it's like I *willed* it to happen or something. I feel awful."

He looked down at her as they made their way toward the door. "Don't. You had nothing to do with what just happened, okay?"

"But I should never have—"

"Tracey?"

"Yes?"

He rested his hands on her shoulders and leaned close to her ear. "You and I both know you didn't wish the man dead," he whispered. "So let that go, okay?"

She pressed her lips together, then finally nodded.

They stepped outside into the throng of folks still milling around in the early evening darkness, all waiting for news about Deacon. The quaint streetlights shone like spotlights on those gathered and others joining them from The Depot across the street. Noah wished he'd thought to exit through the back door to avoid seeing everyone. Right now, all he wanted was a chance to talk to Tracey. Alone.

Suddenly, Stump bear-hugged him. "Noah! When did you get back?"

Tracey stepped away, giving the guys plenty of room. At the moment, Noah's friends seemed anxious to fill him in on all he'd missed, most of the animated conversation involving the council meeting. She noticed that he kept an eye on her, even as she joined her sister across the street in front of the pub. She watched him as well, thankful the Elders were making such a fuss over him.

"Well? What did he say?" Alex asked. "Where's he been? Did he tell you?"

"No, we barely said a word before all this. We'll have a chance to talk later."

Just then, the doors of City Hall flew open again as the paramedics pushed Deacon's gurney outside and into the waiting ambulance.

"I see the chairman survived after all," Alex said sarcastically.

"Alex, stop that kind of talk." Tracey noticed the oxygen mask over Deacon's pale face. "I sure hope he makes it."

Alex folded her arms across her chest. "Well, that makes *one* of us."

Tracey pinned Alex with a glare. "Stop. Please."

The ambulance pulled away, its flashing lights sending a bizarre light show bouncing against the buildings. As it turned the corner at the end of Main Street, the siren blared into the night.

People started chatting again, many making their way into the pub. Tracey looked for Noah again, finding him still across the street, but this time with her father. The two seemed locked in serious conversation. She envied her father, wishing for the same opportunity, but not about to interrupt them.

Everything had happened so fast with so much confusion. And then, in the midst of all the chaos, Noah had appeared out of nowhere. Where had he been? Why hadn't he called? She couldn't help the impatience gnawing at her nerves.

"Let them be, Trace," Alex said, hooking her elbow. "Let's go in and throw some darts or something. How about it?"

"I guess," she answered, glad for something to bide the time. As they turned to go inside, Tracey stopped. "Go on in, Alex. I just want to get Noah's attention and let him know we'll be inside. Okay?"

"Fine. I'll order us some wings." Alex disappeared inside.

As Tracey turned around, a black sedan with darkened windows pulled up to the curb right in front of her, obstructing her view. Irritated, she moved so she could again see Noah.

"Tracey?"

She recognized the voice before turning her head at the sound of her name. *Oh no.*

The front passenger side window continued to lower. "I can't believe I found you," Morgan said, reaching for her hand.

She snatched her hand out of his reach. "What are you *doing* here?"

He pulled on a black Vanderbilt baseball cap and opened the door. Climbing out of the vehicle, he carefully kept his back to the others still standing around. "I need to talk to you. Come, take a ride with me."

"Don't be ridiculous. I'm not going anywhere with you. I can't believe you're here." She leaned to look inside the car where Morgan's driver sat behind the wheel. "Scott. Nice to see you again.

"Hi, Tracey. Nice to see you too."

She didn't miss the awkward expression on his face. *No doubt wishing he was anywhere but right here.* "Scott, you need to take the Senator back to—"

"Tracey, we have to talk," Morgan said, moving closer. That's all I'm asking. A few minutes. I came this far—surely you'll give me at least that much."

Tracey shook her head, furious he had the nerve to show up like this.

"No? Would you rather we make a scene here in front of all these people?"

"Morgan, please. Just go home."

"Five minutes. Give me five minutes then I'll go. I promise."

She blew out a huff then nodded toward the alley beside the pub. As soon as she stepped around the corner, Tracey turned to face him. "You have wasted your time coming here. I'm not coming back. There's nothing you can say or do to change my mind."

He smiled, digging his hands deep in the pockets of his jeans, stepping closer. "Do you have any idea how much I've missed you?" She started to leave, but he caught her arm. "Okay, okay! I'm sorry. I shouldn't have said that."

She looked at his hand still on her arm. "Morgan, please."

He removed his hand but remained close. "I came because I needed to see you. That's it. Pure and simple. Since you left, I can't think of anything but—"

"Stop it! That's enough!" she snapped, raising her hands. "You make me sick, you know that? All that time I worked for you, I believed in you. I believed in your fight for what was right and good and just in this country. I was so grateful that you stood up for the family when no one else would. And now look at you! Groveling in a dark alley, whining like a stupid schoolboy."

"I know, I know!" he shrugged. "It's completely wrong. Don't you think I'm aware of that? Don't you think it haunts me day and night, that all I can think of is the one person on this planet who wants nothing to do with me?" He yanked off his cap. "Tracey, it makes me *crazy*. But I never asked for this! I didn't go looking for someone—it just happened. Surely, you were aware of it too. I could see it in your eyes. Always. You were there, *always* there at my side—"

"No! I never once thought of you as—"

"You can't lie to me," he said, stepping closer. "I know you feel it too. You always wanted us to be more than friends. You'll never convince me otherwise."

"Morgan, SHUT UP! We are done here." She turned on her heel, but he grabbed her, pinning her against the wall, his hands locked on her arms with a strength she never knew he possessed. He kissed her hard even as she jerked her head trying to pull away from him. He kissed her with such force, she couldn't even cry out. As hot tears began to pour down her cheeks, she could think of only one way to break free. She bit his tongue as hard as she could.

He screamed then caught himself, one hand reaching for his mouth, the other gripping her arm and wrenching it behind her back.

"Morgan, LET ME GO!"

"TRACEY!"

Through her tears, she saw Noah rounding the corner in a blur.

Still, Morgan wouldn't let go, yanking her arm up higher until she cried out in pain. Suddenly, Noah cold-cocked the senator right on his nose as the sound of cartilage cracking popped in the night air. Morgan spun backward and fell in a heap on the ground. He tried to lift his head then dropped it, out cold.

"Tracey! Are you okay?" Noah pulled her into his arms briefly, then held her at arm's length. "Are you hurt?"

Tracey couldn't control the sobs wracking her body. She melted into his embrace in a puddle of tears.

At the sound of footsteps, they both looked up.

"Oh no." Scott rushed to the senator's side. "Is he—?"

"No, he's just out," Noah said, still holding Tracey close to his side. "But you probably ought to get the car so we can—"

"I'm on it," Scott said, already taking off for the vehicle.

"TRACEY!" Alex cried, rushing to her side. "Someone told me you'd been—oh my gosh, is that Senator Thompson?!"

Buddy was right behind her. "Tracey Jo, what on earth is *he* doing here?" He quickly knelt down and lifted Morgan's right eyelid then his left. He turned to face his daughter with a proud smile. "Did *you* do this?"

"No," Noah said, "the pleasure was all mine."

Buddy stood up and reached out for Noah's hand. "Then thank you. For Tracey Jo and for me!"

As the black sedan pulled into the alley, its headlights illuminated the scene. Morgan moaned, raising a shaky hand toward his broken nose. "What . . .?"

"Never you mind, Senator," Buddy said as Scott joined them. "Your chauffeur and I will get you back in the car."

"Huh?"

In a matter of minutes, they'd deposited the injured senator into the back seat of the sedan. Scott made his way back to the front seat and started the engine. Just as Buddy was about to shut the back door, Tracey reached for it. "A minute, please?" she asked her father.

"Sure, sweetheart. Whatever you say."

As he stepped out of the way, Tracey leaned into the car. "Scott? Take the good senator home—to his *wife.*"

"Gladly," he answered, shifting to reverse. "Take care, Tracey," he said with a ready smile.

"You too, Scott."

With that, she slammed the door as the car backed out of the alley then disappeared.

Chapter 21

It was close to an hour before Tracey and Noah could finally be alone. Back at the house, they'd patiently chatted with Buddy and Alex before those two said goodnight and went upstairs. With the sudden quiet, Noah felt strangely shy in front of her. They both started to say something at the exact same time.

"Sorry," he said, "you go ahead."

"No, you first."

"I was just going to suggest we go out on the back porch and make a fire. Are you up for that?"

"Sounds nice. You go ahead, and I'll bring us some coffee."

By the time she joined him with two mugs of steaming coffee, he'd managed to build a blazing fire. They settled down on the cushioned wicker sofa—the same place they'd sat not so long ago when they researched the Lincoln teacup together.

She handed him a mug. "It's decaf. I hope that's okay."

"It's perfect. Thanks."

Tracey sipped from her mug, her eyes focused on the fire.

"I was beginning to think we'd never have a chance to talk," he said, placing his mug on the table. "Seems like at least twelve hours since I first saw you sitting in City Hall."

She pushed her hair out of her face. "I know. Strange, isn't it?"

She took another sip of coffee then he gently took the cup from her and set it down. He took her hand in both of his. "Tracey, there's so much I need to say to you, I don't even know where to start."

She smiled, searching his eyes. "I'm not going anywhere."

"And that's a good thing. First, I need to apologize. It was wrong of me to take off and leave you that day on the ride." He paused, searching for the words he'd rehearsed all the way home. "The thing is, you deserved an explanation, but I was so freaked out by the accident, I . . . well, I just bolted. It's what I've always done whenever all that stuff—all those memories from Melissa's crash—starts flooding my mind again. But seeing that little red car and—" He cleared his throat. "What I'm trying to say is, the whole scene made me feel as if I were reliving that day my wife died."

He blew out a quick puff of air, wishing his chest wasn't feeling so tight again.

"Noah, you don't have to tell me right now—"

"But I do, Tracey. I have to. It's never going to get any easier, and you have a right to know. Because I can't have a future with you if I can't deal with my past. It's as simple as that. And up until now, whenever the memories got too vivid or the nights got too long, I'd just climb on my bike and disappear. But this time, I realized how futile, how stupid that is. I was just running away. And not just from my inability to cope; I realized I was running away from any possibility of ever living a normal life again. And while I was gone this time, I realized that's got to stop."

She turned to face him, tucking her foot beneath her leg, her hand still in his. "Then let's make it stop. Together. Tell me what you need to tell me, Noah. If it takes all night, that's fine. Just tell me."

And so he did.

Noah told her every single detail of that rainy day in April. He told her about the arrogant judge who made him late for his appointment with Melissa and their realtor. She'd found the perfect loft in Soho and wanted him to see it. Noah told Tracey about the taxi driver who couldn't speak English, and the traffic jam in midtown Manhattan. He told her of making a run for it in the pouring rain and coming upon the accident. He told her how he felt when he first saw the mangled red Volkswagen and prayed it wasn't Melissa's. How it felt when he spotted the daisies in the car and the vanity plate that read *My Lil' Bug.*

Tracey squeezed his hand, urging him to go on.

"A policeman gave me a ride to the hospital. I kept praying she was okay, but knowing she couldn't be after seeing the damage to her car. They finally gave me a moment with her . . . but she was already gone. My mind was crazy with grief, and I couldn't stop crying. I can still hear the sound of my cries bouncing around in that emergency room."

He stopped, taking a moment to wipe his tears and catch his breath. With a long ragged breath, he continued. "Before I left, the attending physician asked if I wanted to know if the baby was a girl or boy. At first, I had no idea what he was talking about." Noah coughed and blew out another breath. "See, I hadn't known . . . she hadn't told me yet."

"Oh, Noah," Tracey whispered.

"I think . . . well, I think that's why she was so urgent about showing me that loft. I think that's how she was going to tell me—show me where we'd put a nursery. She was always doing things like that. Surprising me." He swallowed hard. "But I couldn't speak, so I just nodded for the doctor to tell me. And he, uh, he said it was a boy." He tried to smile but couldn't. "Later, I decided to name him Bradley—that was Melissa's maiden name. Bradley Bennett. I put that on his gravestone. Next to his mother's."

Tracey laced their fingers, gently squeezing his hand. "It's a beautiful name."

He grew silent, trying to figure out how to go on. He took another deep breath and eased it back out. "Tracey, what I need you to know—what *you* need to know—is that I loved my wife very much. And when I lost her, I completely lost my will to live. Which is why I turned my back on everything I'd ever known and just left. I'd never even ridden a motorcycle before. But one day, on nothing but a whim, I traded my BMW for that Harley out there and just took off.

"And to make a long, long story at least a little shorter, a few months later I found myself working as a roadie in Nashville, met some other bikers, and one weekend took a trip to the Blue Ridge Mountains and met a guy named Buddy Collins."

Tracey smiled. "Ah, the wild, wild preacher man."

"Yes, and that wild, wild preacher man told me about new beginnings and second chances, and how to find *hope again* through a personal relationship with Jesus. He drew me into his group of Elders, and showed me how helping others could slowly bring me out of my grief. He gave me opportunities to take the focus off myself and instead focus on the needs of others. Buddy let me learn for myself how to care again by hammering shingles on a roof or fixing a leaky faucet or mowing someone's lawn.

"And the strangest thing happened. Little by little, I noticed I was starting to feel alive again. That I *cared* about getting up in the morning because there were people who needed a helping hand."

He pulled his hands free for a moment to rub his face and dash away the blasted tears. "I'm sorry, I'm rambling. I think your coffee got cold."

"That's not a problem."

"And the fire needs a little—"

"Noah?"

He looked at her. "What?"

"We're fine. The fire's fine. Go on. I'm listening."

He turned to face her, their knees overlapping as he reached for her hand again. "The thing is—the reason I've told you all this is because, for the first time in a very, very long time—I realized how much I want a chance to love again. You've been so patient with me, even when I didn't deserve it. And when I took off, even while I was wandering all over everywhere and nowhere, in the midst of all that, I couldn't stop thinking about you. It finally dawned on me; I had a reason not to run away anymore. And that reason was *you*."

She smiled, and that was all it took.

"Tracey Jolene Collins, what I'm trying to say is, I'm in love with you."

"Yeah?" she whispered, leaning to rest her forehead on his. "I'm really glad to hear it because I love you, too."

"Yeah?"

"Yeah."

"Then would you mind very much if I kissed you?"

She smiled. "I thought you'd never ask.

And so he did.

Chapter 22

On a brisk autumn morning in late October, Alex and Tracey cut the pumpkin-colored ribbon stretched across the front porch of their new shop to the cheers of their friends, family, and neighbors from town. Above them hung a new sign, beautifully lettered in a quaint, swirly font that made it official—*Second Chances* was open for business.

They spent the rest of the day welcoming their first customers, offering cold apple cider and sugar cookies to all who stopped by. Sales were brisk and compliments poured in along with a steady stream of well-wishers. Noah helped out whenever he could, helping folks carry their newfound treasures to their cars. Out back, the air was filled with the delicious aroma of kettle corn cooking in a big black urn. Buddy and the Elders dished up servings to customers in colorful cone-shaped cups.

Sometime early in the afternoon, Tracey stepped outside for some fresh air. "Daddy, that smells wonderful!"

Gristle chomped on a bite of kettle corn. "I ain't *never* tasted nuthin' like this before! Why you never made none o' this fo' us, Buddy?"

"You never asked," he quipped back. "But where are your manners, Gristle? Hand this to Maleeka for me."

"That's all right, Buddy," Maleeka teased, reaching for the treat. "I'll teach Gregory some manners, even if I have to take him back and make *his mama* slap some sense into him." She took a bite, and her eyes grew wide. "But he's right—why you never made this for us before? I gotta tell ya, this is to die for!"

Buddy laughed. "Well, thank you, Maleeka, but no need to die on my account."

"Hey, speakin'a dyin'," Gristle said, "whatev'a happen to that ol' buzzard Deacon? Ain't seen him round no' more. He do us all a favor and *shuffle off this mortal coil?*"

"Nah, but he had to retire," Buddy said. "After he suffered that massive heart attack at the City Council meeting, he had a stroke while he was still in the hospital. It paralyzed him severely, so he'll be in therapy for quite some time. He isn't able to say much, so I'd say Deacon's days of playing the ruler baron are over."

"Couldn't happen to a nicer guy," a voice behind them mumbled.

They turned to find Lester picking kettle corn out of his cup. He stopped eating and looked up. "What?" When no one said anything, the slightest hint of a smile tugged at his mouth.

They laughed at his reaction, as they often did when he caught them off guard like that.

Buddy stirred the big pot of corn. "Ah now, Lester, let's don't wish Deacon any bad will. He's got a tough road ahead of him."

"There you are!"

Tracey turned to find Mrs. Peterson standing in the back door of their shop. "How nice to see you, Mrs. Peterson. Come out and have some kettle corn," she said reaching up to help the elderly woman down the steps.

"Don't mind if I do, but someone else is here to see you, too." Mischief danced in her eyes as she stepped aside.

There, leaning over to avoid hitting his head on the doorframe, a tall block of a man stepped out onto the stoop. As he straightened to his full height, the stranger stood tall beside the tiny widow.

It took Tracey a second. "Stump? Oh my gosh, it's really you!"

"Holy cow, is that really you, Stump?!" Buddy hooted.

"Who else you know this tall?" Stump teased as he escorted Mrs. Peterson down the steps. Gone was the furry long beard. Gone was the messy, tangled head of matted hair. Gone were the ragged clothes he always wore. In their place, he wore a black sweater over a white oxford cloth shirt and gray slacks—and not so much as a single facial hair.

"Stump, you're positively handsome!" Tracey cried, giving the big guy a hug. "Look at you, all clean-shaven! What a nice smile you had hidden under all that . . . stuff."

He blushed, which was easy to see now with all that hair gone. "I have Mrs. Peterson to thank. I asked if she'd like to accompany me today and she said yes—on one condition."

Buddy laughed. "I guess we can figure that one out. Mrs. Peterson, you are truly a miracle worker."

The diminutive widow stood up on her toes, reaching up to tug on Buddy's ponytail. "Yes, Buddy, it seems I am a miracle worker, and I think I'm looking at my next project."

Buddy gave her a hug. "Well now, Mrs. P, don't get carried away."

Tracey laughed, enjoying the easy banter before stepping back inside. There she found Noah returning from delivering an armoire.

He gave her a side hug, planting a kiss on her cheek. "Don't know if you've realized it or not, but if you and Alex keep this up, you're not going to have a stick of furniture left by the end of the day."

"Which would be an awfully nice way to end our first day, don't you think?" Alex said, rearranging a display on the side counter.

"Bite your tongue, Sis! If so, that means you and I stay up all night refinishing what's left in the back. And I don't know about you, but I'm exhausted.! All I want to do is—"

"Oh, girls! Girls!"

Sadie Woolsey rushed through the front door. "You won't *believe* what's just happened!"

Alex grabbed her by the elbow. "Miss Sadie! What is it? Are you all right?"

"Yes, yes, I'm just so excited, I can hardly contain myself!"

"What is it?" Tracey asked, guiding the librarian to a tall stool at the checkout counter.

Sadie held a hand to her chest as she tried to catch her breath. "Remember those specialists from the Smithsonian who stopped by last week to examine the cup and saucer you found here in these walls? Well, just minutes ago I received a call from them. They said they couldn't reach you at Walnut Ridge, so they called me instead. I explained about the grand opening and asked if I could take a message. Well, lo and behold—are you ready for this? They've validated the pieces to be authentic china from President Lincoln's White House!"

Their cheers filled the room. "I can't believe it!" Tracey said, hugging the librarian.

"Yes, yes, it's absolutely true. And in addition, they said the note from Craggie Collins was authentic as well. Apparently, they have some kind of test they can run to determine the age of the paper it was written on. So they've asked if you would be willing to donate the note in addition to the cup and saucer. Isn't it just wonderful?"

With a hug, Alex said, "I'd say this calls for a celebration!"

Later that evening, long after sunset, the proud proprietors of *Second Chances* celebrated a happy ending to their first day in business—*and* the exciting news about the Lincoln teacup. Noah and Buddy took over kitchen duties, serving up hearty sandwiches and ladles of Alex's baked potato soup. Sadie arrived with two of her famous chess pies, with her trusty camera slung over her shoulder. Most of the Elders had left earlier in the day, but Lester, Stump, Gristle and Maleeka gradually showed up to join the gathering. They all mingled from one room to the next, enjoying a relaxed evening together.

Around 7:30, Buddy gathered everyone into the den to take some photographs of the momentous occasion. Sadie, who fancied herself quite the photographer, took charge and set up each shot—Buddy and his daughters, Buddy and his Elders, a shot of Alex and Tracey, one of Gristle and Maleeka, and a solo portrait of the new and improved Stump. Only Lester refused to be photographed.

"Not happenin'," he mumbled.

They all stared at him, then handed him another piece of pie and left him alone.

"Where's Noah?" Sadie asked. "Let's get him in here and have a shot of him with the girls holding the Lincoln teacup. Perhaps the Smithsonian would like to see the faces behind the historic discovery."

"But you should be in that one too, Miss Sadie." Buddy took the camera from her. "You go stand there with the girls." He looked around. "Noah? Where are you?"

"I'm coming, I'm coming," he said, joining them from the living room. "Alex asked me to get the cup and saucer out of the hutch."

Lifting her hands to caution him, Sadie warbled, "Oh, be careful, Noah. We certainly don't want anything to happen to them. Not after all this time."

"Noah, how about you give the girls the cup and saucer and let them both hold it in front," Buddy said, framing the shot. "Then you step there behind Tracey alongside Sadie."

Noah handed the cup to Alex then stepped behind the girls. "How's this?" he asked, wrapping his arm over Sadie's shoulder.

"Here, Trace," Alex said, holding the cup and saucer. "Let's hold it together like this."

"Okay, on three," Buddy said. "One, two—three!" The camera flashed, and he checked the preview on its small screen. "Looks great, but let's take a couple more. Okay, everybody—"

"Wait," Tracey said, peering into the teacup. "There's something in here." She lifted out a wad of tissue paper.

Noah leaned over her shoulder. "What is it?"

"Oh dear, *please* be careful," Sadie cautioned again.

"Just a wad of tissue paper," Tracey said, lifting it out of the cup.

"Probably just trash," Alex said, taking the cup and saucer from her sister.

Tracey started to unroll the wad of tissue. "No, it feels like—" She turned to look at Noah. A flash caused her to look back at her father, wondering why he took a picture before they were ready.

"Tracey, c'mon—you're killing me here," Alex prodded. "It feels like what?"

Tracey's mouth opened as the tissue fell to the floor. She gazed back at Noah just as he dropped down to pick it up . . . then remained where he was.

On one knee.

"It feels like a ring?" he asked as another camera flash went off.

"Yes," Tracey whispered, staring at the diamond solitaire in her hand. "But—"

"No buts, Tracey," he said, his face beaming with expectation. "I need to ask you a question."

"Uh oh," someone uttered from the back of the room.

They all turned to look at Lester who grinned mischievously.

"Oh my goodness, "Alex breathed as she and Sadie moved over beside Buddy. She carefully set down the cup and saucer then clasped her hands together against her mouth. All eyes returned to Tracey and Noah.

"Tracey Jolene Collins, will you marry me?"

Unable to speak, she simply nodded as a tear slipped down her face.

Noah stood up, slowly sliding the diamond on her finger. "I was hoping you'd say that."

For a split second, no one said a thing. Then spontaneous celebration filled the room, echoing against the rafters of the old house.

Time stood still as Noah and Tracey laughed through tears of joy.

"For heaven's sake, Noah!" Alex shouted, "Give her a kiss!"

And so he did.

Epilogue

Of course, the Lincoln teacup and saucer in my hands aren't authentic. Years ago, Aunt Lucille told me she bought the set in a gift shop at the Smithsonian in Washington. Still, I prefer to imagine the china I'm now carefully placing back in my hutch had originally been a gift from dear old Abe himself. Perhaps young Craggie Collins, or another White House employee like him, had dropped by the Oval Office to say goodbye. And who knows, maybe the President gave him the set as a parting gift. Knowing all too well that the First Lady had already ordered a new pattern since this one hadn't stood the test of time, perhaps Lincoln and Craggie had a brief farewell exchange . . .

> *"Sure sad to see you go, Mr. Collins," Abe says, extending his hand to the young man. "But I thank you for your service these past few years."*
>
> *Craggie shakes his hand as they head for the door. "You're welcome, Mr. President."*
>
> *Beside the door, a tea service sits atop a tall table. The President peeks around the corner then lifts the cup and saucer. "Here, son. As a token of my appreciation. A little keepsake, if you will."*
>
> *"Oh, Mr. President, I couldn't!"*
>
> *Abe motions for Craggie to open his satchel. "Quick, before the First Lady catches me. She's been on a tirade about this blasted china." Safely securing the pieces, Abe closes and latches the young man's leather bag. "Just think of it as a favor you're doing for me." He gives Craggie a wink, then pats him on the shoulder and sends him on his way.*

Or something like that.

I take a deep breath and bask in the faux-memory. Funny, but when I imagine these scenes in my head, I can smell the musty air in that famous old building. I can hear Abe's clock ticking over on the mantel. I can see the dark circles under the President's eyes and the sadness hiding behind his kind countenance. I've never written historical novels, but I have to say it's pretty fun hobnobbing with the movers and shakers of our past. I say that, but then I hear a gunshot ring out on an April night at Ford's Theater . . . and I realize all stories eventually come to an end.

I shake it off, this gray cloud of darker days in our nation's history. Time to change gears and start thinking about my next novella. I've been so distracted lately, I'm having trouble remembering which teacup goes with this new story. The setting is back east somewhere in the vicinity of Boston, I think?

My cell phone rings and I dig it out of my jeans pocket. On the screen I see Mark's picture and my heart does a little two-step.

"Hey, Mark! How's it going?"

"Morning, Luce! There's something I need to know."

"Ask away, big guy," I say, twirling a curl of my hair with my fingers.

"Did Noah man up and come back for Tracey?"

I'm glad he can't see me because my smile is so oversized, I look spastic. I know this because I see my reflection in the glass of my hutch. But how *sweet* is he? Most of the guys I've gone out with in the last decade couldn't care less about my fiction world. The best I ever got was, "Well, uh, you done yet with that, uh, little story . . . thing?" Pathetic.

But Mark? He not only knows where I am in my current project—he *knows my characters' names.*

"I could tell you," I respond, "but then I'd have to kill you. Which would never work because we have plans tonight, right?"

"We absolutely do. And speaking of that, don't forget to wear your crew shirt, okay?"

"It's ironed and ready. Anything else?"

"No. But I can't wait to see you tonight."

"Me, too. You. Too," I stammer, as usual. "Well, you know what I mean."

"Bye, Luce. See you at six."

I drop the cell phone back in my pocket then lean back to look down the hall. There on my bedroom door hangs my brown bowling shirt. Go ahead. Have your fun. Laugh all you want. Me—Lucy Alexander—bowling? I have to admit, I hated it at first. I warned Mark I'd be the laughingstock of the entire UPS fleet in our region. But he was so excited about introducing me to his friends and their significant others, how could I say no? If, however, you're expecting a detailed summary of my efforts to stay out of the gutters at Ten Pin Alley, forget it.

Now, where was I?

Oh, yes. I'm trying to remember which teacup. Then suddenly I see it and remember. It's always been one of my favorites because I have such vivid memories of sipping tea from it all those years ago the summer I visited Aunt Lucille. And oh, what a story it has to tell . . . a story of unrequited love, a mysterious legend, and those who have never forgotten its curse.

I can hardly wait to get started!

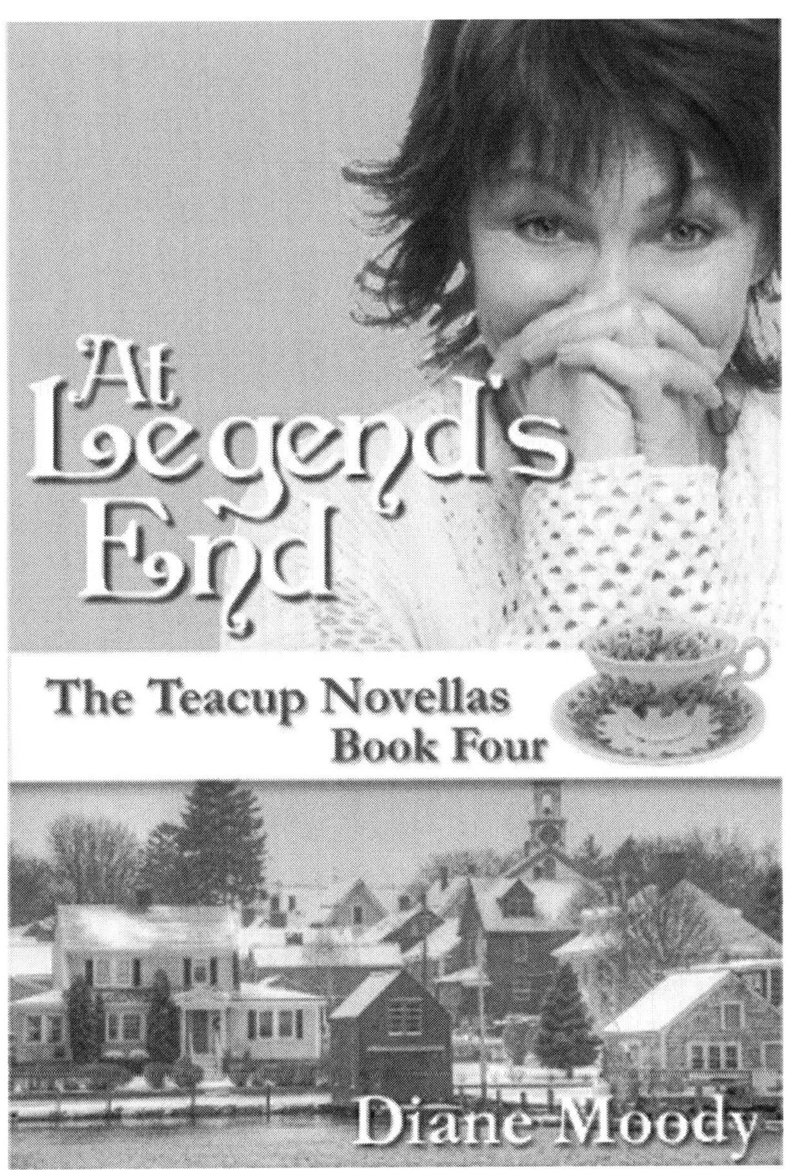
At
Legend's
End
The Teacup Novellas
Book Four
Diane Moody

Love is our true destiny.
We do not find the meaning of life
by ourselves alone . . .
we find it with another.
—Thomas Merton

"For I know the plans I have for you,"
declares the Lord,
"plans to prosper you and not to harm you,
plans to give you hope and a future."
—Jeremiah 29:11

Prologue

"Lucy, I've got to hand it to you. I've never lived anywhere but here in New York, but that last novella had me packing my bags for Tenne—"

I yanked my cell away from my ear as my editor's hacking cough filled the airwaves between us. Again. Always. I'd had the The Talk with her so many times to no avail that I no longer bothered. Right now, as Samantha's body wracked itself in search of a single minuscule breath of non-nicotine-stained oxygen, I knew that she knew what I would say. And I knew that she knew what her response would be. Words were no longer necessary.

"You were saying?" I asked, as the final wheeze afforded me a chance to speak.

"Oh, yes. I was saying I practically had my bags packed for Tennessee. And that's not the half of it. I went online and spent an hour browsing the Harley Davidson website. I'm not kidding you. Did you know they have trikes?"

"What, like a tricycle?"

I remembered the three-wheeled bikes the senior adults in Florida often rode. I have distinct memories of seeing a group of elderly women dressed in their two-piece swimsuits riding those three-wheelers, their bronzed wrinkles flapping in the breeze. Somewhere I had a file full of ideas for a geriatric romantic comedy based on seeing those women sailing along, oblivious to what anyone else might think. I made a mental note to look for that file.

"Lucy? Hello?"

"I'm here. Sorry, Samantha. You were saying something about a trike?"

"Yes, the trike. I have the brochure here on my desk. I think I'll make an appointment to test ride one sometime."

I bit back a giggle. "I don't even know how to respond to that."

"What I'm trying to tell you is, I loved the biker story. Your writing transports your readers into whole new worlds. Which is what I taught you to do when I first signed you. You've come a long way, baby."

"That's really sweet. Especially coming from you."

"Yeah? Well, enough of that. I need you to get started on the next novella and stay on task. I'm leaving town for a few weeks, and I don't want to be worrying about our next deadline while I'm away."

"Now, Sam, you know we've never missed a deadline. Don't worry. Are you heading off on vacation?" I asked, knowing better.

"No, it's Pauleen."

"Is she okay?"

I remembered the picture of the two of them on the windowsill in Sam's office. Pauleen was two minutes older than Samantha, but I'm fairly confident Sam was running her twin's life before they exited the birth canal. Sam had told me they were leap year babies born on the twenty-ninth of February. Which accounts for my yearly confusion as to how old my editor actually is.

"No, her heart's about to give out on her. She never listens to a thing I tell her—"

Must be genetic, I thought.

"—so I've got to take time off to drive up to Maine and see if I can't knock some sense into her before she keels over and dies on me."

I pressed my lips together. So many responses, right there on the tip of my tongue. "Well, give her my best. I'll keep her in my prayers, okay?"

"Forget her. *I'm* the one who needs prayer. My sister can drive me to drink faster than Mario Cuomo."

"I think you mean Mario Andretti."

"Whatever. Listen, I'm outta here. Get moving on the new story. I'll let you know when I'm back in the office. Don't let that boyfriend of yours steal all your time. Got it?"

"Got it. Not a problem."

"Yeah, that's what they all say. Gotta run, Lucy. Ciao mein."

"Right backatcha," I said to a dead line.

Gertie waddled into my office, her pointy tail slowly wagging as she tilted her head and pinned me with those sympathetic doggie eyes.

"I know. You always hate it when Samantha calls." I tilted my head at the same angle. "But enough about her. Time for a walk?"

She took off for the front door, her nails clicking a dance beat on my hardwoods. It dawned on me a while back that God gives dogs to people like me because He knows it's the only way to get me outside for some fresh air. When Gertie was a puppy, I proudly walked her around the block a couple of times a day. Even with those short, stubby Scottie legs, we kept up a steady pace.

But the truth is, now it seems she's the one walking me, forcing me to push back from my laptop and get outside where I can fill my lungs with fresh air, be it hot or cold. Even when I try to talk her out of it, she parks her haunches on the rug by the door and gives me The Look. I'm a sucker for The Look, and she knows it.

Which begs the question—who trained whom?

I snapped the leash onto Gertie's collar, grabbed my windbreaker and off we went. I shouldn't complain, really. Some of my best plot and character ideas pop in my head during these walks. Today was no exception. Something Samantha said was toying with my mind. I knew that Pauleen still lived just outside of Caden Cove, Maine, where they grew up. Sam went through marriages almost as fast as she smoked through cartons of Virginia Slims, but Pauleen had never married. What would that be like? Not just living in the same town your whole life, but being middle-aged and still single. Was there still a stigma against women who'd never married? I'd touched briefly on the subject in my last novella. Tracey's sister, Alex, was completely content with her life. But is that the norm or the exception among women these days?

As Gertie led me around the corner, I looked up just in time to notice a big flash of brown coming toward us. My heart skipped a beat. Who knew a color could spark such a reaction? I grabbed the lip gloss out of my pocket and took a quick swipe at my lips just before the UPS truck pulled up beside me.

The handsome driver leaned out his window. "Hey, lady, I think I'm lost."

"Oh yeah? Where you headed, big guy?" I stepped close enough to catch a scent of his manly cologne.

He reached out and tucked a strand of hair behind my ear. "Anywhere *you* are, sweet pea."

I rolled my eyes for his benefit. "Is that the best you've got? Surely you've got a better pick-up line in your arsenal."

"Sorry, ma'am. It's against company policy to pick up riders."

"I see. Well, then, *sweet pea,* I guess you and your GPS will just have to find your way without me."

He grabbed my hand and squeezed it. "Yes, but where's the fun in that?" He floated me a wink. "Hey, Luce."

"Hey, Mark. How's your day?"

"Better, now that I've seen you. Have you got dinner plans tonight?" he asked, twisting and turning the narrow silver ring on my thumb. It was a habit I'd grown to love.

"Actually, I do. I'm making ziti for this guy I've got a crush on."

"Yeah? I *love* your ziti."

"What a coincidence. I could set an extra place at the table, if you'd like to join us."

He smiled as his eyes danced. "I'd love to—if you think he won't mind?"

"Oh, no. He won't—"

Suddenly, the leash wrapped around my wrist yanked hard, nearly knocking me off my feet. Gertie was in hot pursuit of a squirrel, pulling me along behind her. "Gertie! Stop!"

Behind me, I heard the truck roar to life. "See you at seven, Lucy!"

I turned just in time to see his wave as he pulled away. I waved, hoping he might look back. He did. He always does.

I tried scolding Gertie in my best alpha voice, but she wasn't having it. The squirrel long forgotten, she happily took off down the sidewalk with me in tow. I didn't mind. I was still basking in the moment. I always love it when Mark is in the neighborhood so he can stop by. He'd never go off route, of course, and never come by the house unless he has a package to deliver. He's honest and faithful, even to his employers. I admire him for that. It says a lot about his character. And I'd grown rather fond of his character over the last few months.

As Gertie and I continued our walk, I tried to steer my mind back to my new story. Something was there, just under the surface. I could feel it, but I couldn't seem to connect the dots. "Focus, Lucy. Focus," I chided myself. "Okay, I was thinking about Pauleen. And about middle-aged women who've never married. And—"

Gertie stopped to squat for the fourth time. She looked at me with the sweetest expression on her face. I often imagine her conversations. Which makes sense, considering I'm a pro at putting words in people's mouths. She was in rare form today.

Isn't this fun? Aren't we having fun? Don't we love it out here? There's so much to see! So many things to sniff! Gee, we could stay all day; if you like! Can we? Can we, huh?

And that's when it clicked. All of it, like an elaborate maze of dominoes falling one after another.

Gertie . . . the spitting image of her political canine hero, Barney —the official First Dog of the George W. Bush presidency. We'd mourned Barney's passing a while back, but now all I could see in my head was the famous home of the Bush family there in Maine. I'd spent a weekend in Kennebunkport years ago at a bed and breakfast. I loved the charming coastal town, thinking someday I'd like to move there.

Gertie. Barney. The Bush family estate at Kennebunkport, Maine . . .

That's it!

The perfect setting for my new novella—a fictional town similar to Kennebunkport.

The perfect setting for an unlikely love story between two unsuspecting forty-something characters.

The perfect setting for a not-so-ordinary blue and white teacup.

The perfect setting for a local legend bridging the past with the future.

I took off, racing Gertie back to the house. "C'mon, girl! We've got a story to write!"

Chapter 1

As Olivia Thomas joined the mass exodus of commuters through the thick ribbons of Atlanta's afternoon rush hour, she answered her cell phone. *Right on time.* She and Ellen dubbed it their private Happy Hour, chatting to pass the time as both headed home from work.

"So how was your day?" asked her best friend.

"Exciting. Thrilling. Breathtaking. You know—the usual."

"That bad, huh?"

"No, not really. Just not too many folks applying for loans right now. Such a strange market with this economy. But it is what it is. How about you? Good day?"

"Never a dull moment."

"That good, eh?" Olivia checked her rearview mirror. Some kid in a bright red sports car was riding her bumper, his head jerking in motion to a pounding beat she could feel inside her own car. As his eyes met hers in the mirror, he mouthed off and waved his middle finger at her.

Yeah, you're so tough. See me shaking in my boots?

"You still there?"

"I'm here. Just wishing I was anywhere *but* here. Tell me again why do we do this every day?"

"Do what?"

"Spend an hour every morning and another every afternoon on the road with all these crazies."

"Oh that. But when else would we have this much time to talk?"

"I know, but don't you find it all rather pointless?"

"Hey, Olivia?"

"Yes?"

"What's going on? You've made this commute every weekday for more than twenty-five years. Why's it bothering you today?"

"Just the Monday grumpies, I guess."

"Did something happen today?" Ellen pressed.

"Not really."

"Out with it. You know I won't let up 'til you tell me, so just spit it out and save us some time."

Olivia pictured her friend's inquisitive blue eyes, her fashionable salt and pepper hairstyle, her mischievous smile. They had way too much history between them to play games. Transparency ran deep on both sides. Well, most of the time. She knew Ellen wouldn't stop prodding until she coughed up whatever was bugging her.

But that was the problem. Olivia didn't *know* what was bugging her.

"I'm just so tired. I'm still fighting those eight pounds I put on over the holidays. I still haven't been back on my treadmill. It's been over a month now, but I can't seem to find my motivation. You know the drill."

"Uh huh. And?"

"I don't know. Haven't you ever wondered if there's more to life? If, maybe, somehow we've settled for these ruts we live in, when we were meant for something greater? Something more significant?"

"Well, sure. Who doesn't have thoughts like that? But then I—"

"Then you think about Brent and the kids and your grandbaby on the way, and you think, how could life be any better than this?"

"Stop putting words in my mouth."

Olivia stretched out the kinks in her neck. "But I'm right, aren't I?"

"C'mon, Olivia, that's not fair. Besides, I think *you* love my family more than I do. And I'm quite sure they love you more than me."

"That goes without saying."

"Stop derailing the conversation. Talk to me."

Olivia huffed a sigh. "Okay. Fine. I'll tell you. I went to work this morning just like every morning. And as I walked into my office and turned on the lights, all I could hear was that irritating buzzing sound—you know, when the florescent light tubes try to blink on? I don't know why, but it just got under my skin. And stayed there. All day. Then I realized how much I despise the color of paint on the walls. It hasn't changed in all the years I've been there. It's the color of Band Aids. Who in their right mind picks a color like that for the interior walls of a bank?"

"Someone who likes Band Aids?"

"You're just hilarious. Really. Hear me laughing? No. Then Ted strolled into my office, and he went on and on about the gas grill Rene got him for his birthday. And the whole time, he kept subtly picking his nose. Digging for gold right there in front of me."

"Ew?!"

"I kept wishing I had one of those high-powered water guns so I could just blast that stupid smirk off his face."

Ellen's giggle chirped through the speaker on her cell. "That, I'd pay money to see!"

"Then when I took my break this morning, someone had left a near-empty carafe on the burner, which burned the coffee residue in the pot. The break room reeked. I took it off the burner, set it in the sink, and walked away. I told Marilyn I'd be back in twenty minutes, walked down the street to The Daily Grind, ordered a fresh cup of coffee, and took my break on a park bench."

"Atta girl. Fresh air. Just what you needed."

"I've never understood how grown men with MBAs aren't smart enough to turn the coffeemaker off when the pot's empty. How hard is it? And I'll bet dollars to donuts not a single one of them know how to change the toilet roll when it's out."

"It's because the women in their lives have trained them to be that way," Ellen explained. "First Mommy wipes their behinds and spoon-feeds them until they leave home, then Wifey picks up where Mommy left off. Naturally, they expect their female co-workers to do the same. 'They cain't hep' it,'" she twanged. "'They don't know no better!'"

Olivia laughed. "You have a point, Ellie Mae."

"Of course I do! Hey, it's nice to hear you laugh. All kidding aside, please tell me what's got you so gritchy today."

Out of nowhere, Olivia's eyes began to fill. "I honestly don't know. For some reason, it all just got to me today. And I realized, I'm *so bored* with my job . . . but I'm too old to start over. And what's worse, even if I could start over, I don't know what I'd do. And I just feel so . . . trapped."

"Don't be silly. You can do whatever you set your mind to."

"No, Ellen, I can't. I could never just up and leave my job. Not after all these years. Besides, I've got my 401K to think about, and—"

"Forget about all that for a minute. Listen to me. If you're really serious about this, let's sit down, talk through it, and see what kind of possibilities we might come up with. You're only forty-five, not a hundred and five. Stop thinking like you're old as dirt."

Taking her exit off the interstate, Olivia dashed away her tears. "Oh, don't mind me. It's probably just hormones."

"Doesn't matter. I think we should get together and brainstorm. Who knows what amazing adventures we might come up with?"

She pictured her friend's face, lit up with her signature optimism and wild imaginings.

Olivia sighed again. "Maybe another time. Tonight, I just need some peace and quiet, okay? Preferably, *without* any buzzing florescent lights."

"Or burnt coffee. I get it. But are you sure? Brent's got his photography class tonight. I could meet you at Chili's. Turn your car around. C'mon, it'll be fun!"

"Not tonight, girlfriend. Besides, I'm almost home."

"Yeah, so?"

"Remember when I told you how tired I was?"

"All right, all right. I won't nag."

"Thank you."

"But can I pray for you?"

"I have a feeling you'll pray no matter what I say."

"Got that right. Just promise not to close your eyes unless you're in your driveway."

And as she had so many times through the thirty-something years of their friendship, Ellen prayed for Olivia. She prayed for peace and rest and guidance. She claimed the scripture in Jeremiah 29:11, reminding Olivia of God's promise to give her a future and a hope. She thanked God for their friendship and how much a part of her family Olivia had been all through the years.

"Finally, Lord, whatever's eating at Olivia's heart right now, please let her feel Your arms around her. *Suffocate* her with Your love, Lord. *Astound* her with Your presence. And hey, as long as I'm at it, I might as well go ahead and just ask—feel free to *knock her socks off* tonight, Lord."

Olivia couldn't help the snicker that erupted in a loud snort.

Ellen didn't miss a beat. "And thank you for that amen from the sistah! Thank you, my sistah. And Father God, I don't know *how* You'll knock her socks off—or what that even means? But I believe You can do it. And for that, we'll give You all the glory and the honor in Your precious name. And all God's children said?"

Another snort broke loose as Olivia pulled into her driveway and pressed her garage door opener.

"And yet *another* amen from my beloved sistahhhh!"

"I was wondering when Sister Aretha would show up." Olivia tried to wrestle the odd mix of laughter and tears. "You're certifiable. You know that?"

"Oh, sure. It's why you love me so much."

"Yeah, yeah, I suppose."

"Hey, are you gonna be okay?"

"I'm good. But thanks for asking, Sister Aretha."

Chapter 2

Olivia tossed her mail on the kitchen table and kicked off her shoes. She set the kettle on the stove to heat, then grabbed her shoes and padded down the hall to her bedroom. Changing into more comfortable clothes, she couldn't help wondering why she'd let so many random annoyances nag her over the course of the day. She'd never struggled with depression. She'd always felt blessed and grateful for good friends, a good job, and a cozy home she loved. Others might see her middle-age singleness as a source of sadness, but she never had. She always tried to live her life with no regrets, and for the most part, that's exactly how she'd lived. She especially cherished her quiet evenings at home.

So why, even now as she relaxed on the sofa with a cup of tea and a pile of mail in her lap, did she feel so anxious? Where had these feelings come from today?

Knock it off.

Hoping to block out the doom and gloom, she rifled through her mail. A few bills, an acknowledgment letter from a ministry she contributed to, and a handful of junk mail. She started to toss them all aside when she noticed a letter tucked between a flyer from Dollar General and a page of coupons from Arby's. The return address indicated it was from a law firm in town. Out of curiosity, she opened the envelope and unfolded the letter.

Dear Miss Thomas,

I'm contacting you on behalf of my client, John Emerson Winthrop. He seems to think you won't remember him, but he's never forgotten you. Fifteen years ago, he came to your bank asking for a loan to pursue a business endeavor. Twelve other institutions had already turned him down before he met with you that day. He had already resolved to give up his dream if you refused his loan as well.

As he tells it, you took a pass at first, explaining, "On paper, it just isn't feasible." On a whim, he asked if you'd ever taken a chance on someone, even when it didn't make sense on paper. He said you didn't respond for several moments, so he began gathering his portfolio to leave. That's when you told him to sit back down. And five minutes later, you signed off on a loan to him "in good faith."

You probably don't know this, but Mr. Winthrop used that seed money to produce the first of what's known today as "apps" for the iPhone. I'd try to explain it, but the technology is way over my head, and isn't really significant—beyond the fact of how deeply he appreciates the chance you gave him so many years ago.

Now he wants to thank you for the risk you took on him all those years ago. He has designated a gift for you, and asked that I give it to you in person in his absence. Please contact my office for an appointment as soon as possible so that I can follow through with his wishes.

I look forward to hearing from you.

Charles S. Granston
Granston, Meyers & Breedlove,
Attorneys at Law

Olivia stared at Granston's signature as she lowered the letter to her lap. She closed her eyes, vaguely remembering the young man. She could picture his face framed by a shaggy head of hair, but mostly she remembered the hundred-watt smile on his face when she handed him the check. That, and the heartfelt hug he'd given her on his way out the door.

How odd. How did he even remember me after all these years?

As she drifted off to sleep later that night, she dreamed of a lawyer's strange presentation to her in, of all places, the basement stairwell of an office building. He gave her a Timex watch, a Bic pen, and a plaque with some rambling comments of appreciation scribbled illegibly in blue ink from a Bic pen. Later, as she hung the plaque in her office, she wondered how the kid with the shaggy hair could have remembered the "Band-Aid" shade of her walls and found a frame in that hideous color.

On her break the next morning, she closed her office door and dialed Granston's number. A receptionist answered.

"Yes, Miss Thomas, we've been expecting your call. What time would you like to stop by this morning?"

"This morning? No, I'm at work and—"

"No problem. How about later today? Would you have a few minutes to spare on your lunch break? We're just a couple streets over from your bank."

"My lunch break? Yes, well, I suppose I could do that."

"Excellent. When shall I tell Mr. Granston to expect you?"

Why all the urgency? “Oh, um, well, I could probably be there by 11:45.”

“Good. We’ll see you then.”

Olivia stared at her phone, befuddled. She was about to Google John Emerson Winthrop’s name when someone knocked on her door. She looked up as her boss opened the door.

“Got a minute?” He closed the door behind him then slowly took a seat in the gray faux-leather chair across from her desk.

She tried to refocus her thoughts. “Sure, Cliff. What’s up?”

“Seems we’re about to be bought out. Again. Big surprise, huh?”

For the next thirty minutes, they discussed the details of what would be the sixth buy-out since Olivia started working at the bank a week after her twentieth birthday. It always felt as if someone were shaking the rafters when these things occurred, but after a while they’d settle back into the routine of business as usual. Except for a new name on the signage outside and the checks, little changed.

Olivia leaned back. “Suppose we could talk them into some new paint on the walls this time?”

He gave a quick glimpse around her office. “Still looks nice to me.” He gave her an indifferent smile and left.

Why do I even ask?

She tried to get back to work, but couldn’t stand the curiosity. She called the receptionist at Granston’s office, telling her she’d by right over.

Granston was shorter than she expected, but what he lacked in stature he made up for in congeniality.

“How nice to meet you, Miss Thomas.” He grasped her hand in a firm handshake. “Please, have a seat.” He motioned to a pair of leather wingback chairs in front of his expansive desk.

She sank into the one nearest the door and set her purse on the plush Oriental rug below. “I must say, I was a bit surprised to receive your letter. I hadn’t thought of Mr. Winthrop in years.”

Granston tented his fingers, resting his elbows on his desk. “That’s not unusual for John, I assure you. He’s always been exceptionally thoughtful toward others and extremely generous. In fact, as we speak, he’s on an extended mission trip in the Dominican Republic. He recently established a non-profit agency to provide clean water to some of the bleakest areas in that country.”

"My church helped build a school down there a few years ago. They said the living conditions are heartbreaking."

"It's unimaginable. I joined John on one of his trips down there last year. It was a life-changing experience." He nodded, his kind eyes acknowledging the sincerity of his words. "And speaking of *life changing* . . ." He moved a thin leather folder to the center of his desk and opened it. "I could say the same for you."

"Me?"

"Not long after you helped John secure that first loan more than fifteen years ago, he launched a tech start-up company he named INRS—an acronym for *It's Not Rocket Science.* Five years later, he and his small staff released the prototype for something called the Share Cube. The cubes are about the size of dice. As I said in my letter, the technology is way over my head. But from what I understand, it enables you to share music and video files from one device to another by merely touching the two devices together—a smart phone to an iPod or another phone or whatever."

"I've seen something like that advertised on television."

Granston smiled. "Yes, that would be the Samsung version of the device. Of course, there have been other similar technologies in the past, but John's was the first, and he holds the patent on the device. It's taken all these years to perfect the product, adapting it to the various and rapid influx of gadgets and gizmos on the market. But two years ago, he sold his entire company to Samsung for $900 million in stock and cash."

Olivia felt her mouth fall open.

His smiled broadened. "The Samsung stock has now doubled in value making John Winthrop a very wealthy man."

She tried to conjure up the image of that kid with the messy hair sitting in her office, so thrilled to get a check from her bank for a mere $10,000.

Granston chuckled. "Hard to imagine, isn't it?"

"Yes, it is. I'm in banking, but those numbers boggle my mind."

"I know what you mean. Now to the reason you're here. Believe it or not, my client remains a very humble man. He recognizes everything he's ever been given as 'a gift from God' and as such, he sees his responsibility to pay it forward as often as he can. Or, in your case, I guess that would be paying it *backward*." He smiled, lifting an envelope from the folder. "Miss Thomas, it is with great pleasure that I present to you this check from John Winthrop as a token of his appreciation for taking a chance on him all those years ago."

He stood to hand her the envelope.

Olivia kept her eyes on his, unsure of the protocol for such a situation. Should she tear open the envelope to see how much the check was for? Should she just thank him and be on her way? She glanced down at the envelope as she took hold of it, her hand trembling.

Granston waved his hand as he took his seat again. "Please—feel free to have a look. In fact, I insist."

"Are you sure? I mean, this is all very—"

"Go ahead. Take a peek."

She leaned back, willing her hands to stop shaking. She swallowed against her parched throat then slid a finger beneath the seal. As she removed the check, she found a handwritten note paper clipped to it.

Dear Olivia,

You helped me make my dreams come true. My prayer is that I can now do the same for you.

—John

A sting prickled her eyes as she slowly pulled the note from the paperclip. The first thing she noticed was the numeral five followed by zeros. Lots and lots of zeros. She had to blink several times to see them all. That's when she saw the amount written out on the line below.

Five million dollars and no cents.

Olivia wheezed with laughter, her head falling back against the tall chair as she finally realized what was happening. It took a moment to catch her breath before the air *whooshed* from her lungs again, triggering another round of hysteria. She pounded her fist against her chest.

"I'm so sorry . . . I don't know what I was expecting, but obviously this is some kind of joke, right? Oh! Wait—is this for one of those reality shows on TV?" She looked around for hidden cameras, the last of her giggles still dancing through her voice. "C'mon, tell me. Where are the cameras?"

"I assure you this is no joke," Granston said, still smiling. "Though I wish John was here to witness your reaction just now. The man loves a good laugh."

Olivia's laughter disappeared along with the smile on her face. She looked at the check, then allowed her eyes to track back to the attorney. "Do you mean to tell me—?"

"Yes, I do. That's a check for five million dollars. And it's made out to *you*."

"But . . . but . . ."

Now it was Granston who laughed. "There's just one caveat, and it's important. Mr. Winthrop insists that his gift to you remain private. Of course, you're free to tell one or two of your closest friends or family, but only people you trust. He has no interest in publicity of any sort, so he's quite adamant that this be kept out of the press. I trust that won't be a problem?"

"But . . . but . . ."

He put his glasses back on, folded his hands on his desk, and smiled one last time. "By the way, just so you know—I also handle tax law."

Chapter 3

One week later

Olivia checked the GPS screen in her rental car, following its directions up I-95. With her cell phone on speaker, she laughed again. "I still can't believe I'm doing this, Ellen."

"I can't either. Especially since I'm not with you."

"Don't you dare start. I begged you to come with me."

"I know, I know. But, unlike those with *unlimited funds*, I need my job. Besides, like I told you before, you need some time to yourself to sort all this out. And as much as I'd like to visit Caden Cove again, I still think you're better off on your own for a while. At least until you can get your bearings."

"You keep saying that, but what are best friends for if not for helping their friends find their bearings?"

Ellen faked a huff. "Enough! I promised you I'd come in a couple of weeks if you can't manage without me, and I will. But, my guess is you'll settle into that cozy bed and breakfast, enjoy the beauty of the area, and all that sea air will help clear out the cobwebs. I guarantee it."

"Remind me again how I let you talk me into this? Who visits Maine in the dead of winter? I'm surprised the roads aren't covered with ice or buried under eight feet of snow."

"Y'know, for someone who was just given five million dollars, you sure whine a lot."

Olivia caught a glimpse of herself in the rearview mirror, the same slap-happy grin spreading across her face again. The slow chuckle sprouted until she laughed out loud.

"That's more like it, goofball. It's about time you cut loose and enjoyed all this."

Olivia's laughter waned. "It's still *so* surreal. I still keep expecting to wake up and find out it was all just a dream."

"Hey, it not only happened; you've already taken your first leap of faith by getting on that plane this morning. I kept cheering long after you'd left the main ticket area. Could you hear me?"

"Well, yes—me and everyone else at Hartsfield. But I'm still a little bummed you forgot your pom-poms."

"I know! What was I thinking, leaving the house without them? But hey, if I want to wish my best friend a happy getaway, then let me. I cried all the way home—tears of joy, of course. I want to tell the whole world how happy I am for you!"

Olivia adjusted her sunglasses. "You better not. Except for Brent, you've been sworn to secrecy, remember?"

"You know me. Holder of all secrets and teller of none. I'm just *so happy* for you . . ."

"Oh, not with the tears again? Ellen, I'm thinking my first purchase should be stock in Kleenex and have it delivered to you by the truck load."

Ellen's sniffling filled the miles between them. "Go ahead, have your fun."

"Oh, I plan to."

"Just remember, I'm the one who prayed for God to blow your socks off."

"As if you'd let me forget? You're my Danny Kaye in *White Christmas.*"

"Hey, Olivia?"

She'd grown accustomed to the simple familiar question asked in that same quiet, endearing tone. A mix of words and emotion all wrapped up in a sweet Ellen package. She smiled at the thought. "Yes?"

"I love you, girlfriend. And I'm praying for you to have the time of your life these next few weeks or however long you decide to stay away."

"I told Cliff—"

"I know you told your boss you'd be back by the first of March, but I still don't see why you don't just quit."

"Because it's too much to think about right now. My head's still spinning from all this. Even the attorney advised me not to make any rash decisions right now. I need to think through all of it and make sure I do this right."

"Fine, okay. But promise me you won't short-change yourself by thinking you have to be back by a certain date. Don't be marking days off a calendar like there's a big deadline looming over you. If you never set foot in that bank again, life as we know it will still go on."

"We'll see."

"I hate it when you say that."

"I know. That's why I say it."

"Promise you'll call me after you check in the Captain MacVicar?"

"I promise. Ellen?"

"Yes?"

"Love you."

"Love you too, Olivia."

The hour and a half drive from Boston to Caden Cove passed quickly. The rental's temperature gauge showed 23°, which explained the snow still covering the grassy areas. When Ellen first suggested Maine as a possible destination, Olivia thought she'd lost her mind. Then, after Ellen reminded her of the trips she and Brent had made to Caden Cove over the years, she warmed to the idea. The quaint bed and breakfast inn. The off-season quiet and serenity of the tiny oceanside town not far from Kennebunkport. The perfect place for a person to "find her bearings" after an incredible life-changing bolt of lightning.

Olivia tried to think analytically about her unexpected windfall, but it wasn't easy. She'd always been the sensible one. Dependable. Loyal. Generous. Kind. Considerate. All admirable and complimentary adjectives she'd heard over the years from friends and coworkers. But after a lifetime of self-imposed caution, she couldn't help the wisps of adventure whispering through her veins.

The call to her boss had come easy. "I decided to take a long overdue vacation. I'll be in touch." He hadn't argued. In fact, he'd applauded her for finally doing something so out of character.

She shook off any remaining thoughts of work or obligations and tried to focus on what might lie ahead. Granston had offered advice on her new-found wealth, wisely suggesting she take out a small portion for the time being then let the rest of it earn interest while she decided what she might do. Beyond the personal retreat she'd planned in Caden Cove, she didn't have a clue what she might do or where she might go. But even in the quiet of her rental car, she had to admit she was excited.

So many possibilities! Tuscany. New Zealand. The south of France. The Swiss Alps. How many hours had she spent browsing the internet as she dreamed of international destinations? How many travelogues had she watched on the Discovery Channel, promising herself to one day pack her bags and go?

And now, what was to stop her?

She stretched out a kink in her lower back. What was to stop her? The same thing that always stopped her. She dreaded the thought of traveling alone.

Ellen might join her if they planned far enough ahead. Between family responsibilities and her job as a marketing executive, it was difficult for her to get away. Difficult, but not impossible. Over the years, they'd taken several getaway trips on weekends, a couple of cruises, and even a few mission trips to hurricane-ravaged areas like New Orleans and Haiti. Ellen was always fine the first day or so until she started longing for her home and family. Which curtailed recent trips to overnighters, and to destinations only a few hours away.

It wasn't as if Olivia only had one friend. She knew lots of people, mostly fellow church members. But she'd learned the hard way there was nothing worse than taking off on a trip only to grow weary of her travel companions after a few hours on the road.

But maybe it's time to live a little. Take some chances. Step out of my comfort zone and meet some new people or even travel alone. Who knows, I might even meet someone special along the way . . .

The quirky little nerve in the pit of her stomach stomped a river-dance on her courage. Granston had warned her of men who might charm her right out of her last penny if she wasn't careful. At first, the implication felt like an insult. But with each story he shared about others in similar situations, she began to understand his warning and take it to heart. She had no living relatives, but she vowed to be diligent to guard not only the crisp new bills in her account, but her heart as well.

The one thing she *was* sure about was the opportunity to give generously to several different missions and charities. She'd always tithed to her church and sent donations to a handful of ministries, but Winthrop's gift would enable her to give on a whole new level. She planned to spend time these next few weeks researching causes she might help financially.

Taking the exit off I-95, Olivia felt her heart beat a little faster. The stately homes and quaint scenery seemed to welcome her despite the gray clouds and chilly temperatures. Following the GPS, she drove down the two-lane road onto State Road 9, made a few more turns, then slowly pulled up in front of the Captain MacVicar Inn.

The 185-year-old home was even more beautiful than the pictures on the inn's website. According to the online description, the home was built in 1827 by Captain Jonathan Wade MacVicar for his fiancée Catherine. Since he was often away at sea for months at a time, he had invited other members of Catherine's family to live in the home along with their spouses.

Thankfully, the home had been upgraded and preserved through the past couple of centuries, promising a comfortable stay for its guests. As Olivia walked up the snow-cleared stone pathway to the entrance, she noted the classic Federal design of the two-story home, its black shutters framing windows against walls painted a dark blue. The bright stars and stripes of Old Glory waved from the stoop.

As she walked through the heavy front door, a waft of cinnamon and coffee greeted her. She noticed the rich hues of the hardwood floors beneath her, though a scattering of Oriental rugs and runners softened her footsteps. The old wooden planks creaked alerting her to someone's approach.

A thirty-something woman appeared from around a corner. "Good afternoon!" She wiped her hands on her black pin-striped bib apron and reached out her hand. "I'm Michelle, and I'm guessing you're Olivia Thomas?"

Olivia shook her hand. "How did you know?"

"Easy. You're our only arriving guest this week. I'm Michelle Myers; my husband Trig and I are the innkeepers of the Captain MacVicar."

Olivia pulled off her gloves. "Your only guest? Well, I guess that makes sense for the 'off-off' season."

Michelle slipped behind the long, high desk. "Don't let that spoil your visit. In fact, I always tell our winter guests they're the smart ones. It gets pretty hectic around here during the spring and summer months. February is nice and quiet, as long as you don't mind the cold."

"I love snow! I'm from Atlanta, so it's a nice change."

"Well, then, you'll enjoy your visit with us." She navigated her computer with a wireless mouse. "Yes, here you are. And we have you down for three weeks, correct?"

"That's right. I hope I don't wear out my welcome."

Michelle smiled as she tapped the keyboard. "Not a chance. We're glad you're here. But I promise we won't hover. We're here if you need us, but we won't intrude on your privacy. Okay, three weeks takes you through . . . the end of the month?" She paused for a moment, then glanced at Olivia, a trace of something flickering through her eyes.

"Yes, that's my plan. Is there a problem?"

"No. No. No problem at all." She cleared her throat and focused on the monitor again. "That would be through the twenty-ninth, right?" A brow lifted, though Michelle's eyes remained on the monitor.

"Yes, the twenty-ninth. I hadn't realized this is a leap year."

"Yes, that's right." Michelle eyes stayed glued on the monitor. "And, according to your reservation, you requested a . . . room for one? Single?"

"Yes, that's right."

An awkward silence hung between them, as if Michelle was waiting for some further explanation.

How strange. "Yes, I'm single. That's me, all right. Single."

Michelle slapped herself on the forehead. "Oh, no, please—forgive me. I didn't mean—no, I only meant . . . I'm sorry. It's just that for a moment there—"

Suddenly, Olivia realized what was going on. She nodded knowingly, scoffing a laugh at her own misunderstanding. "You think I look like Martina McBride. I get that all the time. Though most people tell me I look more like Martina's 'heavier, older sister.' Which I find a bit tacky, but I don't take offense. Actually, I consider it a compliment. But for the record, we're not related. I've never even met her. Love her music, but that's as far as it goes. And trust me, you do *not* want to hear me sing."

Michelle narrowed her eyes then tilted her head, studying her. "Martina McBride, huh? Well, now that you mention it, I do see the resemblance."

Olivia's brows drew together. "So, you mean you didn't—"

Michelle waved her off. "Never mind me. Must be those fumes from cleaning the oven this morning. Forget I—well, forgive me. I'm not usually so flighty." She flashed a smile and turned to retrieve a key from a locked cabinet on the wall behind her. She paused, holding it mid-air before slowly turning back around. "You reserved the Catherine Room. It's very nice but since no one else is here, you'd be more than welcome to stay in the Carlton Suite."

"Oh, that's very kind, but I'll be fine in the Catherine. The minute I saw the picture on the website, I knew that's where I wanted to stay."

"But it's really no trouble to—"

"Thanks, but the Catherine is perfect for me." Olivia took the key from Michelle's hand.

Their eyes locked briefly. Olivia wondered if she was checking into the Bates Motel instead of a bed and breakfast.

Michelle started to stay something then snapped her mouth shut and smiled. "Sure. No problem."

The innkeeper gave her a brief tour of the inn then helped Olivia with her luggage, apologizing for her husband's absence. Once in her room, Olivia hung her coat in the armoire and looked around the room. The Catherine was lovely, tucked beneath a vaulted ceiling with windows on each side of the far corner. Flames flickered in the gas fireplace warming the room and its cozy setting. A puffy white duvet covered the four-poster queen-size bed. A blue and white quilt lay folded across the foot of the bed. A collection of needlepoint pillows dressed the head of the bed and beneath, a generous bed skirt made of blue and white ticking reached the long distance to the floor. She was glad to see a step stool beside the tall bed, hoping she wouldn't forget and come crashing out of bed in the middle of the night.

Soft lamplight dotted the room. A floor to ceiling bookshelf flanked the wall in the small area near the fireplace. Beside it, an overstuffed chair nestled in the corner offering the perfect place to get lost in a good book. On the small table beside it, a cut crystal vase held three hydrangeas in muted colors complementing the room's blue and white palette.

She peeked through the wavy-glassed windows which Michelle told her were the originals. The notion filled her with awe, thinking back on the vast history that had taken place since 1827. *America was still young when the cornerstone of this house was laid. I wonder what these walls might tell me if they could talk.*

As she continued wandering through the room, Olivia trailed her finger along the fireplace mantel until she noticed an exquisite glass box sitting on the right side. Inside it, a blue and white teacup and saucer. *Interesting. Did they decorate the room to match the cup? Or did they find a teacup to match the room?* It was a familiar pattern, like dozens of other blue and white transferware designs. She leaned in for a closer look and even tried to open the box only to find it sealed shut.

Well, that's odd. It looks like a thousand other cups you'd pick up at a flea market or yard sale. And even if it was worth something, they surely wouldn't put it in a guest room. She made a mental note to ask Michelle about it later.

Then, feeling sleepy, she kicked off her shoes and climbed up onto the bed to rest her eyes for a while. Relaxing into the luxurious softness, she pulled the duvet over her and fell sound asleep.

Chapter 4

"Good morning, Olivia. Did you sleep well?" Michelle greeted as she entered the small dining room.

"Apparently so. After I checked in yesterday afternoon, I thought I'd just rest for a few minutes before unpacking. Would you believe I didn't wake up until four this morning?"

Michelle laughed as she set a mug of coffee on the table. "That's music to our ears. We love for our guests to relax and unwind. Good for you!"

"Then you must hear lots of good music." Olivia took a seat at the table set for one. "I can't ever remember sleeping that long."

"Even better! Oh, let me introduce you to my husband. Trig, this is Olivia Thomas, our guest from Atlanta I was telling you about."

The tall and lanky young man joined them, placing a small basket of miniature muffins on the table. His tousled brown hair, kind eyes, and ready smile on his handsome face reminded her of Ellen's son, Billy. Trig wiped his hand on his apron and extended it toward her. "Nice to meet you, Miss Thomas."

"And you as well, but please call me Olivia."

"Olivia it is. I'm sorry I wasn't here when you arrived yesterday afternoon. I was helping a friend move. I trust Michelle helped you get settled?"

"Yes, and the room is perfect. Just perfect."

She caught a brief glance between the two innkeepers as she reached for her coffee. A ribbon of yesterday's strange encounter with Michelle flowed through her mind, but she quickly dismissed the memory.

She set her cup back in its saucer. "Oh my goodness, this coffee . . . it's *amazing.* What brand do you use?"

"You like that?" Trig asked. "It's my own blend."

"It may just be the best coffee I've ever tasted. What's your secret?"

"A little this, a little that," he teased. "Can't be giving out the Captain's secrets, now, can I?"

She reached for a muffin. "Guess I'll have to have a word with your Captain."

"By all means. He's buried out back, but you're welcome to pay him a visit if you like."

She slowly set the cinnamon muffin on her plate. "You mean, Captain MacVicar is actually buried here?"

A lopsided grin slid up his face. "Nah, I'm just messing with you. All our guests are live ones. Most of them, anyway." He chuckled as he tightened the ties of his apron. "I'm making omelets today. Any requests? Any allergies?"

"No allergies. How about cheese and bacon?"

"Excellent. Mind if I throw in some minced onions? Maybe a few diced peppers?"

"Even better!"

"Enjoy your coffee. I'll be back with your omelet in a few minutes." He stopped and reached for a newspaper on the side table. "Here's a copy of *USA Today* if you're interested."

"Thanks, Trig."

Olivia browsed the headlines but had little interest in what the rest of the world was up to. After she'd awakened from her twelve-hour nap, she enjoyed a long bubble bath in the clawfoot tub, letting the hot water soothe her from head to toe. It felt strange having so much free time to do as she pleased. She'd blown the sudsy bubbles, allowing herself to simply relax and watch the steam rise, content just to *be.*

And then she closed her eyes and prayed. Longer than she'd ever prayed before. Her heart felt close to bursting, filled with such deep gratitude and appreciation for the extraordinary gift she knew had come from the hand of God. John Winthrop's extreme generosity had shocked her, prompting a desperate need to hug the guy and thank him face to face. Someday, somehow, she would.

She prayed, asking God to lead her. Still overwhelmed, she couldn't begin to visualize what He might have in store for her. She prayed for wisdom in deciding how to help people in need. The idea of making anonymous gifts to people who were struggling thrilled her. Like the single mother of five whose husband was killed in the line of duty. What could she do for them? Or the young man at church whose spinal injury landed him permanently in a wheelchair. How fun would it be to secretly send them monetary gifts to ease the life he and his wife now faced?

So many possibilities. Where do I start? Lord, I'm so confused. I don't want to waste this incredible blessing You've given me. Lead me, Father. Show me what to do.

Now, sipping her coffee as the morning rays of sunlight filled the room, she wondered how to spend the day. When Michelle reappeared with a dish of freshly-cut fruit, she asked for advice.

"If this were your first day in Caden Cove, what would you do? Where would you go?"

Michelle gave her the names of several interesting shops to visit along with some sights to see if she felt like driving. When Trig brought her omelet, he made some additional suggestions.

"Be sure to stop by Molly's Coffee Shop & Pharmacy just off the circle. Very eclectic and charming—as is Molly. You will love her. It's impossible not to. Right, babe?"

"You'll meet her and in five minutes, you'll feel as if you've known her all your life."

Trig continued. "Then just around the corner from Molly's is the Knit Knook, if you're into that sort of thing. But even if you're not, it's a quirky place to visit. And if you're into books, you'll want to stop by Books & Such."

"Definitely," Michelle added. "Trevor has a great collection of first editions, particularly those by New England authors. Lots of history, biographies, that sort of thing. He's a bit particular about his books, so if you're looking for Harry Potter or bodice rippers or any of those vampire books, you'll be out of luck."

"Clearly, I prefer his taste to those you mentioned," Olivia said.

Trig draped a dish towel over his shoulder. "It's a great bookstore, if you can get beyond Trevor."

"Meaning?"

He refilled her coffee cup. "He's a bit of an odd duck. Or I guess I should say he's a bit of a *cold fish.*"

Michelle backhanded his bicep playfully. "Trig! That's not nice."

"Yeah, but get it? *Cold fish*?"

Michelle leveled her eyes at Olivia. "Trevor's last name is Bass. My husband finds this hilarious."

Olivia laughed. "So which is it? Is he an odd duck or a cold fish?"

"Both," Michelle said. "He's rough around the edges, but I'm sure there's a heart somewhere—"

"—under all those *fins*?"

Michelle snickered. "Stop! Don't be so rude in front of our guest."

"I'm sorry. I'm sure you'll find our favorite bookseller to be a real *perch* of a guy."

"Trig!"

"A regular *cod*-mudgeon, if you *catch* my drift."

"Enough!" Michelle stood and yanked at his sleeve. "Let the lady eat in peace. Time to put you back to work, Mr. Myers. Let's go clean your kitchen."

Trig tossed a wink at Olivia as his wife pulled him toward the kitchen. "Sorry. She wants me to *scale* back on my fish jokes. Have a *fin* day, Olivia." He reeled in an imaginary fish before disappearing around the corner.

Olivia couldn't help laughing. Her first morning in Caden Cove and she already loved it. With a final sip of coffee, she decided to make Books & Such her first stop and check out the mysterious bookseller.

Main Street was only a couple blocks over from the Captain MacVicar, so Olivia bundled up and headed down the street. The brilliant blue sky overhead warmed her heart despite the chilly temperatures. She took her time, stopping to enjoy the various architectural styles of the historic homes along the way. She tried to imagine what the interiors looked like. Had they retained the original styles or opted for more modern updates? Obviously the people of Caden Cove took pride in their town as every home appeared to be well-kept. She wondered how they might look when the lush colors of spring embellished these neighborhoods.

Maybe I'll just stick around and see for myself.

She dug her hands deeper into her coat pockets, liking the idea. Which explained the smile she saw reflected in the window of the first shop she came to.

A sign on the door of The Pottery Shoppe read, "See you next spring!"

Next door, a similar sign at Sarah's Closet read, "Pardon our hibernation."

The first "Open" sign appeared a couple of doors down at a small souvenir shop. She kept walking, thinking she'd have plenty of time to shop for gifts later. She spotted Molly's Coffee Shop & Pharmacy at the end of the street and looked forward to meeting the proprietor. But curiosity drove her toward the bookstore.

Rounding the corner, she spotted the quaint shop, pleased to find a brick exterior, a dark green awning, and a handsome carved "Books & Such" sign hanging over the door.

She pulled her knit cap tighter over her ears and crossed the street. The lights glowed from inside the windows like so many warm invitations. She reached for the brass doorknob but found it locked. Only then did she notice the handwritten sign hanging posted in the window: *Be back at 1:00.*

"Well, that's no fun," she muttered, checking her watch. Still, she couldn't help peeking through the windows. She inhaled, imagining the familiar scent of books and lemon-oil, and perhaps a hint of coffee. She cupped her hands against the window pane, delighted to spot a bricked hearth in the corner with a small fire glowing inside.

She could see rows of bookshelves, potted ivies here and there, comfortable chairs beside lamp-lit tables, and a sliding ladder giving access to higher shelving. Disappointed, she decided to kill some time over at the pharmacy until 1:00.

Moments later bells jingled above her head as the entered the pharmacy and coffee shop.

"Good morning!" a voice called from the back of the store. "Be with you in a jiff."

"Take your time," Olivia answered, pulling off her gloves and cap. Stuffing them in her coat pockets, she glanced around the unique shop. Needlepoint pillows, wind chimes, scented candles, bagged coffee, tins of cheese straws and shortbread cookies. The perfect gift shop, including a cluster of tables and chairs near the antique coffee bar. High on the back wall an antique sign lettered in a vintage calligraphy script read, *Ye Olde Pharmacy.*

"Sorry about that, I was just filling a prescription," the matronly woman announced as she made her way up the center aisle. "Oh, hello," she said, seeing Olivia for the first time. "This time of year I always assume my customers are locals. How lovely to see a new face. Welcome. I'm Molly." She extended her hand and Olivia shook it.

There was something strangely familiar about the friendly pharmacist wearing a lavender-print dress beneath a matching sweater and a string of pearls at her neck. With her elegantly coiffed white hair, tiny wrinkles around her eyes, and a gentle smile gracing her countenance, Olivia felt as if she were looking at the perfect picture of an American grandmother.

"I'm Olivia. Nice to make your acquaintance, Molly. Trig and Michelle over at the Captain MacVicar told me to stop in and meet you."

"Oh, aren't they adorable? They bought the inn about eight years ago, and I've loved them since the first day we met. Come in, come in, have a seat," she insisted, motioning toward the coffee bar as she slipped behind the counter. "What do you take in your coffee? First cup is always on the house."

"How nice of you." Olivia took a seat on one of the barstools. "Cream, no sugar, thank you."

"Tell me, Olivia, where do you call home, and how did you find our little corner of the world?"

"I'm from Atlanta, Georgia."

"Atlanta! My goodness, this must be quite a climate shock for you. Hope you like snow."

"I *love* it. We rarely see snow, so I'm thrilled to be here. My best friend and her husband have vacationed here many times. They're the ones who suggested I come up and visit."

Molly passed a steaming mug of creamy coffee across the counter to her then filled one for herself. "We have lots of tourists from Georgia, which always surprises me. I would think Southerners would prefer Charleston or Savannah, not New England. But they seem to really enjoy it here."

"I can see why. It's a lovely town. So very different from the South."

Molly took a seat on a stool behind the bar. "Yes, it is. But you must come back sometime when the weather's nice. Oh, you should see all the flowers in bloom and the sailboats coming and going. It's just heavenly."

"I can imagine. In fact, I've already had the thought of staying a little longer."

"Oh? How long are you staying?"

"My reservation is through the end of the month—the twenty-ninth. Funny, but I hadn't realized until yesterday that it's a leap year."

Molly's eyebrows arched. "Oh? Why, yes . . . the month ends on February twenty-ninth this year." She studied her finger as it traced along the rim of her coffee cup. "Is this a vacation for you?"

Olivia hesitated, choosing her words carefully. "I suppose you'd call it that. I work at a bank, but I'm thinking of taking early retirement. Originally, I'd planned to take a few weeks off, but now I'm wondering why I'd ever want to go back."

"My goodness! Sounds tempting. Do you have family back in Atlanta?"

"No, it's just me."

"Ah."

Ever so slightly, Molly's demeanor changed. Much the same way Michelle's had changed when Olivia checked in.

"I'm curious," she asked. "Is there something I should know? Something about leap year here in Caden Cove? Or maybe something about the MacVicar?"

Molly looked up. "What? Oh, no, dear. Not a thing." She smiled then added, "It's such a lovely place, the MacVicar. What room are you staying in? If you don't mind my asking?"

"I'm staying in the one called the Catherine—"

"Prettiest room in the house," Molly interrupted, still smiling.

"Yes, but I'm curious why . . . well, just now when you—"

"Oh, silly me," Molly said, standing. "I didn't even offer you a cookie. These are my famous cranberry macadamia oatmeal cookies." She lifted the glass dome from a pedestal plate of neatly stacked cookies and used silver tongs to select a large chunky cookie. "Here, you must have one."

Olivia raised a palm. "Oh, I couldn't possibly after such a big breakfast at the inn."

"Oh, of course you did. Well, now. I'll just put this in a bag for you, then you can have it whenever you want."

"I can already tell it's true, what Trig and Michelle said about you."

Molly straightened. "About me?"

"Yes. They said, and I quote, 'Meet her, and in five minutes you'll feel as if you've known her all your life.' They were right."

Molly slid the cookie into a small wax paper bag then handed it to her. "That's so sweet of them. The way I see it, we're all given a few years on this old earth, so we might as well make the best of it. Why waste time carrying a grudge or being grumpy all the time?"

The bell jingled over the door. Olivia turned as a handsome man in a wool coat and gray ivy cap entered the shop.

"Hello, Molly." He nodded toward the pharmacist, then dashed a quick glance at Olivia before heading down the aisle toward the back.

"Speaking of grumpy," Molly whispered, patting Olivia's wrist. "You enjoy your coffee. I'll be back in a few minutes."

Olivia decided to browse the gift area while she sipped her coffee. She wandered the aisles, fascinated by the assortment of locally handmade gifts. As she reached for a uniquely shaped piece of pottery, she turned at the sound of footsteps.

"Pardon me," the same gentleman said as he approached her.

Olivia smiled in return making room for him to slip by her. A faint whiff of musky cologne drifted in his wake. A moment later the bell jingled again and he was gone.

"There you are." Molly joined her. "Sorry for the interruption. Trevor stopped by for a prescription."

"Trevor? The same Trevor who owns the bookstore around the corner?"

"The one and only. I suppose I should have introduced you, but I could tell he was in one of his moods. Why are you smiling like that?"

"Oh, nothing. Just something Trig said this morning."

"Let me guess." Molly grinned. "The fish jokes, right?"

"They were *so bad*, but I couldn't help laughing! Is Mr. Bass really as stuffy as they implied?"

Molly motioned her back toward the coffee bar. "Oh, goodness, no. Trevor's harmless. He's just one of those guys who likes what he likes, disdains what he doesn't, and isn't hesitant to speak his mind. You just have to get to know him. Unfortunately, most of our tourists find him less than amiable, but they still visit his shop."

"Something tells me there's a story in all this."

Molly wiped down the counter. "Not really. Honestly, all kidding aside, he's really a quite interesting young man."

"Young? He didn't look that young to me. I'm guessing he's forty-five? Fifty?"

"The oldest forty-something you'll ever meet—forty-seven going on seventy, if you ask me. His birthday was just a few weeks ago. We had a little party for him at last month's book club." She paused and looked up at Olivia. "You should come! Book club meets tomorrow night. We'd be delighted to have you join us."

"Oh no, I wouldn't want to impose. Especially since I haven't read whatever book you've all read."

"Nonsense. Doesn't matter. It'll be fun! We read Maeve Binchy's book, *Minding Frankie.* Ever read it?"

"I love Maeve Binchy! I've read all her books."

"Then I insist. Tomorrow night at seven."

"You sure he won't mind?"

"Oh, he'll mind. That'll be half the fun!"

Chapter 5

Half an hour later, Olivia took a deep breath before opening the door to Books & Such. Just as she expected, a mixture of pleasing scents wafted through the cozy bookstore. As she closed the door behind her, she heard strains of a familiar Vivaldi tune playing softly in the background. Once again pulling off her gloves, she turned to peruse the books displayed on a round table just inside the door. A paisley tablecloth in hues of deep red, navy, and hunter green hosted titles by David McCullough, Jan Karon, David Balducci, and of course, Maeve Binchy. She reached for the copy of *Minding Frankie,* recalling Molly's invitation.

"Not her best, but an interesting read nonetheless."

His voice startled her, though she knew instantly it was Trevor Bass.

"Oh, hello. Again. I'm the . . . I just saw you over at—"

"Molly's. Yes. I remember. Middle aisle. Georgiana's sculptures. A little strange for my taste, but tourists seem to like them." A touch of arrogance seemed to lift his brow.

Olivia smiled, not quite sure how to respond. It was her first good look at him. She was surprised to find a gentleness in his expression as the arrogance slowly dissipated. A few wisps of gray hovered near his temples complementing a neatly trimmed head of dark brown hair. A day's growth lined his jaw, much of it gray. A line or two here and there graced features she found altogether pleasant.

"It's too early for tourists." He pulled a leather-bound volume off the shelf nearest him and slid it into a different place with the others. "You're not one of the locals, so I assume you're a guest in our little town."

Again, she paused before answering. "Yes. I mean, no. That is to say, I'm not a local. I'm just visiting. Yes. A little getaway. Well, not *just* a getaway. I'm staying a few weeks. Three, actually." She smiled, begging her mouth to stop the babbling deluge. "Three weeks."

His eyes narrowed a bit. He studied her while straightening more of his books.

"Actually, it's one of my favorites," she continued, setting the Binchy book back on its stand. "*Scarlet Feather* is probably my favorite. Maeve Binchy is amazing. I love the depth of her characters. By the end of the book, it's as if you know each of them personally. I was really saddened to hear she passed away last year."

He nodded, but said nothing. She waited, thinking he might say something about the book club, possibly even invite her. Or not. The silence felt uncomfortably awkward. "You have a lovely bookstore. I peeked through the window earlier while you were out."

He turned to face her, his hands still aligning books on the shelf. "Yes, I was out showing some property."

"Oh? You're also a realtor?"

He blinked, furrowing his brow just so. "Yes. Why do you ask?"

Now it was Olivia's turn to blink. The encounter felt more like a ping pong match than a conversation. "No reason. Just curious." She flashed a tight smile, waiting for him to respond.

Finally, he dusted his hands together. "Yes, well. Feel free to browse," he said, stepping past her. "If there's anything I can help you with, let me know." He was halfway to the back of the shop before she could answer.

"Thanks." Olivia bit back a smile. "I think?" she muttered under her breath.

She browsed the aisles, enjoying the ambiance in spite of him. Creaking hardwood floors, creative book displays, and a crackling fire against the backdrop of classical music. *Perfect.* Between the rows of books in the history section, she caught a glimpse of Trevor seated behind a counter at the rear of the shop. When he reached up to rake his fingers through his thick hair, she noted his ring finger was bare.

What's your story, Mr. Bass? Why's a guy like you not—

Olivia winced at the thought. How many times had people asked her that same question? *How come such a pretty woman like you hasn't settled down and married?* The first thousand times, she'd ground her teeth together and tamped down the snarky responses lurking through her head. But at forty-five, she'd long grown weary of it all, choosing to chalk it up to ignorance on their part and let it go.

Yet here she was, pondering the same ignorant question about the bookseller.

Shame on you.

"What's that?"

She ducked behind the books. *Did I say that out loud?*

The sound of his chair scooting against the hardwood floor sent a sickening dread through her. Trevor leaned around the end of the row. "Did you say something?"

"No! No." She shrugged innocence, shaking her head. "Wasn't me."

"Yes, but I'm pretty sure I heard you say, 'shame on you.'" He stuffed his hands in the pockets of his corduroy slacks as he ambled closer.

"You did?"

"Yes. There's only you and me here in the store."

She swallowed hard, feeling the heat glowing in her face. Suddenly, something slapped against her leg.

"AHHH!" she cried, launching herself right into his arms. "What was—"

"Charlie, sit!"

By the time Olivia realized an animal had joined them, she was already extracting herself from his arms. "I'm *so* sorry! I felt something on my leg and I . . . well, it startled me! I'm *so* sorry."

"No, I'm the one who should apologize. I assure you, Charlie's quite harmless." He leaned down, scratching the spaniel behind the ear. "I'm sorry she frightened you."

Olivia tried to calm her racing heart. "She?"

"Yes, she's a King Charles Cavalier, so it seemed only right to—"

"—name her Charlie. Of course."

The gentle dog sat beside her master, her tail wagging against the floor. "She was napping back by my desk, but I guess she wanted to . . . say hello?" A hint of kindness seemed to hide behind his almost-smile.

She swallowed again, though this time it had nothing to do with embarrassing thoughts or a dog's tail thumping against her leg, and everything to do with the bookseller's smile. It changed his entire countenance, transforming this *odd duck* to quite a handsome man. The fact that his nearness allowed her to catch another whiff of his cologne didn't hurt either.

"She's beautiful," Olivia said, kneeling down. She held out her hand for the dog to sniff. "How old is Charlie?"

"She's three. She's also expecting. Aren't you, girl?" The dog seemed to smile, her long tongue spilling out.

Olivia smiled. "Well, congratulations, little mama." She scratched Charlie under her chin sending a back paw in a rhythmic frenzy against the floor. "You like that, do you?" Olivia glanced up at Trevor. "When's the happy day?"

"Not for another four weeks."

She gave Charlie another pat then stood. "I hope she has a healthy litter of pups."

"Are you all right?" Trevor asked, a look of concern in his eyes.

"I think so? Why do you ask?"

He gestured toward her face. "You have tears in your eyes."

"I do?" She brushed her fingertips below each eye. "Oh, don't mind me. I'm just a little—"

"Here." He pulled a handkerchief out of his pocket. "Please."

She pressed her lips together, appalled at the random display of emotions.

"Thank you," she said, taking it from his hand. "I lost my little Sammy around this time last year. She was a Cav-Tzu mix. Her coloring was completely different from Charlie's, but she had those same adorable eyes." She wiped her runny nose, then realized she'd just wiped snot all over his monogrammed initials. "Oh, no. I'm sorry. I'll get this cleaned. I promise."

Compassion filled his eyes. "Keep it. Plenty more where that came from."

"I feel like such a swoon carrying on like this. How silly of me."

"Not at all." He pushed his hands back in his pockets and glanced down at Charlie. "They wrap us around their little paws and there's nothing for it." He studied his shoes briefly. "I'm very sorry for your loss."

He glanced back at her, his eyes warm with understanding. But as kind as he'd been, Olivia wanted nothing more than to rush back to her room at the inn and have a good gully-washer of a cry, as Ellen called them. She took a final swipe at her nose and tried to smile as she raised the wadded handkerchief in her hand. "Thank you. I'll be going now."

As she headed for the door, she heard his footsteps behind her.

"You'd be welcome to join us for book club tomorrow night."

She turned, surprised.

"There's just a dozen or so of us. It's very casual. And since you've read the book . . . that is, if you have nothing else to do tomorrow evening?"

The stupid lump in her throat blocked any semblance of a response, so she smiled as best she could, nodded, then turned again to go.

Hearing the door close behind her, she reached for her gloves and made her way across the street. His words echoed again through her mind.

You'd be welcome to join us . . .

Out of nowhere, the response darted through her mind. "Thank you, Trevor. I'll *mullet* over." Olivia laughed so hard, she had to grab a nearby street light to steady herself. She didn't dare glance back over her shoulder. If he'd seen her outburst, he'd surely think she'd lost her mind.

And quickly rescind the invitation.

"Come along, Charlie. Best we get you back to bed for a rest." The spaniel followed Trevor's footsteps as he retreated to his desk. "There you go, girl. Snug as a bug in a rug and all that."

Charlie curled up on her cozy pillow behind his desk. She rested her head on her front paws then let out a comforting sigh.

Trevor grabbed the mouse beside his computer and resumed his search for a book one of his regulars had asked him to find. He clicked from page to page, then stopped and glanced back at Charlie. "She was different, that one, wasn't she?" He nodded toward the front. "A little strange if you ask me. All that starting and stopping, like she wasn't sure how to put a sentence together."

Charlie eyed him without lifting her head, her tail waving in response. With another sigh, both eyes drifted slowly shut as she settled in for a nap.

"Then again, what would you expect from a tourist who comes to Maine this time of year?" he mumbled. "She should fire her travel agent, if you ask me."

Still, he couldn't help remembering the sadness in her eyes as she spoke of the dog named Sammy she'd lost. He gazed at his own spaniel and couldn't imagine losing her.

It's part of life, of course. You live, you die. End of story.

But Charlie? Well, Charlie had stolen his heart from the moment he laid eyes on her. Three years ago, he'd taken a walk along the beach one summer evening as he often did. The breeze off the water, the cries of the sea gulls hovering overhead, the lap of the water hitting the shore, the pastel brushstrokes painted across the sky . . . it was his favorite time of day and his favorite place to spend it. But as he made his way back to his home on the beach, he noticed a young boy pulling a red wagon along the sidewalk. A woman, the boy's mother, accompanied him.

"Hey, mister! Wanna puppy?"

Trevor wasn't an animal person, so he shook his head as he headed toward his deck. "No thanks."

The boy, who looked to be around ten or so, stopped the wagon and held up a brown and white ball of fur. “Are you sure? She’s *awful* cute. And she’s the last one left.”

“Now, Mickey, don’t be a bother,” his mother said. “Sorry,” she said, waving a hand in apology.

He had waved in response, then the strangest thing happened. He started making his way toward them. “You say she’s the last one?”

The boy’s face lit up. “She sure is.”

“Anything wrong with her?” Trevor asked the woman.

“No way!” the boy said. “She’s perfect. No papers or anything, but she’s a true King Charles Cavalier Spaniel. Tell him, Mom.”

“She is. Her mother is our sweet Charlotte. Her daddy belongs to a family over in Kennebunkport, but neither of them are registered. Just so you know.”

Trevor stood beside them and reached out to pet the pup’s head. “Well, now. She doesn’t seem to mind about any of that, does she?”

Mickey placed the puppy in Trevor’s hands.

“Oh, yes, well ... I’ve never had an animal.” The puppy crawled up against his chest, nuzzling her black button nose against Trevor’s chin. He smiled, feeling the cold wetness against his whiskers. “Well, aren’t you the little flirt?”

“She really likes you, mister. I think you should have her.”

“Mickey, don’t be rude.”

“How much?” Trevor asked, startling himself.

“A hundred dollars? We sold her brothers and sisters for a hundred-fifty, but since she’s the runt—”

“The runt? You said nothing was wrong with her, right?”

“Oh, she’s fine. She was just the last one out, so she’s a little smaller. That’s all.”

“I see.” Trevor held the puppy mere inches from his face. “I’ll admit she’s a sweetheart. I don’t know, little lady,” he said, drawing her closer, “think you’d like to come live with an old guy like me?”

The pup whimpered then licked Trevor right on the nose.

Mickey laughed. “That’s how she says yes. I’m sure of it!”

He’d paid the lad, and thus began the love affair with the pup he affectionately named Charlie. Glancing back at her now, he couldn’t imagine how he’d ever lived without her. As for the day when he might have to say goodbye? No sense worrying about that now. Not with little ones on the way.

He scratched his chin thinking about the tourist who’d just left his shop. What had possessed him to invite her to their book club? It was one thing to invite a canine into his life, but since when did he ask a *tourist* of all people to visit their book club? Theirs was a closed club of locals.

"Oh Charlie, best keep an eye on me. Mustn't go losing my stuffed shirt persona, now can I?"

Chapter 6

"Tell me everything," Ellen bubbled. "How was your day? How do you like the MacVicar? What do you think of Caden Cove? Isn't it charming? What'd you have for dinner? C'mon! Do tell!"

Olivia switched her cell phone to her other ear. "I'll be happy to if you'll let me get a word in edgewise."

"Fine. Just don't leave out a thing."

"I promise. Let me see, where to start . . ."

For the next half hour, Olivia gave her best friend an accounting of her first day in Caden Cove. From her 4:00 a.m. soak in the tub to her breakfast at the inn and her visits to the pharmacy and bookstore, to the unforgettable dinner she'd just enjoyed.

"I had my first lobster roll, and you were right. To *die* for. Ohmigosh, Ellen, I wanted to lick the basket it came in."

"Please tell me you didn't."

"No, but I wanted to. I may have to eat there again tomorrow before—oh! I almost forgot to tell you! They have a book club that's meeting tomorrow night at the bookstore, and I was invited to attend. Not once but twice."

"Wow. Who invited you, the innkeepers?"

"No, they aren't members. And to be honest, they acted rather odd when I told them I was invited. Michelle assumed Molly invited me—you know, the sweet older woman who owns the pharmacy and coffee shop. She was the first to invite me. But when I told them Trevor also invited me, they both stared at me as if I'd grown a third eye."

"Trevor. He's the handsome bookstore owner you just told me about?"

"Yes, but I believe I called him 'nice looking' as opposed to handsome. But yes, same guy."

"Why would that bother Michelle and Trig? Did they say anything?"

"Eventually. They'd talked about him earlier at breakfast, but apparently they think he's full of himself and rather stuffy. Which he probably is, but he's kind of . . ."

"Kind of . . . ?"

"Oh, nothing. Except that he has an adorable King Charles Cavalier Spaniel named Charlie, and she startled me at first, and I—oh, never mind with all that. I'm rambling. It's not important."

"Sure it is. I bet she reminded you of Sammy, didn't she?"

A snapshot dashed through her mind . . . Ellen hugging her as the vet took Sammy's lifeless body from her arms. Had it really been a year now?

Olivia shook her head to dismiss the memory. "Only in her eyes. But Ellen, I just lost it. Not so much at first, but the next thing I knew, I had tears running down my face, and he gave me his handkerchief which I completely slobbered all over—"

"Who? The bookstore guy? He gave you his handkerchief?"

"Yes. In fact, he insisted I keep it. But who could blame him, with it all nasty and—"

"Sounds like he's both handsome *and* kindhearted. Any other descriptions you want to share with me?"

"None I can think of, silly. But I'm still baffled why Trig and Michelle reacted the way they did. You'd think I'd been invited to the prom by Hannibal Lecter or Jack the Ripper. It was bizarre."

"Who knows. Small town like that, there's probably all kinds of drama."

"I guess. I keep getting strange looks and reactions from people here."

"Probably the Martina thing."

"Maybe. Even at dinner tonight at that little pub. I kept catching people staring at me. A guy at the bar actually pointed at me across the room then whispered something in his buddy's ear."

"What kind of bar were you in?"

Olivia rolled her eyes. "Not a bar. A pub. The one you and Brent told me about. It's called Grayson's or Graham—something?"

"Grady's? I love Grady's! It's down some stairs beneath another restaurant out on the water, right?"

"That's it. All kinds of memorabilia on the walls, on the ceiling, everywhere."

"Lot of sports stuff, as I recall. Mostly Red Sox, right?"

"Right. And lots of vintage political buttons and bumper stickers. The Kennedys would have loved it there."

"Which is interesting since the Bush's winter home is just a few miles down the road. Have you been by Walker's Point yet?"

"Not yet. Maybe tomorrow."

"Give Babs my best, okay? And the president too if you see them.

But back to the lobster rolls. Just box up a couple crates of those bad boys to bring home to me, okay?"

"Anything else on your wish list?"

"Silly or serious?"

"Your pick."

"Then I wish for you to have the time of your life. And if your first day is any indication, I'm thinking I might just get my wish."

"Hey, it's only one day."

"Yes, but remember—today is the first day of the rest of your life."

"Ellen?"

"Yes?"

"A little heavy on the cheese there."

"G'night, girlfriend."

"Night, Ellen."

Chapter 7

As Olivia made her way downstairs for breakfast, she pulled on her cable-knit sweater. She couldn't help smiling as she watched a light snow falling outside the windows.

"Morning, Olivia." Trig nodded toward the window. "We ordered some snow for you. Anything to make our guests happy."

"How nice! I'll have to leave a good review on your website. 'Most accommodating bed and breakfast.' Five stars, of course."

"Works for me. Last I looked the temperature was right around sixteen. Brrr!"

"Ellen warned me to pack some long johns. I'm glad I did." She took her same seat at the table, already feeling at home here. "How are you this morning, Trig?"

"Couldn't be better." He poured coffee into her cup. "Though I'm hearing this one might be heavier than the original forecast." He looked back outside. "Not a blizzard but enough to take note, that's for sure."

"Meaning?"

"Meaning we'll stock up more than usual just to be on the safe side. Let me know if there's anything you'd like me to pick up."

"I'm sure I'll be fine. I might stop by Molly's today for a couple of things. When is the worst of the storm supposed to hit?"

"Most likely overnight or early tomorrow morning. It's a cumulative thing, of course." He turned, pointing out the window. "See our snow gauge out there?"

Olivia spotted the marker, a flat metal pole resembling a giant yard stick stuck in the ground. "That green pole?"

"Right. We've already had three snowfalls this year that have buried it by a foot or more."

Olivia slid him a sheepish grin. "Don't hate me, but I *love* the possibility of that much snow."

"Oh, I get that. You're a Southern belle, so this is all fun and exciting for you. But stick around a year or two and you'll take it in stride like the rest of us. Hey, how do Belgian waffles sound this morning?"

"Sounds perfect."

"Cinnamon apples and pecans on top?"

"Even better."

After another mouthwatering breakfast, Olivia enjoyed a brisk walk to the pharmacy making no attempt to dodge the big flat snowflakes along the way, even sticking her tongue out a couple of times to catch a few. It all seemed so magical, as if she were part of a Currier and Ives print. The thought made her smile.

The pharmacy bustled with activity, its narrow aisles congested. Olivia took a seat at the coffee bar, thinking she'd wait for the crowd to thin out before picking up a few things. Nothing she couldn't live without, but she enjoyed watching the locals go about their business. A twenty-something named Cyndi served as barista, telling Olivia she was a part-time employee on busy days like this. She wasn't quite as friendly as Molly, and Olivia had the same feeling the girl was studying her like so many others coming and going. But the girl made a great cappuccino, and for now that was enough.

When the crowd thinned, Molly joined her at the bar, taking a seat. "You'd think I'd be used to this, but snow days always wear me out." She patted her elegant coiffure, then dabbed her forehead with a dainty handkerchief she pulled from the cuff of her sleeve.

"Is it always like this when a storm's coming?"

"Oh yes. Everyone wants to be out and about, whether they need anything or not. We never know when we might be stuck inside for days at a time."

"I can't even imagine."

Molly waved her handkerchief. "Doesn't happen often, but always a possibility. It's the cabin fever that gets you more than anything. So that's why they come." She nodded toward a couple of ladies chatting by the antacids. As she did so, the two stopped talking, gave Molly a knowing glance, then stared openly at Olivia.

She felt the heat creeping up her neck. She turned around to face Molly and lowered her voice. "Molly, could I ask you something?"

"Of course, dear."

"Ever since I got in town yesterday, I keep noticing that . . . well, it seems like everyone is always staring at me or giving me strange looks."

Molly tilted her head just so. "I'm not sure I follow. What do you mean?"

Olivia nodded over her shoulder. "Like those two just now. They stare at me, then whisper to each other."

Molly folded and refolded her handkerchief. "Oh, nothing to worry about, dear. We have so few tourists this time of year. They're probably just curious, wondering who you are, why you're here. That sort of thing."

"No, I think it's more than that. In fact," she began, then paused. "Yesterday when I first met you, I noticed a few peculiar looks in *your* eyes as we spoke."

Molly's brows arched high. "Me? Whatever do you mean?"

Olivia studied her for a moment, wondering how to explain without sounding paranoid. The last thing she needed was a town full of folks thinking she was an idiot. "When you asked if I'd traveled alone. When you asked which room I was staying in at the Captain MacVicar. When you—"

Molly put her hand over Olivia's and closed her eyes for a moment. Olivia waited. When she finally looked up, the slightest hint of sympathy framed her eyes.

"Molly, what is it?"

"My dear, it's nothing really. Just a silly legend that folks around here like to fancy now and then."

"What kind of legend?"

Molly withdrew her hand and got up to pour herself a cup of coffee. "It goes back years and years—centuries, actually." She added a splash of cream then stirred the brew, and took her seat again.

Olivia leaned on the counter. "Tell me about it."

"Bear with me. This may take a while. You see, back in 1826, Captain Jonathan Wade MacVicar was a successful merchant—what was then called a 'sailing master'—whose ships routinely carried supplies from England and Europe to America. He was originally from Boston, but decided to build his home here in Caden Cove after falling in love with a young woman he'd met while waiting out a storm here. Catherine Bennett was the daughter of a fellow mariner with whom MacVicar had been associated for a number of years.

"When Catherine accepted Jonathan's proposal of marriage, he started building a home for his future bride. One where Catherine and members of her family could live while he was away at sea for long periods of time. In 1828, he insisted she and her sisters and their husbands move into the spacious home while he was still at sea, on his way back from England. Then, once he was back home, they would marry in a grand ceremony."

"I read about that online," Olivia added.

"Yes, that much of the story is on the website."

"There's more?"

Her sad smile returned. "Catherine agreed and moved into the stately home, though she insisted on staying in an upstairs bedroom until she and Jonathan were married. Only then would she and her new husband move into the master bedroom on the first floor."

"So Catherine lived in the room where I'm staying," Olivia stated. "The one bearing her name."

"Yes. Perhaps you noticed the lovely shades of blue carried throughout the room?"

"Yes, of course. Blue has always been my favorite color."

"Catherine's as well. And because it was her favorite, Jonathan had the room painted and decorated in pastel shades of blue. But he had another surprise which he'd planned to give her upon his return. While in England, Captain MacVicar met with his friend Josiah Spode II, to select a pattern of china as a wedding gift for his bride back in America."

"I'm familiar with Spode. In fact, I have several Spode Christmas dishes."

"They're lovely, aren't they?" Molly said with a twinkle in her eye. "I have a few myself."

Olivia waved off Molly's offer for a refill, pushing her empty mug aside. "Please, go on. You said Jonathan wanted to surprise Catherine with a set of china. A pretty gutsy move on his part. Most women like to have a say in that sort of thing."

"Yes, but of course those were different times. Plus, I like to think he knew her taste well enough to make the selection. So he met with Mr. Spode, whose father, Josiah Spode I, was the first potter to underglaze blue printed earthenware for the commercial market. It was quite an accomplishment at the time. It's told that Jonathan knew at once which pattern Catherine would like, a lovely new floral design with pale blue flowers on a white—"

"The teacup in my room! The one on the mantel, sealed in a glass box?"

"Yes."

"I've been so curious about it, but I forgot to ask Trig and Michelle about it."

"It's a pattern called *Union Wreath First.* Other versions would follow, but it was the original that the captain picked for his bride. The crate of securely packed china was loaded onto his schooner, *The Merry Martha.* He left the next day bound for America, anxious and excited to return home and marry his beloved Catherine.

"But that day would never come. As they neared the coast of Maine, Jonathan set anchor half a mile off shore. The nearest port was in Boston, but as he'd done every other time, he simply boarded a skiff with a couple of his crewmen to ferry themselves to shore. But the sea is as dangerous as it is unpredictable, even to the most experienced sailors. And as they rowed toward shore, the winds picked up suddenly angering the waves and tossing the helpless little boat as if it were made of mere balsa wood. The splintered remains eventually washed ashore. One crewman's body drifted on shore, but Jonathan and the other crewmen were never found."

"That has to be one of the saddest stories I've ever heard," Olivia said quietly. "This is really true? It really happened?"

"Oh yes, there's no mistake about that. Once the storm passed, *The Merry Martha* sent another crew to shore where they found the crewman's body along with clothes and papers and other debris . . . including hundreds of pieces of broken china."

Olivia waited patiently as Molly dabbed her eyes. "How silly of me. I've heard and told this story so many times, you'd think I wouldn't have a tear left in me."

"Go on."

"Catherine was heartbroken, of course. News of the tragedy spread throughout the entire coastal area, and folks gathered to help search the miles of shoreline. Several days later, while walking the beach three miles south of here, a young man found a saucer—the only piece of the Spode china that was still intact. But when the tragic story was published in a local newspaper, a woman contacted the authorities, telling them she'd found a teacup along the shore where she lived, some five miles south of Caden Cove. And so it was, the cup and saucer were returned to Catherine, the only pieces not cracked or shattered by the storm."

"I wondered why it was kept sealed in that glass box," Olivia said. "With so much history, I'm surprised it isn't kept in a vault or at least out of harm's way. Why do you think it's kept in a guest room?"

Molly sat back. "I'm glad you asked, Olivia. Because the answer leads us to the legend."

Back in her room at the inn, Olivia stared at the cup and saucer on the mantel as she talked to her friend back home. "It was surreal, Ellen, hearing her tell this story that explained so much about this home, and specifically this room."

"I can't believe this. In all our visits to the MacVicar, we never heard any of this before! You'd think they'd have a brochure or something."

"Wait 'til you hear the rest of it. When Molly began to tell me more, at first I was completely into it, hanging on her every word."

"What do you mean 'at first'?"

"It was such a tragic, beautiful love story. Hearing her tell it, I felt like I was right there, witnessing it myself. Right up to the point of the mysterious sequence of events involving lost love and leap years."

"You've lost me."

"It seems the night the captain was lost at sea was February 29th, 1828."

"Okay. It was leap year. So what?"

"Through all the years since that night, a strange phenomenon has occurred. Molly said the MacVicar remained in the family for decades until 1896 when it was sold and converted into a rooming house. When it opened its doors for business, the first guest to stay in the Catherine Room was a young woman named Betsy-something. I can't remember her last name."

"You're not going to recount a list of everyone who has ever stayed in that room, are you?"

"No. Well, sort of. Just hold your horses. I'm getting there. So Betsy was betrothed to a young man named Adam-something, who was killed in a freak hunting accident just days before they were to be married."

"How awful. And what a coincidence that both Catherine and Betsy—"

"Lost their loves?" Olivia added. "But it gets even stranger when you factor in that it happened on *February 29th* of that year."

"Whoa."

"But stranger still, Molly told me, in all the leap years since that happened, there have been five other cases of single women occupying Catherine's room at the MacVicar on February 29th who have also lost love."

"Oh, come on. That's ridiculous."

"In 1912, another young woman was staying in the Catherine Room on February 29th when her fiancé just disappeared. They never found him. Not a trace."

"But—"

"In 1920, after the MacVicar was remodeled as an inn, or today what we'd call a bed and breakfast, another single woman was occupying the Catherine when . . . well, I can't remember what happened to that one. But same thing. Fiancé killed on February 29th. Then another one lost her fiancé on an Italian battlefield in World War II. He died on February 29th, 1944."

"Okay, I get it. They're all tragic love stories that happened on the same day of the year. Yes, it's a bizarre series of coincidences, but what has any of this got to do with *you*?"

"Folks here believe it's much more than mere coincidence, more like a legend of some kind. Apparently, whenever a single woman stays in that room on February 29th, they all watch and wait to see if she'll be the one to break the curse."

"A *curse*?" Ellen cackled. "Surely they're kidding. They can't be serious, can they?"

"That's just it. Molly was completely serious. I'll admit there was a twinkle in her eye, but she never gave any indication it was just a joke. I had a hard time keeping a straight face while she was telling me all of this. And when she was done, I could not stop laughing! I apologized because I think I offended her. As I left, she was sweet, shrugged it off like it was no big deal, but I could tell she didn't mean it."

"But you're not even involved in a relationship! Isn't that a rather important piece of the puzzle?"

Olivia fell back against the pillows on the bed, laughing. "I said the same thing! It's all so absurd, isn't it? But it sure explains all the strange looks I've been getting. I'm just wondering if these folks are all a bit addled, y'know? Maybe all this snow gets to them. Or maybe there's something in the water. Who knows."

"I hope it's not contagious. Can't have you coming home all filled with ghost stories and conspiracy theories."

"Ellen, when have you ever known me to fall for stuff like that?"

"True. You're much too practical. Just don't go falling in love or anything, okay?"

"Because I'm oh-so-prone to falling in love with every man I meet, eh?"

"Yes, but rarely more than twice a day."

"Yes. Rarely. Goodbye, Ellen."

"Later, gator."

Chapter 8

Despite the continuing snowfall, Michele and Trig assured Olivia she would have no problem getting to the book club and back. The sidewalks had been salted and cleared late that afternoon, though another inch or so had fallen in the meantime. She left early enough to grab a quick bite at a small café called Anthony's just around the corner from the bookstore. There she enjoyed a small dinner salad and her first lobster bisque, a soup so delicious she had to talk herself out of ordering a second bowl.

Just before seven, she gathered her things and made her way to Books & Such.

"Thank goodness!" Molly hugged her as she entered the bookstore. "I was so afraid I might have scared you off and sent you packing!"

"Hardly. It'll take a lot more than some strange legend to get rid of me, Molly. I love it here."

Molly took Olivia's hand in both of hers. "Good. Good! Now come in and meet everyone."

A small semi-circle of chairs flanked the fireplace though only a couple of people were seated. Others milled around a table of refreshments and chatted amongst themselves. As Molly led her into their midst, Olivia stifled the urge to react as the familiar curiosity filled their eyes. Now that she was in on the secret, it amused her to observe all their strange looks. Molly introduced her to the odd cast of characters, mostly women.

A retired school teacher named Elise Blackburn. Carla Reynolds owned the bakery called The Fussy Muffin and routinely brought goodies to every meeting. Scott Randolphson, a retired corporate executive from New York, was legally blind. At their introduction, he told her he listened to several books a week by audio. His daughter Mavis rarely left his side. She too was an avid reader, and this month's Binchy selection had been her choice. Mimi Overton ran Little Ones Preschool two blocks over. Mimi, a loud and boisterous sixty-something, wore a velour jogging suit the exact color of Pepto Bismol, though Olivia doubted she'd exercised since Nixon was in the White House. And last was Marilyn Crowder, the proprietor of the Knit Knook, who was already seated and busily knitting what looked to be a scarf from lavender yarn.

Following Molly's lead, Olivia poured herself a mug of coffee, wrapped a warm, soft cookie in a napkin, then took a seat. Trevor appeared from the back of the shop with an additional rocking chair to add to the circle. His eyes met hers briefly.

"Miss Thomas."

"Mr. Bass."

"Now, we'll have none of that," the retired school teacher declared, looking over her half-glasses. "Trevor, this is Olivia. Olivia, meet Trevor. This is Trevor's bookstore."

He took a seat near the hearth. "Thank you, Elise, but *Miss Thomas* and I have already met." He fixed a tight smile and nodded briefly in Olivia's direction.

"Never mind him, Olivia. Mr. Bass likes to put on airs, but I assure you he puts his pants on one leg at a time just like the rest of us."

A handful of chuckles filled the room. Trevor didn't seem amused, instead reaching for his copy of *Minding Frankie.* "Thank you, Elise, for your always delicate choice of words. Now, if we could—"

"Trevor, don't you have an extra copy for Olivia?" Mimi asked, already heading to the display table.

"That's okay, I can just look on Molly's copy here," Olivia offered.

"Nonsense. Plenty of copies available." Mimi placed a hardcover in Olivia's hand. "Now, anyone else need anything? Trevor, you don't have a cookie or coffee."

"I'm fine, Mimi. Take a seat."

"Don't be silly. You go ahead and start. I'll fix you something."

Trevor subtly rolled his eyes and put his glasses back on. "If you insist—"

"I do-oo!" Mimi trilled from behind them.

"Shall we begin?" he asked. "First, I would like to ask that we allow poor Miss Binchy to rest in peace and read no more of her books. As with all her books, I struggled to get through this one, Mavis. With so many extraordinary possibilities out there, I recommend we officially retire Miss Binchy from our book club."

Mavis blushed as she straightened in her chair. "You're welcome to your opinion, Trevor, but I find her characters fascinating and the pacing of her stories an absolute delight."

"Oh my, yes," Marilyn said, looping a stretch of yarn over her clacking needles. "I found *Minding Frankie* such a wonderfully layered book. The premise alone—a young man who struggles with alcoholism suddenly finding out he's fathered a child with a dying woman who's now dying, then finds himself caring for the baby—well, it's such a deliciously impossible situation."

Mimi returned, handing Trevor a plate loaded with cookies as she set his mug of coffee on the table beside him. "Then throw in that busybody social worker who's bent on taking Frankie away from Noel," she added, "and you've got all the components for a drama in the making." She brushed her hands together and took her seat. "And in classic Binchy style, there's a whole network of family and friends who sign on to help care for the little—"

"Yes, and that's *precisely* the problem," Trevor snarled. "She always has such an extensive cast of characters, each of them with their own absurd dramas. It's so confusing, trying to remember who's who. You practically need a cast list to keep up."

"I must agree with Trevor on that note," Scott said, his unseeing eyes roaming over their heads. "Too many characters. She should have entitled this one *It Takes a Village*. Hillary Clinton would be thrilled."

"Oh, for heaven's sake, Scott," Molly said. "Hillary wasn't the first one to originate the concept of friends and family helping to raise a child. Besides, you and Trevor are missing the point."

Trevor crossed his legs, leaned back in his chair, and folded his arms across his chest. "By all means, Molly, enlighten us."

"This is a story of redemption! It's a beautiful portrayal of the roles we all play in each other's lives. Take Emily, for example—the American cousin who moves into this tightknit Dublin neighborhood. Her gifts of organization help weave all these characters together, each one helping the other, using their God-given talents."

When no one said anything, Olivia decided to join the discussion. "I have to agree with Molly."

"Surely you aren't reading some kind of spirituality into this story?" Scott asked.

"Well, no. Not overtly. But as Molly mentioned, we all have gifts and talents and passions that are meant to meet the needs of others. What good does it do if we sit on those, never offering a helping hand where it's needed? Especially if we're able or have the resources to help."

"Good point, Olivia," Mimi added, scooting to the edge of her seat. "Take me, for example. I love children. *Love* them. And since Mr. Right hasn't come along, and I have no kids of my own, I can use my passion for kids by caring for them while their mommies and daddies work."

"And you do a fine job of it," Marilyn said, pulling a long string of yarn from the skein. She turned toward Carla sitting next to her. "And how about our favorite baker here? How would we all survive without Carla's award-winning cakes and pies? Did you all know her Peach Pecan Pie Cake is going to be on the cover of *Southern Living* next month?"

Carla dismissed their admiration with a conspiratorial whisper. "Just don't tell them I'm a Yankee, okay?"

Trevor spoke over their chuckles. "We'll expect a sampling at next month's book club, Carla. Now, back to our discussion."

For the next hour, they argued the merits of the book.

Elise, the retired school teacher, said she enjoyed the book but struggled with the author's constant head-hopping. "Every writer knows you can only write from one point of view at a time. Otherwise, it's too confusing for the reader to figure out who's saying what. Is it Noel who's wondering about Moira's constant invasion of their privacy or is it Lisa? It's one of the fundamental rules of writing."

"And yet, almost all of Maeve Binchy's books were bestsellers," Mavis added. "She may break a few rules, but you can't argue with her success."

"And yet we do," Carla quipped dryly. "Still, for the *uneducated* among us who don't know all those rules and regulations when it comes to writing, we find her work absolutely charming."

Trevor set his coffee back on the table. "Yes, well, good for you, Carla," he patronized. "But it's time to move on to next month's selection. As you know, it's once again my turn to select a book for us to read, and—"

"Trevor, *please* tell us it's not another one of your thousand page, dry-as-dust classics," Marilyn groaned. "I couldn't bear it. Right, everyone?"

Trevor looked over his reading glasses at her. "Now, Marilyn, you'd be disappointed if I chose anything else."

"Oh, no," she groaned again. "Gird your loins, boys and girls. Looks like we're in for it this time."

Trevor pulled a book from behind the small table. "Now, now," he clucked. "Ladies and gentlemen, after the *fluff* of tonight's read—"

"Hey!" Mavis barked.

"—I thought we should exercise our mental aptitude and go substantially deeper by digging into one of the most respected classics of all time. A story so unforgettable, it still thrills readers more than 160 years after it was first published." He held up the thick volume, its title in gilded lettering on the brown leather cover. "This month we'll be reading *The Count of Monte Cristo* by Alexandre Dumas."

"Give us a break, Trevor," Marilyn whined.

Scott tapped his cane against the hardwood floor. "No, quite the contrary! An excellent choice. Who narrates the audio version?"

Trevor grabbed a boxed audio set and walked it over to Scott. "Colin Firth, the British actor." As Scott grasped the set, Trevor patted the older man on the knee. "I took a listen. He does a tremendous job."

"Can't wait to get started. How long does it run?"

"Sixty-seven hours, so you'd better get started tonight."

"You don't honestly expect us to read the unabridged version, do you?" Mimi balked. "Some of us have to work for a living, you know."

"I do, Mimi. And for that reason you'll find both versions available. You'll miss some of the author's brilliance by reading the abridged version, but nonetheless, you'll be able to keep up with our discussion next time."

"Did you ever see the movie?" Mavis asked around. "The one with Jim Caviezel playing the role of Edmond Dantés? It's one of my all-time favorite movies."

"*Loved* it," Carla said, then ducked sheepishly back at Trevor. "But I promise I'll read the book. Honest."

"See that you do, Carla. Some have called this the most perfect literary work ever written. And I'd be inclined to agree."

"Why?" Olivia asked.

"Why?" He turned toward her.

"Why do you agree? What is it that makes *The Count of Monte Cristo* stand out above all others? In your opinion, that is."

He stared at her for a moment saying nothing. Then, as if catching himself, he pasted another tight smile on his face. "Well, Miss Thomas, I suppose you'd have to join us next month to find out. But alas, you'll be long gone by then." He stood. "Very well. Class dismissed, as they say. Grab a copy of the book if you need one. Help yourself to more coffee. Carla, thanks again for bringing your delectable cookies. I look forward to your Peach Pecan Pie Cake next month."

"Don't hold your breath," the baker teased. "Since we're reading the world's longest book and much of it is set in a prison, maybe I'll just bring something more theme-oriented, like molded bread. Or gruel."

Mimi hooted, looping her arm through Carla's. "Bring that for Mr. Snobby Pants over there, but the rest of us want cake!"

For the next half hour, Olivia enjoyed getting to know the others, each spending a few minutes welcoming her and sharing the usual pleasantries. To her surprise, they were all as friendly as she'd found Molly, Trig, and Michelle. Not at all the reserved, cliquish northerners she'd always heard about. Later, back at the refreshment table, Mr. Randolphson visited with her, his eyes aimed above her head. It occurred to her that he was the only one this evening who hadn't given her *the look*. He was a tad formal but asked all the usual questions, chuckling at the appropriate times, always including his daughter Mavis in the friendly chat.

When their conversation came to an end, she was surprised to find everyone else had gone. Looking out the front window, Olivia was shocked to see a wall of white snow—blowing *sideways*.

"Oh my goodness! Look at that!"

"I'd love to, my dear, but I'm afraid I can't."

"Oh, Mr. Randolphson, how thoughtless of me!" Olivia winced, daring a peek at an amused Mavis.

"Call me Scott. I insist." He reached out searching for Olivia's hand and patted it once he took hold. "Now tell me what I'm missing, will you?"

She led him toward the window. "It looks like a blizzard out there! I've never seen anything like it! It's blowing sideways!"

"Oh, that," he scoffed. "Unless it's piled to the rooftop, there's nothing to worry about. Haven't you seen snow before?"

"Well, sure. Not often in Atlanta, but I once had a flight delayed in Amarillo, Texas because the snow was so heavy. Visibility was all but zero."

Scott hooked his cane over his arm while he buttoned his coat. "Texas, was it? Our Maine snows make those out west look like a mere dusting."

Mavis wrapped a wool scarf around her father's neck. "Now, Dad, you can't say that. You've never even been to Texas."

"And I've no desire to, thank you very much." He searched for Olivia's arm, and finding it, gave a squeeze. "It was lovely meeting you, Miss Thomas. I hope to *see* you again soon."

She patted his gloved hand. "Very funny. Good night. Be careful out there."

"We will." Mavis helped her father out the door. "Good night."

Olivia started to follow them when a sudden bark jarred her. Below, she found Charlie gazing up at her, her tail waving wildly. "Charlie, you scared me! Again, I might add." She knelt down to scratch behind the dog's ears. We've got to stop meeting like this, you know."

Trevor caught up with them. "Charlie, leave the lady alone."

"Oh, she's no bother. I was wondering where she was tonight. Let me guess—you don't approve of her taste in books?"

Trevor pursed his lips, but a flicker of humor passed through his eyes. "Charlie has excellent taste in books. But in her condition, I thought it best for her not to get too excited with a room full of people. She's quite the social butterfly."

"Obviously. But I suppose a little caution makes sense." She nuzzled the dog's snout against her chin. "Can't be too careful. Still, I'm glad I got to see you tonight, Charlie." Olivia gave her a final pat and stood again. "Thanks for allowing me to visit tonight, Trevor. I really enjoyed it."

"Good. I'm glad you could join us."

She pulled on her gloves, thinking he was about to say something else. He didn't.

"Okay, then. I'll just be on my way." She opened the door to a face full of snow. "Whoa!"

He reached for the door and pulled her back inside. "You really shouldn't be out in this without the proper shoes." He closed the door.

She looked down at her loafers peeking out beneath her slacks. "I know, but I didn't think to buy some when I got to town. Silly, I know."

"Yes, well, we can't have our only tourist out and about in loafers, now can we?"

"We can't?"

He pointed to the rocker by the fireplace. "Sit. Let me get you some pull-ons you can wear over your shoes."

He disappeared down the aisle as she took a seat in the old rocking chair. Charlie stood, resting her front paws on Olivia's knees. "What's with him?" she whispered, petting the dog's silky hair. "You let me know if he doesn't treat you like a queen, all right? We girls have to stick together."

Just like her Sammy used to do, Charlie smiled a knowing smile, her tail swishing back and forth. Suddenly, she bounded effortlessly onto Olivia's lap and made herself at home.

"Well, now! Aren't you the graceful young lady?" She took Charlie's head in her hands and lifted the dog's snout to her nose, rubbing it Eskimo-style. "I think you're just about the sweetest thing I've ever seen," she cooed. "I might just have to sneak you out and take you home with me. Would you like that?"

"Ahem."

"Oh! Trevor. I didn't see you there. You weren't supposed to hear that."

"No, I suppose not." He joined her, setting a pair of yellow galoshes next to her chair. "I'm afraid I've spoiled her terribly. Charlie, get down from Miss Thomas's lap, will you?"

Olivia held onto Charlie, running her hand down the dog's back. "Oh, please don't. She's fine. Really. In fact, I'm rather loving all the attention."

He took a seat in the chair adjacent to hers. "If you're sure."

"I am." She smiled as Charlie nuzzled her neck again. "Oh, I'm absolutely sure."

"Mind if I ask you a question?"

"Not at all."

"Why exactly are you here?"

Olivia looked over at him. "Here? In your bookstore?"

"No, I mean here. In Caden Cove. It's not often we have tourists this time of year, but especially not women traveling alone."

She narrowed her eyes. "I'm not sure whether to be offended or tell you to mind your own business."

"Oh, no, I didn't mean—that is to say, I . . . well, I'm just curious. That's all. You've only been here a day or two, and yet you've already met half the townsfolk, and you seem almost at home here. Which is absolutely preposterous, insofar as you're . . . you're . . ."

"Has anyone ever told you you're a bit of a snob?"

He sat back. "Me? A snob?"

She turned her head, resting it on top of Charlie's. "You're kidding, right?"

"I don't have a clue what you mean."

She laughed out loud, only slightly embarrassed when her laugh turned to a snort. She held a palm toward him. "I'm sorry! Really I am. It's just that you sounded so innocent just then." She couldn't control the giggles bubbling out of her.

He folded his arms across his chest again. "You're a very peculiar woman, Miss Thomas."

She rested her forehead on Charlie's, then lifted it back up. "I'm sorry. It just seems like you and I—well, it's as if we keep getting off on the wrong foot. Regardless, you have *got* to stop calling me Miss Thomas. It's Olivia, remember?"

He seemed to be studying her for the longest time, but for some reason, it didn't bother her in the least. She cupped Charlie's head in her hands again. "Charlie, what's a girl gotta do to get through to this guy, huh? Any secrets I should know? Any quirky habits? Strange interests?" She raised one of Charlie's ears and whispered into it. "He doesn't play the accordion, does he?"

Olivia darted her eyes at Trevor just as his well-placed reserve gave way to laughter. He shook his head. "Think of me what you will, but be assured I most certainly do *not* play the accordion." He chuckled again then sighed audibly, a contented smile on his face.

The noticeable change intrigued her. How could someone so stuffy and stern have such a warm, endearing smile? The creases that lined his forehead all but disappeared, and for the first time, she noticed a cluster of tiny lines feathering the outer edges of his blue-gray eyes.

"Miss Thomas—I mean, *Olivia*. I wonder, would you like a cup of tea?"

Chapter 9

Over their second cup of tea, their conversation grew more personal. Trevor wasn't sure what it was about this woman that fascinated him so. To him, tourists were a dime a dozen in Caden Cove. For the most part, he played the role of bookseller when he had to, but rarely bothered to get chummy with any of them. Even as a realtor, he kept an arm's length from both buyers and sellers. He knew he had a reputation for being a loner, which didn't bother him in the least. Life was too short for messy friendships and obligatory acquaintances.

The one exception was his book club. Originally, he'd hoped to use it as an effective platform to help these town folk learn a thing or too. To teach them about the classics and thereby educate them at a level far surpassing their routine, daily lives. Of course, the dozen or so men and women who attended month after month weren't as pliable as he'd first hoped. After their first four meetings, several insisted they all be given the chance to suggest which books to read. He'd balked at first, but rather than see the whole thing fail, he'd reluctantly agreed. Yes, they'd studied some interesting books he would never have read on his own. But he'd also endured some of the most inane rubbish ever published. On those months, he wondered why he'd ever started the book club in the first place.

Now, with the snow still blowing outside and the fire crackling beside them, he had to admit he was thankful for tonight's meeting. How else would he have had the opportunity to get to know this stranger in their midst? They'd talked at length about books, of course. But she'd seamlessly moved the conversation to more personal topics. He deflected her questions, preferring to hear her story rather than share his own. And in doing so, he found himself even more intrigued by her.

"Listen to me, rambling on," she said. "I must be boring you to tears."

"No, not at all."

She took another sip of tea then set the cup back in its saucer. "You haven't fooled me, you know. You're very good at deflecting questions I've asked *you*. Enough about me. I want to know what makes you tick. Why all the mystery?"

"Mystery? I have nothing to hide. I'm an open book."

Her smile taunted him. "I bet you say that to all the girls."

"I'm not that clever. And as for 'the girls'—*what* girls? Our little town is hardly a mecca for the singles scene."

"Mimi seems nice."

"Mimi? Oh, please."

"You've never married?"

"No. You?"

She turned to gaze at the fire. "Close, once. But that was a thousand years ago."

He watched her, noticing the carefree, wispy style of her dark hair, a few hints of gray teasing at her temples. He guessed her to be a few years younger than himself. Most singles their age had at least one marriage under the belt by this point in their lives. He was surprised she hadn't. Hers was a smile that lit up the room. He cringed at the cliché, but there it was.

He shook off the boyish thoughts and wondered how to ask her to leave. Just then she turned to face him.

"What?" she asked.

"What?"

"You're looking at me funny."

"I am?"

"You are. And I think I know why."

"You do?"

"Okay, stop answering my questions with a question." She rocked her head slowly, rhythmically from side to side. "It's the legend thing, isn't it?"

"The legend thing?"

"You know—the curse of the single women who happen to stay in the Catherine Room at the MacVicar on leap year? That whole myth about lost love? You told me you've lived here your whole life. Surely you know about it."

"Of course."

She stared at him. "Of course?"

"Sure."

"Sure?"

"Now who's answering questions with a question?"

She smiled. "Sorry. I just thought . . . well, since I've been here, everybody keeps looking at me like I'm some kind of lab rat or something."

Trevor smiled in return. "No surprise there. Every time February of a leap year rolls around, they all go a bit daft, wondering if this could be the year."

"So you *do* know the legend. The curse."

A scoff puffed his lips. "Nothing but a bunch of silly suspicions without a shred of truth to them."

"So you don't believe in them?"

"Of course not. Anyone with an ounce of sanity knows it's preposterous. A handful of coincidences, nothing more."

She leaned back in her chair and sighed. "Thank goodness. I thought I was the only one who thought that."

He flicked his wrist. "Completely absurd."

"Is any of the story true? About Captain MacVicar's demise and Catherine holing up in that room and that teacup—"

"Ah, the teacup. It's tough to say. Stories like these have a way of taking on a life of their own, growing with each telling of the tale, so to speak."

"But what about the captain and Catherine?"

"Well, that part is true, as far as I've been able to . . ." He caught himself, faking a brief cough. "Yes, he was engaged to a young lady named Catherine Bennett."

"Molly told me all about it."

"She did?"

"Yes. In fact she seemed a bit sentimental while telling me about it. I almost wondered if she were related to the family or something."

How much had Molly told Olivia? The fact that Olivia didn't say more put his mind at ease. He plowed on.

"Captain MacVicar was highly respected and extremely successful in his shipping trade, making frequent trips across the sea to English and European ports. His ship, a beautiful three-masted Baltimore schooner named *The Merry Martha,* transported lucrative products like tea, silks from China, spices from the Orient, that sort of thing. Schooners were built for speed more so than cargo space, so MacVicar's was a seasonal trading vessel.

"Early on, *The Merry Martha* carried mail between the continents, but MacVicar hated making the 'packet ship' runs, as they were called. Very risky because they traveled on precise schedules, carrying important documents and 'packets' from embassies and governments along their trade routes. Such predictable time schedules made them easy targets for pirate attacks, of course. MacVicar refused to put his crew in such a dangerous plight, so he soon dropped the mail service.

"Still, I've always been fascinated by those mighty clippers—" He stopped, realizing he'd been chatting away without any regard to his guest. He dipped his head, embarrassed. "Sorry, I tend to get carried away at times."

"Not at all. It's fascinating. I once read a book about a famous clipper that was navigated by the *wife* of the ship's captain—"

"*Flying Cloud: The True Story of America's Most Famous Clipper Ship and the Woman Who Guided Her,* by David Shaw."

"Yes, that's it! You've read it?"

Trevor crossed his legs. "Yes, when it first came out in 2000. I'm sure I have a copy here somewhere. I was familiar with the story, of course, and honestly wanted to like the book. But instead, I was utterly distracted by the imposed fictionalized dialogue. It didn't ring true, somehow."

She tucked a leg beneath her. "Sure, the dialogue was fabricated to better tell the story in a novelization. But I loved Eleanor Creesey's strong spirit and determination, especially in a time period that rele-gated women to cooking, cleaning, and staying out of the way. She was amazing. I've often thought her story would make a wonderful movie."

"Yes, I suppose you're right. An astonishing feat for a woman to navigate a history-making world record like she did. Imagine, breaking the record on the ship's maiden voyage."

"New York to San Francisco in eighty-nine days instead of the previous two-hundred," Olivia added. "And that was before the Panama Canal was built. All thanks to the brilliant navigation—by a woman, no less."

"If you start singing 'I Am Woman,' I'll have to ask you to leave."

She pressed her lips together, mischief dancing in her eyes. "Really? Because I'm fairly sure you want to hear it."

"You'd be sorely mistaken," he teased back.

"But you can't kick me out yet."

"I can't?"

"No. I want to ask you something."

"Fire away."

She took a breath and slowly released it. "I've noticed something about you."

"And what might that be?"

"Your entire demeanor changes when you talk about books. Especially books you love, but even those you don't. You obviously have a genuine passion for books, but I think it's more than just a business for you. Much more. It's as if you come alive when you talk about them. Why is that?"

What kind of a question is that? He clamped his jaw and tried to think how to respond. He tried to read her expression but found only sincerity in her eyes. What was she after? Why was she critiquing him? They'd only met yesterday.

"I hope you don't take this wrong," he began, "but who are you to ask me a question like that? Books are my business. To superimpose anything more is to—"

"It also occurs to me you aren't nearly as formidable as you'd have people believe. Why is that? What's that all about?"

He shook his head, dizzy from her persistence. "I have no earthly idea what you're trying to get at, Miss Thomas."

"It's Olivia. And I'm only trying to understand why you are the way you are."

"Has anyone ever told you you're blunt?" he retorted. "And teetering on the edge of being downright rude."

She relaxed, sitting back in her chair again. "Why, thank you."

"*Thank* you? What . . . I mean . . . are you daft or something?"

"Not at all. See, I've recently come to a point in my life where I'm no longer willing to live in a shell and miss opportunities. And right now I see this as an opportunity to get to know you. I find you extremely interesting, Trevor. But I want to know what's holding you back from answering a few simple questions?"

He felt his face heating again but for the life of him, couldn't find a word to say.

Her eyes still locked on his, she leaned forward to scratch Charlie on the head. "Have you ever thought about writing?"

He narrowed his eyes at her. Again. "Why would you ask—"

"Because I can't imagine you *not* writing. You'd be a natural at it. You have such a unique perspective on so many subjects. You don't run with the pack. Your mind seems to conceptualize things in different ways from the rest of us. It completely sets you apart. Sure, most folks might think you're standoffish, even aloof. But I for one would love to read a book written by Trevor Bass."

He huffed a noisy sigh and clapped his hands against his knees. "You're certainly entitled to your own delusional ideas, but I need to call it a night." He stood up, hoping she'd take the hint.

"Methinks I hit a nerve." She smiled as she gently lifted Charlie from her lap and placed the sleepy dog on the floor. Olivia stood and climbed back into her coat. "Thank you for the tea and a lovely evening."

She may have aggravated him, but he couldn't let her leave in the heavy snowfall. "Let me grab my coat, and I'll walk you to the MacVicar."

"Oh, that's not necessary."

"Sit back down and put those galoshes on." He took his coat from the rack and pulled it on.

She obliged, sitting down before stepping into the oversized boots. "Really, Trevor, you don't have to. It's just a couple of blocks."

He looped a wool scarf around his neck and put on his cap. "Yes, thank you, I believe I know where the inn is located. Can you just do as you're told and not be so stubborn?"

"Stubborn? I'm not stubborn." She stood up, stomping her feet more firmly into the galoshes. "But thanks for the boots."

He motioned toward the front door. "Ready?"

"If you say so."

He opened the door then locked it behind them as he ushered her into the blinding snow. "It can be slippery here and there, so hold onto my arm." He extended his elbow toward her and started across the street.

"Isn't this GREAT?!" she shouted, lifting her face to the blustery night sky.

She giggled like a schoolgirl catching snowflakes on her tongue. He tried to imagine the scene through her eyes; someone who's never been around this much snow before. He fought the urge to smile, still bristling from her nosy questions. Whatever had intrigued him earlier now felt like warning sirens screaming through his head—BEWARE! BEWARE! He vowed to avoid her whenever possible and give her no more opportunities to pry into his personal life.

As they turned up the sidewalk leading to the MacVicar, he realized she'd let go of his arm. He turned to find her stooped with her back toward him.

"What are you—"

WHOMP!

The snowball hit his chest, the surprise of it nearly knocking the breath out of him. "What was THAT?"

"My first ever snowball! I'm so excited!"

"But—"

"Ah, c'mon! Fight with me, Trevor!" She squatted again, rounding up more snow.

"But—"

"Enough with the *buts*, already!" She turned, blasting him with another hit, this one between his shoulder blades.

He reached down, packed a quick one, and spun around to lob it at her shoulder. "Ha! Surprise!"

"You call that a snowball? Come on, buddy, give me your best shot!"

His leather gloves made it easy to pack the white stuff, so he made an even bigger ball. "You want it? You got it!" He threw it hard in her direction just as she turned back toward him. The giant snowball hit her right on the nose and sent her sprawling.

"Olivia! I'm so sorry!" He rushed to her side, sure he'd knocked her out. She lay flat on her back, arms outstretched, her face covered with snow. "Are you all right? Olivia?"

Her breath puffed white clouds above her face. *At least she's breathing*, he thought, though her eyes remained closed. He leaned closer, cupping his gloved hand behind her head. "Olivia? Can you hear me?"

"Huhh . . ." she groaned, her eyes still closed.

"Are you all right?"

She didn't move a muscle. She didn't say a word. Suddenly, a wicked smile split her face, and her eyes flashed wide open as she smashed a handful of snow into his face.

"GOTCHA!"

Her roaring laughter cut through the night, bouncing off the old house as he fell back on the ground. "Oh, you're a real cut up. Very funny." He wiped the snow from his face, trying hard not to laugh. "I thought you were hurt, and *this* is how you repay me?"

"Hey! Is everything okay out there?"

Trevor and Olivia looked up as Trig stood on the front porch wrapping a coat over his plaid pajamas.

"Trig!" Olivia said, getting up. "It's snowing!"

"Yes, I see that, Olivia." He held his hand over his eyes to block the glare from the porch light. "Is that you, Trevor?"

He stood up, dusting the snow from his backside. "Yes, I'm afraid so. Awfully sorry if we awakened you."

Trig grinned. "No problem. Looks like you two are having a good time out here."

Oh, great.

"Yes, well, I'll be on my way now." Trevor waved as he turned to go. "Good evening, Miss Thomas. Mr. Myers."

"G'night, Trevor," Olivia said, still snickering. "Thanks for walking me home."

He said nothing, just raised his hand without turning. As he walked away, he heard Trig's voice carry over the hedge.

"Will wonders never cease? Trevor Bass—in a snowball fight? How'd you manage *that*?"

Thankfully, Trevor couldn't hear Olivia's response.

Now if the ground would just open up and swallow me whole.

Chapter 10

"What did you say?" Ellen asked.

Olivia adjusted her cell phone against her ear. "I've asked Trevor to show me some houses here."

"Just for the fun of it, right?"

"Maybe. Maybe not. I'm thinking about the possibility of buying a house here. I probably wouldn't live here full time. I could rent it out while I'm away."

"Isn't this rather sudden? You've only been there a few days, Olivia. How could you possibly know if you'd want to *live* there? Didn't your attorney advise you not to make any rash decisions for a while?"

"I know, but what harm could it do to look at a few? I haven't signed the dotted line yet. I just want to see what's on the market here."

"What did Trevor say to that?"

Olivia paused, choosing her words carefully. "He didn't seem too thrilled at the prospect, but I'm beginning to think that's his shtick."

"His shtick?"

"Yeah. I think he likes having a buffer around himself, so he purposefully acts obnoxious."

"Sounds like a real gem. Can't wait to meet him."

"Why would you want to meet him?"

"Because you keep talking about him. Every time we talk."

Olivia paused. "Oh, please."

"I'm just saying . . ."

"So, how are things in Atlanta?"

"Stop changing the subject."

"You're barking up a tree that doesn't exist."

"Ha ha. I'm just trying to save you from making a big mistake."

"Are you talking houses or booksellers?"

Silence. Then, "Look, Olivia. You know how much I love Caden Cove. And I can see how it might be appealing—a complete change from here, all that snow, a quaint seaside village and all that. But the whole purpose of you going there was to have a chance to think things through. Make some decisions now that . . . well, now that you have the means to follow your dreams."

"You're such a poet."

Ellen laughed, and suddenly Olivia missed her terribly. "If you're so worried about me making a big bad mistake, why don't you throw your things in a bag, catch a flight up here, and come straighten me out?"

"Don't tempt me."

After three days the snow finally stopped, leaving behind a wintry white carpet more than four feet high. Olivia had enjoyed the respite, spending most of her time reading *The Count of Monte Cristo* in her room or downstairs in the living room. There, Trig and Michelle often joined her, telling her all about life in this quiet corner of Maine. How quickly she'd grown fond of these two and the passion they shared for Caden Cove. She hadn't yet mentioned the teacup or the legend, deciding she'd let them bring it up if they chose to.

She told Trevor she'd wait until the snow cleared to go house hunting. He assured her he was more than capable of driving in such conditions. *No doubt another dig to remind me I'm an outsider.* She could still see the look on his face when she first mentioned looking at houses—a mix of incredulity and disdain. Which, of course, made her all the more determined to pursue the idea.

Oh, the thrill of a challenge. Especially from one so codmungeonly.

Now, waiting for Trevor to pick her up, she fought a nervous anxiousness. If she were honest, she knew why. That night when they chatted over tea after book club, she couldn't help feeling there was something between them. Nothing forthright or obvious, but *something.* A glimmer of possibility? A tiny crack in Trevor's armor, allowing her to see beyond his gruff façade?

Later, during their snowball fight, she'd caught sight of it again in his laughing eyes, warmed by childlike playfulness. A face no longer set in stone, but one crinkled and sparkling with spontaneous abandon. Had she imagined it or wished it so? In the days that followed, the sound of his laughter played over and over in her head. She smiled, pleased to know there was more to Trevor Bass—

"Ready to go?"

Olivia jumped. "Trevor! You startled me!"

"I suppose I should have knocked or something. Trig told me I could find you here."

She busied herself pulling her coat on, avoiding eye contact until the heat in her face cooled. "Yes. I'm here. Waiting for you." She pulled on her gloves, still not looking up. "Are you sure you want to do this today?"

He turned. "Why? Have you changed your mind?"

Olivia straightened her shoulders and finally looked him in the eye. "Not at all. Let's do this, shall we?" With that, she walked past him into the entry hall.

He opened the door for her then held her arm as they navigated the front steps. He hustled them toward the SUV, opening the passenger door for her. Once inside, she turned to thank him but the door shut in her face.

Okay, then. So much for the kinder, gentler Mr. Bass.

He slid behind the wheel, closed the door, and buckled himself in. "I heated the seat for you, but if you find it too warm for your liking, you can adjust it by pressing the button there on your side of the console."

"Oh, how nice. Thank you." She buckled her seatbelt. "Feels great."

"Yes, well, I've selected five houses to show you." He handed some papers to her. "Here are the listings if you'd like to look them over. We'll start closer to town and work our way out toward the beach."

"Sounds like a plan."

He looked at her briefly, then pressed the ignition button and they were on their way.

"I must tell you it's extremely difficult to help you find what you're looking for when you won't give me more specific parameters, like number of bedrooms, price range, square footage. So I assume this is merely an exercise in curiosity more than a viable search for a home."

She turned sideways to face him, adjusting her seatbelt. "Trevor, is there a problem here?"

"What do you mean?"

"Do you grill all your prospective buyers like this? Because I would think it wouldn't help sell houses, coming across so antagonistic."

He stiffened, his eyes on the road. "I have no idea what you're talking about. I simply—"

"The thing is, unless I have to sign my name in blood to assure you I'm serious about looking for a home here in Caden Cove, then I'd expect a little more civility in your approach. Last I heard, most realtors like to schmooze their prospective buyers, not alienate them."

"But that's just the problem," he uttered through clenched teeth. "I don't believe you *are* a prospective buyer. I think you're just looking for something to do while you're here on your 'extended getaway.' I think you're curious about what the houses here look like on the inside. I think you're—"

"How could you possibly know what I may or may not be thinking?" She huffed, shaking her head. "Besides, what difference does it make *why* I'm looking at houses? You're a realtor. I asked you to show me some houses. That's what realtors do. So please explain to me why you're so caustic about it, because I'd really like to know."

He slammed on the brakes, causing the belt to pull tight against her, then turned off the ignition.

"*Now* what?"

He grabbed the papers from the console and got out of the SUV. "You want to look at houses? Fine. Here's our first stop." With that, he slammed the door and disappeared from Olivia's sight.

"Buster, you are *this close* to getting on my last nerve!" she grumbled to herself.

Her door opened, but he didn't wait to help her out. By the time she unlatched her seatbelt, he was halfway up the sidewalk listing off the home's details. "Five bedrooms, three and a half baths, three thousand square feet, hardwood floors throughout, full basement, eat-in kitchen—"

"Stop!"

He halted in his tracks, then slowly turned. "Is there a problem?"

Olivia bit her lip, corralling every ounce of her patience. A litany of sarcastic responses ripped through her mind, but she wasn't about to let him get the best of her. *Breathe in, breathe out.* She closed the door and carefully made her way through the snow drifts to the sidewalk which, thankfully, had been cleared. *Breathe in, breathe out.* She straightened, making her way toward him. Catching up, she leveled her eyes at him. "No problem." She walked past him then headed up the porch steps.

Behind her, he muttered something unintelligible. He stomped up the stairs, unlocked the door, stood back, and while pinning her with a look to kill, threw open the door.

"The home was built in 1899, but previous owners have maintained the home, upgrading as needed. The current owners put a new roof on the home three years ago, and upgraded the kitchen and all three bathrooms just two years ago. But, as you'll see, they did so with an eye toward the original design. Meaning, the house boasts the latest amenities while offering an authentic heritage."

She strolled through the rooms, observing the home's classy features while listening to his well-rehearsed descriptions. Inwardly, she smiled at his robotron tone, aware of its intent. She peeked in every closet, opened every cabinet door, and even took a long look at the contents in the refrigerator, at which point he rolled his eyes with affected exaggeration.

After climbing back up the stairs from the basement, he turned to her. "Well?"

She tapped her gloves against the palm of her other hand, taking one final look around. "No. It's a beautiful home, but *much* too big for me." She flashed him a ready smile and headed for the SUV.

They repeated the routine through three more houses. Olivia enjoyed the variety of architectural styles, the eclectic decorating themes, and the strong sense of community which prevailed while touring the area. It frustrated her not to be able to discuss them with Trevor, but the tone he'd set prohibited any friendly conversation. With a growing sadness, she resigned herself to the futility of their time together.

As they pulled up to the last home on the list, she wanted nothing more than to go back to the inn, put on her pajamas, and read by the fire for the rest of the day.

"I think I've seen enough, Trevor."

He turned off the ignition, looking at her. "What?"

"I'd like to go home now. I mean, back to the MacVicar."

He opened the door. "Nonsense. We're here. You might as well take a look."

She dropped her head with a groan, but she was too tired to fight him anymore. Stepping out of the vehicle, she turned to see the house—a cottage resting on what looked like a knoll of some kind. A chill danced up her spine as she walked closer, following Trevor along a partially cleared path over the slow rising knoll. Beyond the house, the frigid waters of the bay lapped at the rocky beach.

"It's . . . *beautiful*," she breathed.

"What? Oh, yes. The view. Well, trust me; it comes at a hefty price."

He made his way along a winding path toward the door. She followed, already enchanted by the house's cedar siding weathered to a handsome gray patina. White shutters gave it a cozy, enticing appeal. She could hardly wait to see inside.

Olivia's heart skipped a beat as she stepped into the open living area. There, she could see straight through to the bay, included the masts of boats docked a short distance away at a nearby harbor.

"As you can see, the house itself is relatively small—only 1,800 square feet, but with the open floor plan and floor-to-ceiling windows providing an exceptional view of the harbor, it appears much larger. Not to mention the wood-beamed cathedral ceiling. At the pinnacle, it's right at sixteen feet high."

"Oh, Trevor, it's—"

"Note the updated appliances in the kitchen area, all top of the line, stainless steel. Granite countertops. Here's the walk-in pantry." He continued through the charming little cottage, pointing out its special features as well as its shortcomings. "Three bedrooms, all quite small. Only the master is big enough for a queen-size bed. Closets are also small, though the master suite includes a somewhat larger walk-in closet. Still, very little room and not much storage space other than the garage."

Olivia made her way through the room to the French doors. "The master bedroom opens out onto the deck?" She unlocked the door and stepped out onto the deck which ran the length of the back of the house. "Oh, look! Part of the deck is screened-in. What a perfect place to have my coffee each morning."

"I seriously doubt you'd want to sit outside on days like this."

"Sure, but look—there's a fireplace over there. That would take the chill off, don't you think? Hey Trevor, look! There's a stone fire pit out there by those Adirondack chairs! How fun to sit out there with friends and watch the sailboats come and go."

Olivia's imagination bounced from one scenario to another. She dug her hands deeper in her coat pockets. "I've always dreamed of living on the water, but for some reason, I always assumed it would be Florida."

Her laughter seemed to fall on deaf ears as Trevor stepped back into the house. She turned toward the beach below, filled with a sudden, intense yearning to make this her home. It was the very thing she'd been warned against—making rash or sudden decisions. But she couldn't help it. She'd never been so sure of anything in her life.

Right?

She shook her head, dismissing the thoughts as she made her way into the large open living area. Decorating ideas helped her visualize exactly how it would look—not much different from the current owners, but with her own personality.

"Who lives here, Trevor?"

"What difference does it make?" he said without turning around.

"HEY!"

He turned, exuding an air of utter frustration as he crossed his arms over his chest. "'Hey'? Is that how folks in the South try to get someone's attention?"

"It is when the person is acting like a buffoon!"

He scoffed, dropping his arms to his side. "I beg your pardon."

"Oh, enough already with the stuffy britches! Can't you *please* lose the arrogance for just one moment and talk to me? What happened to that kind gentleman who invited me to stay for tea after book club? What happened to that man I had a snowball fight with? Where's that guy? Because *he's* the guy . . ." Did she dare say it?

Trevor huffed, looking past her. "He's the guy you want to drag all over town looking at houses?"

Olivia approached him. "No, Trevor. He's the guy I want to spend time with."

He turned, confusion written on his face.

She took another step toward him. "He's the guy I'd like to get to know better. He's the guy who's crazy about a little dog named Charlie and shows her such *tenderness* . . . but for some reason puts up barbed-wire fences to keep people out."

Her heart pounding, Olivia trembled, surprised at her audacity. She'd never spoken like that to anyone before. Let alone this aloof realtor bent on getting rid of her. But even now, as she searched for a clue in his befuddled expression, she wondered if she'd gone too far.

"I don't know what . . ." he began. "That is to say, I can't imagine—"

"Out with it, already," she said, grabbing his lapels. "What is it you can't imagine?"

He studied her with narrowed eyes, the urgency behind them nearly taking her breath away. "Olivia, I—"

"Yes?"

He cupped her face and without another word, leaned down toward her and placed the most gentle, perfect kiss on her lips.

Olivia felt a rush of relief wash over her, only then realizing how much she'd *wanted* him to kiss her. Her arms circled his neck as he folded her into his embrace.

"Olivia," he whispered against her ear. "How I've longed to hold you, to kiss you . . ."

She smiled. "Then by all means, please don't let me stop you."

Chapter 11

Trevor held her closer, inhaling the scent of her hair and losing himself in the warmth of her returned kisses. Nothing in that moment made any sense, only that she felt *so good, so right* in his arms.

When at last she leaned back to look up into his eyes, he felt a blush warming his face. Still, he couldn't help smiling. "Well, Miss Thomas, I must say I've never had *that* happen at a showing before."

"For the record, *Mr. Bass*, I'm glad to hear that."

"Is that so?"

"I'm not complaining, mind you. I'd just hate to think this was some kind of ruse—bringing unsuspecting women here, dazzling them with the spectacular view and all."

He raised his eyebrows, momentarily looking away. "I assure you nothing could be farther from the truth. In fact, I should apologize for—"

Her kiss silenced his lame backtrack. He laughed as a realization hit him.

"Oh, so now *I* kiss *you,* and somehow you find it humorous?"

He pushed a strand of hair from her forehead. "I find it amusing since we both know my apology wasn't quite truthful."

"Ah. The apology. No need, though I find it rather gallant that it crossed your mind."

"Gallant? No one's ever accused me of being gallant."

"It wasn't an accusation; it was a compliment."

"Yes, well." He suddenly felt awkward, not quite sure what to say or do. He had no practice at this sort of thing, and hoped she didn't find him lacking in the ways of . . . *whatever* this was.

She smiled, placing both palms against his chest. "Oh, Trevor. Thank you for letting me in."

"I show houses. Of course I let you in."

"No, silly." She tapped her finger against his heart. "In here. If only for this moment, thank you. I knew there was a sweet spirit beneath all that gruff exterior."

Trevor started to pull away, but she held firm to the lapels of his coat.

"I'm . . . well, all this is . . ."

"What? All this is what?"

He pulled away, but reached for her hand and tugged her toward the sofa. He took her coat then slipped out of his.

"Wait, are you sure we shouldn't leave? What if the owners return?"

He motioned for her to join him on the sofa. "They won't. I promise."

"How do you know?"

He leaned back. "Because I'm the owner of this cottage."

"What?" She scooted to the edge of the cushion. "You mean this is *your* home?"

"Yes and no. Yes, I own the house, but no, I don't live here. Up until a few weeks ago, I've rented it out. When the economy tanked several years ago, the owners were forced into foreclosure. It was a second home for them, and they had no choice. Wonderful people, but the bank took possession."

"That makes me *so* mad. In most cases, foreclosure can be prevented. At my bank, we bend over backwards to help homeowners stay in their homes. Whatever it takes."

He noted the fire in her eyes. "And I applaud you for that. But not all banks have a heart. In fact, the bank made a pretty penny off this little cottage. But, as a realtor and neighbor, I found out about it before it listed. Made an offer, the bank countered, and we split the difference."

Olivia tucked her leg beneath her, turning to face him. "Wait—you said you're a neighbor? You live around here?"

"No, not 'around' here." He nodded toward the right. "I live right next door."

"Where? Show me." She jumped up and headed for the door onto the deck.

He followed her outside, catching his breath as the biting wind blew over him. "There," he said, pointing to his home fifty yards to the east.

Olivia shielded her eyes from the bright sunlight. "Trevor—it's *stunning*. How long have you lived there?"

"It's been my permanent home for about twenty-one years. My father's family built it more than seventy years ago as a summer home. Of course, I had it completely renovated before I moved back in."

"Will you show it to me?"

"Sorry, but it's not for sale."

"Very funny. It probably has week-old pizza boxes strewn everywhere and smells like dirty socks."

"I'll have you know I've never 'strewn' a pizza box in my entire life. As for the socks—well, every man has his weaknesses."

He grabbed their coats and closed up the cottage before walking her next door. His maid service came twice a month, so he wasn't worried about that. But he couldn't remember the last time he'd brought a woman to his home, and for good reason.

He never had.

"Oh my goodness . . . it's so *beautiful*."

He took her coat again. "I bet you say that to all the guys."

Laughter lit her face. "Hardly. I've never seen anything like this before."

He gave her a tour, enjoying her reactions. He'd lived here so long, he rarely noticed the features she commented on. The framed vintage cloth map of Maine on the wall. His father's collection of clay tavern pipes dating back to the eighteenth century. His eclectic taste in cookbooks lining the shelf in the kitchen. A pair of old rowing oars hanging above the French doors that opened onto his screened-in back porch.

Her hands clasped behind her back, she wandered through the family room. "You spent all your summers here?"

"For the most part. I used to love coming here as a boy, spending time with my cousins. Of course, it was all different then."

"How so?"

He stood beside her at the floor-to-ceiling windows overlooking the water. "We knew everyone. Lots of folks lived here year round, but there were also families like ours who spent the summers here. We were like one big happy family in those days. We didn't have so many tourists back then."

"Ah. Those *evil* tourists."

He turned, surprised at the tone of her voice.

"I'm kidding, Trevor." She smiled, gently rubbing his wrist. "You need to lighten up."

They wandered into the master bedroom. He was pleased she liked the décor, and told her he'd hired a company in Boston to redecorate the entire house just a year ago.

"They did a beautiful job. It suits you. Very masculine. Very classy." She headed into the large master bathroom suite. "Wow. Now *this* is a bathroom. Walk-in shower, soaking tub—with a view, no less."

It felt awkward, escorting her through his personal space. "Let me show you upstairs," he suggested. Just then, a string of whimpers drifted down the hall. "Good grief, I forgot all about Charlie." He headed toward his study.

Olivia followed him. "For some reason, I assumed she was at the bookstore."

"No, I prefer to keep her here at the house when I'm out. Especially with the temperatures so low right now." He leaned over, unlatching the clasp on her crate. Charlie rushed out, yapping happily and tail wagging. Trevor knelt on one knee, giving her a hug. "I'm so sorry, sweetheart. You'll have to forgive my manners. I was showing Miss Thomas our home."

As if understanding, Charlie wiggled out of his arms and pranced toward Olivia who'd also knelt down.

She scratched behind Charlie's ears. "It's all my fault, sweetie. I distracted your daddy. We won't let that happen again." She planted a noisy kiss on Charlie's head. You have my word on that."

"Come along, Charlie. Let's let you get some fresh air." Trevor headed back toward the living area. "What do you say?"

As he opened the back door, she made a mad dash for the grassy area he kept cleared for her and went about her business.

Olivia followed him toward the kitchen and took a seat at the counter. "You keep her crated while you're away? She doesn't mind being cooped up like that?"

"She loves it, actually. When I first got her, I could never get her to sleep through the night. Up and down, all night. Needing to potty, wanting to play, those desperate puppy cries all night long. I was at my wits' end. Then I talked to our veterinarian about it. Celeste suggested I purchase a crate, line it with a nice, soft blanket, and most important, fill a hot-water bottle with warm water, wrap it in a towel, and tuck it inside the crate."

"And it worked?"

"Yes! I couldn't believe it. She cuddled up to that warm bottle and slept for hours. I'd even find her taking naps in there during the day. Celeste said they feel safe and secure to have a place of their own like that."

"Makes sense to me." Olivia rested her chin on her wrist, a contented smile on her face.

He swallowed, wondering why in the world he'd brought this woman into his home without so much as a second thought. He had no experience with this sort of thing! He shifted his weight. "Would you, uh, like some tea?"

"I'd love some, thank you."

"Good." *Good. Something to do with my hands.* He filled the tea kettle and set it on the gas burner which he lit.

"While that heats, would you show me the rest of your house?"

"You mean upstairs?"

She hopped off the stool. "Sure. How many bedrooms up there?"

He waved her ahead, then followed her up the stairs. "Four bedrooms, two full bathrooms."

She stopped, twisting around to face him, her hand still on the rail. "*Four* bedrooms?"

"Yes, four. Why? Is that too many?"

She continued up the stairs. "No, I'm just surprised. That's all. You must have had a big family."

"Plenty of room for aunts and uncles and all those cousins."

"How many brothers and sister did you have? Or were you an only child?"

"Just one brother." He changed the subject, diverting her attention to the upstairs layout. "Jack and Jill bathrooms—one between the bedrooms on that end of the hall, another between those two on this end."

"I love the open loft area. It's like every room in the house has a great view of the water."

She wandered down the hall, strolling through the rooms and the attached bathrooms. "Your decorators did an amazing job, though something tells me you had a hand in the direction they went."

"Well, yes. You must be very firm with them, or you'll end up with bamboo on the walls or stars on the ceiling that glow in the dark."

She turned around, walking backward as she faced him. "I find it hard to believe the people who did your decorating ever once mentioned bamboo walls or twinkly stars."

"Then you must have missed the patch of Bermuda grass growing in the master bathroom. They told me it gave the room a 'spa-like' ambiance."

"As if you'd fall for *that*. You'll have to dig a little deeper to pull one over on me."

The tea kettle whistle blew, so they headed downstairs. As Trevor tended the tea, Olivia closed the back door after Charlie had come back in. The spaniel gave a good shake, her tail wagging constantly.

"Would you mind giving her a treat? There in that glass canister. I always give her a little reward for waiting to do her business outdoors."

"Ah, so Daddy has you trained, does he?" Olivia took a miniature milk bone from the large canister.

"Charlie?" he called. "Where are your manners?"

The dog sat back on her haunches then lifted her paws, a goofy grin accompanying the clever trick.

"Well, look at you!" Olivia gave her the treat. "What a smart little mama you are!"

"That's my girl."

"Trevor, she's adorable. And she clearly thinks *you* hung the moon."

He handed her a mug, the tea bag label dangling over the rim. "I'd invite you to sit outside, but it's a bit chilly for that today."

"Thanks, I'll take a rain check." She followed him into the living area.

He pointed her toward the end of the sofa, then sat adjacent in his favorite chair. It felt safer somehow, with the small table cornered between them. He wished he could relax. She wasn't nearly the chatterbox he'd thought her to be. *She's really quite charming. And genuine.* He liked that. He fought the strange beating inside his chest. Different. Frightening. Wonderful.

His face warmed as he remembered their kiss. Not once in all his life had he done something so spontaneous. But he didn't regret it. Not at all. What pleased him even more was her response.

"So tell me, Trevor. Will you sell me your little cottage next door?"

Chapter 12

By the look on his face, you'd have thought she'd asked him to give her the house free and clear. "It's a simple question. Why the hesitation?"

"Nothing, I just wouldn't have thought . . . I mean, I'm just surprised you'd want to—"

"Live next door to you?"

"What? No. It's not that. It's just that . . . well, you don't even know how much I'm asking for it."

"Oh, *that.*" She chuckled, crossing one leg over the other. "I guess you're right. I need to know the asking price so we can start squabbling over it, counter-offering back and forth. Isn't that how it's done?"

"Yes, but as I told you, the cottage, the view—it all comes at a rather steep price. Not that it's *too* much," he blurted, raising a hand in defense. "It's a fair market value, I assure you."

Olivia laughed again. "Good to know. I'd be bummed to think you were trying to stiff me."

His smile didn't quite reach his eyes. "No, it isn't that. Surely you know that housing prices up here are substantially higher than those where you come from. And it's entirely possible . . . well, I might as well just say it. I doubt very seriously that a bank teller from Georgia could afford such real estate." He paused. "No offense, of course."

Something in his tone irked her, but she let it slide. "None taken. I think?" She shook her head. "First of all, Trevor, I'm not a bank teller. I'm a loan officer at a bank."

"Yes, well, I didn't mean—"

"Second, as much as I've enjoyed getting to know you and our, uh, brief *exchange* over at the cottage, the fact remains you really know very little about me. And that includes my financial status. So I have to say, it's rather insulting to have you sit there and assume I can't afford to live in your little cottage next door."

He released a long sigh, set his mug on the table, and moved to sit beside her. She stiffened. "Well, here I've gone and done it again." Gently, he tucked her under his arm. "I'm so sorry, Olivia. I can't believe I said something so insensitive."

"It isn't that. Well, maybe a little."

He took her hand in his. "I'm afraid you're right."

She looked up into his eyes. "About what?"

"Earlier, you called me a buffoon. Apparently, you were spot-on."

She chuckled, relaxing a little. "Apparently so."

He placed a finger beneath her chin, turning her face toward him. "I'm also an idiot, and I'm so sorry you have to keep finding that out. Over and over—"

"—and over and over."

Their shared laughter felt good. She laid her head against his shoulder.

"What's even more obvious, I'm sure, is my complete ineptitude when it comes to women. All of this is so . . . *awkward* to me. I suppose someone my age should be more experienced, but the fact is, in all my years, I just never found someone who ... well, someone I was interested in. In *that* way. And if you must know, I decided a long time ago I'd rather live my life alone than risk all the heartache."

"Why's that?"

"All around me, I've seen such sadness, such boredom in the lives of my married friends. And family too. Not to mention the rampant infidelity. I grew so tired hearing all of them complain about their spouses ad nauseam. Or worse, hearing them brag about their conquests. And then there was . . ."

She raised her head to face him. "There was what?"

He looked down, his thumb rubbing the back of her hand. "My brother Evan. He was five years older than me. I think I must have idolized him from the day I was born. But then, everyone loved Evan. He was that kind of guy. Then, while he was at Yale, he fell in love and married a girl from Connecticut. Lelia was beautiful, and from the beginning, it seemed as if she belonged in our family. I finally had a sister.

"Both Evan and Lelia graduated and both practiced law. They seemed to have it all. Everything was perfect, right up until Evan found out she'd been cheating on him from the day they met."

"What? How—"

"It's a long story and not worth telling." Trevor pulled his hand free and raked his fingers through his hair. "When Evan found out, he went off the deep end. And who could blame him? He'd never been much of a drinker, but I suppose he was trying to drown away his sorrows or something. A couple days after he found out, some of his buddies from college invited him to go jet skiing in Boston Harbor. Long story short, he was much too inebriated to be out on the water. He crashed into another jet skier. He was paralyzed from the neck down and suffered brain damage as well."

"Oh, Trevor. I'm so sorry."

"The thing is, the brain injury left him aware of his surroundings; cognizant at some level. Meaning, he was aware of his situation but could do little or nothing about it. He felt trapped in a body that would no longer function for him, and it literally drove him mad.

"Our parents had both passed by that time—Dad from a heart attack, Mom from a stroke only a few months later. Aside from some long-lost cousins, I was all the family Evan had left. He refused to come home, demanding to stay there in a facility in Boston. Eventually he quit allowing me to see him, though I kept going for several weeks. But he'd get so violent, I finally quit going, other than an occasional holiday."

He blinked, as if returning to the present, and looked at her sheepishly. "I'm sorry, I shouldn't have told you all this."

"And why not?"

He stood up, walking to the bank of windows. "It's all so sad and depressing. I don't even know why I brought it up."

She joined him by the windows, pulling his arm over her shoulder and snaking her arm around his waist. "I think you were presenting your case for staying away from any kind of meaningful relationship all these years."

"I suppose you're right. Naturally, I blamed Lelia for everything. Regardless, that whole tragedy served as the final straw in my vow to stay unattached."

"Is Evan still alive?"

He shook his head slowly, looking back out at the water. "No. He died three years ago."

She said nothing, not wanting to intrude on his painful memories. After several moments, he hugged her closer against his side, resting his head on hers.

"I think I was wrong, Olivia," he whispered.

"About what?"

He turned, pulling her into his arms. "About love. I was so sure I was better off without all the complications and disappointments and heartache. But then I met you. And suddenly I realize how lonely I've been, living behind these stockades I've built."

She looked up into his eyes, searching, waiting.

"And now I find myself completely and utterly smitten."

Olivia smiled. "Smitten? That's a good thing, right?"

The tension and sadness in his face disappeared as he slowly nodded. "Yes, that's a *very* good thing." He leaned down and kissed her, pulling her closer still.

In that single moment, she thought her heart would surely rupture with joy. *How is that even possible?* Wishing away any further questions, she clung to the here and now and the security she felt in Trevor's arms.

When at last their lips parted, he leaned his forehead against hers. "Olivia?"

"Yes?"

"I'm not quite sure what to do next. In the movies, this is the point where the dashing hero whisks the heroine off her feet and carries her to the bedroom where he makes mad, passionate love to her." He could hardly speak over his laughter. "But I'm quite sure I'd throw *both* our backs out if I attempted something so daring."

She giggled. "I was just thinking the same thing. Can you imagine the two of us trying to explain how both of us ended up in traction?"

His laughter caught in a long wheeze. "We'd never hear the end of it!" He cupped her cheek in his hand. "Olivia, as tempting as that might be, rest assured I would never compromise your good character. You have my word."

She smiled, then touched her lips to his. "I always suspected you were a true gentleman. Now I have proof. And I need *you* to know I'm perfectly happy to stay right here in your arms."

"Is that so?"

"Absolutely. You have my word."

Chapter 13

Hours later, as the sun began to set, Trevor set up shop in his kitchen, preparing dinner. They'd spent most of the afternoon talking, but he couldn't bear the thought of taking her back to the MacVicar yet. Insisting she stay for dinner, he put her to work making a fresh spinach salad. The fact that they never stopped talking astounded him. How could two people keep a conversation going hour after hour without running out of things to talk about? Still, there was so much more he wanted to learn about her. He smiled at the notion while sautéing two chicken breasts in a white wine sauce.

"All right, buster. Out with it," she said, interrupting his thoughts. "Why the goofy grin?"

"Nothing really. I suppose I'm amused by the fact I haven't frightened you away yet."

"Oh, I'm sure you'll think of something."

"We did get off to a rather bumpy start, didn't we?"

She tilted her head just so with a mischievous smile. "That's a nice way of putting it."

He grabbed a handful of the green onions she was chopping and tossed them into the bubbling sauce. "Tell me about your childhood. Have you always lived in Atlanta?"

"I believe so."

"You don't know?"

She sprinkled the rest of the chopped onions over their salad. "Only what my parents told me. I was two months old when they adopted me. My mother always told me how deeply my birth mother must have loved me, to give me up so I could have a better life than she could give me. And literally, that's all I've ever known of my birth mother."

Trevor covered the pan and washed his hands. "Weren't you curious? Did you ever try to find her?"

She shrugged, taking a seat on the barstool. "Not really. I always felt loved and cherished, and for me, that was enough. I suppose it would have been different if I were older when I was adopted. But Mom and Dad were the only parents I ever knew."

He dried his hands on the dishtowel and slung it over his shoulder. "Tell me about them. Are they still living?"

She folded her arms, resting them on the countertop. "No, I lost both of them when I was away at college. It was a freak accident, really. They'd gone for a Sunday drive out in the country as they always did. Only this time, as they crested a hill on a two-lane road, a deer ran into the road. Apparently, Dad hit the brakes, but the impact flipped the car into a ditch. They both died instantly."

He grabbed her hand and squeezed it. "I'm so sorry, Olivia. That must have been heartbreaking for you."

She seemed to study their hands, threading his fingers through hers. "It was awful at the time. It took me years to get over losing them; at least to put it in perspective." She looked up at him. "I know that's why God sent Ellen into my life."

"Ellen?"

"Surely I've told you about Ellen?"

He lifted her hand and kissed the top of it, then let go to check on the chicken. "Is she your sister?"

"No, but we're as close as sisters. Ellen was my college roommate, and we've been best friends ever since. She has the deepest faith of anyone I've ever met. When I lost Mom and Dad, she was there for me. She wrapped me into her family and helped me get through those first days and weeks and months. When she and Brent married and had a family of their own, I became 'Aunt Olivia' to her children. They're my family, in every way that matters."

He turned down the flame on the chicken and put the lid back on. "She sounds wonderful."

"She is. I'd love for her to meet you some day."

"You would?"

Olivia hopped down and grabbed the loaf of French bread from the counter. "Well, sure." She looked at him like it made all the sense in the world.

"Interesting."

"And she's anxious to meet you too."

He stopped in his tracks. "How does she even—"

"Trevor. She's my best friend. We talk about everything." With a silly smile, she shook her head and placed the bread on a cutting board. "Haven't you ever had a best friend?"

He busily stirred the rice pilaf. "I've had plenty of friends. Sure."

"I'm sure you have, but I mean a *best* friend. Someone you call up to talk about your day or discuss the latest Red Sox game? Maybe meet for coffee to catch up?"

He plopped the lid back on the rice pan and faced her, hands on hips. "I'm just not that kind of person. I never have been." He started to say more, then realized the implication of what he'd just said. He pulled the dishtowel from his shoulder and wiped the counter. "Maybe I'm not 'best friend' material. And yes, I suppose that makes me quite a risk for this . . . this *boyfriend-girlfriend* thing." He twisted the towel. "Oh, never mind. I guess I should have come with a warning label, cautioning you—Loner ahead! Beware!"

She took the towel from his hands and tossed it on the counter. "Come here." She tugged at his belt loops to draw him close. "Look at me, Trevor."

He didn't particularly care for all this transparency. It made him feel like such a fool, baring his pitiful soul to her. He bit the side of his lip and glanced down at her.

"I don't care if you've never had a best friend. I'm sorry you've never had the joy of getting to know someone at that level, but it doesn't make you less of a person. God just wired you different, that's all. But who knows, maybe I'll be that person you call up and talk baseball with."

He shook his head, his eyes still on her. "I doubt it."

A flicker of disappointment wrinkled her brow. "Oh?"

"I hate baseball."

"So do I! See? We've got more in common than you think!"

He loved the endless depths of her smile and the sparkle in her eyes. Only now did he notice the tiny flecks of gold in her green-hazel eyes.

"Yes, it seems we do." He fingered the side of her face, tracing it down to her jaw. "And I would be a lucky fellow if it turned out that you were my best friend." He kissed the tip of her nose.

Her silly grin returned. "Wait, go back to the part about the boyfriend-girlfriend thing."

"Yes? What about it?"

"I like the sound of that. I like it a *lot*."

"Why do I suddenly feel like we're back in grade school?"

"We should go steady. I could wear your pin."

"Unfortunately, the only *pen* I have is a 14-carat gold Cross pen that belonged to my father. I don't suppose you'd want me to *pin* that *pen* on your lapel?"

She glanced down at her dark chocolate turtleneck. "Alas, nary a lapel to be—Trevor! The chicken!"

Thankfully, he was able to salvage the chicken, though much of the sauce had cooked away. They sat side by side at the tall counter, his hand cupped over her knee. Over dinner, they chatted nonstop, covering everything from favorite movies and books and music styles, to childhood memories and historic events and places they'd love to travel.

Later, over a shared pint of ice cream, they shared bucket list dreams.

"I've always wanted to see the Aurora Borealis. In person," she said.

"I've always thought how spectacular it would be to take a hot air balloon ride over Napa Valley."

"I like that one!" She scooped another bite of Rocky Road. "Personally, I want to walk where Jesus walked before I die."

He waited, confident she was joking, but the serene expression on her face reflected something altogether different. "You want to go to the Holy Land?"

"Well, sure. Don't you?"

"The thought never crossed my mind. It's not exactly a safe place to travel these days."

She dipped another spoonful of ice cream, this time turning the spoon to him. Sharing a carton of ice cream was one thing; sharing spoons felt so . . . *invasive.* Still, his heretofore stuffy resolve melted away as he drank in the sight of her, those adoring eyes glued to him. He took the bite, never breaking eye contact. Her wink sent a rush of warmth through him.

"I know it's dangerous over there, but I keep hoping I get the chance to go. A group from our church went years ago, but I had to back out at the last minute. I've never forgiven my former appendix for making me miss that trip. Ellen said it was unforgettable, and every Christian should . . ."

He wiped his mouth with his napkin and waited. "Every Christian should . . . ?"

"Trevor, I can't believe we've been talking all this time, and I never even asked you—are you a believer?"

"A 'believer' in what context of the word?"

She set her spoon on top of her napkin. "Do you believe in God? Does He play a role in your life?"

His heart fluttered at the boldness of her question. "Yes, of course. Anyone with half a brain believes in God. I'm surprised you had to ask."

She rested her hand on his. "I know, but lots of people say they believe in God but never give Him the time of day. I'm asking if there was ever a time you asked Jesus into your heart to be your Lord and Savior."

"Well, I'm sure there must have been. As a child, we went to church a couple of times a year. Usually Christmas and Easter. "

She squeezed his hand as a wave of concern trailed through her eyes. "The thing is, Trevor, it's not about going to church. I mean, that's a good thing, of course, but the most important part of being a believer is that initial step of faith, asking God to be Lord of your life. And that's the question I'm asking. Not to be nosy or invade your personal privacy, but because it's so important to me. Besides, what kind of a friend would I be if I didn't tell you about the best thing that ever happened to me?"

He had no idea how to respond. There was no question about her sincerity. She talked about God like He was a close, personal friend.

Olivia took both of his hands in hers and seemed to be studying his eyes, as if searching for answers in his soul. "Hey, we're both tired. Let's talk about this another time, okay? I'm sorry if it feels like I put you on the spot. Just promise you'll give it some thought, okay?"

He nodded. "Sure."

"Fair enough. Now, if you wouldn't mind, *Mr. Bass*, could I impose on you for a ride back to the MacVicar?"

Chapter 14

"That's it. I'm booking a flight today. I'll be there tomorrow."

"Right. Like I believe *that*," Olivia teased. "Ellen, I told you. There's no cause for alarm. Trevor and I are just friends. I promise."

"Friends who've spent almost every waking moment together over the last week or so? Friends roasting marshmallows over a fire pit, surrounded by three feet of snow in the dead of winter? Friends discussing books they love into the wee hours of the morning . . . Have I left anything out?"

"Okay, fine. I admit it's been a whirlwind week."

"Well, I guess so! You've called me every day for the past ten days telling me all about your romantic days and nights with this bookstore Don Juan. Sounds to me like you two need a chaperone at the very least."

"HA! I assure you we've done nothing inappropriate, Sister Mary Margaret. You're also starting to sound like my mother back in my high school days."

"Someone's got to do it, and who better than me? I need to check this guy out. Make sure he's good enough for you. Ask him what his intentions are. You know the drill."

Olivia plopped into the cozy reading chair in her room, and threw her legs over the arm. "Seriously, Ellen, there's nothing to worry about. You're more than welcome to come stay with me. I'd love that! As long as you're not coming just to spy on Trevor."

"Oh sure, take all the fun out of it."

"You're a piece of work. Have I ever told you that?"

"Once or twice. I will say that I love the picture you emailed of you and Trevor standing in front of Walker's Point. Of course, I'd have liked it better if the Bushes were there with you. But Trevor's not at all what I pictured. All this time, I'd been picturing someone more like Cary Grant."

"Cary Grant? Oh, please. Didn't he die fifty years or so ago? For the record, Trevor is *not* a geezer, thank you very much."

"Well, that's how he sounded from all you've told me about him. But now that I've seen his picture, I can see he's younger. Kind of reminds me of Pierce Brosnan. Very handsome. Even debonair. All the more reason I'm concerned."

"Pierce Brosnan? From *Mrs. Doubtfire* or when he played James Bond?"

"Does it matter?"

"No, I'm just curious. I guess there's a slight resemblance, but I hadn't noticed it 'til you mentioned it just now."

"Olivia, it doesn't matter if he looks like Tommy Lee Jones. I love you too much not to be concerned."

"I know." She leaned her head back against the chair. "But can't you just be happy for me? Because I'm really, really happy for the first time in—well, I can't remember *ever* being this happy. He's such a good man, Ellen. You just have to trust me. At least until you get to meet him."

Ellen was silent for several moments. Then, "I am happy for you —at least I'm trying to be happy for you. I can hear it in your voice, Olivia. It's like your whole tone has changed. And I could see it in the picture. Your demeanor is different. You look so carefree and happy, and I want *so much* for this to be the real thing. But I'm also concerned for all the reasons we've talked about before. It's all so sudden. I just don't want you to get hurt. That's all."

"I know."

"Are you sure he doesn't know about the money?"

"How many times do I have to tell you? No, I haven't told him. There's no need. At first, he assumed I couldn't afford a house on the water up here. But that was before we, you know ... realized we had feelings for each other."

"Oh yeah, those 'just friends' feelings."

"Yeah, those. And since then, it just hasn't come up. So to answer your question—no, Trevor does not know about my recent windfall."

"Probably best to keep it that way."

"We'll see."

"Just don't do anything crazy like running off to Maui to get married."

"Maui. Got it. You'll be the first to know."

"Brat."

"Aloha, Mother Hen."

"Aloha-ha-ha, Cinderella."

Olivia grabbed her coat, scarf, and keys, planning to head to Molly's after breakfast. Trevor would be tied up all morning with some online book auction. A collection of first editions had come up for auction from the personal library of someone he'd always admired and respected. Olivia had never heard of the famous historian, but she enjoyed hearing the passion in Trevor's voice when he talked about him. They'd agreed to meet for a late lunch after the auction, giving her plenty of time to herself for a change.

Downstairs, she enjoyed a second cup of coffee after a breakfast dish Trig had made for her. "I never would've thought to put spinach in this egg dish. What a great idea."

"Thanks. There's more. Would you like a second helping?"

Olivia waved her napkin at him. "No! I'm sure I've put on at least five pounds since I got here."

"Well, if so, you hide it well." A funny expression crossed his face. "If you don't mind my saying so, that is. Not that I was checking you out or anything. I just meant that you look, uh . . . great! You look perfect." He sighed. "Oh, you know what I meant."

"Of course I do, but it was entirely too much fun watching you squirm through that one!" Olivia laughed as she set her mug on the table. "I'm about to head over to Molly's. Need anything?"

He picked up the dishes. "Not that I can think of. Say hi to Molly and Trevor for me."

She pulled on her coat, deciding to let him squirm a bit more. "Trevor? Why would you—"

"Oh nothing. I just assumed . . . I mean, I heard you and Trevor have been . . . y'know—"

"Really?" Olivia fought the blush creeping over her face. "What did you hear?"

He shrugged. "Ah, never mind all that. It's a small town. People talk. But the way I see it? It's about time ol' Trevor *reeled* one in."

"Oh no. Not with the fish jokes again."

"Y'know, he's been *floundering* around all these years, until you came along."

"Trig."

"As for me? I'm happy to see Mr. Bass has finally found the *gill* of his dreams."

"All right, I'm outta here.

"Don't forget to tell Trevor hi for me if you get an 'oppor-*tuna*-ty.'"

She groaned, pulling the knitted cap over her head. "Enough! Goodbye!"

Ten minutes later, she was chatting with Molly in the stationery aisle when the front door opened and Mimi Overton's voice sang out.

"Hello, hello! You back there, Molly? You won't BELIEVE what I just heard about Trev—"

Olivia and Molly looked up just as Mimi rounded the aisle and froze. Her eyes widened; her brows jumped high on her forehead as she plastered an exuberant smile on her face. “Olivia! Hi-hello-nice-to-see-you!”

“Well, nice to see you too, Mimi.”

With her smile intact, Mimi looked at Molly, blinked a couple times, looked back at Olivia, then blinked a couple times more. “Yes, well, just stopped by to say hello. I’ll be going now.” She ducked out of sight.

Olivia couldn’t resist. “Mimi, wait! If you need to talk to Molly, I’ll give you two some privacy.”

Mimi thrust her wristwatch up to her face. “Oh my gosh, will you look at the time. Gotta go! We’ll chat later. Bye!”

As the door clanged shut, Olivia exploded in laughter. “Wish I’d caught that on film. Mimi cracks me up!”

She noticed Molly smiled, but wasn’t laughing. She was also avoiding eye contact.

“Okaaaay, how about you and I have a nice little chat, Molly. I’ll even buy you a cup of coffee. Shall we?” Olivia nudged her toward the coffee bar.

“Oh, well, I probably need to get back to—”

“It’ll only take a minute.” She guided Molly’s elbow in the direction of the bar.

“Oh, well then. Okay.”

As Molly poured two cups of coffee, Olivia didn’t take her eyes off her. “Okay, I need you to shoot me straight. What was all *that* about?”

“What’s that?”

Olivia pinned Molly’s hand on the counter. “You know exactly what I mean. Mimi was going to tell you something about Trevor, and by the look on your face, I think you know what she was about to say.”

With a long sigh, Molly took a seat across from her. “Might as well just say it. Word is that you and Trevor are seeing each other.”

Olivia had to bite her lip at the expression on Molly’s face, the perfect blend of guilt and curiosity. “Good grief, it’s not a secret. So we’ve been spending time together. Is there something wrong with that? Is he secretly married or something?”

Molly’s eyes widened until she realized Olivia was teasing. “Gracious, no! It’s just that Trevor’s been an avowed bachelor for so long, we’d all given up on him.” A smile finally graced her face as she reached over to pat Olivia’s hand. “My dear, I for one am happy as a clam to hear such good news. If anyone can brighten his gloomy spirit, it's you."

"That's really sweet, Molly. But it works both ways, I assure you. He's made me—well, he's brightened my life too. It's been years since I've gone out with anyone, but somehow we seemed to figure it out."

Molly patted her hand again. "How lovely. Good for you!"

The door opened as Mavis Randolphson ushered her father inside. "Scott, Mavis, come in, come in!"

"Hello, Molly. Hi, Olivia," Mavis closed the door behind her father. "Brrrr! It's freezing out there today, don't you think?"

"Just another warm day in Paradise, if you ask me," Scott added with a confident smile. "Molly, I've come for some sunscreen. I plan a long afternoon sunning myself out by the pool."

Molly gave him a hug. "Sunscreen, my foot. You came for the prescription you called in. You stay here and chat with Olivia while Mavis comes back with me to settle up."

"Fine, fine." His hand searched for Olivia's. "Tell me, how's our favorite Georgia peach doing today?"

"I'm fine, Mr. Ran—"

"Ah, ah. It's Scott, remember?"

"Of course I remember. I'm fine, Scott. Have a seat." She helped him to a barstool. "Are you enjoying *The Count of Monte Cristo*?"

"Love it. A riveting story from start to finish. Trevor has excellent taste." He leaned forward, whispering conspiratorially. "But I don't have to tell *you* that, now do I?"

Olivia was glad he couldn't see the blush heating her face. "I have no idea what you're talking about."

He chuckled, nodding. "Well, then. If that's your preference, we'll pretend neither of us know. Though I dare say . . ." He wiggled his finger, urging her closer.

"Yes?"

"It's about time our elusive bookman found love," he whispered. "Well done, Olivia. Well done!"

"Scott Randolphson, what shall I do with you?"

"You shall save a dance for me at your wedding!"

"Shhh!' She clapped her hand over his mouth. "Pipe down, will you? You'll have the whole town breathing down our backs if you keep this up. Now, if I remove my hand, will you promise not to say another word about it?"

He nodded like an obedient child then grinned like a Cheshire cat as she pulled her hand away. "Scout's honor." He reached up for her cheek, and she guided his hand, placing her hand over his. "I just want you to know how pleased I am for you and Trevor. I mean that sincerely. For all the years I've known him, I've never seen him so happy. And yes, even a blind man can see that."

Olivia leaned over to kiss his cheek.

"What have we here?" Mavis teased as she and Molly rejoined them. "We turn our backs for two minutes and look what happens."

Scott jostled himself with great effect. "Oh, please, ladies—not a word of this to anyone! Swear on it!"

"Dad, it's a good thing Trevor didn't walk in on you two just now!"

Olivia rolled her eyes. "I give up!" She climbed back into her coat and headed for the door. "What did you all do for fun before I came to town?"

"Nothing!" Scott roared. "That's why we're so happy you're here."

"Riiiiiight. I'm outta here."

The jingling bell on the door did little to stem the flurry of butterflies dancing through Olivia's stomach. *Thank goodness Trevor didn't witness all that.* For the first time, she wondered what kind of fuss folks had been giving him? Did they tease him to his face? Or did they gossip behind his back? She was just a "lowly tourist" to most of them. But Trevor had lived here for years.

She swallowed hard with equal amounts of excitement and nerves battling it out somewhere in the vicinity of her heart.

Chapter 15

"Olivia! Stay right there!"

She turned at the sound of his voice. "Trevor? I wasn't expecting you for another hour."

"I know. Wait until you hear!" He hurried along the snow-shoveled sidewalk to catch up with her, then pulled her into a bear hug. "I got them! The books! I won the auction!"

"Congratulations! That's wonderful!"

"I still can't believe it! It was so close, and I thought for sure Milford Banks would snatch them away at the last moment, but he didn't, and I won them and I can hardly—" He hugged her again even harder. "Oh, Olivia, I can't begin to tell you how *wonderful* it is to have someone to share this moment with! How can I possibly thank you?"

Before she could answer, he kissed here right there for all the world to see.

Her laughter warmed his ear as hugged her again, then swung her off her feet and twirled around. "We have to celebrate!" He set her down again.

"Let's!" She grabbed his hand and turned toward the entry to Anthony's. "A big bowl of lobster bisque! My treat."

He tugged at her hand. "No, not a bowl of soup. Let's go somewhere special. I know—let's go to Boston! I've been wanting to take you there, show you the sights. Let's just do it! All I have to do is put a sign on the door at the shop, and we can be on our way."

"Are you sure? Isn't this awfully sudden?"

"Yes! And that's what makes it so positively delicious!" He hugged her again. "Oh, wait—Charlie. I really shouldn't leave her alone just now."

"Oh? Then maybe we shouldn't—"

"No problem." He grabbed her hand and tugged her along in the direction of the shop. "I'll see if Marilyn can watch her for a few hours."

Olivia had to jog to keep up with him. "Marilyn from the book club?"

"Sorry." He paused, slowing his pace for her. "Yes, you know the one who knits. The woman's always knitting. I think she must knit in her sleep. But she adores Charlie, and often watches her for me if I have to be away for a while."

An hour later, they were on their way. Olivia had changed clothes at the MacVicar while Trevor moved Charlie and her bed over to the Knit Knook. He'd put the *Closed* sign on the front door of Books & Such, then rushed home to change into something nicer. He'd told Olivia they'd be having dinner at an upscale restaurant, requiring the appropriate attire. He wore his navy wool blazer with his gray herringbone slacks and a starched white shirt.

With the icy temperatures, he assured Olivia she'd be fine in a dressy pair of slacks. When he picked her up, she looked stunning in a pair of black wool slacks and a classy silver cowl-neck sweater. A touch of elegant jewelry completed the perfect ensemble.

"You look amazing," he told her, escorting her into his SUV. Later, as they merged onto I-95 south toward Boston, he couldn't take his eyes off her.

"I'm flattered, but keep those eyes on the road, mister."

"Point noted."

But just as he turned his head, a van in front of him swerved into his lane to miss another vehicle that had slowed. Trevor jerked the steering wheel to avoid hitting the van, causing his SUV to rock side to side before catching traction again on the slippery road.

"TREVOR!" Olivia braced herself with a grip lock on the dash. "Slow down! Slow down!"

A frantic rush of adrenaline hammered his heart. "Don't shout at me while I'm driving!"

As he regained control of the SUV, he shot a quick glance finding her face blanched with fear.

"I can't help it! We almost rolled over!"

He forced himself to take a deep breath. "Yes, but you can't—"

"I'm sorry for yelling, but you scared me, Trevor!" She blew out a shaky breath.

He reached for her hand across the console and squeezed it. "Okay. Look, I'm sorry. I'm not used to having a passenger with me. Forgive me for snapping at you."

She stared at their entwined hands. "And I'm sorry for freaking out on you. Ellen tells me I've been hyper-nervous whenever I'm on the road ever since I lost Mom and Dad."

"That's probably quite normal to react that way."

"Maybe, but I'm still sorry."

"Apology accepted."

And it was. But it reminded him that change wasn't always easy. After all these years on his own, making room for someone else in his life would take some getting used to.

They made polite, awkward small talk for the next few miles until they eased back into a more relaxed conversation.

"The curiosity is killing me. Tell me about the books, Trevor."

As they traveled south along the interstate, he told her everything. From first news of the books coming up for auction, to the background of the Maxwell Sullivan estate up near Bangor, to the nail-biting, excruciating final moments of the auction.

"I kept kicking myself, wishing I'd invited you to watch it all unfold alongside me. Then the next moment, I realized how thankful you *weren't* there to witness me acting like a crazy man, pacing back and forth, talking and shouting at myself."

"I would've *loved* to see that side of the reserved and well-tempered Trevor Bass."

"Trust me, it wasn't pretty."

"What about the books? Any titles I would recognize?"

"Oh, sure. These are familiar to just about everyone on the planet. Let's see, where to start." He tapped his finger on the steering wheel. "I assume you've heard of *Alice in Wonderland* by Lewis Carroll?"

"Seriously?"

"A beautifully bound Bayntun in red calf hide, first published in 1866. Stamped and lettered in gilt with blue and green spine labels. Excellent condition."

"Bayntun is the publisher?"

"No, Bayntun is one of the most respected bookbinding companies in the world. Top of the line. Then there's a uniformly bound set of James Fenimore Cooper's *Leather Stocking Tales,* which includes *The Last of the Mohicans, The Deerslayer, The Pathfinder,* and two others you probably aren't familiar with. The set was published in 1823. A rare find, to say the least."

"I don't even want to know how much something like that costs."

Trevor chuckled. "No, you don't. It would take your breath away."

"My thoughts exactly."

"There's also a first edition of Charlotte Bronte's first book called *The Professor,* which was published in 1857. You'll love the cover on that one. Morocco binding dyed a magnificent dark purple-gray, blind-stamped with an intricate floral design."

"What does blind-stamped mean?"

"It's a design that's imprinted directly into the cloth or leather cover of the book. No color of its own. Just an imprint similar to a notary's stamp on paper, only these are on book covers."

"Got it."

"Oh! I almost forgot about the Dickens! I got a Dickens!"

"*The* Charles Dickens?!"

"Yes! *A Tale of Two Cities* in the original wraps!" When confusion knitted her brows, he explained. "Forerunners of the paperback. Early dust jackets, if you will. Before binding, the volume would be sewn together and covered in paper to protect it. Extremely rare to find a nineteenth-century book with its original cover." He shivered with excitement. "Sorry. As you can tell, I get a bit carried away with all this."

She squeezed his hand on the console. "Don't apologize. I understand completely. I'm *so happy* for you, Trevor."

He lifted her hand to gently kiss the peaks of her knuckles. "Thank you. You have *no idea* how much that means to me. "I've . . ." he paused, clearing his throat, "I've never had anyone to share this kind of thing with before. It *quadruples* the fun of it for me in a way I never expected."

She smiled, then leaned over and slowly kissed the back of his hand.

With his other hand on the wheel, Trevor tightened his grip and kept his eyes on the road, trying to ignore the shiver quaking through him at the tenderness of her kiss.

"So that was your biggest find? The Dickens' book?"

"No. It was definitely a thrill to get that one, but my most prized treasure is one you might not think worthy of the hefty price I paid for it. Not that I'll be dropping any figures, mind you."

"No, of course not."

"Care to make a guess?"

"Me? I have no idea. Well, I say that, but I doubt seriously it's a Harry Potter."

"You know me too well. Although I was at an auction in New York earlier this year where someone paid $10,000 for a first edition of *Harry Potter and the Philosopher's Stone.*"

"Ten thousand dollars?!"

"A fair price, actually, but not my cup of tea."

"Trevor, are you telling me some of these books cost thousands of dollars?"

He nodded, glancing at her briefly to enjoy the shock on her face.

"I had no idea. I mean, maybe one or two thousand, but—"

"I know it sounds absurd, but you must realize these books are an investment. Some people play the stock market; others invest in real estate or fine jewelry. For me, it's rare books."

"I get that. But I think you also enjoy the hunt."

"Well, yes. That's half the fun of it."

"So when will they ship the books to you?"

"No, I wouldn't dream of having them shipped. Too much at risk. I'll drive up to get them once the estate is cleared. Hopefully, next week sometime."

"Oh, please let me go with you!"

He thought his heart would surely jump out of his chest. If he were a man given to spontaneous reactions, he would surely pull over, propose, and find the nearest justice of the peace.

Good heavens—where did that *come from?*

"Olivia," he croaked, then tried again. "I'd be honored. I would *love* to have you come with me."

"Good. Then it's a date! Where will we pick them up?"

"About twenty miles this side of Bangor, Maine which is two hours northeast of here. We'll make a day of it."

They chatted all the way into Boston, only breaking the conversation for the bothersome, numerous toll stops. They discussed places they wanted to see, where they might have a light lunch, then dinner at his favorite restaurant, Mistral, in the South End district.

They were both starving by the time they got to town, so opted to grab a bite at The Union Oyster House, the oldest restaurant in the country.

Once inside, Trevor gave Olivia a quick history of the quaint and crowded establishment. "It's been open since 1826. Oysters were all the rage at the time, so the owners built that semi-circular Oyster Bar over there to accommodate the demand. They say Daniel Webster was a daily customer, downing a tall tumbler of brandy and water along with each of his half-dozen oysters—rarely less than six plates of the delicacies per visit."

"It's a wonder he ever had time to write a dictionary."

"Indeed."

"Who else hung out here? Anyone else I would know?"

"Basically anyone who lived or traveled through Boston since 1926. The Kennedys loved the place. There's a plaque on a booth upstairs where JFK used to dine in privacy. We'll pick up one of their booklets on the way out; a virtual who's who of American history."

He watched her savor the indescribable clam chowder, tickled by the groan of pleasure uttered with her first bite. "Wait until you taste the cornbread. I don't know what they do to make it melt in your mouth, but it's the best I've ever tasted."

He laughed out loud when another series of culinary groans of ecstasy filled their booth.

"Oh, Trevorrrrr . . . I might just move in here and spend the rest of my days eating my way through their entire menu." She wiped butter from her lips with a playful look. "Wait—does that repulse you? The thought of me licking bowls of chowder and inhaling squares of this deliciousness called cornbread?"

He chortled, a great honk of a thing which not only horrified him, but made them both laugh so hard they couldn't breathe.

"Stop!" she wheezed hiding behind her napkin. "You're killing me!"

He leaned across the table and lowered his voice. "I'm so sorry! I had no idea I could make such a dastardly noise."

She wiped tears from her eyes, but couldn't stifle the onslaught of giggles.

They laughed and ate and talked until they wore themselves out. Trevor leaned his head back against the booth, trying to remember if he had ever known such a good time in all his life, convinced he hadn't.

When the waiter appeared with an enormous piece of Boston Cream Pie, Olivia raised her hand. "Okay, I'll take one bite. Just one. That's it, because otherwise I'm going to make myself sick."

"Fine. Have it your way." He cut the point of the pie with his fork and extended it toward her. "Here's your one bite. Don't even *think* of asking for another."

She took the bite and closed her eyes, her mouth perfectly still. "Mmm."

"Taste the creamy vanilla custard? The moist sponge cake with the chocolate glaze?"

"Mmm."

"Good, because the rest is mine."

Chapter 16

Over the next three hours, Trevor gave Olivia an abbreviated tour of some of Boston's most famous sights. They started with the New England Holocaust Memorial just across from the restaurant. Olivia stood in awe looking up at the six glass towers which Trevor told her represented the six million Jews killed during the Holocaust and the six major death camps.

"Each tower is etched with seven-digit numbers in remembrance of the numbers tattooed on the arms of the concentration camp prisoners."

On such a bright day, the shadows of those etched numbers covered both of them.

"It's absolutely breathtaking," Olivia murmured.

He tucked her hand under his elbow as they finished walking along the path. "It's a sobering memorial but yes, quite a beautiful tribute."

From there they strolled to Faneuil Hall, called "the Cradle of Liberty" where many of the leaders of the American Revolution first spoke out against British oppression. Their next stop was a tour of Paul Revere's house; then on to Old North Church, the first stop on Revere's infamous "Midnight Ride" on April 18, 1775. They made their way back to Trevor's SUV then drove by Copley Square, Fenway Park, Harvard Square, and many other historic sites before stopping to wander through Granary Burying Ground. There they visited the snow-covered graves of John Hancock, Sam Adams, Paul Revere, members of Benjamin Franklin's family, and many others from America's earliest days.

Trevor looked at his watch. "We're going to have to scoot to make our reservation at Mistral."

"Already? Oh Trevor, I couldn't eat a thing. I'm still stuffed from lunch."

He grinned. "I wasn't going to say anything, but so am I. How about I call and cancel the reservation, and we'll do that another time."

She grabbed his hand in both of hers. "Perfect."

Later, on the way out of town, they stopped for coffee to go, then hopped back on I-95 to head back to Caden Cove. The sun had set, shrouding the road with darkness and headlights. But the interior lights and heated seats of the luxury SUV made for a cozy ride back to town. They filled the time discussing the sights they'd seen as Trevor filled in the gaps of history they'd missed in the brief day's tour.

Olivia marveled at how relaxed and comfortable they'd become with each other in such a short time. It felt as if they'd been close for months instead of mere weeks. Then, even as that thought crossed her mind, a subtle check in her spirit drifted through again. *Too much, too fast.* Stealing a peek at Trevor's profile, she tamped down the echoes of her Ellen's warning.

Oh Lord, I've waited so long. Please let this be okay . . .

"Tell me what you're thinking."

"What?" she asked, startled.

"You were staring at me."

"I was? Oh. Well, nothing. Just . . . thinking about what it's been. That's all."

He glanced at her again. "I see. And what was your favorite part of our—"

"TREVOR! LOOK OUT!"

The glare of red brake lights filled the windshield as cars swerved recklessly around them. Trevor stomped on the brakes sending them into a frantic sideways slide.

Horns blared. Tires squealed. Metal crunched metal. Trevor tried desperately to regain control of the SUV.

"TREVOR!" Olivia cried. "Oh God, help us!"

"OLIVIA! STOP SCREAMING!"

They continued to slide, inching closer, closer to the rear of a yellow Volkswagen Beetle. She held her breath waiting for impact when the SUV finally came to a stop. She quickly twisted to look behind, praying the blur of headlights wouldn't slam into them.

"Oh, Trevor—"

He flashed a rigid palm in her face.

"Wha—"

"Stop!"

"But I—"

"It's called black ice. We drive on it all the time." His hushed, patronizing tone stunned her.

"What?! You're blaming this on *me*?"

He continued, slowly, methodically, as if addressing a three-year-old, his eyes locked straight ahead. "I know how to handle it. Sometimes these *out of state* truckers drive too fast. They cause accidents." He turned, his eyes wild with fury. "But I do *not* need *you* to tell me how to drive!"

"Look, I was only trying—"

He blasted an angry grunt, shoving the palm back at her face. "Not. One. Word."

Olivia gasped, more at the seething tone of his voice than the words themselves. Still trembling from the near-miss, she racked her brain trying to think what could have set him off. The same face that made her heart skip a beat just moments ago, now resembled that of an angry bull—eyes narrowed and nostrils flaring with each carefully controlled breath.

"Stay in the car." He got out, then slammed the door. Others joined him, surveying the pile-up ahead and looking for a way around the mess.

Olivia clenched her jaws, her chest heaving. *Of all the nerve. He almost gets us killed, and somehow that's* my *fault?* She closed her eyes and tried to rein in her emotions. Not once, but twice in one day, he'd jumped down her throat. And for what? Reacting to his reckless driving? He'd apologized the first time, saying he wasn't used to having a passenger with him.

Had she overreacted? Was she the hyper-nervous passenger Ellen labeled her all those years ago?

She pinched the bridge of her nose and squeezed her eyes tighter as they prickled with tears. *Oh please, don't let me crumble. Not in front of him.* She tried to slow her breathing while searching for a tissue in her purse.

Too much, too soon!

Had she put on blinders, unwilling to see the real Trevor, ignoring all those red flags that now rippled with warning?

Frustrated by not finding a handkerchief or tissue, she looked around the SUV. Surely, someone as organized as Trevor would have a box of tissues in his car. She opened the glove compartment and spotted a packet of tissues beneath a small notebook. Olivia pulled two tissues and began to dab at her eyes before blowing her nose. Once under control again, she nabbed one more tissue before putting the packet back in the compartment. Curious about the notebook, she lifted it out and flipped through its pages. It appeared to be a journal of sorts. She snuck a quick look for Trevor, but couldn't see around the vehicle in front of them. Against her better judgment, she thumbed back to the first page. She recognized Trevor's handsome script and couldn't resist reading a few lines before he returned.

July 3, 2009

Upon discovery of the leather-bound MacVicar Chronicles, I found myself fascinated by the family history of those who are, in essence, my neighbors. All that separates us is the passage of time. And while the mysterious legend still haunts our town to this day, I am determined to find the truth of the matter and put the nonsense to rest once and for all. And in doing so—which is the far greater task, of course—I shall begin to write a comprehensive history of our beloved Caden Cove.

"He's writing a book," she whispered in awe. She chanced another peek to make sure he wasn't returning, and thumbed through the handwritten notes and dates and diagrams that filled the leather journal. At first, she was delighted at the discovery. She remembered the night after the book club when she'd told him he should write. He'd scoffed away her suggestion. He'd also brushed off any talk of the legend as nothing but a bunch of silly coincidences. He gave the impression he'd never given it any credence, and yet here was proof that he found it worthy of personal research.

Hearing sirens in the distance, she looked up just in time as he reached for the door handle. With no time to pop the journal back in the glove compartment, she shoved it under her purse on the floor beside her feet.

Trevor rubbed his hands together and blew on them, obviously chilled to the bone. "A semi jackknifed ahead, but there's just enough room on the shoulder to get past all the damaged cars. Otherwise we'll be here all night."

"Is anyone hurt?"

"No."

Olivia waited for more, but there was none. He never turned to look at her. Never asked if she was okay. He snapped his seatbelt and started the engine again, then slowly began inching along until the SUV moved out of the road and onto the shoulder. As they followed other vehicles, Olivia got her first look at the long semi sprawled on its side across both northbound lanes of the interstate. Several vehicles behind it were bent and smashed like so many toy cars accordioned together.

Once around the wreck, Olivia looked back at the flashing red lights of first responders, their sirens a symphony of discord. Turning back toward the front, she made no attempt to engage him in conversation. His insulting tirade still sparked through her veins like a jolt of electricity. She looked out her passenger window and decided to keep silent. It felt ridiculously childish, but she didn't trust herself to speak.

They drove in silence until exiting the interstate onto State Road 9. It gave Olivia time to think. *Too* much time to think. Part of her wanted to thank God for opening her eyes before it was too late—whatever that might mean. She'd been a fool not to take Ellen's concerns more seriously. She knew Ellen had probably spent a lot of time on her knees praying since their last conversation.

Is that why all this happened? Are You answering Ellen's prayers by letting me see this obnoxious, belligerent side of Trevor?

The thought of it grieved her.

A tear slipped down her cheek. She let it fall, not willing for him to see her wipe it away. Instead, she forced her attention back out the side window, noticing his reflection in the glass. She hadn't seen it before. And much to her surprise, he turned briefly to look at her.

Real brave, Trevor. You wait for me to turn my back before giving me so much as a glance? She watched him through the reflection as he squeezed the bridge of his nose, slowly shaking his head. *Well then. That's that.*

As they turned the last corner then pulled onto the graveled lot at the MacVicar, Olivia reached for her purse then looked him in the eye. "Goodbye, Trevor."

"Olivia, wait—" He grabbed her elbow as she opened her door. "Please. There's something I need to say."

She eyed his hand on her arm. "I think you've said quite enough."

"This isn't at all how I wanted this day to end."

"No? Well, I guess that's good to know. But at this point, I'd say it's a little late. Now, if you don't mind—"

"Please, Olivia, I'm begging you."

She pulled free and started to get out.

"Wait. You forgot something."

She turned just as he picked up the journal from her floorboard. He started to hand it to her, then froze. His eyes tracked slowly to hers.

"I . . . I was looking for a tissue and found some in your glove compartment. Then I found that and—"

"You read my journal?"

"But I didn't *know* it was your journal. I didn't know what it was. I guess I was just curious, so I opened it and—Trevor, why didn't you tell me you're writing a book?"

The nerve along his jaw line twitched, and his eyes returned to the journal. "Is there some law that says I have to tell you everything?"

Olivia felt as if she'd been slapped. She stepped out of the SUV, slammed the door, and never looked back.

Chapter 17

Back in her room, Olivia turned off her cell phone. She doubted Trevor would try to call, but she couldn't risk a call from Ellen. Not now. Ellen would never flaunt an "I-told-you-so," but she'd know something was wrong. Olivia needed time to process. After a long hot bath, she climbed into bed and turned out the light. Her pulse quickened with every memory of the past couple of hours, fueling a tangled web of things she wished she'd said, things she knew she'd have to say at some point, and things she desperately needed her heart to hear. She lay there for more than an hour, unable to fight the emotions battling within her until she finally fell asleep on her tear-stained pillow.

The next morning, Trig seemed to understand her need for a quiet breakfast. Over a hot bowl of oatmeal dusted with brown sugar and a medley of dried fruits and slivered almonds, Olivia tried to pray away the throbbing pain in her head. The possibility of packing her bags and heading back to Atlanta kept eating at her, but something inside her heart told her to stay. She'd never run away from problems before. She wasn't about to start now. Still, the chance of running into Trevor caused the pain in her head to tighten like a vise.

Don't be such a drama queen. You're not in high school. He's not your "boyfriend." Stop acting so juvenile and do what you came here to do. You have a new future to plan, so do it.

The thought made her acutely aware of how much she'd lost her way since coming to Caden Cove. How easily she'd been distracted by Trevor's attention. After all these years, she knew better. Yes, it was flattering and wonderful and exhilarating to be pursued. But at her age, she should know better. And deep inside, she did. She'd stopped yearning for romance years ago. If it happened, fine. If it didn't, that was fine too. In her heart of hearts, she knew if God had someone for her, it surely wouldn't be this much trouble.

Still . . .

Sipping hot coffee, she vowed to get back on track and start making the decisions she came here to make. But first, she'd have to get rid of her headache. A quick run to Molly's for some Advil, then she could get down to business. She thanked Trig for breakfast then headed to her room to get her coat and purse.

And prayed she wouldn't run into the local bookseller.

Ten minutes later, Molly rang up her bottle of Advil on the register.

"Must be something in the air today. Just sold one of these to Trevor." She pinned Olivia with a stare.

"Really?" Olivia winced at the croak in her voice. She cleared her throat. "Well, I hope he feels better soon."

Molly closed the register, her eyes still on Olivia. "It's probably none of my business, but—"

"Then thank you for understanding." Olivia closed her purse and turned to go. "I'll see you later."

Molly grabbed Olivia's wrist and held it. "I need a break. Come sit with me. Coffee's on the house."

"I'd love to, Molly, but I really need—"

"It can wait. We need to talk. Have a seat," she said, pointing at the barstool by the counter.

Olivia sighed, then made her way to the counter.

Molly poured two cups of coffee, stirred cream into both, then slid one across the counter to Olivia. "I take it the trip to Boston didn't go so well?"

"Why? Did he say something?"

"Didn't have to. I've known Trevor long enough to read him like a book—if you'll pardon the pun. He doesn't have to say a word. The last week or so, he's been all but giddy. Comes floating through my store, sings my name out like he's on stage at the opera, laughs at the silliest things. Today? He stomps in here like the old grump he used to be. No eye contact. Not so much as a hello or how are you. Just slaps his Advil on the counter with the exact change and off he goes.

"It isn't my business—even though I like to *think* I'm the heartbeat of our little town." Molly smiled. "Mostly, I'm just a mother hen. I'm elated when my friends are happy, and I hurt when my friends are hurting."

Something in Olivia shifted. "Molly. I'm sorry. I'm disappointed, but to be honest, I'm glad yesterday happened. I let myself get carried away. That hasn't happened in years. But I think I was starry-eyed about the *idea* of us, not the reality of us. Life's hard enough without all that complication, you know?"

"Did he lose his temper with you? Snap at you like you're a two-year-old?"

"And *then* some." Olivia nodded with a sad smile.

"Olivia, much as I'd like to, I can't tell you what to do. But I will say this. Trevor's always been set in his ways—"

"That's putting it mildly."

"He can be a real pain at times. But oh, my dear Olivia. The change I've seen in him since he met you? Well, even an old romantic like me can see there's something *special* between the two of you. I've prayed for Trevor for as long as I've known him. I've prayed that God would tear down those walls around his heart and give him a chance at happiness. And I have to say, until you came along, I'd all but given up on him."

Olivia traced the ridge of her coffee mug but said nothing.

"Do me a favor. And you don't have to answer out loud. But ask yourself. Whatever happened yesterday, was it unforgiveable? Was it truly a game-changer, as they say? Or was it something minor or trivial? I guess what I'm asking you to consider is whether you've found in Trevor someone worth fighting for?"

The questions struck somewhere in the vicinity of Olivia's heart. Twenty-four hours ago she would have said yes. In a heartbeat. She'd fallen in love with him. He was the first man she'd allowed herself to fall in love with in twenty years. She'd seen the good in him and adored the time they'd spent together. He was fascinating and funny and kindhearted . . .

But was it enough? Could a few days of companionship and laughter and endless conversations be enough to shove aside all vestiges of the ill-tempered bookseller she'd first met a couple of weeks ago?

No. She'd be an idiot to think the Old Trevor would never surface again.

Maybe it was all just window-dressing. Maybe he'd merely put on a good show for her, looking for a little harmless fun until she left town.

No. That wasn't it either.

She dropped her head in her hands. "Oh Molly, I don't know. I just don't know."

"Then here's what I suggest. Give yourself all the time you need to think about it. Sort through your feelings. And most important, get on your knees and find out what *God* would have you do. I'll be praying for you. And I'll be praying for Trevor as well. Then let's just see what happens. Fair enough?"

Olivia raised her head, pushing her hair off her forehead. She tried to smile. "Fair enough." She reached across the counter for Molly's hand. "Thank you."

On her way back to the inn, she had the sudden urge to get out of town. At least for a couple of hours to find some place to think and pray. Deciding to make the short drive to Kennebunkport, she walked back to the inn, got in her rental car, and took off.

And reminded herself to keep an eye out for black ice.

Trevor closed the shop for an early lunch. With Charlie riding co-pilot, he headed home hoping to clear his mind. His headache wasn't quite as severe, but still an irritation.

But then, what doesn't *irritate me these days?*

He raked his fingers through his hair, shaking off the thought. Once at home, he gave Charlie a treat which she sniffed a couple of times, then ignored. Following her into his study, he studied her waddle, assessing her added girth.

"What's the matter, girl? Not feeling well?"

Charlie's tail took a couple of slow wags before she plodded toward her crate.

"I know the feeling."

He wasn't hungry, opting instead for a nap on the sofa in his study. He watched Charlie circle inside her crate before settling down on her blanket with a hearty sigh.

"Oh, Charlie. What have I done?"

She raised an eyelid, then slowly closed it.

"Precisely."

Trevor draped his arm across his face and let his mind wander. He hadn't slept well last night and wondered if Olivia had the same problem. Had she stayed up kicking herself for having feelings for him in the first place? Had she regretted the time they'd spent together? Did she hate him for his despicable behavior last night?

Probably not half as much as I hate myself for it.

Over his second cup of coffee before leaving the house earlier that morning, he'd had an alarming thought—what if she'd left? What if she'd packed her bags and gone home? Driving by the MacVicar a few minutes later, palpable relief washed over him at the sight of her rental car. And yet, had the car been gone, he couldn't have blamed her.

Now, rolling to his side on the sofa, he tried to figure out why he'd been so ugly to her. She'd brought nothing but joy into his life. For the first time in years, he understood how it felt to love someone. Being with Olivia had knocked down all his defenses. And much to his surprise, he loved how that felt.

And how had he repaid her? By snapping at her. By berating her for a perfectly natural reaction. By speaking to her with such condescension as if she hadn't a brain in her head.

"Oh God, what have I done?"

The question echoed through his mind. Trevor wasn't even sure how to pray. It seemed somehow hypocritical. To be such a stubborn Neanderthal, then ask God for forgiveness? God surely knew he was a lost cause. But even as the thought still drifted through his mind, he knew it wasn't true.

Do it.

What?

Eyes still closed, he shook his head, dismissing the thought. *Nonsense. I must be in that strange place between awake and asleep. If I could just get some sleep . . .*

Do it!

His eyes flashed opened, and this time he knew. Without a second thought, he slipped off the sofa and onto his knees, finally surrendering to the conviction that coursed through his veins with utter abandon.

"Oh God, I'm so sorry . . ."

Chapter 18

Olivia took a final sip of tea then pushed her plate aside. With a tinge of sadness, she realized this would probably be her last visit to Kennebunkport. Midday, after wandering the streets of the famous little town's tourist area, she'd found the cozy pub all but deserted which suited her fine. Seated by a window, she watched the docked sailboats bobbing on the bay's chilly water. There was something peaceful and soothing about the scene; the perfect backdrop for some serious soul-searching.

She couldn't figure out why everything had happened. She wondered why God had let her come up here in the first place. But she was past that now, resigned to make a fresh start.

Again.

Somewhere else. Anywhere else.

It made sense to go home to Atlanta. She would officially resign from her job, then try to stay off the radar from everyone for a while. She needed time to sort it all out without interference. Without all the drama. Without letting her heart get sidetracked . . . She would hunker down and shut out the world until she could come up with a plan, a strategy for the rest of her life.

Why oh why did I waste all this time in Caden Cove? Clearly a mistake, and one I will not *make again.*

With a start, Olivia realized she'd left her cell phone back at the inn. She remembered turning it off before she went to bed, and obviously forgot it when she left that morning. *I don't even want to guess how many times Ellen has called.* Still, she knew her friend would be worried and didn't want to cause her alarm. She gathered her things, paid her bill, and headed back to Caden Cove, praying one last desperate prayer for guidance as she drove.

Give me a sign, Lord.

The sun was setting as she walked up the steps of the MacVicar. After such a late lunch, she planned to skip dinner and stay in for the night. She opened the door, surprised to find Michelle seated at the front desk.

"Hi, Olivia. Have you had a nice day?"

"Yes, thanks. I drove over to Kennebunkport for the day."

"Sounds fun. Oh, by the way, you had a delivery while you were out."

"Me?"

A mischievous grin played across her face. "Trig put them in your room since he wasn't sure he'd see you."

"Put 'them' in my room?"

"You'll see."

"I will?"

Michelle's face beamed. "Trust me."

Olivia headed up the stairs, in no mood for surprises. Opening the door to her room, she gasped. A sea of roses—on the tables, on the fireplace mantel, on the desk, on the floor here and there. Dozens of roses in every color.

"What in the world?"

She pulled the card from the nearest arrangement, stopping first to inhale the sweet scent of its pale pink petals. Tugging the card from its envelope, she read the brief note.

My dear Olivia,
I'm such a fool.
One more chance.
That's all I ask.
Trevor

She made her way around the room, reading each hand-written card.

Can you ever forgive me?
Whatever it takes.
A second chance.
Please . . .

You were right—
I was an absolute buffoon.
If it takes a lifetime, I'll make it up to you.

Olivia, please say yes to us.
If for no other reason . . .
Charlie needs you.

Something between a sob and laugh broke the silence. "*Charlie* needs me? Now you're just playing dirty, mister." She dashed away her tears before reading the final card.

Oh Olivia,
I pray you'll find it in your heart
to forgive me.
I'm home. Please come.
With open arms,
Trevor

She stuffed all the cards in her pocket and rushed from the room, wiping away tears of joy as she flew down the stairs.

"Let me guess. You found the roses?" Trig teased as she rounded the staircase landing.

"I just can't—I've never seen so many—when did he—have you ever seen—oh never mind! I've got to go!"

She grabbed Trig then Michelle for a quick hug. "Thank you! Thank you both! I'll be back!"

Moments later, the car had barely rolled to a stop in Trevor's driveway before she cut the engine and jumped out. She dashed up the stone pathway to the front door then rang the doorbell and pounded on the door.

"Trevor! It's me! Open up!"

Charlie's excited barks grew louder on the other side of the door.

Suddenly, the door opened wide and she flew into his arms.

"Oh, Trevor!"

"Oh, thank God you came! I didn't know if you—"

"I'm here, I'm here," she cried, laughing again. "Trevor, I've never seen so many roses in all my life!"

"I didn't know what color you liked, so I got a dozen of each."

"And I loved them *all.* Every one."

With her arms tight around his neck, he wrapped his arms around her and leaned his forehead against hers. "Does that mean you forgive me?"

"Yes. I forgive you. I forgive you! I was just so *surprised.* I didn't know what to think. What . . . I mean, how did you—"

"Come inside. You're shaking like a leaf." He herded her into the entry hall and closed the door.

Charlie danced around their feet, her tail gently swaying back and forth.

As Trevor took her coat, Olivia knelt down beside Charlie, cupping her head in her hands. "Oh, Charlie, I'm so glad to see you. How are you, sweetie?" She pressed a kiss against her silky head.

Trevor planted his fists on his hips. "Well, that's just great. I buy every rose in the county, and *Charlie* gets a kiss before I do."

Olivia stood and slid her arms around his waist. "All you had to do was ask."

He pulled her closer and kissed her with such passion, she could hardly breathe.

"Olivia, I was so afraid I'd lost you. Afraid I'd scared you away."

"I'm here now. That's all that matters."

He shook his head. "No, there's more to it than that." He tucked her beneath his arm and turned, heading toward the den. "There's so much I need to say. Come sit with me."

Trevor took her hands in his. "I've never been so miserable in all my life as when I left you last night. I acted . . . well, it's *inexcusable*, the way I treated you. I tried all night to convince myself to let you go. To give up what we'd found together and just go back to my pathetic, lonely life.

"But I couldn't do it. In my gut, I knew it would be better for *you*. You deserve so much more than I could give you. You're much too lovely and gracious to put up with an incorrigible grouch like me."

"Trevor—"

He touched his fingers to her lips. "No, please. Let me say this because you need to hear it."

She nodded. "All right."

"I didn't sleep a wink last night. So I closed the shop and came home earlier today, hoping to get some rest. But I could not get you out of my mind. And then . . . I don't even know how to describe what happened. One minute I was whining—for lack of a better word—'God, what have I done?' And the next minute, I heard someone telling me to pray. Twice. Not out loud, mind you—it was more like I felt it profoundly, if that makes sense. And the next thing I knew, I was on my knees pouring out my heart to God."

"Oh, Trevor . . ."

"Long story short, I guess you could say God and I made our peace. I know it sounds absurd, but that's what happened."

"It doesn't sound absurd at all."

He smiled, squeezing her hands. "The crazy thing is how different I felt. Instantly. Like someone had built a fire to warm my heart again. I've never experienced anything like it."

She cupped his cheek and pressed a kiss there. "That may be the most wonderful news I've ever heard."

He placed his hand over hers. "I stayed there on my knees a long time, asking the Lord what to do about you—about us. Olivia, I don't believe any of this is a coincidence. There's a reason you came here. There's a reason we met. I mean, think about it. Tourists rarely come to our neck of the woods this time of year, yet here you were.

And whatever led you here, you quickly became one of us. I've never seen that happen before. Ever."

She arched her brows. "Really? Does that mean I'm one of the locals now?"

"No, but I have connections," he feigned. "I'll see what I can do."

He wrapped his arm over her shoulders and pulled her closer. "When I was praying, I kept telling God over and over that I didn't deserve you—"

"Well, *that* goes without saying."

"Yes, and I'm fairly confident He agreed with me. But I promised if He'd give me one more chance with you, I'd do it right this time. I promised to overcome this stubborn nature of mine. I promised to pull the plug on my pride and anger issues. I *despise* those parts of me, and I'm sick to death of letting them sabotage every good thing in my life. Most of all—you. I promised I'd treat you with respect, and do everything I can to be worthy of you."

She was silent for a moment. A flicker of doubt surfaced again. This was all happening much too fast. Again. An hour ago she was ready to hop a plane back to Atlanta and forget about him. Was she truly ready for a serious relationship with him? Or was she allowing herself to be romanced by the flowers and hugs and kisses and all his endearing promises?

He searched her face. "Olivia?"

Looking into his eyes, she was startled to find something there she'd never seen before—humility and transparency. Oh, how she wanted to trust him!

"I have to be honest, Trevor. After last night, I gave up on us. I spent most of today trying to sort it all out, and I came back to the MacVicar to pack my things. I knew I had to get away from here. Away from you. Because as much as I loved the time we had together —most of it, anyway—I remembered that being single wasn't really so bad. Better single and content than pursuing a relationship that's already—"

"I know, but—"

She pressed her fingertips against his lips. "Ah-ah-ah. It's my turn. Let me finish."

"Okay."

"I knew I'd be better off single than pursuing a relationship that was already on such thin ice—or should I say, *black* ice?"

He grimaced. "Touché."

She flashed him a sheepish grin. "Sorry. I couldn't resist. What I'm trying to tell you is this. In my heart of hearts, I believed you were too much of a risk, and one I wasn't willing to take at this point in my life."

She shrugged. "But on the way back to Caden Cove, I said one last prayer. I asked God to give me some kind of sign. Some kind of visible, in-your-face sign so there would be no doubt left in my mind."

Olivia smiled. "Then I walked into my room and found an ocean of roses. And call me a silly romantic, but I'm pretty sure they were my sign. A great big sign. And a really *good* sign."

He gathered her back in his arms. "To think I almost didn't send them! I worried you might think I'd lost my mind."

He kissed her gently, and Olivia felt the affirmation all over again. "You might have lost your mind, but you found my heart."

"I *love* you, as best as I know how, with all my heart. You are a breath of fresh air in this dusty old bookseller's life." He sat up, taking both her hands in his again. "I know you'll think I'm genuinely crazy, but . . . *marry me*, Olivia. Make me the happiest man on earth. Say you'll spend the rest of your life with me."

Tears pooled in her eyes as she reflected the sincerity on his face. She couldn't breathe. If ever there were a time for a red flag to unfurl, this was it. But with each passing moment, not a single flag waved. No butterflies. No doubts. Not one.

"I love you too, Trevor," she whispered. "Yes. Yes, I'll marry you!" Laughing, she found his lips and kissed him to seal the deal.

Charlie barked and danced at all the excitement and placed her front paws on Trevor's knees.

"Come on up, little mama, and join the celebration." He carefully lifted her onto his lap. "Your friend Olivia here is going to make our family complete. What do you think about that?"

Her tail wagging a constant rhythm, Charlie flashed her goofy smile looking back and forth between them.

"I'll take that as a yes," Trevor said. "Well, then. It's unanimous!"

They talked for hours, exploring all the possibilities that lay before them. Over dinner, they decided an April wedding would be perfect, agreeing to take their vows here in Caden Cove at the Lord's Chapel.

"I'll finally be a local," Olivia quipped. "Though I'm sure they'll think I married you just for the privilege." Her face fell as a thought occurred to her. "Trevor, would you mind terribly if we don't tell anyone just yet?"

"No, of course not. Any particular reason?"

"I'd like to go home and tell my friends first. Especially Ellen. And I need to tell her face to face. In fact, I'd love for you to come back to Atlanta with me. That way, she can get to know you before I tell her."

He smirked. "Why do I feel like I'm going home to meet your parents?"

"They're not *that* old. You'll love her husband Brent. He's the most down to earth guy you'll ever meet."

"What, like me, you mean?"

"Oh sure. *Just* like you."

"I have to admit I'm a little hesitant about meeting Ellen. What if she doesn't like me? What if she doesn't give us her blessing?"

"She just needs to get to know you. She'll love you. I promise."

"Can I have that in writing, please? Our own private pre-nup?"

"If it will put your mind at rest."

"Second thought, never mind. It's a risk I'm willing to take."

Chapter 19

Around eleven-thirty, Olivia returned to the MacVicar, quietly letting herself in the side entrance. She tiptoed up the stairs, tired but giddy, and ready for a good night's sleep. She unlocked the door to her room—and gasped.

There on her bed lay her best friend.

"Ellen! What are you *doing* here!?"

Ellen sat up and stretched with a rigorous yawn. "I heard there was a rose festival so I decided to come."

Olivia threw off her coat and gave Ellen a hug. "I can't believe you're here! When did you get in?"

"Around seven, I think. I wanted to surprise you, but I couldn't stay awake—" Another yawn bit off her words as she sat back down on the bed. "I asked Trig where you were, but he wouldn't tell me at first. Said it wasn't his place. Of course, he was putty in the hands of a professional like me. I laid it on pretty thick and he sang like a bird. Told me you were with *Trevor*."

Olivia felt her face warm. She turned abruptly to hang up her coat in the armoire. "Yes, I was. And I can't wait for you to meet him. I know you'll really—"

"I didn't come to meet Trevor. I came to see *you*. Originally, I planned on coming up for a couple of days just to surprise you. Then I got worried because your phone kept going to voice mail—"

"My phone!" Olivia snatched it off the bedside table. "I forgot to grab it before I left."

"Uh huh. I've been calling for *two* days, Olivia. Are you telling me you haven't been back here in your room for two days?"

"No, no, no—I meant when I was here earlier." She bristled. "Hey, did you just insinuate what I think you did?"

"What? No. Well. Maybe? I don't know, Olivia. You tell me. I had half a mind to drive out to Trevor's house when it started getting so late. I even asked Trig where he lived, but he wouldn't tell me. Which is just as well, because I was in no mood to pay a social visit."

Olivia plopped herself down beside Ellen and draped her arm over her shoulders. "Ellen, you have *got* to chill. Take a deep breath. Let me tell you about the last couple of days and put your mind to rest. It all started when Trevor won some rare books in an online auction."

She told her everything. From the impromptu trip to Boston, the silly conversations over lunch at the Union Oyster, and all the sights they saw while in Beantown. Propped up on pillows, Olivia told her about their drive home the night before, the accident on the interstate, and the awful fight she and Trevor had. She told her about the frigid silence the rest of the way home, and her seething anger that intensified with every mile. And she told her about crying herself to sleep, convinced whatever she had with Trevor was over.

Ellen shoved another pillow behind her head and glanced around the room. "By the floral display, I'm guessing that's not the end of the story. When Trig let me in, I thought he gave me the wrong room. Looked more like a mafia funeral than a guest room."

Olivia couldn't help smiling as she gazed over the colorful bouquets dotting the room. "Yes, there's more to the story." She sat up and stretched. "But it's late and you're probably tired, so we can wait and—"

"Not happening." Ellen pulled Olivia back against the pillows. "Go on. You were saying?"

Olivia turned sideways and propped her head on her hand. "Okay, okay. Where was I? Ah, this morning. Obviously I didn't get a lot of sleep last night, and I woke up with a roaring headache."

She continued, telling Ellen about her stop at the pharmacy and her brief chat with Molly. She told about her drive to Kennebunkport and the resolution she made to go home to Atlanta.

"On my way back, I prayed and prayed, then finally asked God for a sign. I know it's not exactly a leap of faith, asking for something like that. But I just needed to know, Ellen. I had to make sure I wasn't making a big mistake."

Ellen fingered a rose petal on the bedside table. "Then you walked in here and found all these . . . *signs*." She slowly exhaled. "I can see how you might think—"

"Think? How I might 'think' this was a sign? How could it *not* be a sign?" She stiffened at the look in Ellen's eyes.

"We've been over and over this, Olivia. *Nobody* wants to see you happier than I do. You know that! But you're at a crossroads in your life right now and much too vulnerable to start a relationship."

Olivia pressed her lips together. "Then I'm guessing that means you won't be coming for our wedding."

Ellen fell back against the pillows with a scoffing laugh. "Oh, sure. Like you'd marry a guy you hardly even know." She raised her palms in surrender. "All right, all right, I'm sorry—I'll stop playing mother hen. Good one, Olivia."

Olivia didn't react. She simply tilted her head to one side and fastened a knowing smile on her face.

Ellen's laughter waned. "What?"

Olivia arched her brows and looked away, feeling like a guilty Lucy to a suspicious Ethel.

Ellen sat straight up. "Olivia?"

Olivia looked back at her and shrugged.

"Oh-no-you-did-NOT!? Don't play games with me, Olivia. *Please* tell me you're joking."

"I would, but I'm not, so I can't."

Ellen scrunched her face. "Huh?"

Olivia sat up and folded her hands in her lap. "Ellen, Trevor asked me to marry him and I said yes."

Ellen grabbed her hands. "Oh, sweetie, please, *please* tell me you're not serious!"

Olivia broke free of her grasp. "How can you be so dead-set against it when you haven't even met him yet?"

"Because it's just too fast!" Ellen jumped off the bed and started pacing. "I don't care if he's the greatest man who's ever walked this earth! There's *no possible way* you can know all you need to know about him in only a matter of days! Are you out of your mind?!"

Olivia slowly scooted off the bed and went to her, grabbing hold of her arms. "Ellen? You're my best friend. You always have been. But I really need you to calm down and hear me out. I'm not an adolescent child. And I'm certainly not a silly teenager with a crush on the boy next door. I believe with all my heart that this is right. I really do. I know this seems sudden and absurd, and completely out of character for me. But I really do love this man. He's not perfect. Neither am I. But he *loves* me, Ellen. He wants to spend the rest of his life with me. Can't you just try to give him a chance? Can't you at least give me the benefit of the doubt until you've met him?"

Ellen pursed her lips and shook her head. "I don't know," she said sympathetically. "I know you must think I'm such a jerk because I'm not accepting this, but I can't just sit back and watch you get your heart broken."

"And I appreciate that. I really do. But what if he's the one I've been waiting for all these years? Would you deny my chance at happiness without even meeting him?"

"Of course I wouldn't."

"Then can't you please give him a chance? For my sake?"

Chapter 20

Trevor parked his SUV next to Olivia's rental at the MacVicar. He took a deep breath, closed his eyes, and slowly exhaled. She'd called early, even before he'd read the paper or had his coffee. And he knew immediately something was going on by the much-too-cheery tone in her voice. She told him Ellen had popped into town to surprise her, and would he like to join them for breakfast at the inn?

"Are you sure? Wouldn't you rather just have some girl time or whatever?"

"No. No, we'd love to have you join us, Trevor." Pause. "Please?"

The slight quake in her voice was all it took. She needed him, so he would go.

Now, as he approached the inn, he took a deep breath and opened the door.

"Good morning, Trevor," Michelle said.

"Hello, Michelle."

"Olivia told us you'd be coming for breakfast. The girls are in the dining area. Come on, I'll walk you back."

He heard them chatting before he and Michelle entered the dining room. He locked eyes with Olivia and noted the instant relief in her eyes. He tossed her a quick wink just before Ellen turned around.

"Look who I found at the door," Michelle teased.

Trevor gave them his best smile. "Good morning, ladies."

Olivia reached for his hand. "Good morning, Trevor. I want you to meet my best friend, Ellen Thatcher. Ellen, this is Trevor Bass."

He gave her a firm handshake. "How nice to meet you, Ellen. Olivia's told me so much about you."

"Nice to meet you too, Trevor."

The smile on her attractive face was strained at best. As she let go of his hand, he glanced at Olivia, noticing the unmistakable pleading in her eyes.

"Well, then." He rubbed his hands together. "I'm starving. What do you say we have a seat and see what Trig has in store for us."

Right on cue, Trig and Michelle showed up with colorful plates of assorted fruits and a basket of orange cranberry muffins. "We'll let you get started with these while we finish the frittatas," Trig said. Michelle poured each of them a cup of coffee then disappeared into the kitchen behind her husband.

As they unfolded their cloth napkins, a thought occurred to Trevor. "May I?" he asked, reaching for both of their hands.

A wave of gratitude relaxed Olivia's countenance. "Of course. Thank you, Trevor." She squeezed his hand as they bowed their heads.

He uttered a quick silent prayer, trusting God to give him the right words. "Lord, thank You for a beautiful morning. Thank you for allowing us to have this time together. Bless our conversation. And thank You for this meal and the hands that prepared it. Amen."

The moisture in Olivia's eyes matched her uneasy smile.

Ellen gently blew on her coffee. "Thank you, Trevor."

"Olivia tells me you gave her quite a shock when she got in last night," Trevor began.

Ellen sipped her coffee then set it back down and smiled. "Yes, but actually *I'm* the one who was shocked last night. That's quite a room full of flowers upstairs."

Trevor chuckled. "I can't imagine what you must have thought. A little over the top, I suppose."

"Yes, but it sounds as if it paid off." She looked at him with expectation.

Olivia glanced toward the kitchen then back at Trevor. "I told you I wanted to tell Ellen our news face to face," she said, her voice hushed. "I just didn't know I'd be telling her last night!"

"Oh, that's right," Ellen half-whispered. "It's all a big secret, isn't it? Mum's the word and all that?"

He reached for Olivia's hand. "It was important to Olivia that you hear it first, so I'm glad you came. But we'd rather give it some time before we tell the folks here. That will give *us* some time to make our plans without all of Caden Cove chiming in."

"It's definitely a small town," Olivia added. "Word travels around here at warp speed."

"I'm sure it does. Whatever happened about that whole legend thing you told me about?"

Olivia looked at Trevor. Trevor looked at Ellen. Ellen looked back and forth between them.

"A bunch of silliness, nothing more," Trevor said. "Though it occurred to me last night that our marriage might finally put the crazy thing to rest."

"I hadn't realized that either, but you're right," Olivia said. "Who knew you and I would be the ones to 'break the curse'?"

Trig and Michelle returned with their food. "Who's going to break the curse?" Michelle asked, eyeing them with curiosity.

"Oh, nothing." Olivia shrugged. "I'd told Ellen about the legend of the Catherine Room, and we were—"

"—just joking around," Trevor teased, hoping to change the subject. "This smells and looks heavenly. You two have outdone yourselves."

"These muffins are amazing, Trig," Olivia added. "The burst of orange, the tartness of cranberries . . . *so* good. And I love the light sugar crust on top, don't you, Ellen?"

Ellen nodded with a tight smile as she finished a bite.

"Good!" Trig said, wiping his hands on his apron. "The frittatas are right out of the oven, so let them cool just a sec. Let us know if you need anything, okay? Otherwise, enjoy!" he said, following his wife out of the room.

Ellen wiped her mouth with her napkin then placed it back in her lap. "Trevor, I have to admit I was stunned at Olivia's news. And I have to be completely honest with you in that I'm concerned. She told me you've never been married?"

"Yes, that's right."

"And why is that?"

He looked at Olivia then back to Ellen. "For the same reason Olivia never married. The right person never came along." He smiled back at Olivia. "Until now."

"I get that. I do," Ellen said, buttering half of her muffin. "I'm just curious why, after all these years, in a matter of just a few days, you meet Olivia and suddenly decide she's the one. May I ask you a rather personal question?"

"Sure. I have no secrets. Ask away."

"What is your financial status?"

"Ellen!" Olivia coughed. "That's none of your business. How could you—"

"He said I could ask him."

Trevor waved his hand. "It's okay. Really, Olivia. She's your best friend. She's looking out for you. If your father were still living, I'd expect the same kind of questions from him. And I'm sure if I were in Ellen's shoes, I'd be concerned as well."

He gave her his full attention. "I'm quite comfortable, financially. My home is paid for. I have a quite lucrative income from my real estate ventures. My bookstore does well during the season, and I also invest in rare books. So to answer your question, my financial status is good. I should be able to provide for Olivia just fine."

Olivia glared at her friend then stabbed at a strawberry and ate it.

"That's good to know. And thank you for understanding why I asked. I'm assuming she's told you about the m—"

"Ellen!" Olivia snapped, dropping her fork on her plate with a loud clatter.

Ellen raised her hands in innocence. "What? I just wanted to make sure he wasn't marrying you for your—"

"Stop!" Olivia scoffed a nervous laughter. "Who are you, my *mother*? Why are you being so rude?"

Ellen glared at her. "Because I need to know."

Silence.

Trevor held his breath, wishing he could slip from the room unnoticed and let the two of them duke it out. Instead, he folded his napkin and placed it beside his plate. "I'm sorry, but am I missing something here?"

"You mean you don't know?"

"Know what?"

Ellen turned to Olivia. "Surely you told him about—"

"Ellen!" she growled in a low whisper.

"You mean—"

"Yes."

"He doesn't—"

"No."

Both women went silent again. Olivia closed her eyes, shaking her head. Ellen, on the other hand, looked at him—differently. The steely glare seemed to be melting away before his eyes, her features softening. She covered her mouth for a moment then quietly reached over and grabbed his hand.

"Oh, Trevor, forgive me. I'm . . . I just thought that . . . I am so, so sorry."

"For what?"

Ellen shielded her face with her other hand. "Ohmigosh, I'm such a jerk."

Olivia rolled her eyes and offered him a sad smile.

Trevor leaned back in his chair. "Ladies, I have no clue what you're talking about. Could someone please tell me what's going on?"

Ellen sat up, pulling her hand free to push her hair out of her face. "Trevor, I've been *completely* out of line, and I am so embarrassed. The thing is, Olivia is family to me. And last night when she told me she'd accepted your proposal, I thought she'd lost her mind. She came up here to—well, never mind that now. To be honest, I think *I'm* the one who's lost her mind. I couldn't believe, after all these years, she'd finally met someone and fallen in love! But for reasons we won't get into just now, I was afraid you couldn't possibly be right for her. As if *I* had to approve of whomever she gave her heart to! I know that sounds silly, but quite clearly I'm just a selfish shrew who thinks the world should rotate the way I say it should."

Trevor laughed quietly. "Somehow I doubt you're a selfish shrew. Sounds to me as if you were simply looking out for a dear friend. And I find that quite admirable."

Olivia wiped away new tears. "Hush, Trevor. Let her grovel."

Ellen started to laugh, but a sob caught in her throat. "I'm a horrible, horrible person. Olivia, I'm so sorry." She stood up and grabbed Olivia, lifting her into a hug. A moment later she motioned for Trevor to join them. "Group hug. I need to know you both forgive me, or I'll never be able to forgive myself."

Trevor joined them in the awkward three-way hug.

"There now. All better," Ellen quipped, sniffling.

As they took their seats again, Trevor cleared his throat. "I'm not sure what all Olivia has told you, Ellen, but there's something I think you need to know." He reached for Olivia's hand again. "When this beautiful lady walked into my bookstore a couple weeks ago, I had no idea how my life was about to change. She was charming and funny, and not in the least put off by my gruff and sometimes arrogant manner."

"Sometimes?" Olivia asked.

He laughed. "Very funny."

"I thought so. But please. Continue."

"What I'm trying to tell you is that Olivia broke through a barrier I'd carefully constructed around my heart. And what makes that even more astounding is that she wasn't even aware she was doing it. Suddenly, I found myself thinking about her constantly and wanting to be with her. But even more important, wanting to be *worthy* of her." He reached for Olivia's hand.

"But I'm a stubborn man, set in my ways. And after our rather nasty 'bumping of the heads' on the way back from Boston, I thought perhaps I'd just saved myself a lifetime of frustration by putting an end to it. Instead, I was *miserable.* I couldn't eat or sleep. I couldn't even think straight. I was a mess. And I realized I could never go back to being that pathetic man I used to be. I wanted to be worthy of her. Whatever it takes."

He started, then stopped and took a moment to compose himself.

"Before I knew it, I found myself on my knees, asking God to give me one more chance with her," he continued. "I hadn't been on my knees in prayer like that since I was just a kid. And it was as if . . . somehow, in the process, the Lord did something to my heart. He changed me. And for the first time, I realized I wanted nothing more than to surrender my life to Him."

By now, his tears streamed down his face, but he didn't care. "Ellen, it's so important to me that you know how much I love Olivia. And how incredibly honored I am that she's agreed to marry me. And that you never need worry about my devotion to her. Ever. It would mean the world to me—to *us*—if you'd give us your blessing."

By then, Ellen wasn't just crying, she was sobbing. She jumped up, waved him up as well, then bear-hugged him again. "Yes, oh yes." She pulled back then took his face in her hands. "You have my blessing, Trevor." She kissed his cheek then dove for a hug into Olivia's open arms.

"My goodness, was it something you ate?"

They turned to find Michelle joining them with a carafe of coffee.

"No, nothing like that," Olivia said, wiping her eyes. "Just one of those moments in time you know you'll never forget."

"I'll have to tell Trig his frittata was over the top. It'll make his day!" She refilled all their coffees, then cleared away their dishes and headed for the kitchen.

"I have a wonderful idea," Trevor said, wrapping his hands around the warm mug. "As soon as we finish here, why don't we go to my house. We can introduce Ellen to Charlie and—"

"Charlie? She's your King Charles Cavalier, right?"

"Yes, but how do you know about Charlie?"

"I might have mentioned her a few times to Ellen over the phone," Olivia teased.

"I see. What other things have you told Ellen? Anything I should know?"

"In good time, Trevor. In good time."

Chapter 21

After two fun-filled days with Ellen, Olivia and Trevor drove her to the airport in Boston. The three of them talked non-stop until Ellen said her tearful goodbyes and disappeared into Logan International. On the way back, Trevor released Olivia's hand only when they stopped at the toll gates.

And not once did they butt heads about Trevor's driving.

Progress.

"Trevor, this is probably as good a time as any. The other morning at breakfast, Ellen alluded to something I haven't yet told you."

"I wondered what that was all about."

"I know. But it's something I needed to tell you one-on-one."

"Sounds serious."

"It is. But in a good way. Something rather extraordinary happened to me not long before I came up here. Years ago when I first started my job as a loan officer at my bank, a young man came to see me one day . . ."

Olivia told him the story of John Emerson Winthrop, the young man she'd given a small loan to years ago. She told him of the letter she received from Winthrop's attorney, their meeting the next day, and the check he'd handed her at Winthrop's request.

She paused, unsure how to go on.

"Don't leave me hanging. How much was the check for?"

She cleared her throat. "Five million."

His head jerked toward her. "What?!"

"Eyes on the road, mister." She laughed and gently nudged his jaw toward the front. "Don't make me have to take the wheel from you. We don't want to go *there* again, right?"

His bewildered eyes tore away from her as his mouth fell open.

"I know. It's a lot to comprehend, isn't it?"

He nodded slowly curling his fingers around the steering wheel. "Five *million* dollars?"

"Yes. Five million. Granston put it in an interest-earning account for me until I decide what to do. Which is why I came to Caden Cove in the first place. I needed to get away and think about it. Decide what I wanted to do with the rest of my life. Then I met you and everyone else, and I put all those thoughts on hold. Until now."

"Olivia, why didn't you tell me before?"

"I wanted to. I thought about it. But it never seemed like the right time, and I didn't know *how* to tell you. Then you proposed, and I didn't want to spoil the moment. I just wasn't sure how you'd respond. But I would have told you, Trevor. And long before we said our vows. Just so you know."

"Then along came Ellen."

Olivia laughed. "Yes, along came Ellen. But you know what? I'm glad. Her impromptu diatribe at breakfast the other day was just the push I needed. Obviously. And here we are now, finally talking about it."

"Wow." He kept his eyes on the road, his head slowly nodding.

"It's okay if you want to talk about it. I would never want this to be a problem between us. I'd just as soon give it all away than have that happen."

"You would?"

"In a heartbeat. I've always heard about people who win the lottery, and then it ruins their lives. I don't want to be one of them."

"I think I need some time to process it. Don't get me wrong—it's not a bad thing. It's just quite . . . *surreal.* If that makes sense."

"Trust me. I understand completely."

Later, as they neared Caden Cove, he reached for her hand. "A subject change, if that's all right with you."

"By all means."

"I didn't want to bring it up while Ellen was here, but tomorrow I need to drive up to the Sullivan estate near Bangor to get the books I won on the auction. I was actually supposed to go yesterday, but I asked if they could reschedule me for tomorrow. It's the last day the estate is open, so I've got to go. If you'd still like to come, I'd love to have you join me."

"I'd love to! Is it a day trip or will we—"

"It's about a two-hour drive, but we talked previously about making a day of it. I could stop by the inn for breakfast with you, then afterward get on the road. My appointment is at 1:00, so we'd have plenty of time to drive up to Bangor. There are some nice art galleries there and some historic sites you might enjoy. Then if we're hungry, we could grab a bite before heading down to the estate which is twenty miles south. It shouldn't take more than half an hour to settle my account and pack up the books, then we can head back. How does that sound?"

"Perfect. Absolutely perfect."

The next morning, Olivia was putting on her earrings when Trevor called.

"Olivia, I'm afraid we have a change of plans. When the wind blows hard like this, I often lose my power, which is what happened about an hour ago. It wouldn't be a problem except that Charlie is acting a bit strange. In all the excitement lately, I'd simply lost track of her due date, which isn't until next week at the earliest. I remember Celeste—our veterinarian—telling me that small breeds like Charlie can sometimes go into labor early, but . . ."

"What do you need me to do, Trevor? How can I help?"

"Would you be terribly disappointed to skip the trip to Bangor and stay with Charlie today?"

"Not at all. But with your power out, would it be better for you to bring her here?"

"That's what I was thinking. I would take her to Celeste, but she's out of town. Her service said she's due back late tonight. I left a voice mail so she'll know what's going on."

"I'm sure Charlie will be fine here."

Half an hour later, Trevor brought Charlie in her crate to the Captain MacVicar. Trig and Michelle assured him they'd be there to help if there was a problem. Trevor knelt down to gently scratch behind Charlie's ears and promise her he'd be back as soon as possible. Olivia walked him to the door.

"Don't worry, Trevor. We'll go online and see what we need to do if she goes into labor. If anything happens, I'll call you."

"I'm hoping if I get there early, they might be able to squeeze me in ahead of schedule. Otherwise, I'll just wait there until they can get to me. At the latest I should be back by two or two-thirty."

He pulled her into his arms and held her close. "Thank you. I know she's just a dog, but—"

"She's your girl and this is a special time. No apologies necessary."

"You're good to have around, you know that?"

With a final hug and kiss from Olivia, he dashed to the SUV and left.

Trig suggested they leave Charlie in the living room, so they placed her crate in a corner near the fireplace. Olivia changed into comfortable clothes and brought her laptop downstairs with her.

"You just take it easy and get some rest, Charlie. I'll be right here if you need me."

The dog seemed agitated, pawing at her flannel blanket repeatedly before circling around in her crate and settling down. Olivia went online to find out what they might need in case Charlie went into labor. She learned that expectant mothers like to nest and often drag all kinds of clothing or towels into a dark place. Olivia got some old towels from Michelle and a small quilt to put over the crate. Trig went out to the garage to find a large cardboard box in case things progressed. He cut the top off then cut an opening on one side.

"We have an extra thermometer upstairs," he said. "We'll need to watch her temperature. If it drops down to 100 degrees, that'll let us know she's about eight or ten hours away from delivering her pups."

"You sound as if you've been through this before."

"We always had dogs around when I was growing up. Some do great delivering their pups and pretty much do it without any outside help. Others can struggle. I'll feel a lot better when Celeste gets back in town."

The rest of the morning dragged by. It was snowing again, but Olivia found no pleasure in it. She read for a while, then browsed online to catch up on the news. Ellen called just before lunch and they talked for half an hour. Afterward, she stretched out on the sofa not far from Charlie's crate and eventually dozed off.

Around one-thirty, Charlie started whimpering and scratching at her blanket again. Trig decided to check her temperature just to be on the safe side. It registered just below 102° which meant she could go into labor at any time. He and Olivia carefully moved her into the well-padded cardboard box and covered it with the quilt. Charlie circled round and round, pushing the towels here then there, all the while whimpering and panting.

Olivia decided to call Trevor and check in with him. The phone rang several times then went to voice mail. Assuming he was settling up at the estate, she left a message asking him to call when he could. She tried again at two, wondering why he hadn't called and again got voice mail.

"Sometimes it's hard to get cell service when you're on the road," Michelle suggested.

"You're probably right. The estate where he was going was out in the country. I'm sure that's what has happened."

Another hour crept by. Outside the snow was blowing harder. She had the fleeting thought that perhaps Trevor had hit another patch of black ice . . . then rolled her eyes, chiding herself for conjuring up unnecessary fear. She knelt beside Charlie's makeshift bed and watched her sleep, her paws twitching now and then. "Don't worry, sweetie," she whispered. "You'll do just fine."

At three-thirty, Olivia got back online and started searching for a number for the Maxwell Sullivan Estate. She knew the private home number wouldn't be listed, so she typed in "book auctions Maxwell Sullivan" and bingo—a webpage appeared. Scrolling down she found a number for the company that handled the auction and made the call.

After being put on hold several times, she finally got through to the secretary of the auction company and asked how she might reach Trevor Bass who was picking up some books at the estate.

"I'm so glad you called! This is Ginger Fredricks. We've been trying to reach Mr. Bass for several hours. He never showed up for his books, and we're about to close. Do you have a number where we might reach him?"

A haunting wave drifted over Olivia. She held the cell phone against her forehead and tried to think, taking slow, careful breaths. Trevor should have been to the estate by no later than eleven. If he'd had car trouble, surely he would have called. Then again, as Michelle said, cell service could be spotty along the road.

"Hello?"

"Yes, I'm sorry. This is Olivia Thomas, a friend of Trevor's. He left here around nine this morning. He planned to get there early, so I don't understand why he's not there." She shook off the fear knotting in her stomach. "Ginger, let me make some calls and get back to you. Could I have your direct number?" She wrote it down then hung up.

"He never got there?" Michelle asked, taking a seat beside her.

"No, but . . ." She looked at Michelle then up at Trig. "Something's wrong. I have a really bad feeling. What should I do? Who should I call?"

Michelle put an arm around her. "Don't jump to conclusions. I'm sure he's fine. Probably just car trouble or something."

"Let me give Sheriff Sampson a call," Trig said. "Maybe he can tell us what we need to do. Or maybe he can call someone up in that area. I'll be right back."

A few minutes later, Trig returned snaking his arms into his coat. "They said Sampson is over at Molly's. They were going to connect me to him, but I'm going to jog down there and talk to him in person."

Olivia jumped up. "I'm coming with you."

Michelle stood. "You should probably stay here, Olivia. Trig can bring the sheriff back."

"No, I want to go. I have to go. I can't just sit here."

"Okay, if that's what you want to do. I'll keep an eye on Charlie."

Olivia ran upstairs for her coat, overwhelmed by the heavy scent of roses filling her room. She swallowed hard, refusing to give in to her emotion. *God, please keep him safe. Wherever he is, please make sure he's okay.*

Chapter 22

By four-thirty, Olivia was still seated at the coffee bar at Molly's. The sheriff said he would make some calls, but couldn't promise anything since they had no evidence that he was "a missing person as such." Over and over she'd explained how concerned Trevor had been about Charlie going into labor, how anxious he was to get back, and how unlikely he'd go this long without calling. Only Molly's constant assurances kept her from losing her temper with the town's laid-back sheriff before he finally headed back to the station.

"Maybe I should just go look for him myself. At least I'd know *someone* was out there trying to find him."

"Not in this kind of weather, Olivia. The roads will be a mess by now."

She thought back to the night she and Trevor quarreled about the black ice, remembering how the SUV had swerved out of control. "How come Trevor didn't tell me there was more snow in the forecast? Why would he take off knowing there was a chance the roads might ice over again?"

"I don't know," Molly said. "Though it's no secret Trevor's been known to have a bit of a stubborn streak."

"I know, but why wouldn't he . . ."

"Why wouldn't he what?"

Olivia stared at the older woman, though she knew the answer to her own question. Between the long day which ended with his proposal, then Ellen's visit, and all the commotion over Charlie, it probably never crossed Trevor's mind to check the forecast. She swallowed hard.

"Oh, nothing." She turned to look out the windows. "I just wish he'd call."

Her cell chirped and she scrabbled for it in her pocket. The number on the screen wasn't one she recognized. "Hello?"

"Is this Olivia?"

"Yes, it is."

"This is Ginger Fredricks with the Archibald Book Auction Corporation."

"Oh, yes, Ginger! Did he show up? Is Trevor there?"

"No, I'm sorry, he hasn't. I was hoping you'd heard from him by now."

Olivia searched for calm. "No, we've heard nothing. To be honest, I'm worried sick."

"I'm so sorry. I wonder . . . I might be able to pull some strings on this end and get the police here to look into it."

"We haven't had much luck with that on *this* end," Olivia groaned. Sheriff Sampson had returned earlier, trying to convince her that no news was good news. She pinned him with a glare.

"Are you there, Olivia?"

"Oh, sorry. Yes, I'm here, Ginger. What were you saying?"

"My dad is the police chief in Bangor. With your permission, I'd like to call him and—"

"Yes! Oh yes! Please! That would be wonderful!"

"He carries a lot of clout up here, and needless to say, he's in a position to make things happen. If it's okay with you, I'll give him your name and number and have him call you."

"Of course! Please have him call me. And thank you so much, Ginger!"

When she hung up, she filled Molly in on Ginger's offer to call her father. She looked around, surprised to see so many townspeople milling around the shop, all of them listening to her conversation.

Sheriff Sampson approached her. "Miss Thomas, you should have given her *my* contact information."

She ignored him, and turning back to Molly, lowered her voice. "Molly, why are all these people here?"

"Always happens on a snowy day. Plus, I'm sure word has spread about Trevor."

Trig returned from the MacVicar and assured her Charlie was doing fine and not to worry.

Scott and Mavis Randolphson showed up, carrying on about the snow, but Olivia was sure they were here because of Trevor.

Ten minutes later, Chief Fredricks called. Molly motioned her back to her office where she'd have more privacy. For the next fifteen minutes, Chief Fredricks asked her questions concerning Trevor's vehicle, make and model, the last time she talked to him, his planned route to and from the Bangor area, and Trevor's cell number. His kind voice and easy manner helped her relax.

"We'll alert all the law enforcement agencies up here to be on the lookout for Trevor's SUV, and I'll have the Highway Patrol search the roads between Caden Cove and Bangor. I'll have someone from my office stay in touch with you at least once an hour. We'll do our best to find him, Miss Thomas."

Olivia asked Molly if she could stay in her office a while longer. "I still don't understand why all those people are out there. They aren't shopping. Why come out in this weather for a cup of coffee? Don't these people have lives?"

Molly pulled up a chair alongside Olivia's. "They're here because they care about Trevor."

Olivia raked her fingers up the back of her neck into her hair. "I'm sorry, Molly. I've been so blindsided by all this, I guess I forgot that you all have known him a lot longer than I have. How selfish of me."

Molly squeezed Olivia's hand. "You're not selfish; you care for Trevor in a special way. Any fool can see that."

Olivia averted her eyes, brushing imaginary lint from her sweater. "He means the world to me. More than you know."

Mimi Overton burst into the office like a purple tornado, short of breath. "I just heard the news about Trevor! Why didn't anyone call me? The whole town's out there and nobody called me? I was at home watching the news when they said I-95 was shut down because of a twenty-car pileup! I called Marilyn to tell her, and she told me everyone was here. Oh dear Lord, I hope he's not in that pileup!"

Olivia stood. "When? How long ago did the accident happen?"

"Let me think. They said it happened just half an hour ago. Just in time for the evening traffic. And now that the sun is setting, oh my Lord, what a mess. You should see the footage from the news helicopter."

Olivia dropped back into her chair. "Then Trevor can't be involved in that. We first realized he was missing earlier this morning."

"Oh, Olivia. Don't you worry. They'll find him. If I know Trevor, he's probably lost track of time wandering in the library up there. Or maybe he ran into an old friend or just—"

"Mimi, would you mind checking on everybody out front?" Molly asked. "See if you can ask Cyndi to put on another pot of coffee."

"Sure thing. I'll let you know if there's any more news."

"That girl is a whirling dervish if ever there was one," Molly mused as the door closed behind her.

Olivia rubbed her eyes. "I just can't believe this."

Molly sat back down. "Talk to me. It will help. I promise you."

Olivia took a moment then looked up at her. "Molly, we haven't told anyone here but . . . well, the other night Trevor proposed to me." Her eyes filled before the words were out of her mouth.

"Really? What wonderful news! How lovely—for both of you!" She leaned over to give Olivia a hug. "Of course, I had an inkling that something was going on."

"You did?"

"Let's just say, a man doesn't order a dozen roses in every color unless it's a special occasion. We were all dying to know why all those florist trucks kept pulling up to the MacVicar. In a town this small, that's practically front-page news."

"Oh, *please* tell me it's not!?"

"No, not really. Fact is, everyone I know was hoping you and Trevor might find true love."

"Whoa. This *is* a small town. You all need to find some hobbies."

The sweet melody of Molly's laughter eased the ache in Olivia's heart. She leaned her head on Molly's shoulder. "What will I do if they can't find him?" she said, sniffling. "Before we could even say our vows, it feels like he's been snatched away. What will I do?"

Molly rocked her gently back and forth. "There now. Don't you give up on him. Like I said before, your Trevor can be a stubborn one at times. Whatever has happened, you know he'll move mountains to get back to . . ."

Molly stopped rocking. Olivia heard a quiet gasp and sat up. Molly's trembling hand covered her mouth.

"Molly? What's wrong? You look as if you've seen a ghost."

Molly closed her eyes for a moment. "Olivia? Do you know what day it is?"

"Well, sure. It's Wednesday. Why?"

She opened her eyes and reached for Olivia's hand. "No, I mean what day of the month it is."

"It's . . . I don't know, the twenty-seventh? Twenty-eighth?"

"No, dear. It's February 29th."

"Okay. So?"

Molly shook her head. "Don't you remember?"

Olivia studied her friend's worried eyes. "I don't under—" She stopped, then sat up straight. "Wait—this isn't about that silly legend, is it?"

"Olivia—"

"Oh, please," she groaned, standing. "You've got to be kidding me. At a time like this? With Trevor missing? Why would you bring up that stupid myth?"

"It's *because* Trevor's missing that I bring it up. Don't you see? You're still staying in the Catherine Room at the MacVicar. You're engaged to be married. And now, on the last day of February in this leap year, your fiancé is missing."

Olivia dropped her head back and raised her hands in refusal. "Honestly, Molly, just stop it! I don't want to hear any more about that ridiculous curse. Of all the people in this town, you're the *last* person I'd ever expect to be so gullible."

"Yet, of all the people in this town, I have more reason to believe it than anyone else."

Olivia crossed her arms across her chest. "Why? What are you talking about?"

"Sit down. I need to tell you something."

Olivia wondered if the old pharmacist might be losing it. She walked back to her chair and sat down again. "All right. Tell me."

Molly closed her eyes. "When I was twenty years old, I was engaged to marry a handsome young man I'd met at college. Gregory was a couple of years older than me, which meant he was eligible for the draft into the military. So we put off our wedding plans until he finished his tour of duty. Gregory eventually ended up in Vietnam. I don't think I slept through a night the entire time he was there. I was so afraid of losing him.

"He lost so many of his army buddies along the way. It was such a terrible war, as they all are, of course. But not long after the first of the year in 1968, we got word Gregory would be home sometime around the first week of March. I was so relieved. We set our wedding date for March 15th. I could hardly wait.

"Then, the second week of February, a fire burned more than half our family home. The owners of the MacVicar were friends of ours and insisted we stay at the inn until our home was rebuilt." She paused, emotion shadowing her eyes. "Which is how I ended up a guest in the Catherine Room just weeks before my wedding.

"Oh, Molly," Olivia whispered. "I don't think I can bear to hear this."

Molly nodded with understanding. "But you must. You see, just a few days before Gregory was due home, I was awakened with news that he and four others had been killed in a rocket attack on the helicopter ferrying them to the base where they were to catch a flight home."

"And it happened on the 29th?"

"Yes. I was the last guest in the Catherine to lose my betrothed. Yet every four years, when leap year rolls around, we all still hold our breath, wondering—"

"Which is why they're all here."

"Yes." Molly grabbed her hand. "They're all out there holding vigil. For *you*, Olivia."

Chapter 23

Around 6:00, Carla Reynolds brought over several tins of fresh baked cookies from The Fussy Muffin.

"I felt so helpless when I heard about Trevor. Baking is my therapy. Eat up while they're still warm."

Just a few minutes after seven, Anthony sent over half a dozen pizzas from his restaurant with a note offering his prayers for Trevor's safe return.

Olivia appreciated the gestures, but she wished they'd all just leave . . . and then winced at such an unkind thought. They were only here because they cared.

They care, but are they also holding a collective breath about the legend? They might not know she and Trevor were engaged, but they all knew she and Trevor had been seeing each other. They also knew what room she occupied at the MacVicar. It still seemed so ridiculous.

Then again . . .

Exhausted, Olivia felt the weight of her head in her hands. Was it possible the "curse" could be real? Was it merely a coincidence that Molly's story fit the same tragic pattern of so many others who'd stayed in that room before her?

What had Trevor said about it?

Nothing but a bunch of silly suspicions without a shred of truth to them. Anyone with an ounce of sanity knows it's preposterous. A handful of coincidences, nothing more."

How like him to scoff at something so "silly."

And yet, he thought it worthy enough to research for a book he was writing about the history of Caden Cove.

She raked her fingers through her hair again, none of it making any sense.

Trig and Michelle returned, slipping back to the office to check on her. She tried to dam her endless tears, but the mere presence of these two reminded her of the good-hearted townspeople.

"Celeste got back in town about half an hour ago," Trig said. "She came by the inn and checked on Charlie."

"How's Charlie doing?"

"She's okay," Michelle said. "Celeste thinks it could be any time. And with everything else going on, she insisted on taking Charlie to her clinic. Trig helped her transport Charlie over there."

"And you're sure she's okay, Trig?"

"She's in good hands. We took the box we fixed for Charlie—Celeste called it a 'birthing box'—and put her in a dark examination room where Celeste can keep an eye on her."

"That's good. Trevor would be so relieved to know."

"Celeste said to tell you she's praying for you and for Trevor."

Olivia nodded her thanks. She'd never even met the woman.

Michelle grabbed both her hands. "There's something else we need to tell you. Molly told us you know all about the legend of the Catherine Room at our inn. We've always been curious about the legacy of all that, but nothing's ever happened since *we've* owned the MacVicar—"

"Although, whenever someone checks in around the end of February during leap year, we always wonder." Trig added. "Especially someone single."

Olivia glanced at Michelle. "Which explains all those curious looks you gave me when I checked in."

Michelle smiled. "Exactly. Still, we've always thought it's more folklore than an actual curse, but still."

"Up until now, we've thought it was nothing more than one of those mysteries people like to speculate about," Trig continued. "Like where Jimmy Hoffa is buried. Or all those rumors that Elvis is still alive."

"Olivia, what we're trying to say is, we don't think for one minute *any* of that has to do with Trevor's disappearance."

"Thank you. Really. To be honest, I don't know what to think anymore. Especially after Molly told me her story. It's all so bizarre."

Trig scratched the back of his head. "Yeah, when I heard about that, I have to admit I started wondering. I mean, it's *Molly.* If she thinks there's something to it, then . . . ?" He shrugged. "I don't know."

"What can we do, Olivia?" Michelle asked, letting go of her hands. "Anything at all. We feel so helpless."

"Making sure Charlie is okay—that's more than enough."

Olivia's cell phone chirped, startling her. She lunged for it and grabbed it off the table. "This is Olivia."

"Olivia, this is Chief Fredricks. I have good news! We found him!"

"What?!" She turned to Michelle and Trig. "They found him! They found Trevor!"

"Is he okay?!" Trig asked.

Molly rushed into the office. "Is there news?"

"Chief Fredricks, is Trevor okay?" Olivia asked. "Is he hurt? What happened? Where *is* he?"

"Take a deep breath, Miss Thomas. I'll answer all your questions. Are you all right?"

"Yes, yes! Please—tell me!"

"Mr. Bass was apparently run off the road by a tractor trailer outside of Waterville, about a hundred miles from you. His vehicle spun out of control and down a pretty steep embankment—"

"No! Is he okay? *Please* tell me he's all right!"

"He's pretty banged up, but they think he'll be fine. He was conscious when the patrolman finally found him. The officer told me Mr. Bass was pinned against the steering column with the driver's door rammed up against a boulder. He literally could not move."

"Where is he now?"

"He was Life-Flighted to St. Joseph's Hospital here in Bangor. We'll get in touch with the ER over there and have them call you directly."

"Thank you *so* much. I can't tell you how much—" Olivia choked up.

"You are most welcome, Miss Thomas. I'm glad this one had a happy ending."

"Me too," she whispered. "Thank you again."

"My pleasure."

Olivia crumbled into Molly's open arms. "He's alive! He's okay! " she cried. "Oh, God, thank You, *thank* You! He's okay, Trevor's okay!"

The news ignited an explosion of laughter and cheers through the store and beyond. With tears flowing freely, the locals welcomed the news that one of their own was alive and well after all.

Olivia joined them, making sure to thank each one. As she warmed to their hugs, it occurred to her that she was no longer a "tourist" to them. She was one of them.

"I knew that silly old curse was a bunch of bull!" Mimi cried.

"Here, here!"

Chapter 24

Eight weeks later

"I now pronounce you man and wife. Trevor, you may kiss your bride."

He obliged, taking Olivia into his arms and bestowing on her a kiss worthy of the long wait. "I love you, *Mrs. Bass*."

She laughed, her eyes brimming with tears of joy. "And I love *you*, Mr. Bass."

Beside her, Ellen beamed as she handed Olivia her bouquet of pale pink roses and calla lilies. The small gathering at the Lord's Chapel cheered them down the short aisle as the organist's hymn sent them on their way.

Ellen and Brent had come a week early to help Olivia and Trevor with final wedding preparations. To no one's surprise, Brent and Trevor hit it off from the moment they met, and he easily stepped into his unexpected role as best man.

They'd postponed their wedding until mid-May to give Trevor plenty of time to recuperate from his injuries. With a couple of broken ribs and a severely banged-up knee, Trevor was determined to be fully recovered for the biggest occasion of his life.

On that frightening day at the end of February, once Olivia heard Trevor had been found, she gratefully accepted a ride up to Bangor with Trig and Michelle. There they'd found him resting in a hospital room, bandaged and bruised, but alive.

And quite medicated.

"Soupy! You came!" Trevor mumbled, his heavy-lidded eyes locking on Olivia as he waved her over with two fingers.

Olivia laughed, coming to his side. "Soupy?" She kissed his purpled-forehead and for the thousandth time, thanked God he was alive. "I don't know who Soupy is, but I'm sure glad to see you." She kissed his lips and struggled against the gravel in her voice. "Oh Trevor, I was so worried about you. So afraid I'd lost you."

He held her hand, lifting it to his lips. "Now, now. None of that. You can see I'm fine. Just fine." He kissed her fingertips, then nodded toward Trig and Michelle. "Does Emma know that Darcy there is a pompous a—"

"Whoa there, buddy! I think you've got your Austen characters mixed up there, but alas—no Emmas and no Mr. Darcys in the room. That's Trig and Michelle from the MacVicar. You know them, right?"

"Some lazy yummy breakfast crepes filled with hot dog relish."

Olivia turned to them, rolling her eyes and lips pressed together.

"Or is it sauerkraut?" he pondered.

Trig laughed as he carefully shook Trevor's good hand. "Hello, Trevor. Next time you stop by, you'll have to try some of my *mackerel* mousse." He winked at Olivia." Or maybe some *bass* beignets?"

"Oh? Well, perhaps . . . ?"

"How are you, Trevor? You had us all pretty scared."

"I did?"

Michelle patted Trevor's arm. "Yes, everyone gathered at Molly's waiting news of you. It was like that scene in *The Perfect Storm* where all the locals are waiting at the pub to hear what happened to George Clooney and Mark Wahlberg on the *Andrea Gail*."

Trevor offered a goofy smile. "I knew an Andrea once. Dreadful acne. And a wandering eye. Though I don't recall if it was her left eye or right eye?"

Olivia brushed Trevor's hair back from his forehead. "I think someone needs to sleep off his meds."

He beckoned her with his fingers again then whispered loudly. "Aren't you that beautiful girl I'm going to marry?"

"Yes, that's me. Sleep well and dream of tiers and tiers of wedding cake."

Three days later, they transported Trevor back to Caden Cove where the locals smothered him with get well wishes, flowers, and food. Back at home, he welcomed Charlie and her five little pups which proved to be tremendous therapy for him. Of course, he couldn't care for them all on his own. Olivia stayed with him, only leaving for the MacVicar when he was tucked in bed for the night and returning before he woke up the next morning.

Trevor grew stronger with each passing day. He and Olivia took walks as soon as he was able. With her help, he kept abbreviated hours at the bookstore, catching up on business and preparing for the upcoming tourist season. Out of necessity, he hired Mimi Overton to help out the rest of the summer until school was back in session.

At home, they cooked together, played with Charlie's pups, and fell in love a little more every day.

Olivia made a brief trip back to Atlanta to quit her job, wrap up some loose ends, and finalize her wedding plans with Ellen. Back in Caden Cove, she and Trevor eagerly crossed days off the calendar.

Then, the night before their wedding, following a brief rehearsal at the church and dinner at Trevor's for the small wedding party, the groom-to-be walked the bride-to-be out to the fire pit off his deck. There, he surprised her with his wedding present—two tickets for a four-week honeymoon cruise in the Mediterranean, leaving a week after the wedding. Olivia couldn't stop smiling, still finding it hard to believe they would soon take such an unforgettable trip—as husband and wife. She thanked him, kissed him, and buried her head against his chest, still bewildered how it all happened.

But in the deepest corners of her heart, she still wondered if it was all too good to be true. She had waited so long. No, that wasn't right. She stopped waiting years ago, quite sure she would live a long and happy life—alone. She knew it was wrong, this doubt that still niggled through her at the strangest times. Like now. In his arms, the night before they married. Would it really happen? Would they have a long and happy life—together?

And there it was. The faint yet familiar haunting that snaked its way through her veins again and constricted her heart. Olivia had never been a doubter, but no amount of self-talk could eradicate the absurd, lingering fear.

Even worse, she knew where it came from.

When Trevor disappeared on February 29th, the day after he'd proposed, she'd teetered on the edge of a legendary cliff. She'd come *so close* to fulfilling the strange prophecy of those who'd gone before her. Yes, they'd all sighed in relief when he was found and nervously acknowledged the irrationality of the so-called curse. Still, it had planted seeds of doubt in her heart.

Silly, all of it. And yet it burned like an ashen ember not easily doused.

Shaking off the frustration, she grabbed hold of Trevor's hands. "My gift to you isn't something I could wrap. In fact, it's something that requires your approval. But nothing else would please me more."

"Sounds serious."

"It is, but in the best of ways. I've given this a great deal of thought, just so you know. And I've decided to use the majority of the money I was given by Mr. Winthrop as seed money to start a foundation for people suffering from traumatic injuries. And with your permission, I'd like to call it Evan's Place."

He stared at her in disbelief—that much she could see in his eyes. "I don't know what to say . . . how could, I mean, why would you . . ."

"Because what happened to Evan profoundly affected your life,

Trevor. You said it yourself, how his injuries drove him mad, and how helpless you felt through it all. But what if he'd had a caring environment, surrounded by those who know best how to give him another chance at life? What if he'd had faith-based counselors who knew how to help him work through his emotional pain and get him healthy again? No, we can't help everyone like Evan, but we can start by helping a few. We can give hope to the hopeless, Trevor. What a perfect way to use this money!"

She smiled as she brushed away the tear trailing down his cheek. "We don't need all that money. Others do. The possibilities are endless. Please say yes. Nothing would make me happier."

He pulled her into his arms and rocked her gently. "My sweet Olivia. I'm totally speechless."

She held him tight, pressing her ear against his heart. "Then I'll take that as a yes."

Even at her age, Olivia felt like a princess. Through both the wedding and reception that followed, it all seemed like a dream. The simple, elegant décor of the quaint chapel. The intimate gathering of friends. The exchange of vows against the glow of candlelight. The organist's majestic recessional as they made their way back down the aisle.

At the reception under a white tent on Trevor's back lawn, the new bride kept waiting to awaken from her dream. A string quartet provided the perfect background through their catered dinner, and later played a sentimental version of "The Way You Look Tonight" as she and Trevor shared the traditional first dance.

All of it, the stuff of dreams.

But nothing could prepare her for what followed.

After tossing her bouquet, Olivia wondered why Trevor called for everyone's attention. When the murmuring settled down, he announced a surprise ending to the day's festivities requiring everyone's assistance.

"If you'll look just down the beach toward the harbor, you'll notice several boats at the ready, all decked out with strings of lights. I'd like to ask you to join us there where we'll all board a wedding flotilla of sorts. Then, with the captains at the helms of those vessels, we'll make our way out on a short voyage for a special presentation."

Against the curious chatter of their guests, Olivia tilted her head. "Trevor, what's this all about?"

"You'll just have to trust me, Mrs. Bass." He gave her a wink, took her hand in his, and led her toward the paved pathway.

"Come along!" he shouted to the others. "You won't want to miss this!"

Half an hour later, as the sun flirted with dusk, the flotilla arrived at a location half a mile off the coast. The crewman on board each of the boats loosely roped the five vessels together, the back decks forming a bobbing circle. Off the deck of the largest, a yacht belonging to Anthony, Trevor stood before Olivia, holding up a beautifully wrapped box.

"Ladies and gentlemen, Olivia and I will never forget how you honored us today with your presence as we begin our life together. Now, with the waves gently rolling beneath us, it occurs to me that we're all part of a floating 'theater in the round,' if you will. And together in this moment, we're about to make history here off the shore of Caden Cove. What you are about to witness will offer both rest to souls gone by and a blessed peace for our future."

He handed her the box. "Olivia, if you would do the honors?"

With a slight shake of her head, she complied. "Yes, but I have to say, as a little girl dreaming of my some-day wedding, never once did I envision standing on the back of a yacht in the Atlantic." A ripple of laughter scattered on the breeze. She placed her hand over his heart. "I'm beginning to wonder if that accident knocked a few screws loose in your head, Trevor."

He placed a kiss on her lips. "No more talk. Open it."

Olivia pulled the ribbon off the box and handed him the lid. From inside, she removed an object wrapped in thick layers of tissue paper. Trevor held the box as she carefully unwrapped the paper—and gasped.

Along with everyone else.

In her hand, the familiar blue and white teacup from the Catherine Room at the MacVicar.

"Trevor?"

"There's more." From the bottom of the box, he handed her another tissue-wrapped object. As the paper fell away, he placed the matching saucer beneath the cup she held.

"I don't understand."

He cupped his hands beneath hers. "For well over a century, we've wondered about the mysteries that began on February 29th, 1828, when Captain MacVicar and two of his crewmen lost their lives in the general vicinity where we're now moored. As you know, the mysteries have continued to haunt our little town. Over the years, on six different occasions on the 29th of February, tragedy struck the occupant in the Catherine Room at the MacVicar. Their circumstances may have differed, but each of those young women lost the love of their lives.

He turned to his right where Molly stood beside him. "And for some, the tragedy hit much too close to home."

She responded with a nod and a quivering smile.

"Mere coincidence? Perhaps. But the common thread they shared evolved into a legacy of both heartache and speculation about a 'curse'."

Trevor turned back to Olivia. "But today, with these dear friends as witnesses, we shall bid farewell to the legend once and for all."

In one swift motion, he raised their hands up and over the edge of the boat, sending the cup and saucer splashing into the water.

A collective astonished gasp skittered around them.

"Trevor, what have you done?" she cried.

A strangely hushed reverence descended on them, no one saying a word. Olivia and the others leaned over to watch as the cup and saucer slowly disappeared in the water.

Her voice overcome with sorrow, she faced him again. "Why did you do that?"

He tenderly gathered her into his arms. "Because I'm freeing you from fear. I'm freeing *all* of us from fear. And I'm promising you, Olivia, before everyone here, that no myth or curse or legend will ever befall you. And I will *never* leave you."

"Yes, but why—"

"Why?" Pressing his fingers against her lips, he silenced her protests. "Because in times such as these, I've learned the value of releasing that which is of great worth. . . to gain that which is priceless."

Epilogue

The End

I sat there holding my breath, my hands still suspended over my keyboard. Could I really end the story there? *Was* it the end of the legend? They were all there, freeze-framed in my mind, still celebrating in the "floating theater in the round," as Trevor called it.

When he and Olivia tossed the cup overboard, my mind flashed back to the scene at the end of *Titanic* where the old lady version of Kate tiptoed toward the back of the ship, climbed on the rail, and released the "heart of the ocean" necklace into the waters above the wreckage of the RMS *Titanic*. As the brilliant sapphire and diamond jewels of that famous necklace disappeared into the watery grave, so too the *Union First Wreath* cup and saucer floated downward to join the lost pieces of the Spode wedding china Captain MacVicar had bought for his bride.

I pressed my knuckles against my eyes, stemming the pesky tears. I'm such a sap when it comes to these love stories. My brother Chad likes to remind me I'm closer to my story characters than my non-fictional, living and breathing friends. And that's fine. I'm comfortable with these imaginary friends who drift in and out of my life.

But it's always hard to say goodbye. So I pushed back my chair and left the room, already in grief over sending them off to be groomed and tailored for publishing.

As you know by now, this is the part where I normally dance down the hall to the kitchen and break out the ice cream. But if you must know, I'm trying to knock off a few pounds. It's tough for those of us with sedentary careers. Gertie exercises me as often as she can tear me away, but when I'm "in the zone" with my stories, I'm basically superglued to my laptop for days on end. Thus, my ever-expanding gluteus maximus. Which is why I grabbed a carton of peach-flavored Greek yogurt to reward myself for another completed manuscript.

As I leaned against the counter, I purposefully nudged my mind away from Caden Cove. The flora and fauna of the next novella in this series has been traipsing through my mind since the beginning. When I first received the collection of teacups from Aunt Lucille's estate, my writer's block was literally blown out of the water. So many teacups, so little time. Each cup prompting a story, whispering its romantic tale through the muse in my head.

But this one would be different. I'd reserved this particular story as a personal tribute to my favorite aunt and her larger-than-life inspiration in my life. Hers was a love story set against the backdrop of World War II, her handsome fiancé half a world away. I had to get this right. I wanted to give my readers a glimpse into the heart and soul of Lucille Alexander Reynolds. Why? Because she opened my eyes to a whole new world I'd never experienced. Through her gift of storytelling, I learned about colorful characters and personalities, exotic places both near and far, and about the power of love. They became my passion, stretching my imagination to tell my own stories.

The doorbell rang, yanking me back to the real world. I checked the clock on my kitchen wall. Nine-thirty on the nose. Prompt as usual.

"Ma'am, I have a delivery here for a Miss Lucy Alexander. Would that perhaps be you?"

"Why yes, it would," I replied in a sappy Southern belle drawl. I leaned against the doorjamb in my best *come-hither* pose. "How about you come inside, you big brown hunk of gorgeous, and we can unwrap those little ol' boxes together."

He practically doubled over with his guffaw. Have I mentioned how much I like Mark's guffaws? His gasping-for-breath belly laughs? (Though I'm fairly confident that belly of his is ripped. Not that I would know, of course.)

"Oh, Lucy, Lucy, Lucy . . . life was so dull before I met you."

"How's it going, big guy?"

"Pretty good. Finish the geezer love story yet?"

I pinned him with a steely glare. "Forty-somethings are hardly 'geezers,' I'll have you know. They're in the prime of their lives, so cut 'em a little slack, will you?"

He tucked a curl behind my ear. "My apologies. I can't wait to read it."

"Yeah?" I loved that he loved my books.

"Sure. I stocked up on plenty of Bengay and prunes to set the mood when I read it."

I'm quite sure my sucker-punch to his aforementioned ripped belly conveyed my deep appreciation for his sarcasm.

He raised his big mitts in surrender. "Okay, okay! I'm sorry. Just kidding. Listen, I've gotta run. Are we still on for the symphony tonight?"

"Yes, and I can't wait! I'm wearing my sparkly new dress, and I bought you a sparkly new vest to wear, so we can be all matchy-matchy."

Deer in the headlights. I *loved* freaking him out almost as much as I loved his guffaws. Even if it only lasted a millisecond.

"Sweet! Sounds *nifty*. I'll wear my brown leather pants. An ensemble. Trust me, I'll be *hot*."

I shivered, trying to shake that image from my head. "Okay, fine. You win. Score one for the delivery guy."

His dimples took a plunge. "Pick you up at seven?" He gave his usual cursory glance around the neighborhood then gave me a kiss. Can't have the UPS guy kissing on his customers, now can we?

"I'll be ready."

"Good!" He handed me two fairly small boxes, then turned and jogged down the driveway toward his truck. "Oh, and Lucy?"

"Yes?"

"Don't forget your Depends. It's a long program tonight."

I threw Gertie's old tennis ball at him, but it bounced off that big brown truck instead.

I closed the door behind me, still laughing. I decided our humorous sparring must be one of our love languages. We'd taken it to a whole new art form. I adored his sarcastic quips. In fact, I adored everything about my Mark.

I shuffled back to the kitchen and set the boxes on the counter. One was from an Etsy site where I'd ordered a pair of sock monkey slippers. Cute, huh? The other had no return address, so I tore open the outer wrapping. It was a fancy box from a local jeweler.

Huh. That's weird. I don't wear a lot of jewelry. Must be something from Mom. She has a doctoral degree in box recycling.

I opened the box and found another box inside.

A black velvet box.

I'd written too many romance novels. I knew all about little black boxes. Or at least I thought I did. I swallowed hard, blew out a shaky breath, and slowly opened the box.

Inside was the most beautiful heart-shaped necklace made of tiny diamonds on a delicate silver chain. I could hardly breathe. Was it from Mark? Why had he delivered it? Why didn't he just wait for me to open it? Or give it to me tonight?

Inside the lid of the box was a note folded into a tiny square. I set the box and necklace aside and unfolded the card.

When this you see remember me . . .
I love you, Lucy, with all my heart.

Oh my goodness.

The words blurred almost immediately. Mark was kind and sweet and funny and a true gentleman. We'd been dating almost a year. I *loved* being with him. But we'd never taken it to the next level. We often said "I love you" the same way you say it to all your friends —*Love ya! Have a great day!*

But this was new territory. It suddenly dawned on me why he'd delivered this gift the way he did. It's how we met.

He delivered packages to me.

Now he'd delivered his love.

Whoa.

I carefully clasped the necklace around my neck and peeked in the mirror for a glimpse. I'd never owned anything so lovely. Seeing it there in my reflection, I felt adorned in Mark's love.

Whoa.

A flicker dashed through my mind. Something about it seemed vaguely familiar, but I had no idea why. Maybe I'd seen one like it in a commercial. Or maybe in a movie.

I fingered my new necklace as I headed back to my office. Something was prickling me just below the surface. Romantic jewelry notwithstanding, I needed to make some notes for my new story before my thoughts disappeared in the wasteland of my mind.

I'd brought the Christmas cup into my office weeks ago. Don't laugh when I tell you, but it seemed to be calling out to me. Studying it now, I remembered Aunt Lucille's photo album I'd borrowed from Dad. I reached for it and started to thumb through its sepia-tinted photographs when something jumped off the page.

I heard my own gasp. There in the photograph was my Uncle Gary—clasping a dainty necklace around his fiancée's neck—a heart shaped with diamonds.

Ohmigosh . . .

My aunt's necklace! I'd never once seen her without it. Ever. So how did one just like it end up on *my* neck? Mark never met my aunt. I'd never mentioned her necklace to him.

Yet moments ago, my Mark "delivered" one exactly like it.

Whoa . . .

A Christmas Peril
The Teacup Novellas
Book Five
Diane Moody

To Aunt Lucille

"Never be afraid
to trust an unknown future
to a known God."
—Corrie ten Boom

And the peace of God,
which transcends all understanding,
will guard your hearts and minds
in Christ Jesus.
—Philippians 4:7

Prologue

I peeked at the vintage clock on my bathroom wall. Mark would be here any minute. One thing I learned early on in our relationship is that UPS guys are never late. *Ever.* Which is why I'd made such a valiant effort these last few months to be ready whenever he arrived. My natural tendencies concerning punctuality lean more toward the slacker end of the spectrum. But maybe that's part of all that "yucky, mushy love stuff"—stepping it up to do something nice for the love of your life. Going the extra mile with those little things that make him smile.

So worth it. Mark's smile is to die for.

I brushed my teeth and took a swig of minty mouthwash before making a final check in the mirror. I couldn't believe how easy this updo was. Ordinarily, my curly brunette head of horrors caused me grief upon grief whenever I tried something new. But I have to say, that Youtube tutorial was sheer genius. A twist here, a jaw-style barrette there, and voila! A feminine, elegant swoop of curls that surprised even me. I couldn't wait to see Mark's reaction. He's the kind of guy who notices everything. I rather love that about him.

I turned from side to side, pleased with the gorgeous dress I'd found at TJ Maxx a couple of months ago. I'd been shopping for a gift for Mark's sister. Shelly's a gifted architect who's currently staying with Mark until the house she bought is ready. She recently moved here from Sydney, Australia where she'd designed several new schools. I wanted to buy her a welcome-home gift and found the cutest little teacup and saucer. Mark had told me how much she'd enjoyed my Teacup Novellas, so the set seemed like the perfect gift. It was. She loved it.

That day, as I wandered through the clothes section on my way to check out, this amazing dress practically jumped off the rack, calling, "I'm yours! We're perfect together!" Turns out, that little dress was right. She hit just below the knee and fit like she was made for me. I felt beautiful wearing her, and I'm fairly confident the feeling is mutual.

Now, as I made one last check in the mirror, my gaze and my fingers both caressed the heart-shaped diamond necklace glistening against my skin. I smiled, thinking about the charming way Mark had given it to me. He'd delivered it early today like any other UPS box, but I had no idea it was from *him* until after he left. Nor that it held a little black velvet box with a tiny note tucked inside saying, *"When this you see, remember me . . . I love you, Lucy, with all my heart."*

Just thinking about it made my heart skip a beat. So unexpected. So perfect. I couldn't wait to thank him with a kiss. Or three.

But curiosity was killing me. How could he possibly have known my Aunt Lucille had a necklace exactly like this one?

I turned to leave, startled that it was now 7:03. Where was he?

I decided to wait on my front porch, so I gave Gertie a treat, grabbed my long winter coat, and said goodbye. I took a seat on one of my rockers, enjoying the brisk breeze on this first day of December just as my cell phone rang.

Ah, he must have run into some traffic, I thought as I pulled my phone from my small clutch. But Mark's picture didn't fill the screen. It was my cousin.

"Hi, Stephen," I answered, gazing down the street.

"Hey, Lucy! How are you?"

"Good, thanks. And you?"

"Awesome. Just wanted to let you know I got your email questions about Mom and Dad. You won't believe what I found in the attic just now—Mom's diary!"

"Are you serious? Stephen, that's fantastic!"

"You'll find everything you want to know and more. It reads like a love story—literally. Which is no great surprise since Mom was such a gifted storyteller. How about I FedEx it to you in the morning?"

"Could you? I can't wait to see it! But—" I paused, smiling. "Any chance you could send that UPS instead of FedEx?"

"Well, uh, sure. I guess?"

"See, there's this delivery guy—"

"Say no more, Lucy. Consider it done."

"Thanks, Stephen. You just made my day!"

I'd just started outlining my next novella which would be loosely based on my Aunt Lucille's life. Years ago she'd told me how she and Uncle Gary met and bits and pieces of their love story. Over the years, I'd forgotten much of it, and I needed to get my facts straight. Thus, my request to my cousin for help. The diary would be a gold mine of information.

Even now, Aunt Lucille's Christmas teacup sat perched on the shelf above my desk. She absolutely *loved* Christmas, and this particular teacup was part of a holiday setting for twelve she had always used throughout the month of December. I rarely glimpsed at the cup and saucer without a smile sliding across my face as I imagined the magical memories it must have witnessed through all those years.

I blinked away my musings, glancing back at my cell phone. On its screen, the digital numbers showed 7:14. The teacup, the news from Stephen about the diary, and every other thought quickly slipped off my mental horizon as I wondered where Mark could be. It was so unlike him not to call. I placed a call to him, surprised when it rang several times then went to voicemail.

Before I could leave a message, my brother pulled into my driveway and jumped out of his car.

I stood. "Chad, what are you doing here?"

He hurried up the steps toward me. "Lucy, have you heard from Mark?"

"No, I just tried to call him, but—"

"Let's go inside," he said, taking hold of my arm.

I yanked it free. "Why? What's going on?"

He used his key to open the door. Gertie greeted us, barking and doing her usual happy dance.

"GERT! Quiet!"

"Chad, what is wrong with you?"

He wouldn't make eye contact with me. Instead, he made his way into my den and found the remote, clicking it on. I followed him, more than a little ticked at him for the way he was treating Gertie and me.

"You'd better have a good reason for—"

"Shhh," he said, beckoning me with his outstretched hand as he clicked through the channels with the other. "Come here, Lucy."

"No. Not until you tell me what's going on." I folded my arms across my chest.

He finally looked at me and did a double-take. "Whoa, Lucy. You look . . . beautiful."

I tilted my head just so and deflected the compliment.

He blew out a huff and came to me. "Sis, you need to sit down."

I stepped back out of his reach. "Why? Just tell me why."

He palmed his hands in surrender. "Okay, okay. See, I got a call from Gordo a few minutes ago, and—"

"Why would Gordo call you?"

My brother's eyes jumped back to the television and he waved me over. "Because there's been an incident this afternoon."

"An *incident*? What kind of incident?" I moved over so I could see the picture on the television.

He pressed the remote, increasing the volume, as my eyes finally locked on the TV screen. A reporter stood in front of a row of houses in an affluent neighborhood.

"The gunman apparently approached the UPS truck when it made a routine stop here on Waverly Drive at approximately 4:35 this afternoon—"

"Mark?" My breath snagged on a heartbeat. My knees began to buckle. Chad grabbed me, helping me sit down on my sofa.

The reporter continued. "He took the driver hostage, barricading himself and the driver in the back of the truck. We are told the suspect has a sawed off shotgun—"

"NO!" I cried. "Chad, please tell me that's not Mark!"

He squeezed my hands in his and looked me in the eye. "Lucy, Gordo told me his boss called him off his route because they'd lost contact with Mark when this thing went down. It's him, sweetie. I'm so sorry."

No, no, no! This can't be happening . . . I stared at my brother as the reporter's voice invaded the chaos roaring inside my head.

"Police have had no direct contact with the hostage, though they tell us—"

Suddenly, a barrage of gunfire erupted in the background. The camera swung around, clumsily trying to focus on the scene more than a block away as the reporter grappled for an explanation.

"Noooo!" I stood back up and spun around, turning my back to the television, hands over my eyes.

"Hold on, Lucy—"

"SUSPECT DOWN! SUSPECT DOWN!" the reporter cried, as the gunfire abruptly ended.

I turned back around just in time to see the SWAT team rushing toward the UPS truck like so many hornets buzzing the hive.

"What about Mark?!" Chad shouted at the television screen.

I grasped my necklace as a tear dripped off my chin. My prayers had no words, nothing more than frantic yearnings from the depths of my soul, crying out to God to protect my Mark. Chad stood, engulfing me in his arms. I'm sure he was trying to comfort me, but I'd never seen or felt my brother tremble before.

The reporter rambled on, speculating first one thing, then the other. I wanted to slap her for blabbing on and on until she knew what happened. One of the SWAT team guys pointed to something and waved others over to the other side of the truck.

"C'mon, guys!" Chad growled. "Show us the driver!"

And then, as if they'd all heard my brother's command, the same SWAT guy turned and gave a thumbs-up to those in the command vehicle along with a series of hand gestures like some third base baseball coach. A flurry of emergency personnel rushed toward Mark's truck.

Moments passed. I couldn't find a breath. "Chad, is he—"

"We've just received word the hostage is alive," the reporter announced. "The UPS hostage is alive. Medical personnel are attending—"

Chad grabbed my hand, pulling me toward the door. "Let's go. They'll take him to St. Michael's. We can be there in ten minutes."

As we flew out to Chad's car, I prayed this was nothing more than a bad dream. Maybe I was merely lost in some random drama playing out in my mind for a breathtaking scene in a manuscript. Because it couldn't be happening. No way.

My heart told me otherwise.

Chapter 1

"Lucy, wake up."

Someone must have duct taped my eyes shut. For the life of me, I couldn't get them to open even though something or someone kept jostling me.

"Lucy, c'mon. Wake up."

Well, that's just weird. Why is my brother here?

I tried again to pry open my eyelids only to squeeze them shut against the harsh, fluorescent-lit room. "Whoa."

"Sorry, Sis. My arm went to sleep and there was no way to move it without waking you."

I took a deep breath, then wished I hadn't. The unique, pungent hospital scent coursed through my nostrils then raced into my brain, connecting the dots.

Hospital.

I startled. "How long have I been asleep? What time is it? Has the doctor been in? Is Mark still unconscious?"

"Hey, take it easy." Chad stood and stretched his arms over his head. "Oh man, am I stiff. I feel like a truck ran over—" He winced. "I can't believe I just said that. I'm sorry, Lucy."

I stared at him, too tired to string together a sarcastic response. I looked around the waiting room. "Nothing yet?"

"Not yet. I've got to go to the bathroom. Will you be okay?"

"Go."

The clock on the wall showed the big hand on the six and the little hand on the two. It was still dark outside, but I wasn't sure if it was 6:10 or 2:30.

"Lucy!"

Mark's sister rushed across the waiting room toward me, her rolling suitcase in tow. "Shelly!" We embraced in an urgent, awkward hug. "I'm so glad you made it." Shelly had been in New York submitting a proposal of some kind. I'd reached her shortly after we arrived at the hospital.

She pulled back to look at me. "I took the last flight out of LaGuardia. How's Mark? Have you heard anything? Can I see him?"

Before I could answer she pulled me into another hug. "Oh, Lucy, tell me this isn't really happening."

"I keep asking myself the same question. He's in ICU. No, we can't seem him yet, but soon, hopefully. We haven't heard anything in the last couple of hours. Dr. Bradley told us Mark was still unconscious, but he seemed to indicate that was a good thing because they need to keep him sedated to allow the swelling in his brain to go down."

"Brain swelling?" she groaned. "I hear the words, but I can't comprehend that this is *my brother* we're talking about."

"Did someone say brother?" Chad returned, opening his arms to give her a bear hug. "How're you doing, Shelly?"

"Better now that I'm here, but I think I'm still in shock or something."

Shelly was four years older than Mark, but they'd clearly come from the same gene pool. While he stood six-four, Shelly had to stretch to make five-four. Otherwise, they had the same sable eyes, same contagious smiles, and same perfect skin tone that easily tanned. But where Mark's sandy brown hair seemed forever sun-kissed with natural highlights, Shelly's was a rich, natural blonde—the kind women spend fortunes for in salons. And it always looked perfect. Even now, with a pony tail tucked up under a pink ball cap and spilling out the back.

While the physical resemblance was apparent, their personalities were nothing alike. Mark was smart, laid back, and charming. He loved to laugh, and the sound of his unrestrained guffaws was one of my favorite sounds in the world. He loved life, and everyone loved him. Shelly never knew a stranger either, but hers was a more assertive personality. Not a control freak, but she definitely knew how to get things done and never shied away from a challenge. Which came in handy since she was a successful architect in a profession still dominated by men.

"Ladies, let's have a seat." Chad grabbed Shelly's suitcase and parked it behind the seating area where we'd kept vigil for the past seven or eight hours.

Shelly tucked a leg beneath her and folded her arms across her chest. "My flight had Wi-Fi, so I was able to find the video footage online. I must have watched it twenty times, but I still can't comprehend that the guy they wheeled into the ambulance was my baby brother."

"It's surreal, isn't it?" Chad rubbed his eyes. "But all things considered, it's a miracle he wasn't killed."

"Had to be a God thing. How else would you explain it?" Shelly shivered and rubbed her arm. "So catch me up. What's the extent of Mark's injuries?"

"At this point, the main concern is the severity of his concussion," Chad said. "No one seems to know how it is he fell out of the truck. Was he pushed? Did he try to escape? His feet and hands were bound, and his mouth was gagged with several yards of duct tape."

Shelly groaned again, closing her eyes.

"Dr. Bradley said Mark's right shoulder is also shattered," I added, "which may indicate that his shoulder took the brunt of his fall before his head hit. Otherwise, his neck might have been broken." I pressed another mascara-stained Kleenex against my eyes. "Last we heard, they were still checking for other internal injuries. But it's his brain I'm so worried about. What if—"

"Lucy, don't go there." Chad patted my knee. "We don't know yet."

"Chad's right," Shelly said, grabbing my hand in both of hers. "Let's just thank God Mark is alive and breathing, okay?"

Chad patted my knee again then stood up. "I'll go see if I can find some fresh coffee. If Bradley comes back, ring my cell, okay?"

I nodded then watched him head down the hall.

Shelly leaned back on the gray sofa. "I'm so glad he's been here for you."

"Me too. I can't imagine going through this all alone. The UPS folks were here until midnight. Mark's friend Gordo just left an hour ago. They've all been great, but I was glad when they left. I've written about scenes like this in my books, but living it?" I shook my head. "I realized there comes a time in situations like this when you just want to be left alone. Except for family, of course."

"I know. You feel like you have to stay strong and communicative when everyone's gathered around, when all you really want to do is crawl in a hole and be left alone."

"Exactly." I took a deep cleansing breath. "Were you able to reach your parents? Mark told me last week they were on a Mediterranean cruise, right?"

"Yes, and I honestly debated about calling them. They've been looking forward to this trip for over a year, and I didn't want to spoil it for them. But I realized, if something . . ." Shelly looked up at me, her eyes wide. "I mean, if something were to—"

"I know," I whispered, trying to sound braver than I felt. "You had no choice."

"I didn't. I haven't been able to reach them yet. I'm guessing the cell service onboard those cruisers is next to none. In the taxi on the way here from the airport, I finally tracked down their cruise line. I told them we need to reach them for a family emergency, but who knows when we'll hear from them."

I pushed what was left of my updo out of my face. "Good thinking."

"Knowing Mom, the minute she hears them say 'emergency' she'll get both of them packed and demand a helicopter to get off that boat."

"I can't blame her. I'd do the same."

Shelly got up as Chad approached with a cardboard carrier holding three cups of coffee. "Let me help you."

I stood too, though I'm not sure why. She handed me a cup, and I wrapped my hands around it, welcoming its warmth.

"Oh, Lucy—what a beautiful dress."

I looked down, almost surprised to find I still had on my sparkly dress. "Oh. Yeah, it's . . . we were going to the symphony tonight—I mean, *last* night. That's when I first knew something was wrong. Mark was late."

"And Mr. UPS is never, ever late. Gotcha."

"Never." I straightened, willing the knots out of my back. "I guess I'm a bit overdressed for a hospital waiting room."

"Which reminds me," Chad said, still wincing from a sip of the hot coffee. "I thought I'd make a run to your house in a little while. Gertie's probably worried sick about you."

"Oh, Gertie," I dropped into the nearest chair. "How could I have forgotten her?"

"Hey, she'll be fine. Don't worry about it. But I can pick up a change of clothes for you—unless you'd rather go home and get some sleep or grab a shower?"

I shook my head. "No, I'm not leaving."

"I figured. Will you trust me to bring something from your closet?"

"Miss Alexander?"

We stood as a doctor in scrubs made his way toward us.

"Yes, I'm Miss Alexander. Lucy. Um, Lucy Alexander."

"I'm Chris Felton. I'm covering for Dr. Bradley this morning, and he asked me to stop by and update you on Mark's status."

"Thank you, Dr. Felton," Chad said. He introduced himself, then Shelly. "What can you tell us?"

"Mark's resting. He's still comatose, but his vitals look good. Dr. Bradley was concerned he might need to surgically implant a ventriculostomy drain inside Mark's brain to relieve some of the pressure. But at this point, the swelling seems to have slowed considerably, so he's hoping that might not be necessary. He had to set Mark's shoulder with a couple dozen screws. He'll be in a sling for quite a while. We've also put him in a temporary neck brace just as a precaution. He looks pretty beat up, but as Dr. Bradley probably told you, time will tell us the full extent of Mark's injuries."

"When can we see him?" I asked, already weary of the jargon.

"That's actually why I'm here. I'll take you back—well, two of you, anyway. There's a two person limit in ICU."

I shoved my coffee cup at Chad. "Shelly? Is it okay if I come with you?"

"I was about to ask you the same question," she said, setting her cup on the coffee table. "Let's go."

Chapter 2

I couldn't breathe. My fists were clenched so tight, my nails were digging into the palms of my hands. I blinked away the tears, trying to find one single thread of composure.

Before me, Mark lay stretched out like a zombie, almost too long for the narrow bed. His head was wrapped in gauze, much of his face horribly bruised. The neck brace looked uncomfortable, but didn't seem to be bothering him, under the circumstances. His right arm was in a sling against his body. Wires and tubes crisscrossed here and there connecting him to monitors that beeped a steady rhythm. I reached out to place my hand on his before noticing an IV taped to it. Instead, I curled my fingers tightly around his thumb.

"Oh, Mark," Shelly whispered beside me.

I was trying so hard to hold it together. He looked so lifeless, and the mere thought of that possibility crept down my spine. A half-sob slipped from somewhere inside me.

Shelly wound her arm around my waist and pulled me close. "Lucy, he's going to be okay. You know Mark. He's tough as nails. He's not going to let something like a silly hostage situation get him down."

We both laughed. Well, the closest thing to it, anyway. "I suppose you're right."

Shelly reached out and placed her hand on his blanket-covered knee. "So Mark, here's the thing," she began in her business-as-usual voice. "You just need to take it easy for a few days. Give that big ol' knucklehead of yours a good rest. Don't you worry about a thing. Lucy and I will keep an eye on you whenever these nice folks allow us in here, and before you know it, you'll be back in the saddle again. Whatever that means."

I took another deep breath and tried to think what to say. "Hey, buddy. You listen to your sister, okay?" I croaked, which oddly enough, made me smile. Mark always teased me whenever I'd get choked up or croaky. *What's the matter, got a throat in your frog?* Oh, if only I could hear his silly jokes right now. I carefully wound my fingers with his, willing him to hear me.

We stood in silence for a few minutes, Shelly's arm still snug around my waist. It's funny, the things you think of at a time like that.

Like Mark's awkward approach before he tosses a bowling ball down the lane. Gangly and impossible, yet he rarely throws anything but strikes or spares. Or the way he always takes a bite off my plate. When we were kids, if Chad did that, I'd swat his hand away. But when Mark snagged a fry or a piece of fried okra off my plate, I found it endearing and sweet.

I stared at the creases of his dimples. I'd never seen dimples that deep until Mark smiled at me that first time he made a delivery. I caught myself staring at them, thinking they'd be perfect for the handsome hero in the book I was writing. They were so adorable, the one on the right always tugging up the side of his face more than the other, making his whole head appear to lean to one side; like puppies tilting their heads to one side when they're curious.

A nurse quietly appeared on the other side of Mark's bed. "I'm sorry, but it's that time," she said.

I knew our allotted fifteen minutes would go fast, but I would have sworn we'd just walked in.

"No problem," Shelly said. She patted his leg once more and motioned for me to follow her.

I nodded, lifting my hand toward her. *Just one more moment.* She nodded with a smile, raising her index finger—*one minute*— before stepping out of the room. I leaned over and traced my finger down the side of Mark's purpled face. "I love you, Mark. I need you to get better, okay? I'll see you again in a little while."

My throat closed again, so I pressed my lips against his cheek. As I drew back, something glistened on the side of his face. For a microsecond I thought he was crying. That's a good sign, right? But as I brushed away the dampness on his cheek, I realized the tear was one of mine.

Time meant nothing to me as I kept vigil in that ICU waiting room. I despised the clock on the wall, silently, and oh-so-slowly ticking away the yawning four-hour chasms between brief visits back to see Mark. At some point, Chad brought me a change of clothes. I knew I needed to take a shower, but for now the familiarity of my jeans and t-shirt felt heavenly. Thank goodness he remembered to bring my navy hoodie. I have no idea why they keep hospitals so cold. I kept expecting to find a side of beef or two hanging in the corner of the waiting room.

So I was surprised that an entire day and night had passed when Chad showed up again. He handed me a chai latte from Starbucks, and I almost cried at its heavenly aroma.

I stood up, crawling into his outstretched arm. "Oh, Chad, thank you." My voice got all tinny and my eyes watered. Again.

"It's a cup of chai, Lucy. Hardly worth crying over." He hugged me then motioned for me to sit back down. "You, little sister, need to go home and get some sleep."

I knuckled away the renegade tears before taking a sip of my chai. "I can't leave. I won't. Not until he comes around. Please stop asking me to, okay?"

"Okay, okay. By the way, Gertie sends her love."

"I wish you could bring her to see me. I miss her."

"I see people with pets on almost every flight I take these days. Supposedly, they 'comfort' travelers who have anxiety issues."

"Well, I'd definitely qualify for anxiety issues, so go get her."

He reached over and squeezed my hand. "Nah, you've got me here to do that, right? Let Gertie enjoy her stay at Uncle Chad's. I bought her a whole new bag of chew sticks."

"You spoil her rotten. Hey, what's in the bag?"

Chad reached into a reusable grocery bag from Publix. "I found this on your front porch when I stopped by this morning."

He handed me a large UPS bubble-pack envelope. I turned it over and spotted my cousin Stephen's return address label. "Oh my gosh—this must be Aunt Lucille's diary." I tried to rip it open but didn't have the strength. My Eagle Scout brother always carried a pocketknife, so he reached over and slit the envelope for me.

I pulled out the tissue-wrapped book and anxiously starting unwrapping it. My eyes filled again, making me blow out an angry huff. "Honestly, what is wrong with me? I can hardly breathe without losing it."

"Easy, Sis. Cut yourself some slack, okay? So why did Stephen send you his mother's diary?"

"It's for my next novella. I'm loosely basing the story on her love story with Uncle Gary."

"Really?"

I finally freed the diary, letting the tissue paper fall to the floor. Turning the precious book over in my hands, I stopped and closed my eyes. *Oh, Aunt Lucille. How desperately I need to feel your presence here with me now.* I prayed silently—wishing, hoping, longing. Then I pressed the book against my nose and took a deep breath. The faintest trace of her Chanel No. 5 perfume wisped its way into my lungs, filling me with such a visceral sense of my namesake, my Aunt Lucille. Or maybe I just imagined it so.

"Lucy?"

I opened my eyes to find my brother gazing at me with concern. I shook my head, not even attempting to explain the memories swirling through my mind. I clutched the book against my heart and breathed another silent prayer of thanks. Who but God could have orchestrated something like this? A few days ago, while doing research for my new book, I called Stephen to ask him some questions about his parents. He tells me he'd recently discovered his mother's diary. He sends it to me, and it shows up in this hospital waiting room where I'm filled with so much angst about Mark's injuries. Who but God would have slipped this heirloom into my hands, right here, right now?

For such a time as this.

Exactly.

"Miss Alexander?"

Chad and I stood up, turning in sync at the familiar voice of the seven-to-three shift nurse.

"Hello, Kirsten. Any news?" Chad asked.

"Good, and about to get even better. Dr. Bradley has released Mark to a private room up on the eighth floor."

I looked at Chad then back at Mark's nurse. "Are you sure? Isn't this too early? Doesn't he need constant monitoring? What if something happens and—"

"If Dr. Bradley thinks he's ready to move, I guarantee it's because Mark's condition has improved enough to warrant a move. Bradley's a stickler and always errs on the side of caution, so relax. Besides, now you can stay with Mark as long as you like. No pesky limits on visiting hours."

Suddenly my arms were wrapped around her. Believe it or not, I'm not the kind of person who hugs people all the time. But I couldn't help it. Kirsten had just given me the best possible news. Well, *almost* the best.

"I told you it was good news," she said, laughing with Chad as he extricated me.

"So is Mark, uh, is he—"

"Conscious? No, not yet. But Dr. Bradley said the swelling has gone down substantially, and he feels confident that Mark will do better in his own room. He sends his apologies for not telling you himself, but he got called away for emergency surgery. He'll be in to talk to you once Mark is settled."

"And I can stay with Mark as much as I like?"

"Absolutely. If you want to stay 24/7, that's perfectly all right."

"Okay if we go up to his room now?" Chad asked.

"Not yet. You know how things go around here. It could be an hour or so, but I'll let you know just as soon as he's settled, okay?"

The next thing I knew, Chad was prying me out of another Kirsten hug. I didn't care. Mark would be in his own room soon, and I would stay by his side until he was ready to go home. A few days, a couple of weeks—I didn't care about that either. As long as I could be there for him.

As we sat back down, Chad rubbed his hands together. "Well, then. Good news at last. You go ahead and finish your chai. I'll give Shelly a call to tell her."

"Good idea. Thanks, bro."

I took a sip of my chai and started making a mental list of things I wanted Chad to pick up for me at the house. As he placed the call to Shelly, it dawned on me he must have her number already logged into his cell.

Interesting.

Chapter 3

As hospitals go, it took much longer than expected for Mark to get moved. Shelly returned around one that afternoon and convinced me to have a late lunch with her in St. Michael's cafeteria. The place was hopping, but we finally made our way through the salad bar and found a table near the back of the room. I was surprised how good a fresh salad tasted after nibbling on packaged crackers and peanut butter the past few days.

"Lucy, I love that you're wanting to stay by Mark's side, and I totally understand. But I can stay with him too so you can go home and get some rest. We can take shifts or whatever."

I took a sip of iced tea and set the glass down. "Thanks, Shelly. I really appreciate the offer. Maybe after a day or two. I just want to be with him when he wakes up, y'know?"

She nodded, munching on a crouton. "I know. Hopefully that will be soon."

"But you're welcome to stay too. I'd love the company, so please don't think I'm trying to push you out. Because I'm not."

Shelly pinned me with a look. "As if you would? Please. But thanks. You'll probably get sick of me before this is all over."

"No way. I'd love the company."

She stabbed a cherry tomato. "Is there anything else I can do for you? Chad said he's taking care of Gertie and running errands for you, but anything else?"

"Not really. He's bringing my laptop this afternoon, and that'll help. I can catch up on my email and maybe get some work done. At some point I need to call my editor. Last count, she'd left twelve voice mails and threatened to call out the National Guard if I didn't call her."

"Does she know what happened?"

"Yes, I made the mistake of texting her a brief message. You have to know Sam. She loves to be all up in your business, then tell you what *she* would do under the same circumstances. She means well, but she's crusty too. Not a lot of TLC in her skill set, if you know what I mean."

"I had a roommate like that back in college. Her own life was a train wreck, but she always had advice for me on how to run mine."

"That's Sam. I've never missed a deadline, but you'd never know it by her. She starts the pressure before I have a single word on the page."

"Which reminds me. Chad tells me your new book is based on your aunt and uncle's love story back in the forties. I can't wait to read it."

"I've barely started working on it, so don't hold your breath."

"Maybe you can make some headway while you're sitting with Mark."

My cell rang. Kirsten called to tell us Mark was in his room.

"Thank you so much! We're on our way."

An hour later, Shelly took off to run some errands, and I settled in, making myself at home in Mark's room. A constant stream of aides and nurses came and went, but in spite of the numerous interruptions, I was so thankful to be close to Mark. I couldn't stop touching him. Cupping his cheek in my hand, stroking his forearm, brushing the few locks of hair that were exposed beneath his gauze-wrapped head. My eyes always tracked back to his, wondering when I'd find them open again.

A nurse dressed in those comfy scrubs favored by medical professionals joined me by Mark's bed. "Research tells us that coma patients often hear the voices of those around them, so feel free to talk to him."

"Okay."

"I'm Susie Blake, and I'll be taking good care of Mr. Christopher while he's our guest. Are you his wife?"

"No, I'm just his girlfriend." *That sounded so lame.* "I mean, we're very close . . . *very* close. We've been seeing each other since—let me think—over a year now? So I guess you could say we're, uh . . . yeah, I'm his girlfriend. Lucy. My name's Lucy."

I bit the side of my lip. This is precisely why I write books, because I can never seem to get a sentence out without getting tangled up with words. There's a reason God calls some to speak and some to write.

Susie laughed as she checked Mark's monitor, punching buttons and rearranging tubes. "Nice to meet you, Lucy. And I'm thinking you must be pretty special to my patient here, no matter what your relationship is." She smiled up at me as she tucked the blanket in beneath Mark's leg.

"Well, he's amazing. You'll see. He's kind and funny and smart, and never met a stranger."

"Sounds like a sweetheart of a guy. I'll look forward to getting to know him soon. In the meantime, you let us know if there's anything you need. There's a pillow and blanket in the closet there, and that's a recliner, so feel free to kick back when you want to sleep. There's a refrigerator around the corner where we keep some juice and fruit. Popsicles are up top in the freezer. We keep the coffee fresh, so help yourself."

"Thanks. That's really nice."

"Okay, then. I'll check back in a little while."

I grabbed the blanket and pillow from the closet, thankful for some added warmth against the ice locker that was Mark's room. I pulled the chair closer to the bed and covered my legs with the soft blue blanket. I stared at Mark for the longest time before remembering what his nurse just said about coma patients being able to hear the sound of your voice. I tried, but it felt so strange, like I was trying to disturb his nap or something.

I dropped my head in my hands and rubbed my face, wondering why I couldn't just do something normal for a change. Why was everything such a challenge? How hard could it be just to talk to him? Then again, I couldn't remember ever being this tired. Still, I wasn't about to sleep when I finally had time to be with him. To watch over him. To make sure he was comfortable.

When I opened my eyes, I noticed Aunt Lucille's diary sitting beside my purse. I stuck my fingers through the bed rails and gently stroked Mark's fingers. Then, with another glance at his bruised face, I reached for the diary and decided to spend some time with my aunt.

I'd thumbed through a few of the pages, but purposefully refrained from actually reading it until I could give the contents the attention it deserved. For the first time I noticed the ink was green —the same as every note or letter or recipe my aunt had ever written. But who knew green ink was readily available back in the forties? I caressed the familiar handwriting as it beckoned me into its pages.

I was also astounded by the style she'd written. Stephen had told me it read like a love story, but I had no idea she'd used actual dialogue—quotation marks and all. I smiled, thinking how easy that would make it for me to write my novella.

I glanced over at Mark and cleared my throat. I told him about Stephen sending me Aunt Lucille's diary and asked if he would mind if I read it out loud to him. I touched the heart of diamonds resting against my chest as a moment passed. Nothing.

"Okay, then. I'll take that as a yes. Which doesn't surprise me. You would have loved her, Mark. I'm glad I can share her with you. So here goes."

December 1944

Dear Diary,

How perfect. A brand new diary and something new to write about—or I should say "someone" new? The most wonderful things seem to happen when you least expect them. Yesterday, as I boarded the El on my way home from classes, I dropped one of my textbooks in the aisle. Clumsy, but with my coat and gloves and armload of books, it just slipped from my hands.

I turned around and reached down for it just as a handsome young soldier did the same. "Allow me," he said, as we both stood back up, our eyes locked. He slowly removed his cap but never took his eyes off me. It felt as if time stood still. I don't think I took a single breath the entire time. We just stood there—staring at each other. Even now, I've got goose bumps just thinking about it. His eyes were so blue, and his smile seemed to light his entire face. Little lines feathered his kind eyes, and his dimples were surely as deep as the ocean. I'd never seen him before, and yet I felt as if I'd always known him. How is that possible?

He took a handkerchief from his pocket and dusted off my book.

"There now," he said. "All nice and clean." He tilted his head to read the title. "'Teaching High School English.'* Well, now. I bet that's a real page-turner."*

He smiled back at me, and I could feel the heat creeping across my face. "You've no idea," I teased, as I took the book from his hands. "I'm not usually so clumsy, but thank you."

"You are most welcome." The train began to move, jostling us together. He grabbed my elbow to steady me. "I believe there's a seat right here with your name on it." He stepped out of the way and motioned me toward the aisle seat.

I thanked him and sat down, setting my purse on the floor next to my feet. When I turned, he was still standing beside me, his hand gripping the bar above him.

I twisted to look back over my shoulder. "I'm sure there are more seats in the back."

"Oh, I'm perfectly fine where I am. But thank you, Miss . . . ?"

I looked over my shoulder again as I stalled for an answer. I didn't usually give my name to strangers. But he just seemed so . . . genuine. Still, how many times had Father warned me about men in uniform? "Lucille, just because a man is in uniform doesn't mean he's a gentleman. Don't ever forget that." He was right, of course, but—

"Forgive me," the soldier said, placing his hand over his heart. "Where are my manners? My name is Gary Reynolds, Lieutenant, United States Army." His smile crinkled around his eyes again which sent my heart hammering in my chest.

"Nice to meet you, Lieutenant Reynolds."

He held out his hand to shake. "Please—call me Gary."

I smiled, staring at his strong hand as I allowed him to shake mine. "Nice to meet you, Lieutenant Gary Reynolds."

He paused, still holding my hand as he leaned down toward me. "This is the part where you tell me your *name," he whispered close to my ear.*

I couldn't help the shiver skittering down my spine from his nearness, the warmth of his breath against my ear, and the heady scent of his after-shave. I gave him as casual a smile as I could muster.

"Lucille. I'm Lucille."

"Lucille," he said, straightened again. "That's a lovely name. It suits you."

"Thank you, Lieutenant. I'll be sure and tell my parents you approve of the name they gave me."

He laughed, and I could almost feel the sound of it drawing me into his arms. I scolded myself for such a silly thought. But it was such a beautiful sound—a laugh so natural and spontaneous.

"I'm honored! To think, we just met and already you're eager to tell your parents about me. I'll take that as a good sign."

I laughed, still fighting the urge to get lost in those baby blues. "I've always heard soldiers were fast, but that might just be a record."

I looked out the window to my right, noticing for the first time the elderly lady sitting beside me. Her wrinkled face gleamed as she nodded toward the lieutenant, her eyes dancing. I smiled at her, praying he hadn't noticed.

"Hello, ma'am." He extended his hand across me toward her. "You certainly look lovely in that pretty red hat."

She touched the rim of her knitted cap. "Thank you, young man. You obviously have excellent taste." She gave a slight nod toward me, all smiles, and this time even her painted brows were dancing.

I felt the heat in my face despite the drafty December chill in the train.

"Why, thank you, ma'am." He leaned slightly across me, his hand shielding his mouth from me as he faked a whisper to her. "But I'm not making much headway here." He tossed a not-so-subtle toward me. "She seems hesitant to tell me her last name. Any suggestions?"

The woman straightened her back. "A proper young lady never gives her name to a perfect stranger—even if he is a peach of a guy." She gave him a conspiratorial wink.

We all laughed, and I was grateful for a chance to catch my breath. Unfortunately (or fortunately?) she got off at the next stop, shuffling down the aisle in her yellow galoshes. After I stood to let her by, the lieutenant smiled at me as we maneuvered around others coming and going. When I finally took my seat again, a new panic started to waft over me. What if he gets off and I never see him again?

"May I?"

He motioned toward the seat beside me. "Oh, sure." Not sure what else to do, I scooted over to the window seat, giving him mine.

"Thanks. So Lucille, are you from Chicago? Is this home to you, or are you a student just passing through?"

"Both, actually. Born and raised in Chicago—"

"So am I! Where'd you go to high school?"

"Calumet. You?"

"Tilden. Why, we were practically neighbors." He stared at me, gazing up at my hair, my eyes, my lips . . . I felt myself blushing again, so I turned to look out the window only to find it covered with steam.

"Tell me, Lucille." He shifted in his seat, turning toward me and folding his arms across his chest as though settling in for a nice, long chat.

"Tell you what?"

"Everything. I'm home on leave before heading back overseas, I may never see you again, so tell me everything about you. Your favorite color. Favorite flavor of ice cream. Favorite candy. All your hopes and dreams."

"Favorite color, blue. Favorite ice cream, butter pecan. Favorite candy, Fanny May, of course."

"Chicago's best."

"Hopes and dreams? I'll be graduating next spring, and I'd like to teach high school English, preferably here in Chicago."

"What about family? Brothers or sisters?"

"Just one baby brother. He just turned five."

"He's five? You're what—twenty? Twenty-one?"

"I'm twenty. Jack was born when I was fifteen. Mother and Father call him their miracle baby."

"What was that like for you, after being an only child for all those years?"

"I adored Jack from the minute I first got to hold him at the hospital."

"And I bet he thinks you're the cat's meow."

I smiled, remembering how Jack always greeted me every afternoon with happy squeals and hugs. "I assure you, the feeling's mutual."

For the next half hour, as the train drew ever closer to home, we talked non-stop. He told me of his family—just one brother, who was serving with the Army Air Corps in England. He said he was with the 124th Field Artillery stationed in Congleton, England. He hadn't been on the battlefield since his job was assisting the colonel in command of the base. He told me of his dream to be an architect, and how he looked forward to coming back to college after the war. We talked about movies and music and theater, and anything and everything we could think of.

"Lucille, would it be too much to ask—"

"This is where I get off," I said as the train slowed again.

He stood up. "Well, what a coincidence. Mine too. Small world, isn't it?"

I doubted seriously that. What will I do if he tries to follow me home?

And then I wondered what would happen if he didn't. Would I ever see him again?

"Miss Alexander?"

I looked up as Dr. Bradley entered Mark's room. It took a minute for my mind to leap back from 1944. I stood, letting the blanket and pillow fall back in the recliner. "Dr. Bradley, thanks for coming by."

"Sorry to disturb you. I apologize it's taken me so long to get up here and check on Mark. I was in surgery, and it took a lot longer than usual. How's he doing?"

I rubbed my face, then folded my arms across my chest. "About the same. He hasn't moved, hasn't made a sound or even twitched an eye."

"No, and I don't expect him to for a while yet." He shined a small flashlight in Mark's eyes, holding up one eyelid then the other. He continued his examination.

"Define 'a while yet,' if you don't mind."

He smiled, nodding. I'm sure he's asked that question a million times a day. "I'm afraid there's no way to actually know when that might happen. In a case like Mark's, the more he rests initially, the better. We'll keep a close eye on him, and hopefully, when he's good and ready, he'll come around."

"Wait, what do you mean by 'hopefully'?"

He entered something on his iPad, then closed it. I assumed this was the new version of making notes on medical charts. "Don't worry—Lucy, isn't it?"

"Yes."

"The hardest part is the waiting. Your mind wants to jump ahead and explore all the possibilities, the best and worst case scenarios. But every case is different, which means Mark's recovery will depend on how his body and mind respond to the injuries." He closed the gap between us and gently patted my shoulder. "I'll be back in the morning. You get some rest, okay?"

"Thank you, Dr. Bradley."

"Sure enough," he said, exiting the room.

I stretched my legs then stood beside Mark's bed. I wrapped my hand around his, prayed another silent prayer, and wondered when God would see fit to give me back my Mark.

Chapter 4

Chad returned shortly after Dr. Bradley left, bringing me some mail, extra socks, another chai latte from Starbucks, and best of all my laptop.

He also brought an attitude.

"Either you go home and clean up, or I'll throw you in that shower myself." He motioned a thumb toward the small bathroom behind him and leveled his eyes at me. "Which will it be?"

"Is it that bad?"

He rolled his eyes. "The last thing you want is Mark waking up and getting a whiff of you like this. It might send him back into another coma."

"All right, all right." I pushed the recliner upright and took a sip of my chai. Wiping the foam from my lip, I warned, "But you have to stay with Mark until I'm out."

"Hey, do you not see the *Sports Illustrated* I brought? I came to stay, little sister. So hop in that shower before the stink police come charging in here."

"I said I would, okay? You're not the boss of me, you know." It was my favorite go-to line with my brother, but for some reason my snarky quip failed to hit its mark. I was learning that hospitals tend to zap the humor. I grabbed the tote bag Chad had brought, almost afraid to peek in and see what he did or did not remember to bring me. I opened the bathroom door. "Listen, if he so much as twitches his pinky, you bang on the door and let me know. Understood?"

He raised a hand in defense as he plopped into the recliner. "Fine. If he passes gas, I'll call."

"You are so gross and not even remotely funny, I might add. Have a little respect for the coma guy, will you?"

"Go, already."

Fifteen minutes later, I looped the towel around my neck and opened the door. Chad was passed out in the recliner, his head back and his mouth hanging open as he snored quietly. I padded over to the other side of the bed to check on Mark. If only he would wake up. At least now he wouldn't pass out from his smelly girlfriend. Mark loved the scent of my shampoo. *It smells like orange blossoms,* he always said. I leaned over to kiss his cheek, wishing my fresh scent would rouse him.

I towel-dried my hair as I strolled over to the window. Winter was in the air, the wind still scattering the last fallen remnants of autumn's leaves. I shivered, noticing visitors and medical personnel below wrapped in coats and scarves, their breath puffing clouds before them. I wondered if I'd still be in this room when the first snow fell. Would I spend Christmas here as well? I took a deep breath and tried to coax my mind away from all the what-ifs that kept swirling through my head.

The door slowly *whooshed* open behind me. I turned just as my uncle poked his head around the door. "Lucy?" he whispered.

I gravitated toward his outstretched arms. "Uncle Ted? What are you—how did—?"

"Your mother called me," he whispered, noticing Mark asleep and Chad sacked out in the chair. "I came as soon as I heard." He hugged me and kissed the top of my damp head. "Unfortunately, I've been out of town and only found out this morning. How's Mark doing?"

My mom's older brother tucked me under his arm as we walked toward Mark's bed. "About the same, actually. He's still in a coma. Hasn't come around yet." My voice wobbled but I didn't really care. This was my Uncle Ted, after all. He was in the ministry and used to situations like this, visiting people in the hospital under the worst of circumstances.

Uncle Ted was one of my favorite relatives. He loved people, lived large, and knew how to enjoy life—including fast cars. A couple years ago, I rode with him to one of Chad's baseball games. At the time he owned a flashy red Dodge Viper, and I forced myself to quit watching the speedometer when it passed ninety-five. I swallowed my gum as I yelled at him to slow down. Instead, he just flashed me his world-famous grin and pressed the gas pedal harder.

With a head full of hair that turned snowy white back when he was barely in his forties, my uncle always looked the part of a pastor. "Dr. Theodore Wendel" had served as senior pastor at Hickory Street Cathedral for many years until he retired a few years ago. Since then, he's served in an interim position at First Church covering pastoral ministries for that downtown church. A perfect fit.

"Frannie told me about the whole hostage situation. She'd seen some of the footage online and said it was terrifying to see—like something out of a movie."

"It was. You see these things happen on television, and you feel so bad for everyone involved. But you never think it could happen to you or someone you know. It's so surreal."

He side-hugged me again, then put both his hands on the side rails of Mark's bed. "From what your mother told me, Lucy, all things considered, it's a miracle he survived."

"I know. I just wish he'd wake up."

As he leaned over to get a better look at Mark's bruised and bandaged face, a technician knocked softly on the door and walked in with a rolling cart. "Hello, friends and family," she said in a soft, sing-song introduction. "I'm Mishala, and I'm here to borrow a little blood from Mr. Christopher."

I moved out of the way. "Hi, Mishala. Do you need us to leave?"

"No, y'all are fine. I'll be out of your way in just a few minutes." Mishala's warm smile and wide dimples framed her beautiful face, the color reminding me of café au lait.

I motioned for Uncle Ted to move with me to the other side of Mark's bed. That's when I noticed his eyes were wide as saucers, glued on the vials of blood lined up on the compartmentalized cart tray like so many dark red soldiers standing at attention.

"Uncle Ted?"

"Uhhh, I get . . . a little, uh, squeamish at the sight of . . . blood. Maybe I should—"

"Oh my gosh!" Mishala whisper-squealed, clapping her latex-covered hands. "You're Father Ted, aren't you?!"

I watched my uncle make a valiant effort to smile, his eyes still fixed on those blood vials. "Yes, yes, that's, uh, me."

"Well, butter my cheeks and call me cornbread! I see you all the time on TV. Father Ted—it's a real honor." She reached across the bed to shake his hand. "Course, I almost didn't recognize you without your monk's robe." She giggled, tearing off the gloves and putting on a fresh pair. "Oh, I cannot *wait* to tell my kids I met Father Ted today!"

I guess I should mention Uncle Ted's other job. A few years ago he did some radio spots for a local charity. He's got one of those rich, gentle voices that endears him to everyone he meets. The commercials were a huge success, bringing in a record number of donations, so a local TV station hired him to do a number of Public Service Announcements. That's when he did a commercial for a local tire company dressed in a brown monk's robe and sandals. "Father Ted" would look straight in the camera and say, "When driving on life's highways, you know who to trust—Royal Tires." Or something like that. I guess you could say he's a local celebrity. He gets invited to all kinds of grand openings and sales events around town, always giving a blessing in the guise of the famous monk known as Father Ted.

But to me, he was *Uncle* Ted, which is why I'm always caught off guard when people like Mishala makes a big fuss over him.

Suddenly my brother stirred. "Oh, hey, Uncle Ted."

Chad yawned, stretching his arms over his head, the *Sports Illustrated* sliding off his lap onto the floor. "When did you get here?"

Uncle Ted tore his eyes from the tray of blood vials, shook his head a little, then made his way over to Chad. "Just a few minutes ago. How are you, Chad?"

My brother stood up and gave him a hug. "I'm good, thanks. Are you okay? You look a little pale."

"I'm fine. Really." Uncle Ted wiped his forehead. "Is it hot in here to you?"

"Ah, he's okay," Mishala answered over her shoulder. "It's the ones you least expect that can't handle the sight of blood." To make her point, she stuck a syringe into the port taped to the top of Mark's hand, then turned to flash a smile at Ted.

"Okay, I'm outta here." Ted waved and hurried out the door.

"Father Ted! Don't leave!" Mishala called out as she capped off a vial. "Hold up—I wanna get a picture of you 'n me to show my kids!" She snapped off her latex gloves again and looked up at us. "Y'all don't touch anything. I'll be right back." With a giggle, she dug in her pocket for her cell phone. "Father Ted? Wait up. Don't you leave!"

Chad couldn't stop laughing.

"I can still hear you!" Ted sang in protest from the hallway.

"Chad, go out there and take the picture for them. And apologize for laughing at him."

He was still guffawing as he headed out the door.

Chad convinced Ted to go for coffee with him while Mishala finished taking blood. She showed me the pictures my brother had taken of her and "Father Ted," and I couldn't help but smile at the green tint on my uncle's face.

A few minutes later, Chad and Ted returned with a fresh cup of coffee for me. The three of us had a nice visit. Before he left, Ted invited us to pray with him as we gathered beside Mark's bed. Most of the time he keeps us in stitches with his quirky sense of humor. But he's also a gifted man of God with a gentle demeanor and compassionate heart. And just then, as he prayed a beautiful, heartfelt prayer for Mark, it almost felt like he'd ushered us into the presence of God. When he prayed for me, asking God to wrap His arms around me and fill me with His presence, I sensed the most comforting warmth of peace wash over me.

Afterward, he and Chad both said goodnight.

As I settled in for the night, I could tell that Uncle Ted's prayer had changed me. At least I felt changed. More at peace. More hopeful. As I reached for Mark's thumb through the bedrail, I felt a tear track down my cheek. But for the first time, I knew it was a tear of gratitude for what God was going to do through all this. I had no idea *how* He was going to do it. I just knew.

Chapter 5

I channel-surfed for a while, hoping to find a good movie to get lost in, but quickly clicked off the remote when the ten o'clock news flashed a picture of the creep who had taken Mark hostage. I didn't want to know anything about him. I needed to focus all my emotional energy on Mark—not on the anger or outrage I felt every time I saw that man's face or heard an update about what *might* have led him to do it.

I needed a distraction. Quick.

I reached for the diary, pressing my nose against its cover again. "Oh, Aunt Lucille, talk to me. Help me get my mind in a better place. Tell me your story."

I pulled the satin ribbon, opening to the page where I last read. Glancing at Mark, I reminded him of where we'd left off.

"Lucille was about to get off the El at her stop, Gary said it was his stop too, which, of course, she didn't believe, and . . . okay, here's where we pick up."

"I'd be happy to walk you home, if you'd find that agreeable," he said as we stepped off the train. "I realize it may seem rather forward of me—"

"A little, yes." I couldn't take my eyes off his smile. I tried to tell myself this was all wrong, much too fast, and utterly ridiculous, but it wasn't helping.

"I assure you, my intentions are completely honorable."

"Oh? I bet you say that to all the girls."

When his face crimsoned, I wondered if I'd pegged him correctly. Was he just using some tried and trusted litany of pick-up lines?

"Look, Lucille," he said, taking my elbow and moving us out of the path of other commuters. "I like you. I admit it. And it makes me . . . well, it saddens me to think I might not ever see you again."

Was he reading my mind? Was I that transparent?

"Lieutenant—"

"Gary."

I looked into his eyes, so inviting, so . . . sincere? I wanted desperately to believe him, but I knew enough from my years at Northwestern to never trust a guy's sweet talking ways.

"Gary, you're very nice. But how many times have you used that line on other girls? How many times have you told a girl you want to know 'everything' about her? How many times—"

"It doesn't matter, I'm—"

"Yes, it does!" I abruptly started making my way down the station sidewalk.

He rushed up beside me, slapping his cap on his head. "All right—I agree. It does matter." He fell in step with me. "What will it take for you to give me a break? I just want to walk you home. Is that so much to ask?"

I kept walking, the battle between my head and my heart raging on. What would Father say if I walked through the door with a stranger? In uniform, no less! I said nothing, because I couldn't think of a thing to say. We walked in silence for a half block or so.

"Aren't you even going to answer me?"

He sounded so pitiful, I almost laughed. I bit the side of my lip, trying to appear contemplative. What could it hurt to let the lieutenant suffer a bit? Let him stew for a while.

After another block, in my periphery I saw his shoulders slump in resignation along with a weary sigh. Still, he kept pace with me. Thinking he looked like a little puppy tagging along, I had to press my lips together to keep from chuckling.

And who can resist a cute little puppy?

I turned the corner, and he was halfway into the street before he noticed. He rushed over to my side, whistling as though he hadn't a care in the world. When I turned at our driveway, he stopped. I gazed over my shoulder at him as I headed toward my house.

"Well? Are you coming, Lieutenant?"

Once inside, Mother gave him a warm welcome.

"Lieutenant Gary Reynolds, this is my mother, Elizabeth Alexander."

Gary sent a triumphant smile my way, having finally learned our last name. "How very nice to meet you, Mrs. Alexander. *It was such a pleasure getting to know your lovely daughter on the train this afternoon. Thank you for allowing me to stop by for a few minutes."*

Little Jack, always shy at first with strangers, gradually warmed to our guest, sneaking peeks at Gary when he wasn't looking. I had to laugh when I caught Gary making a silly face at Jack, who giggled before hiding his face behind Mother's skirt.

Of course, Mother insisted Lieutenant Reynolds should stay for dinner. When Father arrived home, he gave our guest a more guarded welcome, glancing my direction when he noticed the uniform. But just as Jack had, Father gradually warmed to Gary too.

Later, at the dinner table, he asked Gary about his plans after the war.

"I hope to return to the University of Illinois to complete my degree in architecture."

"And your folks, Gary—do they still live here in Chicago?" Mother asked.

"Yes, ma'am, they're still living in the house I grew up in, over on Yale Avenue."

"I'm sure they must be thrilled to have you home for a visit." Mother handed him the plate of biscuits.

"Yes, ma'am, they sure are." He took a biscuit and passed the plate to Father. "Of course, my mother is worried sick about me heading over to the war. My brother deported last month, and she's not too keen about having two sons so far away."

"I can't imagine," Mother said. "I don't envy her."

Father continued to engage Gary, asking lots of questions, but I could tell he was still checking out the lieutenant from head to toe.

Gary turned to Father. "Mr. Alexander, Lucille tells me you're in management over at Armour."

Father took a sip of tea then dabbed his mouth with his napkin. "Yes, I'm the plant employment manager. I oversee hiring and personnel matters."

"World's largest meat-packing plant. You must hire a massive number of people to keep production moving."

"Yes, but my responsibilities are for the plant only. The administrative and corporate areas are completely separate."

"Still, you must have thousands on your payroll. In your position, do you handle all the union relations as well?"

Father's brows rose a bit. "Interesting question. Do you have union folks in your family, Lieutenant?"

"Oh, no sir. My father isn't a union guy. He can't stand all

the politics." Gary winced, obviously wondering if he'd just stepped into it. For all he knew, Father was a champion for the unions. I suppressed a smile, knowing what he couldn't.

Father's face relaxed. "Then I'm sure your father and I would get along just fine. Seems all I do some days is wade through the red tape those folks keep throwing at us. Worst thing that ever happened to Armour. To the country, for that matter."

"I should tell you Father is a gentle giant," I added. "At six-four, he towers over most of them, but his disarming, quiet spirit keeps them in tow. They constantly try to rile him up over this or that, but he just takes it all in stride, settling them down without uttering so much as a single word."

"A slight exaggeration," Father said with a smile.

Gary chuckled. "With that kind of demeanor, they could sure use you in Washington, Mr. Alexander. Dad says free enterprise will never be the same, thanks to FDR's New Deal."

"He's right. The president bought himself more than enough votes to keep him in the White House, but he'll ruin this country in the long run. Mark my words."

"Well, now, let's talk about something else," Mother said, passing the roast platter back to Gary. "Unions and politics are never good dinner companions."

"My apologies, Mrs. Alexander." Gary wiped his mouth. "You and my mother must be on the same wavelength. She always reminds us that such discussions over a meal are a guaranteed recipe for indigestion."

We had such a nice time. Mother and Father seemed to genuinely like Lieutenant Reynolds. There was no doubt about it—he was full of charm and had a way of drawing you in, as if you'd always known him. So many thoughts wrestled through my mind as I observed him across the dinner table. How fascinating he was. How his eyes lit up when he told stories. And oh my goodness, how handsome he was. There was just something about him that attracted me, but at the same time frightened me more than I wanted to admit. Was he involved with someone? Were there several other "someones" out there, waiting for his call?

After Mother served pie and coffee, Gary thanked her for the delicious meal then surprised us when he stood and began to gather our dishes. "The very least I can do to show my appreciation for such an unforgettable evening is to do the dishes."

"You'll do no such thing!" Mother stood, laughing. "What kind of hostess would I be if I let you wash all these dishes?"

"A gracious and acquiescing hostess, that's who." He grabbed more plates and silverware.

"But Lieutenant, I couldn't possibly!"

He set the stack of dishes back on the table. "Well, all right then. If it would make you feel better, Jack can help me. Right, Jack? You 'n me, little buddy. Here, you grab the crystal and I'll get the plates."

We all laughed heartily as Gary kept the ruse going, as if he and Jack washed dishes together every day. Jack looked back and forth between us, a confused smile twinkling his eyes.

"All right, all right!" I finally said, raising my hands in defeat. "You obviously don't have little brothers, Gary. I think we'll let Jack go help Father build a fire, and I'll assist you in the kitchen. Fair enough?"

Jack hopped down from his chair and made a beeline for the fireplace. "C'mon, Dad. Let's build a fire!"

Mother still wasn't convinced. "But I can't let you—"

"Yes you can, and yes you will." I took her shoulders and pointed her in the direction of the family room. "Go put your feet up. Read the paper. Relax for a change."

She started to protest again, then a knowing smile suddenly lit her face. "Ohhh . . . I suppose you're right, dear." Mother gazed over my shoulder, and I prayed Gary couldn't see her acknowledging wink. "Yes, I think I'll do just that."

As I carried a stack of cups and saucers into the kitchen, I stopped in my tracks to watch Gary tie one of Mother's aprons around himself at chest level. He turned, his hands raised in presentation. "Be honest. Does this pink apron go with my uniform?" He twirled around. "Does it make me look fat?"

I laughed so hard, I barely set the dishes down before doubling over.

His face fell. "That bad, huh?"

My eyes brimmed with tears of laughter as Gary kept the act going. He was such a ham, occasionally breaking into song while we did the dishes.

And oh my, could he sing! His rich tenor traipsed in and out of a number of familiar show tunes; the kitchen his Broadway stage, and Mother's spatula his make-shift microphone. Occasionally he'd draw me into his antics, twirling me across the kitchen floor like Ginger Rogers to Fred Astaire. Though I doubt Fred ever dropped Ginger when he lunged her into a final dip.

"Lucille! I'm so sorry!" He knelt down to help me up.

I could not stop laughing! I've never laughed that hard in my entire life. The sight of him down on one knee, doing his best to help me up with his soapy hands, made us giggle even harder until he finally collapsed on the floor beside me.

"I can't believe I dropped you!" he lamented, lifting the apron over his face. "I'll never be able to face you again."

I wiped the tears rolling down toward my ears, still trying to stop my giggles.

"What on earth—"

Gary scrambled to his feet at the sound of Mother's voice. "Oh, Mrs. Alexander, I'm so sorry!" He reached out both his hands to lift me from the floor, our clumsy efforts regaling me all the more.

Mother folded her arms as she leaned against the counter, but I could tell she was doing a little acting herself. "I heard so much laughter, I just had to come see for myself. I knew it was a mistake to let a man in uniform take over my kitchen."

By then we were both standing again, Gary wiping his hands on his apron, me dabbing at the tears with my thumbs.

He shot Mother a nervous smile. "Mrs. Alexander, I take full responsibility. I made the mistake of trying to entertain your daughter, and I'm afraid I got a little carried away."

She turned to go. "Thank you, Lieutenant."

"Thank you?"

Mother nodded toward the sink. "Nice job with the dishes." The swinging door closed behind her.

Gary's eyes grew wide as he whispered, "Oops?"

As we finished the dishes, I began to dread the moment he would leave. After a brief chat on our chilly front porch, Gary tucked his cap under his arm and slowly made his way to the top of the porch steps. "I should apologize for stealing your entire evening. One moment I was picking up a textbook on the aisle of the train, and the next thing I know, I'm having trouble finding a way to say goodnight to the beautiful girl who dropped it."

Standing at the porch rail, I burrowed my hands into my coat pockets and glanced across the street, suddenly shy. "I'm not sure I thanked you for doing that, so . . . thank you."

"No problem." He stepped closer. "Lucille, I can't remember when I've ever had such a nice evening. I mean that."

"It was fun, wasn't it?"

"Right up until your mother found us sprawled on the kitchen floor. But otherwise? Yes. It was definitely fun." He paused, fingering one of the charms on my bracelet. "More than fun."

I smiled as my heartbeat pounded in my ears. This was the moment I'd been dreading. Would this be goodbye?

"I've got five more days before I head back overseas. I know you're probably busy, but I want to see you again."

I looked at his face, shadowed by the light from the window. Even so, his eyes glistened so kind and serene. "I'd like that. I really would."

He beamed, taking my hand in his. "Good. Tomorrow it is. Shall I just meet you at the train station in Evanston again?"

"No, silly. I don't have classes tomorrow. It's Saturday."

"Even better. How does breakfast sound?"

"Even better."

His dimples deepened as he leaned closer. "About eight?"

"Perfect."

"Eight it is. Goodnight, Lucille." Ever so gently, he pressed a kiss against my cheek.

"Goodnight, Gary," I whispered.

He stepped back, put his cap on his head, and tossed me a wink. Skipping down the steps, he whistled a familiar tune, but I was too mesmerized to recognize it. I touched the spot on my cheek he'd just kissed, wondering if it was all a dream.

As he turned onto the sidewalk, he gave me a quick salute, stuck his hands in his coat pockets, and kept whistling until he was out of sight.

Only later, as I lay my head on my pillow did I remember the name of the song he was whistling . . .

"Let's Fall in Love."

Chapter 6

A lot of visitors came and went with each passing day. Most of them were Mark's UPS buddies, who'd stop by after work. I knew many of them from the bowling league. They were a great bunch of guys, and I knew it would mean the world to Mark when he found out how many came and how often they stopped by.

Mark's boss came every day on his lunch hour. Every single day. I knew Mark had tremendous respect for Calvin, and now I knew why. Calvin was a hulk of a guy who reminded me of Cuba Gooding, Jr., minus the comic effect. Mark told me Calvin ran a tight ship, but had a big, big heart for his employees. He seemed genuinely concerned for me as well, always asking if there was anything I needed. We'd chat for a few minutes, then he'd stand beside Mark's bed, place his hand over Mark's, and close his eyes offering a silent prayer. He'd leave a couple minutes later, his eyes often glistening with tears as he gave me a fatherly hug.

Gordo came every day too and never empty-handed. He knew Mark's weakness for Krispy Kreme donuts, so every morning on his way to work, he'd drop by with a dozen glazed donuts, still warm in the box. "Just like Mark likes 'em," he'd say. I'd share them with the medical staff, allowing myself only one a day. I had to smile when the staff started routinely asking me if the donut guy had stopped by yet.

During that first week, Gordo told me he'd learned an important lesson when his mother was laid up in a hospital for several weeks before she died. "The best hospital visitor is the one who's in and out," he'd said. "Unless you're a close friend or family, patients and those staying with them don't need visitors overstaying their welcome." He told me of people his mother hardly knew who would show up, spend hours on end talking about anything and everything. "Or worse yet, the ones who want to tell you all about their loved one who *died* in a hospital. Like that helps?" Gordo shook his head. "Eventually I had the staff post a *No Visitors* sign on the door. You may need to do that at some point."

I had one such visitor yesterday. Her name was Winifred Small, and she said God told her to come see Mark after she'd watched an update about him on the news.

"God has a word for Mark, and the Almighty has told me to share it with him."

At first, I didn't know what to think. I'd always been skeptical of those who claimed God told them to do this or that—particularly when they're complete strangers. Too often, such a claim was nothing more than someone's self-proclaimed excuse for butting into someone else's business. At least that's what I'd always thought. But I was exhausted and grasping for any semblance of hope, so I welcomed Winifred against my better judgment.

She stood beside Mark, studying him from head to toe, whispering to herself. I assumed she was praying. Suddenly, she looked over at me. "You might want to step outside."

"Excuse me?"

"Sometimes it's difficult to hear truth in times of crisis. I thought you might like to leave while I—"

"No, I'll stay, thank you." I stood up, wrapping my sweater around me tighter.

"Suit yourself."

I opened my mouth to respond just as she began speaking her "truth" to Mark.

"The Lord giveth and the Lord taketh away; blessed be the name of the Lord."

A chill scurried down my back at the tone of her voice as she recited the verse.

"The Lord is calling you home, Mark Christopher. You must stop resisting His call, stop wallowing in this coma, and allow Him to welcome you into heaven."

"No!" I rushed around the bed. "Don't SAY that! God would never tell you that!"

"Oh, He most certainly did."

I grabbed her by the arm. "Get out."

"Not until I'm finished."

"I said, GET OUT!"

"What's going on?"

I'd turned at the sound of Shelly's voice, her face reflecting the tension in the air.

"Would you kindly tell this young woman to let me go?" Winifred pleaded.

"I'll do no such thing." Shelly dropped her purse and keys on the floor, then grabbed Winifred's arm and escorted her out the door. She returned a few minutes later, holding me while I explained what had happened against an avalanche of fresh tears.

"She's crazy, Lucy. Stuff like this always brings the wackos out of the woodwork. But I'm so sorry. If God has a message for Mark, I assure you He doesn't need a complete stranger to tell him."

From then on, we kept the door closed and allowed in only those we knew to visit.

The experience left me uneasy. From then on, Shelly made sure either she or Chad was with me throughout the day. When she tried to insist on staying overnight, I wouldn't have it.

"I'm okay, Shelly. No one ever visits this late."

It took some convincing, but she finally left around ten, promising to be back first thing in the morning. I'll admit, I was a bit jumpy for an hour or so after she left.

Until now, I had never spent a lot of time around hospitals, and certainly never kept a bedside vigil like this. I'd already learned that hospitals are the utter anti-thesis of restful recovery. Time still meant nothing to me at this point, but I'm pretty sure an hour never passed without a nurse, doctor, aide, housekeeper, or orderly stopping by. Even in the middle of the night, the constant flow of medical staff continued; most of them flipping the glaring overhead florescent lights on as they entered the room.

Of course, I was the only one inconvenienced. Mark didn't seem to mind.

Around two in the morning following one such interruption, I couldn't get back to sleep. I finally gave up and made a pit stop, the mirror in the small bathroom a ready reminder of the toll this was taking on me. I made a mental note to take better care of my appearance. I wanted to look my best when Mark came around.

When Mark comes around . . .

He would, of course. There could be no other option.

The day before, Chad had tiptoed into a conversation with me about what he called, "the worst case scenario." I know he was only trying to help. Just in case. Still, I refused to go there. I refused to even consider that possibility. Mark *would* recover. It might take a long, long time, but in my heart I knew he'd be okay. He had to.

I took my seat again and huddled under the blanket before reaching for the diary.

"Okay, the last part we read was the first night, after Uncle Gary followed Aunt Lucille home and stayed for dinner." I looked over the top of the diary at Mark. "Kind of sweet, wasn't it? Him doing the dishes, the two of them cutting up, falling on the floor laughing like that? Then the whole goodbye kiss on the cheek? I always thought Uncle Gary was charming, but he must have dazzled Lucille with all his antics."

I waited, half-expecting Mark to engage in the conversation. Talk had always come so easy for us. Sometimes we spent hours just talking. I *loved* that about him. He never got bored or distracted, even when I chased rabbits on plot lines or story ideas. Some of my most colorful characters evolved from those gabfests.

I felt the familiar ache in the pit of my stomach, missing my big guy who was still stretched out in that hospital bed. I shook off the grief in my soul and tried to push myself out of its grip. I focused on opening the diary and finding my place.

"The next entry is four days later." I flipped the pages back and forth. "That's odd. Lucille wrote a play-by-play account of that first day, then skipped four entire days? Well, I don't know about you, but I'm anxious to find out what happened next." I peeked back at Mark, then started reading aloud.

Dear Diary,

The past few days have been the most wonderful days of my life. I'm head over heels in love with Gary, and I want to shout it from the mountaintops! We've spent almost every waking moment together, which explains why I haven't written here. It's almost midnight, but I'm determined to catch up on paper before I forget the bliss of every single moment—no matter how long it takes.

After our serendipitous meeting on Friday, the next morning we had breakfast together at Mason's Diner. Somewhere between the second and third cup of coffee, Gary convinced me to spend the entire day with him. It didn't take much arm-twisting, of course. I tried desperately to be cautious, to guard my heart and be reasonable, knowing I might never see him again once he headed back overseas. I failed miserably.

With each passing moment, I fell more in love with my handsome lieutenant. Leaving the diner, he tucked my gloved hand in the crook of his arm and escorted me through the most perfect winter day. The air was bitterly cold, but the sky was blue, and I half expected to hear birds singing on such a glorious day.

We rode the El downtown to the Loop, where we strolled along the sidewalks at Marshall Field's and admired the festive window displays. The famous golden trumpets lined above each window seemed to proclaim the news that the holiday season was in full swing.

"Christmas just isn't Christmas without Marshall Field's," I said. "When I was just a girl, we always came here the first week of December. It was a tradition. We'd join all the others, moving in clusters from window to window, and I thought it was the most magical place on earth. Then we'd go up to the Walnut Room where we'd have hot cocoa and Christmas cookies under that enormous Christmas tree that stands several stories high."

"I'm sure we came when I was a kid, but I don't remember much about it."

"Not even the displays with shiny red bicycles and train sets?"

"Okay, I do remember those. And I remember that big tree. I used to pretend all those wrapped presents under the tree had my name on them."

"They were just empty boxes, you know. So you didn't miss out much."

As we stood beneath the famous green clock, the breeze picked up and I shivered.

"It is a bit chilly out here," Gary said, turning to face me. "How about we go inside for a while?"

"I thought you'd never ask."

We took our time wandering the aisles, taking in the fanciful décor and gazing up at the famous Tiffany mosaic glass dome.

"Did you know there are more than one and a half million pieces of glass in that ceiling?" I asked.

"No, I didn't." He twisted his head back and forth to study it. "Makes me a little nervous to think what would happen if they all came crashing down." He looked back at me. "I'm getting hungry. Want to head up to the Walnut Room for a late lunch?"

As we rode the elevator up to the seventh floor, I caught the uniformed elevator operator staring at Gary as she announced the floors on our way up. A tinge of jealousy coursed through me until I looked over and found Gary staring at *me*, oblivious of the operator. I couldn't help smiling.

After the hostess led us to a small round table beneath the elegantly decorated tree, Gary seated me then sat across from me, his gaze inching all the way up the forty-five foot distance to the top of the tree. "I've lived in Chicago all my life, but would you believe this is my first time to eat here?"

"Surely you're kidding?" I spread the linen napkin across my lap. "Mother and I must have eaten here hundreds of times over the years. I can't imagine shopping at Marshall Field's and not stopping by for lunch or a cup of tea."

"Well, there you go. I guess it's more of a gal's thing."

"Then you've missed out." I accepted the menu from the waitress. "And you simply haven't lived until you've had Mrs. Hering's Chicken Pot Pie."

Gary handed his menu back to her. "Might as well make it simple and do as the lady says," he teased. "I'll have the chicken pot pie."

Since we'd eaten such a heavy breakfast, I opted for the Walnut Room Salad with lettuce, mandarin oranges, walnuts, and their famous toasted sesame dressing.

A few minutes later, the waitress returned with a teapot and two cups and saucers. "I've always loved this Christmas pattern."

"Is there anything you don't love?" he asked, a twinkle in his eye as he poured our tea.

"Rude people, mosquitoes, and sauerkraut. You?"

"You mean, besides dishpan hands?"

I laughed. "Yes, Gary, what don't you love, besides dishpan hands?"

He narrowed his eyes in deep thought. "Well, let's see. I'm not too fond of broccoli. I hate the smell of rotten eggs. And . . ." He settled his eyes on mine again. "And a war that takes me away from the most amazing girl I've ever met."

I glanced down into my cup of tea when my eyes begin to sting. "Yes. The war. But let's promise not to talk about it until you have to leave. I don't want it to spoil our perfect day."

He squeezed my hand. "Agreed. No talk of war." He took a deep breath and asked, "Who is Mrs. Hering?"

I shifted my thoughts, grateful for the diversion. "I was hoping you'd ask. It's such an interesting story."

"Then you must tell me." He planted his elbow on the table then rested his chin on his fist. His dimples deepened with his warm smile, and I had to rein in my butterflies just to put a sentence together.

"I'm sure you know the history of the store, dating back before the Civil War."

"I do, but I'd love to hear you tell it."

"It wasn't called Marshall Field's back then, of course. But did you know that Mr. Field was only twenty-one years old in 1856 when he started working for the original dry goods store he would one day own? That's only a year older than I me."

"But I'm sure he wasn't half as pretty."

I could feel the heat in my face. "Well, I wouldn't know about that. But by 1868, the store was moved to its location here at State and Washington. Of course, the Great Chicago

Fire of 1871 leveled it, but not before many of the employees worked valiantly through the night to save the most expensive merchandise and much of the files and records."

"I remember hearing the stories of that when I was a kid. I think someone in my dad's family worked there at the time."

"Here I am prattling on when you probably know more about it than I do."

He took my hand in his and twisted the opal ring on my finger. "I doubt it. Besides, I happen to like listening to you prattle. So please—prattle on."

I couldn't help laughing again. "If you insist."

"I do."

"About the tea room. Back in those days, it wasn't proper for a woman to eat in a restaurant unless she was accompanied by a gentleman. But if a woman was shopping and wanted something to eat, it was an absurd inconvenience for her to go all the way home for lunch then have to return to finish her shopping. Then one day an employee in the millinery department named Mrs. Hering noticed that one of her customers was tired and hungry, so she offered to share her lunch with her client—a homemade chicken pot pie. Soon Mrs. Hering started bringing lots of her pot pies for her customers. Eventually the store opened a tea room to accommodate all their customers, and Mrs. Hering's Chicken Pot Pies have been on the menu from the very beginning. Isn't that a great story?"

As if on cue, the waitress returned with our food. While I enjoyed my salad, Gary devoured his steaming pot pie, groaning with pleasure with each bite.

He wiped his lips with his napkin. "I suppose it would be bad form to pick up the plate and lick it?"

"You wouldn't dare!"

He raised a brow, taunting me, and for a moment I thought he might just do it. Thankfully, he pushed the plate aside and sighed with satisfaction. "That, my dear Lucille, might just be the best thing I've ever tasted."

"Really? Didn't you say the same thing about your pancakes just a few hours ago?"

He leaned in, motioning me closer. "Yes, but that was then and this is now," he whispered.

I smiled at his silliness, wishing I could freeze the moment and savor it forever. I fought the nagging ticking of the clock in my head, already wondering how I'd handle saying goodbye when the time came.

He seemed to pause, his face suddenly growing serious. He leaned toward me again and placed his hand on my forearm. "Tell me something. Is there someone special in your life, Lucille? It only now occurred to me that you might be seeing someone."

I couldn't help but enjoy the concern in his eyes. "Yes, I'm afraid there is."

He straightened and started to say something until I placed my hand firmly over his, entwining our fingers. I gazed down at our joined hands. "If you must know, he's the most handsome guy I've ever known. But the thing that melted me from the very beginning was . . . well, it's kind of corny. Maybe I shouldn't say."

"Please. Tell me."

His sad puppy dog eyes nearly cracked me up. I pressed my lips together, willing away the giggles bubbling around inside me. I reached for my teacup with my other hand. "I mean, he's a nice guy and all, but it was—well, I might as well just say it. The guy loves to wash dishes. And apparently I'm a real sucker for guys in aprons."

Gary's face flushed with relief as he pulled my hand to his lips and kissed the top of it. "Oh Lucille, don't do that. You scared the socks off me!"

I laughed so hard I spilled some of my tea, wobbling the cup back to its saucer. "I'm sorry. I couldn't resist—"

"No! Don't apologize. I may be a tad slow, but I think you just made me the happiest man on earth. Unless you've had lots of guys wear aprons in your kitchen and wash your dishes."

"Only you, Lieutenant."

The rest of the day is still a blur to me. We spent another hour or two at Marshall Field's so Gary could buy Christmas presents for his family. I enjoyed learning more about his parents and brother as we shopped. At my suggestion, he bought a china teacup and saucer—the same holiday pattern as the ones we'd been served in the Walnut Room.

"There's a wonderful story behind this pattern. Back in 1938, the American agent for Spode asked one of their artists back in England to design a new Christmas pattern. The artist—I think his name was Holdway—did so and sent a sample to the American. The plate featured a Christmas tree with presents hanging from its branches."

"That's strange, don't you think?"

"Well, yes. And the American told Mr. Holdway he liked the pattern, but could he put the presents on the floor <u>beneath</u>

the tree and decorate the tree with ornaments. Turns out, Mr. Holdway had ad-libbed the entire concept because he'd never seen a Christmas tree!"

"Hadn't seen a Christmas tree?" Gary laughed. "How is that possible?"

"I have no idea. What's even funnier, he had no clue what went on the top of a Christmas tree, so he painted a Kris Kringle. See it up there?"

"Will you look at that," Gary said, twisting the cup around. "Don't most trees have angels on top?"

"Well, of course they do. Even so, it's become quite famous. They have whole sets of this pattern now, serving pieces and all. I think they're beautiful. Don't you?"

"Yes, and it's perfect," he said, as we waited for it to be gift wrapped. "Mom will love it."

Of course, I had no way of knowing Gary had no intention of giving that cup and saucer set to his mother. Later that evening back at my house, before we said goodnight, Gary suddenly snapped his fingers.

"I almost forgot! I got you something." He rustled through the large shopping bag and came up with a small box—identical to the one we'd had wrapped at Marshall Field's.

"But isn't this—"

"No questions. Just open it."

I couldn't figure out what he was up to, but just as I suspected, inside the box I found the Christmas teacup and saucer wrapped in white tissue paper.

"Gary, I don't understand."

"You see, my mother has more teacups than she knows what to do with. She collects them. When I'm on leave over in England, I always try to find one to send her. Which is why she has little need for another one."

He took the box from my hand, then carefully set the cup and saucer alongside it on the side table. "You, on the other hand, seemed quite fascinated by this pattern and its peculiar history. Which is why I thought it might be fun to give you a souvenir of our day together."

"I don't know what to say. I'm embarrassed to say the thought never crossed my mind to buy you something today."

"Oh, but you gave me the best possible gift."

"What's that?"

"A day I'll never forget."

I placed my palm against his cheek. "I'll never forget it either, Gary."

This time, the clock I heard ticking was the grandfather clock in our entry hall. I chose to ignore it when Gary wrapped me in his arms.

"Lucille, if I could, I'd go AWOL just so I could stay here with you. I'd never go back, never leave you."

"Now, Lieutenant. I could never live with myself if I caused you to be dishonorably discharged."

He smiled, pushing a curl from my face. Then without a moment's hesitation, he leaned down and placed the gentlest of kisses of my lips. As I closed my eyes, I melted into his embrace, and wished, for the second time that day, that time would stand still.

Chapter 7

I closed Aunt Lucille's diary, using the satin ribbon to mark my place. I leaned back and closed my eyes, trying to absorb it all. It felt a little strange, reading her intimate thoughts, as though I was actually there, invading their most private moments. Still, I was hanging on every word, anxious to find out what might happen next.

But my eyes were burning and fatigue washed over me again like an ocean wave. I needed to sleep, even though I kept picturing Gary surprising Lucille with the special Christmas cup and saucer. I smiled at the thought of that same teacup and saucer on the shelf above my office desk. I tried to imagine the joy Lucille must have felt when he gave it to her. Such a thoughtful thing to do, and yet she still barely knew him. I too felt the apprehension she mentioned so many times—wasn't it all too much, too soon?

Something else struck me about the part when they had lunch at the Walnut Room. How Gary twisted her opal ring as they talked. I smiled, knowing just how sweet a gesture that was because my Mark so often did the same thing. I glanced over at Mark and wondered when he would toy with it again. What if he forgot? What if he forgot *all* those little things that told me he cared for me? Like the way he always insists I have the last bite of popcorn or ice cream we share. Or the way he draws figure eights with his finger when he rests his hand on my knee. Or the way he slings my dishtowel over his shoulder when he helps in the kitchen.

Helps in the kitchen. Just like Uncle Gary used to do.

If I thought about the similarities long enough, it might creep me out. No, not really. Nothing creepy in a few coincidences. If anything, these things endeared me to my aunt and uncle even more. As I let myself drift off to sleep, I imagined Uncle Gary and Mark meeting for the first time. As they shook hands, would each notice the other's dishpan hands?

At seven the next morning, Gordo woke me up, arriving right on time with his Krispy Kremes.

"Hey, sleepyhead." He gave me a bear hug as I stood up. "How are you this morning?"

I stretched, knowing I must look like something the cat dragged in. "I'm good. I guess. I must have really slept hard. Never even heard the staff come and go like they usually do, banging around and talking too loud."

Gordo made his way to the other side of Mark's bed. "You ought to go home and get some real rest, Lucy."

"I know." I scratched my head and yawned again. "There will be time for that later."

"How's our boy doing this morning? Any changes?"

I stared at Mark, suddenly realizing how impatient I was to put this all behind us. "No changes."

"I see somebody gave him another shave. You do that?"

I snorted. "Not hardly. That takes a far steadier hand than mine."

Gordo smiled. "Did you know he keeps an electric razor in the glove compartment of his car so he can shave on his way home every day?"

"Really? Why?"

"Says it saves him time, so all he has to do when he gets home is take a quick shower, dress, and head over to your place. He always says the favorite part of his whole day is seeing you."

I smiled, remembering the big goofy smile he always gave when I opened my door for him. "My favorite part too." I swallowed hard to tamp down the lump in my throat.

"Come here," Gordo said, motioning me toward him.

I dashed a tear from my cheek and slowly made my way over to him. He pulled me close to his side, draping his arm over my shoulders. "Lucy, he's gonna make it. You'll see. He'll be up and bossing us all around in no time."

A half-hiccup, half-sob slipped out and with it, a lot more tears. Gordo pulled me closer. "We're all here for you, Lucy. Me and the guys, we've all got your back. And I wouldn't have it any other way. Mark's our brother, y'know? Maybe not kin, but just as close. And when this all blows over, first thing he'll want to know is if we took good care of you."

"I know." I wiped my cheek against my sweater sleeve. "He'd be really proud. And grateful, Gordo."

His kissed the top of my head, a lot like my brother does, then released me. He leaned over Mark's bed and patted his hand. "You take care, buddy. I'll be back tomorrow."

After he left, I went to the bathroom and tried to freshen up. I had just come out when Shelly arrived. I offered her one of Gordo's donuts, but as usual she took a pass. She's much too health-conscious to give in to the sinful pastries. Me? I inhaled mine as we chatted over the Starbucks she'd brought.

A little while later she left, promising to return this afternoon when she picked up her parents at the airport. Apparently the cruise line had moved heaven and earth to help the Christophers get home, but it had taken several days. I was sure Mark's mom was worried sick by now.

And so it continued. One day pretty much morphing into the next, and the next after that.

I was finding it harder and harder to keep my game face on. Oh, the tears came and went. No surprise there. But a foreboding sense of gloom was wending its way through my spirit. Maybe it was just the initial shock wearing off. Or maybe it was the monotony. Either way, I despised it and tried to fight it off however I could. My first line of defense was scripture. I camped out in the Psalms, clinging to them like a life raft in a dark and threatening sea. I reached for my Bible and opened it to Psalm 55.

> *Give ear to my prayer, O God; and do not hide Yourself from my supplication. Give heed to me, and answer me; I am restless in my complaint, and am surely distracted.*

I'm always amazed how God speaks to me through His word. Sometimes it seems like David was reading my mind when he penned those words a few thousand years ago. I am restless in my prayers, crying out to God on Mark's behalf. And I'm definitely distracted by the ever-present fear. I try so hard to shake it but I can't. It feels like an elephant has made its home on my chest. Sometimes I can hardly breathe.

I know I'm helpless. Apart from my pitiful prayers, I know there's nothing I can do to bring Mark around. Most of the time I read the Psalms out loud to him. Other times I have to force my focus on each and every word, willing myself to stake my trust in God even when it feels like the fear will swallow me whole.

I blew out a long sigh and set my Bible aside, then reached for the diary. Scripture soothes my soul—most of the time—but my aunt's journal occupies my mind, keeping me distracted. And this morning, I feel an urgent need for all the distraction I can get.

"Okay, Mark, last we read, Uncle Gary kissed Aunt Lucille for the first time. And I'm fairly sure I saw you blush when I was reading that part, but let's see what happens next."

Dear Diary,

Obviously, I fell asleep before finishing last time. I finally realized I'll never get it all in print at the rate I'm going. Still, I can't bear the thought of missing a single detail, because I still feel like it's all just a wonderful dream. Like I could wake up any moment and be back on that El, picking my textbook off the floor without the help of a handsome lieutenant.

That next day, Gary went to church with us. I had to fight a touch of pride as I walked into the church I grew up in with this handsome man in uniform at my side. Then, as we sang the first hymn, the beauty of Gary's rich tenor voice floated around us like the softest velvet. When I looked up at him, he paused, asking what was wrong. I love that he had no idea why others were looking our way.

Once we took our seats again, he tucked my hand in the crook of his arm and placed his hand over mine—a gesture I'd come to enjoy immensely. I felt protected. Cherished, somehow. For the rest of the service, he never let go. I didn't hear much of Reverend Thornton's sermon, my heart and my thoughts wrapped as one in constant prayer for this human gift sitting beside me. For his safety once he returned to the war. For the precious moments we had left together.

After church we said goodbye to Mother, Father, and little Jack. Gary's parents had invited me for Sunday dinner, and I was anxious to meet them. I found them to be utterly delightful, though much more reserved than their son. Mr. and Mrs. Reynolds made me feel so welcome. To be honest, I was relieved. I still wondered if Gary was a bit of a ladies' man. Had he brought other girls home to meet his parents? Lots of other girls? But those fears evaporated as the Reynolds seemed genuinely interested in getting to know me, asking about my family, discussing mutual friends, and so on.

I asked them about Gerald, Gary's older brother who had recently deployed to England with the 8th Air Force.

"Gerald was anxious to get over there and help with the war effort," Mrs. Reynolds began. "But it was the hardest thing I've ever done—saying goodbye to him. Craig practically had to pry me out of his embrace." She looked across the table at Gary, her eyes glistening. "And I admit, I'm not sure I'll do any better on Wednesday when you leave, son."

Gary stood, rounding the table to give her a hug. "Ah, sure you will, Mom. You and Dad will finally have some peace around here."

"That's for sure," Mr. Reynolds teased.

"Who knows, maybe you'll both take up some new hobbies. Like ice hockey. Or maybe javelin throwing. Hot air ballooning?"

"Very funny," Mr. Reynolds said dryly, laughing with us.

The easy conversation continued for the rest of the meal, then Gary and I did the dishes. (Of course!) Later, Mrs.

Reynolds played the piano as the four of us sang Christmas songs. After a few of the more festive tunes, she played the introduction to "O Holy Night"—my favorite carol. Halfway through the first verse, Gary's father took a seat in his easy chair, pulling his handkerchief from his pocket. He wiped his eyes and nose and glanced up at me with a trembling smile. Finding it impossible to sing, I slowly made my way to the sofa next to his chair. I clasped my hand over his and tried to smile.

As Gary's voice swelled with the reverent, beautiful lyrics and melody, I swallowed hard. I'd never heard anything so beautiful in my life. Just then, I noticed a tear streaking down his mother's face as she continued to play. Gary never stopped singing, but moved to stand behind her, his hands resting on her shoulders.

I knew his parents' tears had little to do with that unforgettable melody or their son's incredibly talented voice, and everything to do with him heading back to war. An odd feeling descended over me, as though I were imposing on an intimate family moment. I looked away, focusing on the gaily decorated tree in the corner of the room and the Zenith console radio on the far wall. I imagined the Reynolds listening to evening broadcasts filled with news of the war, and wondering if their sons were safe. And I tried to imagine what it was like to have not one, but two sons so far away in harm's way.

"Fall on your knees!
O hear the angel voices!
O night divine,
O night when Christ was born;
O night divine, O night,
O night Divine."

I closed my eyes, trying to banish my worrisome thoughts and simply live in the moment.

Later, as we said our goodbyes, I knew something inside me had changed. Maybe it was being in Gary's home or being a part of the impromptu singing around the piano. But considering I'd only known the Reynolds for a couple of hours, I felt strangely at home in their presence. The thought gave me pleasure.

Over these last couple of days, Gary's approaching departure has consumed me. On Monday, he accompanied me on my commute to Northwestern where he strolled the campus while I attended classes. That evening we had dinner at the Continental Room at Stephens Hotel. Afterward we went dancing, and I prayed the night would never end. Oh my, can my lieutenant dance!

This morning (Tuesday), I couldn't bear the thought of sitting in class, and for the first time in my life, I skipped classes so I could be with him.

He tried valiantly to distract me, filling our time with visits to the Field Museum of Natural History and the Adler Planetarium. But even fossil relics and celestial stargazing could not still the dread and angst I felt deep inside with each passing moment.

We spent the rest of the evening here at home where Mother and Father graciously gave us time alone in the parlor. I could never adequately put on paper all the things we talked about—or the many kisses we shared in those final hours together. As my tears began to fall, he busily wiped them away, cradling my face in his hands.

And what he said next quite literally took my breath away—

"Marry me, Lucille," he whispered. "Promise you'll wait for me and meet me at the altar as soon as I come back."

It made no sense. We'd known each other less than a week! How can you really <u>know</u> a person in a matter of mere days? Such a big decision shouldn't be made on a whim, should it?

But of course I said YES!!!

We laughed and cried and talked for another hour. It was almost one in the morning by then. Gary had to report for duty at 8:00 this morning, so we finally said goodnight after a thousand more kisses.

He plans to pick me up at 6:30 after saying goodbye to his folks at home. He assured me they would understand that he wanted those final moments alone with me to see him off at the station. I've felt badly that he's spent most of his leave with me, and worried that they might resent me for it. But at this point, all I can think of is having to let my lieutenant go.

Chapter 8

As I turned the next page, Dr. Bradley entered the room after a quick knock on the door. I set the diary aside and stood to greet him.

"Good afternoon, Lucy," he said, shaking my hand. "How's our patient doing today?"

"The same. Same as yesterday. Same as the day before. The same, the same, the same."

He peered over his glasses at me with an understanding smile. "Have a seat. We need to talk."

I didn't like the sound of that, but sat back down while he pulled the other chair over and took a seat facing me.

"Wait—should I call Mark's sister? His parents are coming in today, but—"

"No, I'll be glad to talk to his family later. For now, I want to assure you we're doing everything we can for Mark until he wakes up."

"But that's just it. What if he *doesn't* wake up?"

"Then we'll cross that bridge when we come to it. Traumatic brain injuries are extremely complicated, which, of course, makes it difficult to predict the short-term and long-term effects, or even how long a patient might stay comatose. Mark's TBI is severe based on the nature of his injury. You've watched me check for his response to light stimuli, waving my flashlight in front of his eyes, and testing voice and motion stimuli. So far we've had no response. But as I've said all along, that's not always a bad thing. Mark's body is trying to heal the injury. Think of it as shutting down all the extraneous activity in order to use every ounce of energy it can to help heal the trauma to his brain."

"I need you to be honest with me, Dr. Bradley," I whispered. I still wasn't sure about the whole concept of coma patients hearing what goes on around them, but I wasn't going to risk it. "Will Mark be the same if—*when* he wakes up? Or will he be . . ." I couldn't say it. The words just sat there, stuck in my throat. "Will he be—"

"Vegetative?" he whispered, pinning me with eyes that understood.

I was thankful he said what I couldn't. "Yes."

He sat back in his chair and folded his arms across his chest. “You asked me to be honest. So yes, Lucy. It’s a possibility. But *only* a possibility. And considering we’re just a week in, I’d say it’s a remote possibility at best. We’ll continue to monitor Mark, run some additional tests later this week.

“But for now let’s focus on the bigger picture, the healing that’s going on. The body is an amazing thing. As doctors we like to think we’re pretty smart and know every intricacy of the human body. But the fact of the matter is, God designed these earth suits with incredible resiliency, with capabilities we still don’t fully understand. Meaning, we’ll do the best we can on our end, and trust God with the rest. Does that work for you?”

I took a deep breath and slowly blew it out. “Yes. I keep trying to remind myself about God’s part in all this. And I truly believe He can heal Mark. I do. But sometimes . . .”

“Sometimes it’s tough to keep holding on, isn’t it?” he said, standing. He patted me on my shoulder. “Keep the faith, Lucy. Let the staff know when Mark’s folks arrive. If I can, I’ll stop by and update them.”

By now he’d made his way to the door. “You get some rest, okay? Doctor’s orders.”

“I’ll try.”

With a wink, he slipped out the door.

I was so tired, so weary of all this. I stood up and stretched this way then that, arching my clasped hands way over my head. I rolled my neck, hearing it snap, crackle and pop. Then I blew out a long cleansing breath and stood beside Mark’s bed. I stared at him for a few minutes, then took his lifeless hand in mine and sat on the edge of his bed.

“Y’know, I think Dr. Bradley’s a good guy, and I don’t doubt for a minute that he and the staff here are providing the best possible care for you, Mark. But the thing is—they don’t know you the way I do. They don’t know how you always go the extra mile for others. They don’t know how you always find the good in people—even the crankiest, nastiest people on the planet. They don’t know how your lopsided smile lights up a room. How it still makes me melt like butter.”

I leaned closer toward him, holding his palm against my cheek. “And they don’t know how much you mean to me. How you’ve changed my life, Mark.” I closed my eyes, willing his to open.

They didn’t, of course.

I felt my cell phone vibrate in my pocket. I kissed Mark’s hand then carefully placed it back on the bed. I dug out my phone and saw my editor’s number on the screen. I couldn’t dodge her again, so I took the call as I headed back toward my recliner.

"Hello, Samantha."

"Lucy? Is that you, Lucy?"

"Yes, Sam, it's me."

"I'm so used to talking to your voicemail, I guess it caught me off guard to hear your actual voice. How are you, Lucy? How's your UPS guy?" Samantha was never good with names, but I didn't hold it against her.

"I'm okay. Mark? Not so much."

"Wow. That's gotta be tough. What's it been now? A couple of weeks?"

"No, just a week. Listen, I'm sorry I haven't returned your calls, Sam. I've just been—"

"No need to apologize. You've got your hands full. And I wouldn't be calling again, but I've got to make a decision about your next novella. We're already under the wire to get it out well in advance of the holidays next year, so I think we might need to put it on the back burner—until this thing with Mark blows over."

I stared out the window, wondering exactly what she was envisioning as "this thing with Mark" blowing over. I dropped my head back and tried to let that go for the moment. I've always been baffled by the publishing process. How it takes a year or more to get a book in print. Sam's explained it to me, but with the whole print-on-demand technology today I still don't get it. But none of that mattered to me right now. And I wasn't particularly interested in fretting about contrived deadlines a year down the road. Not now.

I could hear Sam's long, loud exhale and imagined the cloud of smoke encircling her head as she continued. "It's just that I don't see how you could possibly get this one written in time. You know, under the circumstances."

Now it was my turn to exhale. "I've never missed a deadline, Sam, and I won't start now."

"Sure, sure. I know. But I'm getting pressure from upstairs wanting some conceptual ideas for the cover, a blurb for advertising—the usual. I don't want to harass you with all that while you're—y'know, keeping vigil and all. So I was just thinking we could move it back a few months. Pull it out of the queue and shoot for a later release."

"No. I'm *not* okay with that. Besides, I'm working through my aunt's diary. It's a gold mine of information, giving me so much to work with. All kinds of possibilities."

"Really?"

"Remember how I've always told you what a great story teller she was? Well, her diary reads like a storybook. It won't take that much to tweak it here and there. And it's such a heartwarming love story. You'll love it. I promise."

"I'm sure I will. But the question remains. Can you focus enough to have it ready in time?"

I shrugged. "Piece of cake."

"You sure about that?"

"Positive. I'll get an outline to you by the end of the week." I heard the words come out of my mouth, not quite sure where they came from. Maybe it was my subconscious mind begging for something—anything—to grasp onto. I had no control over Mark's situation, but writing a novella? That I could do.

We said our goodbyes, then I wandered down the hall to get a cup of coffee. The staff were all busy which suited me fine. I didn't have time for the usual chit chat. I needed to make some serious headway in Aunt Lucille's diary.

"Where were we, Mark?" I asked once I was back in the room. I took a sip of coffee and reached for the diary. "Gary proposed to Lucille. Right?" I peeked over at him, choosing to imagine him wracking his brain to recall. "It was their last night together before he headed back overseas."

I opened the diary and noted the date on the next entry—a full week later. I flipped back a few pages, thinking I'd missed something. "That's odd. No way Lucille would see Gary off at the station then not write about it in her diary. Strange, huh? Well, I guess we'll just pick up where we left off."

Dear Diary,

I simply haven't had the heart to write. One moment, my life was full of promise and romance and dreams about our future together. Then the next thing I know, time stood still, and I feel as if I haven't breathed in all the days that have passed.

The morning Gary was to leave, he picked me up at 6:30. He planned for me to drive his father's car back to their home after his train departed. It was freezing cold when we arrived at the station, so we quickly parked the car, intending to spend what time we had left together inside the terminal where it was warm. Gary had just heaved his large duffel bag over his shoulder when we heard someone scream. We looked across the parking lot and saw someone accosting a woman. Suddenly, Gary dropped his bag and cap, told me to stay there by the car, and off he went, racing toward them and shouting at the guy. "Let her go!"

My heart was pounding as I watched Gary scuffling with the man. "GARY!" I yelled. But no sooner had his name left my lips than I watched as the man slammed the butt of a pistol against Gary's head. He dropped to the ground, but I couldn't see where he landed—a parked car obscured my view. "GARY!" I screamed again, this time running toward them as fast as I could.

The man turned to look my way, the woman's purse clutched to his chest, then he bolted around a corner and out of sight. The woman's hysterical cries filled me with dread as I rounded the back end of the car. There on the ground, Gary was sprawled in an unnatural position, his head bleeding profusely. I dropped to my knees and held his face in my hands, saying his name over and over. His eyes found me for a split-second then rolled back in his head.

I was so sick with fear, I couldn't even think what to do. My mind flashed images of a funeral . . . a spray of white roses on a flag-draped coffin. Then the woman's garbled cries snapped me into action. I grabbed the wool scarf from around my neck and stuffed it gently under Gary's head.

"GO FOR HELP! Find a policeman—anyone! Please! GO!"

She stood there trembling, tears running down her wrinkled face as she blubbered something that made no sense, and it was only then that I realized she spoke another language. Italian? Polish?

I tried to remember the words. "Polizia? Policja?"

Her hysteria increased as more of the foreign words flooded from her mouth.

I went positively blank, unable to think what to say, and I could feel the panic rising in me.

Then suddenly others were there to help—a group of travelers coming from the station who must have seen or heard us. They called for help and in a few moments the wail of an ambulance siren filled the air.

Even now as I write about what happened, it still seems like a nightmare . . . as though I'm totally disconnected from reality, though I have only to look up to see Gary lying in that hospital bed to know the nightmare is real. We've been here a week now and—

I slammed the diary shut and sat up as an icy chill sent long shivering fingers down my back. How was this possible? I'm sitting in a hospital beside my Mark who's been in a coma for a week now . . . and I'm reading words written by my aunt as *she* sat in a hospital keeping vigil beside Uncle Gary.

"Whoa." I let the diary drop to my lap, my mind spinning. I rubbed my eyes. "This can't be right. I never heard about this before. Why didn't Aunt Lucille ever tell me? Why didn't Dad—"

I scrambled to dig my cell phone out of my pocket and called home.

"Lucy!" my dad answered. "We were hoping to hear from you. How's—"

"How come you never told me about Uncle Gary being in a coma?"

"What?"

"The day he was supposed to leave to go back to the war. He was trying to stop a mugger from attacking an old lady, and the guy cracked his head open with the butt of his gun. Why didn't anyone ever tell me about this?"

"Lucy, what's going on? Has something happened? Is Mark all right?"

I huffed. "He's exactly the same, Dad. He's in a coma. It's been a week now. And I'm reading Aunt Lucille's diary and just read about this, and frankly, I'm a little miffed that no one ever told me about this!"

"Okay, sweetheart. Just take a deep breath for me, will you?"

I imagined my father pulling off his readers, running his hand through his thinning hair, and trying to calm me down. I could see this in my mind because it happened so often when I was growing up. Especially during my teenage years. Which probably accounts for most of those missing hairs on his head.

So I took a deep, exaggerated breath for his benefit. "There. Okay? Start talking."

"First you need to explain to me why you're so upset. Where did this come from?"

"I don't know, Dad. It just feels like something was kept from me. Something so pertinent to what I'm experiencing right now. And I guess I feel like Aunt Lucille should have told me! All those years, when she used to tell me stories, she never once told me about this. All she ever said was that she'd met Uncle Gary when he was home on leave during the war. Why would she leave this part out?"

"Did you ever ask her? Ask for more details about their courtship?"

Dad's question caught me short. "Well . . . no, I guess I never did. Which is odd, actually. Because I was always so mesmerized by the two of them. How they still acted like a couple of young lovebirds after all those years."

Dad chuckled. "That's true. Gary treated Lucille like a queen. Always did. And Lucille pampered him something terrible."

"Whenever I was with them, it was almost like watching a love story on the big screen. Know what I mean?"

"I'd never thought of it that way, but you're right. Course, I was just a kid when they married, so that kind of thing didn't really register in my mind at the time. But later—oh my goodness, they not only doted on each other, they spoiled me rotten."

"Which is why you adored your sister."

"Still do, Lucy. Still do. I miss her more than you know."

"Me too, Dad."

Chapter 9

Shelly and Mark's parents arrived shortly after I got off the phone with Dad. I have to admit, I had mixed feelings about them coming. As selfish as it sounds, I was feeling a peculiar mix of territorial jealousy. I'd been with Mark since the whole hostage incident. Others came and went, but this room, this vigil—it was mine. And I wasn't sure I wanted to share it with Mark's mom and dad.

I was so wrong.

When Lisa Christopher walked in the room, I heard her gasp. I watched her hands cover her mouth, her brow wrinkling as she took in the sight of her son stretched out in the hospital bed.

"Oh, Mark," she rasped as she slowly moved toward the bed.

I started toward her but stopped myself. My ridiculous territorial jealousy disappeared as I put myself in her shoes—seeing her grown up baby boy looking so pale, bruised, and lifeless.

"Oh, sweetie," she whispered edging closer to him.

"Lucy." Brian Christopher approached me with outstretched arms. I'd been so focused on Mark's mother, I hadn't even noticed Shelly and her dad walk in.

I started to respond but couldn't find my voice. He engulfed me in a bear hug and the dam inside broke. Again.

He kissed the top of my head and turned, his arm still over my shoulders. "How's he doing, Lucy?"

I pressed my lips together then croaked, "Pretty much the same. I'm so glad you're here."

He hugged me again then moved aside as Mark's mom approached me. "Oh Lucy, how are you?" She hugged me so tight. I tried not to slobber on her coat before pulling back to face her.

"Um, I'm okay. I guess. All things considered."

She leaned her forehead against mine. "How can we ever thank you enough for taking such good care of Mark? Shelly told me you haven't left his side since the day he was admitted. You have no idea how much that means to us."

I tried to shrug it off, but she had no idea how much her words meant to *me*. I felt such a tremendous relief just having them here—the complete opposite of what I'd expected.

For the next half hour, we talked. I tried to reassure them of Mark's prognosis, telling them what little I knew. I stepped out briefly to ask the nurse in charge to page Dr. Bradley. He arrived twenty minutes later and took the Christophers down the hall to a room set aside for consultations.

While they were gone, I made an unexpected decision. Maybe it was utter fatigue. I don't know. But I sensed such an intense compassion toward Mark's parents after watching them see their son for the first time. And I realized, if I were Mark's mom or dad, I'd be *desperate* for time with him. Alone. Time to process. Time to come to terms with the reality of what had happened. What might still happen.

Which is why I told them I'd like to go home for a few hours to rest. Shelly looked at me like I'd grown a third eye, then a moment later she mouthed—*thank you.* I told them I'd like to come back later after dinner and stay with Mark overnight, if that was okay with them.

"Lucy, that's perfectly okay with us," Lisa said. "We're both exhausted from jet lag, so a good night's sleep in our own bed will be heavenly. As long as you promise to call us if anything happens?"

"Mom, we've been at this for a week now," Shelly added. "Lucy knows the drill."

"Absolutely," I said. "And the same applies to you—you'll call me if anything happens while I'm gone, right?"

"Right," Shelly answered, giving me a side hug. "Now go home. Get some rest."

The Christophers hugged me on my way out. I knew it was the right thing to do. To give them time alone with Mark. But still—it felt *so* weird to leave. As if I'd left my heart back in that room. Which, I supposed, was exactly what I'd done.

I realized I was fingering the heart necklace Mark had given me as the elevator dinged its arrival. As the doors opened, there stood my uncle.

"Lucy! I was just coming to see you." He gave me a hug as I got in the elevator with him. "Is everything okay?"

I pushed the button for the first floor. "The Christophers just got here. I wanted to give them some time with Mark."

Uncle Ted leaned back against the elevator wall. "That's nice of you. Can I buy you a cup of coffee?"

"Okay if I take a rain check? I haven't been out of this hospital in over a week, and all I want to do is go home and go to bed."

"I don't blame you a bit. A rain check it is."

"Oh, wait. I just realized I don't have a car here. Could you give me a ride to my house?"

"My pleasure, Lucy."

We chatted on the way to Uncle Ted's car in the hospital parking garage. It wasn't until I saw his Buick sedan that I realized what I'd gotten myself into. My uncle's driving was the stuff of family legend.

"Oh, Uncle Ted, I, uh, forgot that—"

"Hop in, Lucy." He unlocked the doors with his remote and motioned me toward the passenger side.

I uttered a quick prayer for survival, too tired to grapple with finding another ride home. I'd just fastened my seatbelt when he peeled out of the garage, leaving a patch of rubber on the pavement behind us. Which is why I uttered a second prayer.

Oblivious to the blur of wintry scenery flying past us or the possibility of ice on the roads, Uncle Ted carried on a one-sided conversation while I tried hard to stifle the multiple warning cries piercing my mind.

"You like Mark's folks? Y'know, it's important to have a good relationship with a prospective mate's parents. It's also a good idea to make a keen observation of his relationship with his parents. Find a man who admires his father and honors his mother—not just in word, but in deed—and that's the guy you want to marry."

There were so many responses I could make, but speaking was impossible given the fact that my teeth were tightly ensconced on my lower lip. My half-hearted "uh huh" would have to suffice.

"Now take your own mother and father. Those two sweethearts have tremendous respect for each other. Not to mention the way your father loves and adores my sister. And I don't have to tell you what a goner she is for him!"

I closed my eyes for my third prayer. *Oh Lord Jesus, forgive me of every sin or possibility of sin or even the tiniest inclination toward sin—just please let me get home in one piece!* I peeked just in time to feel the sharp thrust of my shoulder against the passenger window as Uncle Ted made the final turn onto my street. The neighbors' houses rushed by at warp speed, and I began to panic—*will he stop at my house or will I have to eject myself outta here as he flies past it?*

His tires squealed in protest as he slammed on the brakes, our heads jerking forward as the vehicle of death came to an abrupt stop in my driveway. He put the gear in Park and turned toward me.

"And what's so wonderful about that is, when Mark recovers and you two get back on your path to marital bliss, Mark will easily note that your parents have given you a legacy of a home filled with warmth and love and respect—which all add up to making *you* a great catch."

Still panting from the Grand Lemans trip home, I stared at my uncle, wondering how my calm, sensible mother could possibly have come from the same womb. Then, unbuckling my seatbelt, I opened the car door and paused before getting out.

I looked over my shoulder at him. "Uncle Ted?"

"Yes, Lucy?" His eyes gazed at me with rapt attention, a smile of expectation on his lips.

I shook my head again and decided not to address the whole "path to marital bliss" issue. "Thanks for the ride home."

"Anytime, kiddo."

I nodded, then got out just as he revved the engine. My "goodbye" was lost in a flurry of exhaust.

Inside, my house felt strange, much like it feels after being away on an extended vacation. Everything looks the same, but the soul of the structure seemed to keep me at arm's length. I cringed at the pathetic metaphor, but there it was. I'd been gone a week, not months. And without Gertie's nails tapping on the hardwoods to welcome me home, I felt as though I were intruding somehow. I thought about calling Chad and asking him to bring Gertie home, but even in my sleep-deprived fog, I knew that was silly. I'd only be home a few hours.

I ignored the pile of mail on the table beside the door and shuffled my way down the hall, dropping my coat and kicking off my sneakers along the way. Half an hour later, after a long and hot bubble-filled soak in the tub, I set my alarm and climbed under the covers of my bed.

Turns out I slept through two alarms. Which is why it was close to nine o'clock when I drove back to the hospital. I was still groggy, but those few hours at home made a world of difference. The urgency to check on Mark kept tapping at my heart, but each time I remembered Lisa's expression when she saw her son, I knew he was in good hands.

On a whim, I stopped by Chad's to see Gertie for a few minutes. Hospitals should make it a practice to allow pets in patient rooms. Fifteen minutes of love and affection from my sweet Scottie was good medicine. The best. Mark loves her as much as I do, and I imagined sneaking her in and letting her lie on Mark's bed alongside his legs. He would love that.

The Christophers had just finished sharing a pizza when I knocked on the door. They insisted on leaving the last piece for me plus some humongous chocolate chip cookies Shelly had picked up. We chatted for a few minutes before they left, and I quickly noticed how reticent Lisa was to leave her son. How well I knew that feeling. I assured her I'd keep a good eye on him and call if anything came up.

I felt so much better as I settled back in my "lair" as Chad now called it. Clean from my bath, clean hair, clean clothes, and even a clean mouth—flossed and sparkling. I sat on the edge of Mark's bed, asking about his visit with his parents. I told him Gertie sent her love, and how I wished I could have brought her with me. Holding his hand between both of mine, I wished for the ten-billionth time that he would wake up. I needed to see those warm sable eyes of his and his lopsided dimples. And oh, how I needed to hear his laugh.

I kissed his hand and gently placed it back on the blue hospital blanket next to his leg. He seemed to prefer it there.

Once back in the recliner, I reached for Lucille's diary, suddenly anxious to find out more about Uncle Gary's coma—and wishing Lucille would talk to me through the decades and tell me how to handle all this. Did she teeter back and forth between anxiety and faith like I did? Did she fret over the possibility that Gary wouldn't make it? Did she pray for hope when it seemed there was none?

And did she feel the same guilt I felt whenever I asked God to *take* Mark rather than leave him a "vegetable" or forever lost in a coma?

Of course, I knew what she didn't at the point I'd stopped reading. I knew Uncle Gary would survive and marry her. I knew their marriage would be magical and romantic for decades to come, until they stopped counting anniversaries when Uncle Gary died. As I opened the diary, I prayed Mark and I would have another chance just as they had.

"Okay, big guy. I know you enjoyed spending time with your family, but it's time to get back to the story. I still can't believe Uncle Gary was so brutally attacked like that. He was just trying to help that little old lady!" I looked over at Mark. "And don't you find it ridiculously bizarre that he ended up in a hospital bed in a coma—just like you? It's so crazy. I always felt a special bond with Aunt Lucille. You know how much I adored her. But that doesn't even come *close* to what I feel now, after discovering what they went through and how much our situations are alike. I mean, it's almost a little creepy, don't you think?"

I waited for the answer that didn't come. "Anyway, let's see. Where did we leave off? Oh—here we go. I'll pick up the last paragraph before we got interrupted."

Even now as I write about what happened, it still seems like a nightmare . . . as though I'm totally disconnected from reality, though I have only to look up to see Gary lying in that hospital bed to know the nightmare is real. We've been here a week now and nothing has changed. The doctors keep telling us to give it time, to hold on, to not lose faith . . . but each hour that passes fills my heart with so much sadness, I can hardly breathe at times.

Whoa. The hairs on the back of my neck just prickled. Talk about creepy. I'm reading Lucille's description of how she felt—using many of the *exact words* I've thought myself, day after day since we've been here. I'm not sure anyone else could understand these emotions except for my Aunt Lucille. Strange. Unbelievably strange.

I glanced at Mark then found my place again.

Gary's parents come every day, of course. I've grown to love them both so much. They seem truly grateful that I'm willing to stay with Gary around the clock. I'm so glad this hospital allows loved ones to stay with patients as long as they like. It's a good thing because I would have fought them on the matter.

Mother comes every morning. She leaves Jack with our neighbor, Mrs. Trussell, so she tries to stay no more than half an hour. I suspect she keeps it short so she doesn't impose on the Reynolds' time with Gary. In a peculiar way, my parents and Gary's have gotten to know each other fairly well over the past week. He'd be so happy to know they genuinely like each other.

I want so desperately to tell them about Gary's proposal the night before all this happened. But I can't do it until he comes around—I mean, WHEN he comes around. I don't want to share such special news without him.

A nurse reminded me today that Christmas is the day after tomorrow. I was absolutely stunned. Time has stood still since that morning at the train station. It's strange—the way I felt when she told me. I remembered the beautifully decorated windows at Marshall Field's, and how we shopped that day so Gary could leave presents for his family when he left. I remembered the tree in the corner of the Reynolds' living room, the lovely lights and garlands of cranberries and popcorn.

I've always loved Christmas. It's my favorite holiday. And yet, when the nurse asked about my plans for Christmas, I wanted to slap that starched cap right off her head! I didn't, of course. I tried to keep a kind tone in my voice when I told her we'd be spending Christmas at Gary's bedside. She stopped and looked at me, her eyes moist with tears, then reached for my hand and squeezed it, asking me to forgive her for saying something so insensitive. I thought that was sweet of her.

Still, I can't shake the added gloom of knowing Christmas may come and go without Gary coming around. I smile, remembering his constant medley of Christmas songs in the days we spent together. He can be such a ham at times! Oh, how I miss those carefree days of Christmas carols and dancing and laughing so hard, our sides ached.

But those happy memories last only a few moments before the gravity of all this sneaks back under my skin. I look at his face, hardly recognizing it without his contagious smile and those sparkling blue eyes. Oh Gary, please come back to me.

Mother prayed with me this morning before she left. We stood by Gary's bed, our hands covering his. Mother prayed for God's healing hand to reach down and touch Gary. She prayed for his doctors and nurses and those who bathe him each morning and keep his room clean. I never would have thought to pray for those people. How I wish I had my mother's faith.

And then she prayed for me, asking God to keep me safe in His care. Asking Him to calm my spirit and help me learn to trust Him completely. When her voice failed, she squeezed my hand, urging me to continue her prayer. Instead, I turned and wept on her shoulder.

I'm so blessed to have a mother who loves the Lord with all her heart. I only wish I had half the faith she does.

Chapter 10

Later—

The strangest thing happened this afternoon. The hospital visiting hours began at 2:00 p.m. Around 2:45, someone knocked on the door to Gary's room. A man I'd never seen before opened the door and asked if he and his mother could come in. Of course I said yes, and when he stepped aside, I recognized her immediately—the woman Gary had tried to rescue in the parking lot at the train station. Her face was filled with such unmasked sorrow.

"My mother doesn't speak English, but she has been most anxious to find out about—" he paused, glancing over at Gary then back at his mother—"to find out about the man who saved her life. We have tried for days to find him. Only today would the police tell us his name, and that he was here, brought to this hospital. My mother has been—uh, most, uh—anxious to know how Mr. Gary Reynolds is." He nodded as if to assure himself he'd said it right. I recognized his heavy accent as Italian.

"Please come in," I said, extending my hand to her and then to her son. "I'm Lucille."

"Yes, please. Nice to meet you. I am Marco Bertolucci, and this is my mother, Abelina Bertolucci."

Mrs. Bertolucci mumbled something to her son.

"She said she remembers you from that day. You are Mrs. Reynolds?"

"No, I'm not—I mean, he's not my—well, we're engaged, but no one knows about that yet. I'm his fiancée."

"Ah," he said with a hint of a smile that quickly faded. "I am sorry for your, uh, for his injuries. Is he going to be . . . okay?"

I started to say something but couldn't find my voice. I motioned for them to join me closer to Gary's bed.

"Oh—" Marco held his index finger to his lips and whispered, "He is sleeping. We do not wish to disturb him. We will go—"

"It's all right," I said. "I admit, I prefer to think that he's just resting, but the doctors tell us he's actually in a coma."

Marco translated for his mother. "Co-ma?" She looked between us.

"Coma, yes. Think of it as a deep, deep sleep."

He translated again, then his mother asked a question through her son. "She wishes to know if he will wake up."

I blinked away the tears stinging my eyes. "Yes, we hope so. Soon."

After Marco translated, Mrs. Bertolucci lifted her gnarled hands toward me, cupping my face in her palms. She uttered something barely over a whisper, her brows arched in sympathy as she spoke.

Marco continued. "My mother wishes you to know that God will take care of this man, her hero, who saved her that day. She knows this because God told her to make him her famous Christmas Cannoli Siciliani. And God would not tell her to do so if Mr. Reynolds were—uh, if he was not able to, uh . . . eat."

I felt my lips quivering as I tried to smile. "That's so sweet, and I know Gary will love them."

Mrs. Bertolucci reached into the large bag over Marco's shoulder and lifted out a silver tin with a red and white checked bow tied around it. She handed it to me with such care, as though they were the crowned jewels instead of pastry.

"Thank you, Mrs. Bertolucci. This is—"

Another exchange. "She wishes for you to call her Abelina."

"Abelina. Thank you."

We couldn't communicate with words, but I hoped she could see the joy she'd given me reflected in my face. "Abelina, I will look forward to sharing these with Gary. And when he wakes up, I want him to meet you. Promise me you'll come back." I nodded toward Marco, anxious for him to tell her.

A broad smile creased her face as she chuckled, mumbling again as she clutched my hand.

"My mother says she would like that very much. Very much."

"As would I. Marco, could you write down your telephone number so I can call you when that happens?"

As Marco jotted his number on a scrap of paper, Abelina motioned for me to join her beside Gary's bed. She held my hand and placed her other hand on Gary's. I smiled, remembering how my mother had done the same thing just a few hours ago. Abelina smiled at me then closed her eyes. In her native tongue, I could tell she was praying. Marco joined us, quietly sharing her prayer with me.

Moments later, they left. I returned to Gary's bedside and took his hand in mine. I felt it immediately—the heaviness that had shrouded me seemed to have lifted. And for the first time I let myself hope—truly hope. I glanced over at the tin of cannoli and smiled.

"Gary, Mrs. Bertolucci said God told her to make those cannoli for you. And she said He wouldn't have told her to make them if you couldn't eat them. Isn't that something?"

I kissed his hand and set it back down. I made my way over to the tin, curious to take a peek. But as I started to untie the homespun ribbon, I stopped and peeked back at Gary.

"Okay, okay. I'll save them for you. But just so you know, it's a tremendous act of sacrifice on my part. I'll bet you those cannoli are absolutely divine."

As I sat back down, an idea started to form in my mind. Why stop with Mrs. Bertolucci's Christmas cannoli? What if we celebrated Christmas here—right here in Gary's room? I looked around, my mind suddenly racing with ideas. I dug a small notepad out of my pocketbook and started listing them all.

I finished half an hour later just as Mr. and Mrs. Reynolds arrived.

I practically jumped up to see them. "I'm so glad you're here! Wait until you hear my plan!"

"Hey, Sis? What in the world are you smiling about?"

I snickered out loud as I threaded the satin ribbon to mark my place in the diary. "Hi, Chad. Just lost in Lucille's world for a while. She's come up with some kind of plan to have Christmas right there in Gary's hospital room. Crazy, huh?"

Chad dropped his coat on the other chair and sat on the edge of Mark's bed. "I don't know. Sounds kind of fun. We could do that."

"What?"

"Well, face it, Lucy—Christmas is just a few days away. And unless your Sleeping Beauty here decides to snap out of it tonight or tomorrow, I think Lucille might just be on to something."

I stared at him, my mind already bouncing back and forth between a 1944 hospital room filled with Christmas decorations and brightly wrapped gifts and the room I was now sitting in. A row of floral arrangements lined the window sill, including some wilted purple mums I didn't have the heart to toss out. I'd taped all the get-well cards Mark had received on the wall opposite his bed. Otherwise, the room looked like every other hospital room I'd ever seen. Plain and dull, and terribly depressing.

I looked back at my brother. "Y'know, I think you're right. We could *totally* do this."

"Sure we could." He plopped his size-13 Nike on his other knee. "School's out now so I can be your gopher. Just tell me what you want."

I stood up and stretched, realizing I hadn't been out of my chair in a couple of hours. "Good grief. I think my body has started molding itself to this lovely mauve vinyl."

"Why don't you go home for a while? I can stay as long as you need me to. Go take another soak in your tub."

"Thanks, but I'm okay." I wandered over to the window, looking out into the darkness. I shivered, watching the trees bend sideways in the blustery wind. "Looks frigid out there."

"Coldest December on record. They're saying we might actually have a white Christmas this year."

"Seriously? I can't even remember the last time that happened."

"I think you were still in diapers, if I recall."

"Diapers, huh?" I pinched that tender spot between his neck and his shoulder. It was my favorite sibling target zone.

"Ouch!"

"Wait—" I stopped and looked back out the window. "If it snows, how would we get everyone here to the hospital on Christmas? You know what happens when it snows in this town. People freak out and completely forget how to drive."

Chad leaned back against Mark's legs. "We'll just have to work it out. I can borrow Pete's van and haul everybody up here. But we probably ought to get a move on it with the planning. You thinking food? Tree? Decorations?"

My head started spinning. "Whoa, buddy. You've got the

cart *waaay* before the horse. I haven't even had a chance to find out what Aunt Lucille pulled off in Uncle Gary's room."

"So why not start there?"

He blinked at me with those incredibly adorable eyes. It was an old trick he used to play back when we were kids. I'd get mad about something, he'd tilt his head just so and blink rapidly, pinning me with that look of his. I fell for it every time —well, not *every* time. There was that whole mess with the charcoal fluid in Dad's shed. No need to bring that up now.

I shook my head. "Start where?"

He got up, grabbed Lucille's diary and handed it to me. "Let's see what dear ol' Aunt Lucille had up her sleeve."

"You want me to read to you?"

"You read to Mark, don't you? At least I'm lucid." He leaned over to whisper in Mark's ear. "No offense, big guy."

Chad pulled the other chair over and took a seat. He stretched out his legs and folded his arms across his chest. "Fire away, little sister. I'm all ears."

I rolled my eyes for effect and opened the book. "Okay, the last thing we read before you so *rudely* interrupted us—"

"My bad."

"—was when Lucille finished her list of things to do just as Gary's parents walked in." I looked up at my brother. "I don't remember ever hearing much about Uncle Gary's parents, do you?"

"Lucy, they were dinosaurs by the time we came along."

"Hey—have a little respect, will you? They played a pivotal role in Lucille and Gary's courtship. Not to mention the heartache they must have experienced through all this. Think about it. Their younger son is overseas flying bombing missions over Europe. Their oldest son comes home on leave, falls in love, then tries to help an old lady in distress, and ends up comatose in the hospital." I shivered. "Chad, every time I think about the similarities of what happened to them and what's happened now with Mark, I still can't believe it. I mean, what are the chances?"

"I'll admit it's bizarre. Especially when you factor in Steve sending you Aunt Lucille's diary—"

"—so that I received it just a day after Mark landed in a hospital in a coma." I shivered again. "If this were a book I was writing, the reviewers would nail me for it—'Ridiculous!'" I fingered air-quotes. "'Too convenient to be plausible!' 'Absurd!' Oh, they'd have a field day with it. I'd be lucky to get anything above a one-star rating on Amazon."

"But weren't you planning to write Uncle Gary and Aunt Lucille's story? Isn't that your next novella in your teacup series?"

I stared at him. "Yes it is. Which presents the dilemma of whether to portray their love story accurately, or take some creative license and tweak the story here and there."

"Don't look at me. You're the writer."

I shook it off. "I know. Okay, stop interrupting me or I'll never get through this."

He raised his hands in surrender.

Chapter 11

At Chad's urging, I picked up where I'd left off. "Gary's mom and dad had just arrived. Okay, here we go."

After updating them, I told Mr. & Mrs. Reynolds about my idea to have Christmas right there in Gary's room. I was elated when they both loved the idea and offered to help in any way they could. We sat down and went over my list, dividing the tasks. I would ask the nurses if they might allow us to use the lounge area down the hall for our buffet. Mrs. Reynolds came up with a marvelous idea to bring enough food to share with the nursing staff on Gary's floor.

I must admit it seemed rather strange with all of us bustling about and Gary still lying there, completely unaware of any of it. I fought a constant battle inside my heart. On the one hand, I felt relieved to have something to do, something to look forward to. But on the other hand—for lack of a better word, I felt guilty. As though I were ignoring Gary. Such peculiar mind and heart games.

Father found the cutest little Christmas tree which we placed on the wide window ledge in Gary's room. Mrs. Reynolds brought some small ornaments and short strands of cranberries and popcorn. Mr. Reynolds brought a radio and found a station that played nothing but Christmas carols—a welcome relief from all the war news.

Mother Nature cooperated with a lovely snowfall; pretty enough for a picture postcard, but not so much that would interfere with our families coming to the hospital for our festivities.

On Christmas Eve, Mrs. Reynolds insisted on staying with Gary overnight so I could go home and freshen up for our party. I was exhausted but at the same time energized with anticipation. Still, once I had everything ready and crawled into bed, I fell sound asleep for hours.

The next morning I put on my emerald swing dress with a large green-and-white pinstriped bow overlapping the square collar on the right shoulder. The full A-line skirt fell a couple inches below my knees. It was my favorite winter dress, perfect for the holidays. I arrived at the hospital at 7:00. Mrs. Reynolds said Gary had a restful night. I could tell she was trying hard to keep a light heart, but I recognized the sadness in her eyes. A few moments later, she left for home, assuring me she and Mr. Reynolds would be back with Christmas dinner in a few hours.

I could tell the housekeeping staff had stopped by, leaving a fresh clean scent in their wake—a welcome relief from the strong aroma of bacon and eggs wafting through the hall as food services delivered breakfast to Gary's neighbors on the floor. It always made me a little sad, catching a whiff of those meals, whether it was breakfast, lunch, or dinner. Gary loved to eat. "Food is much more than mere nourishment, Lucille!" he'd once proclaimed. "A well-cooked meal is to be celebrated! Enjoyed!"

I'm not so sure he'd say the same about those meals rolling by his door.

I stayed busy adding some last minute decorations. I placed some of my favorite nutcrackers on the ledge beside St. Nicholas. Mother had insisted I bring "the Christmas candle," a strange old thing that had been photographed in every family Christmas picture for as long as I could remember. I set it on the small table beside Gary's bed. I turned it this way and that, apologizing to Gary for how pitiful it looked.

I lingered, slowly taking a seat on the edge of Gary's bed. I brushed back a lock of hair from his face, then traced my finger along his strong jawline. A twinge of sadness crept back in, so I kissed his stubbled cheek and looked for something else to do. Spotting the radio, I decided a little music would surely help keep my spirits up. As I adjusted the knob, an orchestral rendition of "The First Noel" played quietly.

Perfect.

I still had some time before the others would start arriving, so I reached into the bag I'd brought and pulled out the small box. I took my seat there beside Gary again.

"Obviously, I didn't have time to get you a present. I trust you'll forgive me, Lieutenant, especially since you weren't even supposed to be here for Christmas. If I'm completely honest, I have to admit I'd rather you were thousands of miles away and healthy than to be here with me like this. I try not to think about that too much." I shook my head. "Anyway, this morning before I left the house, I saw this sitting on my dresser and decided to bring it with me."

I opened the lid and lifted out the teacup and saucer—the Christmas set Gary had surprised me with that day at Marshall Field's. "I haven't used it yet, and I decided I want you to be the first to drink from it. I know it's silly, but I don't care. It meant so much to me when you gave it to me that day, and I just thought . . . well, I guess you could say I'm putting all my hopes into it. Hoping you'll wake up and celebrate Christmas with all of us today."

I set the cup and saucer on the table beside the old candle. "It will be our tradition. Years from now when we're old and gray, we'll share a cup of Christmas tea together on Christmas morning. Who knows, maybe we'll collect a whole set of these dishes. Wouldn't that be fun? And each year we'll remember how—"

"Good morning, Miss Alexander."

I turned to find Gary's doctor approaching us. "Merry Christmas, Dr. Pembleton. How are you?"

"Fine, thank you. The nurses told me about your plans today. I think it's a wonderful idea. Looks nice in here."

"Thank you." I stood, smoothing my skirt. "It's helped having something to do. Something to look forward to."

I watched as Dr. Pembleton started his routine examination of Gary. When he finished, he tucked Gary's chart under his arm and started heading back toward the door. He smiled—the kind of smile doctors give you when there's nothing new to report, nothing encouraging to say. I didn't bother asking.

"Well, I for one think it's a great idea to have your Christmas here. Always good to keep a positive outlook. Especially during the holidays."

"You're welcome to join us."

"That's most kind, but I'll be heading home once I make my rounds. We've got a house full of relatives and a lot of gifts under the tree waiting to be unwrapped."

"Do you have children? Grandchildren?"

"No grandchildren yet. Our two daughters and their husbands arrived last night. Our twin sons are both overseas. Josh is stationed in England with the 8th Air Force, and Justin is on the USS Saratoga somewhere in the Pacific. We're trying to carry on as usual, but we miss them terribly."

"I hope they'll be home soon. I hope all our boys over there can come home soon."

He smiled briefly. "That would be the best Christmas present of all, wouldn't it?"

"Yes, it would."

He opened the door. "Take care, Miss Alexander. I hope you and your family have a nice time today."

"Thank you, Dr. Pembleton. You too."

Over the next couple of hours, our families arrived with armloads of our favorite holiday dishes—turkey with all the trimmings, cranberry salad, fresh-baked yeast rolls, and enough desserts to feed an army. I was so pleased the hospital staff eased their rule about underage children for the day, allowing Jack to join us. When he first laid eyes on Gary, his little chin trembled as he asked all about his injuries.

"Can he hear us, Lucille?"

"I don't know for sure, but I'd like to think so. I talk to him all the time. Would you like to say something to him?"

Jack shook his head and backed up against me. "No."

"That's okay, little buddy. How about you and I go take a peek at some of those yummy pies and cakes in the lounge area?"

All things considered, in spite of the circumstances, it was a wonderful Christmas. It truly was. What had been an afterthought—inviting the medical staff on Gary's floor to share our Christmas meal—turned out to be such an unexpected blessing. A double blessing, actually. I'm sure most of them would have preferred to be home with their families instead of working a holiday shift. So for us, it was a chance to thank them on this special day for taking such good care of Gary.

"There's your answer."

"Chad, I'm not finished reading this section."

"I know, but you've read enough for now. You wanted to know how Aunt Lucille moved the family Christmas up to Uncle Gary's hospital room. Now you know."

I closed the diary and pinched the bridge of my nose. "I don't know. I'm not sure we should try this."

"Why not? Have you got someplace else to be on Christmas?"

"Don't be such a brat. Of course I'll be here. But I'm not her, Chad. Aunt Lucille's hostessing skills were legendary. She was the poster child for multi-tasking before anyone even knew what that was. It's like she had the Midas touch for making ordinary situations into extraordinary celebrations. To her, *everything* had possibilities. The simplest, most mundane activity was reason enough to celebrate."

"Makes you wonder if all that might have started right there." Chad pointed to the diary in my lap. "Maybe she learned the importance of celebrating regardless of the circumstances. Regardless of the inconvenience or how scared you are about something."

I just nodded, trying to make sense of it all.

Chad leaned forward, resting his elbows on his knees. "And maybe, just maybe," he began, a lazy smile curling his lips, "your beloved namesake is offering you some hope in a hopeless situation. I'll admit, it would be a whole lot easier to think of that book in your lap as a work of fiction as opposed to such a freaky coincidence traveling through time."

"I know! Look at me—I've got goose bumps just thinking about it."

"But the thing is, I learned a long, long time ago that there's no such thing as a coincidence. Someone once said coincidence is God's way of remaining anonymous. I think there's a lot of truth in that."

"Whoa . . . I love that." I scratched the back of my head. "I could write a full-length novel based on that concept."

My brother laughed. "Yeah, you could do that in a heartbeat, Lucy. All I'm saying is, let's look at this as a *providential gift* from Aunt Lucille—and just run with it. Why not?"

I jumped up. "You're right, Chad. Why not?" I grabbed my laptop and powered it up. "This is good. This is really good. It'll keep my mind occupied. Just like Lucille. It'll give me something to do. Okay, let's come up with some ideas and then divvy up the list."

I shuddered. Like a 3.5 on the Richter scale.

"You okay?"

"Yeah. It's just—that's almost verbatim what Lucille wrote in her diary after coming up with the idea. When Uncle Gary's parents showed up that morning, she sat down with them and divided the list."

"Fine, let's just keep the earthquake references to a minimum. We've got enough to deal with as it is."

Chapter 12

Over the next couple of days, I tag-teamed with Shelly and the Christophers, taking turns staying with Mark so we could get everything ready in time for our own version of a hospital Christmas. I had to admit it was good medicine. I couldn't remember a Christmas I'd looked more forward to. Strange, isn't it? My boyfriend is in a coma, and I'm baking cookies and rounding up decorations and strings of Christmas lights. It felt a lot more like business as usual, even if it wasn't. And after all we'd been through, I welcomed it like a soothing balm on the craziness of the past few weeks.

After Mark's parents left on Christmas Eve night, I finally had a chance to sit down and relax. I insisted on staying overnight with Mark. Even with all the distractions, I kept getting emotional at the most random times. Like this afternoon when I realized I'd forgotten to pick up some Poppycock—the gourmet popcorn that comes in clusters with a caramel glaze. Mark *loves* Poppycock, especially the pecan praline flavor. I went to four different places and they were all out. Said they'd been sold out for a week and didn't expect to get any more in time for Christmas.

The rational voices in my head assured me it was no big deal. All things considered, it was probably the last thing Mark would think about if he was awake. And let's face it, Poppycock is amazing, but it's a dental nightmare. With all the other holiday treats and cakes and cookies, it was just another cavity waiting to happen. Right?

Those were the rational voices. The emotional voices had an altogether different tone. Which is why I found myself at the Publix cash register at closing time, bawling like a baby. You know, the ugly cry with mascara tracking down my cheeks and snot running down my chin? Yeah, that was me. Utterly inconsolable. Naturally, that was the precise moment when my cell rang and, blubbering fool that I was, I answered it. Samantha was at JFK on her way to some chateau in the Alps for the holidays and wanted to wish me a Merry Christmas. Patience isn't one of Sam's strong suits, which is why she kept yelling at me, trying to find out why I was crying so hard and couldn't talk. Then she shrieked, sucking in the loudest emphysema-laced breath on record.

"OH, LUCY—PLEASE TELL ME YOUR UPS GUY DIDN'T DIE?!"

The Publix cashier—*Bethany,* according to her name tag—actually got down on the floor next to me and wrapped her arm around me while I wailed. Later, when my brother showed up (Bethany called him for me), he informed the kind grocery staff that I had apparently and unfortunately hit a point of critical mass.

"I think she held it in as long as she could, then BOOM! Sorry you all had to see this."

The store manager held my hands as Chad helped me up. "She said something about that UPS guy who was taken hostage. Said she needed some Poppycock for him. I'm sorry, but we're all out. I called the other stores in town and no one has any left. We didn't know what else to do."

"Oh, wow. That was really kind of you." Chad herded me toward the doors. "Thanks so much for your help. She'll be okay."

After making such a spectacle of myself, I didn't want to argue with Chad. But I wasn't sure I'd ever be okay again. He took me home, pulled my sneakers off, and tucked me into bed. Then, because he's the best brother on the entire planet, he stayed with me. He took a seat in the shabby chic easy chair there in my room, and stayed there until I woke up several hours later. He let me shower and pack up the last of my cookies, then drove me to the hospital.

Now, a couple hours later, with everyone gone and the lights in the hospital corridors dimmed, I settled in to spend Christmas Eve with my Mark. I wasn't proud of my very public Publix meltdown. But sometimes there's an odd sense of serenity that follows a good cry. A cleansing, of sorts. And that's how I felt as I took a few moments to relax.

I let the gentle ambiance of the decorations comfort me. The heady pine scent coming from the miniature tree. The strings of tiny white lights on the tree and along the window ledge. The soft Christmas music playing on my Pandora playlist. The heat of my snickerdoodle latte warming my insides. All of it, helping me relax and just . . . be.

When I finished my latte, I reached for the box in my oversized bag. It filled me with an almost reverent peace as I mirrored the same thing my aunt did on that Christmas Eve seventy years ago. I unwrapped the Spode teacup and saucer and held them in my hands.

"Mark, I still don't know if you can hear a word I say. But I need to share this with you. I feel so honored, so strangely content. Which makes no sense, if you think about it. Yet here I am, holding the same teacup Aunt Lucille held that Christmas Eve so long ago as she kept vigil with the love of *her* life. Remember when I read to you about the vow she made to have tea with Uncle Gary on every

Christmas morning thereafter using these cups? True to her word, she eventually owned twelve place settings in this pattern. And I'm so glad to know the history behind these cups and all those dishes. Who knows, maybe I'll try to twist Stephen's arm and see if he'll let me have his mother's Christmas dishes."

I set the Spode teacup and saucer on the bedside table and reached for Mark's hand. I pushed away all the fears and doubts and slammed the door on my ever-present worry. Tonight I wanted nothing more than to be with Mark. That's all. No strings attached. No if-onlys. No demanding prayers.

We were together. And for tonight, that was enough.

A little later I decided to finish reading Lucille's diary. Not the whole book; just the part that covered that Christmas in the hospital. I wanted to know when Uncle Gary finally came around. I wanted to know what happened next.

"We left off on the afternoon of Christmas day," I told Mark. "Lucille wrote how thankful she was that the hospital staff could join them. Remember? Okay, here we go."

I was so thrilled that everyone stayed around after we ate. Even the nurses would stroll back through on their breaks. I'm guessing they too wanted to feel a little "normal" on this most blessed of days. Later in the afternoon, as the snow continued to fall outside, it was just us—Mr. and Mrs. Reynolds, my parents and Jack and me. We'd brought in extra chairs from the lounge and placed them in a circle around Gary's bed. We chatted quietly for a long time while Father's radio softly played Christmas carols. Jack had fallen sound asleep in Mother's arms.

My father was talking to Gary's father when Craig suddenly turned his head and raised his hand. In the background I heard the soulful strains of "O Holy Night" playing on the radio. I watched as Craig gazed at Patricia, and I knew they were remembering the Sunday we sang in their living room. They were remembering, as I was, the moment when our voices fell away until it was only Gary singing—his smooth tenor voice bringing such a sacred richness to that unforgettable melody.

Craig reached over and grasped Patricia's hand. With only the glow of the Christmas lights, I could still see the tear that spilled down her cheek. I looked away, not wishing to invade on their shared moment. As I'd done a thousand times that day, I glanced over to check on Gary . . . and my heart stopped when I found him staring at me!

"Gary?" I gasped as I rushed to his side. "GARY! Can you hear me?" I grabbed his hand with both of mine and squeezed it hard.

Suddenly his bed was surrounded as they all gathered around, all speaking at once, saying his name over and over, all of us waiting and holding our breath as one.

He said nothing at first. His eyes slowly tracked from one to the other, his mouth moving as though he was trying to talk— or remember how *to talk?*

"Sweetheart, can you see us?" Patricia cried. "Can you hear me?"

His eyes locked on her, but showed no immediate recognition. He turned his head to the other side of the bed and looked up at his father.

"Son," Craig said, his voice graveled with emotion. "It would be awfully nice right now to hear your voice and let us know you're here with us."

With my free hand, I wiped tears from my eyes. The movement must have caught Gary's attention as he looked back at me. His eyes seemed to change a little—barely a trace, but there nonetheless. As though they were trying to smile even if his mouth wasn't.

Then, ever so softly, he began to sing, his raspy voice accompanying the music still playing on the radio.

Right in time. And right on key.

"Sweet hymns of joy
in grateful chorus raise we,
With all our hearts
we praise His holy name . . ."

His voice gave out, too weak to reach the higher notes that followed. He closed his mouth, a flicker of sadness dashing across his face. "Am I dead?" he croaked.

We exploded—all of us—in laughter and tears and hugs of joy.

My father dashed toward the door. "I'll go get the nurse!"

Patricia kept kissing Gary's hand, holding his palm against her face. Neither she nor Craig could speak, but the joy on their faces was unmistakable.

I leaned down. "Gary! Oh Gary—you came back to us. You finally came back to us!"

"Where did he go?" Jack rubbed his eyes as he leaned back from Mother's shoulder.

Gary looked at my brother. "Hi, Jack," he whispered.

A shy, sleepy grin warmed my little brother's face. "Hi, Gary."

We all laughed and hugged each other all over again. Gary gave my hand a gentle tug, and as I leaned closer, he smiled.

"You look beautiful," he whispered.

I laughed, taking his face in my hands. "Not half as beautiful as you. I was so worried I'd never see those baby blues again." I kissed his forehead.

The slightest smile curved his lips just as his chin began to tremble. He squeezed my hand as a silent sob shook him.

The head nurse made her way into the room ahead of two others. "Well, well! Look who decided to show up for Christmas!"

Gary stared at her, still struggling with his emotions.

"It's very nice to see you, Mr. Reynolds. How are you feeling?"

He took a shaky breath. "My head hurts."

I let the diary fall to my lap and buried my face in my hands. It was too much—it was all too much. Somehow our parallel universes were colliding, and I felt like I'd literally stepped back in time. I was right there in Gary's room. I had felt the electricity in the air, the same crackling surge they'd surely felt. I'd cried tears of joy along with them and shared in their hugs of celebration.

For those moments I became Lucille, overwhelmed and giddy with relief that the love of my life had *finally* come back to me—

Right up until reality slapped me hard across the face and shoved me back into *this* room with the love of *my* life—who remained still and unconscious. I bit down on my knuckles and stood up, letting the diary fall to the floor. I clawed at my sweater, pulling it tighter around me as I turned my back on Mark and made my way to the window.

Get a hold of yourself, Lucy.

The rebuke felt like another slap. How could I be so naive? Of *course* Gary woke up—I'd known all along that he would. I'd been in his home! When I was ten, he let me drink my first coffee. He showed me how to dead-head petunias so they'd keep blooming. We'd spent hours singing Broadway show tunes, Aunt Lucille and I standing beside the baby grand piano he played so masterfully. Gary had come out of his coma and married Lucille and had a son named Stephen and lived a full life. It wasn't just some made-up story.

So why was I so angry? Why did I feel like biting somebody's head off?

I took a deep breath and blew it out, shaking my head. Stupid, stupid questions. I knew *exactly* why I was angry—I'd been reading a story knowing all along how it would end. As if I'd skipped to the last page in the book and sneaked a peek at the ending. These reading sessions merely filled in the blanks. They simply told me "the rest of the story."

And deep in my heart, I knew that Lucille and Gary's happily-ever-after didn't guarantee the same for Mark and me.

I plucked some tissues from the nearest box of Kleenex and wiped at my relentless tears. I was sick of them. Sick of the emotional roller coaster. Sick of losing control at the slightest bump in the road. Sick of all of it.

I stood there staring out at the snowfall for the longest time. Silly, but I didn't want Mark to see me like this. These are the mind games one plays with a coma boyfriend. But in spite of all I'd learned, this was one story I had no desire to write. *Ever.* Lucille and Gary's story would fill the pages of my novella, but I would surgically detach myself from what was happening to Mark and me. I would type every word from Lucille's perspective and leave it at that.

The serenity of the gentle snow falling outside my window slowly began to drain the angst inside me. I made a conscious effort to breathe in, then breathe out. Over and over, I let the calming breaths do their job. And as they did, I caught the sweet words of the familiar carol drifting through the room. How long had I stood here, tuning out the music playing on the radio? The age-old lyrics tugged at my heart, beckoning me to a Bethlehem stable two thousand years ago.

Silent night, holy night.
All is calm, all is bright.
Round yon virgin, mother and child.
Holy infant so tender and mild.
Sleep in heavenly peace—

My heart stopped even as the reverence of the beloved carol continued.

Sleep in heavenly peace.

I looked over my shoulder at Mark and watched his chest slowly rise and fall, just as it had for the last couple of weeks. He looked so serene. So peaceful. And yet his peace had delivered unspeakable fear to those of us who loved him. Was it possible for us—for *me*—to experience such peace in the midst of such a horrific nightmare?

I knew the answer to my own question. I'd memorized the verses as a child.

And the peace of God,
which transcends all understanding,
will guard your hearts and minds
in Christ Jesus
—Philippians 4:7

Peace I leave with you;
My peace I give to you.
I do not give to you as the world gives.
Let not your hearts be troubled.
Do not be afraid.
—John 14:27

I could hardly remember the child I was when I learned those verses. They meant little to me then, just a bunch of words I memorized to earn stickers on a Sunday school chart. Later, I would understand why it was so important to learn scripture. Back then, I learned those verses because it was what we were supposed to do. It was expected. But oh my goodness, how thankful I am to know them now. Like so many life rafts in a raging sea of fear.

Silent night, holy night
Son of God, love's pure light
Radiant beams from Thy holy face
With the dawn of redeeming grace . . .

I closed my eyes and prayed.

Oh Jesus, thank You. It's only through You that I can fathom such grace. To be redeemed to You through a mercy I can't even begin to understand. But I believe in You. I trust in You. And I'm clinging to Your promises as if they truly are life rafts in a dark and stormy sea.

When I finished praying, the strangest thought came to mind. I've always woven threads of faith through the books I write. I'll never be a preacher or a missionary, and I've never felt called to lead a Bible study or even teach kids in Vacation Bible School. But I never once doubted God's call to use the passion He gave me for writing to tell of His unconditional love and mercy and grace.

So was *this* the faith thread of my own personal story?

The assurance of God's presence even when I can't feel it?

His promise of peace even when it seems to elude me at every turn?

The legacy of hope that defies understanding?

And the greatest gift of all—His precious Son born in a manger on that silent, holy night . . .

I glanced at the snow falling outside the window and took another cleansing breath.

And then?

I smiled.

Chapter 13

On Christmas morning, Chad and Shelly woke me up.

After my late-night heart-fest with God, I'd fallen sound asleep. Maybe the most restful sleep since this all began. I stretched and smiled and hugged them both.

"Merry Christmas, Chad. Merry Christmas, Shelly."

"Right backatcha, Lucy," my brother said, holding me another moment. "For someone who slept in a chair all night, you sound rather chipper."

"Me? Chipper?"

Shelly unwrapped the scarf around her neck and studied my face. "Chad's right. You seem different somehow. Relaxed. Everything okay?" Her countenance drew together and she quickly turned toward Mark. "Is he—"

"No. No change. Sorry."

"Don't be silly. I just—" she tilted her head and stared at me again. "Are you sure you're okay?"

I felt like I was looking at Shelly through a different lens. I realized how much I'd grown to love Mark's sister. She was smart and beautiful and sincerely compassionate toward everyone around her. Including my brother. I'd picked up little nuances between them now and then. A look. A lingering smile. The fact that he'd saved her number in his cell phone. The fact that they arrived here together. On Christmas day. I wondered what else I might have missed and made a mental note to have a heart-to-heart with Chad about it later.

The staff scooted us out the door so they could bathe Mark and shave his whiskers. I was rather fond of those whiskers—not permitted in the UPS employee guidelines—but cute, nonetheless. We took the opportunity to go downstairs and grab some breakfast in the cafeteria. A far cry from the Christmas mornings of our childhood, but it would have to do.

The rest of the day felt eerily similar to Lucille's Christmas. Lots of relatives showing up, and lots of good food streaming in. I felt a little guilty seeing the parade of scrumptious holiday dishes coming in juxtaposed against the trays of grayish-looking fare showing up from the hospital's food service.

I half-expected to see Lucille come around the corner, wearing her emerald green swing dress with the pinstriped bow, carrying the strange old "Christmas candle" to put on Uncle Gary's bedside table.

But thanks to my unexpected encounter with the Lord last night, I felt strangely calm. At peace. As though I were finally given a glimpse into that heavenly sleep my Mark was experiencing. And just as Lucille noted in her diary, ours was truly a wonderful Christmas. I think it helped that I didn't allow myself too much hope or expectation. I was okay with having our families together, blessing the hospital staff with a taste of home cooking, and basking in the peace I'd accepted in the wee hours of the morning.

Some of the UPS guys stopped by later. Oh, how Mark would have loved to see those characters filing in. Gordo and several of the guys from the bowling team showed up bearing gifts. Lots of chocolate, lots of crossword puzzle books (Mark always quizzed the guys first thing every morning at work), some Krispy Kremes with red and green sprinkles on top, and even a Josh Groban Christmas CD. I love my big guy, but unlike Uncle Gary, Mark's singing could make every dog in the neighborhood howl. The fact that he was off key and constantly fumbling the lyrics only egged him on. Which was why he often belted out Groban-esque serenades along with all those crossword quizzes at the UPS station. I loved seeing the guys, and knowing they'd taken time away from their own families to stop by on this Christmas morning made it all the more special.

Mom and Dad called from Tulsa. They apologized for not being here with us, unable to make the long trip on such short notice. I'd completely forgotten about the airline tickets we'd reserved to head home for Christmas. We'd sort all that out later.

Thankfully, the Christophers helped fill the parental void. Over the past few days, I'd grown to love Mark's mom and dad even more. I decided their "love language" was compassion. It motivated everything they did and bled into every conversation. Now I knew where Mark and Shelly got it.

We ate, we visited, and we opened silly, last-minute gifts Chad and Shelly had rustled together. A FedEx hat for Mark—ha ha. Fake cruise tickets for Mr. and Mrs. Christopher for a trip down the Arkansas River. For me, a framed photo of Gertie wearing her Velcro elf ears, along with some falsified adoption papers she'd supposedly signed over to Chad. It felt good to laugh again.

The weather was getting worse with predictions of roads icing over, so we said our goodbyes around seven that evening. Mark's mom and dad offered to stay overnight, but I could tell they were really tired. Even if they'd stayed, I wouldn't have left. I couldn't bear the thought of leaving Mark. Not on Christmas night.

As much as I'd enjoyed the day, I was glad to have Mark to myself again. We'd all tiptoed around the unspoken hope that Mark would wake up just as Uncle Gary did on that Christmas day so long ago. With everyone gone now, I let down my guard and realized how exhausting it was, clinging to such a fervent wish while knowing the odds were against me.

I grabbed a cup of coffee down the hall then settled back in my recliner. Around eight, one of the nurses told me there was a Mormon Tabernacle Choir Christmas concert on PBS. I'm so glad she did. It was the perfect ending to an almost-perfect day.

For the first time, I hesitated to pick up Lucille's diary. I'd read enough. Still, I wanted to know how their story ended. Tomorrow I planned to write a rough draft of the outline for my novella. I'd promised Sam she'd have it by the end of the week, and I intended to stay on deadline. Even if she didn't have good wireless connections in Switzerland, my outline would be waiting in her inbox whenever she got to it.

I looked over at Mark and studied his face as he slept. "I'm thinking we should read the rest of the story tonight. Are you up for that?" He didn't object, so I found my place and started reading.

Over the next few days Gary still wouldn't let me out of his sight, except when he was wheeled downstairs for tests. He passed all his examinations with flying colors surprising all of us, including Dr. Pembleton. He asked several of his colleagues to stop by and see what he called his "miracle patient." They were quite intrigued, pelting Gary with their endless questions. I could tell Gary was growing impatient, wanting nothing more than to be released so he could go home.

We were especially relieved to learn that Gary's mental faculties were strong and unencumbered by the long days he spent in a coma. He began asking more questions about the attack that put him there in the first place. We evaded the subject at first, until one evening after everyone else had gone home. He insisted I tell him everything, so I did. I gave him a minute-by-minute account as I remembered it. He seemed pleased to know the elderly woman he rescued was all right, and said he looked forward to meeting her and thanking her for the Christmas cannoli he'd inhaled.

The Army had kept in touch, of course, and eventually sent one of their own medical doctors to confer with Dr. Pembleton. Apparently they were trying to decide what to do with Lieutenant Reynolds. Oddly, they didn't ask my opinion on the subject.

Then one morning, Gary's parents arrived with unusually bright smiles, acting rather mysterious. His father set up a tripod for his camera. His mother helped Gary sit up in bed, stuffing pillows behind him, then helped him put on his robe she'd brought from home.

The curiosity was killing me. "All right. What's going on?"

Craig took a peek through the lens of his camera then stood back up. "Lucille, how about you move over there and take a seat in the chair next to Gary's bed."

"Why? What's this all about?"

"Oh, come on, Lucille," Patricia said, stepping out of the way. "Let us have a little fun, will you?"

"Gary?" I groaned playfully.

"Don't look at me. I'm just a guy coming out of a coma."

I laughed in spite of myself, looking back and forth between them as I slowly sat down. "Okay. I'm sitting. What on earth are you all up to?"

Patricia joined Craig behind the camera, their silly smiles still puzzling me. Gary reached under the edge of his blanket and pulled out a small box. I recognized the Marshal Field's Christmas wrapping paper.

"Lucille, you know, I'm not supposed to be here."

I grimaced, concerned where such a statement might be heading.

"No!" He reached for my hand. "I didn't mean I was supposed to be dead! I meant to say I was supposed to be overseas for Christmas. That day we shopped at Marshall Field's, I found something I wanted to give you for Christmas. You'd wandered into the ladies lingerie department, and if you recall, you sent me away."

"Well, of course I did!" I teased. "A lady doesn't shop for those things with a fella she just met."

He laughed. "Yes, I think that's what you told me at the time. We agreed to meet in fifteen minutes back by the elevator. Remember?"

"Yes, I remember."

He twirled the opal ring on my finger. How I'd missed that simple, intimate gesture.

"While you were shopping for 'those things' as you call them, I strolled over to the jewelry section. And that's where I

found the perfect Christmas gift for you. I asked the lady to set it aside for me to pick up later. I had it gift-wrapped then brought it home. Before I left the house that last morning, I put it under the tree and asked Mom to give it to you on Christmas Eve."

I glanced over at Patricia who shrugged in feigned innocence.

"That was my plan. But, as you know, things didn't go as planned, and I've been a bit indisposed, as it were." With his index finger, he pushed the box another couple of inches toward me. "So, along with my sincerest apologies, I'd like to finally—FINALLY—give you your Christmas gift."

Gary gave me a wink as Craig kept snapping pictures. "Go on. Open it."

"For a guy who 'just came out of a coma,' you're quite the crafty one."

"You have no idea."

I carefully unwrapped the paper and set it aside. Then, lifting the lid from the small box, I found a smaller black velvet box inside. I couldn't breathe and didn't even try to say anything. Instead, I opened the box and found the most stunning heart-shaped necklace made of diamonds.

"Oh, Gary. It's beautiful," I whispered.

"Do you like it?"

"I absolutely love it!"

"Here, let me help you put it on." I gently removed the necklace from the box, then handed it to him and turned my back so he could clasp it for me. The clicks of the camera came faster and faster.

"There," Gary said, patting the clasp in place. "All set. Hey, Dad—easy with that thing, will you? I'm still recovering from a pretty serious headache here."

"Ah, these are great shots! Wait until you see them. Okay, you two give me a pose. Lucille, can you sit on the edge of the bed beside Gary?"

I turned around, my hand over the diamonds resting just below my neckline.

"Let us see those diamonds sparkle, Lucille. Oh, that's perfect. Okay, ready, set—smile!"

He took several more shots before Gary begged, "Enough!"

That's when I turned back to face him, took his face in my hands, and kissed him right on the lips. "Thank you. I've never seen anything so beautiful in all my life. I'm speechless."

"Somehow I doubt that," he teased, kissing me back.

Patricia approached us. "Here, let me get a better look." I stood up so she could see my necklace. "Oh, son, you were right. It looks truly lovely on her." She hugged me then pressed a kiss on my cheek. "A belated Merry Christmas, Lucille."

"Oh, wait—" I turned as Gary wrestled with the blanket. "I think there's something else under here."

Craig waved Patricia out of the way. "Honey, you're blocking the shot."

"Oh, here it is." Gary handed me another box, wrapped exactly like the other one.

"I think a heart of diamonds is more than enough, Lieutenant."

"On that, we must disagree. Go ahead. Open it."

"I feel terrible, Gary. I didn't get you anything."

"I know. You didn't know I would still be hanging around for Christmas. No apologies needed."

Still shaking my head, I tore the paper off the box to find another, smaller black velvet box. I slowly opened the lid. "What have you—"

"I'd get down on my knee if I could."

My mouth fell open as I stared at the large solitaire diamond ring. I slowly looked up at Gary.

He slipped the ring from its slot and held it, taking my left hand in his. "I've already proposed, but let's make it official. That is, if you don't mind marrying slightly damaged goods. Lucille Alexander, will you marry me?"

Against a backdrop of furious camera clicks, I kissed my lieutenant again and again. "Oh yes! I will, I will!"

I set the open diary on my lap, toying with its satin bookmark as a smile warmed my face. I leaned my head back on the recliner and looked over at Mark.

"What a perfect love story. Don't you think? Can't you just see the twinkling in Aunt Lucille's eyes when she realized what was going on? First he surprises her with the heart-shaped necklace. Then, as if that wasn't enough, he pops out an engagement ring? I'm telling you, this is the *perfect* romance. With this diary, the novella will all but write itself. I'll have it done way ahead of schedule. Samantha won't know how to handle herself."

I heard a soft knock on the door and looked just as Uncle Ted poked his head around it. "Are you awake, Lucy?"

"Of course I'm awake," I said, climbing out of my chair. "Come in! What are you doing here? It's almost midnight." I gave him a big hug, the icy cold fabric on his coat giving me a sudden chill.

"I couldn't sleep. Too much coffee or too much sugar. I'm not sure which."

"How did you even get here? When the night shift came in, they all said the roads are covered with ice. They said there were accidents all over town."

"Oh, you know me. The more hazardous the driving conditions, the better. I even stopped over at the high school and did some donuts in the parking lot. It was a blast! The faster the spin, the bigger the adrenaline rush!"

I motioned him to pull over the extra chair. "No hard feelings, but I'm so glad I wasn't with you."

He pulled off his coat and wool scarf and took a seat. "Ah, but you would've loved it."

"So the caffeine and sugar kept you up, huh?"

"Oh, that reminds me." He reached into the pocket of his coat and pulled out a bag of Poppycock. "We always have a round of Dirty Santa at my in-law's on Christmas. I won this, and I thought you might like to have it."

I couldn't help the laughter that sprung out of me.

"What? You don't like Poppycock?"

I waved him off. "No, it's not that."

"Look, this is even the good stuff. Praline Pecan!" He tore open the bag and held it out to me. "Try some."

I laughed even harder before explaining my meltdown at Publix.

"Hey, all that stress has to eventually come out. It was probably the best thing that could have happened to you."

I took a handful of clusters and munched a few. "I think you're right. As embarrassed as I was, I have to admit it felt like a tremendous release after all this tension. I'm just glad there weren't too many folks around."

"I'm sure they've seen worse." Uncle Ted tossed a handful of Poppycock in the air and caught it in his mouth.

"The employees were great. See that gigantic poinsettia over there? They sent that along with a note saying they were praying for us. Cool, huh?"

We chatted a while longer. I was so glad he'd come. Uncle Ted always seems to know when someone needs a little extra TLC. I suppose it's part of his ministry DNA.

Before he left, he said there was one more thing.

"What's that?"

He leaned over, his elbows on his knees. "Lucy, I was praying for Mark this morning while I shaved. It doesn't happen often, but a verse came to me out of nowhere, and I knew it had to be from the Lord."

"What verse?"

"I thought you might ask." He pulled his iPhone from his pocket and opened his Bible app. "It's Psalm 62:8. But after I finished shaving, I looked it up and read it in context, starting with verse five."

"My soul, wait in silence for God only,
For my hope is from Him.
He alone is my rock and my salvation,
My stronghold; I shall not be shaken.
On God my salvation and my glory rest;
The rock of my strength,
my refuge is in God.
Trust in Him at all times, O people;
Pour out your heart before Him;
God is a refuge for us."

He tucked the phone back in his pocket. "Primarily, it's a reminder that God is always, always there. He's our rock, our strength, our refuge. And when we can't find even a miniscule trace of His handprint in what we're going through, He's reminding us that He's still there. And He always will be. No matter what."

I let the verses roll around in my head, and told my uncle about my heart-to-heart with God the night before.

"Kind of feels like God sent you here to affirm all that."

He rubbed his hands together and smiled at me. "It sure does. Maybe it wasn't so much the caffeine and sugar keeping me up after all."

"Thanks, Uncle Ted. I'm really glad you came."

He stood up and nodded toward Mark as he pulled his coat back on. "Any change?"

"No, not today. But I'm learning to take it one day at a time."

He hooked his arm around my neck and walked me back toward Mark's bed. "Come pray with me."

A few minutes later he was gone. I prayed he'd skip the ice donuts on his way home.

I gradually made my way back to my chair and pulled the blanket around me. I reached for the diary and caressed the smooth leather cover. I felt confident there was more to Lucille and Gary's story, but I was tired and needing sleep, so I reached over and turned out the light.

As I drifted closer to that fine line between awake and asleep, I kept thinking about the last entry I'd read. I leaned my head back and closed my eyes, fingering my necklace.

"The thing is, Mark, I still don't know how you knew about Aunt Lucille's necklace. I never talked about it. And yet the one you gave me is *exactly* like hers, so it can't just be some random coincidence."

I took a deep breath and slowly exhaled, then closed my eyes, ready to call it a night.

"The photo album."

I snuggled deeper beneath the blanket, wishing the voices in my head would knock it off.

"Under the coffee table."

I couldn't believe how fast I'd fallen asleep. Still, I welcomed the sweet sound of Mark's voice in my dream.

"It's not rocket science, Lucy. I saw the picture in a photo album."

I glanced over at dream-Mark and found him staring at me. I marveled at how much I'd missed the sound of his voice.

"Hi, beautiful."

"Hi, Mark."

Wait—did I just say that out loud?

"Did Gary have to go back overseas to the war?"

I blinked. Twice.

"Lucy?"

"Mark?!" I rubbed my eyes, fighting to wake myself up.

"So did he?"

My eyes flashed open. I shoved the recliner upright and vaulted myself to his bedside. "MARK! You're awake?!" I flipped on the overhead light.

He blinked against the brightness, and I grabbed his face in my hands. "Can you hear me? Mark, say something!"

"Hey, Lucy." That goofy lopsided grin tried to find its place.

"MARK! You came back! You came back to me!" I blubbered through the gush of happy tears streaming down my face. "You came back!"

He closed his eyes for a moment, then started looking around. "Back from where? Where am I? What happened?"

I smothered him with kisses. "I thought you'd never ask."

Epilogue

Dear Diary,

Before he left the hospital, Mark went online and ordered this beautiful leather-bound journal for me. It's one of the things I love most about him—how he always knows the perfect gift to give. He wanted me to have it so I could write our *love story.*

It's still so hard for me to comprehend that he was listening all those weeks while I read from Lucille's diary. They'd told me coma patients could often hear the sound of voices around them, but the skeptic that I am, I didn't really believe them. Which is why I was gobsmacked when Mark started asking me questions about Lucille and Gary's story; things he could not have known otherwise.

In answer to Mark's persistent question, Uncle Gary was sent back to complete his tour of duty in England. Thankfully, the war ended soon after, and he returned home in early June. He married Lucille in a lavish ceremony at Drexel Park Presbyterian Church.

As much as I loved the journal Mark gave me, I couldn't bring myself to start writing in it right away. I didn't want its opening pages to be filled with the haunting, surreal story of what had happened to Mark.

Which is why I've waited until now. A full six months later.

Two days ago, I walked down the aisle of First Church on my father's arm, carrying a bouquet of pale green hydrangeas as a stringed quartet played Pachelbel's "Canon in D." Ahead of me stood my handsome groom, his face beaming as he waited alongside Uncle Ted who married us moments later. Chad and Shelly served in our bridal party. I'm fairly confident there will be another Alexander and Christopher wedding in the not so distant future.

Ours was a perfect wedding, as was the reception following.

We stayed in town that first night, then flew here to Paris. Yes, PARIS! Maybe it's the jet lag, but I'm sitting here on our hotel room balcony staring at the Eiffel Tower, and not quite believing I'm actually here. We've given ourselves an extra day to rest before heading out to see the sights.

We are newlyweds, after all. And that's all I'm going to say about that.

I'm so ridiculously happy, I can hardly bear it. Happy to be Mrs. Mark Christopher. Happy to be here in the most romantic city in the world. And most of all, happy that my new husband is alive and well.

I've had so many random thoughts about what happened to us, bringing us here to this moment in time. Looking back, it's easy to see God's hand through all of it. Even for a sometime-skeptic like me.

I've always believed things happen for a reason. Like the fact that Mark has always been physically fit. Granted, in his job at UPS, he hustled all day long, delivering packages. And if that wasn't enough, he worked out at the gym faithfully, four times a week. Which is where he met my brother Chad. Who, it turns out, gave Mark that final nudge to ask me out.

For someone who writes love stories for a living, I never saw it coming. Who knew my happy-go-lucky UPS guy had a crush on me?

The fact that Mark was in such great shape physically facilitated his speedy recovery, surprising all of us, most of all his doctors. That his weeks-long coma left no lasting effects on his mental faculties was truly miraculous. All things considered, he was a lucky, lucky man. No, I take that back. "Luck" had little to do with it; God, on the other hand, had everything to do with it.

I can also see God's handprints on the timetable of Aunt Lucille's diary arriving when it did. It still baffles me how eerily similar Uncle Gary's and Mark's attacks were. Stranger still, that I read Lucille's account of Gary's prolonged hospital stay even as I kept vigil beside my Mark. What was it Chad told me? "Coincidence is God's way of remaining anonymous." Indeed.

Then, shortly after Mark left the hospital, the insurance carrier for UPS offered him an astronomical "pain and suffering" payment. Mark's dad is a financial wizard, and he helped Mark invest the money wisely. To be honest, I was surprised when Mark decided to take the money and walk away from his job. Then, one night while he was still at home recuperating, we had a long talk.

"Promise you won't laugh?" he said.

"Me? Laugh at you? Never."

"Like I believe that?"

"Go on, big guy. Give it your best shot."

He glanced down as though unable to face me. "The thing is, I've always had this crazy dream of becoming a professional bowler."

I stared at him, swallowing hard as visions of a life spent in tacky bowling alleys flashed through my mind. "Oh?" I croaked. "Really?"

He nodded, still looking down. "Really."

"Well, I'm, uh . . ."

"Lucy?"

Did his voice just crack or did I imagine it? "Yes?"

He finally leveled his gaze at me. "I'm kidding."

I swatted his arm as he rocked with laughter. "Don't do that! I believed you!"

He tried to wrap his arms around me. "Sorry. I couldn't help it. You're such an easy target."

I pulled back. "Go ahead. Have your fun. I'm used to it, you know."

He raised his hands in surrender. "I'm sorry! I was only kidding." He tugged at my hand and laced my fingers with his as his laughter subsided. "I've actually given a lot of thought about this windfall. How it came out of the blue—"

"You mean, out of the brown?"

He laughed again. "Duly noted. Good one."

"Go on."

"The thing is, I want to do more with my life than deliver packages. Not that there's anything wrong with it. UPS has been great. But after everything that happened, I can't help but think it's the right time to start a new chapter in my life. Do something different."

"Such as?"

"I'm not sure yet. But it's exciting to think about the possibilities. Believe it or not, I've always wanted to learn how to paint. Oils and watercolor."

"Seriously? You?"

"I know. Crazy, isn't it? I'd like to try and see if I'm any good at it. And I want to learn to cook. To bake bread and pastries and make all kinds of delectable desserts."

"How come you never told me any of this before?"

"I don't know. Maybe because I never gave myself permission to dream those kinds of dreams before. Weird, huh?"

"Not really. I think it's wonderful, Mark." I curled my fingers over his. "So what will you do? Start taking lessons? Cooking and painting? Both at the same time? One at a time? What's your plan?"

"I don't know. I haven't gotten that far."

"Then what will you do in the meantime? Until you decide?"

"That much I do know. Two things."

"Two?"

"First, I want to travel. I've always wondered what it would be like to go places I've only dreamed about. New Zealand. England. Austria. Paris. Rome. I actually had a dream the other night that I lived in an old villa on a hillside in Tuscany with rows of vineyards stretching in every direction."

"Yeah?"

"Then I woke up because I heard Dean Martin singing 'That's Amore.'"

"Why would that wake you?"

"Because he was standing there in my courtyard with a drink in one hand, serenading us. In person. As in, alive.*" Mark shivered. "Dino's been dead since 1995."*

"Well, yeah, I can see your point."

"But at the same time, I realized how at home I felt there. Weird, huh?"

I gazed over at Mark's fireplace and watched the flames dance as I tried to imagine him living in Italy—with or without Dean Martin. But something else bothered me. Something he'd said but I'd already forgotten. It was there, but not.

Mark placed his finger under my chin and turned my face back to his. "Of course, that could never happen unless . . ."

"Unless?"

"Unless you come with me."

I searched his eyes, unsure I'd heard him right. "But—"

"Marry me, Lucy."

"What?"

"Marry me. We'll travel the world, then we'll decide where to live. Together. You can write your books, I can paint or cook or make wine—as long as you're there with me, it doesn't matter."

I felt my chin begin to tremble as the familiar pin-prick in my eyes triggered the first tears I'd cried in weeks.

Mark smiled as he thumbed away my tears and held my face in his strong hands. "Marry me, Lucy. Let's write our <u>own</u> love story."

I placed my hands over his and kissed him over and over.

He leaned back. "Can I take that as a yes?"

I nodded. "Oh, it's a definite yes!"

And that's how it happened.

That's how we ended up here in Paris, our first stop at the beginning of an extended honeymoon.

That's why I'm sitting here on the balcony of our hotel, watching the golden rays of the sunrise reflecting off the Eiffel

Tower, and writing in my new diary with the quiet snores of my new husband serenading me in the background.

As for living in a villa on a hill in Tuscany—who knows. Someday, we might have a home on this side of the Atlantic. But for now, we're content just to be here.

Together.

At the beginning of our very own happily ever after.

Acknowledgments

With every book comes help from old friends and new, and Lucy's novellas are no exception. On her behalf, I would like to thank the following:

First and foremost, I want to thank my Lord and Savior Jesus Christ. I am so profoundly humbled to be used as a vessel for sharing Your unconditional love, mercy, and forgiveness on the pages of my books. Writing may now be my profession, but I can never adequately express in words the unfathomable honor I feel to be a child of Yours. To God be the glory, great things He has done!

Eternal thanks to my beloved aunt, Lucille McKeag Hale, whose gift of vintage teacups inspired the stories of this novella series. How I would've loved to share these stories with you!

To my best friend and husband, Ken. I'm convinced I'd never write a single word without your constant encouragement. Thanks for all those brainstorming sessions over fajitas and chimichangas at El Jardin, for your exceptional expertise in marketing, and your Midas touch in Gimp Land. There's still a golf cart in Maui with your name on it. Let's do it. Let's go. Have I told you lately how much I love you?

To Glenn Hale, for his incredible knack for catching those elusive typos. It only goes to press after ol' Eagle Eyes has a look. Thanks, Dad. Ninety never looked so young. Love you always.

To Sally Wilson, Cyndi Hollman, and my favorite Aussie, Bev Harrison, for giving my stories their extra sparkle. I couldn't do it without you.

To my amazingly gifted daughter Hannah for designing the cover for *The Teacup Novellas Collection.* I will never forget than rainy November afternoon in New York when we cozied up with chai lattes in the corner of that Starbucks and I witnessed your incredible gifts as a graphic designer. I am so proud of you and so glad God let me be your mom. *muwa*

Tea with Emma
To Teresa, my prayer "sistah" and dear friend. Thanks for being such a faithful cheerleader. And thanks for the special tea party that early morning we watched the Royal Wedding together. Your tea and scones surely rivaled those of the palace!

Strike the Match

To Katie at *The Vintage Teacup* on Etsy. Thanks for the beautiful picture of the gorgeous Lomonosov teacup and your willingness to share its beauty on my cover. If you're ever in the Nashville area, we must have tea! I adore your Etsy shop and trust my readers will stop by often, as will I: http://www.etsy.com/shop/TheVintageTeacup

To Dan Logan for his spectacular log cabin fire photograph, taken in Crown Point, Alaska. The moment I found your picture, I knew I'd found my cover shot. Thank you for your generosity in allowing me to use it. You are a gifted photographer, my friend. Check out more of Dan's stunning pictures at: www.flickr.com/photos/dcsl/sets/

And to Sally Wilson. Yes, I know—I dedicated this book to you, but I can never thank you enough for the trail you have blazed for me and others in this passion we call writing. From the first time we met at the ACFW conference in Houston, I knew we were kindred spirits. I am so blessed to know you, to brainstorm over panini with you at Red Tree, and to experience life with a true blue, albeit quirky friend who lives "just down the road." You are one of my most cherished friends, and I thank God for you.

Home to Walnut Ridge

To my favorite biker babe, Terry Young, and her wonderful husband, Ivan. Thank you for educating this motorcycle-challenged author and making sure I didn't embarrass my characters with any misguided faux-Harley lingo. I hope I got it right. I've gained a whole new appreciation for those who love the open road. Love you ttmab.

To Sharon Jacob and Julie Harrel of *Vintage Shabby Chicks,* whose shared passion for restoring "used, discarded, and sometimes broken furniture and giving it new life," was the inspiration for Alex and Tracey's new business. Thank you for a business model that so flawlessly mirrors God's promise to give us new life through Jesus Christ. Sharon, thanks for taking time to educate me on your painting magic and showing me so many of your beautiful transformations. To learn more, check out Sharon and Julie's website at: http://www.vintageshabbychicks.com

A special thanks to Marian Parsons—a.k.a. Miss Mustard Seed—for permission to include her fabulous *Miss Mustard Seed Milk Paints.* To my readers, you can visit her website at:

http://missmustardseedsmilkpaint.com.

Take my word for it, you simply must pamper yourself by ordering a copy of her beautiful book, *Inspired You: Breathing New Life into Your Heart and Home.* I guarantee you'll be inspired!

Also, special thanks to my new favorite artist, David Arms. In January of 2013, God surely led me into your quaint barn gallery in Leiper's Fork, Tennessee just after I began working on this story. The moment I saw it, I knew this was the perfect setting for Tracey and Alex's converted smokehouse, both inside and out. Thank you for graciously allowing me to borrow its charm for my cover art. To my readers, I invite you to spend some time visiting David's website. There you can read his story, visit his studio, learn about his unique use of symbolism, then treat yourself by browsing through his amazing portfolio. I know you'll find his work as unforgettable as I have. Visit David at: http://davidarms.com

At Legend's End
Thanks to Erin Pechtel for allowing us to feature Rufus, your adorable King Charles Cavalier Spaniel, for the interior section breaks. Rufus, you rock!

In memory of Linda Brewer, my sister Morlee's dear and precious friend who found love again later in life—living proof that the best things in life really are worth the wait.

A Christmas Peril
To my cousin Allan Hale for sharing so many wonderful memories of his parents, Harold and Lucille Hale. Thank you for allowing me to use their photograph on my cover. All these years later, I still miss them so much.

And finally, with deepest appreciation for my readers whose emails and reviews have warmed my heart in ways I'd never dreamed. You are the reason I write.

About the Author

Born in Texas and raised in Oklahoma, Diane Hale Moody is a graduate of Oklahoma State University. She lives with her husband Ken in the rolling hills just outside of Nashville. They are the proud parents of two grown and extraordinary children, Hannah and Ben.

Just after moving to Tennessee in 1999, Diane felt the tug of a long-neglected passion to write again. Since then, she's written a column for her local newspaper, feature articles for various magazines and curriculum, and several novels with a dozen more stories eagerly vying for her attention.

When she's not reading or writing, Diane enjoys an eclectic taste in music and movies, great coffee, the company of good friends, and the adoration of a peculiar little pooch named Darby.

Visit Diane's website at www.dianemoody.net and her blog, *just sayin'* at www.dianemoody.blogspot.com

Copyrights

Tea with Emma

Front cover photo: © Angela Ostafichuk | Dreamstime.com
Front cover photo: © Petar Neychev | Dreamstime.com
Front cover photo: © Christopher Nuzzaco | Dreamstime.com
Interior teapot image: © Aerobaby | Dreamstime.com

Strike the Match

Front cover image photo: © Photoeuphoria | Dreamstime.com
Front teacup photo: Katie at The Vintage Teacup on Etsy
Front fire photo: Dan Logan | Flickr
Interior lighthouse image: © Daniel Dupuis | Dreamstime.com

Home to Walnut Ridge

Front cover photo: © NadyaPhoto|iStockphoto.com
Front cover barn photo: used with permission
from David Arms, of the
David Arms Art Gallery,
Leipers Fork, TN
Teacup photo: public domain

At Legend's End

Front cover photo: © SerrNovik | iStockphoto.com
Front cover photo: © DenisTangneyJr | iStockphoto.com
Interior: "Rufus" | King Charles Cavalier Spaniel

A Christmas Peril

Front cover tree photo: © HannamariaH | iStockphoto.com
Front cover "Lucy" photo: © FurmanAnna | iStockphoto.com
Front cover couple: Harold and Lucille Hale

Other Titles From OBT Bookz

From Author Diane Moody

The Runaway Pastor's Wife

Blue Christmas

Blue Like Elvis

Confessions of a Prayer Slacker

Tea with Emma
The Teacup Novellas (Book One)

Strike the Match
The Teacup Novellas (Book Two)

Home to Walnut Creek
The Teacup Novellas (Book Three)

At Legend's End
The Teacup Novellas (Book Four)

A Christmas Peril
The Teacup Novellas (Book Five)

From Author McMillian Moody

Ordained Irreverence
Elmo Jenkins (Book One)

Some Things Never Change
Elmo Jenkins (Book Two)

The Old Man and the Tea
Elmo Jenkins (Book Three)

The Elmo Jenkins Trilogy

Made in the USA
Monee, IL
19 January 2020